ALSO BY JANET FITCH

Paint It Black
White Oleander

THE
REVOLUTION
OF
MARINA M.

JANET FITCH

LITTLE, BROWN AND COMPANY
LARGE PRINT EDITION

Copyright © 2017 by Janet Fitch

Hachette Book Group supports the right to free expression and the value of copyright. The purpose of copyright is to encourage writers and artists to produce the creative works that enrich our culture.

The scanning, uploading, and distribution of this book without permission is a theft of the author's intellectual property. If you would like permission to use material from the book (other than for review purposes), please contact permissions@hbgusa.com. Thank you for your support of the author's rights.

Little, Brown and Company
Hachette Book Group
1290 Avenue of the Americas, New York, NY 10104
littlebrown.com

First Edition: November 2017

Little, Brown and Company is a division of Hachette Book Group, Inc. The Little, Brown name and logo are trademarks of Hachette Book Group, Inc.

The publisher is not responsible for websites (or their content) that are not owned by the publisher.

The Hachette Speakers Bureau provides a wide range of authors for speaking events. To find out more, go to hachettespeakersbureau.com or call (866) 376-6591.

All poetry from the Russian, including the epigraph selection from Anna Akhmatova's *Northern Elegies* and Marina Tsvetaeva's "We shall not escape Hell," is translated by Boris Dralyuk, except for the lines from Mikhail Lermontov's "A Prophecy," which is translated by Anatoly Lieberman. Used by permission.

ISBN 978-0-316-02206-4 (hc) / 978-0-316-43994-7 (large print)
LCCN 2017935938

10 9 8 7 6 5 4 3 2 1

LSC-C

Book design by Marie Mundaca

Printed in the United States of America

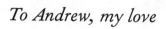

To Andrew, my love

I, like a river,
Have been diverted by the ruthless era.
My life was switched. It flows
Into another channel, past strange lands,
And I no longer recognize my shores.
          —Anna Akhmatova, *Northern Elegies*

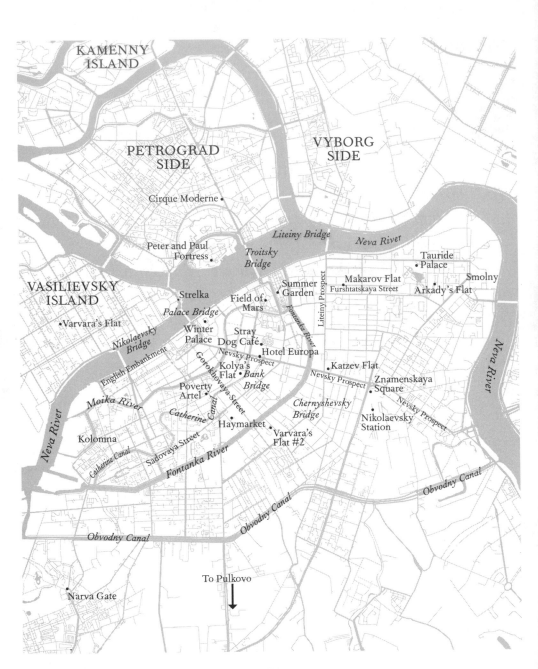

PETROGRAD
1917

THE
REVOLUTION
OF
MARINA M.

New Year's 1932, Carmel-by-the-Sea

ROCKING ON THE RAZOR-MUSSELED bay, lulled by the sleepy toll of buoy bells, the music of rigging, the eloquent stanzas of the waves, I wait for news from the sea. No boys and girls play on the deserted beach now, only a few stoic fishermen huddle on upturned buckets. The slow labor of the poet building himself a stone house at the cove's south end makes for mild entertainment. If I knew him better I'd tell him the danger of trusting to solid things. It's an illusion. All one needs is a rented cabin, a decent stove, a small boat, a garden gone to seed for winter. I watch the lanky form of my landlord's son crossing the shingle, coat collar up, stopping by to collect rents. I have the money in a cigar box back in my cabin, most of it anyway. It's only five dollars, the shack's not built for winter. I don't complain, there are shutters to block out a storm, and an iron stove with a solid pipe. In a few minutes, I will beach my boat on the pebbly shore and give him his due—we'll share a bottle of homebrew, or perhaps he comes with a flask. No liquor on the premises just now—though it will come soon, down from San Francisco. Those who love poetry, even my unreadable foreign brand, are a tender breed. *Why don't you write in English, Marina?* asks my friend Elizabeth. *You speak it so well.*

My dilemma. My English is good enough for the little stories I publish in pulp magazines, but for poetry one needs one's native tongue. The voice of the soul is not so easily translated. Though to say "soul" here is already wrong. We say *dusha,* meaning not just the spiritual entity but also the person himself.

A tug on the line. I pull in a shining perch, shockingly alive. I add it to a rockfish in my pail and row back to shore. I have a motor but spare the gas when I can. At times like this I surprise myself, how I've managed to create something of a life on this foggy shore out of the broken pieces of myself, scavenged from the sea like flotsam. Or is it jetsam...it irks me not to know the difference. I will have to consult my oracle, the giant moldy *Webster's* I've acquired since my arrival here, the very edition we had in my childhood home that lived on a stout shelf along with the *Nouveau Larousse Illustré,* the *Deutsches Wörterbuch,* and Dahl's *Explanatory Dictionary of the Living Great Russian Language.* When I was very small, I had to sit on my knees to read these great books. *Why do you not write in English, Marina?* Because when you are flotsam, or jetsam, you cling to what is yours.

After the landlord's lanky son leaves—*a roll in the hay,* that delightful image—I lay my *Webster's* on the scrubbed table in the lantern light, to learn that *flotsam* is the debris left from shipwreck, while *jetsam* is merchandise thrown overboard from a ship in crisis to lighten the load. *Ship in crisis.* That it was. The difference seems to be tied to the fate of the ship. Did it survive after shedding those such as myself, tossing us overboard—*jetsam*—to lighten the load, or did it founder, to be torn apart, mastless and rudderless, the planks and boards washed ashore—*flotsam*—perhaps one bearing the ship's name. And the name was...*Revolution.*

I can hear her half a mile off, Elizabeth in her clattering jalopy. I've made cornbread in my iron pot, a *Dutch oven*...always the Dutch, showing up in surprising places. I will have to look that up. I dredge the pink-gilled perch in cornmeal and fry it with a hunk of salt pork. My mouth stirs these tasty *k*'s, the *t*, the *p*—*hunk of salt pork*. My friend has brought a crate of artichokes down from Salinas and Polish vodka—Smirnoff. Where did she find it? The Americans prefer their native bourbons and ryes. Such a blessing after all these years of bathtub hooch. Her company is so sweet—this lovely girl with lines to grace the hood of a luxury car. Yet she treats me as if I were the exotic one—her movements careful and calm. What have I done to deserve to be treated so tenderly? Am I so *dikaya*—wild—that I might startle and take flight like a red deer?

After dinner, she showers me with gifts, H.D.'s *Red Roses for Bronze* and the new Wallace Stevens, books she, a student of literature at the university at Berkeley, can ill afford. And now she's hiding something else behind her back, her hazel-gold eyes bright, anticipatory. I pour more vodka into our jelly-jar glasses and pretend not to notice. Finally, she holds it out, a gift wrapped in a sheet of the San Francisco paper. I flex it—thin, paperbound—and try to guess. "A layer cake? A phonograph?" Then tear open the wrapper.

Russian. *Kem byt'?* A book for children—*Who Will I Become?* by Vladimir Mayakovsky. My heart catches in my throat like fingers in a slammed door. Mayakovsky, dead two years now. Dead by his own hand. Or maybe not. You never know. But dead just the same.

"Do you know it?" she asks, eager to have surprised me.

I shake my head, remembering the last time I saw him, in Petrograd at the House of Arts, a robust and charismatic man, full of swagger. *Who Will I Become?* Inside, the same stepped verse he came to favor. This is the ship that sailed on without me: *1928, Government Press.* And here are the child's choices: doctor, worker, auto mechanic, pilot, streetcar conductor, engineer. But no Chekist. No *apparatchik.* And nowhere a poet. Nowhere a cloud in trousers.

I get very drunk that night in the little cabin and recite

aloud everything I know penned by Vladimir Vladimirovich. I sing it as he did, that thrilling bass voice, booming like the waves, so Elizabeth can hear the music. When I run out of his poems, I move on to Khlebnikov, Chernikov, Kuriakin. My pretty friend cannot believe how many lines I know by heart, but this is nothing. There's no end to the flow once the gate is opened. Here they teach children to think, but they don't train the memory. I suppose they cannot imagine what a person might be called upon to endure, when a line of poetry can mean the difference between strength and despair. I drip candle wax into my glass, watch the drops swirl and adhere. "What are you doing?" she asks.

"It's something we used to do, to tell our fortunes." I recite for her:

On St. Basil's Eve, cast the wax in water.
At midnight cast the wax.
Sing the songs the girls have sung
Since ancient times.
Prepare, my dear,
If you dare, my dear,
To see your future.

Part I

The Pouring of the Wax

(January 1916–February 1917)

1 *St. Basil's Eve*

MIDNIGHT, NEW YEAR'S EVE, three young witches gathered in the city that was once St. Petersburg. Though that silver sound, *Petersburg,* had been erased, and how oddly the new one struck our ears: *Petrograd.* A sound like bronze. Like horseshoes on stone, hammer on anvil, thunder in the name — *Petrograd.* No longer *Petersburg* of the bells and water, that city of mirrors, of transparent twilights, Tchaikovsky ballets, and Pushkin's genius. Its name had been changed by war — *Petersburg* was thought too German, though the name is Dutch.

Petrograd. The sound is bronze, and this is a story of bronze.

That night, the cusp of the New Year, 1916, we three prepared to conjure the future in the nursery of a grand flat on Furshtatskaya Street. From down the hall, the sounds of a large New Year's Eve soiree filtered under the door — scraps of music, women's high laughter, the scent of roasted goose and Christmas pine. Behind us, my younger brother, Seryozha, sketched in the window seat as we girls prepared the basin and the candle.

Below in the street, harness bells announced sleighs

busying themselves transporting guests to parties all along the snow-filled parkway. But in the warm room before the tiled stove, we breathlessly circled the basin we'd placed on the old scarred nursery table, its weathered apron ringed with painted sailor boys, waiting for midnight. I stroked the worn tabletop where I'd learned to make my letters, those shaky *A*s and *Б*s and *B*s, outlined the spot where my brother Volodya gouged his initials into the tabletop. Volodya, now fighting in the snows of Bohemia, an officer of cavalry. And we brand-new women in evening gowns waited to see our fortunes. I close my eyes and breathe in the scent of that long-ago room, beeswax and my mother's perfume, which I'd dabbed on my breasts. I still see Varvara in her ill-fitting black taffeta gown, and Mina in a homemade dress of light-blue velvet, and myself in russet silk with an olive overlay, my hair piled on my head, sculpted that morning by M. Laruelle in the Nevsky Passazh. My artistic brother, with his long poet's locks, sported a Russian blouse and full trousers stuck into soft boots in shocking defiance of wartime custom, which dictates that even noncombatants strive for a military air.

I was a month shy of sixteen, the same age as the century, my brother one year younger. Waiting for midnight, our three heads converged over the basin of water: Varvara's cropped locks, the dusty blue-black of a crow; Mina's, ash blond as Finnish birch, woven into that old-fashioned braided crown she couldn't be persuaded to abandon; and I, with hair the red of young foxes crossing a field of snow. Waiting to see our fortunes. *Kem byt'?* indeed.

A sun, a seal, a wedding ring.
A house, a plow, a prison cell.

It seems like a scene in a glass globe to me now. I want to turn it over and set the snow to swirling. I want to shout to my young self, *Stop!* Don't be in such a hurry to peel back the petals of the future. It will be here soon enough, and it won't be quite the bloom you expect. Just stay there, in that precious moment, at the hinge of time... but I was in love with the Future, in love with the idea of Fate. There's nothing more romantic to the young—until its dogs sink their teeth into your calf and pull you to the ground.

On St. Basil's Eve, we cast the wax in water.
And the country too had poured its wax
In the year of the 9 and the 6.

What sign did I hope to receive that night? The laurel crown, the lyre? Or perhaps some evidence of grand passion—some ardent Pushkin or soulful Blok. Or maybe a boy I already knew—Danya from dancing class, Stiva with whom I'd skated in the park the day before and dazzled with my spins and reckless arabesques. Or perhaps even an officer like the ones who lingered before the gates of our school in the afternoons, courting the senior girls. I see her there, staring impatiently into the candle flame, a girl both brash and shy, awkward and feigning sophistication in hopes of being thought mysterious, so that people would long to discover her secrets. I want her to stay in that moment before the world changed, before the wax was poured, and the future assembled like brilliant horses loading into a starting gate. *Wait!*

My younger self looks up. She senses me there in the room, a vague but troubling presence, I swear she catches a glimpse of me in the window's reflection— the woman from the future, neither young nor old, bathed in grief and compromise, wearing her own two eyes. A shudder passes through her like a draft.

Midnight arrived in a clangor of bells from all the nearby churches, Preobrazhenskaya, St. Panteleimon, the Church of the Spilled Blood, bells echoing throughout the city, escorting in the New Year. Solemnly I handed the candle to Mina, who pushed her spectacles up on her nose and bent her blond head over the basin. Precise as the scientist she was, she dripped the wax onto the water as I prayed for a good omen. The lozenges of wax spun, adhered, linked together into a turning shape, the water trembling, limpid in candlelight. To my grave disappointment, I detected no laurel wreath, no lyre. No couples kissing, no linked wedding rings.

Varvara squinted, cocking her head this way and that. "A boot?"

Seryozha peered over our shoulders. Curiosity had gotten the better of him. He pointed with a long, graphite-dark finger. "It's a ship. Don't you see—the hull, the sails?"

A ship was good—travel, adventure! Maybe I'd become an adventurer and cross the South Seas, like Stevenson...though the German blockade sat firmly between me and the immediate realization of such a heady destiny. Or perhaps it was a metaphor for another kind of journey. Could not love be seen as a journey? Or the route to fame and glory? Try as I might to tease out the meaning, it never would have occurred to me its final dimensions, the scope, the nature of the journey.

Varvara poured for Mina. The wax coalesced—a cloud, a sleigh? We concurred—a key! She beamed. Surely she would unlock the secrets of the world, the next Mendeleev or Madame Curie. No one considered that a key might lock as well as unlock.

And Varvara? The swirling dollops resolved themselves into—a broom. We shouted with laughter. Our radical, feminist, reader of Kollontai, of Marx and Engels, Rousseau and Robespierre—a housewife! "Maybe it's a torch," she said sulkily.

"Maybe it's your new form of transport," Seryozha quipped, settling himself back into the window seat.

She sieved the little wax droplets from the water and crushed them together, threw the lump in the trash, wiped her wet hands on a towel. "I'm not playing this stupid game anymore."

Seryozha refused his turn, pretending it was a silly girl's pastime, though I knew he was more superstitious than anyone. And behind us, in the red corner, the icon of the Virgin of Tikhvin gazed down, her expression the saddest, the most tender I had ever seen. She knew it all already. The ship, the key, the broom.

With no more future to explore, and Varvara sulky with her news, we abandoned the peace and timelessness of the nursery to rejoin the current era out celebrating in the salon. No one had noticed our absence but Mother, who glared briefly but sharply in our direction, irritated that we'd missed the New Year's toasts. Vera Borisovna Makarova wore a Fortuny gown with Grecian pleats and a jeweled collar, a Petersburg beauty with her prematurely silver hair and pale blue eyes. Mother took her social responsibilities seriously, orchestrating her parties like a dancing master, quick to spot a group flagging, a woman standing uncomfortably alone, men speaking too long among themselves. Our New Year's Eve party famously brought together my father's jurists and journalists, diplomats and liberal industrialists with Mother's painters and poets, mystics and stylish mavens—in short, the cream of the Petrograd intelligentsia. Did this impress me? The British consul flirting with the wife of the editor of the *Petrogradsky Echo*? The decadent poet Zinaida Gippius in harem pants taking another glass of champagne from

Basya's tray? It was our life. I didn't realize how fragile such seemingly solid things could be, how soon they could vanish.

In the dining room, we picked at the remains of the feast laid out on yards of white damask—roast goose with lingonberries, salad Olivier, smoked salmon and sturgeon and sea bass, the mushrooms we'd picked that autumn. Blini with sour cream and caviar. No *boeuf* Wellington as in past years, *boeuf* having disappeared with the war. But Vaula's Napolcons glistened, and the Christmas tree exuded its resin, which blended with the smell of Father's cherry tobacco, imported all the way from London by friends in the British consulate. Yes, there he was, in the vestibule, lounging in his tailcoat, his shirt a brilliant white. Handsome, clever Father. I could tell he had just said something witty by the way his dimples peeked out from his neat reddish-brown beard. And beside him on the table lay his gift to me in honor of my upcoming birthday—my first book of verse. I'd been obsessively arranging and rearranging the small volumes all day around a giant bouquet of white lilacs. I admired the aqua cover embossed in gold: *This Transparent Twilight*, by Marina Dmitrievna Makarova. It would be a parting gift for each guest. The poet Konstantin Balmont, a friend of my mother's, had even reviewed it in the *Echo*, calling it "charming, promising great things to come." I'd had more sensuous, grown-up poems I'd wanted to include, but Father had vetoed them. "What do you know about passion, you silly duck?"

Still, I agonized when anyone picked up a volume and paged through it. What would they think? Would they understand, or treat it as a joke? By tomorrow, people would be reading it, and around the dinner tables, they'd be saying, *That Makarov girl, she really has something*. Or *That Makarov girl, what an embarrassment. Well, at least her father loves her.* I tried to remember the ship, the South Seas, and told myself—who cared what a bunch of my parents' friends thought? Varvara took glasses of champagne off Basya's tray and handed them to us, "To Marina's book and all the tomorrows." She drank hers down as if it were *kvas* and put it back on the tray. Our maid scowled, already unhappy in the evening uniform she loathed, especially the little ruffled cap. She'd been on her feet since seven that morning.

The champagne added to my excitement. My father cast me an affectionate glance, and a sharp one of disapproval for my brother. He'd so wanted Seryozha in school uniform, hair shorn, looking like a *seryozny chelovek*—a serious person—but Mother had defended him, her favorite. "One night. What harm could there be in letting him dress as he likes?"

In the big salon, couples whirled and jewels flashed, though not so garishly as in the years before the war. In the far corner, the small orchestra sweated through a mazurka, and people who shouldn't have, danced. A red-faced man lowered himself into a chair. My head swam in the heady mix of perfume, sweat, and tobacco.

And now, a slightly fetid sweetness like rotting flowers announced the approach of Vsevolod Nikolaevich, our mother's spiritual master, pale and boneless as a large mushroom. He took my hand in his powdery soft one. "Marina Dmitrievna, my congratulations on your book. We're all so very proud." He kissed it formally—the lips stopping just short of the flesh. He dismissed my friends at a glance—Varvara in her purple-black, Mina in homemade blue—as people of no consequence, and zeroed in on my brother. "Sergei Dmitrievich. So good to see you again." He proffered his flabby hand, but my brother anticipated the gesture and hid his own behind his back, nodding instead. Unflappable, Vsevolod smiled, but took the hint and retreated.

Once the mystic was out of sight, Seryozha extended his hand floppily, making his mouth soft and drooly. "Wishing you all the best!" he snuffled, then took his own hand and kissed it noisily. It took many minutes for us to catch our breaths as he went through his Master Vsevolod routine, ending by reaching into a bouquet, plucking a lilac, and munching it.

I swayed hopefully to the music, my head bubbling like the champagne—French champagne, too, its presence in wartime negotiated months in advance—and watched the sea of dancers launch into a foxtrot. I was an excellent dancer, and hated to wait out a single number. Having removed her glasses, Mina squinted at what must have been a blur of motion and color while

Varvara examined the Turkish pants and turbans of the more fashionable women with a smirk both ironic and envious. One of the British aides had just smiled at me over his partner's shoulder, when a vision beyond anything I could have wished for up in the nursery swam into view: a trim, moustached officer with uptilted blue eyes, his chestnut hair cropped close, lips made for smiling. Heat flashed through me as if I'd just downed a tumbler of vodka. Kolya Shurov was back from the front.

Was he the most handsome man in the room? Not at all. Half these men were better looking than he was. And yet, women were already smiling at him, adjusting their clothing, as if it were suddenly too tight or insecurely fastened.

Kolya was coming this way. Mother was leading him to us!

"Enfants, regardez qui en est venu!" she said, glowing with pleasure. She always loved him—well, who didn't? *Look who's here!* "Just in time for New Year's."

He leaned in and kissed my cheeks formally, three times—for Father, Son, and Holy Ghost—and I caught a whiff of his cologne, Floris Limes, and the cigar he'd been smoking. He held me out at arm's length to examine me, beaming as if I were a creature of his own invention. The blood tingled in my cheeks under his scrutiny, the warmth of his hands through the thin sleeves of my dress. My face flushed. I could hardly think for the pounding in my chest. "Look how elegant you've become, Marina Dmitrievna. Where's the skinny girl disappearing around corners, braids flying out behind her?"

"She disappeared. Around a corner," I said, an attempt at wit. I wanted him to know that things had changed since he'd last seen me. I was a woman now—a person of substance and accomplishment. He couldn't treat me like that girl he used to whirl around by an arm and a leg. "It's been a while, Kolya."

"How I've missed beautiful women." He sighed and smiled at Mina—she was blushing like a peony. My God, he would flirt with a post!

Now he embraced my brother, clapping him on the back, ruffling his hair. "And how is our young Repin? Nice shirt, by the way." That shirt, which Seryozha had sewed himself and which my father had mocked. Kolya took him by the shoulder, turned him this way and that, examining the needlework. "I should have some made up just like it." Who didn't love Kolya? None of Volodya's other friends ever paid us the least attention, but Kolya wanted everyone to be happy. No one escaped the wide embrace of his nature. "Are you still waiting for me, Marina?" he said into my ear. "I'm going to come and carry you off. I told you I would." When I was a scabby-kneed six-year-old and he a worldly man of twelve.

Was this the ship, then, the wax sails? Kolya Shurov? Blood roared in my ears. The intensity of my desire frightened me, I wanted to put words between us, like spikes, to keep myself from falling into him like a girl without bones. "You're too old for me, Kolya," I said. "What do I need a *starik* for?" But that was wrong, too, horrible. Oh God, how to be! I imagined myself a woman, but at times like this, I could not find my own outlines. For all my hours of mirror gazing, and the poems addressing my vast coterie of nonexistent lovers, I was a mystery to myself.

"Not so old anymore," he said. "When the war's over, six years' difference will be—nothing." He chucked me under the chin, as if I were ten.

"Kolya brought a letter from Volodya, children," Mother said. Shame surged up where peevishness had been. How could I have forgotten to ask about my brother? What a self-centered wretch I could be. She produced an envelope and removed the contents, a sheet of long narrow stationery covered with my elder brother's strong handwriting. We crowded around her as she read. *"Dearest Mama and Papa, Marina, Seryozha, I hope this reaches you by Christmas, and that everyone's well. I miss you profoundly. Feed my messenger and don't let him drink too much. He has to come back sometime."*

Kolya lifted his glass of champagne.

"I have to admit, the war doesn't go well. Heavy battles daily. I pray all this will come to an end soon."

I could well imagine the cold, the wounded and the dead, the scream of the horses and the creak of wagons under the guns. This party now seemed a mockery, the whirling people dancing while my brother huddled in some miserable tent with his greatcoat wrapped about him.

"*But Swallow*"—his horse—"*is doing well. He's found a girlfriend, my adjutant's mare. It's funny to see how they look for each other in the morning.*"

My mother wiped her eyes on her handkerchief, and gave a small laugh. "At least the horse is happy."

"*Brusilov*"—the general of the Southwestern Army—"*keeps our hopes alive. I admire him more than any man alive. The men are tough and true. With the help of God, we must prevail. Thinking of you all makes me feel better. Say hi to Avdokia for me. Tell her the socks are holding up. I kiss you all, Volodya.*"

Mother sighed and folded the letter back into its envelope. "I don't know how he can bear it. I really don't."

"His men would follow him off a cliff," Kolya said. "You should be proud of him."

She leaned on his shoulder. "You've always been such a comfort." Then she spotted something—a quarrel brewing—that set her hostess antennae quivering, and she excused herself to attend to her guests.

Meanwhile, Kolya approached the table of books, picked one up and riffled through the pages, stuck his nose in and sniffed the verse. "Genius," he announced. "I can smell it."

"What does genius smell like?" Mina asked.

"Lilacs." He sniffed. "And firecrackers." He unbut-

toned the chest button of his tunic and slipped the little
book inside, pressed it over his heart, looking to see if
I'd noticed. How could I not have? "I'll read this on the
train, and think of you."

Yes, yes, think of me! But what did he mean, on the
train? Was he leaving so soon? "Maybe you can just
sleep on it, save you the trouble of reading."

"That's the best way to learn anything. It's how I got
through school." He grinned. "So organic. Excuse us,
ladies." He took my arm. "I need to talk to our poet."
He led me away, leaving Mina yearning toward him
like a sunflower, blinking without her glasses, and Varvara regarding him uneasily as if he were an unsteady
horse I'd seen fit to ride. Where were we going?

He pulled me after him into the cloakroom and
closed the door behind us. It was warm and close and
full of the guests' coats and furs smelling of snow. The
transom let in only a filtered light. I could feel his
breath in my ear as I stood pressed against someone's
sable, leaned back into the softness. Everything about
me had gone both soft and prickly as if I had a rash. I
felt like a fruit about to be bitten. I wanted to call out
like a child, *Kolya is going to kiss me!* For once, no one
was watching. No Father, no Mother, no governess or
nanny, not even the maid or the cook.

I breathed in his strange scent. When I was a child,
I actually stole one of his shirts and kept it on the floor
of my closet behind my skates, to smell it when no one
was looking, a smell like honey. How many years had

I waited for this moment, imagining it? Since the day Volodya brought him home, a lively, chubby boy who became our Pied Piper. You could say it went back further, maybe I'd been a greedy, lustful little zygote. But the moment had been prepared like dry straw in a hayloft, waiting for a spark. And when our mouths met, I knew exactly why we had never kissed before. If his mouth, his tongue, were the only food left on the planet it would be enough. I would have let him do anything, right there in my parents' house, standing among the furs. I had always considered Kolya out of reach, but impossibly, unbelievably, here he was in my arms, his face, his breath. His arms around my waist, my mother's Après l'Ondée rising from my breasts, mingling with the honey of his body.

"Are you going to wait for me, Marina?"

"Don't make me wait too long," I whispered. "I'm not good at it."

"I'll hurry then." He was unbuttoning his tunic. Were we going to make love right here among the coats? But he removed something from inside his uniform, a velvet pouch, which he pressed into my hand, still warm from his body.

"What else do you have in there?" I joked, hooking my finger to the open cloth, pretending to peep in. "Tolstoy?"

"Only Chekhov," he said. "He's smaller."

The cloth of the little sack was soft when I rubbed it against my face, my swollen lips. "What is it?"

"Open it."

I tried to work the cord, but my hands weren't quite attached to my wrists. Inside, there was something hard — a large circle. I held it to the light. A bangle, white or some pale color, enameled, with arabesques of gold and black. "To remember me by." He rubbed his lime-scented cheek against mine. "Don't forget me, Marina."

As if I ever could. Even dead I would remember him. I held up my forearm to admire the gift. How perfect it looked around my pale wrist. I could wear it without attracting too much attention — clever Kolya. A ring or a valuable jewel might have elicited parental scrutiny. Was this my arm? The arm of a woman who had received love gifts? I felt the way a goddess must feel when worshippers deposit sheep and bags of grain at her feet.

We fell into another kiss — his mouth, his honey, the length of him pressed to me, the furs around us — when the cloakroom door swung open, the light illuminating us. It couldn't have been that bright, but it felt like a policeman's searchlight. "What the devil?" I only had time to catch one glimpse of Dr. Voinovich's surprised face — my father's colleague at the university — as Kolya and I lunged past him, pretending we had not just been all but making love among the guests' coats. I avoided my friends' questioning faces. I didn't want to share this, see myself in their eyes, I wanted this moment just for myself.

In the salon, the orchestra had launched into a tango. I had never danced the tango outside of dancing class, but I could have followed Kolya through a Tibetan minuet. We found a place amid the couples and away from the hall, where I expected Father to appear any second for a cross-examination. Kolya held my right hand in his left, the other decorously pressed to the small of my back — yet I knew the decorousness was only a ruse. I could feel him appraising the curve of my spine, the flare of my hips, knowing how his touch filled me with heat.

We began to move together. The tango was suddenly no longer a series of awkward turns and memorized motions from dancing class, one's dress becoming damp from a partner's nervous palms, but a love affair, proud and challenging, a drama. How perfect for us. He wasn't a showy dancer, but easy and sure on his feet. Although I knew some of the dips and fast turns, I saw that they were unnecessary — that *this*, the silent conversation, the question and answer between man and woman, was the real dance. Although I had never danced with him before, I could feel his every intention, the tiniest signals. What must it be to make love with him — the firestorm of passion we'd engender. I prayed the orchestra would never stop, but too soon Mother descended to take Kolya away to meet some of her people, consigning me to my friends, who suddenly seemed so very young. My ship had already slipped its moorings, the sails rising to the wind.

2 *The Stray Dog Café*

FROM THE WINDOW OF my salmon-pink bedroom, I watched the snow whirl and worked on an aubade to that cloakroom kiss—the fur, his scent. *What do you know about passion, you silly duck?* I kissed the bracelet on my arm. How would it have been if we had shed our clothes in the cloakroom, and made love among the furs? I unspooled scenarios in my mind: Kolya and I in years to come, separated by some circumstance—tragic—then him catching sight of me across a room, like Tatiana with Onegin. How he would remember that moment in that long-ago cloakroom, how he would yearn. I wept just imagining it.

I thought of Kolya reading my poems on the train today, on the way back to his unit, seated among the other soldiers. Would he recognize himself in the figure of the ringmaster with his shiny moustache and his gleaming buttons? That poem was a love letter. I knew there was danger in showing too much of my passion—it frightened people, like it had the boys I'd kissed in stairways and at children's parties. I shrugged the shawl from my shoulders—it was so hot in here—opened the *fortochka* window, and paced, stopping for the hundredth time to look at myself in the vanity mirror: my red hair, the round dark eyes of a *Commedia* Columbine, the freckles and blush in my cheeks. My fat lips, still impressed with his kisses. *"Lyubimiy,"* I whispered. *Beloved.* I could smell him in my hair. I wondered if he could smell me, too—I wished I had a scent of my own and not Mother's, but it was a little late for that. I could only find peace by imagining myself a few years hence, looking back at all this as if it was already done. I sat back down at my desk and wrote:

> *You talk to the night.*
> *I was her first, you say.*

Someday it would be me who'd be quoted in girls' diaries. Lovers would recite my verses in the depths of the night. I would be *Makarova* by then, the way people said *Akhmatova* or *Tsvetaeva.*

> *And you'll say*
> *You knew me once*
> *When my dress was made of autumn leaves*
> *And my hair a smoldering fire*
> *As you smoke your cigar*
> *Sip whisky with its peaty smoke.*
> *Memory fades, but never that.*
> *A kiss among furs,*
> *Another kind of fire.*

Akhmatova would do it with a gesture. *And I put my left glove onto my right hand...* Above my head, her profile hung in a frame between the windows. Seryozha had cut it for me from black paper. My muse, my light-house, with her Roman nose and bundle of long hair done up the way I wore my own. I imagined her at Wolf's bookshop—maybe even today!—picking up my book of poems. Would she remember the girl she'd met one night at the Stray Dog Café? Under the glass of my desk, I kept the calling card she'd signed—the fine clear hand, the letters unconnected, the writing running uphill: *To Marina—Bravery, in love as in art. A.* I touched that *A* with my fingertips. Was I brave enough?

That Stray Dog world had already ended. I'd squeaked through the doors just as they were closing and managed to get down that famous staircase behind the Hotel Europa. How many afternoons I'd spent in the square, sitting on a bench under the statue of Pushkin, my sights on that subterranean entrance, hop-ing to catch a glimpse of her graceful figure, tall, stately, dark-haired, wearing a black shawl and her fa-mous black beads. But I never saw anyone come in or out except men carrying crates on their shoulders. THE STRAY DOG ARTISTIC CABARET was a place of late night carousal, where the gods drank and smoked and re-cited, where they fell in love.

Mina and Varvara often kept me company in my vigil, attempting to appear blasé and sophisticated while eating nonpareils from paper cones. Varvara smoked her cigarette boldly in the open air, daring passersby to comment, meeting their disapproving eyes. Then came the autumn afternoon she'd had enough of my torment. She crushed her cigarette into the stone and said, "Why don't we just go there sometime? This mooning around's getting on my nerves."

"They'd never let us in," I said, but my heart already thumped with the possibility. Could we? They'd throw us out, but just for a moment, even an instant, to enter the holy of holies? It was like a door that I'd always believed to be firmly secured—and now she was questioning if it was even locked at all. "When would we go?"

"Tonight," she said.

"We can't," Mina said, dropping a candy onto the pavement. "We have two tests tomorrow."

But tests and grades were the furthest thing from my mind, which flew this way and that like a bird caught in a gallery, searching for an exit. Mother and Father were attending a party with the British second secretary and his wife... it would only be a matter of getting around Miss Haddon-Finch, our governess. Our nanny, Avdokia, wouldn't tell. She enjoyed our small rebellions, sometimes even collaborated when she felt Father was being harsh. The Russian peasant is, at bottom, an anarchist.

First I had to set my trap. On the way home, I stopped at Wolf's bookshop and bought Miss Haddon-Finch a special gift: *Penrod,* by Booth Tarkington, the latest arrival from England, having miraculously made it through the blockade. Not cheap, but it would be well worth it.

"Why, thank you, Marina, dear. What a thoughtful gesture," she said that evening, stroking the cover of the book.

Seryozha was onto me instantly. He pounced the moment she left the nursery, forcing me to tell him what I was up to. I explained why I couldn't take him—at fourteen, slender and small-boned, he was often mistaken for twelve—but he threatened to tell Father if I left him behind. He didn't care about poetry, but the interior of the Stray Dog had been painted by Sudeikin, who'd designed sets for Diaghilev. Seryozha had to see it. "If I don't go, you don't go," he said, and I could not persuade or bribe him.

That evening, with Mother and Father off with the British and Miss Haddon-Finch in bed with her book, we dressed in our most grown-up clothes and made our way to Mikhailovskaya Square. The night tasted of the coming frost, and the trees were already bare. Varvara stepped out of the shadows, and with her, Mina, who'd come despite her misgivings. She hated to be accused of being a grade-grubber and a baby. I held the finial of the stair rail, rubbing it with my palm as if I could receive an impression from it of all those who had touched it before me. At the bottom of the stone stairs, the black door called to me. It was one thing to dream, another to actually barge in upon one's gods at play.

I took a step down, and another. A line occurred to me: *In Petrograd, you go down into heaven.* I took it as a sign, inspiration already arriving. How long did it take to traverse those dozen or so steps? The worn egg-shaped doorknob fitted itself to my hand. I trembled as I pushed it open.

No absinthe-reeking netherworld awaited us, no flocked walls or tufted sofas, no hookahs. Instead, we found ourselves in a smoky cellar, walls and ceilings covered with Sudeikin's folk-style birds. People drank perched on straw stools at small tables, or along the banquettes that lined the walls. Smoke hung thick as fog, and on a bare stage a lithe dancer performed an angular modern choreography on top of a large mirror. "Karsavina," my brother whispered excitedly. The great ballerina, on whom Fokine had launched so many of the Diaghilev ballets. We'd seen her at the Mariinsky Theater that season in *Swan Lake*, and here she was dancing on a mirror, one dark-haired Karsavina above and an upside-down one below, as if floating in midair.

We huddled in the entryway, trying to take in as much of the scene as we could before the portly owner, busy with the two gentlemen in front of us, could notice the presence of a quartet of underage spies and toss us out. Luckily, there was a disagreement over the admission price. "Hey," the first man said, "you didn't charge the people who came in just before us."

"Yes, but they're artists," said the proprietor. "You're pharmacists. Twenty-five rubles."

I prayed they would argue until dawn. Those brilliant legs in their tights, multiplied by the mirror, formed a flashing kaleidoscope—she was close enough for us to see her little earrings, the pearls dangling. Although the pianist played a complex composition, to my ears cacophonous, she was able to find the line of it, while the audience members talked and watched and drank and cheered and stamped their feet.

Now came our turn to pass the Cerberus of the place, who scanned us with a jaundiced eye. "What have we here? Aren't you a little young, kiddies?"

"This is Marina Makarova, the poet." Varvara shoved me forward. "She just had a poem in the *Echo*." It was true, though it was in the Children's Corner.

He rubbed his moustache, tugged at his beard. "Give us a poem then."

Which poem would open the cave of wonders?

I recited my "Waiting with Pushkin in Mikhailovskaya Square":

A pigeon picks and pecks
In the poet's brazen palm.
He weighs it like a merchant.
Which is heavier, my brother?
Your sweet immortal song or the
Living bird that nests upon your hand?

"All right," said the proprietor. "No drinking. You, sign the book."

He motioned me toward the Stray Dog register. I eagerly scanned the pages, the names, the names! *Blok*. *Mandelstam*. *Tsvetaeva*. Accompanied by scraps of poetry, little drawings. I signed, and my brother sketched a fast likeness of me underneath, impressing our host despite himself. A harried waiter with a moustache set us up at a tiny table squeezed into a corner by a coatrack.

"Absinthe all around," Varvara ordered with an imperious sweep of her hand. Knowing I would be forced to pay, if push came to shove, I was grateful when the waiter replied, *"Kvas,"* that slightly alcoholic brew. But we never did get a bill. We were Artists, even at that age. Superior to the gawkers and tourists.

Seryozha already had his sketchbook open on the table and was furiously drawing, trying to capture everything all at once: patrons, waiters, Karsavina. I did the same in my own way—memorizing, trying to stuff my eyes like a suitcase. Meanwhile, Varvara, unimpressed but pleased with herself, rolled a cigarette and lit it, posing, as Mina waved the smoke away. Sprawled with some other odd characters on stools sat the great Mayakovsky. The futurist poet was unmistakable—enormous, broad-shouldered, ferocious, towering over his friends even while sitting down. But where was his famed yellow blouse? He had dressed simply tonight, disappointingly conventional in a plain jacket, shirt, and tie. My brother was seized with admiration. Turning the page, he rendered the man's brooding form, his dark brow and heavy jaw, his massive back and profile.

And then I saw her. *Anna Andreevna Akhmatova*—all those marvelous *A*s. Like sighs. Her shawl, her profile, the glossy black hair, her fingers gracefully looped into her beads. She sat with the poet Kuzmin, whom I recognized by his sleepy eyes, his thinning hair. On her other side lounged a beauty with golden curls who looked like an actress. She whispered something into Akhmatova's ear, making her laugh. I was shocked—I hadn't imagined the Tragic Muse could laugh. She was actually quite lively. I couldn't stop staring, while my brother's pencil flew and Mina fidgeted nervously. "We still have those exams, they're not disappearing." Varvara pretended she came here every day of the week, sipping her *kvas*, exhaling smoke.

Now Seryozha was sketching a hulking boy with tawny longish hair who sat by himself in another corner—shapeless jacket, scarf around his neck—watching like a great hungry bear. I'd never seen him before, but recognized one like myself. I knew that hunger. His eyes were only for Vladimir Mayakovsky. His hand went into his pocket every thirty seconds or so, pulled out some pages, put them back in again. *Poet.*

After Karsavina, the great futurist loped up to the small, curtainless stage. It took him about four steps. I'd read his manifesto: *Through us the horn of time blows in the art of the world. The past is too narrow. The Academy and Pushkin are less intelligible than hieroglyphics.*

Throw Pushkin, Dostoyevsky, Tolstoy etc. overboard from the Ship of Modernity. What an egotist! Throw Pushkin overboard? Pushkin loved freedom more than anybody. Mayakovsky confused me, upset me. I, too, believed in the Future, but this kind of sweeping dismissal frightened me. Secretly it made me feel like I, too, would be thrown from the ship someday. Yet if he thought so, why did he come here? The place was filled with the very artists his futurist manifesto had so viciously attacked. Yet none of them seemed to give it a second thought. That night I realized that poetry was a brotherhood—that you could be furious at your brother and yet enjoy his company more than the company of most.

But Mayakovsky didn't read polemical work that night. Rather, he recited a long, complex love poem. Now I learned how vulnerable a man could be, even a terrifying man like that, protesting that he was only *a cloud in trousers,* proclaiming that love could turn his maddened flesh to sweetness. I tried to imagine being the recipient of such a passion. Would it frighten me?

"Look—it's Vera Kholodnaya," Mina whispered. Suddenly her fretting about the exams and her parents was forgotten as she watched the star of our silent *kinofilm* taking a seat near the stage. The most famous woman in Russia after the empress herself. The actress watched the poet, enraptured, and I saw that unconsciously, Mina sat up straighter, held her head more gracefully.

Next, an improvised play unfolded, the actors making fun of the gentlemen who'd paid their good money to see Karsavina and the immortal poets bestow their gifts—the so-called *pharmacists*. Two of them came to the stage to play soldiers in foxholes, and everyone laughed, including the men themselves. No hard feelings.

After the skit, *she* took the stage, her shawl wrapped about her, her long white hands, the grave white face. The voice that emerged from her lips was like that of a cello, a medium, and sent shivers through the audience. I had hoped she would recite her poem about this very place—"We Are All Carousers and Harlots"—but instead she recited poems about the war in a voice like time itself:

> *Give me bitter years of fever,*
> *Choking, sleepless suffering,*
> *Take away my child, my lover,*
> *My mysterious gift of song—*
> *Thus I pray after Thy Service,*
> *After many anguished days,*
> *So that clouds which darken Russia*
> *May be lit by glorious rays.*

Such bravery—to offer Fate such a sacrifice. To give anything, even her lover, even her gift. I would never have had the nerve to tempt the gods that way. I was too greedy. My sticky-handed heart wanted everything—

lovers, lyres, and laurel wreaths. Why did she have to show me the impossible heights? Her words tore my soul to shreds. The whole assembly, even Mayakovsky, thundered their applause as she returned to her seat, flinging appreciative shouts like garlands. Then she turned back into her other self, laughing and relaxed, as if she hadn't just dared heaven to destroy her.

Gathering myself while I still had the courage, I wove my way to her table and stood before her. No sound would come from my mouth. Her eyes were very blue—blue and full of light. I'd thought they were brown. I managed to say, "These are for you," and thrust out a fistful of carefully copied-out poems.

She considered me and my outstretched offering, her arm resting across the banquette behind her friend. Her eyes were mischievous and gay. "Recite one for me."

Right here in front of Kuzmin? She was waiting—I couldn't refuse her. Should I pick one that was most technically correct? Or the one I'd written about her? My voice hoarse, my lips dry, I began:

O blessed bird of prey
With curved beak and eye of jet
Who sees each tiny creature dart
Sweeps him up, his sweetness pulsing . . .

Her pretty friend applauded when I was done, and Kuzmin lit a cigarette and squinted against the smoke. But *she*, the poet, the eagle, simply nodded and extended a hand for the pages. *"Marina Makarova,"* she read from the page. "Are you in love, my dear?"

I nodded. *How did she know?*

"Is it going well?"

I laughed. What could I say? "He barely knows I'm alive." She took a card from the table, the card of the Stray Dog Café, and signed it: *To Marina — Bravery, in love as in art. A.*

Now, in the salmon-pink bedroom, I began again the poem of the kiss, the furs, the fire, the snow.

3 *The Coming of Varvara*

VARVARA — FOREVER PUSHING ME ahead, opening doors I was afraid to pass through, even though behind them were things I desperately wanted. I try to remember how it was before she came, when it had been just Mina and myself. My life had been sweet and dull, a normal bourgeois Petersburg girlhood: studying, going to the *kinotheater* on Nevsky Prospect — at first accompanied by my governess but later with my brothers, with Mina. We watched detective films, westerns, romances, Kholodnaya in *Children of the Century* and *Her Sister's Rival*. With her clear eyes and round face, Mina would grow to resemble her, though not back then, when she was still a chubby, bespectacled mama's girl. Away from school, she and I spent most of our time together, but at the Tagantsev Academy, we kept to our own groups. I drifted restlessly between cliques—the literary set, those melancholic Ophelias, and the drama girls, livelier and more flamboyant but also histrionic and full of vicious gossip. Rather than follow me into such exhausting company, Mina retreated with one or two other misfits to study for the next exam and secretly eye the popular girls with an air of wounded longing.

Then Varvara came, the volatile reagent that forged of us a third element. We'd heard she'd spent the fall at the Catherine Institute, a school for the daughters of the aristocracy, but had been asked to leave after a month or two. Before that, they said, she'd been living in Germany, a residence already exotic and questionable, but had to return home because of the war. At the academy, Varvara quickly polarized girls into advocates and detractors—mostly the latter. But how brilliant she made us feel, how advanced. She galvanized us. I abandoned my theatrical crowd, and Mina her drones, and we began to spend all our time in one another's company. While I had been reading *Idylls of the King*, Colette, and Dostoyevsky—and Mina her eternal Dumas—Varvara was already tearing through Hegel, Engels and Marx, Kropotkin, Gorky, and Chernyshevsky's *What Is to Be Done?*

I remember the first time I brought her home for tea, secretly hoping she'd say something shocking, so I could be a rebel-by-proxy—but she'd been irritatingly polite, her dark eyes glittering at the sight of the sandwiches. She'd praised the light streaming through the tall windows, the excellence of the cooking, the warmth and tidiness of the flat. But eventually she grew more talkative, telling Mother about her aunt in Germany, with whom she had been living when war broke out and the Russians were called home. "Really, it's a shame we're at war. We've got so much more in common with Germany than with England." She had no idea that we had Volodya serving under arms or that Father was a sworn Anglophile.

"Weak or strong?" Mother asked, so picturesque in her blue silk blouse, pouring tea from the silver samovar.

"Strong," Varvara said.

Mother asked casually, "And where does your family live, Varvara? Are you near here?"

In Petrograd you never had to ask, *What does your father do? How much do you live on a year? What are your prospects in life?* You only had to ask, *So where does your family live?* My mother was a master of strategy, a Suvorov of manners.

"On Vasilievsky Island," Varvara said, accepting her tea, which was served in a cup and saucer, English style, rather than in glasses. She dropped two cubes of sugar into it. Three. Four. My mother's good breeding wouldn't let her stare. But Seryozha kicked me under the table, rounded his eyes.

"Is your father at the university?" Vasilievsky Island could be elegant near the Neva, especially in the vicinity of the Twelve Colleges of the university, which looked across the river toward St. Isaac's Cathedral and the Winter Palace. But away from the river it became more working class, slummier as you moved north and west, toward the factories and shipyards. Mother's mind was a social card catalogue, narrowing, calculating. *Vasilievsky Island. Four sugars! Bobbed hair. Terrible shoes. Widely traveled, lived in Germany, well spoken. Such horrible opinions! Professor's daughter?* I could hear the cards clicking. "Does he teach?"

"*Il est mort.*" She dropped the words onto the cutwork tablecloth like dropping a rat there, then reached for another sandwich. "Measles. We got it, too, but we recovered."

"*Ah, kak zhal',* " Mother said. *What a pity.*

Afterward, we retired to my bedroom. Varvara immediately fished a sandwich out of her pocket and wolfed it down. "Where do they get all the food?" she asked. "You have contacts in the country?"

I'd never thought about it. "Maryino..." Our estate near Tikhvin. "But it's mostly timber. I don't know...Vaula goes to the shops."

"There's nothing in the shops," Varvara said, trying my bed, bouncing on it. "We haven't seen butter in months. It's fifteen rubles a pound if you can get it. We're eating horsemeat, not minced pork and salmon. Come out of your dream world."

I flushed. At fourteen, I never really considered where our food came from, not until that very instant.

I was not a callous girl. I knew there were poor people, sad people—I wasn't blind. But the mechanics of our own family, how we tied into the general suffering, wasn't anything I thought about.

"Women work twelve hours a day in this city. Just a few blocks from here." Now Varvara was prowling around my room. She opened my wardrobe and began examining my dresses as if she were thinking of buying something. "Old ladies, pregnant women. On their feet. Breathing lint, breathing mercury all day in the tanneries. You really don't know, do you?" She pulled out a frock, deep green velvet with a large collar of Belgian lace, and held it up to herself in the glass. "Then they stand in the queues." She must not have liked the effect, for she wrinkled her nose and shoved the dress roughly back into the wardrobe. "And when the shops run out, they're out. Except for people with the *kapusta*." Cabbage. Money. "For people like you, things appear by magic from under the counter, from a back room. I've seen it. It's disgusting."

I could feel tears welling up. Why was she attacking me? She turned her attention to my bookcase, pulled out a small volume—Coleridge. When she saw it was verse, and English to boot, she stuck it back on the shelf. "The police hold the lines back for you people," she continued.

"Don't say *you people*."

"They take one look at your cook and let her go right in ahead of everyone."

I tried to make a joke of it. "Maybe next time, we'll dine *chez vous*. I've never had horsemeat."

She plopped my white fur hat onto her unbrushed hair. "I'll make sure you receive an invitation."

I took her up on it, in that first bitter winter of the war. I knew I was a sheltered girl, spoiled even, but she shamed me for it. For instance, I'd been to England, and Baden-Baden and Venice, but not to the poor districts of my own city—say, the Lines of Vasilievsky Island. But Varvara did it every day, and though Miss Haddon-Finch made me promise not to take the streetcar with all the soldiers, the militarization of the city being what it was, I would be damned if I would insist on a cab and be ridiculed by Varvara again.

We got on the streetcar at Nevsky— it was already filled to capacity with soldiers, and more kept jumping on—and I noticed to my astonishment that not a single one paid the fare. The conductor didn't demand payment, either. If these officials of the tram system were afraid, who would keep order if something happened? I clung tightly to my book bag, as Varvara had instructed, and tried to see out the windows, which were completely steamed over. It was impossible in any case, we were crammed in so tight. Snow had been falling all day, obscuring the city like a veil.

The tram groaned and squealed across the Neva, and Varvara pushed and shoved our way off near the university. My relief at being free of the rough hands patting me down faded as we began to work our way west past the wide streets called lines, once intended as canals but never dug. They formed long ugly blocks perpendicular to the Neva, and grew worse as we walked away from the university toward the docks in the four o'clock twilight. Men followed us, shoving one another. Some called out, "Hey, sweetie! Hey, darling!" *"Krasavitsa moya!"* *My beauty.* "Hey, Red, here I am. Give us a kiss!" Frankly terrified, I tried to swing along at the same pace as my long-legged friend, telling myself that Varvara encountered this every day. No wonder she exuded confidence. Nothing else would seem intimidating by comparison.

We passed a long red apartment house, where dirty children played in the wet snow and women loitered in the doorways, their drawn faces watching us pass in our school uniforms. "That's a brothel," Varvara said.

Prostitutki. I thought of Sonya Marmeladov in *Crime and Punishment.* The women called out to workmen and university students from their doorways as snow fell on bits of their ragged finery—a worn astrakhan coat, a hat with a drooping feather. A ragged child watched us as if we were queens, wiping his nose on his sleeve.

"This way," Varvara drawled. "That is, unless you want to meet them. They're stupid as chickens."

She led me through a dirty courtyard and into a back building, up some dark, sour stairs, then down a hallway to a battered door. She used her key. *"Avanti."*

She gestured, and I found myself in a dreary room taller than it was wide, dense with old furniture and decorated with pictures in ornate frames—gloomy oil paintings, several lithographs of Volga landscapes.

The place smelled of mold. Two dusty windows facing the yard provided a bit of illumination. In the red corner, an icon of St. Nikolas the Wonderworker hung behind a smoky blue icon lamp. And a portrait of our emperor, Nikolas II of All the Russias. I could hardly believe what I was seeing. The emperor presided over Varvara's home. We had a few icons, but never that.

"I know," she said, following my astonished gaze. "I can't believe it myself."

A woman in rusty black silk sat in a chair so quietly that at first I didn't see her. She gazed out the window, a book in her lap. That it was Varvara's mother was obvious—she bore exactly my friend's features—the high bridged nose, the sharp cheekbones, the black eyes—but with all the life drained out of them. Her mother didn't turn her head, or acknowledge us in any way. I wondered if she really was a countess—hard to know given Varvara's sense of humor. A maid came in, wearing a dirty gray apron and carrying a battered samovar. She had one white eye. We sat at a small table and allowed this pitiful creature to serve us tea weak enough to be mistaken for dishwater in etched tea glasses delicate as frost on a windowpane. She rolled as she walked, like a sailor. Varvara passed me a small sugar pot filled with little tablets. "Saccharine," she said. "It's sweet. But don't use too much."

She dropped the little pill into her tea, and I followed suit. Fascinating. Already a new world. The woman served some bread and hard cheese that tasted of nothing at all. That eye haunted me, like the vulture eye in Poe's story. *I loved the old man . . .* The maid brought Varvara's mother a glass of tea as she sat in her chair by the window. "When I was a girl," the mother suddenly said in a cracked voice unsteady as the round wooden table, "my mother had a French laundress — Marie. And all she did was press pleats. Only pleats." She imitated a laugh, like paper crinkling. "Now all we have is poor Dasha. *Comment tombent les puissants . . .*"

Varvara snickered, and her mother turned to her with the impossibly sad expression of a Byzantine saint. "That hair," said her mother. "You look like a guttersnipe."

"I am a guttersnipe," Varvara said.

Her mother sighed and addressed the portrait of the emperor, or perhaps the saint. "You see what I must endure? Death will be a blessing." She went back to contemplating the ruin of her life out the dirty window.

"Tell Marina about your matched team of white trotters," Varvara said. "The countess was always particular about her horses."

"Orlov trotters," her mother said, her voice like leaves blowing across an empty square. "Polkan and

Yashma. They were smarter than people. Which doesn't take much."

After another pale glass of tea, the servant brought out supper. The countess did not join us for a rotten cabbage soup with bits of some sort of chewy, gamy meat, but was served separately on a table before the window, with a napkin as a tablecloth and a small vase with a silk flower in it. Varvara nodded at me as I ate. *Horsemeat.* This beast in my mouth had once pulled a wagon. I chewed and chewed, the gristle preventing me from thoroughly masticating it. Finally, as discreetly as I could, I spit out the rubbery bit in my napkin.

Afterward, Varvara asked if I'd like a tour of the flat. It surprised me that she wanted to show me more of this squalor. Very seriously, she began with the windows, introduced in turn as left and right. The table. A narrow wardrobe holding her few clothes. Her bookcase, overflowing with historical and political texts, dictionaries in German, English, French, Latin, and Greek. The divan on which she slept at night—*"Ma chambre"*—over which she'd hung pictures carefully cut from journals. I made out Engels, Kropotkin, a wood engraving of Delacroix's *Liberty Leading the People*—which seemed in rebellious confrontation with the two Nikolases in the red corner. A small kitchen, in which we disturbed the servant at her own tea.

She indicated another door as *"La chambre de ma mère"* but did not, thank God, open it. I worried there might be a coffin hidden inside.

The conveniences were at the end of the outer hall, shared with the neighbors. "I'd recommend leaving that to the imagination."

After that, my friend was eager to go. I approached her mother, mustered my best dancing-class curtsy. "Thank you for having me." Varvara glared at me. Her mother returned my gesture with a reluctant nod of the head. "It's good to see *some people* still exhibit a modicum of breeding."

We walked quickly away from her building in the stunning cold and darkness. Varvara strode at double speed, still angry at the curtsy. We had to hook arms together against the stinging wind, the hard bits of snow jabbing our faces. I didn't know whether to apologize for not believing her when she'd said she ate horsemeat, or express my sympathy at the way she had to live. I felt ashamed of my new warm coat, my white fur hat, my parents, our big tiled stoves, our bathroom, and that I never once thought them extraordinary.

We walked in silence down to the Nikolaevsky Bridge, where I could wait for the tram to take me home, although I planned to get off at the first stop and find a cab. The streetlights revealed nothing but snow falling and the rough white surface of the Neva. "So now you know," she said.

What should I say? *I'm sorry that you're poor?* "If only your father had lived."

"Oh that." Her breath was white, the snow building up on her black tam. "That's just a joke. My father's very much above ground, sad to say. Count Razrushensky—you've never heard of him? Union of the Russian People?" An archreactionary group, part of the Black Hundreds. The nemesis of liberals like my parents. "The People's Will tried to assassinate him in '06. Failed. Too bad. Bet your mother's heard of him. She kept giving me those looks."

The wind whipped around us as we arrived at the tram stop. It was hard to see anything now in the darkness, and the cold was punishing up here on the river. We clung to each other for that small bit of shelter. "But even if he's reactionary, surely he would help his own daughter."

"You don't understand," she said, speaking through her scarf wrapped around her nose and mouth, our backs to the wind. "It's a game. Who will win. You really don't know this?"

I shook my head. "Should I?"

"It's sort of a well-known scandal." She kicked one overshoe against the other to knock the snow off and keep some feeling in her feet. "He moved one of his women into the house with us. Told the countess to divorce him if she didn't like it. Of course she wouldn't. Too devout. But not too devout to spite him for the rest of his life." We leaned on the frozen rails, staring up the Neva toward the Winter Palace, the lights pretty through the sifting snow. "So he's on Millionnaya Street, living with his mistress—or one of them—and we're on the Sixteenth Line, eating horsemeat."

Other people's lives were so confusing. "But why? Aren't they still married?"

"No, of course you don't get it." She took my hand. "Sweet Marina. They hate each other, don't you see? She's doing it to punish him. To shame him. Living on the few rubles she gets from her tired old estate and parading her misery around Petrograd, you should see the pleasure she gets from it. It's like something from Dostoyevsky." She leaned into me. "And he loves seeing her suffer. Loves it. You can't shame him. He doesn't care what people think. I ran away to see him once. The servants wouldn't even let me through the front door—left me sitting on the step like an orphan selling matches." I could see her face, wild under the streetlight. "I wish they'd both die."

Snow sifted through the rails of the bridge, onto the tails of the iron seahorses. I leaned against her, put my arm around her waist, rested my head against her shoulder. My stomach rumbled with the unaccustomed foulness of the meat I'd eaten. "There's nobody who can help? His family? Hers?"

"Well, that's the hell of it," she said, turning around, pressing her back to the railing, scowling at some passing men, wiping her eyes with the back of her knitted glove. "We're all so very proud, aren't we? She won't take a kopek from his family. Hers doesn't have anything." She pulled her scarf up higher, so there was only a slit in it for her glittering eyes—was she going to cry? "His brother once offered to take me to his crummy estate outside of Tver, but I'll be damned if I'm going to be raised by a bunch of reactionaries in the middle of nowhere. That's why I ended up with my aunt in Germany. But then the war had to come along. So here I am."

I slung my arm around her shoulders as she started making terrible sucking noises. She didn't even know how to cry properly.

A few minutes later, I got on the tram by myself. It was less full than it had been, but I was still squashed in with everybody else, hanging from the strap as soldiers took up all the seats. They asked if I had a boyfriend, how old I was, where I lived. They wouldn't stop talking to me, some standing right next to me, pressing up against me, but I would not get off, I would take it all the way. I felt that I owed Varvara that much, to understand what it was to be her.

Finally, I made it home, back to our comfortable flat, with Basya straightening pillows and the scent of Vaula's cooking wafting in from the kitchen. Mother came down the hall, perfumed and dressed for the theater, hooking a pearl earring in place. I could have wept.

4 *The Hospital*

LETTERS FROM KOLYA APPEARED following New Year's—addressed to my family: "Dear Makarovs," with a few cheery anecdotes. Nothing for me. Couldn't he have written to me separately, or at least enclosed a private note? Was he ashamed of his interest in me? Where were the love notes I'd been so eagerly expecting? I wrote poems about him, about trees come to flower and then withered by ice. A man at the front imagining home, a faithless lover, a walk into bullets. I wrote letters to the regimental address. *Why don't you write? I'm waiting but I'm not good at it, Kolya.* I wrote poems about fever, I wrote about mud, I wrote about the sloppy end of winter, the thawing Neva heaving from the pressure of spring, so that it sounded like gunfire. My passion, once aroused, was difficult to dampen.

Wait for me, you said.
Then left me alone in the echoing world.

Late in the spring, I received a letter. It looked as if it had been mauled and then dropped in the mud. Its date: January 1916.

My darling Marina,

I still feel your touch, smell your hair. How do you intoxicate me so? What am I doing on this train? Should I jump? I don't know when I will see you again. I've been reading your book constantly. Some of the fellows want to borrow it, but I won't let them touch it, only Volodya. I don't want anyone's eyes sliding along the

contours of your mind. I want you all to myself. Stay
home, see no one until I return.

Ever your Ringmaster, K.

And a little line drawing of a fox in a ringmaster's
shiny boots and top hat.

That summer the Russian army broke through the
Austro-Hungarian lines on the Southwestern Front, a
stunning advance that took pressure off the French and
the British at Verdun and knocked the Austrians out
of the war. Called the Brusilov Offensive, it proved
the Entente's greatest victory. And yet the flood of the
Russian wounded, the terrible numbers of the dead, un-
dercut any mood of rejoicing. For the city was more
than the imperial capital, it was the great staging area
of the war—whole districts devoted to barracks, to
shipbuilding and munitions factories. Soldiers drilled
in the middle of boulevards, and crowded every tram.
We could watch the country's lifeblood pouring into
the war like water onto sand. We had front-row seats.
The stores, as Varvara had told me that first year, were
stripped to bare shelves, but the hospitals were full, and
new ones were opening all the time. Even the Winter
Palace housed the wounded.

Mother's friends and their daughters donned the
short white veil of the volunteer nurses, a brave red
cross sewn upon the apron, but Mother couldn't bear

the sight of wounded men, not with Volodya at the front. Every amputee reminded her of the danger. In lieu of nursing, she organized a sewing circle among her friends, making swabs and rolling gauze for use on the battlefield. My school friends knitted scarves and socks. I tried, but I was no Seryozha. My scarves resembled great tangles of hair.

It was Miss Haddon-Finch who suggested that she and I could help the war effort by assisting the British embassy with its program of distributing parcels—clothing and tools, boots and underwear, evaporated milk and sugar—to wounded Russian soldiers returning home to distant villages. "The British want to show their appreciation for their sacrifice," she said. I quickly agreed. Anything was better than sitting on a summer's day rolling gauze. A young adjutant at the embassy gave us a list of questions we should ask the men. They seemed awfully dry, more like a census—name, region, district, and so on. *Profession? Married or single? Number of children? Literate?* But I supposed they gave married men more than the single ones, and something for the children, books if they could read. Our job was just to take the information. The packages would arrive upon discharge.

My dread grew with each block as we took a cab up to the great military hospital on Vasilievsky Island, grim in the summer heat. Its vast foyer echoed—even there, beds had been set up. I wasn't a squeamish girl, but I still remember my terror at seeing wounded men lying right in the open, soldiers moaning, hobbling on crutches, their heads encased in bandages. My governess had that English confidence, though, young as she was, and I followed her brisk steps as she approached the desk where a formidable nurse wrote in a ledger.

"*Izvenite,*" said Miss Haddon-Finch. The woman refused to acknowledge our presence. She tried again, louder. "Excuse me, please? I'm here to visit the soldiers. We were sent by the British embassy. For the discharge packages."

"What packages?" the woman snapped. "I don't know what you're talking about."

Miss Haddon-Finch again explained our purpose in halting Russian, but it just irritated the big nurse all the more. "I don't have time for this," the woman fired back. "Escorting British ladies around like it's an exposition. Do you think this is a museum? I've got dying men to think about. We don't even have enough beds. Are the English going to give them to us?"

My governess couldn't understand such rapid speech, but she certainly could guess that her request wasn't being properly received. It brought out her military side, this plain young woman in shirtwaist and boater, daughter of a colonel in the Indian army. "I beg your pardon," she said in English, the way the British did, which was anything but a plea for forgiveness. "I'd like to speak to your superior. I'm here on behalf of His Majesty the King. I resent being treated like a beggar."

I translated quickly for her, proud of her starch, and the irritable nurse got up and found a soldier into whose hands she could deposit us.

I explained our purpose to him, showing him our forms and questions. He asked a heavier man, perhaps a doctor, who shrugged—*What's it to me?*—and the soldier led us up the wide stairs, through some swinging double doors into a great airless ward that smelled of carbolic and human waste. The heat! And the stench. Once you have smelled the stink of decaying bodies, you never forget it. The cheap tobacco the soldiers smoked was a blessing. Both my governess and I stood a few feet inside the doorway, afraid to move another foot closer. There were so many men, a vast stockyard of the wounded—a row against each wall with an aisle down the middle, long as a soccer field. Those who were not in too much pain stared at us, calling out for help, for attention. *"Barynya!"* *Miss!* "Water, there's no water." "Help me!" The smell, and the shouting...I grew woozy and turned back to the door.

"Stop it," my governess said, grabbing my arm. "Imagine your brother. My brother. Don't be afraid of them. They're in pain."

She started at the first bed, by the door on the right. She tried to speak to the man, who had some sort of box keeping his yellowed sheet from his feet. "What happened?" she asked in her halting Russian. "Trench foot, *barynya*." he said. Clean-shaven, but a peasant, his lined face, his short nose, his bright eyes.

Puzzled by the Russian phrase, she turned to me to translate.

I was burning up, and the stink made me queasy. I could smell his decaying feet. It was dead summer. Why didn't they open the windows? "Are you hot, soldier?"

"Better than being cold, *barynya*."

"This lady has some questions for you," I said. "The English are giving packages on discharge. To thank you for fighting."

"They're going to thank us for fighting," he told the man lying next to him, whose head and left eye were swathed in soiled bandages. "Why don't the tsar thank us?"

"Thinks he already did," said the man beyond the one with the bandaged head. "One less arm to wash." They all laughed their way into coughing fits.

"Sorry, miss. I shouldn't joke around. Just been in this bed awhile," said the first.

The man across the way groaned rhythmically. "Help me...help me..."

"What's wrong with him?" my governess asked.

"Gangrene, miss," said the first man.

She shuddered, touching the little locket around her neck that held a picture of her brother, fighting in France somewhere, probably Verdun. "Maybe we should just find out which ones are being discharged." She was a great one for systems. She would have made a good soldier, despite her weakness for romantic novels. She stopped a small nurse carrying a pan covered with a cloth. "Can you tell me which men are to be sent home?"

"How should I know?" the nurse said. "If they get better they go back to the front. If they get worse..." She shrugged. "The amputees go home. Why don't you start there?"

"But how will we know?" she called after the woman, already bustling away.

"It's on the chart," the nurse called back over her shoulder.

Despite the noise and the heat and our confusion, we began to go down the row, studying the charts that hung at the foot of the beds. *Trench foot, shrapnel, bayonet. Amputation. Gangrene. Bullet in the head, bullet lodged in the spleen, in the spine, in the groin. Paralysis. Amputation.* "We'd better split up," she said. "It'll go faster."

Talk to them myself? To the man groaning on the other side of the row? "But won't you need me to translate? What if they don't understand you?"

"I'll do fine," she said. "Go." She gently pushed me toward the other row.

I took my forms and my pencil and, quietly terrified, approached the first bed. "Water," begged the man with gangrene. He smelled awful, his thin face yellow with fever.

A nurse bustled by. "Excuse me. This man is thirsty," I said.

She stared back at me with the white eye of a startled horse. "Water's in the hall. Get it yourself." I didn't know what to do, I wasn't a nurse. But I got his cup from the side of his bed, took it out in the hall—at least it was cooler there—filled it from a large urn, and took it back. I tried to hand it to him, but he couldn't sit up. He just lay there, calling for water. There was nowhere to sit. What should I do? I could feel my helpless tears welling up.

"I'll give it to him, miss," said the man in the next bed. He sat up in his dirty nightshirt and I saw that he'd lost a leg. I tried not to stare, but I didn't know where else to put my eyes. He took the cup from me, reached across the narrow gap between beds, and held up the soldier's thin head, his neck like a flower stalk, and began dripping water into the fevered man's mouth.

An amputee! I remembered what I was doing there. "I'm taking information," I said. "For packages. For men who're going to be discharged."

"Theotokos be praised," he said. "Not a moment too soon."

Name? Region? District? Profession? Married? Children? Mardukov, Foma Fomanovich. Peasant. From Irkutsk Oblast, Cheremkhovsky District, village of Kuda. I laughed. "Really?" *Kuda* meant "which way."

"Yes, if you go there, you'll be asking, too," he said. His whole demeanor brightened at the small contact. I'd thought he was fifty but he gave his age as thirty-five, married with four children. "She wrote to me, *barynya.* Look." He reached into his boot—his one boot, standing by the bed...where was the other, with his leg? Did they bring the leg with him or leave it on the battlefield? I could feel that other boot calling to this one. He handed me a soft piece of paper, grimy from handling.

I opened it. It wasn't a woman's handwriting. Lettered, not cursive, full of misspellings. *My dear Fomusha*...I didn't know if I really should be reading it. I tried to give it back to him, but he indicated with a rolling of his hand for me to keep it. "Read it to me, miss. I'm a poor simple man, I never learned how."

I read his own letter aloud to him. *"My dear Fomusha, I pray that this letter finds you well. We are fine. The goat had twins, at last."* I glanced at the date—February 1915. Over a year ago. *"Little Vanka cut a tooth, he's been bawling about it for weeks."* And soon Foma would hold him, he'd be walking by now, wouldn't he? Talking? I didn't know much about children.

"She's a wonderful woman, my Rozochka." His lined face smiling, the creases like the rays of the sun.

"The Krylovs' izba burned down last month. Is it cold there? The winter's been terrible here. You should see Grisha—he looks just like you."

"He's almost six now," said the soldier.

"Sonnechka had her baby, a girl. The rye looks good, and the wheat, too, though harvest's the devil without you."

He examined his remaining foot, thick-nailed, and sighed. "At least I'll be home. A thousand thanks, miss." He took the letter and folded it, put it back into his boot.

I moved to the next bed, the occupant already waiting for me. All of them had something they wanted to tell me, more than *region, district, village, profession, married, children*. They showed me letters, pictures. They were shy about discussing their wounds, but their bodies spoke for themselves. Trench foot spoke of water-filled ditches where they stood for days and weeks. Their coughing told stories of battlefield gas. Suppurating wounds under dirty bandages gave testimony to the lack of care the nation gave its conscripts. How could we make wounded men sleep in such foul surroundings, such narrow beds? With stale sheets and pillowcases. Everything yellow and gray—walls gray, the floors yellow. And the inescapable heat. My dress was already soaked. I kept thinking that these could be the very men Volodya described in his letters. He spoke of their bravery, their camaraderie. I tried to flag nurses as they bustled about so importantly, yet no one had time to change a man's bandages, get him a glass of water.

Though filthy and neglected, the men who were not racked with pain or delirious with fever were for the most part surprisingly cheerful, happy to share their information, whether they were likely to be discharged or would be healed only to be sent back. I tried to get them to talk about the war, but they wanted to talk about their villages: Kuda and Polovodovo, Tarkhan-skaya Pot'ma, Sosi, Gus', Veliky-Dobrovo. A soldier from Ryazan Oblast, patched about the head and left eye, asked if I might write a letter to his wife. He was exceedingly polite: "A thousand pardons, miss, but it would mean everything to her." I had an entire ward to get to—Miss Haddon-Finch was already way ahead of me—but I saw no point in bustling around like these nurses, too busy to get a man a glass of water. We would finish the ward today or we'd come back tomorrow. Meanwhile, I would attend to this man. I tore a sheet from my own notebook and took his dictation. He watched me, head cocked to better view the page, the way children watch a magician performing.

Annoushkha, little bird—

I'm here in the capital, I got caught between the devil and an Austrian. That eye's never going to be any good, but God be praised I'll be coming home soon. Don't worry about a thing. I think of you…

He paused. Awareness of my youth and station prevented him from saying more. "You say the rest."

"*I think of you every day, the sun in your hair,*" I said.

"Yes, say that. *The sun in her hair*…she's got such pretty hair, too. Blond braids like that." He showed me with his big hands, his fingers could hardly close around them.

"How should I sign it? What does she call you?"

From the expression on his face, the sly grin, it was probably dirty. "Say *Senya*."

"With all my love, Senya."

I continued to the next bed, and the next. Men from villages whose names sounded like fairy tales told me their specifics. How sheltered I'd been. I could really see how Volodya must have changed since leaving us to fight with these men, for here was Russia, here in these beds. These eyes, clear or red or yellow or bandaged, these men young and not so young. The giant wounded body of Russia. What did I know of these lives? I felt my privilege, my foreignness as a girl from Petersburg, with its quays and canals, its classical buildings, its foreigners and colonnades, its seafront. Compared to the Russia of these men, this was Finland, Paris, a polonaise, a tango, dueling pistols at dawn. It was silver and lilac, Great Peter's dream.

Big men tossed in fever or lay listless, laughed off the loss of a leg, an arm, yet still believed in the emperor and the healing power of the holy icons worn beneath their dirty shirts. I thought about the poet Walt Whitman, whom Balmont had translated into Russian. It was said he'd served as a field nurse in the American Civil War.

My comrade I wrapt in his blanket, envelop'd well his
form . . .
And buried him where he fell.

Where was our Whitman? I wondered, imagining he was here somewhere, in a trench or a hospital like this one, putting it all into words that would reach across time to break your heart. Maybe this Brusilov Offensive would be the thing to break through and end the war. But the looks of this ward made me wonder. I asked a few of the men about the offensive, how it seemed to be going, but none of them had any idea. They went where they were told; they trusted in God.

I gazed back at the crowded ward, like a terrible mirror house. How many men lay mangled in wards like this in Russia right now, their bodies ruined? Could we really afford to lose so many? Wouldn't we run out of arms and legs? Though they said we were winning, I couldn't help wondering what losing would look like. I thought of Volodya...but there were no officers in these wards, only common soldiers. Bad luck to think it. *He'll be fine...*

And why did I think *Volodya* and not *Kolya?* He could have been shot just as easily. And yet somehow I felt he would be protected—if not by God or the Virgin or spirits then by his own buoyancy. Surely he, if anyone, would know how to evade the bullets and grenades. Yet I knew this was childish thinking. Kolya Shurov was only a man like any of these, blood and muscle, with arms and legs that could be lost, flesh that could be torn, eyes that could burn. Charm couldn't dissuade bullets or bayonets, land mines or poison gas. But still, I couldn't quite believe it. Volodya was heroic, an officer of cavalry, the type who could be killed defending somebody else, could trip a land mine. He would be the one to lead any charge. I prayed God to bring him back, safely and soon.

When I told Varvara what I was doing with the wounded men, she shook her head slowly, said the only cure for what was going on in this country was to end the imperial nightmare and agitate for a socialist state. She told me to read *Das Kapital*. "Better to work for change that affects everyone." I knew she was right, yet what about the man in this bed, groaning, his body in plaster? Sometimes simply holding someone's hand was better than all the Hegelian dialectics in the world. Varvara had not seen the glow in a man's wounded face as I approached his bed, how happy he'd been to be asked the most mundane questions, how glad to simply have been sought out and addressed as a man.

I moved to the bedside of a soldier with a blond beard. His leg had been amputated at the knee, and the smell was nauseating. Sick as he was, his letter to his sweetheart brimmed with affection and humor:

Dearest Olya,

I'm here in the capital enjoying the fine life. Only the big tankards of kvas, the dancing girls. They send us violins to sing us to sleep. If I hadn't lost that leg, it'd be a holiday.

The man in the next bed smoked a twisted cigar. "She's probably sleeping with the foreman, brother," he interjected. "Women don't wait, and that's the truth."

I flushed, thinking of the boys I'd kissed when I thought Kolya had forgotten me. *Wait for me...*

"Shut up, Yid," the blond man said.

"I bet you get back, there'll be another kid who looks nothing like you." The cynic was reading a book. The first literate man I'd seen here.

"Keep it buttoned, or I'll shove your face in," said my soldier. "She's a treasure, *barynya*. She's my angel."

"Should I put that in?" I asked. *"My treasure, my angel?"*

"Yes, write it all down."

I added these to the other phrases. "What else?"

A tear rolled down his cheek into his beard. "Tell her I'll be back soon, I'll warm her up and how..." Then he remembered who he was talking to, a sixteen-year-old *studentka*. "A thousand pardons, *barynya*. Forgive me, I'm not used to fine company."

I wanted to see the title of the volume the other soldier held in his hands. "What are you reading?" I asked him.

"Nothing for you," he sneered. *"Barynya."*

My eyes watered as though I'd been slapped in the face. The other men had been so grateful...he obviously had a poor opinion of women.

"Bedbug! Louse. Don't listen to him, *barynya*." My

bearded private defended me, though he could barely lift his head for fever. "If I could get out of this bed, I'd beat his Yid head in."

Finally I could see the title of the man's book. Chernyshevsky's radical *Chto Delat'? What Is to Be Done?* It made me all the more curious about this rude fellow to see that he was reading the same book Varvara was so fervent about. "You're not an officer?"

"Don't be stupid," he said, smoking his twisted cheroot. "If I were an officer would I be here? No, I'd be in Tsarskoe Selo on a featherbed, eating eggs on toast."

"You got that right," said my bearded man.

I finished his letter and moved to the bedside of the literate man. The smell of his cigar was sharp and bitter.

"Mind if I ask you some questions?" I asked. He wasn't an amputee and probably would be sent back to the front, but he interested me.

"Why not?" the man said. "I have a few moments." He put his book on the gray sheet, his cigar stuck between his teeth.

His name: *Evgeny Isaakovich Marmelzadt. From Petrograd. Unmarried. No children. Profession, typesetter. Literate.* "Why aren't you an officer?"

"Steblov, tell her why I'm not an officer."

"'Cause he's a Jew, *barynya*. Who'd follow him anywhere except to the pawnshop?" The blond-bearded soldier laughed.

Marmelzadt took his cigar from his teeth. "I rest my case."

An odd little man, rude and yet willing to talk. Thinning sandy hair, a wide bony jaw. Unlike the other men, he wasn't intimidated by my clean clothes and educated speech. In fact I had the feeling he considered himself superior to me. "Excuse me, Evgeny Isaakovich, can I ask you one more question?"

"Maybe. Let's hear it."

"Do you think the offensive will succeed? That we'll win the war?"

He smiled a rancid little smile, reading the tip of his cigar as if a joke nested in its glowing nib. "Everyone's going to lose this war, little missy." He squinted, sticking it back between his teeth. "Walk away from your pretty streets, your Nevsky Prospect. Stop looking at yourself in the mirror long enough to take a good look around."

"But Brusilov——"

"Forget your Brusilov. He can't save it. This whole country is sinking like a stone. It's rotten, everything in it is rotten. These poor fools can hang on to their saints and their tsar as much as they like, but when this offensive fails, then you watch. You heard it here first. Thank me later."

I felt his disapproval like a lash—especially the part about looking at myself in the mirror, which of course I did constantly. But I needed to know what someone other than my father thought. I wanted to argue with him—his words cast such a chill, even on a hot day. As I moved on, I felt his gaze following me. I thought of him as we took a cab all the way back to Furshtatskaya Street.

5 *Fathers and Sons*

AUTUMN. THE BRUSILOV OFFENSIVE died and crumbled in the mud of Galicia—just as the sour-faced soldier had predicted. Not enough support at the right time, Father said. Territoriality, shortsightedness, and squabbling among the generals had undermined our best hope for victory. Gloom pervaded the house—gloom at school, irritability in the street and in the classrooms. Mother decided to cheer us one night by pulling out an old photo album with silver hasps. We curled up with her in the little sitting room that served as our library, me on one side, Seryozha on the other. Above her hung the Vrubel portrait of her as Igraine, all sea and mist. Near the Russian stove with its blue tiles, Miss Haddon-Finch worked on a jigsaw puzzle while Avdokia sat on a little rush-bottomed chair mending a hem. The scent of cherry tobacco wafted down the hall. All was as it used to be when we were small, and we sat next to Mother, watching her turn the big black pages of the old album like pages in a book of fairy tales. For a moment, I could forget the war, the men, even Kolya, just to dwell there, a little girl, smelling Mother's perfume.

Verushka and Vadik, Maryino, 1879. Two small children, regal in their little chairs in a garden shaded by an arbor, having their tea under a much younger Avdokia's watchful eye. "We were considered the prettiest children in St. Petersburg," Mother said, as if it were a simple fact, like days in the week or the orbit of Mars. "People used to stop us in the street to admire us."

Our nanny, now old and stooped in her little chair, smiled down at her mending. "Such a pair. Little Vadik—akh, there was a handful. And you weren't so easy yourself. Our little tsarevna."

Old photographs tipped in against the large black pages, each image titled in white ink, first in Grand-mère's spidery writing, then later in Mother's pretty Catherine Institute hand.

"Your brother, where is he now?" Miss Haddon-Finch paused, a piece still in hand, above her jigsaw puzzle—the Houses of Parliament. Father had it sent from England for her birthday. She had a bit of a crush on him.

"In America." Mother sighed, turning the page. "Last we heard. But the war..." We hadn't seen him since the summer he'd taken a dacha on the Gulf of Finland, ten years ago. He didn't come back when war broke out, and Father saw that as tantamount to trea-son. In Vadim's last letter—sent from California— he'd included a photograph of himself painting on a stony beach. Dressed in a pair of pants tied at the waist with a rope, he was lithe and finely sculpted as an As-syrian bas-relief.

"You must miss him very much," said Miss Haddon-Finch.

Vera and Vadim, The Lido, Venice, 1891.

"Yes, I do," Mother said.

Young, on a boardwalk, Uncle Vadim in a white suit with a straw hat, looking exactly like Seryozha. And Mother, simply garbed in a long white dress, carried a hat as big as a carriage wheel. How relaxed and happy she looked that long-ago day, like a Manet, her hair in the breeze. She always looked happiest with her brother. In pictures with Father, she appeared elegant but always slightly tense. In this picture, she was sixteen, just my age. Two years later, she married Father. It gave me a haunted feeling, that someday I would see pictures of myself as I'd been this year and turn the page to find myself at university. And then what? A wedding picture with Kolya? Posing with a group of fellow poets on the Black Sea? Living on foreign shores, like Uncle Vadim? I imagined the album would end with me, fat and gray-haired, my descendants gathered around me.

Dmitry and Vera, St. Petersburg, 24 June 1893. Their wedding portrait. They stood side by side: Father, the young lawyer, his gaze leveled at the camera, with his well-modeled face and clever dark eyes, hair combed back, sensual lips—before the beard shielded them—in a bit of a smile, and Mother ethereal in her wedding *kokoshnik,* the Russian-style crown threaded with pearls. Her expression was a bit more guarded in her oval face, her large clear pale eyes. They were both so supremely confident for such young people, gazing out from the picture as if they knew they would be the center of whatever circles they found themselves in. But gone was the freedom my mother embodied in the picture with her brother in Venice two years before. This photograph spoke more of ambition than affection or affinity.

"Your school called today," Mother said to Seryozha as he turned the page, toying absently with his unruly blond hair. "Unfortunately your father was home to take the call."

Seryozha winced. Mother's disapproval was one thing, but Father's was of a different order of magnitude. Father had done well in school and loved every moment of it. He had been president of the debating society, the geography club, the English club, and editor of the school literary journal. He'd dismissed Seryozha's tales of boys who mocked him, tripped him, made sure his books fell in the mud, and the jaded or aggressive schoolmasters from whom little help was forthcoming when this bullying was reported. As a woman from minor aristocracy, Mother didn't care much about academics and liked having her youngest at home, sketching, amusing her. Consequently, my brother had developed a repertoire of mysterious ailments, most of which required a great deal of bed rest.

"I think I have that disease they have in Africa, where they fall asleep right where they stand," Seryozha said, turning the page. "In the middle of walking to work or milking a goat."

"Oblomovka," she said. Oblomov, the hero of the famous Goncharov novel, about a useless young nobleman who can't get out of bed. She kissed him on the cheek. She never petted me or Volodya this way, but Seryozha was the baby of the family, her special pet. For my part, I would rather go to school every day of the year—even if I were beaten bloody—than sit at home day after day. If it had been me, I would have taken up Father's offer of boxing lessons. But avoidance was Seryozha's way, and there was no talking to him about it. His stubbornness was a strange bedrock beneath his seeming weakness and passivity. He could not be forced into anything.

A strong waft of cherry tobacco entered the room, followed by Father in a dark red-and-blue dressing jacket and slippers of Morocco leather. He settled into an armchair and flicked on the reading light. We all tensed a bit, watching as he unfolded his paper and began to read with an exaggeratedly casual air. A lawyer at heart, Dmitry Ivanovich Makarov liked to surprise his prey.

"I've been talking to Konstantin Guchkov down in Moscow," he said, shaking out the page. "He's offered to arrange a spot at the Bagration Military School. Just as soon as we're ready."

Seryozha kept his head down and pretended to study a photograph of Volodya on a rocking horse.

"The school tells me you've been absent four times in the last month," he continued. "Really, it's got to stop."

Miss Haddon-Finch rose and excused herself for bed. She didn't care for family quarrels. Avdokia, however, remained stubbornly in her chair.

Father put down the paper and took out his gold Breguet pocket watch, which Mother had given him as a wedding present, and checked the time against the clock on the wall. He wound it, placed it back in his pocket. "Lying in bed when good men are at the front. It's a disgrace."

I could see the life draining out of Mother's face. "He needs time to develop," she said. "Surely certain allowances can be made. You know how horrid those boys are."

Father turned the page of the newspaper on his knee. "All boys are horrid. Trust me, my dear. He's got to get used to it. The best thing about this Moscow idea is getting him away from you. You coddle him as if he were six." He nodded at us on the settee. "Look at him. Do you think that's good for him?"

It was hard not to see it from Father's point of view: the three of us tucked up over sweetened tea and butter cookies, petting Tulku, Mother's little greyhound, and examining old photographs, while men slogged through the mud of Galicia and the Ukraine, leaving their arms and legs behind. "He'll be sixteen soon, and clearly he's not university material—"

"I'm going to art school," my brother said, sitting

up, putting a little space between himself and Mother. "I've decided. Golovin will recommend me." Mother's cousin, the scenic designer for the Alexandrinsky Theater.

Papa studied his youngest son over his pipe, removed it. "You're talented enough, son, but I don't see you with the ambition to launch a career. You'll expect people to intercede on your behalf, open doors, make exceptions, do your talking for you."

Mother turned the page in the photo album, her foot circling, like a cat twitching her tail. He had boxed us in, for which of us would dare speak up for Seryozha when to do so was to illustrate the correctness of his view?

"The sad truth is that there are only two people here who can make sure you find your way in the world, son. Yourself, and me. And as far as I can see, only one of us is taking that responsibility seriously."

I ached for my brother—my father was always picking on him—but on the other hand, I couldn't disagree. Seryozha could be both lazy and impervious to argument, his own worst enemy. Lying there, looking at picture albums...compared to those men in the Oborovsky Hospital, where I'd spent my summer, their stoic good humor, even when missing a leg or an eye—or even compared to Kolya or Volodya—he was a disaster.

Father took his pipe tool from his pocket and dug the ashes from the bowl, knocked them into the heavy

ashtray. I gave Seryozha a look that meant "Say something." If he didn't want to be shipped off to military
academy, he had better defend himself.

Seryozha tried his voice. "Look at Uncle Vadim.
He's got a career." Our uncle traveled the world painting, taking photographs, illustrating articles in
magazines—exactly the kind of life both Seryozha and
I dreamed about.

"Vadim," Father said disgustedly. "These are grave
times. We need serious men now, not globe-trotting
dilettantes."

My mother blanched, closed the big album. "I find
it…reprehensible that you would take out your feelings about my brother…on our son." I knew what it
cost her to state her feelings so openly. Propriety was
as much a part of her as her own skin.

Seryozha set up very straight. Avdokia, behind my
father and out of his view, crossed herself.

"We will not be raising any Vadims, my dear," he said
crisply, packing his pipe from a roll of tobacco he kept in
his pocket. "Your brother has shirked every responsibility except for his own pleasure since the century turned."
He lit up with a flourish, puffed self-righteously, and sat
back, gazing at her with the hard, cool expression he normally reserved for legal adversaries.

Mother sat very still, very erect, her mouth in a thin
straight line, smoothing the cover of the album in her
lap, a soft green calfskin.

But Seryozha heard the threat of the Bagration school

quite clearly. "I can do better," he said. "Two more years at Tenishev, and I'll be out of there—it's not so long, really. I guess I can stand it."

"You *guess?*" Father's eyebrows peaked.

"I mean, I will." My brother stood. "Really, I will."

Father let him stand there awhile, fixing him with his butterfly-pinning stare. "Give me your solemn word—as my son—that you will stop shaming your brother and the men who are out there dying for our country. I won't have it."

"I'll go every day. I swear." Wiping his hands on the sides of his pants.

"Good." He shook out his paper with a snap. "Avdokia, I'd like some tea now."

6 *Bread, Give Us Bread*

A BITTER COLD BUT windless day, a light snow sifting out of the fog like confectioner's sugar. After school, the three of us were on our way to see a new Vera Kholodnaya picture. We passed a bread line outside a bakery—every day they seemed to get longer. So many sad, tired people, weary shoulders drooping, waiting for their daily loaves. The city had become a waiting room—the part not already a barracks or a hospital. Ever since the offensive broke in September, a gloom of hopelessness had fallen over the city. Strikes had become a regular feature of life.

Varvara stopped to talk to a woman near the head of the queue. "How long have you been standing here, Grandmother?"

The woman gave us a keen assessment with her small colorless eyes. "She asks how long we've been here, the little missy." The women standing around her laughed. "Only since eight this morning, sweetheart," she said sarcastically. *"Nichevo." It's nothing.*

"Worse every day," said a sweet-faced woman in front of her in a badly knitted rose shawl. "Soon I won't bother going home. I'll just bring a cot and a stove and a chamber pot and have my mail forwarded."

"It's the Jews," an old woman said. She pulled something from her handbag, held it out to us. A pamphlet, worn and badly printed: THE JEWS ARE PROFITING FROM YOUR BLOOD AND SWEAT. THEY BOUGHT OFF THE DUMA! SHUT DOWN THE JEWISH DUMA!

As a Jew, Mina turned away, disgust and a trace of fear on her face. I, too, felt the assault. Father was a member of the Duma—a legislative body of limited powers dominated by businessmen, landowners, and aristocrats. It was hardly a "Jewish Duma," and shutting it down wouldn't do anyone any good. But neither of us said anything.

Varvara held up the leaflet and shredded it slowly before the woman's eyes, letting the pieces fall like big, untidy snowflakes. "What garbage." She sniffed her glove. "Protopopov's stink is all over it." The emperor's reactionary minister of the interior, a well-known anti-Semite. "The government waves the Jews in your faces to distract you. Can't you see? They don't want you to think about how the war's going. It's the government that's sending all the food to the front, and the hell with us. This line wasn't here two years ago, was it? It's all going to the war."

The women glanced about them uneasily. To have someone speak like this on the street was dangerous for all concerned. But Varvara persisted. "Yes, your husbands, your sons. For what? Do you know what this war is about? It's a big land grab. The tsar and the king of England, the kaiser—all cousins, squabbling among themselves. Dragging us along behind them. Ask yourself, who's making the money here? Nobel, Putilov, Westinghouse, Dinamo." The big factories, manufacturing munitions. "They're the ones who want this. They don't care how hungry you are."

These women were actually listening to her. It did my heart good to see that old harridan chewing her cheek in fury.

"You want to shut down the Duma?" my friend scolded her. "Fine, shut down the Duma. Cut your own throats while you're at it."

The woman in front of the anti-Semite, a blond housewife with dark circles under her eyes, spoke up. "They say he's got syphilis, Protopopov. That he's completely insane."

"Protopopov's not going to stop until there's no food

left in the country," Varvara said. Funny, Father had said the same thing just the night before.

The old hag chimed in. "They say the Germans are giving the Jews a million rubles to get us out of the war."

"I'm leaving," said Mina, her gray eyes burning behind her glasses. "I'll see you at the theater."

But Varvara barely heard her. She was just getting started. "The Germans don't have to pay anybody. Are you joking?" she shouted. "We're losing the war all by ourselves!"

Behind her, a raw-boned *baba* with a mottled face leaned in. "I heard the grand dukes are sending all the gold to Germany—in coffins of dead prisoners of war. For when Germany wins the war." I hadn't heard this one yet. The rumors never ceased to amaze me.

The old Jew hater revved up again. "If only the tsar would come back from the front. He doesn't know what's happening here."

"He doesn't?" Varvara spat. "With police spies everywhere? Nothing happens in this country he doesn't know about."

With the mention of police spies, the women quickly dropped their gazes and clamped their lips together.

Suddenly, a woman shouted back to the queue from the bakery's doorway. "They say there's no more bread. They're completely out."

The women pressed closer. "Sure they are." "Hoarders!" "Thieves!"

"They've still got food!" "Speculators!" "If we had a fat wallet, they'd find some!"

The women crowded forward as someone inside struggled vainly to lock the doors. The women beat on the metal, shouting, "We want bread!" "Hoarders!" "Scum!"

I thought that we should leave, too. Something was about to break. Women put their shoulders to the door, ten of them, twelve. They heaved against it—one, two, three—and finally burst into the shop. In a moment, they dragged the owner out, a tubby, bald man in an apron, bellowing and threatening, waving his meaty arms to try to free himself from the crowd of babushkas. "There's nothing, I swear on my children's heads! You can't squeeze blood from a rock!"

"Yes, but you can squeeze our blood!" a woman cried out. "Speculator!" Someone hit him over the head with her handbag, and they began to claw at him. It was terrible. The poor man could hardly help it that he'd run out of bread. Others who'd rushed inside wrestled a big bag out into the doorway, tore it open, and began scooping flour into upturned skirts and aprons, into purses and hats. There was flour after all! There was flour—and sugar, too! Here were more women, more sacks, everything covered in flour. Women hunched over, scurrying away with their prizes. How stupid, how credulous I'd been for having believed the man when he said he had nothing, for having worried about him! *For people like you, things appear by magic from under the counter, from a back room. I've seen it. It's disgusting.* He had been holding back flour for the rich, who could pay double, quadruple the price, just as Varvara had said. A speculator! In wartime!

The melee spread out as the infuriated women broke into other shops. "We want justice!" "We want bread!" Varvara was out of her mind with excitement, shouting, "Bread and justice!" I knew she thought of this as a righteous demonstration of legitimate anger. Maybe in the abstract I might have thought so, too, but right now it was becoming a dangerous mob. I pulled her into a doorway where we could watch without being arrested if the police started rounding people up. Varvara's burning eyes memorized the scene. She trembled like a warhorse, thrilled and alert at the mayhem. I could feel how she itched to run out among them, breaking windows and flinging flour and dry goods into the arms of the crowd.

Constables soon arrived, sorely outnumbered. The women moved around them. One grabbed a woman and punched her. Right in the face! In broad daylight. I clapped my hand over my mouth and shrank back deeper into the doorway as other women surged to her defense, grabbing him, tearing at his uniform. He'd lost his hat. Another constable knocked a woman down, then kicked her again and again with his heavy boot. I was paralyzed. Could this be real? Could this be happening in my Petrograd? I clung to Varvara in the doorway. "We should go."

"You go," Varvara said, her eyes glittering. "This is history. We're watching history."

Then I heard the clatter of horses' hooves on the cobbles, and eight mounted Cossacks burst into view, plowing headlong into the crowd. The women screamed and scattered, running in all directions. The sound—hooves, and blows, and the cries of women...right here on Liteiny Prospect, where my mother bought flowers. This was the reason the people never protested, I realized, watching the Cossacks strike human flesh—unarmed women—with their cudgels. This was the reason people put up with so much. This was the whip at the end of the arm.

At last we fled, the two of us slipping around the corner into a courtyard, then into the courtyard behind that, unshoveled, an uneven rut of a path leading us through. I rarely went this far off the main boulevard. After a few courtyards, I didn't even know where I was anymore. We came to a dead end in a tiny ten-by-ten courtyard, where a pasty-faced woman lounging in a doorway with a young girl drenched us in her laughter. Something hit a wall behind us. We didn't turn to see what it was. We turned and scrambled back until we found an opening onto a quiet side street—no one running, a dog sniffing at a pile of snow, a horse pulling a wagon piled with rags.

Varvara hugged me, twirling me off my feet, kissing my cheek, as if we'd just passed a school exam. "They're not sitting still for it. Oh God, did you see?"

I thought of the baker's bloody face. The way the policeman kicked that woman. Had Varvara incited it all, ramping the women up about that ugly pamphlet? Her delight frightened me. People had been hurt! Why was she dancing around like a lunatic?

We found Mina sitting alone in the third row of the theater, eating Jordan almonds out of a twist of paper. "I didn't think you'd make it," she said, moving down in the row. Now she eyed us more closely. "What happened?"

"It was a riot," Varvara said. "You should have stayed."

I sat with my friends, facing the flickering screen, but I didn't even notice Kholodnaya's performance. I was still vibrating with the violence I had just seen—not a shooting in a detective *kinofilm,* but right in front of me, blood and flour and the music of smashing glass.

One didn't have to get very far from Nevsky Prospect after all. The war was coming to us.

7 *A Sleigh Waited*

OUTSIDE THE TAGANTSEV ACADEMY, a sleigh waited. In the low passenger seat, a young officer sat with a rug across his lap, snow piling on his astrakhan cap and the shoulders of his steel-blue army greatcoat. We were accustomed to the sight of young officers waiting for senior girls. The horse stamped, the bells of its harness cheering the dull, powdery air. Small puffs of vapor rose from its dark nostrils. I froze in place on the steps. Varvara collided with me, and Mina dropped her book. This was not just any officer. That rosy, well-shaved face with its frosted-over moustache did its best to maintain its casual air and not burst out laughing.

I didn't let myself run to him. I had waited enough—he could wait for me now. "What are you doing here?" I called from the steps.

He unhooked the bearskin rug. "Thought you might like to go for a spin. Join me in a cup of hot chocolate. A soldier's dream of home." The horse stamped in the cold. Who else would know it was my favorite color of horse —dappled gray with dark, intellectual eyes? The driver on his high seat dusted himself off. I could feel the girls behind me whispering. It would be all over school by tomorrow. *Did you see Makarova with that officer?* I had never inspired any gossip, it was about time I did. Let them talk about me for a change.

Varvara gave me a skeptical look: *You're not falling for that, are you?* while Mina scrambled to pocket her spectacles, the better to be seen. The horse switched its tail. I could feel my ship tugging at the dock, impatient to move out to sea. Kolya Shurov was waiting to carry me off, as he promised he would. Was I one to shirk the call of adventure? I was not. I walked to the sleigh, let him take my book bag, settle me into the small seat. We decorously kissed cheeks—*an old family friend*—and I caught a whiff of his cologne, Floris

Limes. He hooked the rug over us. *"Davai, davai!"* he shouted to the coachman up on the box. *Let's go!* The broad-backed driver slapped the reins, and the sleigh lurched forward, breaking free from the ice.

How warm it was under the bearskin rug, the snow tickling our faces, the song of the runners. "I wrote to you constantly," I said. "Why didn't you ever respond?"

He put his arm around me, pressed close. The smell of him, I almost fainted.

"I wrote when I could. In wartime you have to know it's hit or miss." I couldn't tell if he was lying or not. But that letter from January didn't get to me until April.

We trotted up the Fontanka, past the Ciniselli Circus and the Engineers' Castle and across the end of the Summer Garden with its famous fence of gilt and iron. "On nights in bivouac, I imagined us just like this. This sleigh, this snow, this light." He closed his eyes and recited, *"O madman, tell me—when, where, how / Will you forget them, in what desert? / Ah little feet, where are you now?"*

He was reciting Pushkin for me. I was witness to a Kolya I'd never seen before, a Kolya come a-wooing. It was intoxicating. He was trying to seduce me—*an old family friend* no more. I saw that he thought of himself as a Pushkin—romantic, spontaneous. He caught my indulgent smile and knew he'd been caught at it. He took off his glove, slipped his hand inside my muff. We intertwined fingers, our hands a new creation.

Soon we entered the open Field of Mars, where he and Volodya had paraded with their regiment two years ago August before they'd shipped out to the front. "Faster!" he called to the driver. "Let's fly!" And we sailed through the lilac shadows of the winter afternoon—the city powdering itself in snow like an old empress before her dressing table. We flew up Millionnaya Street, where Varvara's father lived, and out onto Palace Square. "Around!" he called, and we circled the Alexander Column as though we were in a crazy chariot race, then left behind the red Winter Palace and the yellow General Staff Building and the Admiralty with its gilded steeple, to cross St. Isaac's Square with the cathedral dome blurred in the falling snow and past the *Bronze Horseman*—Peter forever rearing, facing the river.

We slowed and turned southward, as did his hands under the rug, tracing my thick woolen stockings up to the long bloomers, inching above the garters, finding naked flesh. He was shameless. Such pleasure. I let my head rest on his arm, my eyes closing. Oh God, the moan that escaped me—I hoped the driver was discreet. When I opened my eyes, I saw the impish look on Kolya's face as he undid the bow at the leg of my knickers. How far would he go? I tried to stop the progress of his hand, but it was like trying to stop the assault of an army. I felt the honey dripping from me—I had to admit that doing this in a sleigh right in public made it all the more exciting.

"Tell me you love me," he said. "Tell me what was in those letters." Cupping my bottom in his hand.

"You better stop," I said.

"Why?" Kolya said. "Don't you like it?"

There was no answering that. Onward we went, and I realized I must have seen couples do this a thousand times. What a child I was not to have noticed. I groaned again as he caressed the soft skin, my wet warmth, and I clung to him, to his heavy overcoat, to a bucking release that I'd only experienced in the slightest bit alone with my legs wrapped around my pillow. Who was shameless, after all?

"Driver, a left." We turned onto the Catherine Canal Embankment. "Third door."

"You said we were going for chocolate," I sighed.

"I'll make you some," he said.

The sleigh pulled up in front of an apartment house near the Bank Bridge, where the griffins grinned with their golden wings, bridge cables in their teeth. "Whose house is this?"

"A friend." He unhooked the rug on my side. "They've left it to me."

I'd been by this building a thousand times. The windows looked haughty to me, judgmental, staring down at my wobbly-legged, flushed-face condition, my hat all askew.

People were walking by on the embankment. I wondered if anyone could tell what we were about to do. If anyone would recognize me. Kolya squeezed my shoul-

der. "Are you afraid? I can take you back if you want."
Bravery, in love as in art. No, there was no turning
back. He would soon return to his unit, or something
else would intrude. I knew this afternoon would never
come again. He heaved himself out of the sleigh, took
my arm. I noticed I was almost as tall as he was now.
Had I grown in a year? I raised my fur collar against
my burning cheeks as Kolya paid the driver. And it
struck me in this moment what a timeless scene this
was—the man paying the cab as the woman waited,
half hidden in the collar of her coat. How many men,
how many women had lived this exact moment? I felt
so at one with them, through time. Now I was the
woman, and he was the man. Our time and place, now.

Together we walked to the building's front door and
up a short flight of stairs. I would tell no one about
this—not Varvara, not Mina. Part of being a woman
would be to have just such secrets. He unlocked a door
on the second floor. We hung our coats and hats in the
entry. He removed his tall boots, and I my slushy overshoes. I threw my book bag in the corner. Inside, a
warm sitting room awaited us, with small side chairs
and a wide divan covered in olive velvet. Would it happen here? My heart pounded so hard I missed what
he said. He repeated himself—"It's too hot, don't you
think?"—and opened the *fortochka* in the tall casement
window overlooking the Catherine Canal. The delicious coolness mixed with the heat was like a cold cloth
in a fever. He bent over and touched my heavy coiled

hair, breathed in the scent as if it were a flower. I offered my lips, but he only touched them with a finger, rolling the lower one down ever so slightly.

I hadn't even noticed the gramophone with its green bell until he went to it and, after cranking it vigorously, lowered the arm. Strains of the tango from New Year's Eve emerged into the air. He held out his hands to me, he in his cavalry uniform, khaki tunic with gold buttons, blue breeches with their double red stripe, standing in his gray socks, perhaps knitted by one of my classmates. His cropped brown curls lay flat to his scalp, the moustache he sported nestled into the corners of his upturned mouth like twin commas, those clever blue eyes alight...

We began to dance. Not the relatively decorous tango of that New Year's salon, but pressed together from breast to knee. I felt him hard against me, the full length of him. Now it was not the suggestion of lovemaking, but the thing itself. He pressed me back, our feet turning but deftly, never tangling. I surprised him with a tango kick. He laughed. *Better watch me, Kolya.* I could follow, but there were other sides to me as well, even as a sixteen-year-old virgin. The play of the gaze—the look away, then suddenly, nakedly, back. The very air leaned against us like a dog hoping to be petted.

"I knew it would be like this," he whispered into my hair. "I could dance with you to the end of time. Remember how you danced *Swan Lake*?"

I was seven years old. I'd just seen the ballet, had to show everybody the white swan and the black. "I'm a glutton for attention."

"You believed it—that's what I loved. The way you threw yourself into it. I knew you were those swans. I saw how you would be someday. Glorious. I've been waiting for you, Marina."

I had been waiting as well. All this time, masquerading as a nice, well-bred girl when I was a stream in flood, a length of fire, the fall of a hawk. And he knew me—he had always known this lay under school uniforms and children's party clothes, inside the camisole with the blue ribbon. He knew me at six, had waited for me as a peasant waits for the pears to ripen in summertime, watching that tree all the time he goes about his hoeing and reaping. Now he would reap the rewards of his patience.

He pulled a tortoiseshell hairpin from my coif, then another. My hair started to fall, uncoiling heavily over my shoulders, the great mass of it, a Niagara of russet. I had never imagined inspiring the look on a man's face that he beheld me with right now, the wonder with which he touched my thick locks, lifting them in his palms like a bouquet of roses. He hadn't seen my hair down in years. He buried his face in it, his hands. It was going to be hopelessly tangled—I helped him tangle it more. It would be a nest for us, like two thrushes in a thicket.

He unbuttoned my brown school dress, pushed it

from my shoulders, let it fall to the floor, and traced my bared, lightly freckled shoulders with his fingertips. Touching the ribbon on the front of my slip, untying it, pulling it from me, kneeling before me. I stepped out of it and he pressed the fabric to his face. I thought I would faint with the pleasure. When had I ever seen anything so erotic? He ran his hands up my thick wool stockings, pressed his cheek against the plush of my Venus mount. I held him there, knew he could smell me through the cotton lisle. He rubbed his face, his head, like a cat in catnip. I wished I had worn newer underwear.

Suddenly he lifted me up and threw me over his shoulder—the Rape of the Sabines!—and carried me, laughing and shrieking, into the other room. He dropped me onto a white eiderdown with enormous pillows. The brass bedstead knocked on the wall. Outside, snow fell into the frozen canal, onto the griffins of the bridge, and beyond, softening the lit windows of the Assignation Bank Building. I felt sorry for those people bent over their ledgers. Poor everyone who wasn't us.

Kolya sat on the edge of the bed, untied the bow of my corselette. Finally, fear came licking at me, as I perceived for a moment the seriousness of my position. I rolled away from him, sat up. "You won't make me pregnant? I would die. I'd kill myself."

He put his fingers across my lips. "I wouldn't. I'm not some sweaty ignoramus. I never leave it to chance."

He reached into his tunic and pulled out small square packages, put them on the bedside table. *Rezinky. Preservativy.* I knew what they were, I'd seen them in my father's drawer. "I'll never hurt you, Marina, I promise you that."

I got up and stood before him, suddenly serious— grave, even—and undid the buttons of my corselette, watching him as I opened them one by one. To hear him inhale as he saw my breasts, I knew they were beautiful. Not apple-round, like the Venus de Milo's, but wide set and full at the sides. Now I unbuttoned his tunic, then his shirt, pulled it off. The intoxicating smell of him, warm honey and musk, rose from his chest. He was hairier than I had imagined, gold and curly. I ran my hands over him, the miracle. I pulled him to his feet so I could press my breasts against him. So many textures—the cropped hair, the shaved face, that curly moustache, the softness between his shoulder and chest, the nubs of nipples standing up now, yearning for mine. I brushed against them with my own.

We shucked off the rest of our clothes, which tangled and gripped us as if they didn't want to allow the final frankness, but soon we achieved our undressing— admiring one another in flesh so long guessed at. Of course I had two brothers, so the male member was no mystery to me, but never had I seen one rampant, not in life. I had once stumbled on a book of Japanese pornography in the library of one of my mother's arty friends. That shock, the giant hairy mollusks of the women and the stair banisters of the men. Kolya was, happily, neither outsize nor frightening but rather thick, in a nest of golden brown. I thought it would be hard to the touch, but it was velvet, like the inside of my arm, or a horse's nose. Veined and soon moist. He pushed my hand away.

"Don't you like it?"

He laughed, rolling his head, his eyes to the ceiling with my ignorance. "Yes, but a man can only take so much before he goes off."

So much to know. We knelt on the bed, thigh to thigh, our kisses deep and hungry, while a kaleidoscope of sharp feelings tumbled within me: Would it hurt? Would it be the same after? Would he boast? Laugh at me? Ah, but I had waited my whole life for this pleasure, my bottom in his hands, the bright universe of his touch, this lively desirous body, the muscular flesh, the intensity of my own sensations as his fingers moved, guiding me in the tiniest tango, my body impulsively kicking and gripping as he talked to me as though I were a skittish horse. "You're so passionate. I knew it would be like this. Don't stop, I want to see you…" A warmth passed through me, so explosive he had to hold me up.

What is virginity? Is it innocence? Ignorance? Fear? Unripeness? I was his pear, dragging down the branch with all my ripeness. I wanted his teeth to burst my skin, his hot mouth to tear me apart. And yet he ate slowly, with exquisite attention.

There was no end to the surprises. I lay upon the hill of huge pillows, and watched him smooth the *preservativ* over himself. He traced me like an artist with his brush. While his fingers had been surprising, his sex felt enormous—would it really all fit? He pushed, then stopped and rubbed me gently. I didn't care if it hurt, I wanted him. I pulled him down onto me. I wanted to feel his full weight on me, embrace the length of him, his chest flat against my breasts. Was I too small? It turned out I was equal to the task. A sensation not like anything in a book. Stretched beyond myself, intense, not wanting to stop, wanted him all inside me, not just his member but his whole body. Who needed flesh if it was going to keep me from merging with absolute sweetness? Now we rolled and switched places, me on him, urging him with my hips as I'd urge a horse from trot to canter. Then the darkness took me again, a sparkling wave from groin to head, and gasping, I sagged onto his chest like a drowned woman flung onto a beach.

Afterward, we lay together, his flagpole clad in the *preservativ* bright with my blood. He handed me a towel with which to clean myself, but I was too lazy. I wrapped my legs around it and lay there with my head on his shoulder, drunk with the smell of him and the slow ticking of my body unwinding. So much for those gleanings from novels, from paintings, as if love were a matter of posing in picturesque *dishabille*. No. You went into it as a tiger encountering another tiger. You went into it like a person jumping off a bridge. I dozed, inhaling him—the scent came from his armpits, that honey musk smell, and a muskier one from the nest down below. I fell asleep wrapped in my own hair.

He woke me sometime later. He'd lit the lamp, was passing a box of chocolates before my face like smelling salts. Swiss chocolate, a big red box. I took one, and it was all part of the afternoon, the chocolate melting in my mouth, the fragrant bed, the liquid between my legs, the reflection of us in the bare window. My hair was an explosion of tangled red. It looked like we'd fought a war on the white sheets, completely untucked from the striped mattress ticking, the puffy eiderdown crushed, everything soaked with our sweat.

"We have to go soon. Come on. I've drawn a bath for you." He kissed the top of my head, got up, found his shirt on the floor, put it on.

It was almost six by the clock on the bedside table. If I missed dinner, my family would wonder what had happened to me. "I could call them, say I'm going to be late."

"You don't have to eat every chocolate in the box." He squeezed my breast, slapped my bottom.

I took another chocolate, just for that. "Everybody always says that. But let's stay here forever and eat every chocolate in the world."

"I adore you, Marina," he said, buttoning up his tunic. "But I've got some people I'm meeting in a few minutes. It's why I'm in town. Not just to explore delectable young women."

"What could be more important than that?" I wanted more. I wanted to take up residence in the nexus of pleasure called Kolya Shurov. "Take me with you."

"It's army business. I hardly think you'll pass muster."

Reluctant to move, yet knowing I must, I shuffled into the small bath perfumed with the fragrance of milled soap. I gingerly lowered myself into the water. It was just as well we had stopped when we did. My body probably couldn't have stood another assault. I washed, wincing at the abrasions, dried myself off using the one bloodied towel in order not to shame the maids too much. The face before me in the mirror was bright, smudged, a little stunned. *Who are you?* I asked, touching my fat lips, gazing into my stupefied dark eyes. *This is what a woman who has just made love looks like.* The next room of the self.

"When will I see you again?" I asked, attempting to brush my tangled hair with the help of some borrowed brushes, my clothing mostly restored. Propriety was pure disguise.

"I'll send you a message," he said. "Wear a red ribbon in your green coat after school so the messenger will know you."

Was Father looking at me strangely? Did Mother really not know? Couldn't they smell him on me? Couldn't they tell? I ate quickly and tried not to look at Sery-ozha. I was sure he'd noticed a change, if only because of the waves of happiness rising off me. Luckily Av-dokia ate in the kitchen with the cook and Basya. My nanny was clairvoyant—she wouldn't be fooled for an instant. I watched plain, good Miss Haddon-Finch debone her fish and wondered if she'd ever had such an afternoon. Or my parents, for that matter, seated at their two ends of the table. Had they ever been capable of such ardor? The shrieks, the groaning, the sweat, the torn-up bed. I doubted it. They didn't even sleep in the same room.

Seryozha caught my eye, cocked his head. *What?* I smiled like the Mona Lisa—perhaps this was her se-cret. Father spoke of a conference with members of his political party, the liberal Kadets. Something about the tsar. "We're offering the emperor a way out," he said to Mother, spearing a piece of sturgeon and some potato on his fork. "Constitutional monarchy. He could preserve his crown, but he won't see it that way…"

"Surely he will," she replied.

I was usually quite interested in politics, especially after the bread riot—not to mention the rebuke from Marmelzadt and Varvara's constant agitation—but tonight all I could think of was the feeling of my bare breasts pressed to Kolya's chest, all the ways we ex-plored our love in that white bed. I finished my meal as fast as I could, and excused myself. I would write a real aubade this time, an ode to those cropped curls, all the textures of him. I knew I would love hairy men for the rest of my life.

I sat at the vanity table in my salmon-pink bedroom, brushing my hair. It still smelled of him. Beneath the glass lay a picture of Kolya and Volodya taken in the south two years before, sitting on a rocky hillside. Such confident young officers in the pure hot sun. I was about to kiss his sweet face when Seryozha entered. He closed the door, stood behind me sternly, as if he were Father. "Who is it? Tell me."

I coiled my hair back into its decorous coif, replaced the pins. There was no point in trying to conceal my love. I was too eager to talk about it. "It's Kolya. He's here on leave. He was waiting for me after school in a sleigh with a gray horse."

My brother's sternness softened, replaced by uncertainty, a flicker of pleasure, then envy, and back to uncertainty. "Did you...?"

I nodded.

He came closer, crouched to look over my shoulder, eye to eye with me in the vanity mirror. "Are you all right?"

I nodded. He put his head on my shoulder and we stayed that way for a long time. When he stood, I saw he was weeping, though whether it was from losing me and childhood or envy, it was hard to say.

*   *   *

I could not stop thinking about sex. I imagined everyone naked—Vaula, the *dvornik*, people in the street. I imagined them making love and tried to decide which ones were still virgins. My new eyes caught couples who had clearly just made love saying goodbye at cabs and couples on street corners preparing for an assignation. Their energy set them apart, brightness bursting from them like little colorful suns. I imagined who would be prim and who would be passionate. I felt my way into the lives of old couples strolling along, fires dampened but still slightly warm. The ugliest sight: couples who had not made love for years. You could see it by how they walked together. No affectionate touch. No *tango*. How could they bear it, linked to a person for whose body you didn't yearn? No one escaped my scrutiny—bourgeois men and women, my own father and mother. The unemployed, my teachers, people in the shops.

How loathsome suddenly became the routine of schoolgirl life. Geometry, French, Russian literature, English. Voice lesson with Herr Dietrich, dancing class with M. Dornais. It seemed like a joke. Although I enjoyed being handled by those nervous boys in dancing class as much as I ever did. Perhaps more. I felt them so keenly now, the hands on my skin, a glance to my bosom. I imagined undressing Danya Bolechevsky, pimply but receptive, and Sasha Trigorsky—his erect carriage, what else might be erect? Men in the streets, at Wolf's bookstore—no one escaped my lascivious scrutiny.

Every day I wore a red ribbon through the buttonhole of my green coat no matter how bitter the cold: twelve degrees below zero. It had been a terrible winter, but I was a furnace. I emerged through the school gates in a fever, head held high, so the ribbon would be visible. Walking down to Mina's apartment, or to Konditerskaya Sever on Nevsky for chocolate, I waited for his summons. Who would it be today? He liked to use the most outlandish people he could find, it was part of the surprise. Would it be the cripple dragging himself along on a sledge? The freezing newsboy? The man with a great red birthmark? I stopped on the Anichkov Bridge, where the four bronze statues of horse tamers struggled with their mounts—two of them were very much in danger of being trampled. And I wondered who I was in this drama—horse or a groom? Straining at the bridle or trying not to be trampled as I attempted to turn that great passion to my own purposes? Everything seemed like a metaphor these days. I was wide open to the world, waiting for the one who would stop me and hand me a small white envelope. At last, a Nevsky prostitute approached and handed me an envelope with a red seal. I tore it open—his paper, the finest, from Michelet's. Just like Pushkin's.

Today is impossible. I'm devastated. I can't stop thinking of you, Marina. I see you everywhere. Think of me with you right now. Tomorrow, I promise.

Underneath the words, a little drawing—a nude girl dancing with a bushy-tailed fox. I had to laugh, though the message wounded me. How could he not be as eager as I to spend every moment in bed? Still, when we did meet, my anger would be quickly absorbed in the unfolding desire. Our passion took more weight and dimension each day, like a fast-growing young bear.

One night, our family attended the ballet—with our parents' friends the Gromitskys. It was Karsavina in *Les millions d'Arléquin*. Both Seryozha and I had been besotted with her, ever since that night at the Stray Dog. "I wish we could have *The Firebird*," Mother complained to Madame Gromitsky. "It's not right that the French should get all our moderns." The Mariinsky Theater, under imperial patronage, had to follow imperial taste, and thus far the tsar only endorsed the classics. Even the Harlequin was a stretch. Balletomanes like Mother resented the fact that the Parisians were able to delight in the bright creations of Diaghilev's Ballets Russes—productions never staged in Russia.

Karsavina, I decided, had definitely torn some bedsheets.

In the interval, Seryozha and I remained in our seats. I hated breaking the lingering trance and Seryozha was finishing some sketches. Now Mother exclaimed, "Oh look, it's Kolya. What a pretty girl—Kolya!"

My lover was coming up the aisle escorting a beautiful woman in a low-necked black gown, his hand on her back. I wanted to vomit. As they approached, I held my hand over my eyes as if to cut the glare of the lights. Where could I hide myself? *Go away, Kolya!* How could he? So much for the fox and the girl. Was this what he was doing instead of meeting with me? If I hadn't been caught in the row, I would have run away weeping. Shamelessly he approached, broke out in a grin. Now he was greeting my parents, introducing this creature, Valentina somebody. I tried not to look, but how could I not? It was like an overturned cart, an auto wreck. And the beast winked at me! As if we were in collusion. As if this were all a great joke! As if I were so sophisticated that I would know it was still the two of us and not give a thought to the exquisite woman he stood next to. "Are you enjoying the ballet, Marina Dmitrievna?" he asked me.

The nerve! "I *was*," I said.

He leaned past Seryozha and pressed a note into my hand, rolled my fist around it. A page torn from the program. *Tomorrow at 4. Without fail.* And a drawing of a fox in jail, its nose sticking out from the bars, tears dripping from its eyes.

8 *No Gentleman*

ON THE STEPS OF the school, Varvara showed us a pamphlet from her schoolbag, glancing around to see that no one was looking over our shoulders.

WHY IS YOUR HUSBAND AT THE FRONT? TO FIGHT THE
TSAR'S WAR! WHY IS THERE NO FOOD IN THE CITY?
IT'S DISAPPEARING INTO THE WAR! THE TSAR'S ON
HIS WAY OUT. *REMEMBER BLOODY SUNDAY. WE'LL
FINISH WHAT WE STARTED. BREAD FOR ALL!
EQUAL RIGHTS FOR ALL. DOWN WITH THE WAR.*

"You're going to end up in prison," Mina said.

"They say you're not a real revolutionary until you've served time," she retorted.

It was 3:30. "I have to go. Kolya's waiting for me," I said. Already my eyes ached in the vicious cold, my lashes coated with ice. How could Varvara even think of standing around in this weather handing out leaflets?

"Yes, run to your lover. Go on," Varvara sneered, wrapping her scarf around her head and neck. "When people ask where you were in January 1917, what are you going to say—*I spent it in bed with Kolya Shurov?*"

But there would always be more textile factories, more miserable women. I was flopping, drowning in air after Kolya's appearance at the Mariinsky. I needed his apology, an explanation, reassurances that I was still the one.

He answered the door in the apartment on the Catherine Canal. Food and flowers crowded the table in the sitting room behind him, but I remained rooted in the entryway, my overshoes leaving a puddle on the parquet. He tried to take my coat, but I shrugged him off.

I was not letting him touch me until I got a straight answer. If I let him get close, I wouldn't be able to concentrate on my fury. "Just tell me one thing. Are you sleeping with her?"

"Who?"

Such innocence. "Just don't."

"Oh, don't be like that." He returned to the divan, to the table spread with the feast, as I remained in the anteroom. "At least have a glass of wine before you cut my head off," he said, seating himself. "And these macaroons are divine."

Persephone ate six pomegranate seeds in hell and was doomed the moment they slid down her throat. "Tell me now."

"Take off your coat. You're making me sweat."

It was terribly hot in there, it was true. But I didn't dare. I had to resist, keep anger alive, get to the truth. "What am I to you, Kolya? Am I another name in the roll call of seducible schoolgirls? Is it me in the afternoon and Valentina in the evening and Katerina before breakfast?"

He sighed and rubbed his face with one hand.

"Is she better than me? More exciting, a woman of the world?"

He laughed. "No one's better than you, and that's the truth," he said. "Valya's—just someone I know. I'm doing some work for her. I didn't sleep with her, I promise."

"Do go on," I said, and it sounded just like Mother. It just came out.

"She wants to get some things out of the country. That's all, I swear to you." He laid his hand over his lying heart.

"I saw you. I saw how you touched her. You have slept with her."

"A long time ago. She was Volodya's girl. We were just doing some business, I swear to you. She wanted an escort to the ballet, and I figured, what's the harm? I can't exactly take you."

"Why not?"

"Why not? Imagine your parents. Your father. I don't want him putting two and two together too soon...God. But listen, I have something to tell you—I didn't want it to be like this, but I've been recalled. I'm leaving tonight."

My anger ebbed with this blow. He couldn't leave now. I needed time to sort out this Valentina thing, to forgive him. But there wouldn't be time. And the truth was that I ached for him. My arms ached, my breasts, my body was a mass of frustration and yearning. "Swear, Kolya. Swear you didn't sleep with her. I'll never forgive you if you're lying."

He stood, held my hands, pulled me into the room. Looked deep into my eyes, his blue ones, for once, not laughing. "She's just an old friend. I swear."

He unbuttoned my coat, hung it on the back of a chair, knelt and pulled off my galoshes, led me to the feast.

Persephone was doomed with only six pomegranate

seeds, but I ate macaroons and drank sherry wine and devoured the feast I had come for—his flesh, the red-gold fur, making love in four different ways until we lay exhausted on the mattress.

We rested our heads on the heaped pillows, listening to the wind roar outside, shaking the windows. He opened the *fortochka,* chilling the room. I pulled up the eiderdown. Briefly I thought of Varvara, out there on Vasilievsky Island, standing before the gates of a factory, handing out those incendiary leaflets, and felt guilty for abandoning her. I ran my fingers through the hair on his chest, traced the line down to his navel, lower, to the leonine forest of him.

"And what were you going to do for her, your friend Valentina?"

"An export job," he said, linking my fingers with his, biting them systematically at the knuckles. "She has some things she wants sent out of the country. Actually, your father should do the same. Time to close up the bank accounts, pack up the silver, convert cash to jewelry and art. Get it out to Sweden. England, even."

They're smuggling the gold out in coffins. "It's really that bad? Did you tell Father?"

"Let's just say he wasn't amused. He practically called me a traitor." I could see that had hurt Kolya. He was only trying to be helpful.

"Brave of you," I said. To advise Dmitry Makarov to prepare to abandon Russia, especially now, when he was working around the clock, writing speeches, articles, meeting with the Kadet party? Foolhardy. The Kadets had been trying to persuade the emperor to accept a constitutional monarchy, ever since the death of Rasputin. But the tsar was unable to see that it was the only way to keep his crown while allowing the country to move forward. An absolute monarch, he felt that sharing power was as bad as abdication.

I examined our fingers entwined. Someday would we wear matching rings? "Every day, I think today's the day that the revolution will come. But it doesn't. The people just keep suffering. Striking, protesting—it keeps going on."

He reached past me to the bedside table, fishing out a cigar from the ashtray, relighting it. "Watch the soldiers," he said. "When the army goes over, then you'll see your revolution. The monarchy will collapse like a thatched hut. I just don't want to see your family trapped inside. You Makarovs mean a lot to me."

He was starting to scare me. "What about your assets, Kolya? Are you taking them out? Or is that just for others?"

He pulled me to him, cradled my head in the hollow of his shoulder, kissed my temple, worked his hand into my hair. "I come from a long line of gamblers, *milaya*. The factory went under years ago. The estate was gone before I was born. My only assets in the world are the ones you like so well."

Was Kolya poor? I hadn't ever thought about how he supported himself. He couldn't be flat broke, could he?

He did all the things Volodya did—bought uniforms, dined in restaurants, went out carousing. But when I thought about it, I realized that he didn't have an apartment. At university, he'd lived with Volodya. We took him on vacation with us. Did my parents know he was poor? They must. It was only I who had missed the clues. I, who thought I saw everything and complained that others were insensitive. I was as guilty as anyone. Poor Kolya!

"I tried talking to Vera Borisovna," he continued. "She reassured me, 'Russia is built on stone, Nikolasha, the stone of the Russian soul. Never forget that.' But the thing about stone," he said, stroking my bare thighs with his fingertips, "is that water seeps into the cracks. And when it freezes, the stone splits and crumbles to dust. Stone's of no use in times like these. We need to be flexible, like the little birches trembling in a summer breeze."

Honestly, I was shocked to hear him talk like this. In my family, we spoke of honor, of country, of duty. Of holding steadfast to certain virtues. "What kind of Russian are you, Nikolai Stepanovich?" I asked, only half in jest.

Kolya calmly gazed at the tip of his cigar. "I'm the citizen of a country of exactly one." He reached for his ashtray, put it beside him in the bed. "Shurovistan. But you're welcome to visit. I give you a lifetime visa."

Wind blasted the windows. I thought of the workers in this cold, the women queuing for bread. "Varvara says there's going to be a general strike. Surely that can't be ignored."

"Oh, it will be. They'll get double barrels for their trouble. The emperor won't give an inch."

"Not even a general strike? It's been terrible. You haven't been here, you don't know."

He crouched over me, playfully growling like a bear. "Not even a general strike."

I fought not to let his proximity distract me. "They're going to start rationing bread, Kolya! The people won't stand for it."

He bit my neck just above the shoulder, sending shoots of pleasure down into the soil of me. "You're out of your depth, Marina," he whispered in my ear. "Let the workers take care of themselves."

I pushed him away. "What am I supposed to do, play Marie Antoinette in the sheepfold?"

He knelt, waving his pole at me. "Baaah."

"They're chaining them to the workbench. It's illegal to complain. If you do, it's to the front with you."

He groaned and flopped into the eiderdown, which inflated around him like a cloud. "No! Right from the Tagantsev Academy to the front?" He was laughing at me. "Will they give you a chance to change clothes?"

I pinched his nipple, and he grabbed for my wrist. We struggled until he had me pinned on the mattress, damp and fragrant. He straddled me, his face hovering above mine. "So now you're a radical? Do I address you as Comrade Marina?"

"Yes!" I tried to roll out from under him.

"So it's the workers you love now, not Kolya and his rapier?" Which was already alive again.

"I'm serious, Kolya." But my claim sounded ridiculous even to me, lying there wet with my arms pinned, Kolya rubbing himself against me.

He switched to holding my wrists above my head with one hand while he put on a fresh prophylactic with the other. "I can see how serious you are. I'm so impressed."

I struggled to throw him off me. "Stop it! Listen to me. This is important."

He groaned and rolled off me. "Is this what you want? My last night? Okay, here it is. All the emperor cares about is the war. Workers in Petrograd are starving? *Nobody cares.* As long as they produce, to hell with them. And if it takes chaining them to their benches, that's what will happen."

I felt desire's sharp ebb. The shock of what he'd said propped me on one elbow. "That's what you think? Are you really so indifferent? I thought you were a good man."

He got his cigar lit, exhaled the fumes, a man of the world. "Good or bad, it's what's happening. Nobody's asking me."

I sat up, looking down into his face. "I'm asking you."

"As long as his armies are supplied, the emperor will send the country to the devil. And my job in this mess is just to see that the army's supplied." He exhaled away from me.

"Well there's a safe job. When men are losing their lives." I didn't know what I was arguing about now, only that I wanted to hurt him for being so callous about the fate of the people. Or was it to punish him for taking Valentina to the ballet? Or because he was leaving me again? "Maybe you're speculating yourself, while Volodya's fighting in the cold."

His rosy face went hard then. He started collecting his clothes. "You want me to get my head blown off? You're asking me what I think—I think this country's as corrupt as old eggs and I'm just trying to survive it." He found his underpants and got into them, buttoned his shirt. "Do you believe it's a valiant thing to die? I've seen this war. You haven't. It's a communal grave for valiant young men. And reluctant ones, and ignorant ones too. They all die the same. Where are my damn pants?"

I'd hurt him. I never knew I could do that. I'd thought he was impervious. "I'm sorry, Kolya, I'm sorry. I don't know why I said that. It's not what I think at all." I had his pants and clung to them, I wouldn't let him take them away.

"I won't die for this country," he said. "Not for God and not for you. If you're a Bolshevik, you'll at least understand that much."

But I didn't understand. Heroism was a very real value in our house. Patriotism. Volodya was at the front, absolutely ready to die for ideals, for country, and this was what was admirable about him, although perhaps all wrong—his unquestioning valor. Kolya's relativism, his pessimism—I didn't know what to think. Logically he was right, but there was something upsetting about a man without loyalty, without an idea of honor. I wept. I was only sixteen, and I loved him ferociously. How could I ruin our last hours together trying to figure it out? What I wanted was his love, his body, his smile, his scent, his weight. I threw his pants under the bed, held my arms out to him. "Sorry, sorry..." Holding him, rocking him. Kolya, my fox, generous, clever man. He was not evil, not an abstract symbol of indifference to suffering. Who didn't have contradictions?

And I more than he, as it turned out.

9 *Do Not Awaken My Memories*

HE RETURNED TO HIS regiment, leaving me as sad and useless as a single glove. People, once lively, now flattened to puppets, mouths opening and closing unconvincingly. My ears were stuffed with wax, my eyes smeared with grease. I couldn't find a place to put myself. I eyed every cripple and dwarf. I put away my green coat. I could barely brush my hair. Our fight left a stone in my breast. How could I have accused him of such crimes on our very last afternoon?

In front of the school, everyone stopped to wrap scarves tighter around their necks and draw them up around their mouths and noses. Varvara and Mina had been doing their best to cheer me up, each in her opposite way — Mina by letting me talk about him endlessly, commiserating, wanting to hear every detail, and Varvara by jeering at my lovelorn fog. "Yes, yes, he's gone. The world doesn't revolve around Kolya Shurov's sky-blue eyes."

"She's heartbroken," Mina said, drawing me close. "Leave her alone."

Varvara hoisted her schoolbag on her shoulder. "Come with me," she said. "Talk to some people worse off than you."

"Don't listen to her," Mina said. "You'll get yourself arrested. Anyway, it's got to be ten below. Let's get some hot chocolate."

"Come on, Marina." Varvara twined her arm through mine. "Let's make ourselves useful. You'll feel better. Remember when you went to the hospitals? We need you. You need to see what's going on. Mina, you coming?"

"I'm getting chocolate. Marina, it's dangerous up there."

But maybe the danger would help wake me up out of my funk. I let Varvara trundle me onto a tram going north across the Liteiny Bridge into a grim working-class neighborhood on the Vyborg side of the Neva. Vyborg, where the big factories were, with the workers' tenements crouching in their shadows. We got off and walked past the Finland Station and into the backstreets within clear view of the Crosses—Kresty Prison—and the Arsenal plant. It summed up everything—the elegant palace side of the river could have been a thousand miles away. We entered a gloomy courtyard. I was glad just to be out of the wind. But then I saw the women, ragged, blue-faced, queuing up for a single water pump. The ice, their wet shoes. It was a disgrace.

Varvara helped them pump, for which they were grateful, and got them talking. The stories made me shiver with pity. *Nobody cares,* said Kolya. Husbands at the front, sick children, food shortages, no fuel. Horrific tales of the granny in the building who took care of the babies of the working women when they were at the factories. "She waters down the milk and keeps the money herself," a youngish woman told us, her eyes black with weariness. "I'd go to work, too—my old man's not well—but I can't leave the kids with an old witch like that. You might as well put them out on the river."

I let Varvara ask them questions—not *name, district, region* but rather about their lives—while I pumped their water, the cold biting my hands as my gloves grew wet. At least I had galoshes. She talked to them about the militarization of labor, about socialism, about the war. Mostly they were worried about bread rationing. "They say it'll be just a pound per person," said a

woman with anxious eyes and sunken cheeks, a soldier's wife. "My husband's fighting for what? A pound
of bread a day? How are we supposed to live?"

I pumped her water and let my sorrow over Kolya spill
into sympathy for this wretched woman. I was no good
at agitating, but I could do this, stand in the icy dark
courtyard of a tenement under the walls of the Arsenal
and listen to half-starved women complain about bread.
Their misery had to end. My problems with Kolya
seemed laughable compared with trying to keep a tenement warm, the rent paid—some families didn't even
have the whole flat to themselves, just a corner of it.

Two days later, we returned to stand at the gates of the
Belhausen knitwear factory. Varvara pulled a sheaf of
leaflets from her school satchel.

SISTER WORKERS! FIGHT SLAVERY AT THE WORKBENCH!
SUPPORT THE PETROGRAD WORKERS COMMITTEE!

The flyer was illustrated by a simple graphic woodcut of workers—women and men marching shoulder
to shoulder as a frightened owner tumbled away. For
the literate, a more detailed argument accompanied it
below. The wind shuffled the flyers in Varvara's gloved
hand.

But the members of the Workers' Committee had all
been arrested. It had been in the papers. Where had
these flyers come from? Who gave them to her?

"Better you not know," she said mysteriously, trying to impress me with her radicalism. "That way if we're arrested, you can't tell them anything."

"We're not going to be arrested," I said. "Varvara, tell me. I can't be arrested. My father will crucify me." If talking to the women in the courtyards was suspicious, leafleting factories was flat-out illegal. I'd be expelled a semester short of graduation. I'd never see the university.

"Do you want to help these women or not? Look—stand over there." She pointed to a streetlamp around twenty feet away, ducking her head against the wind. "If you see cops, start singing. Put those voice lessons to work."

The cold reached everywhere—inside my scarf, inside my nose, freezing the hairs. This was insane. The light was already fading. I had no idea where I was—in front of some factory in Vyborg on a rough, uncleared lane. I would have left, but I feared losing my way in a dangerous slum. "What do you want me to sing?"

"How about 'Do Not Awaken My Memories'?"

A song about a seduced and abandoned girl. "Very funny."

But I thought of those women at the pump, their blue faces, their ragged clothes, and Kolya's callous statements, and took my place under the streetlamp to keep watch, my eyes stinging in the cold, my nerves thinner than a violin E string. At five o'clock, a whistle blew, signaling the shift change. Women began to file out of the factory through the big gates. Varvara stood at the gate, holding out a leaflet. Some eyed her and shouldered past, while others were too beaten down even to look. But several accepted Varvara's pamphlet. Each time felt like a triumph. One woman took half the stack and put them under her coat, scurrying away into the dark, reminding me that other women took far bigger risks than we did.

The city was on the boil. Strikes and bigger strikes, on the Vyborg side, on Vasilievsky, on the Okhta side, and in the south at the big plants—Putilov, Nobel, Arsenal. There were lockouts, bread riots. And absurdly, I turned seventeen right in the middle of it all. Ridiculous. An insult to celebrate such a thing when the whole country was sliding into the abyss. Yet Mother insisted on a party. "I can't," I told Father. "It seems so hardhearted. When people have so little."

"I know," he said. "You're a good girl. But we still have to live our lives. We can't go about in horsehair and ashes. Leave this to the politicians. You should have your party."

"It makes me sick," I said.

He stroked my hair, smiled. "How many times will you turn seventeen? Enjoy it. The country will still be here to worry about the day after."

I felt like an absolute fool, standing among well-dressed schoolchildren with my hair done up like a fancy cake, eating Vaula's "larks"—crispy pastries that looked like small birds—and talking about a skating party in the Tauride Gardens. This was no longer me. I'd had my first love affair. I'd waited in the cold at the Belhausen factory gate, braving arrest, agitating on the Vyborg side. Right now, soldiers' wives were freezing in their corners, their children were drinking watered-down milk, workers were being forced to labor despite horrendous conditions, bread was being rationed. What was I doing playing children's games and drinking hot chocolate? Mina stayed with me, trying to make me laugh, while my hapless brother fended off the forays of flirtatious girls. Varvara ate four pastries and got into an argument with Sasha Trigorsky. I missed Kolya like fire. Did he even remember my birthday? Although it shouldn't have mattered. I didn't know who I was, didn't know what to feel. It took everything I had not to throw a tantrum, as if I were seven and not seventeen.

Afterward, in my bedroom, I felt just like the wind blowing from all four directions, every possible emotion, one minute coldly furious, weeping the next. I wrote a poem.

After the cake
The chocolate and the lemonade
The children return to the sleighs
To kisses and Mama and supper.
A girl turned seventeen

The coldest day of the year.
Birds fell frozen from the sky.
A man at the front counted his cards.
All men are gamblers, he said.
She entered the world like a mole.
She entered the world like a spy.
She entered the world the queen of hearts.
Her hair a flame.
Her bones bleaching white
While he gambled her away.

Part II

My Revolution

(February 1917–October 1917)

10 *International Women's Day*

IN THE MIDST OF that terrible winter of 1917, after weeks of twenty, thirty below zero, the weather suddenly turned fair. Overnight, thermometers soared from four below to forty degrees, just in time for the International Women's Day march. Had the weather not cooperated, who knows whether events would have unfolded as they did? That short warm spell changed the world.

What is history? Is it the trace of a footstep in wet cement? Is it the story of important men in smoky rooms and on battlefields? The inevitable outcome of great impersonal forces? Or is it a collision of chance events—like the sudden rise of the mercury on February 23, 1917, in the midst of a hungry midwinter and a ruinous war? The day before, Putilov locked out its thousands of workers—the owners claiming there wasn't enough materiel to keep the factory running, though it was more likely in retaliation for striking. So the essential ingredients happened to come together on that one day—thousands of unemployed and striking workers, warm weather, and the Women's Day march.

I'll tell you this: history is the sound of a floor underneath a rotten regime, termite-ridden and ready to fall. It groans. It smells like ozone before a storm.

But up on Furshtatskaya Street, it could have been any Thursday morning. An old woman walked her dog, which trotted ahead, visiting huge piles of snow. A wagon clattered by. *Dvorniks'* brooms swept passages and pavements in front of chic apartment buildings. Father, leaving for the Duma that springlike morning, briefcase in hand, had a swing in his step. He wore his fedora instead of a fur *shapka*. When he was gone, I shook Seryozha awake. They'd closed school in anticipation of huge crowds turning out for the march, hoping to keep the children off the streets—though of course the opposite was likely. My sleepyheaded brother slunk further under the covers, his tangled blond hair on the pillow. I shook him again. He rubbed his eyes, stretched, peered at the clock, groaned. "You go. I hate crowds. Anyway Papa said to stay in."

"We're not staying in. Get dressed." I threw his clothes at him. Father had warned us last night, "There's likely to be trouble," but what were the chances I'd stay home with eighty thousand women, strikers, and soldiers' wives coming out to demonstrate? I fetched the water pitcher from my brother's dresser and prepared to anoint him with it. A half hour later, we emerged onto Liteiny Prospect, already teeming with people marveling at the mild weather—shopkeepers chatting with customers, the florist with the greengrocer. The air vibrated with life. Of course

Seryozha dawdled, having to admire every window display—the antiques shop, the stationer's. Like a cop, I took his arm and marched him forward to Mina's flat on Nevsky Prospect.

The Katzevs' apartment at the corner of Liteiny and Nevsky smelled of kasha. Mina was still finishing breakfast, but Varvara already had her coat on and she paced like a caged leopard. Mina's mother, Sofia Yakovlevna, poured us glasses of tea and insisted Seryozha sit down and try a savory *cheburek*. Everyone there petted Seryozha. It was a boyless family, and how they spoiled him—Mina's two younger sisters vied for his attention, her mother plied him with snacks and praise. Then Mina's father, Solomon Moiseivich, a bearish, jovial man, appeared from the photography studio off the sitting room carrying a big box camera, tripod, and case. He squeezed my brother's skinny shoulder. "Ah, my young assistant's arrived. I can use the help today, believe me."

A rapturous look replaced Seryozha's former sulkiness. He loved this old man—a real artist who praised my brother's sketches and silhouettes and brought him into the darkroom whenever he could. Seryozha picked up the heavy camera case in which Papa Katzev kept his film, though I'm sure it weighed thirty pounds. But he would walk through hell to protect Katzev's film, even if his arms fell off.

"You children stay with Papa," Sofia Yakovlevna called after us. "If anything happens, come right back up."

Solomon Moiseivich kissed his wife on her plump cheek. "They'll be fine, Mama. I'll keep an eye on them."

A skeptical smile edged along her maternal face. It was highly unlikely that the photographer, under a black cloth, could keep an eye on anyone, let alone four young people. The younger girls clamored to be brought along, wheedled and protested at being kept inside, but she would not be budged.

In the street, the sun splashed the storefronts, gilding churches and washing the faces of apartment houses all down Nevsky Prospect to the Admiralty needle. It poured over idle office workers and sleepy clerks, haulers and porters. It felt like a holiday. Carrying the big camera, Solomon Moiseivich shouldered and *Excuse me*'d his way to the curb, and we four filled in right behind him, Seryozha guarding the camera case as if bandits would come and rob him of it.

Around us, the crowd thickened—well-heeled ladies, gentlemen smelling of cedar chips, pale shopgirls and carters, carpenters and doormen, schoolkids on their day off, laughing and shoving. Even a few drunks came out to soak up the sun. A vendor moved among us selling sunflower seeds. "Watch your purse," a young man told his pretty wife.

A sudden whiff of cigar smoke made me think of Kolya. "Look, here they come." A man who looked like a poolroom sharp in his checkered coat and flat cap pointed toward the Admiralty.

At first I saw nothing. Then, way up at the end of Nevsky, a black dot appeared. A bit of red. As I watched, the dot grew into a bobbing mass, adorned with small smears of scarlet. Now a noise, faint, like the whispering of waves on a pebbly beach, a low gravelly chatter, arose and soon echoed off the buildings and rolled down the boulevard. The marchers were chanting but we weren't close enough to hear the words.

"They said there might be a hundred thousand out today," said the man in the checkered coat, chewing a handful of sunflower seeds and spitting the shells on the ground.

Varvara squeezed my arm. I squeezed back. We felt the shimmering possibility that things could be different. No—they were already different. This column of black coming toward us felt like history itself. Mina chewed her chapped lips and eyed the policemen shifting nervously from foot to foot, holding their truncheons behind them. If her father hadn't been three feet away, she would have bolted. The presence of the police made my stomach hurt. What if they went wild, as they did the day the women stormed the bakery?

Closer the marchers came. So many women…my eye had only beheld such numbers on the parade ground of the Field of Mars. But these weren't soldiers. They were simple workers, mouths open, chanting, *We want bread*. Bread! Was that too much to ask? Now we could read the banners: DOWN WITH HUNGER. BREAD AND JUSTICE! WE WANT BREAD AND THE EIGHT-HOUR

DAY. There would be no more pretending that the city didn't see them. Their footsteps resounded on the wooden paving blocks, their high voices begging for justice. I was too young to have witnessed the Revolution of 1905, when the poor had come to petition the tsar and were slaughtered. Their reward? Twelve more years of hunger and oppression, and a few crumbs of concession to the middle class, like the powerless Duma. I prayed this time would be different.

Now they were upon us.

Such faces! Bathed in morning light, on this miraculous day, it was as if God himself had blessed the procession, had dipped in gold their banners, their shabby coats and worn scarves. Shy women marched arm in arm, in fours and fives, tens and twenties, unused to such boldness, following behind their more determined sisters holding the banners. What desperate bravery at a time when it had been declared that any two people assembling in public could be arrested. How must this feel to them—to emerge from their dark airless slums, hidden away in the shadows of the factories on the outskirts of the city, to walk in the sunshine down the most glittering street of them all? To bear witness to all they had suffered and demand that justice be done?

I wished Mother could be here, Father, too, so that they could see this woman. This one, with the white scarf pulled low on her forehead marching along with her friend with the large bruised eyes. They smiled, awed by their own audacity. These women stitched our boots, wove the cloth we wore, cut our coats, fashioned the buttons, knit our underwear and our hose. These women—and men, too—wouldn't stay hidden with their suffering one more day. Meanwhile, Seryozha expertly handed frames of unexposed film to Solomon Moiseivich and stacked the exposed ones into the case, his fears forgotten. If Kolya could only see all this, surely he wouldn't be able to maintain his cynicism about the people's cause.

Now a group of stylish women passed by under the banner: SOCIALIST WOMEN STAND FOR NEW LIVES. I could well imagine myself among them. A young woman in a tricorn hat and bobbed hair could be me in a year or two. It was their march to begin with, but their movement had been joined not just by a phalanx but by an army.

A tram running alongside the marchers braked to a stop, its female driver getting out and leaving her tramload stranded. Her car blocked the one behind it, and soon the smell of static electricity and the screech of hot metal stained the air. How comical the passengers looked, peering out the windows, confused to be so at the mercy of the working class. Varvara laughed. "You're not going to make that appointment," she called to the bewildered passengers still in their seats.

OKHTA TEXTILE ON STRIKE! WE WANT BREAD AND THE EIGHT-HOUR DAY!

Then came the families of the soldiers, solemn as a religious procession. FEED THE CHILDREN OF THE DEFENDERS OF PEACE IN THE HOMELAND begged a banner held by a woman in a blue scarf, surrounded by soldiers' wives with their half-grown children, old people, mothers and fathers. They seemed even more unsure of themselves than the workers did, unpracticed in the art of public protest, driven by desperation. INCREASE THE FOOD RATION FOR SOLDIERS' FAMILIES! FOR THE DEFENDERS OF FREEDOM AND THE NATIONAL PEACE!

We all felt the sea change, even Mina. "Feed the children!" we shouted. "Feed the soldiers' families! *Urah!*"

"Look, Marina!" Varvara nudged me. "It's Belhausen."

Belhausen knitwear! I even recognized the woman who had taken the stack of flyers from Varvara that night. Their banner proclaimed: IF A WOMAN IS A SLAVE, THERE WILL BE NO FREEDOM. LONG LIVE EQUAL RIGHTS FOR WOMEN! We waved and called out, and perhaps they recognized us, but in any event, the woman raised a hand in salute.

A song began among the textile women. Varvara knew the words:

Arise, arise, working people.
Arise against the enemies, hungry brother!
Forward! Forward!
Let the cry of vengeance
Sound out from the people!

Mina took a step back. She caught my eye—
vengeance?

The rich, the exploiters, deprive you of your work,
Tear your last piece of bread as the stock market rises,
As they sell conscience and honor, as they mock you.
The tsar drinks the blood of the people.
He needs soldiers, so give him your sons!

The police, so vastly outnumbered, could do nothing but bounce on the balls of their feet.

"They said it wasn't time," shouted a sharp-chinned woman holding a banner on a pole that seemed too large for her hands. PUTILOV WORKERS SUPPORT WOMEN'S RIGHTS! "Our brothers told us it wasn't time. But when the women say it's time, it's time! A pregnancy only lasts nine months, brother—the baby comes whether you say so or not."

The women cheered, and we joined them. Suddenly, a well-dressed couple stepped back from the curb. Then other onlookers began pressing back toward the buildings. Mina instinctively took my arm. "What's happening?" A buzz of anxiety arose from the crowd, and then someone shouted "Cossacks!" "Seryozha!" I called, but my brother remained at Katzev's side, handing him another frame of film. Mina pulled me toward their door as the Cossacks—the knout of the tsar—emerged from Liteiny Prospect mounted on flared-nostriled horses.

Mina stood on tiptoe. "Papa!" she shrieked.

I dug my nails into Mina's arm. Solomon Katzev didn't move and Seryozha remained steadfast beside him. The mounted men gathered at the edge of the march, and their officer urged his horse into the mass as you would urge it into a river. Whip raised, the bayonet of his rifle gleaming, saber at his side. I clung to Mina. We could smell the sweat of their horses as they passed, heard the creak of their saddles, their black capes flung behind them. One by one, the Cossacks waded into the frightened column. Poor women, little boys, old men, all edged backward to give these fierce men passage. But the whips stayed on their shoulders, rifles on saddles, savage sabers at their sides. Not one Cossack lifted a hand against the demonstrators. They simply rode through.

Urah! It was a miracle. Everyone—protestors, onlookers—threw their arms in the air and cheered, wept. The sound made the horses wheel, white-eyed, necks lathered from fear, but the Cossacks kept them well in hand. Sobbing, shouting, I embraced Mina, Varvara, and a woman in a sealskin coat standing behind me. One of the riders nodded at the crowd, touching his shaggy hat in the flick of a salute. Solomon Moiseivich came out from under the cloth, and I saw him squeeze the bulb of the shutter.

"You should have been there, Mama," said Mina, slurping up the golden broth swimming with noodles as steam coated her glasses. "They didn't fire. I couldn't believe it."

"We saw it all from the window," said her sister Dunya.

"Nothing happened anyway," said their little sister, Shusha. "You should have let us go."

Sofia Yakovlevna shook her head. "You could all be murdered."

We drank our rich, fragrant soup while Varvara imitated the woman from Putilov. *"A pregnancy only lasts nine months, brother—the baby comes whether you say so or not."*

"Well, this pregnancy's lasted twelve years," said Mina's old uncle Aaron. "The baby's going to be huge." Like everyone today, he was thinking of the failed Revolution of 1905.

"Three hundred years, if you ask me," said Aunt Fanya, a tiny hunchbacked lady with Mina's sharp sense of humor.

After the meal, Papa Katzev and my brother retreated to the darkroom. While we waited to see what they had captured of the day, Mina's aunt taught us to play American poker using buttons from the sewing box as chips. I loved the names—her aunt used the American words: *hold, call. Aces and eights.* Of course Mina, our mathematician, won handily, but gradually the rest of us caught on. As we played, Uncle Aaron talked about his days in New York organizing garment workers before being deported. I had no idea that Mina's family was so political.

I was raking in my first pot when Seryozha appeared in the studio doorway, his hair damp and hanging over his eyes, accompanied by a strong draught of vinegary chemicals. "We're ready."

We pressed into the close confines of the darkroom—like a little theater—arranging ourselves around the wooden sinks with their enamel trays. I never tired of seeing an empty sheet of paper become a scene, a portrait, that magic, although my eyes smarted from the fumes. "Everybody in?" said Solomon Moiseivich, then he turned out all the lights but one, coated in red paint. He placed a large negative onto a square of white, shut the frame, and turned on the light. "One," he slowly counted, "two, three," then turned it off again and slid the paper into the first tray of chemicals.

Before us bloomed an image on the white page—the first line of marchers, the empty cobbled street ahead of them, their dark figures entering from the right, as if from the past, walking onstage, their mass dividing the sheet in half. I could see history's footprint in that moment. I had been there.

11 *The Two Mariyas*

TWO DAYS LATER, I sat with Mother at a table for six at the Hotel Europa, a spacious room decorated in the art nouveau fashion. All around us, soignée women lunched, well-dressed families fussed over pretty children, and business associates tucked into steaks and roasted chickens. At the end of the long room, a string quartet stitched a Bach concerto onto the fragrant air, while not five hundred yards away on Nevsky Prospect, strikers milled behind a cordon of soldiers. How ridiculous to be waiting here for the appearance of Great-Aunt Mariya Grigorievna and elderly Cousin Masha, visiting from Moscow.

Mother removed her gloves, slowly and beautifully, a small performance in itself, glancing about to see if she knew anyone, and of course she did. We ordered tea, which came in traditional glasses with silver holders. I studied the waiter, a somber long-faced man who resembled Pasternak. He looked like he'd been born old, as if joy had never crossed that masklike face. Did he hate us? Did he secretly hope we would all choke on our sturgeon in cherry sauce? This dumb show of privilege — the quartet, the stylized flowers of stained glass, the illumination of the skylights. Yet it was beautiful. Did beauty have to be shameful? I wished there was someone I could ask. But who? Not Mother. Certainly not Great-Aunt Mariya Grigorievna, whom I could see approaching, regal in an old-fashioned hat decorated with a crow's wing, followed by dour, sharp-faced Cousin Masha in a purple velvet beret.

We exchanged obligatory kisses, for which I had to hold my breath — my great-aunt smelled of roses kept in a box with dried bones and vinegar. Masha smelled of violet eau de toilette and an illicit cigarette. The host seated my great-aunt and placed her snuffling pug in her lap. "What is happening to this place?" she spluttered. "Your local orators have been holding forth all morning. We've almost converted to Bolshevism and it's not even lunchtime."

Mother laughed. The traitor! She supported Father's dreams of a constitutional monarchy, but when she visited her family, sometimes her politics grew hazy.

Cousin Masha, a small homely woman with the rabid self-righteousness of someone who'd taken up plainness as a cause, thrust out her sharp chin. "Don't laugh, it's perfectly horrid. 'We demand a Workers' Soviet. We demand ice cream on Tuesdays and an automobile for every scrubwoman.' Our nerves are worn to a thread. To a thread!" Now I couldn't help laughing, and she glared at me, as if it had been me protesting under her window. I was glad we had a seat between us. Cousin Masha was a pincher and a tattletale, eager to spot one's sensitivities and air them in public.

The waiter handed us menus, large and tied with a golden cord and tassel. Mother turned pages. "Mitya hopes the unrest will pressure the emperor to agree to parliamentary concessions."

Good for her. She hadn't forgotten us entirely. Great-Aunt Mariya snorted. "Dmitry Ivanovich won't be satisfied until the Union Jack flies over the Winter Palace." She set her dog on the chair between herself and Mother and opened her menu. "Thank God it's still Russia—or at least it was the last time I heard. It is Russia, isn't it, Masha?"

"One might wonder," Masha said, scowling at a fat businessman who was laughing too loudly behind her.

"The emperor's father would know what to do with those demonstrators," said my great-aunt. "They'd be on their way to Siberia by now."

Why was I here, dressed up in navy silk like a fool to flatter the vanity of this old party? Just because she was a rich relation without children? It was intolerable. Only the day before, I'd helped lead a walkout at school. How exciting it had been to speak out for freedom, for the eight-hour day and the end of labor militarization, instead of suffering through geometry and Milton. The teachers either sympathized with us or retreated in the face of our agitation, and in afternoon history class, Varvara led a vote to strike. It passed unanimously. Even Mina, when she saw that it was inevitable, voted yes. News spread like a fire from classroom to classroom that the senior girls were walking out. The junior girls voted to join us, even the lower school. It was hardly a tools-down strike at Putilov, but we felt part of the great upheaval.

And now, I had to listen to what the emperor's father would do to the strikers. My freckles felt like they would burst into flame.

"Would you like some tea?" Mother asked her aunt. "Or wine? Mitya and Seryozha should be along soon, but we should go ahead and order." She summoned the long-faced waiter with a nod.

"Tea. Ceylon." My great-aunt petted the snuffling Potemkin. "And some milk in a dish."

"And a little Madeira," Masha added, smoothing her curled collar. "I think I've earned it, don't you?" I imagined she must secretly dream of Spain. A scarf tied gypsy style over her forehead, guitars in a star-filled night. I imagined her drunk and humming the "Malagueña" in their big dark apartment in the Arbat.

"Really, we're grateful the police have kept their heads so far," Mother said. "The Kadets are cautiously confident that the emperor will come around, as long as no violence occurs." She stroked her napkin as if it were a nervous cat. "If he doesn't feel it's a defeat."

"The Kadets should come to my hotel room," said Masha. "They could listen to the speeches without waiting for the newspaper."

"They're calling for abdication." Mariya Grig-orievna's jowls trembled. "Fifty yards from the Winter Palace. It's treason."

Abdication? That hadn't been among the demands of the International Women's Day march. My God, how far things had come since Thursday. I writhed with impatience to finish this visit and find out what was going on in the street. The collar of my dress rubbed against my skin, making it itch.

Where were Father and Seryozha? They had decided to walk, but it was taking longer than it should. Or rather Father had wanted to walk and invited Seryozha along. The truth was, he didn't want to spend too much time with the two Mariyas. "Too nice a day to ride," he'd said. Seryozha had been pleased but wary, like a boy befriended by a bear.

They didn't appear until we were finishing the soup, Seryozha trailing behind Father with a head-down sulky look. They must have quarreled. My brother let himself be kissed and dropped into the empty chair between me and Cousin Masha, his mood dense and volatile, like the atmosphere on a hot, cloudy planet. Father greeted the old ladies with false heartiness, taking the chair between Mother and Mariya Grigorievna after my aunt removed Potemkin. Though Father despised the bug-eyed dog, he disliked Cousin Masha even more. "You're both looking well. Quite hale and hearty. Sorry we're late. Ran into a bit of trouble on the way."

Mother glanced over at her gloomy son with alarm. "The strikers? You should have come with us."

"Just some hooligans. It was nothing." Father glared at my brother, who pretended to study the menu. His lips trembled, I could tell he was trying not to cry. "If it had been Marina, there would have been a bloody nose or two now."

Now I noticed the dust on Seryozha's school jacket, the torn sleeve. He'd gotten into a fight—how could that have happened with Father right there? Were they boys he knew? Or just street boys attracted to his long poet's locks and vulnerable, dreamy face? He must have been dawdling, looking in a shop window. Father would have had to go break it up—how furious he would have been at having to rescue his son from little toughs. *Nobody's going to fight your battles for you, son*...yes, I could see the clench of his jaw under his red-brown beard.

"Was he in a brawl?" asked Mariya Grigorievna, pressing her hand to her throat, as if Seryozha were a dangerous thug instead of an artistic fifteen-year-old.

"Hardly," Father said drily. "But he attracts it. Walking around like that. He might as well have a sign around his neck."

Mother glanced across me, sympathetic but helpless. "But you're all right?"

My brother wouldn't look at her. His nose was red. He stared down at his menu. "Just fantastic," he replied.

Mother wiped her mouth, sipped her Riesling, and nervously rearranged her silverware. Father ordered a glass of vodka and veal cutlets and took up his charming self like an actor stepping into a familiar role. He asked the old ladies whether they had anything special planned for their stay and how things were in Moscow. Meanwhile, Seryozha took out his notebook and began to caricature them—Masha with her cunning face, sipping her wine, her hat like a dripping egg. Father with his pipe. Jowly Mariya Grigorievna and her jowly dog—as they talked about the wisdom of sending money out of the country.

Father allowed himself the passion of his disapproval. "You can't be serious. It's unpatriotic. In the middle of a war."

"I'm as patriotic as you are," my great-aunt said, stiffening. She, who had wanted the strikers sent to Siberia. In Seryozha's drawing, her hat looked ready to fly away with her. "But one must also be practical." My brother wrote that as a caption below, *One must be practical.*

We were all relieved when the main course arrived. As I thought of the strikers, the sturgeon stuck in my throat—too fatty, too sweet, and the quartet sounded treacly, like putting lip rouge on Bach. The diners tucking into their meals seemed repellent, callous and greedy. Now Cousin Masha launched into a critique of modern child rearing, which started as an excoriation of my brother but ended as a rant about Mother and Uncle Vadim and how spoiled they'd been. Her spite hung in the air like oily smoke. "My parents said nothing good would come of it. That it would come back to haunt you in the end."

"*Les enfants terribles,*" agreed Mariya Grigorievna, but in a tone of indulgence, even approval. "With all your little tricks. You used to absolutely plague that nanny—do you still have her?"

"Avdokia? Oh yes, she's very much with us." Mother was happy to turn to more pleasant family memories. "Still the same. Inventing ever more elaborate curses for the insufficiently devout."

"Your father just gave you everything you wanted." Masha wouldn't let it go. She was on to her second Madeira, and little patches of red bloomed on each bony cheek. "Praised you for putting the right shoe on the right foot, as if you'd done something miraculous."

"My father was a kind man," Mother said, quietly but firmly. I remembered Dyedushka's huge eyebrows and muttonchop whiskers, his French walking stick. The way he teased you. The candy in the little drawer in his desk.

"And look where it got you," said Cousin Masha with an extra jab of malice.

Mother blotted her mouth with a snowy napkin. "And where is that, Masha, dear?"

The old cousin shrugged as if it were obvious, cutting her chicken eyes at Father. His prestige in Petrograd—his articles, his law practice, his teaching at the university, membership in the Duma—meant nothing to her. Father didn't come from *dvoryanstvo*. He worked for a living, so family legend had it that Mother married beneath her. Impoverished Masha, who'd sponged off Mariya Grigorievna for years, took great solace in that prejudice. She was an incurious woman, uninterested in the world, in other people, new ideas, progress, or change. Only the workings of her own social class and her tenuous foothold in it drew her. She feared that Mariya Grigorievna would leave her fortune to Mother instead of Masha, her deserving companion.

Father clamped his pipe between his teeth and made a show of patting himself down for a means of lighting it. "Excuse me, ladies, I must find some matches." Leaving us alone with the two Mariyas.

"Gone to the bar, most likely." Mariya Grigorievna fed a shred of rabbit in sour cream to Potemkin off her fork. I could hardly watch it, but Seryozha's pencil flew, making skritching noises on the paper. I wished I could follow Father's lead and abandon ship, but I felt sorry for Seryozha, didn't want to leave him alone with the Moscow harpies.

Now that Father was gone, their attention turned to me. My great-aunt asked about my plans for the future. Mother spoke up. "Marina will be entering Petrograd University in the fall," she said with some pride. "She's been admitted to the department of philology."

So there.

The old lady tucked her chin, making many of one. "You should save the money. A girl hardly needs that kind of education. It will only give her ideas."

I couldn't keep still one more minute. "I believe that's the point," I said.

Seryozha snickered. Encouraged, I continued. "In your day, it was enough to look pretty and know what fork to use. Today we want to do things, not just sit there like painted dolls."

Potemkin's eyes regarded me with horror, just like his owner's. "In my day, a young lady at least knew how to comport herself and not go running around contradicting her elders."

I felt Mother's hand on my arm, stilling me, but I had the bit in my teeth. "A month from now, you won't recognize this country. Our lives are about to change forever, while you're talking about comportment and feeding rabbit to your dog."

She picked up another piece of meat and held it to the small beast's mouth. "A whole month? I don't recognize it now. And if I feed him rabbit, why shouldn't I? It's my money, my dog."

"You see, Vera? You see?" Cousin Masha finished her second glass of Madeira. "Mother was right—*sow the wind, reap the whirlwind.*"

Mother rubbed her temples. "Masha, dear, your mother was a horse's ass. That's what *my* mother used to say."

Great-Aunt Mariya Grigorievna laughed out loud. "So true. Forgive me but she really was."

Masha's face turned dark with fury. I was glad not to be seated next to her. She would have pinched me. "Waiter!" she called out. The man with the long face was at her side in a moment. "This fish has gone off." She pushed her plate away from her. The man took it without comment, though she'd eaten half.

At last Father returned, white-faced, his pipe trailing the scent of his tobacco. "There's been some trouble down by Gostinny Dvor. Shots fired. We should all avoid Nevsky for the next few hours."

"Who shot? The soldiers or the strikers?" How could I get around my parents and find out what was going on?

"I'm ready to avoid the entire mad city," said our great-aunt, placing her napkin on the table, signaling the end of the meal. "We've met with our bankers, I see no point in lingering, do you, Masha, dear?"

"I should say not," said our disgruntled cousin.

"We can be back in Moscow by morning." The old lady stuck her face nose to nose with the pop-eyed pug. "What do you say, Potemkin? Let us leave the asylum to the inmates. Maybe next year they'll have come to their senses." She stood and we rose to kiss her and Cousin Masha. Mother embraced her old relative with an affection that surprised them both, knocking their hats together.

It was the last time we ever saw the two Mariyas.

12 *Incident at Znamenskaya Square*

IN THE WATER-GRAY first light, the sidewalks already exuded a bristly, nervy energy. I hurried after Seryozha. For a change, he was the one who'd woken early, rousing me from sleep, determined to spend the day at the demonstrations—with Solomon Moiseivich. I understood. After our luncheon at the Hotel Europa, I needed no urging.

Fresh posters had been stuck to the walls overnight, and groups of people stood around reading them.

FROM TODAY FORWARD, ALL STREET ASSEMBLIES WILL BE DECLARED OUTLAWED AND SUBJECT TO ARREST. TROOPS WILL FIRE TO MAINTAIN ORDER. ALL WORKERS ARE HEREBY INSTRUCTED TO RETURN TO THEIR FACTORIES BY TUESDAY MORNING, FEBRUARY 28, OR SUFFER CANCELED MILITARY DEFERMENTS AND BE INDUCTED INTO DUTY ON THE FRONT LINE. BY ORDER OF THE MINISTRY OF THE INTERIOR.

"Guess you better go home now, kids. Papa's mad," joked a man in a corduroy cap.

"This time we're ready for Papa." His friend rattled a bag in the palm of his hand. It jingled, full of metal.

"The reserves don't want this fight any more than we do," said an old man with hands the size of dinner plates. "They'll come over to our side."

"Yeah? You saw 'em yesterday. *Move along. Bugger off.*"

Seryozha, halfway down the street, called to me to hurry. But I wanted to hear what the workers were saying. "What happened yesterday?" I asked the man in the corduroy cap.

"Police fired on the crowd up near Gostinny Dvor."

I was glad Seryozha couldn't hear that. "Are you worried? About being sent to the front?"

The man with the metal said, "Nobody's going anywhere, *devushka*. It's them's going somewhere. Straight to the devil is where."

*   *   *

As we approached Nevsky, we could see the demonstrators already crowding the boulevard. At the Katzevs' building Varvara had just arrived. She rushed up to us. "They're rallying out in the districts. Bigger crowds than yesterday. The government's raised the bridges—as if that's going to do any good." Raising the bridges on the Neva was a time-honored tactic but an iced-over river in February was not much of a barrier. "Everyone's running across. The police don't dare shoot. They know the least spark and—*babakh!*" She flung her hands upward and out. I could picture the workers, their dark coats and caps, running across the frozen expanse. Small figures against white like living sheet music. The city was coming together like two halves of a brain—what the reactionaries feared most. "It's beyond protest now," she said. "It's revolution."

Revolution. The great brazen sound of the word rang in my bones, resounded in the bell of my chest. It had us hypnotized, promising resurrection, a cleansing, after which Goodness and Future would emerge like the shining city of God.

We climbed to the fifth floor—Seryozha running ahead—but by the time we got to Mina's, her father had left. "Come in, have breakfast," her mother urged, but we grabbed Mina and fled back down to the street, resisting her sisters' pleas to take them along. Sofia

Yakovlevna let loose a skein of warnings that trailed after us like scarves.

The rising sun fingered the tops of the buildings as we came out onto the street. A crisp winter day. The soft snow that had fallen during the night gave the gathering crowds a holiday spirit. The transparent blue of the sky arched above us like the dome of a church. Seryozha raced ahead, not caring that he was alone, watching for Solomon Moiseivich. Varvara thought he was most likely to be photographing workers crossing the river and gathering at Palace Square. Sullen-faced soldiers clustered on corners and mounted police trotted in the streets. I fell back with Mina, who was having trouble keeping up. She stopped to catch her breath, bent over at the waist, bracing herself on her knees. "Do we really have to run? Won't they be coming this way?"

In a gathering chorus, church bells rang out. It was Sunday. Kazan Cathedral, the Lutheran church, the Armenian church, the Church of the Spilled Blood all sounded their benedictions. A good sign.

"Listen." Varvara stopped us with outstretched arms. She didn't mean the bells. Yes, from the direction of the Neva they came. Little black figures, the swaying red banners. Steam rose from the assembled mass, so many lungs, and as the bells faded, the sound grew deep and wide, a song. At first you couldn't hear words, but then they became clear. *"Arise, arise, working people. Arise against the enemies, hungry brother!"* Homemade ban-

ners and signs from factories swashed overhead, METAL
WORKERS NO. 14, ADMIRALTY SHIPYARD ON STRIKE! But
also newer, more militant slogans: DOWN WITH THE AU-
TOCRACY! RUSSIA OUT OF THE WAR! SOCIALISM MEANS
STRENGTH OF THE MANY! It thrilled me to see their demands, right out in the open. *The emperor's father would
know what to do.* At the curb, we caught up with Seryozha, his sketchbook open, attempting to capture the
flow of humanity. A man, skin burned by some kind of
chemical work. A tall woman in a white scarf, a chin
like a doubled fist, leading a chant: *Give us bread! Give
us peace!* Faces Kolya might have picked to be his messengers.

Suddenly Varvara grabbed my arm and stepped into
a passing line of strikers.

My brother and Mina stood frozen like two rabbits
on the curb. "Come on, Seryozha!" I called. But he
pointed in the direction of the river and Solomon Moiseivich, and soon I lost sight of him as the marchers
swept us along in the opposite direction, east, away
from the river and toward Gostinny Dvor. Varvara was
practically jumping with excitement. "Where are you
from, brothers?" she asked the men marching with us.
A blond man with a big moustache and a thick patched
coat black with grease replied, "Ericsson." The big
manufacturer of telephones and other electronic de-
vices. These men were taking a tremendous risk
striking—it was one of the militarized industries.
They weren't just putting their jobs on the line. Their

strike was tantamount to treason. Their bravery made me feel very young and frivolous, like a colt who'd decided to follow its mother in harness. People at the Hotel Europa stared at us from the window as we marched by. I wondered if the two Mariyas were still in Petrograd, if they could see me.

A young worker with elfin ears wedged himself between me and Varvara, draping his arms heavily over our necks. "What are you girlies here for? Bit of fun?" He smelled sharp and bitter—he'd been drinking. I didn't know what to do. I didn't want to be a bourgeois missy. He was "the people," after all. But Varvara had no compunctions. She shoved him off, sent him staggering into the men behind us, shouting at him, "Where's your discipline? This is a strike, not a social hour!"

The Ericsson men laughed. "That's the way, little sister," said the blond man with the moustache, while our would-be Romeo shrugged, wiped his nose on his coat sleeve, and spit—not quite at us, but close enough.

A wave of song reached us from up ahead. We followed with our own wave, hearing the same melody from various sections of the boulevard like a rolling echo. Soldiers leaned out the window of a military hospital, waving handkerchiefs—my soldiers! Businesses were mostly closed, the streetcars abandoned. Some of the strikers were trying to turn one of the trams over. People stared at us from the cafés. No one had told them that the revolution had arrived. *Arise, arise, working people*...

As we approached the intersection at Sadovaya Street, cracking sounds echoed off the buildings. I stopped, confused, but people around us began to turn, break off. They were shooting at us! Or someone was shooting, it was hard to tell who. We followed the Ericssons, dodging behind Gostinny Dvor, the great department store, zigzagging past the Assignation Bank and around to the Chernyshevsky Bridge, then back onto Nevsky. The excitement! Our blood was up and I could understand how soldiers were able to run into the gunfire of enemy troops. When we rejoined the demonstration, there were more strikers than ever. Workers in an upper-story tailor shop waved red flags.

At last we poured into Znamenskaya Square, the plaza before the Nikolaevsky train station. And I saw that we were just one of many streams flooding in from all four directions to meet in the grand circle surrounding the statue of Alexander III, the emperor's father, on his flat-footed horse, the tsar's expression equal parts indigestion and disgust.

So many people, and they kept coming, pressing us farther into the square. No one could scare us away now—we were too many. How glad I was that Seryozha and Mina hadn't come after all. They would have been apoplectic at the gunfire and panicky at the size of the crowd, whereas Varvara was thrilled and singing at the top of her lungs. And I was at one with these brave people, ready to change the fate of a nation.

Speakers climbed onto boxes to address the demonstration. "The old order has led the country to ruin!" shouted a gray-haired woman, hatless in a simple coat and dark skirt, pointing up at the statue. Her voice would have been the envy of a regimental sergeant major. "This is not the war to end all wars. It guarantees there will be more! It strengthens the autocracies! Forced annexations cause hatred among the peoples! Only socialism can guarantee a lasting peace."

"Russia out of the war!" responded a handsome bearded student who had appeared at my side. He flashed a brilliant smile at me.

"Up with the people's socialism!" Varvara shouted.

The gray-haired woman ceded the soapbox to a younger man. "We call for the return of the Soviet of Workers' and Soldiers' Deputies! We call for the arrest of the tsar's ministers." He pointed back up Nevsky, the way we'd come. "They're huddling right now in the Mariinsky Palace. They're rolling down the shades, they're putting out 'for rent' signs!"

"Down with the autocracy!" "Arrest the ministers!" We cheered him on. "We demand abdication!"

I could taste it. It was so close, the new world. It was right at my lips like a red, red apple. We would make a new life for Russia with our own hands. What a day! Just to express such thoughts in broad daylight! Surely the revolution had arrived.

Then something happened in the crowd. I stood on tiptoe trying to understand. The blond Ericsson man pointed. Mounted Cossacks had arrived on their excited horses. We all stood as still and silent as Alexander III above us, waiting for what would come. I was afraid to breathe. "Steady," said the Ericsson next to Varvara. "We've been here before." My skin prickled under my coat. I clung to my friend as the horsemen rode by in double file, stitching their way through the crowd like thread through black cloth. I could smell the horses, hear the jingling of their spurs so close, the horses' metal shoes scraping the pavement.

As at the Women's Day march, they did not strike us. They had not given in. Shouts rose up from the crowd—"Comrade Cossacks!" "*Urah!*" And the sky seemed flung over us like a bright bolt of silk on a seamstress's table, like a banner of heaven.

The speakers resumed their exhortations, the crowd more excited and confident than before. The student and I and Varvara exchanged quick bursts of conversation between speakers, praising this orator or that for a turn of phrase or a bit of information. What a day! I thought about this handsome student, just the kind of boy I really should be going with, instead of the opportunistic Kolya. He was at the university, studying law. I didn't ask if he knew my father.

Now the crowd lurched forward again, sending me crashing into a striker. I clutched his belt to avoid falling. "Volynskys!" someone shouted. One of the elite Life Guard regiments, the tsar's most loyal troops. Oh God. A bespectacled Volynsky officer on a nervous chestnut horse pointed his saber and sent a detachment of mounted guards into the crowd. "If they come close, put your coat over your head," said the striker ahead of us. He took off his cap and showed us the metal sheet he'd put inside. "We've learned a few things. You'll be fine."

Then they came, riding at a slow trot. People shrieked and tried to move away. "Brother soldiers!" the striker called toward the horsemen. "We're on the same side!" They unsheathed their swords, but after a moment it was clear they didn't want to use them.

"Disperse!" a mounted Volynsky called out. "All you people! Please! We don't want to use force! Please leave."

"Hold your ground!" demonstrators cried out all around us. Varvara took my arm. She linked her other arm to that of the Ericsson man next to her, and the bearded student took mine. "Brother soldiers!" The strikers were calling to the mounted Volynskys. "Join us!" The tinny taste of panic settled in my throat. The crowd lurched again and I stumbled, cried out, falling, skinning my knees, then was grabbed back to my feet by Varvara and the student. The officer on his wheeling horse called again for the demonstrators to disperse. "You have two minutes to clear this square!"

An orator still on his soapbox called out, "We're not clearing out! You clear out!" He turned to the line of soldiers, reaching his arms out to them, and shouted, "Brothers, we're your comrades! We're your brothers, your wives and fathers. Soldiers, don't fire on your family! We're hungry—we're not your enemies!"

"One minute!"

There was no chance of clearing this enormous demonstration. I couldn't have taken a half step to the left or right. It would be now. Either they would let us go as the Cossacks had, or we would die today in Znamenskaya Square. I held my ground among the Ericssons, gripping Varvara and the bearded student until my arms were numb. I could see a few of the Volynskys' faces, hard, thin-lipped, pale.

The officer let his horse turn and raised his saber. "Fire!" he shouted.

I closed my eyes as the first shots were fired. They sounded like crackling wood in a hearth. Screams. But everyone held fast. Then a cheer rang out. *Urah!*"

"They're firing into the air," shouted the bearded student.

We loosened our grip on one another and shouted out, "Brother soldiers!"

People were throwing things at the officer. "Go back to your tsar!" "Here's a warning!" "Your day is over!"

A bugle sounded. I felt like a warhorse, my nostrils flared with excitement. Was this it? Had the revolution really come? The man on the box shouted, "Up with the Republic!" and another wave of shots rang out. This time he crumpled, fell to one side, disappeared.

"Hold your ground!" "Run!" "Don't panic!" shouted voices all around me, barely audible over the screaming. People were pushing and pulling. I held on to the student, but where was Varvara?

"Sons of whores!" "Here they come." "Hold your ground!" The crowd lurched again and I stumbled, falling, grabbing at people who were also falling. The student's shoulder caught my jaw. Then we saw the horsemen, charging. I couldn't hear my own screaming in the roar around me. How enormous were those steel-shod tons as they knocked people to the ground. A demon bay with a nasty wide stripe down its nose and blue eyes charged us. A woman in its path tried to run, but somebody pushed her down in his own terror, and she fell under the horse's hooves. She curled into a ball trying to protect herself, her hands up around her head. The soldier did nothing to turn the horse away but let it rear and trample her. I screamed. People tore at the rider's stirrups, but he wheeled around for another charge. With outstretched sword, he rode at us—those blue eyes, that blaze, the thunder. The saber entered the chest of the bearded student at my side, piercing him through like an olive. The soldier lowered his sword so that the student fell off by his own weight, then spurred his mount forward to the next victim.

I knelt by the young man who had stood by me for the previous hour. His dark eyes held all the surprise and anguish in the world. Blood guttered in his mouth as he tried to speak. It gurgled from his chest and pooled into the snow around him. "Shh…" I kept saying. *"Tishe…"* I held his hand between my own as my dress soaked up his blood, and watched his face grow paler. I couldn't breathe. My mind simply could not comprehend what was happening.

"Marina!" Varvara jerked me up by the arm. "Let's go!" But I didn't want to leave him. What if he was trampled? "He's dead, Marina," she said. "They're coming back!" She dragged me away, and we ran, slipping and staggering toward the north side of the square, away from the train station. Another assembly of soldiers at Suvorovsky Prospect picked people off as they fled.

We stumbled into a café that was filling with fleeing demonstrators, and huddled with the startled customers—travelers and tarts with their finery and cheap jewelry. The waiters had closed the curtains, but I peered between them out at the street. A worker held a cloth to his neck while blood poured through his fingers. All through the vast square, people scattered, leaving behind bodies in the snow like so many bundles fallen off a cart.

Varvara wrapped her arm around my waist, her head pressed to mine. Through the parted curtains, we watched men—workers and students with red crosses on armbands—dart back into the square to retrieve the wounded, slinging them over their shoulders and carrying them away. How naive I'd been, thinking I knew what a revolution was. Thinking that we could demand change and it would be given to us because we asked. I shivered, seeing the student's blood on my dress, my coat, my shoes. His face, the way the sword impaled him. The blue eyes of the horse, the rider. I couldn't stop shaking.

"You're all right." Varvara held me by the shoulders. "Look at me, Marina." Her face swam into view. "We'll get those bastards back. This isn't the end. It's only the beginning."

But it seemed like the end to me.

13 *The Autocracy Has Spoken*

I DIDN'T REMEMBER COMING home, whether people stared at me, covered in blood. Avdokia was there, her soft wrinkled face gray with worry. She laced her arm around my waist and walked me to the bathroom. She got me out of my things, though I was shaking, shaking…took off my coat, my dress, my shoes, soaked in his blood, sticky. I lay in the deep white tub, hot and pink. My lungs ached, my body ached. How could I have thought we could win our freedom? That things could be different? I should have known the weight of what held us down. How thick the walls. How final, how useless.

My old nanny wrapped me in thick towels, put me into a nightgown and a robe. She sat me at my vanity table and combed out my wet hair. Framed in the mirror's reflection, a perfect fool. No heroine, no revolutionary. Only a pale, frightened girl, so much younger than I thought I was. The picture of Kolya and Volodya smiled up at me from under the glass. It meant nothing to me. Like something from another world.

She tsked and tugged at my wet hair, her little gnome face gazing at me in the mirror over my shoulder. Questions struck me like hard bits of snow, like sand. *Where*s and *why*s, *how*s. I didn't want to talk, only to be cared for like a child. She led me into the nursery, where we knelt together in front of the icon of the Virgin of Tikhvin, who knew everything. The lamp flickered in the dimness. My nanny prayed for me, thanking the Virgin for bringing me home safely. I didn't have to pray. The Virgin knew what had happened. It was too late to pray for the student. Time flowed but one way. I only thanked her that Seryozha had not been there. Then she put me to bed.

Later, I heard my parents come in, speak to the servants. I heard Avdokia telling them I wasn't feeling well and had fallen asleep. After a while, Seryozha slipped in, sat on my bed, held my hands. He knew what had happened at Znamenskaya Square. "Forgive me," he kept saying. I could tell he felt cowardly, as though he'd abandoned me. But there was nothing to say. I squeezed his hand. I missed him, I missed the way it had been when it was just the two of us in our beautiful child's world. Games in the bushes and trees in the Tauride Gardens, our secret language, Rakuku. I missed my own life as if it were already over.

Mother opened the door, dressed for a party, smelling of Après l'Ondée. Her gown rattled with crystal beads like hail on pavement. And here was Father, in tailcoat and brilliant white shirt, threading cufflinks into his cuffs. Soldiers had fired on starving workers and they were going out to a party. What kind of a world was this? I thought of the way the young speaker had fallen from his box, shot like a duck on the wing. I remembered how the soldiers prevented people from leaving the square by forming two lines, the front on one knee, the back standing, and picking us off as we fled. After they were gone, Avdokia came and sat by my bed and stroked my hair. "Marinoushka, what do you have in that head of yours—straw? Don't you know if anything happened to you, I couldn't live one day?" I held her hand pressed next to my face and wept.

I dreamed of horses, of being crushed, of falling under a carriage, my leg caught in the traces, being dragged along the ground. I dreamed I was riding a horse over a jump and it caught a hoof, threw me, then fell on me. I wept because I had died and hadn't even had time to live yet.

Gunfire awakened me. I thought I had dreamed it, but no, there it was, the now familiar crackling. Whom could they be shooting now? Surely the workers had gone to bed long ago. Was it people they'd arrested—

could they be executing them? I sat up, turned on the small lamp. Three a.m. How I wished that Kolya were here, someone I could really talk to. But he would never understand me. He would never understand what it felt like to take another's cause as his own — or, rather, to see his own in another's. Volodya would understand, but he was far away, in the snows of Galicia.

Instead, I padded to my bookcase and picked out an anthology of poetry, to see if anyone had something to say to me tonight. I kept thinking of Akhmatova's poem, the one she read that night at the Stray Dog. What would I give now for the people to have their wish? Yes, my happiness, yes my laurel wreath. What a child I'd been.

I sat up in bed, reading, seeking consolation from poets to whom none of this would have been a surprise — Pushkin, Lermontov — when I noticed my door silently opening, as if pushed by a ghost. Was it the student? "Hello?" I whispered.

"It's me." Varvara slipped in, carrying an old portmanteau bag. She dropped it onto my bed. "She kicked me out, the witch."

The high prattling of gunfire still rang out. She'd come all the way from Vasilievsky in this? She sat on my bed, sniffed the lavender cloth with which Avdokia had wiped my face, threw it back in its bowl. I didn't want to see her. Her being here brought it all back — the stifling crowd, the horses, the woman curled on the ground. "Who let you in?"

She grinned, bouncing on the bed. "I bribed Basya to leave your back entrance open. Don't be angry. Of all nights, we should be dancing for joy!"

She had lost her mind. We'd been in a massacre. It could have been us. I'd seen a beautiful young man bleed his life out on the stones of the square. I turned over and put the pillow over my head.

She pulled it away from me and threw it on the floor. "The soldiers are in mutiny, Marina. It's moving among the barracks like a grass fire. Can't you hear it? They're rising up. They won't do it anymore."

The soldiers who had shot at us today? *Please, Holy Mother . . .*

"After the attack today, the strikers went to the barracks and talked to the soldiers. The Pavlovskys broke out to see for themselves. They clashed with the police. We're not talking strikers now. There's no going back. It's mutiny." The Pavlovsky regiment. The soldiers were fighting with the police. *Watch the soldiers,* Kolya had always said. I found myself shaking again. Varvara reached into her boot and pulled out a bent *papirosa,* the cheap cigarettes comprising an inch of bad tobacco and three of cardboard holder. She opened the *fortochka* and smoked, blowing the fumes out into the night. I could hear the gunfire louder on the clear air. "They're all coming out. The Volynskys, the Pavlovskys, even the Preobrazhenskys." The most prestigious Life Guard units. She exhaled a stream of smoke. "Just think, Marina—a quarter of a million soldiers are stationed right here in Petrograd. Add that to a city full of striking workers. That's storing your powder next to your kindling."

I thought of the soldiers in Znamenskaya Square. Could they have changed that quickly? Shooting workers at noon, then supporting them at midnight?

"They've voted to join the revolution," she said. "They don't want to fight the people. Shoot women, children. You saw them today. They hated what they were doing."

"You mean they're out there running around? A quarter million soldiers?" I wanted them to support the workers, but I thought of the soldiers on the trams and imagined the havoc they could wreak. "What if they break into the wine shops?"

"No, no, no. You still don't understand." She threw her head back impatiently. "They're forming soldiers' councils—soldiers' soviets. They're voting for deputies. They're shooting their officers." She flicked the end of her cigarette out the window, kicked off her boots, and got into bed with me. She smelled of tobacco and pencil shavings. "There's no turning back. If it doesn't succeed, they've signed their own death warrants. Better get some sleep, Marina. It's going to be quite a day tomorrow."

14 *In the Land of Red*

THE NEXT THING I knew, Varvara was shaking me. The clock read 7:00 a.m. Still dark. She'd already dressed—her coat buttoned, her hat on. "Come on," she whispered. "Get dressed." There would be no school today, and I'd imagined I would spend my hours quietly reading, writing, trying to recover my soul.

"I can't. Not after what happened."

"Listen." She gestured, finger in the air. Nothing. An absolute silence had replaced the percussion of the night. She sat down on the bed next to me. "This is it. It's mutiny if they fail. But if they succeed, it's revolution. For that student—let's be there. His death was for a reason, Marina. He believed in it. How about you?"

I didn't want to see anybody else die. Yet what kind of coward wants to see justice but isn't willing to stand up for it? The Lermontov lines from last night's reading returned to me:

A year will come—of Russia's blackest dread;
Then will the crown fall from the royal head . . .

Perhaps this was the moment.

I found an old dress and some boots and followed her

down the hall. Seryozha poked his head from his room. "Where are you going? You're not really going out today?"

"You don't have to come."

"I'm not a complete coward," he said.

"It's not a test," I replied.

Outside, the streetlamps glowed, eerie halos of yellow, and my eyes stung from smoke. The three of us crept through the shadows to the end of our block, where soldiers fortified a barricade with sandbags and metal braces. The mannequins in the milliner's window goggled at the strange sight of soldiers loitering, rifles slung over their shoulders, their officers snapping orders. Seryozha dug out his notebook and sketched the unlikely juxtaposition of the heads and the dark silhouettes of the servicemen.

"I thought you said they'd got rid of their officers," I whispered to Varvara.

"You'll see. Follow me."

We doubled back, cutting through dim courtyards, startling a group of drunks sharing a bottle around a small garbage fire. One of them threw an empty bottle after us, laughing as it shattered.

Below Basseinaya Street, a luxury motorcar roared around the corner in the snow, twenty soldiers impossibly balanced on running boards and clinging to the bumpers, standing on the seats. They held their bayoneted rifles out like porcupine quills. Flags flew from

the car's hood, and some men fired into the air for
no reason other than to hear the revolutionary music. Seryozha and I dived back into the passageway,
where other people had taken shelter. Varvara, however, remained unprotected at the curb, enthralled by
the danger and the chaos. In the crowded passageway,
I rested my head on Seryozha's shoulder. I could feel
him trembling. "Let's go back," he whispered.

Honestly, I had been thinking the same thing, but I
would not dishonor that student's death by spending
the day with Mother looking through photo albums
and writing odes. "We could go to Mina's," Seryozha
said. "It's closer, and we don't have to cross the barricades."

I understood—he didn't want to be left alone on the
street. He wanted me to see him to some safe harbor. I
owed him that much.

The black door opened. Still in shawl and nightdress,
gray braid over her shoulder, Sofia Yakovlevna appeared in the lamp's glow. "What on earth?" She pulled
us inside the familiar apartment, smelling of kasha and
the coats hanging in the anteroom. "What are you doing here? Don't you know what's going on?"

"The soldiers have broken out of barracks," Varvara
said. "It's revolution."

Gunshots echoed off the tall buildings on the Liteiny
side, illustrating her point. "So I hear," said the older
woman.

Seryozha craned to look past her. "Is Solomon Moiseivich..."

"He got a call from a friend at the *Echo*. He left like there was a fire." Worry rose from her round figure like heat from an oven. "He'll either be shot or have photographs to live on the rest of his life."

She led us into the parlor, where a sewing project covered the table under the milk-glass bowl of the chandelier. Seryozha picked up a scrap of the fabric, a pretty rust-colored wool with a small paisley print, and fingered it appraisingly, like a tailor. "It's a dress for Dunya," said Mina's mother. The middle daughter, Dunya, the family beauty, with her shining dark hair and eyes. "She's growing so fast. Like a sunflower."

I wondered how my mother would describe me. Certainly not as a sunflower. I thought of Sofia Yakovlevna, sewing here in her robe in the early hours. How she welcomed us in. Mother wouldn't have answered the door in her nightdress if the end of the world were at hand.

The older woman lit the spirit flame under the samovar just as Dunya came out from her room, tucking up her braids. "Give them tea, Dunechka. I'll finish dressing and get breakfast started."

"We're not staying," Varvara said bluntly.

"Surely we have time to eat," I said. I was in no hurry to leave the warmth of the flat for soldiers driving around shooting in the air.

Seryozha found a loose scrap of the fabric and a

threaded needle and began to sew—a sight that would have given Father a seizure. As Dunya prepared the tea, I examined the photographs that decorated the walls. Writers, actresses, singers, the most famous artists in Russia—all of them had sat for Solomon Moiseivich. Maxim Gorky as a serious young man, surprisingly handsome in a dark Russian blouse. Chaliapin, big and pale-haired, with luminous eyes above a dark fur collar. Mendeleev as an old man, his long ragged beard and wise eyes. And what would today bring?

The telephone rang. It sounded like an explosion. Dunya ran to the hall to grab it before it woke everyone. "Oh yes, Dmitry Ivanovich." We could hear her high voice. Seryozha gazed down at his handiwork as if he'd never seen it before. "They're right here. Marina?" It was up to me. Dunya rounded her eyes in alarm as she handed me the receiver.

"Yes, Papa?"

He didn't bother to greet me. "I thought as much. It's an insurrection, a military insurrection, and you're out wandering the city? I can't pick you up, I'm going to the Tauride Palace. The emperor has suspended the Duma. You are to remain at the Katzevs'."

I traced a stripe of their rose-and-green wallpaper with my finger. "Yes, Papa."

"You are not to move until I can send someone. Do I have your solemn promise, whatever it's worth these days?"

"Yes." In a way, I was relieved by his abruptness. He wasn't asking for an explanation. There was no need to lie or beg forgiveness.

"I don't know what you're using for brains, but I suggest you try something else. It's inexcusable to impose on the Katzevs, but there's nothing for it. Let me talk to Sofia Yakovlevna, and for God's sake, stay put."

Mina's mother stood in the hallway, dressed now but with her gray hair still undone. She took the receiver reluctantly. My father at the best of times intimidated her. "Yes. Of course...it's no trouble, really. As long as necessary. Don't give it another thought, Dmitry Ivanovich." She paused. "And good luck—all our hopes are with you."

It struck me again—this was real. Even my father was part of it.

Varvara knelt on the window seat to look down into the intersection. "Now that's a beautiful sight," she said. "Now that's poetry." I peered over her shoulder. In the warming light, the streets had been transformed. Red rags hung from windows and from streetlights. Red flags decorated commandeered motorcars and festooned the fronts of abandoned trams. Red had been tied onto horses' bridles and around the coat sleeves of workers. *Krasniy, krasiviy. Red, beautiful.* Twins.

Mina emerged from her room in a thick sweater and skirt, her ash-blond plait still untidy from sleep. She knelt on the cushions of the window seat and pressed her face to the cold glass. "Why aren't you out there, Robespierre?" Her new name for Varvara.

"We're just getting something to eat," she said. "You coming?"

"Sure," she said. "Who wouldn't want to be shot by some drunken soldier?"

Soon the phone started ringing and did not stop. A friend reported that a police station on the Vyborg side was on fire, another that there was fighting on the Liteiny Bridge. Mina's youngest sister, Shusha, improbably dressed in a revolutionary ensemble of red flannel nightshirt and a red ribbon tied around her forehead like a fillet, found a set of old brass opera glasses through which to better examine the insurrection below.

Sofia Yakovlevna, carrying in a bowl of steaming kasha, stopped to admire Seryozha's embroidery. They were sunflowers, for Dunya. "Is there anything you can't do?"

He smiled wryly, painfully. Their perception of him was so different from the prevailing one in our household.

We ate breakfast with the whole family, Mina's aunt and uncle—awake and dressed now—jumping up periodically to take the glasses from Shusha and monitor the situation below. As we finished our tea, our young sentry reported, "Something's happening at the police station."

Varvara leaped up and grabbed the glasses, focused, pressed them back into Shusha's hands. "They're breaking in. Let's go!" She dashed to get her coat. I only hesitated a moment before I followed her.

Mina stared after us. "Are you crazy?"

Sofia Yakovlevna stepped in front of me. "Marina, your father! Don't make me a liar."

I loved her, this kind, worried woman, but I couldn't spend the day embroidering as the revolution was being born. I wanted to breathe its air, see its beautiful wings unfold. "I'll come right back, I promise." I didn't want to shove her out of my way, but I feinted left and darted right and ran past her, putting on my coat as I went.

Down at the station, a group of soldiers rhythmically hurled themselves against its locked doors as others urged them on. "Come on, boys!" "Heave-ho!" "*Eyy ukhnem . . .*"—the song of the Volga boatmen. Strikers and ordinary citizens pressed in to watch.

My heart was flying in my chest, thinking of yesterday's massacre. What if the police came rushing out? But I hadn't seen a policeman since we'd arrived on this side of the barricades. At last the doors gave way, tearing at the locks. The black maw of the station gaped like a mouth in an O. But now the soldiers hesitated, clustered on the steps, speaking among themselves.

"What are they waiting for?" Varvara shouted. "Why don't they go in?"

"It might be a trap," replied a soldier with a pale face and bloodshot eyes. "They could be waiting for us. Leave this to us, little comrade."

Finally, a small group of soldiers decided there was nothing for it but to go in, rifles leveled, bayonets fixed. In a moment, a second group followed them. Then workers entered, pouring through the gap like water through a sluice. Varvara flashed a grin, tipped her head toward the opening. She wanted us to follow them. I backed up to join the crowd of the less determined as she vanished through the broken doors. After yesterday, I preferred my blood inside my skin. I knew Sofia Yakovlevna was watching from the windows, so I turned and waved. She could honestly say she'd never let me out of her sight.

After a few minutes, people reappeared in the doorway. They were handing out boxes of papers, dumping them onto the sidewalk. I joined the human chain. The piles grew. As we waited, I picked out a piece of paper from the mass. *Boris Vissarionovich Agazhanian.* A report from a police agent. His address, his place of business. They were dumping police files, the hated surveillance that all Russians suffered. The country was riddled with agents—every *dvornik* was paid to report on the comings and goings of the house. And if you were involved in public life, nothing you did would go unnoticed. For a prominent critic like Father, an outspoken Kadet, frequent contributor to liberal journals, it took day-to-day courage to go about his business. He knew every word and action would be recorded, reported, anything could be used against him. Varvara probably had a dossier by now. Maybe I did, too. We threw hundreds of these files onto the pavement. A young, nimble striker lit the corners of the pile with a seriousness of one lighting a candle in church. Black smoke feathered up. I set *Boris Vissarionovich Agazhanian* onto the flames, set him free from his petty sins, the gossip of his neighbors, the political innuendo. He and the others. A spark fell onto a woman's skirt and she quickly batted it out. When the bonfire grew too hot, we threw the files in from a distance.

Then a man appeared in the broken doorway. He stopped on the step and gazed bewildered at the crowd. Others emerged, like ghosts from the underworld. Two, three, then a dozen, wearing gray pajamas. They were letting the prisoners go.

"It's your lucky day, Comrades!" an old man shouted out to them. "You're free!" One after another, they began to realize that their situation had changed for the better, and they melted into the crowd. Znamenskaya Square was not the end, after all, but only the beginning.

After dark Solomon Moiseivich returned to the Katzev flat, ash from the fires dusting his greatcoat, smearing his face. Seryozha jumped up to take the camera and tripod from him. Sofia Yakovlevna ran to him, smiling with relief as she helped him out of his coat and brushed at soot with vigorous blows.

"They broke into the police station," Shusha clamored. "Varvara went in."

"Telephone's out," Mina said.

Shusha twirled on the parquet, her red ribbon flying. "Look, I'm a mutineer."

"Greetings, Comrade," her father said with a laugh. He sat heavily in his chair at the table.

His wife went to get him his dinner while Dunya pulled off his boots. "Korolenko down the hall says the emperor's sending troops from the front. Is it true?"

"There's a lot of territory between here and the front," the big man said, sighing with pleasure as the boots left his feet and his slippers replaced them. "Many things can happen before then, child. Every hour it's something new." He pulled Shusha toward him, kissed the side of her head.

"They broke into the police station. Marina was there! They let the prisoners out."

Sofia Yakovlevna gave me an exasperated look as she set her husband's soup before him. She was still angry at me for not coming back after the police station. Instead I'd followed Varvara up to the Arsenal. We'd heard that soldiers had broken in and were handing out rifles and pistols to the strikers like prizes at a fair. If the people were armed, surely the revolution would not be put down so easily. They would defend themselves. They would not be mowed down again. I saw it for myself: soldiers passing crate after crate to the crowd, the people breaking the wooden boxes open. Even though I knew it had to be, it was a chilling sight—the wartime arsenal of Russia delivered into the hands of the revolution. I hadn't seen Varvara since then, she'd been lost in the crowd.

Now the bearish photographer squeezed Seryozha's skinny arm. "I hope you're rested. We're going to have a long night. Ready?"

It was one in the morning when Seryozha woke us. No one had gone to bed, we slept in the parlor. Too much was at stake. We crowded, bleary-eyed, in the darkroom, our faces painted red from the safety light. Solomon Moiseivich's deep round voice rang out in the dark. "I got a call early this morning. Vasily Rodionovich from the *Echo* said the Pavlovsky regiment was breaking out of barracks, headed for the Winter Palace. Marching behind their regimental band. I dressed so fast I almost forgot my shirt." Into the bath went the first print. The photograph bloomed: a ragged parade crossing Palace Square.

He indicated with a flick of his fingers for Seryozha to transfer the paper to the next tray while he took down another square of processed film, exposed the next shot. I could hear Uncle Aaron's wheezing. The chemicals were hard on the old man's lungs, they stung the eyes. Mina shoved her glasses back up on her nose. Seryozha poked at the paper with tongs.

A line appeared…a roofline bisecting the paper, studded with the familiar statues decorating the Winter Palace. We stared into that sink as if into a scrying basin. And against the glowing white of the sky, clear as ink on rice paper, a tattered banner flew, dark against light. I knew it was red. History was emerging from its shell like a chick from an egg.

"And the emperor?" Sofia Yakovlevna whispered.

"Still at Stavka," her husband replied. Stavka, staff headquarters at the front. "But they took the Winter Palace. The sentries surrendered without a fight. They all but handed over the keys to the tsar's washroom."

Without a fight. I thought of those guns handed out today. I no longer believed in miracles.

A new page hit the developer. Upon the familiar stone steps of the Tauride Palace, seat of the Duma, a man harangued a large crowd. I recognized the long, equine face and squarish head of cropped hair— Kerensky, the radical lawyer and Duma member. Father considered him a rabble-rouser, vain and emotionally unstable. But he got results. He wore a military tunic instead of the usual frock coat and tie, and the photo caught him midbreath, giving an impassioned speech. "What did he say?"

Solomon Moiseivich indicated with lifted palms for Seryozha to keep agitating the print. "He called for seizure of the telegraph, the railway, all the government offices. He demanded the ministers be arrested."

Other elements in the Duma were moving ahead of Father. The telephone was already out, they must have taken it. Again, I felt the thrill of the burning police files. This was really happening. And we were all part of it, together, the whole country moving into the unknown.

My brother pulled the photo into the stop bath as the big man continued his story. "Kerensky's playing liaison between the Duma and the Workers' Group. It's now called the Workers' Soviet. He shuttles between them like a tennis ball. The Duma'd better do something, or the Soviet will." *We demand a Workers' Soviet. We demand ice cream on Tuesdays and an automobile for every scrubwoman.* So they had their Soviet now. What else might have happened while we dozed in the Katzevs' parlor? I could not believe how fast the world could change once it started to move.

In the tank, a hall with pillars and red flags appeared on the sheet, hundreds of pale faces. "This is the Soviet. Think, Mama, this morning these people were prisoners in the Peter and Paul Fortress. Now they're meeting with delegates and writing proclamations."

Sofia Yakovlevna covered her mouth, her eyes glittering but unsure.

"But which one is the government?" Shusha asked. "The Soviet or the Duma?"

"It remains to be seen, my dove," her father replied.

As we settled down to sleep that night, all of us stinking of the darkroom chemicals, there was one image I could not get out of my head. A rough band of common soldiers, eighty men or more, posing for Solomon Moiseivich around a commandeered automobile, grimly defiant, each face fiercely focused. Men who just yesterday had been about to be shipped to the front to fight in this hopeless war were suddenly masters of their own fate, history thrust into their hands. What would they do with such unexpected power? You could see it in their eyes, behind their defiance—a terrified confusion. Today they were for the revolution, but what about tomorrow? They themselves did not know.

15 *Visitors*

GUNFIRE SOUNDED THROUGHOUT THE following day. Whoever was shooting—police, officers who'd escaped the mutineers, workers—it was clear that the regime wasn't handing over the keys to the tsar's washroom quite so easily. Varvara never returned, and gunfire or not, Seryozha had left with Solomon Moiseivich, propping a note on the divan where he'd slept, a drawing of him bearing the film case behind the bearded photographer, followed by a parade of armed mice.

I did my best to be cooperative, to make it easier and more fun for everybody to be locked up in the apartment. I played poker with the girls and Aunt Fanya, rounds of chess with Mina. I even let her win. She was a sulky loser and hadn't had Dmitry Makarov to teach her the moves of the masters. I taught Dunya to waltz as her little sister banged out *Tales from the Vienna Woods* on the piano. I won a bet with young Shusha by walking on my hands all the way down the hall. All this was to make it up to Sofia Yakovlevna for defying her the day before. She was always so kind, so tolerant. But she was accustomed to her own girls, who did exactly what she said.

I even offered to help with lunch. I stood in the small kitchen, chopping cabbage inelegantly before a tall window filled with plants in pots. I'd never cooked anything in my life. Sofia Yakovlevna chopped onions the way a gambler shuffles cards, not even looking at her hands and the flashing knife. "You let that girl influence you too much," she scolded me as we worked. "We love Varvara, but such an angry girl I've never seen. You be careful. She's going to bring such trouble down around her. I can see it as if it were written on her face."

"She's more bark than bite," I said, sucking my finger where I'd nicked it with my knife—it was scalpel-sharp.

The older woman wagged her head, neither yes nor no. Lifting the cutting board over a pan smoking with oil, she scraped the onions in with a whoosh and a sizzle, the delicious smell blooming. Steam coated the window. Broth boiled in another kettle. "You're wrong," she said. "Listen to me. I know she's your friend, but she's going to bring misery to everyone around her. You keep doing what you're doing. Go to school, write your poems. You're not a revolutionary—you're a girl from a good family who has such wonderful prospects if she doesn't get swept away by all this."

She looked at my pile of mangled cabbage and
sighed. "Like this." She took the knife from me, cut
an even wedge from a second cabbage, and began slicing it so thinly you'd think she was shaving its face.
She watched me as I tried again, using the blade as
she'd showed me. Uniform shreds of cabbage peeled
off the wedge. Her smile worked its way from behind
her sternness like sun from behind a cloud. "See?
You're not so hopeless. You should get that cook of
your parents' to show you a few things—someday you
might have to live in this world."

Just the words I'd thrown at my great-aunt.

We sat down to lunch, jumpy from the sound of gunfire
in the street. Suddenly shots rang out above our heads.
Were they shooting from the roof? Now it was returned, and bullets shattered the masonry around our
windows. One broke an upper pane. Dunya screamed.
"Get down!" Uncle Aaron shouted, and we all dived
under the table, grabbing for each other's hands.
Dunya was crying. Her aunt held her. *"Tishe, tishe..."*
Sofia Yakovlevna prayed a Jewish prayer. I had never
heard her speak in the language I assumed was Hebrew.
We waited to see if there would be more gunfire, but
it seemed to be over. We had just begun crawling out
from under the table when we heard the thunder of
booted feet in the hall. Fists pounded on the door, then
something harder—a rifle butt.

"Oh God, here they come," Mina whispered and we

crawled back under. "Shh," her mother whispered. "Maybe they'll go away."

"Search party," a man called out. "By the power of the Military Revolutionary Committee, open this door!"

"I'll get it," Uncle Aaron said, crawling out backward. I could see his feet in their worn slippers, the heels he never pulled up when he donned them. "Coming, Comrades!" Cold air wafted in from the hall, and heavy boots stamped into the flat, all we could see from under the tablecloth.

"Are you here alone, Grandpa?"

"The family's under the table."

"Tell them to come out."

Dunya and Shusha were crying. Mina held my hand tightly as we came out to face five unshaved, grim soldiers, three with rifles, bayonets fixed, two with pistols, drawn and ready. Crude red armbands decorated the sleeves of their patched greatcoats. It was one thing to see mutineers on the street busy breaking into a police station or throwing rifles to a crowd, but quite another to have them just a few feet away pointing their guns at you. Mina was crushing my hand.

"Someone's firing from these windows," shouted the eldest, with a squared-off beard and close-set eyes, his cap cocked back on his head. "Hands where I can see them."

We held our hands in the air. "Please...there's no one but us, Officer," begged Sofia Yakovlevna. "I swear to God."

The man laughed harshly. "No more officers now, Mama. Only men. Spread out, boys. Rykov—you watch them."

A red-eyed boy who looked like he hadn't slept in days pointed his pistol at each of us in turn as we all listened, following the crashing progress of the searchers through the flat. I silently prayed we would live through this. The gun jerked from me to Sofia Yakovlevna to Shusha in her red ribbons—as if any one of us might attack him if he blinked. He was going to kill us by accident. "We're not going to hurt you, son," said little, hunchbacked Aunt Fanya. "You don't have to keep pointing that thing at us."

"You shut up, Grandma, unless you want to eat a lead sandwich," he said.

Then we heard it. Gunfire, directly above us. Whoever was shooting had made it to the roof. The mutineers emerged from the rooms at a run and thundered back through the front door. "Sorry, citizens!" shouted the square-bearded one as they flew from the flat.

It took a moment for the blood to return to my head. I felt dizzy. My hands shook. They'd only been in the flat a minute, two at most, like a vicious thunderstorm. We could hear their boots on the roof. Shots. Scuffling, screams. It went on and on—what were they doing to him? Finally, we saw the body, flung off the roof and down into the street. Now the sound of their boots, clattering back down the staircase, and the slam of the door as they left the building.

Uncle Aaron and Aunt Fanya went back to their bedroom to lie down, and Sofia Yakovlevna moved the rest of us into the photography studio with its black curtains, its windows facing away from Liteiny, where most of the gunfire was coming from. She built a fire in the studio stove to take off the chill, though our mood was damp as the Baltic. I peered through the gaps in the curtains, watching people moving along the sidewalks. One group was busy breaking into a food store. Soldiers came out of a wine shop, their arms full of bottles. I felt less like the girl who'd burned the police files and more like I had yesterday—vulnerable, overwhelmed. Uncle Aaron thought the shooter was an officer enraged at the mutineers, deciding to revenge himself on the disloyal troops.

I thought about Volodya, handsome in his fur-lined greatcoat. What would he do if his troops mutinied? Would he bend, like the little birches? Would he understand the great sea change that had come, that the masses could not suffer anymore, that they'd risen up? Or would he insist on discipline? *O Holy Theotokos*, I prayed, *let him be wounded…not really wounded, just a graze, or a touch of fever…lying in a tent, out of the way in some field hospital. Let him not be telling his men to get back in line, to salute and march on.*

Shusha curled up in an armchair and mournfully ran her red hair ribbon through her fingers, sucking her thumb as she hadn't done for years. Mina went into the darkroom to investigate the damage. Dunya sat with her mother, staring sad-eyed at the door. I could still hear the man's screaming. What was he thinking, shooting at the soldiers? How many of them did he think he could kill? A whole revolution? Yet I would never forget the vicious reprisal, either. One death did not salve another.

We could hear Mina sweeping up glass, the delicate clatter as she deposited it in the waste can. I knew Sofia Yakovlevna was thinking of her husband, in the thick of it with his camera. And my brother, having at last found something he would die for.

Dunya started weeping again. "They didn't have to kill him."

"It's out of our hands, Dunya, dear."

Dunya wrapped her arms around her mother and pressed their foreheads together. I envied them.

"Shushele, why don't you get the magic lantern? We haven't seen that in a long time."

The girl jumped to her feet and ran to the shelf where the lantern and the slides were kept. Yes, it was exactly what we needed. The Katzevs had a marvelous collection of hand-painted glass slides from their mother's own childhood — of Afanasyev fairy tales and Jewish stories and travelogues. As Shusha set up the old projector, Mina emerged from the darkroom, smelling of the vinegary stop bath. "Aren't we a little old for this?" she said when she saw the projector.

"You don't have to watch if you don't like it," said her little sister. "Dunya, you choose."

It was nice of Shusha. After the afternoon's incursion the gentle middle sister seemed the hardest hit.

"Vasilisa the Beautiful," Dunya said softly.

It was my favorite, too. "God, the one's sucking her thumb, the other's talking to magic dolls," Mina said, leaning next to me by the curtained windows.

Sofia Yakovlevna ignored her, waiting for Shusha to put in the first slide, which depicted a pretty little girl and a stout father in a long boyar's caftan. She began telling the story of Vasilisa, whose dying mother leaves her a magic doll. "*Zhili-buili*, once upon a time, there lived a merchant who had a daughter named Vasilisa the Beautiful..." The slides were exquisitely painted, sharp and vivid, not like the factory-made things one saw in most people's nurseries. "When she was nine, her mother fell deathly ill," she continued in a voice both soft and rich. "She called Vasilisa to her side and gave her a doll. Not just any doll, mind. A magic doll. She told her daughter that whenever she needed help, she should take the doll out and give it a little to drink, a little to eat. And then the doll would tell her what she needed to do."

Shusha was having trouble removing the slide. "Oh let me do it," said Mina impatiently. "You're going to break it."

That made me smile. Even our scientist wanted the reassurance of a story, her mother's voice, this tale of a girl who has a secret way of finding help in a wild world. I was sorry Seryozha wasn't here. He'd never heard Sofia Yakovlevna do her slide show, and these were wonders he would appreciate. But I thought of him on the streets of Petrograd at Solomon Moiseivich's side and knew he needed to be there. Father always accused me of not letting him grow up. Maybe it was true at that.

Halfway through the story, the flat's doorbell rang. "Pretend we're not here," whispered Dunya.

"I'll go," I offered, but Sofia Yakovlevna shook her head vehemently. "You girls stay out of sight."

But when she opened the door to the flat, it was Varvara's voice we heard, already in the parlor talking to Aunt Fanya. She followed the old lady in, her bobbed hair matted, her clothes wrinkled. "What are you doing back here in the dark?" she said, then saw the slide on the wall, Vasilisa feeding the doll to help her with the witch Baba Yaga's impossible chores. "Really? Fairy stories, today of all days?"

"The soldiers broke in," Shusha said. "Someone was shooting. They threw him off the roof. It was horrible."

Mina's glasses picked up the light from the magic lantern's flame. "The one guarding us almost shot us."

"I'm sure they weren't looking for chubby chemistry students," Varvara said cheerfully. Her good mood seemed tasteless, as out of place as a polka at a funeral.

"They didn't spare him," I said.

Our gloomy faces should have told her how bad it was, but she just shrugged. "It was a risk he took."

"You didn't hear him," I said.

"You're not asking me why I'm here." She grinned, fairly dancing on the balls of her feet.

"You got hungry?" Mina guessed.

On Sofia Yakovlevna's face, a mixture of fear and curiosity. "Would you like some *shchi?* Marina helped me make it."

Varvara's smirk told me what she thought of my embryonic culinary skills. "Oh she did? Very domestic. No, I'm fine. *Dandy.*" She used the English word. Now that she had our attention, she went to the studio costume rack, plucked a tricorn hat with a plume off the shelf, and dropped it onto my head. "Your Imperial Majesty!" She bowed. "Where are you right now?"

"Stavka," Shusha said. "That's what Papa said."

"A good guess, my kitten, but in this case—wrong." Varvara took my hand as if we were dancing a quadrille and led me to the velvet armchair where Solomon Moiseivich so often photographed clients. She seated me in it, then handed me a vase as a scepter. "His Imperial Highness is on his special train, returning to Petrograd."

"*Bozhe moi,*" said Sofia Yakovlevna. *Good Lord.*

"Accompanied by a trainload of loyal troops."

This was it—the tsar would crush the revolution. The mutineers would go to the firing squad or to the front, and all would be back to the way it was before.

"Yes, you've decided to end this revolt business once and for all." She shook the plume, tickling my nose.

"Show us who's boss—or so you think. But here's the thing. What you don't know is that the telegraph workers are on our side. They report straight to the Soviet."

"How do you know this?" Mina demanded, folding her arms across her chest.

"I've been spending time at the Tauride Palace. At the Soviet. And as we speak, it seems, the railway workers are shifting and shunting His Imperial Highness around like a badminton cock. 'We're so sorry, *Gospodar*, there's snow on the tracks. We'll have to send you to Petrograd by way of Pskov! Such a nuisance, I know! But there's nothing for it.'"

The genius. It took my breath away.

"And listen," Varvara said, squeezing my shoulder. "Wherever he stops, his soldiers—his most loyal troops—get wind of the revolution and melt away like cheap candles. He'll be lucky to have a footman left by morning."

Sofia Yakovlevna opened the dark curtain behind her, letting in the afternoon sun and dispelling the last of our dreaminess. Her face looked older in the winter light. "What about the other troops? The ones they sent when the mutiny broke out?"

"That's the best of all," Varvara said, perching on the arm of my chair. She smelled sharp and stale—how long had it been since she'd bathed? "Evidently some of the tsar's advisers think a slaughter would look bad to the Allies. The troops have been told not to come into Petrograd. They're sitting at Dno, waiting for orders—which aren't going to come." The crooked grin widened. She looked like a child at Christmas who actually received the pony he asked for. "Check and mate."

And it occurred to me then that my friend had been born at just the right time. More than any of us, me or Mina or even Father, she was in exact alignment with the times. Its dangers weren't dangers to her; its violence matched her own.

Mina's mother paced, her hand to her mouth, trying to understand what it would all mean for her family. She and Aunt Fanya began to talk, and Mina joined them.

"You stink," I said to Varvara. "Where did you sleep last night, a kennel?"

"At your house, actually," she said. "I hope you don't mind." Was she joking? "Basya let me in."

Though Varvara was my friend, I was absurdly irritated with our maid. It wasn't very loyal of her. But Basya was a sly character, always looking for some gossip, some trouble to stir up. She probably just liked putting one over on the *baryn*.

My dismay must have been obvious, because she added, "Are you upset? Where else was I supposed to go?"

"You could have stayed here," I said.

"Too far." She added in my ear, "And I don't think Mama Katzev likes me very much. Look at her."

Mina's mother stood with her arms crossed, exactly

like Mina, anxious-eyed, as if Varvara had swept in a bit of gunpowder on her skirts. "She's okay," I said. "But I wish you wouldn't use my place. Father'll go crazy if he finds you there."

"He sleeps late. We're out by six, me and the comrades."

I turned so that Sofia Yakovlevna couldn't see my face. "What?"

Varvara laughed. "You have something against the comrades? The Ericssons? The women from Belhausen? You might have to wash your hairbrush, but—"

"Tell me you're joking." Would she really do that, bring the devil knew who into my parents' flat? Into my bed? "Varvara, you didn't."

"Come on. Be a sport. You want me to sleep in a doorway?"

I wanted to strangle her. "Listen, you can stay, but don't bring anyone else. Promise me." She was laughing. "Varvara! It's not funny!"

But she clearly thought it was. "What's the matter? You marched with them, you braved arrest. We're talking about a bed you're not even using."

Was I being hypocritical? I would march with strikers but not allow one to sleep in my bed? Then I thought of the soldiers, the screams of the man on the roof. And frankly, just the thought of unwashed strangers...

"Just promise. I'm serious." I pulled a lock of her

hair, twisted it around my finger. "Or our friendship is done."

Her eyes grew glossy with unexpected hurt. Her mouth worked, pressing back a tremble. And I realized with a shock that I was all she had. She had no family, no close friends…if she lost my confidence, she would have no one at all. I let her go.

She gave one shuddering sigh and embraced me. Kissed me as though she was going away, searched my eyes. "You know you're being completely selfish and ridiculous—but I promise. I was just kidding, anyway. But don't say things like that." She took my hands. "Still love me?"

"Of course," I said. "You might have a wash, though."

"*Burzhui*. Look, I have to get back to the Soviet—I just wanted to tell you about the railway. I miss you. You should come with me."

But I would not.

When she turned back to the others, she put her swagger back on, like a favorite coat, hitched up her skirt revealing the gun in the waistband. "In five years we'll all look back, and today will seem like another century."

On March 2, our fourth day at the Katzevs', Father came to fetch us. It was just after breakfast, and I'd made the kasha myself. He wore a fresh shirt and smiled like a man who, having walked through a storm, feels the sun drying the clothes on his back. He followed Uncle Aaron to the table, the old man still in his robe and slippers. In his arms, Father held a sack the size of a young sheep. He wouldn't sit down. His brown eyes glittered, laughter in them, and amazement.

"What do you hear in the Duma, Dmitry Ivanovich?" Sofia Yakovlevna asked. "Is this going to end?"

"He's abdicated," Father said. "He's signing today."

Abdication. The tsar was removing his crown, setting it down on the grass, and walking away.

Abdication, a great brass bell, solemn, resonant, deafening.

Abdication, the word that had sounded so treasonous that day at the Hotel Europa. So radical when the strikers had called for it that day in Znamenskaya Square.

We gazed at each other like simpletons, and every face bore the same expression as our sluggish minds struggled to absorb the sound, the sense, the moment we learned we were free.

A Russia without a tsar. I sat very still, questioning my arms, my legs, my feet resting on the soil of a land that no longer had a ruler. The light filled the windows as it had the morning before, one still broken—the same light, but without a tsar.

"What about the tsarevich?" Uncle Aaron asked.

Father shook his head. "He abdicates in favor of the Grand Duke Michael, but Michael won't take the crown without assurances, and he's not going to get them."

The crown of Russia had gone from most precious object to poisoned apple, a rotten, stinking potato nobody wanted.

Again, that grave smile. "The Duma Committee's forming a Provisional Government," Father said. "Prince Lvov, Miliukov…Kerensky, of course. I don't know by whose authority, but what else is there? The reins are dragging on the ground."

Sofia Yakovlevna closed her eyes and inhaled as if a fresh fragrance had entered the room. "Did you think you'd live to see it, Dmitry Ivanovich?"

"Something in me always believed," he replied. "Though I never imagined it would come in this way."

Shusha twisted and squirmed in curiosity. "What's in the bag?"

"Go ahead, open it," Father said. "From Vera Borisovna and me, a small token to thank you for your kindness, keeping the children so long."

Shusha began removing packages from the sack, Mina and Dunya carefully peeling their wrappings away. "Oh my God, it's butter!" Mina exclaimed. A pound of butter wrapped in cheesecloth. A small sack—sugar! Dunya licked her finger and stuck it in the bag, then it went right into her mouth. Her eyes closed. They'd been using saccharine for two years. "Oh, it's too much, Dmitry Ivanovich," their mother said, eyeing the whole chicken he'd included. Marmalade. A dozen eggs, individually wrapped in gauze. Aunt Fanya held up a bottle of cognac. "*Santé*, Dmitry Ivanovich!"

"I think we've taken up enough of these good people's time, Marina. Get your brother."

I hesitated, looked over at Sofia Yakovlevna. I didn't want to be the one to tell Father that his son had found another father who understood and appreciated him, that he'd defied orders to follow him into the dangerous city.

"He went out with Solomon Moiseivich," Sofia Yakovlevna said simply. "He's helping with the camera."

My father nodded, as if my brother's absence were the most natural thing in the world. Now I saw how stunned he was, how truly off his normal balance. The workers, the soldiers, the Russian people he'd fought for but never trusted had just handed him his dearest wish. He'd been surprised into power.

16 *Resurrection*

VOSKRESENYE, WE SAY. RESURRECTION. We awoke to discover that what we had thought to be eternal, the absolute dictatorship of the Romanovs, had turned to sand. Snow fell that following morning, but by afternoon, a brilliant sun came out, dazzling us. I walked through the neighborhood just to see what the world looked like without a tsar. The air tasted sweeter. The stately houses on Furshtatskaya Street seemed newly washed. A religious feeling welled up in me, that life had been transformed, not just politically but spiritually. It felt like Easter, and I wasn't the only one who sensed it. People smiled and greeted one another: "Good day to you!" "Good day to you, too!" "Do you believe it?" "Could you ever guess?" On a whim, I bought a huge bouquet from a shop on Liteiny exactly where I'd seen barricades just a few days earlier, and walked around handing out flowers—spicy red carnations and little chrysanthemums. People tucked them into their buttonholes and hats. They seemed euphoric but dazed, as if they were walking in a dream or had been deafened by a blast. I saw that miracles were shocking, as overwhelming as disasters.

On street after street, people broke the Romanov double-headed eagles from fences and buildings. They wrapped them in ropes and pulled, and if they didn't come loose, they'd smash the stone with crowbars and hammers. "Do it!" the crowds cheered. "Heave-ho!" Pulling off those eagles, with their savage beaks and claws, was like pulling the nails from our own hands. We climbed down from our cross. We were risen.

The new Provisional Government took its first steps away from the rule of autocracy. Under the august leadership of Prince Lvov, a dedicated liberal and the central figure of Father's Kadet party, eight basic resolutions became the law. I was amazed how far these liberal gentlemen were willing to go. The document granted freedom of speech and assembly, the right to strike, a constituent assembly elected by universal and secret ballot, men and women alike. It provided for the dissolution of the police "and all its organs" in favor of a militia whose officers were elected and controlled by the city. It declared amnesty for political prisoners and authorized protection for the soldiers who had mutinied, giving them the same rights as civilians when off-duty. It abolished rights based on religion, nationality, and social origin. A daring piece of work.

Kadet Paul Miliukov, the new foreign minister, asked Father to join the foreign office. "You know, I'd rather help draft the constitution," Father had said that evening, though I could tell he was thrilled at the posting. "But I'll go where they need me." They knew he had foreign contacts, and doubtless saw that as more valuable than his legal skills. I thought of Great-Aunt Mariya Grigorievna. *Dmitry Ivanovich won't be satisfied until the Union Jack flies over the Winter Palace.* But we were ahead of the English now. Unlike them, we had no king.

But there was another government in Russia as well. The Soviet of Workers' and Soldiers' Deputies, elected by the factory committees and the army units, met in the opposite wing from the Duma in the Tauride Palace. Which was the real government? Each body thought it was in charge. The Provisional Government behaved more like a ruling body, with its statesmen and sense of decorum. It continued the war and made policy. But without the support of the workers and the soldiers, its power was only hypothetical. How galling Father found the situation—the Soviet calling the shots, when he himself wasn't sure the Provisional Government even had the right to govern.

Instead of police, now armed militias called Red Guards patrolled the streets. Neighborhood committees sprang up that were responsible for everything from food distribution to house maintenance. Without police, Avdokia darkly predicted mass drunkenness and looting, but instead—for the most part—you saw a determination to prove that we didn't need an emperor to govern ourselves as modern, civilized people.

Everyone was part of the revolution now, from bankers to textile workers, even our schoolmistresses—all moving forward together on the same great ship, which had finally left port. It reminded me of the legend of Kitezh, the holy city that sank beneath Lake Svetloyar to keep it out of the reach of Tatar invaders. Legend had it that one day the spell would break, and the city would rise again. That's how we felt—the three-hundred-year Romanov siege had been broken and the city was rising from under the waters.

The Soviet's first act in power was a call for elections in the army. From now on, soldier committees would run their units, not officers. Father was apoplectic. "Command isn't a popularity contest," he fumed. "We're still running a war out there!"

"They're organizing themselves," I said. "Would you prefer them running amok? If it wasn't for the soldiers, we'd still have the tsar." I stirred my morning kasha, which I preferred these days over Western eggs and toast.

"Marina. Don't let your idealism run away with you," he said. "I'm all for democracy, but war can't be won by soldiers' committees. There has to be discipline, and there has to be expertise." Vaula brought him his boiled egg in its cup. He cracked the egg smartly, lifting the top off like a brain surgeon, making sure it was properly cooked, with a runny yolk. Mother was sleeping in, but Seryozha and I were back in school.

"Lucky Volodya's popular," I said. "Maybe they'll elect him."

Father wiped his mouth, checked his Breguet watch. "That's something to be hoped for. The one silver lining is that these hundreds of so-called soldier delegates are now full voting members of the wise and beneficent Soviet. They're descending on the Tauride Palace en masse. It's a mess. They outnumber the workers ten to one. There aren't enough chairs." He chuckled, finished his English tea. "The Soviet can't get a thing done. It's going to give us time to put our own house in order."

The rage for elections and committees was contagious. At the Tagantsev Academy, we voted in student committees on policy, curriculum, maintenance, and food supply. The teachers had their own committees, but we got an equal voice—just as in the government and the Soviet. Varvara—and surprisingly, Mina—sat on the academic policy committee, while I signed up for food supply. *A provisioning unit*. These were exciting times, and I forgot about Kolya for days on end. It was the food supply committee's responsibility to walk to the district food depot early in the morning and collect the school's bread and milk. A special perk of the job—we were often accompanied by boys from the nearby Herzen School, which made the assignment far more attractive than arguing over whether there should be calculus in the mathematics curriculum. One boy in particular, Pavlik Gershon, caught my eye. He helped me carry the big milk can, and we talked about Baudelaire. He asked me to go skating after school. "Why not?" I said.

Varvara was the one who heard about the revolutionaries returning from Siberia, where many had been in exile for decades. We bought flowers and trooped down to the Nikolaevsky station—now called Moskovsky—to wait for them. Znamenskaya Square was full of people holding flowers and banners and singing "La Marseillaise." It still made me queasy to be here, I couldn't stop seeing the dying student, the snow scattered with bodies. I wished I had known his name. I wished I could tell him that today we would welcome the exiles home and that his death had been part of that. I wished I could tell him I would never forget him, never.

We worked our way through the crowd to the station

only to find that the militia was keeping spectators out. Standing to one side, we watched groups of dignitaries arrive. I recognized Kerensky—now the minister of justice—with his military tunic and brush-cut hair. Varvara elbowed me as a handsome old woman in a big fur hat was ushered inside. "Vera Figner," she said. She'd been part of the conspiracy to assassinate Alexander II, an act Father thought had done more to hurt progress in Russia than anything Nikolas II could have dreamed of. But Varvara stared in wonder. "Twenty months in solitary in the Peter and Paul Fortress," she said. "Twenty years in the Shlisselburg."

Now a good-looking but rather messy woman with a cigarette in her mouth approached the guards. Her appearance raised cheers from the crowd. "Vera Zasulich, the writer," Varvara shouted in my ear. I recognized the name—a radical writer whose work my friend admired, one of a group of Marxist socialists who'd broken with their Bolshevik brothers and joined the more inclusive Mensheviks. Behind her, a group of young people demanded entry. "Delegation from Petrograd University and from the polytechnic college," their leader announced, unfolding some papers. The militiaman studied the documents with the elaborately thoughtful expression of someone who could not read. "Pass," he said, and in they went.

Suddenly Varvara was on the move, her arm linked in mine. I clutched the flowers I'd brought and Mina clung to the belt of my coat. "Delegation from Petrograd Tagantsev Gymnasium," my friend shouted over the din, and showed what looked like a hall pass. The militiaman glanced at it, then at us—at me with my flowers; at Mina, the intellectual, with her glasses; at Varvara, confident with her red armband—and waved us inside.

Following Varvara like ships behind an icebreaker, we threaded our way through the throng and out onto the platform. The station was less crowded than the square outside, but it teemed with people holding bouquets and banners, civilians and students and soldiers alike. The dignitaries spoke cordially among themselves on the platform. Paul Miliukov and Vera Figner eyed each other nervously. We could hear the crowds outside singing.

At last a train came rumbling in, brakes screeching against the great iron wheels filling the air with hot ozone, the cars grimy with mud and soot, the windows frosted over. The crowd pushed forward in anticipation of the doors being opened. Then the exiles emerged holding their pitiful sacks of belongings. Thin, worn, exultant, each stopped in the doorway for a moment as he or she took in the size of the welcome. I could see they were overcome with emotion. These men and women had been exiled for ten, twenty, thirty years. Now they were home. Not only home but welcomed by an entire city. Lovers who had not seen one another in half a lifetime embraced. Families and old comrades pounded one another on the back. I held my gloved hand over my mouth and wept as people around me shouted and cheered.

An elderly woman emerged from one of the cars, pausing on the step.

"Urah!" the crowd roared. Varvara shook me, pounded my back. "It's Breshkovskaya!" This was the one we'd all been waiting for. The Grandmother of the Revolution, the newspapers called her. This squat, wall-faced woman, born to nobility, had already spent twenty years in Siberian exile by the time I was born. In her few short years of freedom, she'd founded the Socialist-Revolutionary Party—the SRs, the original party of radical rebellion—just before she was rearrested, in 1905. She'd been in Siberia ever since. And here was Kerensky, kissing her three times. I'd forgotten he was an SR. As justice minister, he was the one most responsible for this amnesty.

"What an ungodly idea," my father had said. "Bringing the revolutionaries back to Petrograd. That man is a menace."

How old she was, standing in the train doorway, her white hair under her crushed hat. What a life she had lived. What courage, what fortitude. She waved to us with a white handkerchief clutched in one hand, carpetbag in the other. And so the revolution emerged from the train to meet the revolution. I felt as though we were her brilliant child, showing our fine work to our teacher, bathing in her esteem. *We did listen,* the crowd was saying. *We never forgot you.*

17 *White Swans and Black Sheep*

EVERYTHING AT THE MARIINSKY Theater spoke of the new era. Workers and soldiers I'd marched with now sat on gilded chairs, shoulder to shoulder with my bourgeois family, waiting for the performance of *Swan Lake*. Mother chatted self-consciously with our guests, the English second secretary, his wife, and an attaché, but I noticed she'd left her sealskin coat on, so she would not have to reveal the cut of her elegant clothes. The bones of her face stood out anxiously, and small lines grooved her mouth. The group exchanged commonplaces about mutual friends, as if nothing in the least bit extraordinary was happening, while the shabbily clad women workers seated in front of us estimated aloud how much fabric it must have taken to create the ornate curtain. I tried to imagine how it must feel to enter this gilded hall after a long shift at Okhta or Belhausen. Their factory committees had evidently distributed free tickets. "I thought it would be bigger, didn't you?" said one in a red scarf. An older woman examined the tiers of loges. "Glad I'm not up there. I'd be afraid to open my eyes."

I felt suddenly protective of the ballet. Would they like it? Would they find it stilted and ridiculous? What if they didn't understand? Would there be a riot? Or would they love it, these workers, these soldiers, who might only have ever heard a guitar or a wheezy accordion? I couldn't wait for them to witness the power of the orchestra, the artistry of the dancers. This was their culture, their birthright. I prayed the introduction would go well.

Seryozha, next to me, drew the trio of women before us in their scarves, posed against the backdrop of the baroque curtain's swags and tassels. *I Thought It Would Be Bigger,* he titled it. Behind us, the imperial box, whose coat of arms lay shrouded in white, was filled with the exiles I recognized from the train station: Breshkovskaya, in the same crushed hat she'd worn when she arrived. I couldn't stop turning and staring, so miraculous to see them in seats just a month ago reserved exclusively for the imperial family.

The soldier next to Father chewed handfuls of sunflower seeds and spit the shells on the floor. My father surreptitiously kicked them off his shoes while keeping his careful composure. I understood why the man did it—to show that the place didn't intimidate him, when clearly it did. Suddenly, the attaché flinched, as if stung by a bee, and recovered a paper airplane that had hit him in the back of his head. We turned to see who'd thrown it. Pavlik Gershon waved from the balcony.

My brother eyed him. "What happened to Kolya?"

"You mind your own business," I said.

The lights dimmed. People called out as if some trick was about to be played on them, and the jarring notes of the orchestra tuning added to their anxiety. But with the tapping of the conductor's baton and the first wood-wind notes of the overture, they quieted down, and at last the curtain rose. First there were gasps, whispers, then laughter as the new audience beheld the stylized movements and the men in hose. The soldier next to my father hooted merrily, "Hey, Prince, you forgot your pants!" The dancers in the corps bravely forged ahead despite the catcalls. Father's face betrayed nothing, but if Mother had been a horse she would have bolted.

Soon the grace of the ballerinas began to charm the newcomers, and the jester's athletic leaps drew vigorous shouts of approval. What a thrill for the dancer—knowing that this was a spontaneous, visceral reaction to his art! Audience and performers were getting to know each other, minute by minute gaining respect for one another. When the soldier next to Father called for the dancers to drink from their goblets instead of twirling around—"You'll never get drunk that way, Ivan!"—others shushed him. Yet I sensed the orchestra rushing, trying to get through it. When the curtain closed, Mother sat back as if she'd just run a mile and fanned herself with the program.

I prayed that the second act, with its brooding music and mysterious dark woods, would be more gripping. The sighs as the curtain rose were as sweet as music to me as the viewers beheld the blue enchanted trees, the lake of the stage. The company's von Rothbart performed in fine, defiant form with bravura leaps and

wonderfully evil wings. Poor Prince Siegfried, however, was catcalled for his handling of the hunter's bow.
At last Karsavina entered as Odette, the enchanted
swan. Oh, her slim white-clad figure with its crown of
feathers, so pale against that otherworldly background.
She balanced *en pointe* on those impossibly slender legs,
alone in the center of the big stage. Even the soldier
who had been spitting sunflower-seed shells on Father's
shoes stopped to gape. I watched the returnees. Had
they ever dreamed, in their prison cells and cold nights
of exile, that someday they would watch *Swan Lake*
from the tsar's own box, the workers and soldiers of
Petrograd all around them?

"I didn't think I'd survive that," Mother sighed, tipping
back her champagne flute. "'Hey, Prince, you forgot
your pants!'"

"I thought it very democratic," said Mr. Sibley, the
British second secretary, taking blini from Basya's plat-
ter. "I've always supported audience participation in
ballet."

I refused to laugh along with the rest of them. Those
soldiers didn't have chandeliers and dining rooms waiting for them. Those workers weren't drinking champagne and sneering at anyone, they were curled up on
thin mattresses, trying to snatch a little sleep before
their shifts in the morning.

Seryozha pressed his hands to his cheek, fluttering
his eyelashes, and nodded over toward Miss Haddon-

Finch, who was doing her best to flirt with the attaché. She looked almost pretty tonight, with high collar and cameo pin, as she tried to engage him in conversation. But his answers were short, perfunctory. Instead, he set out to flatter me, the daughter of the household and presumably a more useful connection. "That dress is lovely, Miss Makarova. The blue sets off your hair. It's like a painting."

How I hated a snob. "But it's not blue. It's green. A beautiful Irish green."

Seryozha snickered. Even Miss Haddon-Finch smiled. Mother glanced at me with twitchy-tailed irritation. *Stop it.*

Getting nowhere with me, the attaché turned his attention to Father, and the two of them reminisced about Oxford. Sibley, too, was an Oxford man, and Father launched into recollections of the year we spent at Christ Church while he was lecturing on international trade law. Seryozha mimed falling asleep in his plate. He ate a potato and asked to be excused. "Sorry— homework," he said. I prepared to follow suit, but before I had a chance, Mother shook her head. *Don't even think it.*

Square-jawed Mrs. Sibley, congenitally cheerful, brought up the newly completed Trans-Siberian Railway, which took travelers all the way from Petrograd to Vladivostok. "What an adventure, don't you think?"

"Two weeks on a train, to end up in Vladivostok?"

My mother laughed. "What could be better?" She'd returned to her witty self.

The Englishwoman turned to Father. "Dmitry Ivanovich, surely you would be interested in seeing the vast hinterlands of your country."

Father smiled, amused at the very idea. "I'm afraid I'm in rare agreement with my wife." He tapped the lip of his flute to signal Basya to pour more champagne. "However, the Trans-Siberian's more than a mere outing, Mrs. Sibley. It's our hope for the future. Siberia holds eighty percent of our wealth—our grain, our ore. Alas, the rail system's a shambles. Without it we can't get the raw materials to the factories, food to the front. I don't have to mince words with you, Sibley. We have everything we need to push the Germans back to Berlin but workable rail stock." He shook his head before taking a bite of Vaula's golden trout.

Sibley sprinkled caviar on a blin with a small bone spoon. "I do hope you'll persuade Miliukov of the urgency. It won't be difficult to secure our help."

I bet not. The British would sell their own mothers to keep Russia in the war. The British had declared their support for the Provisional Government within hours of the abdication. They didn't care who was running things as long as the Russians kept throwing bodies into the machine.

"This new coalition—what's the feeling about the commitment?" asked Sibley. "The SRs especially."

"La guerre, toujours la guerre." My mother traced a

plume in the air, as if she could clear the war talk from their minds with the impatient gesture. It was spoiling the effervescence. "We're educated people. Surely we can talk about—the weather?"

"It's not our war," I blurted out.

Father turned on me as if blackbirds had flown out of my mouth.

Now I was in for it, but I couldn't stop myself. "We had no say in it. The people want peace. They're demanding it. It's why they toppled the tsar."

Miss Haddon-Finch flushed, red creeping up her ears. "Men serving in other countries are depending on Russia," she said tremulously. It wasn't like her to express a strong opinion on politics in our house, but I'd forgotten about her brother, fighting in France.

Mother said to Mrs. Sibley, "Our eldest, you know, is with Brusilov, at the Southwestern Front. Cavalry."

"And his men favor a fight to victory," Father said, his eyes leveling at me. "It's only our local untrained reserves who talk about retreat. Where are you getting your ideas, Marina?"

As if I hadn't seen the banners, hadn't noticed the queues.

"The people have no idea what they want," Father continued. "Remember the signs? On one side they said, 'Down with the war,' and on the other 'Down with the German woman.'" The guests all chuckled. "They just don't know what's involved. We have alliances, as Miss Haddon-Finch so kindly pointed out."

The Englishwoman blushed, pleased to be noticed by Dmitry Ivanovich, in whom she placed much more store than in any wet-lipped attaché.

I suddenly saw my father through the eyes of the Ericssons, through the eyes of the women at the pump. The arrogance of him, when it was the courage of those people that had brought him into power. "How can you say you know what the people need if you're not listening to them? They can't fight anymore. They need the war to end."

"Marina, that's enough," Mother said.

Father's fury was apparent in the tightness of his mouth, the way he looked away as he sipped his champagne.

But he would hear me out. "What about our soldiers—fighting without guns, without boots? What about our own hungry workers? They didn't agree to those alliances. But they pay the price."

Mother arched her neck in a slow, resigned circle, her eyes closed. All she cared about was that I was ruining her party.

"Everyone's suffering, Miss Makarova," the British diplomat replied gently. "France has been a battlefield for three years."

Father picked up his napkin ring and dropped it gently on the tablecloth, tapping it, something he did when he was concentrating. "If Russia pulls out, millions will die. You want that on your conscience?"

I heard in my voice that horrible tremolo it got when

I felt passionate about something. "You've seen the queues." I addressed the second secretary. "The people work all day and queue all night. There's no bread. No fuel. Boys drilling on Liteiny are barely Seryozha's age. How much longer can you expect us to hold out?"

"It's complex," said Mr. Sibley. "Is this what young people are thinking?"

"Russia will not abandon its allies," Father said firmly. "A commitment's a commitment. And I've seen your marks for German, my dear. They've never been that good." In Russian he added, "One more word and you'll take your meal in the kitchen. You're being insufferable."

I collected my plate, my knife and fork, and stood with what gravity I could still muster. "I'm afraid you must excuse me then."

In the kitchen, the servants looked up from their tea Vaula cutting a cake, Basya with her feet up, waiting to clear and bring out dessert, Avdokia mending my nightshirt. Clearly I'd interrupted a juicy bit of gossip, probably about us.

"I've been exiled," I said and put down my plate among them.

"At least it was a short walk," said Basya. Avdokia frowned. Vaula tried not to laugh.

18 *Cirque Moderne*

SUCH FREEDOM, TO WALK alone in the evening with friends, unhampered by parental rules, participating in the serious discussions that had become daily life in the city. Everywhere people were arguing, voicing opinions, joining committees, trying out lines of reasoning, flexing political muscle. We were talking about the war as we drifted across the Field of Mars in the enchanted, unearthly northern spring twilight. "The Germans will bring back the tsar," said Pavlik. "They'll reverse everything we've achieved."

In the half-light, it was still bright enough to see the color of the girls' spring coats. Also the heavy length of Pavlik's eyelashes. The trees smelled fresh and the square glowed, the long yellow buildings dizzying in perspective, an uninterrupted pattern of columns and windows. Seryozha lagged behind, thinking his own private thoughts. Here on these broad parade grounds, we'd sent Kolya and Volodya off to war. Here we'd buried 184 martyrs of the revolution just two months ago, a solemn day. I would never forget the sight of those coffins next to their resting places, imagining the student in one of them. And our parents walking in procession with members of the Provisional Government, everyone singing "You Fell Victim" until your heart would burst.

"That's a spurious argument and you're a capitalist dupe, Pavlik, like all the Defensists," Varvara called over her shoulder. "If we stop the war, the German workers will win their soldiers over, just like we did, and the kaiser will fall. We have to stop the shooting, and bring them over to the revolution."

I wasn't really in the mood to argue tonight. The beauty of the evening made me think of my fox, my real lover. If he were here, we wouldn't be talking about the war, wasting the spring twilight. We'd stroll in the fragrant air, our footsteps matching, and stop to kiss on the bridge over the Winter Canal. We'd be in bed before the hour was out. What I would give just to press my forehead to his, drink in the honey smell of his skin once more.

"What do you think of this new Bolshevik?" asked a girl from our school, Alla, trailing behind us. Recently, Vladimir Ilyich Lenin had returned from exile, and his April Theses had just run in the Bolshevik newspaper *Rabochy Put'*. "They say he's against the Republic."

Varvara sighed, as if Alla had woken up in the third act of a play and asked for a précis. "First, he's not new," she replied. "And second, he's not against the Republic. He's against a *parliamentary* republic, a bourgeois republic. Your papas, thinking they speak for the people. He wants a *soviet* republic—by direct representation."

"What we need are free communes," said another Herzen boy, Markus, an anarchist. "Lenin talks about the 'withering away of the state,' but the essence of the state is that there's never a good time to wither."

"The Bolsheviks will do it," Varvara said, sticking her chin out.

"I'll believe it when I see it," Markus said.

They were two of a kind. They stopped to light cigarettes together, sharing a match. I thought he would be perfect for her, but she'd scoffed when I suggested it. "Anarchist utopian."

We crossed at the Trinity Bridge over the black water of the Neva, passed the brooding bulk of the Peter and Paul Fortress, and the art nouveau Kschessinska Mansion, now the headquarters of the Bolshevik Party. The ballerina Mathilde Kschessinska had received it as a gift from her lover Nikolas II. I wondered where she'd gone. Paris? The tsar himself was under arrest, somewhere in the Urals with his family. Oddly, since his abdication he'd quickly become irrelevant. Nobody clamored for his head on a pike. Aside from a few aristocrats who might secretly dream of restoration, no one thought about him anymore. Varvara examined the windows of the mansion, probably hoping to catch sight of Lenin's big bald head.

Our destination loomed into view — the vast, rickety hall of the Cirque Moderne, *the* radical venue for speakers of all left-leaning political stripes that spring, and a magnet for students from all over the city. Where once the Stray Dog had been Mecca, now it was this old wooden hall on the Petrograd side of the river. Pressing inside, we joined the thousands already listening to the orators in the cavernous smoky gloom. It smelled like bodies, wet wood and cheap tobacco, old boots. About five dim bulbs lit our way as we clambered up into the rickety tiered benches surrounding the stage on all sides. We had to climb nearly to the ceiling. I imagined what the woman who'd worried about the loges at the Mariinsky would think of this. I could tell that Seryozha was nervous as we squeezed in among the university students, workers, soldiers, retirees, and wounded veterans. Pavlik climbed in next to me.

Down in the very center of the hall, a common soldier, stocky, square-shouldered, was addressing the crowd, speaking about the war in the name of his comrades. "Show us what we're fighting for," he shouted up to us all. "Is it Constantinople? Or a free Russia? Or the people on top? They're always asking us for more sacrifices, but where is their sacrifice?"

If only my father could hear this. If only he'd listen more to the Russian people and less to his friends in the British embassy and the Kadets and industrialists. *Where are you getting your ideas, Marina?* Pavlik handed me a chocolate, smiled. He really was very sweet. How infinitely better this was than wandering the lengthening evenings thinking of how little Kolya cared for me. He never responded to my letters. My brother took out his notebook and sketched the soldier, and the next one who ventured to speak.

The best speaker was a small fiery man with wild

black hair and a pince-nez named Leon Trotsky. They all had something to say, but I had waited for this one. What a speaker! He'd been the leader of the Soviet of 1905 and had just returned from exile. Trotsky made us understand that this moment was a fuse and that we held the match, that the whole world was on the brink of revolution. All we had to do was light it. He was a cauldron melting the crowd into a single substance, and we threw ourselves in.

"Russia has opened a new epoch," he called to us, "an epoch of blood and iron. A struggle no longer of nation against nation but of the suffering oppressed classes against their rulers." The roar of applause in that barn left no confusion as to what it meant to believe in revolution. He talked about the achievement of the revolution, our impact on the world.

I'd always thought that once the tsar was gone, the wheel would stop, or at least pause, giving us a chance to get used to things, but now I could see that the revolution was just beginning. It would become a way of life as people clarified and changed their perceptions of what they thought could and must be done. Already, between February and May, my father's superior in the foreign office, Paul Miliukov—a constitutional monarchist and one of the leading lights of the Kadet party—had been run out, replaced by Mikhail Tereshchenko, a nonparty beet-sugar magnate from the Ukraine. Now there was a new coalition of ten capitalist and six socialist ministers. The socialists, still trying to find common ground, had committed to continuing the war and calming the masses. But like Lenin, the man onstage had another idea. "Only a single power can save Russia—the Soviet of Workers' and Soldiers' Deputies! All power to the Soviet!"

What was the government waiting for? Here was a clear message, impossible to misunderstand: end this war, redistribute the land, feed the people, and achieve peace.

After Trotsky, another man took the stage, a pro-war Defensist, but he didn't stand a chance—it was like having to sing after Chaliapin. "The war is Russia's face to the world," he argued to the enormous crowd. "If we retreat, we'll be putting out the welcome mat! With the tsar we were subjects, but with the kaiser we'll be slaves. The worker will be back under the lash. The only way to establish ourselves in the world as a true power is to continue the war and uphold our alliances."

I had heard this argument before and had never been able to counter it. People booed and hissed, but others shouted, "Let him talk!"

Up in our section, something was happening behind us. "The poet!" "Go on, kid." A big young worker stood on his bench and began to speak—no, he was reciting a poem! Lucky for him he had a deep actor's voice and was able to create a pool of attention around himself. His poem likened a burning police station to a garbage incinerator, then to the blast furnace of a great factory, and finally to the gaping mouth of a lying old man. His shock of tawny blond hair looked familiar. Suddenly I recognized him—the boy from the Stray Dog Café! The one who wanted to show his work to Mayakovsky. Tonight he wore a carrot in the button-hole of his jacket, the long green ends dangling, and he signaled the end of his poem by unthreading the carrot and biting off the end. Had I imagined it, or had he grinned right at me as he sat down? I felt it all the way through my coat, my layers of clothes, directly into my body. I quickly turned and faced front, my heart thumping around in my chest like a bird in a hallway, looking for an exit.

Onstage, an older woman now addressed the hall. I tried to concentrate and not to check if the poet was still looking at me, but when I managed to see past all the heads, he was gone.

The soft deep voice in my ear startled me. "Not her again." The boy had moved down to a seat right behind us. I could hardly hear through the thunder in my ears, my freckles were on fire. "She looks like a teacher I once had. I keep thinking she's going to give me a whipping."

It would hardly do to let him see how thrilled I was. "Maybe you need one," I replied, not turning.

Seryozha laughed over the drawing in his lap. Pavlik glanced back over his shoulder, annoyed with this interloper. The Tagantsev girls watched the whole thing closely, storing up gossip for the next day.

"If it was you, who knows? I might let you."

Varvara made her black eyes bulge with exasperation. *Can't you leave off for a moment?*

He held out the feathery end of his carrot, tickling my nose. "Here's the whip."

I laughed, brushing the leaves away.

"Kuriakin. Gennady Yurievich." The poet held out a giant hand. My hand vanished in it, and yet we shook. It was a softer hand than I had expected, more flexible. "Call me Genya." *Genya.* I shivered.

"Do you mind?" Pavlik said.

Genya stuck his big face between Seryozha and me and ignored every signal from Pavlik that he was unwelcome.

"Makarova. Marina." Then I added, "This is my brother Seryozha." Surely I couldn't be accused of flirting if I introduced my brother.

Down on the stage, the woman argued not only for the end of the war but also for the end of state power and for worker control of the factories. Markus shouted his approval, pounding on his knee. "Yes! Exactly!"

Genya eyed the sketch my brother was working up. Now I saw that it was of the poet reciting over the heads of the crowd. He cocked his head for a better angle. "I even look halfway intelligent. Most appreciated." How heroic he was in Seryozha's eyes, broad-shouldered, chin tilted up, soldiers and sailors gathered around him. "Look, let's get out of here, Makarova Marina," he said. "Let's go for a walk. It's hot in here, and I've had enough of the sermons."

Pavlik crossed his arms peevishly as I left with the boy from the Stray Dog Café. "I'll be back," I whispered to Seryozha as I climbed over him. "If not, go home with the others." His face was still red from being caught admiring the handsome young poet.

Outside, the air was fresh and the night finally dark, splashed with stars like flour slung into the sky. In the absence of police, all sorts of sinister people scuttled in the shadows, but who would bother me with this giant, this Genya Kuriakin? He was like a figure from a folktale, an indomitable Ilya Muromets. And the way he'd chosen me, plucked me from the crowd as a boy picks a flower from a meadow—it was so easy. As simple as destiny. *Genya,* a name like grain on the tongue, like a gift in the hand. That hard *G* grabbed you, the *ya* declared itself again. *Ya,* I.

We strolled along the Petrovskaya Embankment, where the river sparkled, shattering reflections of the lights from the bridges and the Winter Palace. The whole right side of my body turned rosy with this boy's proximity. Walking with him was like standing next to a furnace. "I've seen you before, you know," he said. Had he seen me that night at the Stray Dog after all? I didn't reply. There was time. We had all the night ahead. "At Wolf's bookstore. You wore a green coat and a white hat, and you were looking at poetry."

I must have been hunting for my own book, seeing if any had sold. I wanted to tell him that, but it would seem like I was trying to impress him. And he probably wouldn't consider my stuff poetry anyway—it wasn't very futuristic. But this was poetry, too—this, the fragrance of sex and possibility. It was a scent that surrounded me ever since I'd started up with Kolya. As if I'd passed through a mirror and found I'd become beautiful, or interesting, something other than myself. It was foolish and vain of me, but right then I felt as if I could stretch out my arm and the bridge itself would sidle closer, rub up against me like a cat.

Genya Kuriakin leaned against the balustrade and reached out toward my face. I stood very still as he carefully picked up a lock of my hair that had fallen loose and tucked it back in. "Yes, a green coat and a white fur hat, a ribbon in your buttonhole. I wrote a poem about you. Do you want to hear it?"

"If it's any good," I teased him.

He stepped away from me and began:

You touch my poems
as if testing my eye
with the tip of your tongue
seeing if I'm something good
to eat.

And decide—against.

No, don't go!
Am I really so tasteless?

Too salty?
Too tough?

Really I'm tasty as can be.
            Feast on my heart, my liver
Take my tongue, my brain, my limbs
      What use have I for arms
           unless you take them?

        You think me kitsch?

The red ribbon in your buttonhole . . .
What valor have you shown,
        what valedictions on what battlefields?
      What monsters have you slain,
          Tsar-Maiden?

My poem fails to stir.
        I may as well jump.
          Tear out my eyes.
            Fall on the tracks.
       Cruel beauty.
       Have you already eaten
         some other poet?
       Are you full?

The smell of your smoke
        lingers in the aisle.

Poor poet. I could well imagine his anguish as I examined his book, then put it back, unread. With that red ribbon in my buttonhole, waiting for Kolya. It was for valor in bed, Genya—*that* battleground. "Yes, I remember."

He kissed my palm, as if he were drinking from it. "No, you don't. But that's all right. You can remember this instead."

We continued walking along the quay. The stars were winking on, and the warmth of his arm around my shoulder made my coat unnecessary. Then the moon began to rise, fast, illuminating his face, his eyes. Were they green or brown? His nose was long and bumpy, it had been broken. When we stopped again, I pulled the carrot from his buttonhole, took a bite, and threw the rest into the water. He kissed me then, suddenly, carrot still in my mouth, with all the awkwardness of unstudied desire. This was what young people did, I thought—simple and open, not a practiced seduction. Not hidden away in some stranger's decadent flat. I felt younger than I had before, lighter, as if I'd been allowed to go back and try a new path.

He talked and talked. He'd come from a town in the Volga called Puchezh, north of Nizhny-Novgorod, where his father was a priest. Genya was a Bolshevik, he'd been to jail or so he said, he hated religion. He lived with a group of poets in a flat near Haymarket Square, and contributed to a journal called *Okno*—*The Window*. He considered himself a futurist. He loved

Mayakovsky and Khlebnikov, and with bashful pride he admitted that his *Okno* friends had published a volume of his poetry called *The Brief Memoir of a Clay Pigeon,* the very book I'd picked up and put down again.

I didn't volunteer any information about my own family—it was too embarrassing to say that my father was a Kadet member of the Provisional Government, that my mother was a Golovin, that we lived in a twelve-room flat on Furshtatskaya Street. Instead, I told him about the poets I loved, that I was graduating soon, on my way to university. "I write, too. Poems. That's what I was doing at Wolf's that day. Seeing if any of my books had sold."

"I should have known. I felt it. More than just a beauty." He leaned his back against the balustrade, folded his arms. "Well? Let's hear one."

I loved that he assumed I could just rattle one off, that he assumed it would be worth hearing. But which? The poem I'd written about the death of the student at Znamenskaya Square? That would impress him with my revolutionary fervor. But instead, I recited one written by the girl in the white fur hat, so we could be formally introduced.

Insomnia

My window gazes onto night,
alone and sleepless-starry.
Down Furshtatskaya, a single light
shines from the topmost story.

Who is this comrade untouched by sleep?
Does she rock a newborn baby?
Does he pine for love and weep?
Does she mourn for vanished beauty?

Another soul who can't find peace.
I will not douse my light
and leave them in emptiness
to pass the wine-dark night.

As blissful souls drift blissfully
inside their peaceful homes,
dear stranger, you and I must ply
our oars till morning comes.

I couldn't see his face in the dark. He was too quiet. I'd embarrassed him. Oh I should have done one about the insurrection. "You think it's kitsch."

He laughed, wrapping his heavy arm around me, resting his cheek against my hair. "No, it's perfect. Just right. I was afraid you would be clever, all hard and brilliant. I hate cleverness. Without blood and bone, there's no poetry—there's nothing."

What gods had favored me with this chance meeting? I felt I was teetering on top of a needle twenty feet in the air. The Neva flowed deep and wide before us, plashing, speaking its indecipherable truths, like Fate itself, unknown. Everything I'd thought about the future was dissolving in my hands. As Mina would say, I'd not taken variable x into account. And here he was, variable x. Genya plucked at my coat. "Why don't you wear the green one? And the furry hat?"

"It's spring," I laughed. "And ermine would scarcely do for the Cirque Moderne. Trotsky would hardly approve."

"He'd make an exception for you. Haven't you heard of Marina Makarova, Comrade? The poet with the head of fire and the voice of flame? Surely you can't begrudge her a hat. No? I didn't think so. He says it's all right."

Who would have guessed it? A romantic. A man who wrote poems about burning police stations, a Bolshevik. He held me tight, buried his face in my neck. "I love you, Marina Makarova."

How my body missed a man's embrace. Kolya had never said he loved me. No one ever had. "You can't love me. You just met me."

"I don't care. I love you. Just say my name."

"Genya Kuriakin."

"Say it again." He picked me up as if I weighed nothing, as if I was a child, shouting, "Say it! I want to feel the syllables climbing your beautiful throat, the corners of my consonants stuck in your teeth, my vowels sticky on your tongue!" He spun me around, making me dizzy. His silky hair smelled of trees, of hay and meadows. When he slid me down his body, it was like sliding down the trunk of an oak.

He pressed my palm to his lips as if his face were freezing and my hand the only warmth. "Marry me, Marina. You will, won't you?"

I laughed out of sheer happiness, the lunacy of it all. "But what shall be our wedding ring?"

"How about Saturn? He's got rings to spare." He reached up and pretended to grab Saturn out of the starry sky in one enormous fist and slid the ring onto my finger. "A perfect fit."

And so we were wed.

19 *At Haymarket Square*

How could I have lived in the same city as Genya all these years and never seen him with his pack of fellow poets, conferring in cafés, reading on street corners? They called themselves the Transrational Interlocutors of the Terrestrial Now. They were everywhere, reading under the General Staff Building arch, in Haymarket Square, and on the banks of the Pryazhka River right under the windows of the great Alexander Blok, which is where I first met them. It was a clear provocation, one generation of artists trying to outrage their elders. A young man of twenty-five or so was reciting a *zaum* poem to the perplexity of the passersby — transsense language poetry invented by the avant-gardists Kruchenykh and Khlebnikov, whom I already knew Genya adored.

A girl in a worn skirt and wrinkled blouse handed around a cap, but the haphazard audience, two sailors and a whore, only made fun of the poet. After he was done, Genya introduced us. The poet was Anton Chernikov, the editor of their journal and the leader of their group. I was dismayed by his look of frank horror as he took in my neat shoes, my hat, my hair, and the kiss Genya planted on my neck, his arm around me. I knew I had little hope of ever winning him over. His sneering face would never accept me, the bourgeois miss. More personable was a tall strapping paint-splattered blond, Sasha Orlovsky, an artist, and Gigo Gelashvili, an earnest, shock-haired Georgian poet. He had a gift for rhyme, and a little crowd gathered as he recited—a woman selling *pirozhky*, a drunk, and two dockworkers. I looked up to see if Blok would appear in his fifth-floor window, but the curtains remained drawn.

The girl with the cap was called Zina Ostrovskaya. She said nothing at all when Genya introduced us, just stared in disgust. She reminded me of a small vicious animal, like a mink or a ferret. Her poetry, when it was her turn, proved sharp and political. But Genya was their star. People heard him a block away and came to investigate. Idlers stopped to listen in the warm afternoon. The whores especially admired him. He incorporated everything from *zaum* to the language of the street, biblical cadences and Russian mythology. As a finale, he sang a sailors' song to the tune of the Orthodox liturgy, which brought shouts of encouragement and a clattering of coins from the loitering sailors and longshoremen.

Afterward they lounged in the sun and counted their money, ate sandwiches out of their pockets. It seemed that the Transrational Interlocutors, or at least their core group, lived together near Haymarket Square in a place they called the Poverty Artel, an *artel* being a small factory, which in this case produced poetry. "We pool our poverty and divide it among our members," Genya joked. I wondered if these street-corner performances were enough to live on.

"Oh, we do all kinds of things," he said. "Painting houses, putting up handbills. Anything people have for us."

And how had they managed to avoid the draft? He shrugged. "Gigo and Sasha have student deferments. I'm an only son. Anton here was discharged for mental instability."

"Unsuitability for service," corrected the scowling avant-gardist, crushing out a cigarette.

"The apartment's in Anton's name." My new love tossed a piece of his sandwich to a strutting seagull. "Nobody's registered but him, just in case the government changes its mind. Makes us a little harder to find."

I wanted to visit the Poverty Artel, but Genya was oddly shy about letting me come over. I couldn't understand. I had no compunctions about being alone with him, about moving on from kisses to love. I even made Seryozha go to a drugstore and buy condoms, over his vociferous protests. I had to bribe him with a set of pastels. What was Genya waiting for? "It's a flophouse," he said. "You don't want to see that." And when he walked me home to Furshtatskaya Street that day, and we kissed in the parkway under the bright-leaved trees, I asked him to come up with me. He gazed at the fancy plasterwork and the iron balconies, at a woman coming out to walk two matched Borzois, and shook his head. "I'm not going in there."

"Come in the back way then. That's what Varvara does." And then into my salmon-pink boudoir.

"I don't go in the back way," he said stiffly.

I was mortified. I had offended him, suggesting he use the servants' entry. "Well, come in the front, then, and meet my mother."

"Some other time," he said, chastely kissing my temple.

Yet later from our windows I caught sight of him, loitering in the park strip under the shade of the burgeoning trees.

I sat at my place at dinner, imagining how this would all look to Genya: Mother in her filmy summer organza; Father relating amusing anecdotes about the foreign office; Tripov the art collector, his fat fingers bedecked with rings; the Gromitskys quarreling about their visit to Capri; Basya in a starched apron and cap, handing around asparagus. How Genya would mock all this, and rightly so. The chatter and clatter of silverware seemed almost unbearable to me now, the ludicrous epergne spilling over with roses, the chandelier whose crystals Basya had to disassemble and soak one by one. These days it was becoming dusty. She did as little as possible, and with ever greater insolence—Mother was becoming afraid of her. The revolutionary feeling was growing in the city, even in her own home. I could see my mother's eyes stray from time to time to the chandelier, to the little strings of dust, and I noticed that she avoided looking into Basya's face as she offered more wine. I missed what people were saying as they tried to draw me out. I was further and further away, thinking about Genya waiting for me in the parkway, in the silvery White Night. Tonight I would make love with him. Even if it was behind a statue in the Summer Garden.

Finally the dishes were cleared, and I seized the moment to flee. I threw on a light shawl and ran down to Furshtatskaya Street. It was almost ten, a warm June evening—bright enough to read a newspaper. The leaves cast shadows on the ground. For a moment I thought he hadn't come. But there he was, standing under a tree in the eerie dappled shade of the northern summer evening. I ran to him, kissed him breathlessly, tilting my face up to him as if I were trying to kiss the sky.

We walked together slowly through the cool silvery streets toward the Summer Garden. He kept stopping to look at me, or walked backward in front of me. How different it was to be with Genya. When I'd been with Kolya, I'd been the moon, and he was the sun: he could give me his warmth or withhold it, pursue me or forget me. Genya bent toward me as if I were the source of light. Strange—for once I didn't feel the impulse to show off for him. Mother always scolded me for my blurtings, my "antics," my tendency to tell people more than they ever wanted to know. "One attracts others with mystery," she said, "not by turning one's pockets inside out." Genya treated me as if I were as mysterious as a hidden spring. I loved seeing myself through his eyes. Everything around us shimmered in this dream light. I felt drunk, though I'd only had one glass of champagne. "You're like a ghost in that dress," he said.

"I'm a corpse—is that what you're telling me?"

"Not a ghost then. A sleepwalker. In a white nightgown," he said. "Barefoot, with a candle in hand."

I'd worn a white dress intentionally. I wanted to glow in his memory, to haunt him, yes, the way Kolya had once haunted me. I hummed the dreamy grand waltz from *Sleeping Beauty*, taking his hand and turning under his arm.

In the Summer Garden, the unearthly twilight shifted through the old trees, illuminating the mossy sculptures lining the gravel paths. Every lover in Petrograd was out tonight, breathing with us the green of the linden trees as birdsong tumbled liquid through the air.

"I want to do something astonishing," Genya declared. "Something heroic. Kill myself in your honor. Swim to Antarctica. Fight a duel." He mimed fencing an imaginary adversary on my behalf. He bit the shoulder of my thin dress, tugged at it like a dog. "I'd like to tear this off with my teeth," he said in my ear.

"Please! Not in front of Diana." Clutching demurely at my bodice, I pointed at the glowing bare-breasted huntress with the moon in her sculpted hair.

"She doesn't like me," said Genya, resting his cheek on top of my head. I wasn't a short girl but he towered above me as we gazed at the glaring goddess, poised with bow and arrow.

"She doesn't like men."

"And why should she? Why would any woman?" He rubbed his stubbly cheek against mine. "Big hairy protuberant fellows. Always knocking something over or giving a speech. If I were a woman I'd have nothing to do with any of us." His breath was sweet and smelled of fennel seeds.

As a schoolgirl, I'd imagined I'd walk here someday with a lover in summer just like this...though I always pictured characters from Pushkin: a man in a swallowtail coat, me in a summer gown and bonnet. The idea of Genya in breeches and a swallowtail coat made me laugh. A bearskin and bast boots were more like it. Or chain mail.

"Come home with me tonight," he said, in the shadows of a lesser path, leafy and fragrant. "I wish I had some better place to take you…but I told the boys to clear off. We'll have it to ourselves."

So it had come at last. I passed my hand back and forth, so that the shadows of the linden leaves cast their shapes on my palm. His proposal was certainly better than the idea of bringing him into my fussy bedroom with its trinkets and albums, the vanity table with all the pictures, the crocheted bedspread. He simply would not have fit.

Sadovaya Street was thick with people strolling, taking in the magical night. Haymarket Square was bustling with its long lines of stalls—vendors of *pirozhky* and ice cream, old clothes and hats. A potbellied man had a bear on a leash and was making it dance. Watching the bear lumbering on its hind legs—the leather collar on its neck, the chain—Genya's eyes filled with tears. "Poor thing," he said. "You can see how he hates this. The revolution should take bears into account."

Suddenly, someone in the crowd behind us screamed, "Thief! He's got my handbag!" Other people took up the cry. "Catch him!" "Get him!"

A skinny young urchin flashed by with the woman's purse. There were no police anymore, so the crowd went running after him, men and women, baying like hounds. They soon caught the culprit—oh the shouts and the curses! They boiled up like noxious gas as they beat him, others soon joining in. *Please stop it*, I prayed, tears dripping down my face, clinging to

Genya. It reminded me of the day of the bread riot, and how the baker had been beaten and the woman punched. "Someone's got to stop it," I said. The boy disappeared in their midst like a small fish in the center of a sea anemone.

Then Genya was shoving his way through the horde, pulling them out of his way, into the ugly inner circle. Their faces were so puffy with fury and a horrible glee that they were unrecognizable as human. He grabbed people by their collars and flung them aside to reveal a boy about Seryozha's age, broken on the stones. "Isn't that enough?" he shouted at the crowd. "Didn't she get her miserable purse back?"

A man with a face like a knobby potato kicked the boy one more time. "That's what we do with thieves. He'll remember that the next time he thinks of stealing something."

His face streaming with tears, twisted in pity, Genya picked up the limp and bleeding body, lurched to his feet, and carried the boy on his shoulder away from the crowd. I followed him through the square and he turned down a passage into a courtyard. A woman pumping water into a pail glanced up at us with little interest, as if we were hauling coal. Genya carried the battered boy up a steep stairway, arriving in a dark, dirty hall. I had to reach into his pants pocket for his key, at which he gave me a ghost of a smile. The boy moaned. I unlocked the door.

Here it was, the Poverty Artel. Three windows over-

looking a courtyard. A divan and a cot, some mismatched chairs and stools, a table covered with manu-
scripts. Newspapers plastered the walls. But the divan
had been neatly made up with sheets and a pillow.
Genya lay the thief there, the boy's purple face already
swelling, his eyes shut tight as a newborn's. "Stay with
him. I'll get some water." My would-be lover grabbed
a jug.

I sat next to the boy, praying he wasn't terribly hurt.
The thief keened and moaned. I took his hand—hard
and dirty—and hummed a song my mother used to
sing when I was small. *Fais dodo, Colin, mon petit
frère…* While we were waiting for Genya to come
back, the boy turned and squinted at me through terrible swollen eyes. "I don't want to die. I'm afraid," he
whispered through his split lip, his broken teeth.

"You won't," I said, and tried to shape my face into
a reassuring smile. "He's getting you something to
drink." All I could do was hold his hand.

I thanked God when Genya finally returned with the
pitcher of water. The urchin's head was swelling into
something unrecognizable. We switched seats. Genya
took a rag—no, a nightshirt—and sponged the boy off.

"I hate people," he said, wiping the urchin's face with
the rag. "Animals are more noble. Look at this boy.
He's poor and desperate, but can they see it? Can they
pity him? No. They should embrace him. They should
save their kicks and blows for the bastards who keep
them so poor, who set them on each other like dogs."

I sang for a while, low, sad songs, until the boy's breathing slowed. *The bird nests, but I am an orphan, I have no home...*

We spent the rest of the night watching him sleep, like worried parents. Was he asleep or unconscious? "Shouldn't we get a doctor?" I asked. "What if he..." But I didn't want to say *die*...dying was a matter for professionals, not poets.

"There's no doctor," Genya said gently.

"We could fetch him to the hospital..."

"They wouldn't take him. Look, we'll think of something in the morning."

He held my hand, and recited the poem I had written about the light in the window—he remembered it. All we could do was keep this boy company. So that's what we did. I couldn't help but imagine how it would be to watch a child who was ill, a little boy with a fever. This was what was meant by love   not passion, not a game of pleasure.

I fell asleep on the cot, on top of the blankets—the sheets were far too grimy—but Genya stayed awake all night in the chair by the divan, putting cold compresses on the boy's swollen head.

When I woke in the morning, Genya stood at the window. "He's dead." The frail lifeless body, the purple battered head, a pink stain on the pillowcase. "I'm going to take him down. Let them look at their handiwork." He lifted the small form, the head flopping. I opened the door for him and locked it behind us, followed him down the narrow, foul-smelling stairs out into the courtyard, then the lane. As we walked, Genya began to sing "You Fell Victim," the song they'd sung when they buried the martyrs of the revolution. People stared as he carried the fragile corpse through the workaday streets and into Haymarket Square, moving through the stalls selling hats and fruit and cucumbers, past tinkers and candle makers. His song gathered a crowd. He propped the boy up against a post and addressed them. His voice carried far into the square, reciting a poem he must have written while I slept:

> *Citizens, comrades, you,*
> *the new elite!*
> *this is the boy*
> *you beat last night.*
> *You were wolves*
> *snapping*
> *as he ran*
> *your jaws red with justice.*
> *This is the boy*
> *who committed a crime*
> *for a few kopeks*
> *he has given his life*
> *he needed four kopeks*
> *no one asked—whose child are you?*
> *No one asked*
> *what terrors he'd seen.*
> *White Nights*

are romantic, dearies,
    just right for killing
        a boy with no name.
Our sweet revolution means nothing to you
      You're gorged with truth
with justice
        he should have run faster.
He should have just starved
    more quietly.

The onlookers were silent. A middle-aged woman clutched a handkerchief to her mouth. A man in a leather apron took off his cap.

Genya left the boy to them and walked me back to Furshtatskaya Street.

20 *Into the Countryside*

THE SMELL OF PIPE tobacco lay thick in the hall that morning. I was hoping to go straight to my room—I was dead tired and smelled from sleeping in my clothes on that squalid cot—but Miss Haddon-Finch flew out from the salon and stopped me from getting any farther than the vestibule. "Marina!" Red-eyed and rumpled, she pressed a handkerchief to her mouth. "Where have you been? We're all beside ourselves...your mother...your father! We thought you'd been murdered. Seryozha told us about the boy...what were you thinking? With everything else Dmitry Ivanovich has to worry about?"

"I'd like to go wash up now," I said. "It's been a terrible night."

"He wants to talk to you. He's in his study."

They must have wrestled it out of my brother. He'd never have shared this unless coercion was involved. Well, they knew now. All right, so what? It wasn't as though we'd done anything, much as we'd wanted to. Ironic. But even if we had...I was a grown woman now. I'd seen four people die right in front of me. I supposed I could face my father's disapproval. I straightened myself, took a deep breath, wiped my hands on my coat.

He was waiting in his study, his cheek on his hand, elbow propped on the green leather top of his desk. Dressed, but not carefully. His collar was askew, and his skin looked rough and bloodless. *This is what he'll look like when he's old.* "Close the door," he said.

I did. I decided to speak before he could, so he couldn't draw out the suspense. "A boy was beaten last night on Haymarket Square. My friends took him back to their room, and we tried to save him. He died this morning."

He gazed at me wearily across an open book... Dickens. I recognized the volume, one of a set. His eyes the same brown as my own, though this morning his were drooping and bloodshot, yellow in the whites. "Friends, you say. Your brother told us you've taken up with a self-proclaimed poet, some young roughneck you met at a radical meeting. Is that why you took off so quickly last night that you could hardly push in your chair?"

"Yes. But not the way you're thinking." Though it was, of course.

He rubbed his eyes, pulled his palms down his face, as if he could wipe off the sight of me. But there I was again. "Well, you're a graduate now. A young woman. I just thought you had more respect for yourself. An awareness of your position in life." He gestured for me to sit in a spindle-backed chair.

Were we really going to have this conversation? My position in life? I would not sit down. This was going to be a very short interview. "We sat with the boy, and that's all."

He tapped his letter opener on the desktop, turned it, tapped, and regarded me from under his curly eyebrows. "If you don't understand what I'm saying, I don't know how at this late date to convey it to you."

I felt like I was being slowly rolled in slivers of glass. My palms sweated. My neck sweated. I could smell myself—I stank. "You can't. It's too late."

"You didn't think for a minute what a turmoil your behavior would cause." He steepled his hands, matching fingertip to fingertip.

"I'm sorry. There was no telephone—"

"All that education, the talent, the brains—our confidence in you. For what? So you could run around the streets of Petrograd like a cheap slut?"

I was too tired to defend myself. I struggled not to cry. "Everyone grows up, Papa."

"Running around with God knows what kind of hooligan—someone you picked up at the Cirque Moderne." He snorted as if that was the rudest irony of all. "All those years of care, and you throw yourself away with both hands." He'd never looked at me with such despair. It was like watching a carriage toppling over. I could do nothing to stop it. "It's my fault, I know. We're all so very modern now. Don't discipline the children. It's simply not done." His mouth hooked downward in its nest of brown beard like a mask of tragedy. "Do we need to go out and get you a yellow card?" The document prostitutes carried to show they'd registered with the police.

I imagined Seryozha, cowering in his room, sick with shame at having informed on me. And Mother, too, nowhere in sight. I'm sure there had been a terrible fight. Father began to call me names—old-fashioned names, *trollop, jade*—trying to make me cry, his voice louder and louder.

I wanted to hurt him back. "What is it that you object to most? That I'm not virginal or that he's not one of us?"

Suddenly he was himself again, Dmitry Makarov, the lawyer. "I thought you said you hadn't done anything with him."

"Oh, so now you believe me."

"There have been others?" His complexion was ashen.

I had no apologies, no argument to make. This was my life. Someone so out of touch had no right to dictate its shape or content.

"I'm not your father," he said. "Women like you are fatherless."

The father I knew could never say this to me, never. Waves of nausea flooded over me. I was too shocked to weep. "Is it all right if I go now?"

"Go. It disgusts me to look at you. Stay in your room until I decide what in the world's to be done with you."

I went. How clean it was, the freshly made bed. It smelled good and light streamed in through the lace curtains. I washed, then sat at my vanity. *Slut. Jade. Trollop.* Those words, coming from my own father's lips. What did they even mean? I looked in the mirror. I looked...pugnacious. Was I a slut? I certainly liked being handled by men. Sex, the life of the senses, it was very strong in my nature. I didn't want to hurt my father, but women like me always hurt their fathers, because we couldn't stay little girls. Funny, when I really had been sleeping with someone, he'd never known it.

Avdokia woke me in the afternoon, coming in with soup and a cucumber salad, cold chicken on a tray. "It's the big worker boy who hangs around, isn't it?" she whispered. "I've never seen Dmitry Ivanovich in such a state. He went off to the foreign office on an hour of sleep, poor man. I hope you've learned your lesson."

"And what lesson is that?" I said, clearing off the

desk so she could lower the tray. "We tried to save a boy's life, a pickpocket being beaten by a mob. Papa's jumping to conclusions."

"A pickpocket." She shook her head, sighed, sighed again, as if there were no more oxygen in Petrograd, as if it had been raised to Himalayan heights and she had to labor to fill her lungs. "May the Holy Theotokos have mercy."

"We sat with him all night. He was young. It was terrible. His head was as big as a watermelon."

"Eat some soup, sweetheart." I took a hot mouthful to placate her, but eating was the last thing on my mind. I could still see the crowd's savage glee, the boy's battered head, the way he hung limp in Genya's arms. My father's face. I might never eat again.

"Dmitry Ivanovich is a changed man since joining the government," my nanny said, hanging up my clothes. "You can't waltz around like it doesn't matter anymore. He's been working so hard, he's got so much on his mind. Oh, why did you have to go off last night? They were having a nice party here. That boy—it's not going to go well."

When I tried to go out to the toilet, I found the door of my room had been locked. So it had come to this. He didn't know what to do with me, so he'd locked me up until he could formulate his plans. I couldn't bring myself to pound on the walls. It was hardly the Crosses. I used the chamber pot, sat down to write. After a while, I heard knocking on the wall from the nursery next door. Seryozha. *Fais dodo*... trying to apologize. I didn't knock back.

That evening I heard my father and mother quarreling: *Reputation. Your daughter. That hooligan.* Part of me wanted to announce that I'd sacrificed my precious virginity not to *that hooligan* but to Kolya Shurov, trusted family friend. Would he like that better? What was worse, my class treachery? Or that I'd ruined his perception of me as a pure vessel, inert and worthy to be passed along to an approved husband? Either way, I'd proved to be a stony field, an intractable horse, useless for the task assigned it.

Avdokia came and went with food and the chamber pot, her eyes red from weeping. "Pray, Marinoushka. Pray for forgiveness."

On the fourth day of my comfortable imprisonment, Miss Haddon-Finch let herself in. "I'm here to help you pack," she said briskly, no nonsense. "We're leaving. For Maryino."

The country? We never went this early. "It's only June."

"It's been decided." She opened my wardrobe, began taking out summer clothes, piling them on the bed. "This has all been very hard on your mother, not to mention Dmitry Ivanovich. They've decided it will be better if we got away for a while. We could all use a little peace and quiet."

But she forgot to lock the door. I shoved past her and marched down to the dining room, where they were eating breakfast. Mother was still in her dressing gown, Father ready for work at the foreign office. Seryozha, also up and dressed, tried not to look at me.

"What if I won't go?" I said.

"Are you moving in with your hooligan?" Father asked, sipping his coffee. "Is he ready to support you?"

I didn't know what to say to that. Did he have to be so extreme? Move in with Genya in that squalid room of his or break it off with him? Out of sheer defiance, I wanted to say yes, I'll move in with him. But that was going too far, even for me. I had to think. Did I really want to move in with Genya? Even if I tried it for the summer, what would I do about university? I possessed no money of my own. Father had me in a corner. He wanted me to see that I had no choice but do what he said. To recognize *my position*. In other words, surrender.

"I'd prefer to stay here," I said.

"But you love Maryino," Mother said in her filmy morning coat. "We all could use some time to re-flect—"

"The answer is no, you cannot stay here," Father interrupted her. "You'll go with the household or you'll find some other accommodation. You can't come and go, doing what you like with whomever you like, and come back here. It's not a bordello."

There was no point in arguing that a bordello was

the very opposite of the freedom he described. "I could live with the Katzevs," I said. "Surely Sofia Yakovlevna would let me."

"Forcing them to house and feed you for months at a time? They're not wealthy people, Marina. For someone who claims to be so sensitive to the plight of the common man, you're embarrassingly self-involved. The Katzevs have children of their own to think about. Consider the example you're setting for the younger ones. No, you pride yourself on being an adult, but you're still thinking like a child. Now, you'll pack, and tomorrow you'll accompany your mother to the country-side."

Yes. I saw there was no other way. "At least let me say goodbye." I had to tell Genya how it stood with us, that I wanted him, but I had to go.

"There's the telephone. Be my guest," Father said, gesturing to the hall.

Mother sighed, stirred her tea. Seryozha twisted in his seat, his face red and blotchy, guilty as a dog who'd eaten your shoes.

"You know he doesn't have one," I said. "Let me see him once more, and I'll go."

"Write him a note and I will mail it for you." Buttering his toast.

I couldn't very well say I didn't know Genya's address. So I wrote a hurried note, telling him that my father was sending me into exile in the country for the summer but I would be home by fall. *I'll wear Saturn's ring, and I'll think of you.* I addressed it to *Gennady Kuriakin, Grivtsova Alley, east-side courtyard, second floor, room 8.* I'd have to pay Basya to deliver it. The idea of Father intercepting it was too grim to imagine. And what if he decided to confront Genya face-to-face? Hideous. I hated to let Basya know such intimate details of my life, but it was better than Genya's never knowing.

While I packed, Seryozha slipped into my room. He was crying. "I'm sorry. I just didn't know what to say. They were so worried——"

"You could have said I was at Mina's."

"They called Mina's."

I sighed, folded nightgowns. "Well, I guess we've got a long summer ahead of us."

"You maybe. Not me." He ran his hand over the eyelet lace of my summer bedspread. "I'm going to Moscow. I'm leaving in five days."

I stopped folding.

"For Bagration Military School."

I clutched the ruched cotton of my nightgown. "He can't do that." My brother pretended to count the bands on my bedpost with his thumbnail. I grabbed him, turned him around, tried to force him to look me in the eye, but he wouldn't. "You can't. You've got to tell him right now you won't go."

"But I want to go." He twisted away from me. "I need to. I need to start my own life."

I held my hands to my mouth, as if something were

about to fall out. My heart maybe. "Seryozha, you've heard them talking at the Cirque Moderne. You know what's happening out there. Don't get on the wrong side of this!"

"It's already been decided," he said. My little brother. It was just what Miss Haddon-Finch had said. But *somebody* had decided—it wasn't Fate. It could still be undone.

"No." I batted the neat piles of clothes off the bed onto the floor. "Let's run for it. We can go, right now."

"Don't be stupid," he said, sitting down at my vanity. "What are we going to do, sell newspapers?"

"Maybe Solomon Moiseivich would give you a job. Apprentice you. You can't let him do this. You're not cut out to be a soldier." The idea made me dizzy with terror.

He bristled. "How do you know? People survive it. Look at Volodya. Papa's right. I have to stop dodging these things."

I knelt by his side, took his hands in mine. "Please, I'm begging you...this is not a fight you want to join."

He was about to cry, this would-be officer. "Don't say any more." We stayed like that for a long time. I wept, I think he did, too. After a while, he stood, then I did. We kissed three times, formally, and I had to let him go.

It rained the morning we left, a real soaker. In the first-class compartment, I sat with Avdokia, her arm around me, her smell of yeast, my head on her shoulder. Out the fogged-up window, the slums of the Vyborg side rolled past, the very seedbed of the revolution. Mother, with her hands folded in her lap, occupied the forward-facing seat alongside Miss Haddon-Finch and her little Italian greyhound Tulku. He stood on her lap to look out the window, leaving his nose print on the glass. But Mother's eyes were closed, shutting out the sorry scene rumbling by, factories and tenements, as well as the squalid one inside the compartment—namely, me.

Miss Haddon-Finch wept quietly, dabbing her eyes with her handkerchief, her spectacles fogging up. I couldn't tell whether they'd held her responsible for my supposed "disgrace." Was she afraid she was going to be dismissed? I hardly needed a governess anymore—but there wasn't time for arrangements to be made, and Mother would need some adult companionship. She couldn't exactly dine with Avdokia and her half sister, Olya, every night. Or was the Englishwoman frightened at the prospect of a long summer alone with Mother in the depths of Russia, without her Dmitry Ivanovich?

It was the one positive note—I wouldn't have to see Father all summer. His arrogance had grown worse now that he was in the Provisional Government. I couldn't stop thinking of Seryozha at the Bagration Military School and all that it meant. I knew what kind of boys these officer cadets would be, sharpening their cruelty on the softest in their midst. After a few months of torment, he would prefer the enemy at the front! Or the unthinkable could happen—he could become one of them and call it growing up.

And my sweet Genya—how long would he wait for me? Would he write poetry for some other girl, someone he saw on a bridge, drawn to her shape reflected in the water? I tried to remember the feel of his arms, his body, the taste of his lips, his smell of hay and fresh wood. We had never even made love. It made me cry all over again. Avdokia petted me, murmuring, "We're in God's hands, Marinoushka. *Tishe...*" Quiet now.

21 *Maryino*

WE SPENT THE NIGHT in the market town of Tikhvin, in a small hotel near the station, and the next day, we rode up to Maryino. The weather was dusty and hot. I was sullen, and Mother had a headache. We drank tepid water from a flask, and Miss Haddon-Finch tried to teach us a game, spying something beginning with a certain letter, but no one wanted to play. Only Avdokia was in a holiday mood, her little eyes brightening as she pointed out familiar landmarks. "I have cousins in this village, Verushka. Remember Mishka, with the wall-eye?" She was coming home.

After we'd endured hours of heat and airlessness and being thrown about, the landscape started to look familiar to me as well. Then we were passing through our village, Novinka, with its rambling cluster of izbas, its blacksmith shop, its silvery wooden church with its birch domes. Mangy dogs barked after our coach. The peasants watched us, but no one waved. We jounced out past the fields, the long strips of the peasant allotments. The oats had been cut, now wheat grew green under a bright blue sky.

The road to the estate itself brought us up a hill, and then down through a linden allée my mother's grandfather had planted, using dynamite to assure that the roots had room to grow. They were taller than any trees in the area. Now the house appeared, dark wood with white carved moldings around the windows. This beloved place. But dill and Queen Anne's lace and thistles crowded the yard, and one of the shutters hung crookedly.

The old steward, Grigorii, came to his feet slowly, as if he were just stretching. A sturdy, stout peasant with a long beard, he didn't remove his cap as the coach stopped before the porch—that was new. His smile was warm but his bow was brief and even a little ironic. But roses still rambled up the side of the house in bright red bloom, pretty but unpruned, and insects buzzed like tram wires before a rain.

"We just heard you were coming," he said to Mother. No *barynya*. No *Vera Borisovna*. She was visibly rattled and tripped alighting from the carriage. She had never become used to revolutionary treatment and certainly hadn't expected it here.

Avdokia steadied her while upbraiding her cousin. "Where are your manners, you stupid sot? You're still living here, stealing everything not nailed down. Have some respect."

He took off his cap, scratched his head, then embarrassed at having taken orders from this old woman, put it on again defiantly.

To gain time Mother removed her gloves, her hat, touched her shining silver hair with an unsteady hand. "Where are the others?" she asked.

"Oh, they're around. Except for the young ones. Army took seven of 'em." It was a small village, no more than fifty souls. Seven young men was a huge loss. "Yegor got killed last August." He hocked, as if to spit, then thought twice when he caught Avdokia's fierce eye. I remembered Yegor, a rock thrower who kicked the cows. But now he was dead.

"How awful," Mother said. "Such terrible times. Our Volodya's stationed on the Southwestern Front."

"Officer, no doubt," Grigorii said.

"Yes, he's grown into a fine young man," she said stiffly. "And Annoushka? How is your wife?"

"She's fine, praise be to God," Grigorii said. "She'll get herself elected to the zemstvo soon enough." Unlikely—the zemstvo was an all-male peasant organization led by landowners like us. But he was letting us know that things had changed. Putting us on notice.

"Yes, that's good." Mother brushed her forehead, as if trying to whisk away a fly. But the fly was the new era. The moment went on and on. What was he hoping, that she'd pick up her own bags?

Grigorii finally hoisted her trunks into the house. I'd have called it a draw.

Mother settled into Grandmère's old boudoir. Miss Haddon-Finch was put into my childhood room, which had also been Mother's. I took Grandfather's old study at the head of the stairs. Avdokia went in with her half sister, Olya, and Olya's daughter, Lyuda, behind the kitchen. Lyuda, my age or maybe a year older, unpacked my things. She handled them slowly, fingering my clothing, smoothing the cottons, the silks, as if she were shopping.

Over the following weeks, Avdokia treated me as if I were recovering from a horrible shock—which I supposed I was. She made me lie down with cold compresses of water steeped in lavender, sent me out to pick strawberries, blackberries, rowan berries, chamomile. I knew everyone thought me angry and peevish, but I didn't care. I was helpless and useless and saw no point in being stoic about it. I plunged into my trunkful of books, played lackluster rounds of cards with Miss Haddon-Finch, who invited me to call her Ginevra, and wrote dozens of letters to Genya, which Avdokia refused to mail.

Dearest
I write these letters

Send them into the abyss.
How long can I endure
Mother, nanny, peasant cousins, village gossip.

Too many women in the soup.
Death by fire would be quicker.

The river mocks me, flowing on.
The birds fly west.
I try to join them but
My waxen wings won't hold.

In the kitchen, the Revolution's arrived.
The peasants set their place at the table.
But where is the Revolution
To spring me from this green prison?

I slashed at the heads of shoulder-high weeds with a walking stick I'd found in the hall and cursed my father for his stupidity, my brother for his passivity, and the entire country for its idiocy. Ginevra trailed behind me, her skirts caught in the weeds as I made my way down to the river. The water was wide and slow, light skittering across the surface like gold coins. I took off my shoes and stockings and climbed out onto a large old birch that had fallen almost horizontally out over the water. "Be careful, Marina!" she called out to me. "I can't swim!" When I was a child I could walk the entire length of this trunk, imagining I was a world-renowned aerialist, the Great Esmerelda. The crowd marveled at my grace and daring. Below me, water grass waved under the surface of the river, hiding pike and perch where I had once imagined tiny mermaids and orphans played. I could almost feel the warmth of the water. Blue dragonflies flitted. I stripped out of my light dress.

"What are you doing? Marina! Someone will see you!" Her voice rose as I took off my slip and my corselette. "Come down immediately!" I dropped my bloomers, and plunged into the green water.

This was what I'd forgotten—the sweet embrace of the river, the feel of it slipping over my naked flesh. Even its murky taste was wonderfully familiar. I turned over in the current, my red hair dark and streaming over my shoulders like a rusalka, the river spirit.

I could hear Ginevra, but I was lost to her. Above me floated boughs of birches and elms, dark proud spruces. Fat trout patrolled the deep hole at the riverbank's edge. All my rage to return to the city dissolved, and I was just a fish swimming among the water weeds. Suddenly I heard giggles. Some little boys fishing on the opposite bank jeered, throwing pebbles, my nudity exciting and confusing to them. Let them look and imagine what they might have for themselves one day.

Afterward I dried my freckled skin with my dress and put it back on, lay in the soft grass under the birches as Ginevra scolded. *What would happen if you'd drowned?* and so on.

"I've lived here all my life," I said. "I'm not suddenly going to put on a corset and play the fine lady."

"Then I wash my hands of you. You heartless thing!" She wept as she marched off. Oh, the blessed quiet as she was gone! As if a tear in a fabric had been stitched closed. The humming of bees swelled and ebbed. I wrung out my hair and braided it. I felt Maryino recognized me as the same child who'd collected flowers and climbed these trees. I missed Seryozha. *Where is the other one?* the big maple asked. But he was gone, lost to the land of men. Why did everybody want a boy to hurry up and become a man, but nobody wanted a girl to become a woman? As if that were the most awful thing that could befall her.

Ignoring the harshness of the twigs and rocks underfoot, I walked barefoot to the springhouse, drank the icy water from my hand. The bathhouse lay buried in vines, which Seryozha and I used to pretend was Baba Yaga's hut turning around and around on chicken legs. *Turn and face us.* Maybe Genya and I could come here someday, clear out all those vines. We could bring the Transrational Interlocutors and create our own Commune of the Future. Though Genya detested the countryside. To him it represented every backwardness. It made me laugh—he and my father shared at least that.

Back at the house, I uncovered a sickle in the garden shed—a bit rusty—and decided to mow the overgrown yard. I was tired of sitting around all day with a book and a compress on my face, the bourgeois miss. I took the little blade and began to slash at the thistle and fennel where we'd normally have set tables and chairs and eaten under the canopy of trees. The work proved harder than I'd expected.

"Marina! What do you think you're doing?" Avdokia flew out onto the veranda. She must have seen me from the window. "You're going to cut your foot off!"

Blisters were already forming on my palms. My arms itched, the sun was hot, and my nose ran from the pollen.

"When I was your age, I would have killed not to have to mow one more inch." She pulled the sickle from me, examined the little crescent of steel. "Look how dull that blade is. Shame. Lyudochka! Lyudochka!" Her niece appeared in the open doorway, wiping her hands on her apron. "She's going to cut her foot off. At least sharpen the blade for her." The old woman sighed deeply. "That Grigorii's got it coming."

The girl led me back to the shed. On a shelf she found a stone, dark and heavy. She sat on a stump and drew it along the blade. "I've got the laundry or I'd help you. The old lady's right—when you're not here, Grigorii and Annoushka don't do anything but sit on the porch on their asses drinking *kvas*. Your grandfather would have put the fear of God into them. He was a real *baryn*, that old man."

It smelled like rain. I could hear it in the heavy metallic thrumming of the cicadas. I cut weeds for a while longer. Though the urge to do it had gone out of me, I knew Lyuda was watching. It certainly was much easier with the sharp blade. Soon I'd cleared a scrap of yard. Then I sat on the steps admiring my work and staring at my blisters with pride.

Lyuda brought me a glass of cherry water and we gazed out at the wind rustling the hazelnut bushes and the larch, fingering birch boughs like an invisible hand combing through a girl's long hair. A long way off, I could see Ginevra and Mother coming back from a walk. They looked like a painting together, dressed in white blouses with their white parasols, and I felt a wave of intense nostalgia, as if I were already looking at a past time. How precious all this was, how soon it might be gone. It only made it more poignant and beautiful in my eyes.

One afternoon Mother received a letter—a group of her friends was planning to visit. Such joy! Suddenly she remembered that she was the mistress of Maryino and not just a pale captive. She summoned the steward, waiting for him in the salon at the little writing table exactly where her father and grandfather once sat, and I noticed that upon stepping inside the doorway, Grigorii reflexively removed his cap. She told him that guests were coming, that he must clear the yard and the path to the aspen grove, fill in the worst of the potholes on the drive, "and for God's sake repair that shutter." Not a quiver in her voice or the slightest apology.

Soon long tables stretched underneath the trees, and

the rooms filled with guests. The house itself seemed happy, and though I still tried to portray myself as the despairing urbanite, the longer I stayed the happier I grew. I noticed the art collector Tripov among the guests who arrived from Petrograd. Perhaps it was he who had organized the excursion as an excuse to pay court to Vera Borisovna.

Now my mother had friends to walk with through the pines and the aspen grove, to show off the village church to and play cards and guessing games, to ride in the wagonette to other estates. We sat at night at the long table covered with white tablecloths under the trees, and my mother laughed as her guests shared their gossip—who was having an affair with whom, what had happened at so-and-so's birthday party, a neglected painting that turned out to be a Rubens, a remarkable man who taught spiritual dances and had such an original point of view. Mother wore a long gown of lilac linen. She glowed in the unearthly summer twilight, which would go on until the sun briefly dipped below the horizon before returning in an hour or so—like a child who will not go to bed.

"How has Dmitry Ivanovich fared in this auto-da-fé?" Ilona Dahlberg asked, her crimped gray hair in its elegant chignon.

"He's managed to keep a toehold," Mother replied. "You know he's the most stubborn man. He says Tereshchenko's an excellent minister, though he's no Pavel Nikolaevich." Paul Miliukov, a true *intelligent*, still led the Kadet party, but he'd become increasingly counterrevolutionary in his views.

"Dmitry Ivanovich had better hang on tight," said the art dealer Ryazanovsky. "It's not over yet."

"It seems my husband's excellent on the high wire. Who knew? Maybe he has a new career," said Mother, making them all laugh. She tinkled her fork against her wine glass, lifted it. "I'd like to propose a toast. To long summer nights with good friends. And no more politics. *Toujours gais, mes amis.*"

Avdokia got wind from somewhere that the *barynya* had been swimming au naturel and deputized her niece as my watchdog. "And if anything happens to her, you'll wish you'd never been born," she'd warned her. I could imagine Lyuda's mockery as soon as my nanny's back was turned. A strong, spirited girl, she was delighted to be freed from making beds, doing laundry, and clumsily serving meals. Now her only responsibility was to tramp the countryside with me and make sure I didn't run off with a deserter or drown in the Kapsha. She was not afraid of swimming, though she paddled with her head above the water like a dog.

And at last I found a postman for my letters. Because I still didn't know the address of the Poverty Artel and couldn't address them to "a murky courtyard off Grivtsova Alley," I addressed them all to Mina, with instructions on how to deliver them.

"What is it?" Lyuda asked, weighing the package in her hand.

"Letters. For my boyfriend in Petrograd," I said.

She touched the address written on the brown paper. "And this says where it goes?"

I showed her the word, *Petrograd*. Held out the silver ruble. "This is for the postage, and you keep what's left. Will you do it?"

"Sure, why wouldn't I?" She tossed the coin in the air and snatched it as it fell, fast as a snake on a rat. Could I trust her? She could easily throw the letters away and keep the ruble for herself. But who else did I have? She was more trustworthy than Grigorii. She took the package and put it in the basket with our lunch.

We stopped in the shade of a small copse of birches, where the grass was high. She spread out a tablecloth and we sat. I emptied my skirtful of daisies and began to weave them into a chain for my hair. "What's Petrograd really like?" She spoke of it as if it were the sunken city of Kitezh, not a place one could travel to in two short days. "Bet you people wear different clothes for breakfast, lunch, and dinner, eh?" We could hear the bells of the village cows grazing close at hand. "They say even the workers eat roast beef."

"We haven't seen beef since the war began," I said. "You probably have more here than we do." I wove the green daisy stems together, breathing their bright, bitter smell, staining my fingers. "In Petrograd the bread queues stretch around the block."

The dappled sun caressed her broad face and her blond plait. "Is that why you're here? For the food?"

I wiggled my bare toes dark from dirt, noting with satisfaction the calluses forming on the bottoms. "My father doesn't like my boyfriend. He's trying to break us up." When I said it that way, it seemed so simple. The world's oldest story. "That's why I need you to mail the letters. I don't want him to forget me. My father hates him. He's so sure he knows what's best for everyone."

"You know what I remember?" she said. "Him bawling out Annoushka because she overcooked his eggs. *Three minutes. I gave you a timer. What have you done with it?*" What a perfect imitation! "And it had to be served in a little cup, or it went right back to the kitchen. *The Englishman*—that's what your grandpa called him." She dropped her voice, brushed her jowls to suggest Dyedushka's bushy whiskers, and pounded her fist into her hand, the way Grandfather used to punctuate his pronouncements. "*Why can't the Englishman eat kasha like everyone else?*"

"He's still like that," I said. "Teaching the world how to live."

"So tell me about the boy." Her wide-set blue eyes were eager for gossip.

"He's a poet. A worker and a poet. He calls himself a bargeman-Keats."

"What's a Keats?" she asked.

I recited Keats's love poem to Fanny Brawne, one of my favorites, and translated it roughly for her.

O! let me have thee whole, —all—all—be mine!
That shape, that fairness, that sweet minor zest
Of love, your kiss, —those hands, those eyes divine,
That warm, white, lucent, million-pleasured breast,
Yourself—your soul—in pity give me all,
Withhold no atom's atom or I die . . .

She fell back on the tablecloth, pretending to swoon. "He really talks like that? The blacksmith can barely open his mouth. But why a *bargeman*-Keats?"

I pulled out the sandwiches Olya had made, black bread with smoked fish, handed her one. "Bargeman-Keats means that when people look at him, they see the bargeman, but not the Keats. He's a giant. He could pull a plow without a horse. My father wants a son-in-law who will fit in his egg cup."

Lyuda laughed open-mouthed, her head thrown back. What a fine-looking girl she was, wide hips and heavy breasts. More a match for Genya than I was. "All our boys are gone," she said. "There's only a bunch of ugly old men, halfwits and peewees. Why isn't your bargeman-Keats in the war?"

There were several answers to that. Draft dodger, only son, Bolshevik. "He doesn't believe in the war," I said.

"Who does? It's just that our lot can't get away with it." She licked her lip, a bit of sour cream from her sandwich escaping her mouth. "My mother thinks I should marry the blacksmith. What do you think? He makes a good living, but he's old, thirty at least, and stupid as a sheep. Maybe I should run off to Petrograd," she said. "Get a job in a factory, go dancing all night."

I imagined those women at the pumps on the Vyborg side and the Belhausen women. Many had started out as peasant girls themselves. "You might not want to go dancing after standing in a dark barn all day, working at a loom until your legs swell and you can't breathe for the dust in your lungs."

"You think this is any better? Stuck with kids and old geezers, trying to bring in a harvest? Sending our money to you lot so you can drink champagne and eat roast beef?"

My face went fiery red. Before the revolution she wouldn't have dared. But she was right. It was unfair, unjust, and yet it was how we lived. I never really explained that part to Genya. I lay back and watched the spruce boughs in their circles soughing in the wind. Maryino wasn't just a beautiful retreat. It was a means of production, as Varvara would say. How Lyuda must hate me.

"Akh, don't look like that." She brushed crumbs off her lap, threw a bite of bread to the birds. "I'm just saying it's pretty but no paradise. You'll see me in Petrograd soon enough."

I chewed on that as I ate my sandwich, then shimmied up the tilted trunk of one of the old birch trees, where I could sit in the fork about eight feet above ground over Lyuda and drop catkins down on her. The breeze sent the bright green of the boughs into motion.

   She pulled the letters out of the basket and was looking at the words again. Running her fingers over the
address. "Look, here's something you can do for me,"
she called up into the trees. "Teach me to read. Do that
and I'll send your letters for free."

I'd brought a trunkful of poetry, but even I could see
that none of it would be suitable for the purpose.
Mother's cache of Blavatsky and Steiner, doubly useless. If only Ginevra's Austen and Dickens were in
Russian, that would have been ideal. In the end I wrote
a ballad for her myself, the story of a cow from
Novinka who came to Petrograd to make her fortune.
I had the cow fall in love with one of the horses on the
Anichkov Bridge and become a singer at the Stray Dog
Café. I was proud of how fast she caught on. Soon she
was reading everything—labels on tooth powder, tins
of sardines. It wouldn't be long before she was reading
my letters, if she hadn't started already.
   Replies began to arrive from Petrograd, from a
"Nadezhda Lyubova"—Hope of Love.

Smuggler
   thief
            red-headed
               -handed
      where are my lips?
Where is delight?

*   *   *

The house seemed so empty once Mother's guests departed, leaving behind a slight air of mourning, though summer was still high. After dinner, we sat on the porch listening to the nightingales, Mother curled in Grand-mère's rocking chair, Avdokia with her pipe, Olya on the old bench by the door. Ginevra wrote a letter by lamp-light, waving the moths away, while Mother rocked, her eyes half-closed, humming, then began to sing in her pure, lovely voice, *"Au clair de la lune / Mon ami Pierrot, / Prête-moi ta plume / Pour écrire un mot…"*

The tune enveloped me. She used to sing when I was young, but rarely did anymore. I listened, then quietly, hoping she wouldn't stop, started to accompany her. My voice was lower than hers now, and she began to improvise harmony above, her voice embroidering itself through my melody like silk thread through plain cotton. I could recall how fiercely I had once loved her, the most beautiful of all the mothers, the most talented, the most sophisticated. The other girls envied me. She invented games for us, fashioned puppets and creations in paper—it was how Seryozha got his taste for constructions. She read to us, and sang. If she had not settled for becoming an ornament, a fashionable wife, she might have been an artist herself. Tonight she let down her talent, like the hair of Rapunzel. We sang "Gentil Coquelicot" and "Fais Dodo, Colin," as the crickets chirped and fireflies winked in the long grass.

Lyuda joined us on the porch after the washing up, and she and Olya sang an old song about sweethearts parted by war, how youth would be wasted and lovers would die, the world would ever come between them. When Avdokia sang with them, their harmonies blended with hair-raising beauty, like one woman at three stages of life. Their song shook tears from me. Then Annoushka started one, even sadder—"I Walk Alone upon the Road"—and each woman, joining, added her own unique timbre and temperament. In the glowing half-light, we drank from the ancient spring that ran, deep and sweet and cold, beneath us all.

22 *The Harvest*

SUMMER EDGED TOWARD FALL, filled with checkered lilies and cornflowers, and still we remained at Maryino. I'd lost Lyuda to the hard labor of the wheat harvest and began to wonder if Father was ever going to bring us home. Letters arrived for Mother from her friends in Petrograd, and for me from Nadezhda Lyubova. *I can't think about anything but your hair.* But bad news came from Father. His letters complained about Kerensky and the difficulties faced by the new government: coup attempts first by Lenin's gang, then by the rightists led by General Kornilov. *Kerensky's appointed himself commander in chief*, he wrote. *It's Alice down the rabbit hole. The Kadets resigned en masse, but*

I continue in harness. I'll stay until I'm fired. Boycotts and walkouts make a splash, but then where are you? Tereshchenko manages to navigate the zigs and zags, but the situation's volatile. A Bolshevik demonstration was recently fired upon, and of course they're making political hay of it. I recommend that you stay in Maryino until things settle down.

Mother and I strolled along a path that had already begun to close in now that the harvest was taking priority. The wind set the aspen leaves to rustling on their white branches. "You don't put your hair up anymore," Mother said, touching the long braids I wore. "You look like a little girl again. Sweet years…"

I laced my arm through hers. Her perfume was still the same. But now we were two women, the same height, though she was the slimmer, the more ethereal. "A little change is a good thing, Marina," she said. "But one needs tranquillity to absorb it. Too much change and it's just a hurricane. We don't have time to make sense of it as we're tumbling down the street." She peered into a thicket. "Those blackberries are ripe. Pick some."

I went into the deep grass and picked the black ones into my old straw hat, trying not to let the wicked thorns tear at me and avoiding the wasps growing drunk around the burst fruit. "Mama, what is it you think Papa is so mad about? Is it Genya? Or is it me? He's not really a worker, you know. He's a priest's son and a poet."

The wind in the trees was an ocean's rumble, that wide, many-voiced murmur—like a rumor moving through a crowd. She sighed, pushing her hair back under her hat. "Can't you see how impossible it is? Although I'm sure it's exciting…the lure of the forbidden. You're curious. You were always sensitive about the lower classes. Worrying about the coachmen out in the snow, remember? And there's the revolutionary cachet…"

She thought I was in love with Genya because it was fashionable. But he was hardly representative of "the lower classes" as she so horrifyingly put it. I popped a blackberry in my mouth, sweet and sour, and brought the rest to her. She ate them as we continued our walk.

"Was there no one before you and Papa married?" It was something I'd always wanted to know but never dared ask.

The trees shimmered in a sudden burst of wind. She had to hold her hat to keep it from taking off like a gull. How could she still be so beautiful, that elegant profile with the straight, sculpted nose, the finely turned mouth? "A boy came to visit one summer. He was staying on the Zarkovskys' estate. Grisha, his name was. He played tennis very beautifully. He moved like it was music." She frowned. "But relations between men and women are overemphasized, in my opinion. It's not as important as you think it is right now."

I'd never heard her speak about anything so personal. Though I couldn't have disagreed with her more, I wanted to hear what she actually thought about love. "What is important then?"

"Harmony," she said. She stroked her fingertips along a white aspen trunk. "Nature. One's feeling for deeper things." Tulku disappeared into the bushes—after a rabbit most likely. "Your father never cared for the country. I wouldn't mind staying on here." She reached down and plucked a dandelion, held the head without blowing the floss, twirling it in her hand. "Actually, I'm dreading going back into that hurricane. It's so peaceful here. Don't you feel it? It reminds me of so many things."

I felt it myself, this nostalgia, but I waved it away. "You'd miss your friends if you didn't go back."

"They can take care of themselves," she said.

I ate a blackberry, but it was too sour. I spit it out. "I start university in a few weeks, remember?"

"If there's a university left," she said.

Whether or not there was a university, there was Gennady Kuriakin. *My* university. *My* Petrograd. Nadezhda Lyubova, my hope, my love.

I sat in the kitchen watching Annoushka make bread, the room dim compared to the brightness outside. She was a fount of information, had opinions about everything. "What if we just stopped paying taxes? What's Russia to us? What's this war to us? Nobody asked us what we thought." She turned the loaf over, kneading it, pummeling it. "When is this repartition going to happen? That's what I want to know. The tsar's gone. What are they waiting for?" It was on everybody's mind, the division of the land. She stopped to wipe sweat from her brow with the back of a floury hand. "What does Dmitry Ivanovich say?"

I knew exactly what he would say because I'd asked him that myself. *These things take time. The landowner has to be compensated.* If she and the others were looking for the land to be seized and distributed into peasant hands, they shouldn't be looking to the Provisional Government. Even the SRs in power now didn't have the nerve. "I don't think they're any closer," I admitted. "Only the Soviet is talking about it seriously."

"Well, bless you for telling the truth," she said, turning the loaf over and punching it down. "We've heard the peasants in Ryazan are taking the land and the hell with the landowner. They're burning them out down there. Killing them in their beds, so they say." Annoushka cut her wicked eyes at me, just to make sure I got the message, then fell dutifully to her task.

Ever since the tsar's fall, the peasants had been waiting for the redistribution of the land. Soldiers were deserting so they could come home and be part of it. They believed that if they weren't physically present when the land was parceled out, they wouldn't get their share. They were deserting by the tens of thousands. I watched Annoushka finish the bread and slide it into the oven with a paddle. Although I didn't believe she and Grigorii were going to slit our throats as we slept, change was in the wind.

Sooner or later, I saw, we were going to lose Maryino. We were living on borrowed time.

I asked if she'd heard anything about the food situation in the capital. Were provisions from here getting into the city? Something had to relieve those bread queues. Father said the Provisional Government could do nothing because the railways were so poor and the army was eating most of the bread. Anything that got on the trains came off before it got to us in the city.

"It's all going to the army, isn't it?" Annoushka said, wiping the table down. "The pirates. They come and take what they want, pay us a few kopeks. Over in Alekhovshchina, they refused to go along with one bunch. Cut off their heads with scythes, they say." The musky scent of yeast and the wood burning in the big oven smelled like home—yet the terrible things she was saying took away all familiarity.

I thought of Kolya and his provisioning unit. Was that what he was doing all this time—robbing the peasants for the army? Yes, I imagined that was exactly what he was doing. He was completely capable of seizing a village's grain if they refused to accept the price he offered. I had seen the toughness behind the charm.

I had to get back to Petrograd. Somehow I had to tear Mother away from her nostalgic dream—though first I had to put it away myself.

As the light changed and the days shortened, we still heard nothing from Father, and my urgency grew sharper. Mother began to talk about having our winter clothes shipped to us. I had to do something or all would be lost. One afternoon I found her on the porch, where she sat in Grandmère's rocker, listening to the harvest songs coming from the fields with a pleasure deeper than joy. How could I rob her of this? Yet it had to come. It would have been so much easier if we'd been quarreling, but I felt closer to her than I had in years. "I hope Father calls us home soon," I said. "Annoushka says the peasants are speaking out against the estates."

She said nothing, just kept rocking.

"The deserters are coming back. They're tired of waiting for the repartition. They're taking the land on their own. Annoushka says they're burning the manor houses."

"Annoushka's imagination is running away with her," Mother said.

"It's already happening in Babayevo." Babayevo was a hundred versts away — hours on horseback, yet close enough for ideas to spread.

Her eyes slowly opened, the long lashes just like Seryozha's. "Our peasants won't do that. We've known them for four generations. They can barely sharpen a scythe let alone take over Maryino."

I shrugged. "The revolution's not just in the city. It's in the izbas, in the fields. They're talking about it. They've been waiting since Emancipation."

Mother shaded her eyes against the glare. The pines

rustled behind me, throwing their patterns of sun and shade on the side of the house. "You're on their side, aren't you?"

"You can't support the peasant in the abstract and deny him in fact," I said. "This is the reality — the soldiers are coming back and they're armed. They want the land."

I saw how she clutched at the pendant around her neck. "Even Kerensky said that there would be no expropriations."

She'd become too attached to the illusion of safety, as if Maryino could sink beneath the waters and life could continue as it always had been. Illusion and nostalgia surrounded her like a fog. I felt it myself, but I had to shake it off. "The peasants are tired of waiting. The deserters are taking matters into their own hands. Annoushka said they're nailing the landlords into their manor houses and setting them on fire."

"Wishful thinking," she said. But she was sitting up straight now, brushing off her skirt in irritated little gestures. Probably remembering all the insolences of Grigorii and the coachman and the way the peasants didn't bow when she rode through the fields.

"We don't want to be here when the division comes, Mama. We can't stop them, but we don't have be here when it happens."

We heard the dog barking at something in the woods. She clapped her hands and called until he broke from the trees and raced onto the porch. She petted his narrow head. "Your father would never expose us to any danger," she said, but she was only reassuring herself. "He would have sent for us."

I was about to mention that he'd sent Seryozha to Moscow, too, recklessly, but Mother looked so pained every time I brought that up. "He's distracted. He's got the whole country to think about. But you see how they look at us—Grigorii, Annoushka. They're already thinking it's theirs."

"Stop it." She lifted Tulku onto her lap and kissed his hard little head. "They've got their revolution. What more do they want?"

A woodsman was felling a tree somewhere. She flinched at the resonating blows of the ax.

"If we were murdered, Papa might not know for weeks," I added.

"Don't exaggerate," she snapped. But the skin had drawn tighter over her cheekbones. Her nose seemed suddenly sharp.

That night she penned a letter. I watched her at Grandfather's desk, stopping to wipe her eyes with a handkerchief, blow her nose. It had finally sunk in that she might well be losing Maryino. She scratched out a passage, rewrote something on the back, took out a new sheet, recopied. I think she was trying for a reasonable tone to plead our case, one that would convey the seriousness of our situation here without opening her up to ridicule. Then she started crying again, her forehead against her balled-up fist. I wanted to run to her, embrace her, and tell her I'd made it all up. But everything was true, except for the bit about Babayevo. And who knew? That, too, could be true by now. There was no helping it. All the signs said it was time to go.

In the morning, she called Grigorii and gave him the letter, even said "please" when she sent him off, coins jingling in his pocket, to catch the first post.

23 *Return to Petrograd*

I WAS NEVER SO happy to see the slums of the Vyborg side as I was that September day. The autumn sun shone on the gold spire of the Peter and Paul Fortress, and the panorama as we crossed over the Neva at the Liteiny Bridge was more breathtaking than ever. A tram rattled by—trams! This wonderful noise—traffic, crowds, shops. How I loved this city, the smell of its smoke, the throngs milling on the wide sidewalks, the shimmering canals. My city, my Petrograd.

But on Furshtatskaya Street all that awaited us in greeting were twelve slightly dirty rooms and Basya. "Where is Dmitry Ivanovich?" Mother asked as our bags were carried in.

"At work, missus," Basya said. "Where else would he be?"

Missus. Mother took her hat off very, very slowly, put it on the hall table, removed her gloves finger by finger. Surrendering to this new rudeness by quarter inches.

"It's only a cold dinner I can get you," the maid continued, as if she hadn't noticed a thing. "He doesn't eat at home now, and we weren't expecting you till tomorrow."

"Yes, all right," Mother said. "I'll take it in my room." She retreated to her bedroom, closely followed by Avdokia, muttering curses under her breath. Ginevra, however, sighed with pleasure at the end of our journey. I supposed she had found the separation from the city harder than even I had. The *dvornik* and his son carted our trunks in. I slipped out to the kitchen, where Basya was resting, watching Vaula chop cucumbers for a salad, and eased past them, heading for the back stairs.

"Look at the little chit," Basya said. "Going out already. Go then. Don't mind me."

"Murders on this very block," Vaula said, looking up from her cutting board, her round blue eyes drooping a warning. "Things have changed since you left. You might not want to go out there by yourself."

"Maybe I've changed a little, too." I stole a slice of cucumber from the board. "Anybody come looking for me?"

"Who could the girl be talking about?" Basya said to the cook.

Vaula laughed, salting the sliced rounds.

"You know very well who." I would have twisted her scrawny arm if I thought it would help.

A bell rang on the bell board: my mother's room. Basya snickered as she passed me, her breath smelling of cinnamon and tobacco. "Ivan Tsarevich, you mean? That big hooligan shouting poems at the windows? Sure, he stood out there caterwauling until your father threatened to call the police on him if he ever saw him again. The idiot came back a few more times just to be sure. Foma saw him out there after midnight, at two, maybe three in the morning, watching your windows."

I kissed her on both cheeks and ran out the back door, down the stairs, into the courtyard, and out to the street.

The city was even shabbier than I remembered it—perhaps I'd sprinkled it with a bit of Lyuda's imagined glamour in my mind. But it was still Petrograd and I loved every dirty beggar as I ran toward Sadovaya and Haymarket Square. The noise, the shops, the miraculous automobiles rushing through the streets. It was September, and the cool river air had swept summer from the pavement. I ran all the way to Grivtsova Alley, racing up the stinking stairs to the Poverty Artel. I knocked, called out. "Genya! Open up!" I could not wait for him to touch me, to feel his arms again, his kiss. I knocked again. Nothing. This was it, wasn't it? The worn door—number 8.

But there was no one home. They'd probably gone to shout their poetry from the rooftops, I told myself, but anything could have happened. They might have been drafted or evicted. The mail took forever to arrive. Yet why should they be home this time of the evening? Genya had no idea I was returning today. Still, I could not keep tears from rising. The mountains I'd had to climb to get here, the plots I'd had to orchestrate! I descended the stairs at half the pace I'd flown up them. Out in the courtyard, women waiting to pump water followed me with their eyes. I called to them, "Do the boys on the second floor still live here? The poets?"

"Who else would have them?" one of the women called out and the others laughed.

I couldn't run around Petrograd looking for them. Instead I stopped in at the one place where I was certain someone would be home. From the hall, I could hear lively hands playing ragtime on the piano. Shusha's skills had certainly progressed since spring. I knocked hard and Dunya answered the door. She was wearing a rust-colored dress with an embroidered sunflower on the pocket—Seryozha's handwork. I burst into tears.

She threw her arms around me, pulled me inside. The smell of soup, of kasha embraced me as ever. Shusha jumped up from the piano—"Mariiiina!"—and hugged me hard. "Did you hear me? It's the 'Maple Leaf Rag'! Mama just got it for me." She sat back down and began again.

Now I saw Mina—she'd been hidden behind a heap of books like a barricade. She rose and kissed me. "She can't stop playing it. I could kill her. Look at you—you're a peasant now." She tugged at my braid, which I hadn't bothered to put up before I ran out of the house.

My friend looked older, prettier, in a crisp white blouse and necktie, her hair worn in a fashionable coil instead of its old-fashioned crown. A *studentka*. I realized with a surge of panic that she'd begun university. I'd come home too late. But I refused to mourn. I was back, that was the thing. If Genya was still in Petrograd, if he still wanted me, that would be enough.

"Marina!" Now I saw Solomon Moiseivich on the divan with his foot up on a stool. "I'd get up but gout's got me. I thought it was the province of kings, but Fate says, 'For you, Solomon, we'll make an exception.'"

Sofia Yakovlevna bustled out from the kitchen. "Marina! Welcome home, welcome back." She wiped her hands on her apron, and then gave me a squeeze and a kiss. "We were wondering whether you'd come home. Your letters didn't say. Look how healthy you are! Brown as a nut. Where's your brother?"

"Yes—how's my favorite assistant?" the photographer inquired.

They didn't know. I looked again at Dunya's dress, thinking of how he'd sewn those flowers. "They sent him to Moscow, to a military school. To become an engineer."

"You're joking," Mina said. She pushed her glasses up on her nose, the better to study me. I shook my head.

Solomon Moiseivich rounded his eyes at his wife, speaking whole treatises in that single glance. "Well. Engineering's a good trade."

"I'm sure Dmitry Ivanovich has his reasons," Sofia Yakovlevna said quickly, then patted my shoulder. "Sit down, Marina. I'll get you a glass of tea." But a note of worry hung in the air.

I took a chair next to Mina. "So you've started without me." I picked up one of her heavy books—chemistry. I would not cry. I was home, that was the important thing. "How is it?"

"Lots of work." She shrugged, pretending it was all such a burden, but I could tell how proud she was. "Rumor has it they might cancel the term because of the food shortages. I'm trying to get as much done as I can."

I laid the book back down on the pile. "It's that bad?"

She nodded. "People are leaving every day. Going south. Going abroad. We were wondering if you'd even be back."

"Did you deliver my letters?" I asked under my breath.

Mina smiled, showing her pretty small teeth. "What do you think, that I'd stand in the way of true love?" She tugged at my long braid again. "Actually I didn't even need to deliver them. He comes by with his friends—at dinnertime, naturally. Dunya's got a crazy crush on the painter."

"Oh, so I've got the crush." Dunya threw a wadded-up paper at her. "Tell her about Nikolai Shurov."

Mina's cheeks blazed.

I could feel myself go pale in equal measure. "What about him?"

"He came to town is all," Mina answered, studying her smooth hands, the little sapphire ring she wore. "I ran into him at the pharmacy." She shrugged again. "He'd gone to your parents' looking for you."

A sudden tightness in my throat, down to my solar plexus. Why should I care, when I had Genya? But on some level I still did. Look at her face. Had he made love to her? No, he wouldn't have. Though he couldn't resist an admiring female, even if she was chubby and wore glasses and talked about integers and valences. And she had beautiful skin, and her gray eyes were shaded by long, white-tipped lashes. In fact, she wasn't even fat anymore. She looked...pretty.

She gazed toward the hall that led to the kitchen, where her mother had returned to her cooking; to her father, reading on the divan; to her sisters; then back to me, pleading with me not to say anything more.

I lowered my voice. "Is he here in Petrograd?"

"No," she whispered. "He went back to the front. That was months ago — in July, before the offensive."

I could feel my eyes stinging. He'd been here, while I was out in the country mowing weeds.

"Do you mind?" she whispered, touching my sleeve. Her bottom lip trembled.

"No," I said and tried to smile. What was done was done, and anyway I had Genya. In just a few minutes, I would see him. The hell with Kolya.

"I told him about Genya. Was that right?"

"Of course." A soothing thought. He deserved that, for leaving me alone for all those months. Did he think I would wait forever?

Sofia Yakovlevna asked us to clear the table for dinner. I knew I should leave—not impose myself on their hospitality—but Genya might be coming, so when she asked me to dinner, I agreed with alacrity. I was going to see Genya. And Kolya? Kolya was the past. Ancient history. I telephoned home, told Ginevra where I was, that I'd be home later. I was in no hurry to see Father, and had seen enough of Mother and my governess to last a decade.

We sat down to eat, dragging Solomon Moiseivich's footstool into place so that he could keep his foot up. It was so good to see the whole family again. Mina told me about all the people who had come to pose for photographs since I'd been gone—Tereshchenko and the chairman of the Petrograd Soviet both! Kerensky himself had come the day before yesterday. "Talked without stopping," said Solomon Moiseivich. "He's due for a nervous collapse, if you ask me. But the picture turned out well."

A pounding interrupted us in mid-meal. I jumped, recalling the day that revolutionary soldiers burst in to search the flat. But this time Dunya raced to answer the door. In a moment, she returned with Sasha Orlovsky, and behind him, my own sweet Genya. Did I fly? Or had he crossed the room in one step?

I leaped into his arms, and we kissed in front of God and all the Katzevs.

Anton Chernikov squeezed past us. "Oh, look. The rusticated cousin returns."

I breathed in Genya's scent, like fresh mown grass and the harsh *makhorka* tobacco he smoked. Everyone was watching, but this was more important than finishing dinner. I breathlessly thanked the Katzevs, and together we ran down the stairs as if the building were burning.

Out in the street, we floated above the city, cartwheeled over people in shoes and coats. We walked sideways along pastel buildings glowing in the twilight. We used the trees for toothpicks. "I heard Father threatened you with the police."

His laughter, rich, huge. "And let me tell you, the Red Guards came right away. How dare I shout love poems at such an important man?" He tugged on my braid, pulling me closer. "This was what you looked like at nine, isn't it? God, I wish I had been there." He cupped my face in his palm and kissed me. I didn't know if people walked around us or if they simply had vanished. "How was it out in the boonies without me?" he whispered. "Horrible and dusty and ridiculous? Were you ready to die of boredom?"

"Every day. Twice sometimes." I rubbed my cheek against his hand. "They had to keep the knives out of reach. Take me home, Genya. While they're all still at Mina's."

Haymarket Square seemed strangely empty this evening, the stalls closing up early, though the weather was fair. Was there some new curfew? We crossed the luminous Catherine Canal at the Demidov Bridge and raced up narrow Grivtsova Alley, the tops of the buildings still in light, up the dark stairs two at a time. Today we would make right what had gone wrong then.

Inside, the Poverty Artel smelled of turpentine and smoke. A section of wall was in the process of being painted, cubo-futuristically, over the tiling of newspapers. I took off my coat. So this was what it usually looked like—unmade divan, unmade cot, chairs piled with papers and paint, ashtray overflowing, sunflower-seed shells crunching underfoot. He bustled about, pulling the sheets up on the divan, picking up clothes from the floor. "Forget about that," I said. I pulled him down next to me, took the clothes from his arms, and tossed them back onto the floor. So much time had passed between us. I didn't care how dirty the room was.

I could feel a hesitation on his part, a new shyness. "What is it?"

He gazed at me, worry in his hazel eyes under the shock of tawny hair. "There wasn't anybody else, was there? Out there?"

Oh, was that it? I tried not to laugh. "Who? The twelve-year-olds? Or the old uncle with the beard halfway to his knees?"

He laughed, but the uncertainty remained. It had to

be slain, this dragon of time and distance. I took his hand and kissed it, slowly, biting the knuckles each in turn, then kissing the palm until he groaned. I planted my fat lips on his, and our kisses began in earnest, his big fingers fumbling at my buttons, his floppy hair longer than ever, falling into his eyes. I pushed it from his face.

"I swore I wouldn't cut it until I had you back," he whispered into my neck. "I would have grown it as long as a Sikh's."

I raked my own hair free of its braid, pulled it apart so that it flowed over my back and shoulders, and he buried his face in it as if it were a wonderland. The room was cold but I took off my dress and tossed it aside, helped him out of his old jacket, his shirt. He looked at me so uncertainly. Why? The beauty of his body was Atlantean, his smooth wide chest hairless, so large, so different from Kolya's pelt of chestnut fur. How warm he was. I pressed my cheek to the muscle right over his heart to listen to the blood surge inside him. It was like a Niagara. With my finger, I traced the dip above his rib cage. He was big and bulky and warm, his heavy arms laced with sinews like a ship's rope. He tried opening my corselette, fumbling to work the buttons far too tiny for him—or was it that his hands were trembling? I pushed him away so I could unfasten it myself and let him see me, my breasts and shoulders dotted with summer freckles, his expression better than any mirror. I opened his worn trousers and slid my hand in. He groaned. He was huge, and ready—so that wasn't what was making him shy.

"I don't want to hurt you," he said.

"You won't," I said. I didn't care if he did. I produced a condom, hoping it wasn't too small, but he managed to roll it down over himself. Would he think I was a trollop, a jade? Would it break? I'd take that chance. I wanted him. I pushed him back onto the gritty sheets and lay over him, my hair a crimson tent.

Oh, the bliss of that hour. It had been months since I'd slept with Kolya. Before the revolution. We made love and it was far more serious business than it was with Kolya. We were naked in our feelings, stopped and started again, then lay wearily in each other's arms as the last light faded from the room. I felt as though I were rocking on a barge, on the Volga with my bargeman-Keats, the river so wide you couldn't see both banks.

Finally the Interlocutors returned, banging on the door. "Open up!"

"Go away!" Genya shouted back.

More kicks from the other side. "Pigs," we heard someone shout. We grunted like swine, making ourselves laugh.

Genya insisted on escorting me home, arm in arm in the dark. I could feel the uneasiness of passersby now, a tangible wildness in the air. I thought of Vaula's warning, how things might have changed since I'd been gone. Yet seeing Genya, who would have the nerve to disturb us? The lights reflected in the canal for us alone. We crossed at the Bank Bridge, with its gold-winged griffins glinting, so close to the flat where Kolya and I...I pressed into Genya's side. All that seemed like another century.

When we turned onto Furshtatskaya, our flat was lit up like an ocean liner. I knew they were waiting up for me. We kissed a long time, my lips swollen and raw, my body still tender, my hair a cloud of tangles. After that, I felt I could face anything.

The younger *dvornik* stepped out of the shadows with a lantern, but seeing it was me with Genya, he waved genially and went back to his cubby, where he was playing cards with a friend.

"I really should go."

Genya released me but as I moved away, he snatched me up again. "Don't. Don't ever go." His arms tightened around me. "Don't go to them. I can't stand it. I hate them. I want to fight a duel with your father. I want to have him on the ground under my boot. I'll show him no mercy."

I searched for his mouth again.

"Marry me," he said. "Come live with me. You don't have to go back."

I thought of that room, the divan with the dirty sheets, Anton pounding on the door. "But how shall we all sleep? Standing up like horses in a stall?"

"We'll levitate. Sleep in midair. The night will be our eiderdown."

I had to kiss a mouth like that. I rested my fingers on his lips, memorizing them like a blind girl. And then I left him there, watching me, the dry leaves whirling about his feet.

24 *The Coming Storm*

PIPE TOBACCO GREETED me when I returned. I walked past the doors of my father's study, straight to my room, wondering if it was too late to take a bath. I began to peel off my hastily assembled clothing—I'd misbuttoned my dress. It made me laugh. How I would have loved to spend the night in Genya's arms, in that little flat, even with its fleas and Anton writing his articles. But I couldn't be greedy. It would have been too strange if the Interlocutors had returned while we were lying together in the wash of fragrance and sweat, talking about childhood, about rivers and birds.

Sitting before my round vanity mirror, I began to brush out my hair. What a crop of snarls. I still remembered it flowing down, framing Genya's face in a red waterfall. The enamel bangle fell back from my wrist. Why did I still wear it? It seemed a sign of something, a delectable complication. I was not too young to have had a past, I thought with a certain pride. That's how young I was.

In the hall, a shuffle. A quiet knock. The door cracked open. Ginevra, still fully dressed. I returned to my toilette. My face was smooth with satisfaction. Hers, on the other hand, was worried and drawn. "Your father's been waiting. He wants to speak to you."

"He told me he never wanted to speak to me again. I'm taking him at his word."

"Marina, don't be a child."

If I were Mother, I would pretend I had a headache. But I was not her. I would rather face the firing squad and get it over with. I threw a shawl over my nightgown, hoping I didn't stink too badly of lovemaking, and followed *the English* down the corridor, preparing for a brawl.

I found Father at his desk, in the room I'd always loved, with its soft green striped wallpaper covered with photographs, its masculine smell of tobacco and leather and wood smoke. The big leather-topped desk with its spindle corral kept his papers from running away. The light from the green-shaded lamp washed over the bookcases on the walls, making Tolstoy and John Stuart Mill my witnesses. My father looked the same as always, only with a harder edge, his crisp, wavy hair even crisper, his neat beard more sharply trimmed. He stared me down. "You couldn't wait twelve hours to go running off to your…factory boy?" he said.

I should have expected this. No one grants freedom—it has to be won. Our revolution had taught us that much. "That's right. I went to see him. He's not going to disappear. I'll leave if you want me to, but I won't be a prisoner."

He fiddled with his tobacco pouch, packed the bowl of his pipe. His delicate fingers scrabbled, uncertain, in the curly threads. "Don't I have enough to do without you running around the city like a bitch in heat? It's disgusting. I should have left you at Maryino."

Although I told myself I cared not at all what he thought, this characterization struck me with force, and my tears came. As if it was his right, as if he owned me. "Is that your answer? Move the women to the country, your son to military school?"

I noticed a subtle shift in his expression, a slight smile. He could see he had landed his blow. But there was something more. "Sorry to disappoint you, but in fact your brother is adjusting quite well."

"I don't believe you."

"He's made friends. He even won a prize in mathematics." He opened the right-hand drawer of his heavy desk and took out a small packet of letters, set them on the leather desktop. He tipped his chair back, clasped his hands behind his head.

The letters were addressed in Seryozha's handwriting, although I did notice the flourishes had been subdued. Already changing. The postmark was Moscow. I wiped my eyes on the back of my hand, and opened one of them.

My bunkmate's name is Pyotr Gagarin. He's from Suzdal. He's pretty funny. I'm learning to fence. It's strict but not impossible. And nobody compares me to Volodya. I miss Petrograd, but Moscow's impressive. They let us out in the afternoons. I love how old it is. The bells are incredible.

Another letter. I let my eyes drift down the page. He was playing poker and had not lost his spending money yet, had even won a few rubles.

Though I make sure to lose some afterward so the others won't think I'm a shark. I won a prize in geometry, if you can believe it. They're sure my draftsmanship will get me into the engineers. I'm starting to think that's not such a bad idea.

He was learning to ride. They had given him a horse named Flea with three white stockings, "a most intelligent fellow." I couldn't put any of this together with the boy I knew as well as I knew any human being on earth. A horse? He'd always been terrified of anything bigger than our mother's dog. And here were drawings: a quizzical bay, presumably Flea. Moscow, the church domes of every shape and size. A little crooked lane, a marketplace. Boys at meals, sitting very straight, their backs not touching the chairs.

I folded the letters into their envelopes, trying not to show any emotion. It couldn't be real. "He's faking. He's just trying to please you."

"Why don't you want to believe that your brother

is doing fine without you? That while you're making a mess of your life he's actually straightening himself out?"

Doing all right. Making friends. Doing all the things boys do. Trying to be the boy our father wanted him to be. Doubt shook me by the neck, like a terrier with a rat. If Father was right about Seryozha, what else was he right about? He thoughtfully cradled his pipe in his palm. "I called you here because I've made a decision. About your future." He made me wait while he lit up again—his lawyer's trick. "I will send you to England to complete your education."

He caught me so off guard that I couldn't formulate a response. I had just gotten home a few hours ago.

"Miss Haddon-Finch will accompany you," he continued in a puff of fragrant smoke. "Some of my contacts have already made the arrangements." Just like when he sent Seryozha to Moscow. *It's all been arranged.* "You'll stay with Mrs. Sibley's sister in London this fall, take some time to get to know the city. Then in the spring you'll apply to St. Hilda's."

Oxford. I'd dreamed about it ever since the year we spent in England, when he was lecturing at Christ Church. Clever, clever Father. He was offering me Oxford in exchange for the revolution, in exchange for Genya. My father hadn't forgotten about university at all. He'd just made it impossible for me to attend here while offering an attractive alternative.

How different life would be if I took him up on this

offer. I pictured myself moving through the cloisters of Oxford, talking about Shakespeare and Keats. Tea with the dons, rowing on the Thames with those shining girls. It all seemed so retrograde to me now. Could I really see myself going off to Oxford to study dead English poets when there were living poets here in Russia I called by their first names? My country was transforming itself beyond anything England ever hoped for. St. Hilda's had been the dream of a ten-year-old girl. I was a Russian poet, a woman. I would make my own life, to suit myself, and my future was here. "You still don't see—I'm not your pawn, to be moved here and there to your liking. I believe in the revolution, and I intend to be part of it."

My father's face flushed dark against his curly reddish-brown beard. "Just because you're here doesn't mean you're part of it, and just because you're running around with a loudmouthed hooligan doesn't make you a revolutionary. Only a trollop. And an idiot to boot."

I was surprised how little it stung. "Go ahead, call me names. But I'll continue to see that so-called hooligan. He's an artist and a revolutionary and we're very much in love."

"The triple disaster," my father said. He sighed, pressing his hands to his eyes.

As we glared at each other across the broad expanse of the desk, locked in that showdown, I saw we were exactly the same—our stubbornness the same, our brown eyes, his reddish-brown hair concentrated into my flaming red. I was more his child than he knew. But my womanhood had put a permanent barrier between us. He didn't know how to be the father of a woman, and womanhood could not be undone. The future already a fact.

I left dry-eyed and gracefully, without so much as slamming the door. I felt strangely that I had won and yet lost.

My room already felt different to me, as if it belonged to someone else, someone who treasured trinkets and keepsakes and pictures in silver frames, a girl with lace-collared dresses. I had always loved the salmon-pink walls, but now they were cloying. I knew that whatever happened to me, to us, I would not be here long. Whoever this woman was that I was becoming, she would not live in a room like this.

September 1917. A crispness in the air, frost at night. In Mother's era, this would have been my season. I would be preparing for balls, having gowns made, fitting my dancing shoes. Instead, with no classes to attend, I wandered the city streets with my poet's notebook, my poet's ears and eyes, breathing the living city. I watched the fishmongers of Haymarket Square, the freight haulers, the cabmen and the shopgirls, and wrote about them, wrote about the city, imagining my way into its secrets. My time with Genya only inspired me to dig deeper into the life around me.

One afternoon I turned a corner to find Varvara standing on a crate opposite a bread shop, making a speech to the women in the queue. "Far from improving the situation of the common people, the revolution in February has only increased your suffering," she said from atop her rickety crate, which probably had held bottles of beer. So she had finally made it, a crate of her own. I hung back so as not to interrupt her. "The situation is worse than ever. The government is powerless to do anything but argue and pass resolutions in favor of the captains of industry." She saw me, and the hint of a smile crossed her impassioned mouth, before she plunged back into her fierce harangue. "And still the war keeps grinding on! They say we have to stay in to seem strong to the imperialist allies! We, the Bolshevik Party, say down with the imperialists! Winter is coming, and it's time to end the war! It's time to bring the food and the soldiers home!"

"About time," the women murmured.

"What did we have this revolution for?" she shouted. "To keep dying? To keep starving? We asked for bread and peace, and what did we get?"

"Just a bunch of yak," a woman who had almost made it to the doors called out. In a bread queue, the closer to the head of the line, the more irritable and aggressive people became.

"It's always the same," grumbled a stout woman with a big mole on her cheek. "Whoever gets in, they pad their own nests and the hell with you."

"Who wants this war?" Varvara called out. "You?" she pointed to the woman with the mole. "You?" She pointed to an old man.

"It'll bury us all," the old man said.

"Not if the Soviet has any say in it. All power to the Soviets!" She finished, got off her beer crate, and hurried over to hug me. "I thought we were going to have to go out to the hinterlands and drag you home." She began handing out pamphlets down the line. It was wonderful to see her again, her messy black hair, her long stride.

"So you're a Bolshevik now."

She handed me a stack of pamphlets. "All the revolution has done is allow people to complain without being arrested," she said. "The Provisional Government's a joke. Look at this." She tilted her chin at the queue. "They're actually sleeping in line now." What that woman joked about last year had come true. "You are the source of all power," she told the women. "The Soviet represents you." The pamphlet's damp ink stained my gloves: *All Power to the Soviets*. "The Soviet is the future of Russia. Stand with the Bolsheviks. Get out of this war."

I admired her, so energetic and modern compared to the tired women in their scarves. I noticed since I'd been back that women in the city were cropping their hair the same way Varvara did. Changes and more changes. Helping her hand out her crude pamphlets, I felt part of the electricity of the city. Since I'd been home, I had noticed a flood of new newspapers, broadsides, and pamphlets, kiosks were plastered with news, pavements thick with opinions. No one clicked their tongues at us now for handing them our leaflets. They read them boldly.

We walked across to Vasilievsky Island over the Nikolaevsky Bridge, with its shell-and-seahorse railings, the fresh wind on the Neva whipping up whitecaps. "So you're back at your mother's?" I asked.

"No. I've got another place." How quickly she walked, hands in her pockets—I'd forgotten about that. "You going to move in with the poet?" she asked.

"Not just yet. But I might. To be honest, I don't know what I'm doing yet."

"Hold on, I need to do a little business." We stood before a modest apartment block on the Seventh Line that had a boarded-up shop on the bottom floor. As we climbed to the second story, the noise of machinery, rhythmic and heavy, rattled the building. She knocked at a drab, peeling door. Our entrance silenced a group of serious-looking young workers talking around an oilcloth-covered table. I recognized one of them. Marmelzadt, from the previous summer in the hospital ward. His lips twisted into the imitation of a smile when he recognized me. His hands were black with ink.

"Well, it's the little *barynya*," he said over the clatter of the press.

"Glad to see you looking well, Comrade," I said. "Guess the army's getting along without you."

Deserted or discharged? I wondered. Kerensky had announced the death penalty for deserters, reneging on one of the Provisional Government's basic promises, the abolition of capital punishment in the army. Yet soldiers were still walking away from the war by the company and battalion. "You know each other?" Varvara seemed startled. There were things she didn't know about me, too. I liked that.

"You see, I've taken your advice," I said to him.

"Kraskin?" Varvara asked. So he'd taken a revolutionary name. *Ink.*

He watched me, his expression a blend of superiority and suspicion. What was the *baryshnya* doing invading their Vasilievsky Island revolutionary cell? As before, I found him provocative: he was irritating, yet somehow I wanted his approval. He turned his back to me and gave Varvara another stack of pamphlets to hand out:

THE PROVISIONAL GOVERNMENT IS IN THE POCKET OF THE IMPERIALIST WEST. STOP THE WAR! THE REVOLUTION MUST CONTINUE! ALL POWER TO THE REVOLUTIONARY SOVIET OF WORKERS' AND SOLDIERS' DEPUTIES! BREAD AND PEACE!

On the way back, we passed a barbershop on Bolshoy Prospect in the heart of Vasilievsky's working-class district. I stopped to watch the barbers at their labors, pulling out my notebook. Barbershops always seemed like such dignified places, quite different from the cloying, slightly bullying ministrations of women's hairdressers. There was something so esoteric and philosophical about these minor priests with their ointments and jars, bestowing a temporary princehood upon every man as he sat on his throne for a trim and a shave.

On impulse, I caught Varvara by the sleeve and pulled her inside. We squeezed into seats on the bench among the men, ignoring their outraged stares in response to their precinct's violation. Today I would rid myself of the equivalent of salmon walls—this great mass of hair I was constantly at war with. A modern woman should have better things to do with her time than spend hours brushing and washing and putting up hair. What oppressive beauty.

When it was my turn in the barber's chair, I removed my hat, took out my hairpins, let my hair fall. The blue-eyed barber, a Hungarian with a curly moustache, looked stricken, threading his fingers through my heavy red locks, which hung over the back of the chair to my hips. "Don't ask me to cut this," he said. "It would be a crime."

"It weighs a ton, and it's always in the way. It gives me headaches. Cut."

"You're breaking my heart, *devushka*." He pressed his fist to his mouth.

"Girls today," said a man in the next chair. "Used to be women liked being women. Now they want to be men. Cut off their hair, smoke, wear pants…"

Varvara, hovering to my right, smoked a rolled cigarette in an inky hand. "Used to be men liked being
serfs, too…but somehow they came to their senses."

The Hungarian mournfully stroked my hair.

"Just a line." I indicated where he should cut with the
edge of my hand, an unbroken cut from nape to jaw.

He sighed, twisted my long hair into a tail, and cut
straight across. He could hardly bear to look. I hadn't
had more than a trim in my entire life. My hair now fell
to my shoulders, uneven. It looked like a madwoman's.
The amputated length of it hung in his hand like a dead
fox. "You could keep this," he said, offering it to me
over his arm.

"You keep it," I said. "I'm not sentimental."

Seeing that the worst was over, he got to work, shaping. When he was done, my head felt light, liberated,
modern, my newly exposed neck thin and embarrassed.
I gave him a smile with his ruble. The men shook their
heads as we left.

Out in the parkway on Bolshoy, we sat on a bench
and I asked Varvara to teach me to roll a cigarette. I
managed to roll a sad twisted version, and we walked,
smoking, modern, very proud of ourselves, down to
the university along the Neva embankment, handing
out her pamphlets to the students. Most took them with
curiosity, but one crumpled it and threw it at me. It
bounced off my chest. "We're not interested in your
defeatism," he said. "Bolshevik scum."

If I hadn't cut my hair, I don't think I would have

stared at him as boldly as I did. "Wait until they get rid of the student deferments," I spat back at him. "Then you'll be singing a different tune." I was no longer that girl from the Tagantsev Academy, straddling the worlds, Papa's darling. I was a visitor from the future.

After our pamphlets were gone, we walked the windswept Strelka, the eastern tip of Vasilievsky Island, and sheltered in the lee of the Rostral Columns. The wind was unaccustomedly cold on my newly bare neck. Before us, the hulk of the Peter and Paul Fortress rose upriver—fortress, prison, cathedral, mint, all in one. Everything you needed to found a civilization. I considered the great beast of the Neva and the clotted clouds moving in overhead while Varvara eyed the Winter Palace across the black swells. "What's going on at the foreign office these days?" Father's offices had moved from the Duma to the Winter Palace since I'd been gone.

I shrugged. "I'm not exactly kept abreast anymore. I eat in the kitchen. But there's always a steady stream of foreigners coming through, making their deals."

"What kind of foreigners?" she asked, still watching the palace.

"English and American mostly."

"What kind of deals?"

I wrapped my scarf higher around my neck. "Father and I go our own ways. We don't even talk anymore."

Varvara exhaled. The wind smelled of a coming

storm. "But you could. You're in a position to know far more than you do. Why don't you play nice for a while?"

It took me a moment to understand what she was asking me. "You want me to spy on my father?" Surely she wasn't serious. Did she really see me as some kind of Charlotte de Sauve?

"All you'd have to do is sit there and eat your cutlets. It's not like you'd be breaking into the safe at the foreign office." She'd thought of this as I'd been getting my hair cut. As I'd been handing out pamphlets for her. That mind never rested. "But it could help hurry the peace, to know what they're up to."

I thought of the way Father and his friends bandied the future of Russia about as they passed the fish, the butter. The memory irritated me all over again. Though it was my family she was talking about. Betraying my own father.

"Kerensky's beating the invasion drum like mad," she said. " 'The Germans are in Riga! The Germans are going to take Petrograd! They're going to cut in front of you in the bread lines! They're going to work your twelve-hour day. Oh, we can't give you justice—the Germans won't let us!' They're trying to move the garrison out of Petrograd so they can have their way with the workers. We need to know what else they've got up their sleeves."

"What will you do with the information?" I asked softly.

"Get us out of the war. But we need to know what's going on."

I had no love for the capitalists and industrialists who frequented our table—the way my father spoke as if he and his Kadets *were* Russia when he was only in power because the people brought about a revolution. These foreigners made no secret of their beliefs. Why shouldn't I help Varvara if it would help move power into the hands of those who had made the revolution? "It's just table talk, though," I warned her. "Nothing very startling."

"Just keep your ears open. Listen for anything about the war, anything about industry or treaties, oil, railroads. Mostly their plans for our future."

At the Cirque Moderne, it was never hard to spot Genya, even in that crush. As I neared, he noticed my newly cropped hair, and his smile vanished. I pressed my way to him and saw that his eyes were full of tears. He touched the shorn strands with bewildered fingertips. As if I had lost an eye. "Oh, Marina, why?"

He hated it. My sentimental revolutionary. It made me laugh. "I thought you were a futurist," I teased him. "This is the future." He laughed at himself then, at his own sentimentality. He gathered me up, lifting me off my feet. "No, it's good. Out with the useless trappings of the pampered life! Out with bustles and skirts on pianos. Freedom for heads and necks of the beautiful women."

I took some woodcut broadsides Sasha Orlovsky had printed and began to distribute them to the crowd:

REVOLUTION
IS IT THE THUNDER?
NO, IT'S THE WORKER
CLEARING HIS THROAT.
——KURIAKIN

I loved handing these to people in the wooden hall, watching them moving their lips, slowly reading the words, reading it aloud to others. This hall was the university of the poor. They weren't going away; they were learning, moving into their power. I could imagine Lyuda here. They were readying themselves to steer their own destiny, and my father and his cronies be damned. And what would I do? What was right and necessary, even if it frightened me, even if I knew others might not understand. I had to bet my soul on it. The important thing was to get out of the war and rebuild the country, repair the devastation, and see what the future would hold.

25 *Big Ears*

WHO WAS THIS GIRL in aubergine silk, with pearls once again in her ears, chatting with such important men that October? It was my *season*. A season of betrayal, without parties or carriages or young men in evening dress joking behind their programs. Only late dinners with diplomats and businessmen, trade representatives, Kadet diehards, Moscow journalists, American envoys, British railroad and mining representatives, British banking interests. The talk was of the war, the collapse of the French army, the German advance on Riga, barely a hundred miles away. The talk was of the future of the government and its ability to resist the Germans. And that night, the talk was of the letter that had appeared in *Novaya Zhizn*, written by someone in Lenin's own party, claiming that Vladimir Ilyich himself was planning the immediate overthrow of the Provisional Government. Evidently Lenin had been in hiding abroad since the summer, when he had been implicated in the failed Bolshevik coup in July. The others in his party were blaming him—many of them had been arrested, but Lenin escaped.

"Not likely they'll be able to go through with it now," Father said, smoking his pipe, gloating. "I believe it would be missing the element of surprise."

"Nothing would surprise me at this point," said Vladimir Terekhov of the Russo-Asiatic Bank as he smugly sipped his claret. I tried to memorize everything that was said. I had an excellent memory, although this was a novel use for it.

"One can't help but be reassured that the comrades are squabbling," said Mr. Sibley, my English soon-to-be host—or so he thought. I'd told my parents I'd

broken it off with Genya and was reconsidering the offer for Oxford.

Mother had long since given up trying to turn the
conversation to matters other than politics. The wives
no longer came at all. Many had already been sent out
of Russia for their safety. She and I were often the
only women at the table, and the topics resisted her.
Tonight, however, a handsome British naval attaché
named Captain Cromie had accompanied Mr. Sibley,
and his presence brought her to life. *Captain Cromie.
British naval attaché.* I made a mental note. Also,
Terekhov had miraculously procured a standing rib
roast, inspiring Vaula to prepare an entire English style
dinner, down to the Yorkshire pudding and horseradish
sauce. This while the bread of Petrograd was rationed
to less than a pound a day per person.

I did my best to be agreeable, to insert an intellectual
comment or two, to show that I was "taking an interest." "How do you see our situation, Mr. Sibley?"

"It's a game of nerves, isn't it?" said the diplomat.
"The Bolshies are weak but they're fantastic at sounding the alarm. And the right vibrates to the least disturbance. The Provisional Government has to keep a firm
hand on the tiller."

"And you must miss your wife."

"She sends her love to all of you, by the way. She
can't wait for you to join us in London."

How happy Father was with my new compliance.
He gazed down the table at me with proprietary plea-

sure, delighting to see me put away my proletarian brown dress and don a silk gown, my hair cleverly marcelled by Mother's hairdresser into elegant waves. Mother was also glad to see me "back to my old self." Their very happiness was maddening—that they preferred this falsehood, this *thing* I was portraying, to the girl they well knew me to be. Exactly as they preferred my brother's "assimilation" into the military academy. They wanted to believe this charade.

It made for a strange cynical pleasure, to pretend I was one of them, to smile at their jokes at the expense of the people—something only Kolya, with his love of trickery, could really appreciate—while storing away the choice scraps for Varvara.

That night Terekhov and Mr. McDonegal of Sheffield Steel discussed Kerensky's new legislation establishing martial law in the factories. It had been one of the causes of the revolution in February, and here we were again. "We'd never get away with it back home," said McDonegal.

"Nobody likes it, but absentee rates are through the roof. Eighty percent, more," said the banker. "If the Russian worker wasn't so busy playing politics, he might have time to put in a day on the production line." He blotted his lips and pushed away his greasy plate.

It took all my self-control not to pick up the water pitcher and pour it over his head. And when would that be, Mr. Terekhov? After sleeping overnight in the bread queues? In between locating a missing load of iron and tanker of fuel? The workers themselves were the only ones keeping our factories open.

"Will the government finally move house?" asked Captain Cromie. "Somewhere safer?"

"Like Japan?" Mother quipped, making the others laugh.

"Kerensky and his Moscow bankers," Father sighed. "They're pressuring him to move down, but we're doing our best. It would give Germany altogether the wrong signal. Put out the welcome mat. Whatever you've heard about our Petrograd garrison, Cromie, I can promise you they are solidly anti-German. They'd never give up Petrograd. The only problem is that they'll defend it in the name of the Soviet instead of the government."

All Power to the Soviet. It was getting closer every day.

"I don't know which is worse," said Terekhov.

Cromie was full of questions. "Is the Soviet really calling the shots?" An attractive man with chiseled face, military bearing, and excellent Russian, Cromie had won over the others, but I didn't trust him. There was something more to him...the way he weighed the others' statements before he spoke. What was he really doing here?

"My dear Cromie," said Sibley. "I'm sure the government's got them well in hand."

"We've heard that Kerensky's going to send the garrison to the front and replace them with reliable troops," said the attaché. "In case there's anything to this insurrection talk."

"Which would be fine, if only he wouldn't broadcast his every whim," Father said grimly. "Every time Kerensky manages to make a decision, he makes a splashy speech about it, and then he's countermanding it before the ink is dry. It's undermining the little confidence anyone has in us."

"What do you think of Lenin?" asked Cromie. "Does he have the sway people say he does?"

Father stoked his pipe, spoke carefully. "He's not the great speaker of the movement—he leaves that to Trotsky and Zinoviev, that Cirque Moderne crowd. But he's absolutely relentless. Without him the Bolsheviks would have compromised long ago."

"He's doing a fine job of keeping the agitation going," said Mr. Sibley, lighting up an after-dinner cigarette. "Even from hiding. Whenever the fires seem to die out, he gets the bellows out and fans them up again. I'd say the Germans are getting their money's worth." He chuckled drily.

I'd always been sure it was a lie that the Bolsheviks were being funded by Germany, but Sibley was in a position to know. Was that something Varvara would want to learn? *English believe Lenin's in Germany's pay.*

"That's the thing you have to remember about the Bolsheviks," said Terekhov. "These are the dregs of society. Look at their leaders: Jews. The dregs of the Jews at that. Their own people won't even have them.

Trotsky, Martov, Zinoviev? These aren't Robespierres. They're little Jewish businessmen. All this talk about taking power. I don't see it." Anti-Semites weren't all monarchists; the Kadets were crawling with them. Terekhov was exhibit A.

"*Peace without annexation or indemnities* — that's the German formula," said Sibley.

Peace without annexation hardly meant winning to these people. They wanted a hunk of the Ottoman Empire as a prize and to bill the loser for the whole mess.

"But there won't be a separate peace?" Cromie said.

"No separate peace, no negotiated end," Father said. "We won't bend on that."

Nods all around the table. But the people wanted us out of the war, and the Bolsheviks would do it without dithering for a second.

"If you could only get your hands on this Lenin," said McDonegal. Basya came in to clear the table. He let her clear his plate but hung on to his wine glass. "He seems to be the one stirring the pot. I'd do a house-to-house search if I were you."

Father watched Basya piling plates on a tray, and Mother frowned at her cap, sliding off her head. Basya kept clearing, her face impassive, as if she had no idea what Mother's frown was about. She did it on purpose, the provocateur. She loathed that cap. I winked as I handed her my plate.

"Why don't you people just pick him up?" said the British steel man. "It can't be that hard. Surely hundreds of people know where he is. Pick up some other Bolshie and sweat it out of him."

"You might find having Lenin is as bad as not having Lenin," Sibley said thoughtfully. "Tiger by the tail. Arresting him could be the spark that sends the whole thing up."

Father watched Basya depart, the door swinging closed behind the starched white bow of her apron. "We're monitoring the situation quite closely. As we speak."

Something about the look on his face, the way he tucked his chin toward his collar, caught my attention. They knew where Lenin was.

"How closely?" Cromie asked.

"We know he's moved back into Petrograd," Father said.

"Are you confident?" Cromie asked.

"We have a good idea," Father said. "Let's just say we'll know where to find him."

The government knew where Lenin was. Or at least the foreign office did. My breath stilled. I wanted to ask more, but I was afraid my questions would be too pointed. *This* was why I had spent all these evenings listening to dull, self-important men at this gleaming table.

"Well, that is good news. Nab him in his sleep—if a scoundrel like that ever does sleep," said McDonegal.

"But why..." began Cromie, raising my hopes, only to fall silent again when Basya returned to collect the remains of the meal. She must have been aware of the tinkling of glasses, the pointed glances, but she took her time at it.

Finally, when she had gone, Father explained. "While there's still a schism among the senior Bolsheviks, we need to wait. Lenin's continuing to battle resistance. It's still possible that Kamenev and his more sensible colleagues might prevail in the Soviet."

"But how long are you going to wait?" Cromie asked. "My God, the man's advocating overthrow."

"Not much longer, I imagine," Father said. "But as soon as we arrest Lenin, we'll lose our source as well."

They had someone inside the Bolshevik organization itself. My mouth ran dry. I stared into my empty water glass but was afraid to pour myself more and betray my shaking hands. When I looked up I noticed Cromie examining me. I smiled back, as if I thought he was just admiring the shape of my eyes, my brow, the style of my hair, instead of asking himself the same questions I was asking. *Who are you? Why are you listening so closely?* Father sat back in his chair, and I well knew the look on his face: the bland gravity he got just before he moved a piece for a checkmate.

I lay in bed in the dark, listening to my heart pound. I imagined them closing in on Lenin as he slept. How could I wait until morning? But Varvara had warned me against ever coming near her apartment on Vasilievsky—it would mean the arrest of them all. I wondered about that shadowy figure working his way into the Bolshevik camp, willing to risk all to report to the Provisional Government. What on earth could be his motivation—or hers—to risk Bolshevik reprisal in order to support this strange agglomeration of liberalism and cravenness, wild disorganization and indecision, ego and oratory?

I rolled over on the hot sheets and thought of Father. I couldn't help remembering how he'd looked at dinner, smug, so sure he knew what was right for Russia. Yet what I was about to do left me queasy. I had more in common with that shadowy figure on the other side of the political fence than I had with him, so confident that his actions reflected his ideals, unable to see the chasm between them. Excited and angry and defiant, eluded by sleep, I read until daybreak.

In the morning, I stood outside Wolf's bookshop, reading the handbills pasted onto a kiosk, anxiously checking for anyone watching me. What if the Bolsheviks were watching me? Maybe they'd been watching me all along. I hadn't thought much about that. Or maybe the government, though I doubted that. Who would spy on us?

And it occurred to me: what if it wasn't Varvara who was collecting my notes? Maybe she had handed me on to some other Bolshevik who wouldn't understand why I was doing this. The idea made my stomach churn. I realized as soon as I thought it that it was probably true.

She'd never promised it would stay just between us, I had simply assumed it. But I couldn't walk away now. I had the note in my pocket, something essential for the revolution. It wasn't personal. It was bigger than I was.

I waited a bit longer, saw nothing suspicious, so I stuck a pushpin into the door jamb of the bookstore, low down—my signal that there was a message—and entered the shop. At the sound of the little ringing bell, the clerk glanced up. I nodded and wound my way back through the rooms to a dusty alcove where the complete works of Plato in Greek awaited. Varvara and I had picked them as the books least likely to be purchased. I pulled out book 10 of the *Republic*—her sense of humor—and opened it to the section where Plato inveighs against poets, claiming that poetry disorients men and that the only poetry he'd allow in his ideal state would be hymns to the gods and the praise of famous men. I parted the book and inserted my note—

You have a spy. Either at Smolny or among the Bolsheviks. Govt knows Lenin's in Petrograd, knows where.

New guest: with Second Secretary Sibley, Captain Cromie. British naval attaché. Seemed very interested in local affairs. His Russian suspiciously good.

Govt believes there will be no insurrection.

Then I reshelved the book out of order. The next time I returned, it would be back in its proper place.

With studied casualness, looking around again, I retreated to the history room, where I located *Great Russian Discoveries in the Arctic and the Pacific 1696–1827: Accounts of Nautical Expeditions to Siberia and Russian America* by F. G. Popov—another volume unlikely to find a buyer. I prayed there would be something in it for me that was not about treachery.

Inside, in Genya's big, barely legible scrawl, a poem:

*Who sentenced me
            to this jail?
The vandal
the thief
                        she jokes with fools
over salmon and wine
Leaves me to
                    yowl
with the cats.*

*Burn
            the house down
                        with your arson-prone hair
                            and fly to me, fly!
I'm drowning in air like a fish
            flip-flopping on deck.*

*Pity my lips.
In the agonies of waiting
                they froze and fell off.*

If you see them,
please send them back.
Pity my lungs
That can't even whimper
Air does them no good
Kiss me alive again.
Madness is you
Somewhere that's not here.

Sweeping the room once more for any suspicious loiterers, I stuck the poem in my pocket. Madness was me, just about anywhere.

In the hushed, scented precinct of Madame Landis's boutique in the Nevsky Passazh, Mother and Madame were locked in discussing the minutiae of hats: the nostalgic virtues of yesterday's styles—broad brims, egret plumes, veils—versus the utilitarian casquettes, turbans, and tricorns of today. Tricorns! The fashion of revolution secure on bourgeois heads. I kept touching the poem in my pocket. *I am drowning, too, Genya, in this endless drivel and perfume and imposture.* I had to see him, feel his solid form around me, talk honestly to someone.

I glanced at my watch and feigned surprise. What an actress I was becoming. "It's almost four? I almost forgot—my friend Veronika's family is leaving for Odessa. I told her I'd pay a call. Mama, take the tricorn. That's the best."

"So many leaving," Mother sighed. "Soon we'll be

rattling around by ourselves, like buttons in an empty drawer."

"I'll be back by dinner," I said, patting Tulku's elegant little head.

"Remember we're going to Viktor Vladimirovich's." Tripov's. In the face of Father's increasingly long working hours and the growing unrest, the all-night debates at the Pre-parliament—the new Duma—she expected me to be her evening escort.

Freed, I dashed down the glass arcade of the Passazh and out into the rain, crossed Nevsky Prospect, and dodged a tram, the angry driver ringing her bell at me. I raced behind the Gostinny Dvor department store toward Haymarket Square. In the absence of police the number of robberies had been rising all fall, and I looked a perfect fool in my bourgeois finery. But if someone wanted to rob me they'd have to catch me first. I pounded up Grivtsova Alley in my heeled shoes, up those wretched stairs two at a time, knocked, and tried the battered door. It opened, but it was only Anton, reading on the divan, a coat thrown over him as a blanket. He pretended not to recognize me. "Is it rent day already?" he asked, turning a page. "I don't have it. Check back on Friday."

I finally found Genya at a corner table with Zina and his other friends in a workingman's café on Gorokhovaya Street, the greasy windows steamed over. Loath to go in dressed as I was, especially with Zina there, I tapped on the glass with the edge of a coin. When he saw me, he rushed out into the cold without his coat, wrapping himself around me in an enormous embrace. His jacket smelled of the café, greasy *pirozhky* and rough tobacco, cabbage and tea. "Look at you. You're making me jealous of all those English diplomats. I'll kill them one by one, dump them in the canal. You won't be able to move a boat there'll be so many of them."

I could feel Zina staring through the restaurant window, seeing him with the Enemy in full regalia. I linked my arm in his. "Let's take a walk."

We strolled along the Catherine Canal in the miserable October drizzle. Gone were the colors: the pinks, the golds, the blues. The scene had washed out into gray. The bare trees brooded in expectation of winter. "I missed you," he said. "Why can't your mother do the spying? Or the old nanny or somebody? Nobody would suspect her of passing secrets."

"She'd be perfect, except she never tells what she knows. You'd have to dig it out of her."

Soon this canal would start to freeze. Winter on the way. I clung to Genya. Even coatless, he exuded warmth, and I sheltered in his lee like a skiff at anchor. Three young girls passed us on the embankment with their bags and books, heading perhaps to the ballet school at the Mariinsky, their gait marked by the duck-walk of little ballerinas. They crossed over the bridge, giggling at us, two mismatched lovers, my head tucked into the hollow under Genya's jaw.

In the shelter of our bodies, our hats, I pulled off my soft suede gloves and rolled a messy cigarette, which made him laugh. With my elegant clothes, my cropped hair, and my hand-rolled smoke, I was neither old nor new but caught in midtransformation. He rolled his cigarette far more deftly, and we leaned together with our elbows on the balustrade, smoking.

"Come back to the Artel with me," he said. "I can't stand being with you like this." He spat a tobacco flake.

I rubbed my face against his sleeve. I would have loved to go back to the Artel and make love with him, but I could just imagine coming back rumpled and stinking from sex to encounter Vera Borisovna dressed and perfumed and ready for me to accompany her to Tripov's salon. "I have to get back in a minute," I said. "I shouldn't even be here. Someone might have followed me from the milliner's."

"I hope you're getting something worthwhile," he said miserably, his arm heavy around me. "Sometimes I think it's just Varvara trying to break us up."

That made me laugh. "Why would she do that? She adores you."

"She tolerates me," he said, his eyes the same color as the gelid green water. "But she'd rather not share you with anybody."

Yes, it was true, she was possessive of her friends. But she was also completely dedicated to the cause, far more than I could ever be. Memorizing the names of English coal barons and American envoys was hardly agitating in the factories and the barracks. I hoped she'd be proud of me. I'd finally proved useful, shown her I wasn't just a romantic poseur with my lovers and poetry, irrelevant in the wider crisis.

"I need you more than the Bolsheviks do." His big hand lay on my bare neck. His hazel-green eyes reflected every feeling—Genya Kuriakin would be the worst spy ever. "I'm going crazy. I can't sleep, I can't think, I can barely breathe. I draw pictures of you naked and kiss them—it's pathetic. I can't hold out much longer. Are you sure we need to do this? Is it making any difference at all?"

He wanted reassurance, revelations, disclosures. But something in me was surprisingly secretive. I wanted to keep these worlds apart, the dark life I was living on Furshtatskaya Street and the bright one Genya and I had. I didn't need to prove my loyalty to him in any case. Only my love. I considered lying, telling him I hadn't found out much of anything, but then what would be the point of our suffering? "I've heard some things that could make a difference. But don't ask me to tell."

"You don't trust me?" He gave me a hurt look, like a little boy's. "*I'm* the Bolshevik." Then he realized he was yelling and tried to contain himself. "You think I'm going to write it on a placard and hang it around my neck?"

I cradled his cheek in my cold, ungloved hand, warming my palm on him the way one might put one's socks on the radiator. "I have to do this my way." We stood shoulder to shoulder, watched the sluggish water flow under the Stone Bridge, where once People's Will terrorists had planned to blow up Alexander II. This long and torturous history.

"You're right. You're doing the right thing," he said, his arms coming around me, his chin resting on my head.

"I'm afraid he'll find out," I whispered.

He held me tighter, trying to build a wall of himself around me. "He won't. And so what if he does?"

I could only shake my head. My love, so kind, so tender, but he had no family feeling, and no divisions within himself, where I had nothing but. How I could make him understand how it felt to be caught between who I was—my history, my class, my family, the *barynya* I'd been raised to be—and the revolution, what I hoped for Russia and for myself? I was *between two stools,* as we say.

26 *October*

EVERY DAY I WENT out to update the *Republic* and *Great Russian Discoveries* and to test the mood of the city. A certain pressure was building in my sinuses, a tingling in my hands and the soles of my feet. Tides of people, restless, flowed from corner to corner, looking for news, reading the proclamations and appeals plastered on every wall. They asked the workers and soldiers to stay home and support the government. I bought a pamphlet with stamps we used for small change—WILL THE BOLSHEVIKS BE ABLE TO HOLD THE POWER?—written by Vladimir Ilyich Lenin. He was of the opinion they'd be able to. Throngs filled every corner, soldiers arguing with students, workers with carters. I bought all the socialist papers and read them one by one under my dripping umbrella. They all said the same thing, that the soldiers' section of the Soviet demanded that if the government couldn't or wouldn't defend Petrograd, it should either make peace or make way for a soviet government. *Rabochy Put'* said the northern soviets had sworn to defend Petrograd's soviet against the government if that were to become necessary.

The time was coming. I could smell it in the air.

Eleven o'clock on a foggy, drizzly morning, the 24th of October. I stood on the street corner waiting for a tram. I'd been suffering from a toothache and had made an appointment with the dentist. Ginevra volunteered to accompany me, but Mother had persuaded her to stay home. I felt sorry for my governess, stuck waiting for our departure for London. I wished I could warn her: *Make your own plans, and quickly,* but that was impossible.

The mood on the damp street that day was surly and a peculiar nervous intensity clung to the crowds. Only the bourgeois newspapers were on sale. No *Rabochy Put'*, no *Soldat*. So Kerensky had done it, had closed the socialist presses. An opening salvo. A wall poster warned THE SOVIET IS IN DANGER! I read as I waited. GENERAL KORNILOV IS MOUNTING COUNTERREVOLUTION! THE PEOPLE SHOULD PREPARE TO DEFEND THE SOVIET. It was signed, THE MILITARY REVOLUTIONARY COMMITTEE. The big Bolsheviks, in other words.

The dentist, a small fussy man in a second-floor office overlooking the Kazan Cathedral, had his own opinions. In fact I wished he wouldn't have been quite so excitable as he plied his sharp tools and drill. "I think Kerensky's trying to goad the Bolsheviks into violence." His thick glasses magnified his eyes, which looked huge and slightly deranged. "They can't possibly hold power, so it's an invitation for the generals to come in and take over. But my wife thinks it's just incompetence. The result's the same either way. Black Hundreds. Pogrom."

But why couldn't the Bolsheviks hold power? The Soviet had the troops, and the workers... anything was possible.

With the metallic taste of cocaine running down my throat, and my jaw swollen and numb, I returned to Nevsky Prospect an hour later to notice a change, people swarming the newsboys, grabbing up their wares. As I got closer, I saw why. They were selling the Bolshevik papers again. While I'd been reclining in the dentist's chair, the presses had been liberated. Kerensky had just lost a critical fight. I pushed into the crowd, not worrying about my jaw. I wanted to get one of those papers before they sold out.

I scanned *Rabochy Put'* under my umbrella, but was disappointed to find nothing about insurrection, just a big dull article by Lenin about the peasant question and an editorial by Kamenev making the usual threats, which could have been published two months earlier. Although I did note that Kamenev, author of that letter in *Novaya Zhizn,* was back in the fold. I was learning how to read between the lines. So the MRC senior leadership had buried their squabbles. That had to mean something.

Just then, a group of mounted cadets rode past, heading toward the Winter Palace. A bourgeois woman clapped with her gloved hands. "Bravo. Bravo! Those brave boys." I saw nothing to cheer about. We had used up all our men, and now we were starting on boys. I thought of Seryozha's learning to ride. He was only sixteen. Would they use him for guard duty in place of troops the government considered unreliable? But by their blue uniforms, I knew these boys were from the artillery school, training to be gunners and marksmen. Surely they wouldn't use a bunch of drafting students to guard the government. While I clambered onto the streetcar, I couldn't stop thinking of the lunacy of Father's enrolling Seryozha in military school during these revolutionary times.

*   *   *

As soon as I entered the vestibule, Mother rushed in. "Marina, the servants are gone." Her voice was high and tremulous. "Basya, Vaula too. They're not in their rooms. They're nowhere!"

I did my best to soothe her. "They're just frightened. They want to be with their families."

It was getting close. The radical press was working again, and the servants had disappeared. Mother was wound tight as a tin soldier, pacing, her dog at her heels, peering out the windows of the salon, which overlooked Furshtatskaya, holding her arms as if it were freezing, gazing down as if troops of maids and cooks were going to come marching down the parkway to overthrow bourgeois apartment buildings. "After all we've done for them. I never want to see them again. Traitors."

My lungs hurt at the mention of the word *traitor*.

For dinner, Avdokia brought us some snacks and soup, which we ate in silence at the card table in the salon. Ginevra played patience, while Mother directed her fears into the intricate patterns of Scarlatti on the ivory keyboard of the big Bösendorfer. Scarlatti wrote more than five hundred sonatas for a Spanish queen, and it seemed that my mother intended to play every last one. Avdokia knitted a scarf of soft gray wool for me. I thought of the cadets on their horses, the poster put

up by the MRC. Large shapes moving in the night. I
prayed that Seryozha was safely out of this. I could
picture him on the floor by the divan, throwing small
balls of wadded paper for the dog. He had been gone
so long—five months. I wondered what he looked like
now. Short-haired, harder, warier? Would I even recognize him?

Around ten, we heard the crack of gunfire, instantly
recognizable, and not so very far away. Mother took
her hands from the keyboard and sat silently with them
folded in her lap. It was here. The moment we had
all expected, or dreaded, or hoped for, was beginning.
But what would it mean? We waited to hear if it would
quiet or grow worse. Avdokia crossed herself and
prayed. I felt the creak of the wheel, the heavy strain of
the timbers, the first faint ringing of gongs.

By midnight it was clear that Father wasn't coming
home, even though he had promised Mother he would.
"We should go to bed," I said.

"Go if you like," Mother said, meaning the opposite.

"Verushka, you're tired," Avdokia said in the voice
she used for children, cajoling, humoring. "He'll work
all night. Just lie down a little, Marina can sleep in your
room. You won't be alone."

"I'll wait. I'm too worried. I just couldn't…"

In the end, we all stayed where we were, I on the
divan, Ginevra at the card table in the wing chair, Avdokia leaning against the wall on her bench, snoring,

Mother pacing and then playing at the Bösendorfer, taking small glasses of vodka for her nerves. Scarlatti and scattered gunfire filled my dreams. I don't know what it was that woke me—the sound of the piano bench pushing back? My mouth tasted of dust and my jaw hurt. Mother stood in the dimly lit room. "Mitya?" she called out. The grandfather clock in the hall said half past one.

My father entered wearily from the hallway, hair wet with rain, and sagged into an armchair by the door, too tired to make it all the way in. He leaned forward, his face in his hands, elbows propped on his knees.

Mother raced to his side, knelt by him, touched his face. "Mitya. What's happened?"

He made a disgusted *"Tcha."*

She pressed her cheek to his thigh. "I'm so glad you're home. I was afraid something awful might have happened. We waited up for you."

He sat back and rested his hand in her silver hair. "You didn't have to." I wasn't used to seeing them so intimate with each other. It was almost embarrassing.

"There's such a bad feeling in the air."

"Indeed."

"Is it insurrection?" I asked.

A glance at the windows. Another sigh.

Mother rose, wiped her eyes, tried to compose herself. "You must be hungry. Let Avdokia get you some dinner."

"I had a sandwich at the Winter Palace. I could use a

whisky, though." He was hoarse. He sounded like he'd caught a cold. "Or three. Or just hit me over the head with the bottle."

Mother rose and poured him a drink, indicating to Avdokia with a tip of her head that she should get him something to eat anyway. I could smell the peaty, scorched scent of Scotch. She pressed the glass into his hand. "The servants are gone."

He took a deep draught. "That's the least of our problems. They've got checkpoints set up on Million-naya Street. I was lucky to get home at all. Fortunately my driver knows another route."

Now Ginevra awoke in her armchair, her face creased from sleep, her coiffure lopsided. "Oh, Dmitry Ivanovich, we're so glad you're home!"

"And I as well, Miss Haddon-Finch. Thank you."

"What checkpoints?" I asked.

"The Military Revolutionary Committee," he said. "Oh Christ, where to begin? Kerensky cut their phone lines last night after we all went home. Decided to close the Bolshevik papers without telling anyone and decreed the arrest of the MRC and the leaders of the Petrograd Soviet. He made a long speech at the Pre-parliament to get it all rubber-stamped. He got a standing ovation, but after four hours of caucus, the parties came back with a vote of no confidence: 126 to 103. Kadets, too. He didn't see it coming. God, what do we do now?"

The government was crumbling under its own ineptitude, the outpouring of rhetoric leading nowhere, Kerensky whipping himself into hysteria.

"We heard shooting," Mother said.

"The bridges are in dispute," Father said. "The utilities, the telephone, telegraph—it's all up in the air." He rubbed his face, dug out his pipe from his jacket pocket. He finished his drink, put it on the floor, packed his pipe, and lit it with unsteady hands. He leaned back with his eyes closed, concentrating, as if that pipe were the sole object in the world.

"You'll find a way," Mother said soothingly. "You always find a way."

Avdokia came back with a plate of food for him—some cold potatoes in sour cream, herring and onions, black bread—and set it down on the card table.

Father picked up his glass and moved to the table, lowered himself into a seat. "Maybe I'll snatch the guns of a Red Guard and 'go out blazing' like a Zane Grey cowboy. *Shootout at the Pre-Parliament*—think it'll be a bestseller?" Managing a mordant laugh. His face looked so haggard, the lines had become fissures.

The Provisional Government was on the brink of collapse. I thought I would feel triumphant, but what I felt was a terrific uncertainty and hope and most of all tenderness and pity for my father's sake. All his hopes and plans, all his work, first with the Kadet party and now for the Provisional Government, ending in this.

Although he said he wasn't hungry, he began to eat mechanically, his head hanging over his plate. I believed he was weeping. Mother poured him another glass of whisky and sat at the table with him. Tulku laid his head on her knee.

A loud knock on the half-open salon door startled us all. A familiar tall black-clad figure—wind-whipped, scarf-shrouded, wet from head to toe—stood in the doorway, eyes sparkling dangerously. How did she get in? It was as if she had materialized out of the very air. "Greetings from the Future!" She grinned, swayed. Was she drunk? My parents stared at her as if she were three-headed Cerberus himself. Her nose and cheeks shone rose-red, while the rest of her face glowed frost-white in the dimness. Her black hair hung in wet tendrils. "Why so glum, citizens? You should be celebrating!"

I jumped up and ran to her. God, of all times to appear. I tried to pull her away, down the hall. "What are you doing here?" I hissed.

"Tell her it's two in the morning," Father called out. "This is a private home, not a tavern."

She broke away from my grip, whirling past me into the salon. "Am I too late? I've got a secret for you, Dmitry Ivanovich. It is too late! Too late for you! You and your cronies, your English thieves, your bankers and warmongers! You should have listened to the people when you had the chance."

I had said it myself, but not tonight. Had she no pity? Had she no decency at all?

He straightened, blinking, at a rare loss for words,

trying to focus on this noisy, untidy, threatening creature who stood in front of him.

She laughed as if she were in fact quite mad. "I'm going to give you a little friendly advice. I'd stay away from the Winter Palace tomorrow if I were you. Maybe even sleep away from home for the next few nights." She took off her scarf, shook it, leaving little puddles of rain all over the parquet. "We've got the bridges, we've got the telephone, the telegraph, the Nikolaevsky station. The ministers are next."

"I'm sure I don't need the advice of a deranged schoolgirl," my father said coldly. In his rising anger, he seemed less weary, coming back to himself. "In fact, I've never been so sure of anything in my life." He wiped his mouth, and stuck his pipe back between his lips.

She wiped her face on her sleeve. "Maybe you don't need my advice, but maybe you do." She began wandering around the room, hands behind her back, like a museum visitor, examining things as if she'd never seen them before. She stopped before the portrait of Mother painted by Vrubel. "By morning your ministers will be in the Peter and Paul Fortress. The garrison's already come over to our side."

My father might have already been arrested if he hadn't found a way around that checkpoint.

"It's been a very long day, and I've had about enough of this," he said. "I'd like you to leave now."

"You're not going to invite me to stay?" She laughed.

"There's gratitude." She put her hands on her hips and tossed me a theatrical glance.

His reserves of patience were finally drained. "Gratitude? I'll have you deposited on the sidewalk with yesterday's garbage."

"And who's going to do that?" She grinned her lopsided grin. "Look around, Dmitry. Your *dvornik*'s gone, your maid, your cook. I'm just giving you a head start. For Marina's sake."

I couldn't believe she'd just called him Dmitry, like he was a schoolboy. Couldn't she see how devastated he was? I didn't want to approach her, didn't want to be seen siding with her at all, but I had to get her out of here. I stood in front of her, so she couldn't see him and vice versa. "Varvara, you need to go."

"But I'm trying to do your old man a favor." She said it even louder, to make sure he heard.

"If I ever need your help, I'll make sure to come find you." Father returned fire, waving the stem of his pipe in her direction. "I happen to have sources of information far better than yours."

"Yes, I know," she said. She turned back to the Vrubel, examining it. "I'll give you that much. You've been a regular font of information."

I felt a jolt of electricity race upward from my spine to my head.

She didn't even look in his direction. "Thanks to you, we know lots of things. Things we'd have missed otherwise."

I was afraid to say a word. The look she gave me then frightened me more than anything I had ever seen. A dangerous glee. She took a bronze-colored chrysanthemum out of the vase Mother had arranged and stuck it behind her ear. "You've been ever so useful—you don't even know."

"I have no idea what you're jabbering about," Father said, downing the last of his whisky Russian-style. Standing, he took Mother's arm, helping her up. "We're going to bed."

It should have been enough to put the subject to rest, but Varvara had the devil in her that night. She would not stop until the job was done. "No, you wouldn't have any idea. Captain Cromie, the English spy? British Second Secretary Sibley? The railroads? The intentions of the British and the banking community? Thanks to you, we discovered a leak on the staff of our own Central Committee. For that alone, our humblest thanks." She delivered a clumsy curtsy.

A slow horror spread over my father's face as the picture began to come into focus, its shapes coalescing in his mind like an exposed photograph. He turned to look at me, his daughter, his own little girl. I burned, I twisted. Why? Why did she want to hurt me? What was in it for her? Couldn't Varvara just have been happy with the success of the Bolsheviks? I couldn't breathe. I was hoping I could just faint, but no such luck.

"You've been working for them?" he asked in that ruined voice. "For the Bolsheviks?"

If only I could have gone up in a puff of smoke, leaving nothing but a greasy smudge on the parquet. I had never thought I'd be put in a position to explain myself. Put there by Varvara—whom I had trusted! Not only trusted—the one I had betrayed him to please. The sharp, bitter object in my throat felt like a fist of rusted iron.

My father took a step away from me. "Who are you? I don't know you." My mother, too, was staring, as if I had risen from the grave.

How revoltingly happy Varvara looked with what she had done. *She wants you all to herself.* Was that it? She would even ruin my place in my family for that? "Dmitry Makarov," she said, gloating. "The great chess master himself, moving everyone around the board like so many little pawns. The one thing you didn't consider was that your pampered little darling would have a mind of her own."

"You little gargoyle. You witch." He took a threatening step toward my friend, my enemy. "Take your pestle and broom and get out." I thought for a moment he would strike her, but instead, he pointed violently to the door. "Out!"

His fury made her laugh and dance around him. She truly looked demonic. "Yes, think of it. Right from your dinner table to Smolny." I thought he would have a heart attack, a stroke. Avdokia attempted to grab her by her coat but Varvara backed away. "I'm just returning the favor, giving you a running start before the Red Guards get you. It's your lucky night!"

His face looked so white it could have been powdered. I'd betrayed him, his love, his confidence. And now I in turn had been betrayed.

"Out!" His voice was grated, almost gone.

"I'm going, I'm going. Hey, see you around, Marina." She saluted with the chrysanthemum — "Thanks for the help!" — and tossed it at him. It bounced onto the floor.

In her wake, the smell of ozone stained the air. The big clock ticked out our silence. In the distance, rifle fire. My father stood in the middle of the parquet floor, adrift as a man fallen overboard in a stormy sea. I could feel him staring at me as if I were a stranger. How could I, a girl who wouldn't have stolen so much as an egg or a kopek, have done such a thing? I had stolen his secrets and passed them to his enemies. I dared myself to look in his eyes. All the weariness in the world was there.

"Why? To punish me?" he rasped, staggering a bit, steadying himself with a manicured hand on the back of a chair. "For breaking up your love affair?"

"It had nothing to do with that," I said.

"You hate me so much?"

And he'd thought this the worst night of his life when he came home. Now he knew it was. "It was never about us," I said, managing to get the words around the clutch of razors in my throat. "You were selling our future, night after night, while the country begged for peace. I wanted Russia to have a chance."

"Good Christ!" He threw one of the little wooden

chairs across the room. It skidded across the parquet and hit one of the silvery blue walls. "Don't you have a brain in your head? You expect the Bolsheviks to give Russia a chance?"

The urge to beg forgiveness passed, and outrage rose up in its place. "If we left it to you it would be like the revolution never happened. You had the chance, and look what you did with it. You and your Kadets. The government, Kerensky. All of them."

Mother was silent. Ginevra held her hand over her mouth. Avdokia, palm to her forehead. No one would defend me.

"I'll give you half an hour to pack and leave," he choked out. "I never want to see you again."

I could smell the smoke in the room. As if a bolt of lightning had come through the roof and struck us all down.

It was after two. A dark, rain-filled night peppered with gunfire. The Englishwoman bravely stepped forward. "You can't send her out there. Surely she can wait until morning." I could have kissed her. It would have been brave enough if I'd been innocent, but the bravery to stand up for the guilty demanded a special depth of character. I couldn't look at either one of them.

And my father had turned his back on me. "I cannot have her under my roof. Not one more second."

The world was cracking—I could hear it—like ice that had grown too thin to hold us, and we were falling in: this apartment, the Bösendorfer, the clock. I'd never dreamed it would end this way. I wanted to help the revolution, but at what price? "Papa…don't hate me."

"Dmitry Ivanovich," Ginevra tried again. "I beg you to reconsider. You can't send a young girl out onto the street—"

"Let her go to her Bolshevik friends. Or to the devil for all I care." He was crying. He wiped his face on the back of his hand.

I thought my deeds would be forever hidden, that only good would come of them. As I walked past, he turned away. Mother whispered to him, her arm around his shoulder.

I didn't remember walking down the hall. I just found myself in my room. I put a suitcase on the bed and stared into its lining of mauve watered silk. What did one pack on a trip to the devil? A warm coat, fur on the inside. Hat, sturdy shoes. A warm dress or two, heavy stockings. I wavered over my jewelry: pearl earrings, a ring with a small emerald from Grandmère, a gold bracelet with my name engraved on it, carved amber beads. Only the enameled bangle was really mine. I left the rest piled on the vanity table. I would start from nothing, like other people. I took Seryozha's silhouette of Akhmatova and my book of poetry. A brush, my clock. I left the photographs of Volodya and Kolya. What would Volodya say when he heard? If he heard?

No one came to watch me go, not even Avdokia.

Outside, it was completely dark, the streetlights all

extinguished. Gunshots echoed off the buildings. I'd been determined to go to Genya's, but my nerves failed me. I was no revolutionary, no Varvara with a gun in my waistband. I was only a thin, tired girl with a small suitcase and my father's curse in my heart to keep me company.

Like an abandoned cat, I slinked back into the archway. The lights in our flat had gone out. In a bit of hardscrabble luck, the door to the *dvornik*'s cubby wasn't locked. I crept in and curled up under the counter on the dirty floor among newspapers and old tools, out of sight. I leaned against my suitcase and let my tears catch up with me. What had I done? I wrapped my coat tighter around myself and waited through that long cold night, the most miserable girl in Petrograd.

Part III

The Terrestrial Now

(October 1917–Early Spring 1918)

27 *The Dawn*

I STOOD IN THE cold hallway of the Poverty Artel at the return of daylight, shivering in the silence. It was too early, but what choice did I have? I tapped on the door, waited, tapped again. I knocked. In a moment, Zina's round face appeared, her hair rumpled, a blanket wrapped around her. Her sleep-soaked glance sourly took in my suitcase, my woolen scarf, and she turned away without even a "hello," leaving me standing in the hall. I followed her in, closed the door.

It wasn't much warmer inside. The stale air smelled like feet, like ashtrays and people. In the dimness, I could only recognize rough shapes. Dawn hadn't yet managed to penetrate the courtyard. "Genya?"

I heard someone turn over, call my name. "Over here." I followed the voice, bumping into chairs in the close, stinking air, inching along stepping on things — a mumbled curse — to find my lover propping himself up on a pallet on the floor. He opened the covers, and I crawled in, boots and all, as if I could bury myself in his side, as if I could return to his body like Adam's rib. "What happened?" he whispered. "Come on, don't cry." But I couldn't answer or stop my tears.

I just wanted to hold him. I was here, I was safe. He rocked me, stroking my hair. Eventually I fell asleep in his arms.

Sometime later, something woke me, a cough, a slammed door—and the first thing I saw in the dim room was Genya on one elbow, watching me. I smiled and touched his mouth. He kissed my hand. Then the shame of my exposure, the grief returned to me in a wave. "Varvara told him everything." I shielded my eyes—I didn't want him to see me crumble.

"I'm glad," he whispered fiercely. "Now you're here."

I pressed my head to his chest, just listened to the steady hammer of his heartbeat.

"How touching," a voice grumbled.

"Don't be an ass," someone else hissed.

The skritch and flare of a match. Cigarette smoke. Someone yawned. People began to move. A blanket-wrapped figure on lined-up chairs became Sasha, heavy arms stretching. Across the room, on the cot, someone groaned, sat up. Legs appeared in their white winter underwear, feet shoved into boots. Anton. From the divan above our heads, Gigo's black eyes studied me. "Thought so." Another floor sleeper stirred nearby, under the table—a feminine voice cursed. Zina.

One by one, they sat up, lit cigarettes, smoked, coughed, struggled into clothes. Sasha went outside, presumably to use the convenience. But Genya didn't move. He lay next to me, gazing at me as if he had wished for a pony and had opened his eyes to a soft nose and long whisking tail. He was all I had now. I had never expected to be so fully in someone's hands. I only hoped he was ready for this.

Anton poked the fire, letting a trickle of smoke escape into the room. He looked the perfect cartoon of an avant-garde poet—unshaved, scowling, his black hair sticking straight up as he clomped around in unlaced boots. "She's not staying," he said, shaving off pieces of kindling with a hatchet. "No women."

"What does that make me?" Zina sat up in her quilt, her dark hair matted from sleep.

"No sweethearts. No *innamorate,* consorts, or girl-friends," said the editor, letting his smoke express his feelings.

"Anton doesn't like people to have girlfriends," explained Sasha, closing the door, taking a chair, stretching his bony wrists out from his raveling sleeves. "He thinks it distracts us from our misery."

"And misery is to poets as milk is to babes," pronounced Gigo, his face above mine, sticking over the side of the divan. "Why keep it all to ourselves?"

"Don't listen to him," said Genya, kissing my temple, pulling me close. "You're staying and that's it. She's got nowhere to go, Anton. Her parents threw her out."

"That's why they invented bridges." Anton lit a spirit lamp with a match, set a kettle on it. "For bourgeois girls…to jump. Off. Of. It's my flat, and I say no."

"Vote." Genya sat up, raised his arm. "Show of hands. All in favor."

Hands went up. Genya. Sasha. Gigo. Zina's black eyes flashed from me to Genya, calculating. She loathed me but pursued Genya's favor like a starving dog. "Why can't she go to a hotel? She's got money. It's already too crowded."

"She's one of us," Genya said. "She was working for the Bolsheviks. That's why they gave her the boot."

Reluctantly, Zina raised her hand—halfway.

Anton slammed the screechy stove door. "What's next—elephants? Giraffes? High-wire walkers?"

Genya grinned triumphantly, kissed my brow. "You see?" With a mixture of relief and apprehension, I surveyed my new home. No more napkins and polite handshakes and marcelled hair. A new life. A life of poetry—wasn't that what I'd always wanted? With Genya? And I would show Anton just who was a poet.

A rare autumn sun bestowed benedictions upon a huge armored car blocking the entrance to the telephone exchange building and the soldiers surrounding it. They eyed passersby mistrustfully. But where were their loyalties? To the government or to the revolution? "All Power to the Soviets!" Zina shouted, and a young soldier nodded. Revolution. Just as they'd done in February, the soldiers were taking the communications points. Only this time they weren't going to beg any bourgeois politicians to lead them. *Oh please, Mr.*

Lawyer, Mr. Banker, Prince Lvov, Paul Miliukov, show us the way. This was the real revolution, the one we'd been waiting for.

Theater Square gleamed under a tender frost. Sun glanced off the bayonets of Red Guards, burnished the gold dome of St. Isaac's in the distance. We watched members of the Pre-parliament arrive at the Mariinsky Palace for the noon session. But I thought the government had fallen. Had Varvara's imagination gotten the better of her? Gigo stepped in front of one of the delegates, who wore a high white collar and regarded the pale, excitable poet with alarm. "What's the order of the day, sir?" the mad Georgian asked. The man glanced at the rest of us and his face composed itself into a weary amusement, but he regarded the Red Guards more soberly. "I believe we'll be discussing procedural issues," he said, his mouth twisting into a wry smile. "We may be adjourning early."

We moved up into St. Isaac's Square, bristling with Red Guards. They seemed to be coming from the Nikolaevsky Bridge. The cathedral drew up its gold cap like a dowager pulling away from a pack of clamoring beggars.

But the most astonishing sight by far awaited us on the Neva shore. The embankment teemed with people in the sea wind—soldiers and sailors, workers and students. And opposite the Winter Palace—a warship. The *Aurora*, she was called. The Dawn. Huge, with her three smokestacks and two masts, rows of portholes, her seven big guns leveled at the Winter Palace. I couldn't get my mind around her presence. A battleship in the Neva. Poised to fire. Would they really do it? Blow holes in the palace's half mile of Italianate flank? Nothing much seemed to be happening on deck, yet the mere fact of her meant that our naval base at Kronstadt was already in the hands of the Soviet. Kerensky had thrown down the gauntlet and the Kronstadt sailors had picked it up.

On impulse, Genya clambered onto the narrow em-bankment railing and balancing there, shouted at the steel bulk, his hand outstretched.

> *Aurora!*
> *let loose your thunder!*
> > *Awaken all these sleepwalkers*
> *Free us*
> > *From yesterday's nightmare and all the*
> > *little tsars.*
> > > *We're ready for your fury*
> > > *Those with ears to hear*
> > > *awaken!*

He teetered and almost fell, jumped down to finish his poem on solid ground. His seaward lines rolled like waves hitting granite cliffs on a northern shore. Gigo and Zina each took a turn reciting, then Genya pulled me forward. The crowd watched me expectantly, happy to be entertained while they waited for the revolution to begin. I gave them my poem about the massacre at Znamenskaya Square, but I had nothing to follow it with. I had to put something more up into the air. So I began to sing the first song that came into my mind, "Dubinushka." Little Hammer. *"Strike harder, strike harder, da ukhnem!"* My singing teacher, Herr Dietrich, would have had a heart attack if he heard what I was doing with all that training, but some listeners tossed coins, which my friends picked up from between the cobbles.

A strange moment, entertaining the revolutionary crowd with their own work songs, receiving their hard-earned kopeks in return. For the sailors in the crowd in their flat white caps and striped jerseys, I began another—"The Boundless Expanse of the Sea." *My friend, we're on a long journey, far from our dear land we go…* A blond sailor came forward and pressed a silver ruble into the palm of my hand. His hatband read AURORA.

I wish I could say I still had that ruble, but we spent it on dinner.

In the afternoon, we tramped out to Smolny, a good three miles away, to see what the All-Russian Congress of Soviets was doing about the insurrection. Delegates had converged from soviets all over the country, but the start had been delayed and delayed again and the delegates were getting restless. Gunners stood poised at their machine-gun stations flanking the entrance to the building, exactly where tenderly brought-up young noblewomen once walked when it was a convent school. The gardens teemed with armed workers and rough men in red armbands—Red Guards—who had come on their own to help with the insurrection. Thousands of them were camping out, waiting for instructions. There were too many—we heard revolutionary soldiers trying to send them home, but few left. The tension was thick. Evidently the Bolsheviks had announced they were pushing back the starting time for the congress yet again. We tried to talk our way in, to no avail, and now the sun was going down. I was tired and hungry but I had no home to go to besides the Poverty Artel, and the poets were in no mood to abandon the streets. Genya certainly showed no signs of flagging. We ate in a nearby café, lingered over our tea, then set out again. I drifted along in a fog of exhaustion, Genya's arm around me the only thing between me and collapse.

The first cannon shot came around ten. We converged on the English Embankment with the excited, slightly menacing revolutionary crowd to watch the firefight. It wasn't the *Aurora* after all. Stranger than that—it was the Peter and Paul Fortress firing across the wide Neva, pummeling the Winter Palace. To a native of this mirrored city, it was a sight unthinkable even twenty-four hours earlier. Like the fork running away with the spoon. *This is really happening,* I had to keep reminding myself.

"The Bolsheviks have to take the Winter Palace tonight," said Zina, leaning on the parapet, vapor escaping her lips. "They'll want to report a victory to the Congress of Soviets. That's probably why they're holding off the start. But they can't keep the delegates waiting another day—there'll be a riot."

Gigo stamped his feet, put his collar up.

The rapid fire of machine guns added to the great boom of the cannons, a symphony. I shivered and pressed into Genya for warmth. If only we could just go home. I didn't know if my trembling was from fear or exhaustion, but I couldn't make it stop. Sweet Sasha asked if I was all right, if I needed to go home, but I shook my head.

Another burst of machine-gun fire—too loud, too fast, too close—made me jump. Above me, my lover's nostrils flared, drinking in the smell of gun smoke. I could tell he wanted to get closer, to go right up to the cordon. I couldn't stop seeing Znamenskaya Square, the bodies, and the men with the Red Cross armbands carrying away the wounded. I was in over my head, thinking I could keep up with Genya Kuriakin. I wanted to be like him—brave. I wanted him to think of me as worthy of his love.

Anton had had enough. They weren't taking the Winter Palace fast enough for his liking. "I'm going back," he said. "Let me know in the morning how it turned out."

I could go with him. But I would not leave Genya. I

wanted to see what he saw, go where he went, to prove I could, to myself as much as to anyone.

We didn't return until early next morning. We stumbled in, laughing, bumping into the furniture as we tried to shed our coats and boots, stoke the fire. "Anton, wake up." Genya kicked his bed. "They did it! While you were here keeping your fleas warm."

I laughed. I was drunk—on wine and on our insane bravery. If I hadn't been so tired, I never would have done it. Never would have had the nerve. But I was standing strangely outside myself. We had gone into the Winter Palace, had drunk its wine, had plumbed hell itself and returned.

"We got inside," said Zina, bouncing on her heels. "All of us. Genya first."

The soldiers were first, breaching the firewood barricades, hundreds of soldiers pouring in, and then Genya was up ahead, waving for us to follow him. *Marinoushka, what do you have in that head of yours—straw?* Yes, but it had been wonderful, strange beyond imagining, to enter the violated palace.

"It was fantastic. Pure madness," Gigo said, turning a chair the wrong way around and lowering his slight frame into it.

"You should have been there," Genya said, wrapping his arm around Anton's neck where he sat up in his cot. The editor reached for the clock. It was around five. He groaned and let it fall to the floor.

I sank onto the divan, remembering all those corridors. The fine paintings, the Malachite Hall. Ballrooms used for barracks, dining rooms for offices. Everyone was lost—the soldiers, the cadets; people shot at each other out of sheer nerves and confusion. A revolutionary soldier dropped a grenade down a staircase—why? My ears still hadn't stopped ringing.

Anton shoved his friend's heavy arm from his shoulders. "Then you got drunk to celebrate?"

Sasha pulled up a chair to the messy table. "The soldiers broke into the tsar's wine cellars. We heard they lost a whole battalion down there. They sent another in after them and they disappeared, too. They won't be coming out anytime soon, either."

Genya reached under his jacket and pulled out three bottles. Sasha produced four more.

Zina goggled. "So that's where you were."

We'd gone down just to see it. Now I would never get the picture out of my head, that Blakean hell: drunken soldiers bashing the necks off vintage bottles, lying on the floor as their mates poured wine into their open mouths. The cellars went on and on, a labyrinth under the palace, and the soldiers turned into animals before our eyes, like Odysseus's men on Circe's isle. The drunken men were more frightening than cannon fire. I slipped in the spilled wine and fell, cutting my knee. Genya and Sasha grabbed bottles and we departed, fighting our way back upstairs against a tide of descending celebrants. I looked at the tear in my stocking, the jagged sore, but it seemed like someone else's leg. I still couldn't feel it.

"Wine?" Genya held an old bottle against his forearm like a sommelier. It was a Madeira, 1848.

"A good year," I said.

He handed it to Sasha, who began working its cork with his penknife, as Genya continued his story about our adventures conquering the Winter Palace. "We found the meeting room where the ministers were holed up. The Red Guards were just marching them out when we got there."

Actually we hadn't seen them. Genya was painting a picture now. We came upon the room by accident, wandering among soldiers and looters grabbing plumes and statuettes, clocks and miniatures, the Red Guards trying to stop them. *These things belong to the people!* Shots firing, people running, smoke. We passed through ruined chambers that had been used as barracks. Suddenly we found ourselves in a dining room, rather plain compared with the outer galleries, its long table scattered with pens and pads bearing the scribblings and drafts of proclamations. The ministers had been trying to find a course for themselves and the country up to the last moment, when the Red Guards had arrived to arrest them. Waiting for the inevitable. What a fitting finale it was for the Provisional Government. True to form, they'd conferred to the very end. Talk, that was their forte, while they waited for someone else to act. But I wondered what had happened to one dignified gentleman in particular, a man with a reddish-brown beard and eyes like my own. I prayed he'd listened to Varvara, but I doubted he did. Perhaps going down with the ship seemed more noble than what had occurred that night on Furshtatskaya Street.

Finally Sasha got the stopper out of the bottle. Zina found glasses of varying sizes and degrees of cleanliness. We poured and toasted the revolution, the sailors, and, finally, poetry. I thought of those hundreds of soldiers swilling priceless wine as if it were *kvas*. Some bottles probably dated from the reign of Peter the Great. Then I shook myself. Who had tears for vintage wine when men were still dying in a war nobody wanted? Let them drink. I raised my glass, the oval of Madeira like a fine red fire.

Genya held his hand behind his back. "Guess what I found," he said, his eyes shining but a bit blurred by drink.

"The Orlov diamond?" Anton ventured, squinting against the smoke spewing from the stove.

"The tsar's truss," suggested Sasha, sniffing the wine.

Genya brought his big hand around and displayed on his palm...an ordinary fountain pen. He grinned, triumphant. "Kerensky's pen."

"How do you know?" Anton asked. Despite his blasé air, he was intrigued. He grabbed it, tried it out on a scrap of paper. There was still ink in it.

Genya snatched it back. "It was at the head of the table, wasn't it?" He held the pen before my eyes.

"With this pen, I swear I'm going to write the most revolutionary poems the world has ever seen."

Sasha divvied up the rest of the Madeira, which had been waiting for us in that bottle since before Alexander II freed the serfs. "To Kerensky's pen."

Then it really struck me, the gravity of what we had seen, where we had been, what we had done. The Soviet had taken the Winter Palace. Dual power was over. My father and the government, our class, the liberals, had had their moment and had bungled it sorely. Now the Bolsheviks and the workers would have their chance to drink that wine.

"You think the ministers will be all right?" I asked. "They won't shoot them, will they?"

"They're probably becoming poets and moving in here," Anton sighed. "Along with the Kronstadt sailors and Lenin's mother."

Genya sat down heavily next to me on the divan. "Someone said they took them to the Peter and Paul Fortress. But there was an explosion, maybe a grenade, and a bunch of them scampered off."

"And the cadets?" I whispered. Those boys, guarding the palace.

"I see them more as essayists," Gigo said. "I don't think they're much for poetry."

"A whole group of them left when we went in," Genya said, nuzzling me. He knew what I was worried about. "I heard the rest came out after the ministers. They're fine. No one's going to shoot a bunch of kids."

They opened another bottle. I'd never drunk wine so fine. It sent its dizzying thickness all through my tired body. After that, all I remember was Gigo singing the Georgian national anthem and Zina demonstrating the cancan. Genya offered up a toast. "To the revolution! May the last be first and the first be damned."

28 *Grivtsova Alley*

THE WHEEL OF REVOLUTION whirled on with a speed that made our heads spin. Within hours of the fall of the Winter Palace, the Congress of Soviets had already named the new ministers, to be called commissars. And what a list! Lenin, chairman; Trotsky, foreign affairs; Rykov, internal affairs; Kollontai, public welfare; Lunacharsky, education; Stalin, nationalities; and so on. I laughed as I read the names in the afternoon papers. Many were familiar to me from the Cirque Moderne, people I'd never have imagined would one day be running a nation that encompassed one-sixth of the globe. A woman minister—Varvara's beloved Kollontai! And Trotsky as foreign minister. Changes were coming that would make the February Revolution look like a snoozy afternoon in a gentlemen's club.

Not everybody was pleased with the success of the Bolshevik insurrection. As we staggered out into the daylight, blinking and hungover, we saw walls bearing pleas to RESIST THE BOLSHEVIK TAKEOVER! "A bit late for that," Genya said. We bought all the newspapers. Gorky's *Novaya Zhizn* called for a new government that would unite *all* socialist parties and criticized the SRs and the Mensheviks for walking out of the Congress of Soviets, letting the Bolsheviks have the field. I thought of Father's letter, criticizing the Kadets for walking out this summer: *Boycotts and walkouts make a splash, but then where are you?*

But *Pravda*—the paper of the Petrograd Soviet, remade from *Rabochy Put'*—shot back, saying that the people had struck down the tyranny of the nobles in February and now the tyranny of the bourgeoisie was at an end. The Kadet paper predicted that the Bolshevik coup would last a mere day or two before it crumbled under its own ineptitude. "They would know all about that," Zina said.

Within twenty-four hours, the Decree on Peace and the Decree on Land were adopted by the Congress of Soviets, proving that the Bolsheviks had the will to do what the government had endlessly debated but had not been able to accomplish. In a single day, the assembled delegates legislated three basic popular demands: they called for immediate negotiation for peace, without annexations or indemnities; they ordered confiscation of all land from nobility, landlords, and clergy for distribution to the peasants; and they set a date for elections to the Constituent Assembly—November 12, three weeks away. It felt like a dam bursting.

*   *   *

For my part, I was having another revolution. For the first time I lived as others did, standing with my bucket in the courtyard pumping water, using a shared toilet on the landing of the stairway. I stood in line for bread. I often literally sang for my supper, varying my repertoire as seemed appropriate—work songs, sea chanteys, love songs. And I never complained, tried never to show myself as the bourgeois miss. I had finally gotten off Nevsky Prospect, Comrade Kraskin.

But there was one aspect of life on Grivtsova Alley that nobody seemed to notice but me: roaches, fleas, bedbugs. Genya never said a word about the infestation. I didn't want to be the *girlfriend* focusing on such trivialities when we had the Future to forge on the anvil of our verse—or vice versa—but it was hard to think about anything else for more than a few minutes at a time when you were being eaten alive by small voracious creatures.

I studied the other women in the queue for water as I moved forward on the plank that crossed the icy puddle in the courtyard. There must be something they did about it that eluded the poets of the Artel. Some secret. But whom to ask? The rangy woman in front of me worked the handle of the pump, briskly filling her bucket. I asked if she had bugs in her flat and what we could do about them.

"Why not read them some poetry?" she said, and the

women behind me snickered. She switched out her full pail for an empty one and glanced up into my face. Her demeanor softened. "You don't know anything, do you, *devushka?* Not a thing." She snorted. "Tell those boys to drag the bedding down here and beat the devil out of it. With shoes if you have to. Scrub the place down and put the legs of the beds in kerosene. That'll fix you right up." I watched her pick up her pails and straighten slowly under the weight.

Bozhe moi, was that what they were doing? I hoped the neighbors didn't smoke in bed. Now I was glad we slept in our clothes. It would make for an easier getaway.

Not only were we infested, but everyone smoked *makhorka,* and Anton spat his sunflower-seed shells right onto the floor, daring me to say something. One cold November day, I couldn't stand it anymore. "All right!" I yelled. "All right! Fine! Beautiful!" And I grabbed everything from the floor, piled it onto the table—papers, shoes, socks, books, shirts, slippers— and swept the room with a savage broom I borrowed from the woman next door. Boiled water on the stove, threw it on the floorboards and into the corners, and scrubbed it with a brush and a scrap of lye soap I had managed to buy. I didn't care how much the others teased me, calling me "housewife" and "Mama." It was worth it. All of us were covered with bites and boils. I berated myself for my naïveté. I'd brought books and a silver-handled hairbrush from home but hadn't thought to bring a towel or soap or, God help me, a set of sheets. Any working-class housewife would have known better.

Genya and Sasha dragged the mattresses, bedding, and divan cushions down to the yard for me and we beat them with slats of wood. Feathers flew. When we brought the clean bedding back to the clean flat, no one said a word. Although I was sure everyone appreciated the lessening of the infestation, they had to feign indifference so they wouldn't jeopardize their bohemian cachet. Anton pointedly restored the gritty underlayer as soon as he could.

I developed new respect for housewives—what a lot of work even the tiniest bit of cleanliness entailed. To wash, you pumped water, brought heavy pails up the flights of stairs. If you wanted it hot, you boiled it on the small stove, and sometimes it tipped over—what a mess. To wash clothes was a monumental task. Anton loathed seeing female laundry strung across the room. The domestic aspects of life must have recalled some childhood indignities for him. He believed somehow he'd emerged full grown from literature via some sort of immaculate mental conception. He held up my newly washed panties for general inspection. "Are these the drawers that launched a thousand ships?"

And yet despite the dirt and the cold, the battle with bugs and the spartan diet, life in our small room was ferociously interesting. We read and talked and argued and read some more. On the shelves, Apollinaire and Khlebnikov and Mayakovsky pressed up against *The Lay of Igor's Campaign* and Balmont's translations of Poe and Arthur Conan Doyle. Dostoyevsky faced off with Rimbaud. They even had my little book, *This Transparent Twilight*.

"I wouldn't fall in love with just anyone," Genya said when I'd first noticed, putting his arm around my waist, burying his nose in my hair.

"Baaah," said Gigo. They snorted and whinnied and oinked. Any sign of tenderness or lust brought mockery from our fellows. Only Sasha tolerated us—like Genya, he hid a romantic heart inside his futurist breast.

The difficulty of maintaining a love affair in a room occupied by anywhere from four to eight talkative poets couldn't be overestimated. Genya and I slept most nights as chastely as Tristan and Isolde. The frustration! His chest against my back, we furtively made love while the others slept—and God knew whether they really did. If the divan creaked the smallest bit, Anton would call out, "Lo, the turtledove shits on my head!" And I was not by nature a quiet girl in bed. How ironic—in the gold and green room on the Catherine Canal, I could keen and moan, but in this liberated milieu, I had to stifle my cries in a pillow. A wonder that the poor got children at all. Though we knew that coitus interruptus was not the most efficient method of contraception, we didn't always have the money for *preservativy*. And if I became pregnant? It would be Genya's child—the ultimate futuristic improvisation.

But these difficulties and irritations were small sacrifice compared to the camaraderie and improvisation of our artistic life. I felt liberated. I'd made the leap, left my family and that old world behind. No more straddling stools. Such a relief to be wholly myself, to live without lying, to reach out, to try new things, to let curiosity unfold. Every day was an adventure, and I rested my head on Genya's broad chest every night. He always smelled good to me, of grass and wood.

But still I itched—my hair, my groin, my armpits. I smelled so bad that I sometimes woke myself up at night. I'd never been so dirty in my life. And what would I do when my period came? Everyone in the room would know. I could ask Zina, but she hated me so much.

"Can you smell me?" I whispered to Genya.

"The *banya*'s right around the corner." He shifted behind me, pulled me against him, his breath in my ear. I was mortified at his evasion.

The *banya*…akh, I knew where it was. I went by it every day, a windowless storefront on Kazanskaya Street. I didn't want to tell him that the idea terrified me. I'd never been to a public *banya*. I knew they would laugh at me if they knew. *What kind of Russian are you?* But Father was strictly opposed to them, felt they were unsanitary, breeding grounds for disease. The toilet on the landing was bad enough, but at least you were alone in there.

"It's not so bad," Genya said. "Zina can show you."

"Zina can show you what?" she asked from the table. No such thing as privacy in a Poverty Artel.

Somehow Genya assumed that Zina and I would become friends. What he didn't know about women. He never realized that Zina had considered him hers, that in her overheated imagination, I had broken up their love affair with my false bourgeois charms and sexual tricks—though Genya swore there'd never been anything between them. She dogged me, trying to diminish me in his eyes, like a little terrier, more aggressive to compensate for her small size. Sometimes I'd catch her studying me, as if trying to figure out where to slip in the dagger. I'd be damned if I would admit my squeamishness to her.

That dull gray November day, people shouldered past me—a man hurrying by with a shabby briefcase, a woman fighting the raw wind with what looked like a huge sack of doorknobs. I couldn't stand there forever in the cold. I steeled myself and pushed open the battered green door marked ZHENSHCHINY. *Women.*

Small and windowless, the anteroom was clad in peeling wallpaper the color of bread mold. No one sat at the counter. I didn't know what to do next. "Hello?" I called out. An attendant, a female dwarf, stormed in from the other room. Then, taking a second look at me, she smiled. I supposed my coat and hat were of better quality than what was usually seen here. She instructed me on payment—fifty kopeks for the *banya*, fifty for soap and a towel—calling me *milaya*, pointing out the reasonable fee, "not like those fancy places on Sadovaya." She led me into a dressing room, indicated the hook where I was to put my clothing, and waited—for a tip. But I could only give her a few small coins. She scowled when she looked at them, shoved me toward a wooden door.

On the other side it was—Goya. Twenty, twenty-five naked women crowded together in a large wet wooden washroom. A hideously fat woman scrubbed her neighbor's bony back. A toothless granny held up the flab of her stomach to get at her hairless *zhenshchinost'*. Wrinkled, contorted feminine forms of every variety—hair, no hair…I wanted to run for the door, but I'd already paid my hard-earned ruble, and the dwarf would know what a coward I was. I would never be able to show my face here again.

The sight of them blistered my eyes. I'd seen a hundred paintings entitled *In the Bath*, where rosy beauties waded knee-deep in picturesque rivers and washed their long hair. Brown soap never appeared in Rubens. This was the thing itself, the squalor of human life. Age and decay. It was one thing to see bent backs under brown shawls, sagging stomachs faintly suggested by full dresses, breasts swinging low under bodices and aprons, genitals quite invisible, and another to see them revealed in their horrific variety. Bodies covered with wounds, with sores, rashes, bruises, welts, and worse. Bandages kicked into a corner. I could just imagine what Father would say, with his concern for public health. And Mother... I couldn't stop looking at their tragic feet, their twisted toes like the claws of some horrible bird. I could see why Jesus would want to wash the feet of the poor.

Woman. How could one not pity her, with that forked stem, that tube for food and babies? This one— expanded like overyeasted bread. That one— contracted like a fallen soufflé. Emptied out, gouged like clay, clawed, bruised, imprinted with the devastation of gravity and years. I felt every inch the foreigner, visiting not from abroad but from the land of youth and beauty. They stared at me, too, at my smooth, pale flesh with its constellations of freckles, the wide-spaced breasts Genya found so stirring. The flame of my hair above and below. Conspicuous as an albino on safari. I moved to the buckets by the tap in the wall, filled one, and found a place on a bench where I could wash, concentrate on the steaming hot water and not the Rabelaisian sight all around me.

Hot water! Such luxury. I would not have imagined in my earlier life that someday it would make me weep with gratitude. I washed with the small bar of lye laundry soap the dwarf had sold me, imitating the others, squatting with the bucket between my legs, modestly scrubbing, then sudsing my neck, my short hair, rinsing again and again—what divinity, what bliss. I felt sorry for the women wrestling with their long skeins of hair. They must have to run home with it wet and dry it over the stove before they caught cold. Why didn't they cut it?

But slowly, as I watched them patiently, proudly comb it out, I realized that lives so brutally hard might need such impractical beauty, that this little indulgence—long flowing hair—might be their sole grace note, to be savored rather than suffered.

I knew so little about life.

A cloud of billowing steam escaped from a wooden door. A woman staggered out, lay on a bench, pink as a salmon, steam rising from her skin as from a dish of noodles. It seemed there were more infernos to explore. I gathered my fortitude and my towel and pushed through into the mystery.

Searing steam, fragrant with the smell of green wood, revealed only vague smears of pink and motion, the sounds of rustling slaps as women flailed one another with bundles of birch twigs, leaves still attached. Through the mist, I found an empty place on a lower bench. My fellow bathers gradually materialized out of the blistering fog, like a photograph in a tank. An immense woman encased in fat like a walrus took center stage, flanked by an old woman who looked like a melting candle and a younger one whose shoulders and breasts revealed the shocking marks of repeated beatings—some bruises still livid, others already faded toward green and yellow like a forest floor. On the upper, hotter bench, shriveled old *babas* sat with backs like question marks, bent from a lifetime of standing over stoves, brooms, children.

A strapping girl with long black braids and full ripe breasts like blue-veined planets emerged from the steam to throw a ladle of water onto the stove. It spat and hissed and clouds obscured the scene. I liked it better that way, though the heat was phenomenal. I felt less glaringly out of place. Just when I'd begun to relax and enjoy the feeling of being clean and safely invisible, the fat woman hawked and spat on my foot. Had she really? I stared at the thick yellow glob of phlegm oozing down my instep. *"Burzhui,"* she sneered. "I could eat you for breakfast." The others tittered, waiting to see what I would do.

I'd been to a girls' school—I knew she would keep it up unless I stopped her. I got up and washed it off with the dipper. "So that's how you got so fat."

The women hooted. The fat one narrowed her piggish eyes.

I sat back down. "Watch out for her," said the woman to my left under her breath, a rangy woman of late middle age, long breasts scarred vertically—from nursing, I imagined. I recognized her. The woman from my courtyard. *Put the legs of the beds in kerosene.* "She runs a booth in the Haymarket. She's mean as a bucket of snakes."

"She lives with all those poets on Grivtsova," said a

voice down the bench. "They're all crazy as bedbugs."

I was shocked. I hadn't imagined anyone knew who we were. No one ever talked to us.

"She take them one at a time or all at once?" said a woman in a felt hat. I would have liked a hat like that—my ears were burning up.

"In that dog kennel they live in?" said our neighbor. "It would have to be all at once. No place for the queue."

Everyone laughed—even me, although the joke was at my expense.

The girl with the globelike breasts squealed. "Ooh, the blond—that's my idea of a man." I wondered if Sasha knew he had an admirer in the neighborhood. I hoped for Dunya's sake he didn't. Those breasts could smother him outright.

I slicked my hand down my arm, the sweat pouring. Was I getting dirtier or cleaner? I couldn't resist licking it, tasting the salt.

"Give me the big one," said a woman twice the girl's age. "Prince Ivan. Now *that's* a man."

Sage nods all around. Clearly they knew whom she was talking about. *Prince Ivan*. I imagined how Genya would laugh.

How strange, though…they *knew* us. They had *ideas* about us. Here we thought we were living in a world of our own making. It never occurred to us that it was a fishbowl, that others saw everything, drew conclusions, too. We lived in a real world where our futurist experiments meant nothing, where nobody cared about Victor Shklovsky.

"One more bastard in the courtyard by summer—you heard it here first," said the rangy woman, elbowing me goodheartedly. "Take my word for it and kiss those pretty girls goodbye." My breasts.

Unlikely. It wasn't easy to make love in the Poverty Artel, four or five people listening to your every breath. "In the future," I said, "there won't be bastards. People won't even know what that means."

The way the women stared, I wished I hadn't spoken, that I'd just enjoyed the sweating and let them think what they liked. Now I had to explain myself. "Children won't be the property of fathers. All children will be the same. The whole property basis of marriage is obsolete."

"Intelligentka," one said with a laugh. "Vote list number three!" another called out from the steam. List number 3 was the Bolshevik slate in the upcoming election.

Their disdain was a challenge. Who was a *burzhui* now? "Kollontai said that for a woman, love should be no more important than drinking a glass of water." Something I remembered Varvara quoting.

"What, are we men now?" the spitting walrus demanded.

"Who drinks water anyway?" said a woman in the steam, her words punctuated by the slap of birch twigs. "Too much trouble. Pump and boil..."

A tiny babushka on the bench above me patted my shoulder. "I've been married three times. I'd rather have a glass of water."

"I'd rather have a drink of vodka than a man," said a blond woman combing her hair. "Though I hardly remember either one."

"I'll take Ivan," said the woman in the felt hat. "And he can bring the vodka."

"Actually, he's mine," I said. "But you can have one of the others. How about the tall skinny one? He could use a girlfriend."

They howled. They all knew which one I was talking about. "He's the craziest one of all," said my neighbor. "I have to keep the milk covered when he goes by."

I wondered if Anton knew that he'd been passed over by the wives of Grivtsova Alley.

"He goes with whores," said a woman sitting on the bench across from me. Her thighs looked like they'd been eaten by mice. "I've seen him up the street."

My big ears knew a piece of ripe intelligence when they heard one.

"Who else would take him?" said the woman from my courtyard. "He's so sour, he scares the vinegar."

"He's got that limp," said a woman savagely slashing at herself with a birch flail. "Must be why he's not in the army. But the others—what's their excuse?"

The birch twigs thwacked disapprovingly, making it hotter. The green scent permeated every inch of the room, whose walls I hadn't yet seen.

The girl with the braids threw another ladle on the stove. Instantly the heat redoubled. The women disappeared. Suddenly the girl was right in front of me. "You don't believe in love?"

I was grateful for the change of subject. "When women have to trade on love, it's an offense to love. Worrying about who will take care of us—that's not love, is it? In socialism, marriage will be untainted by commerce."

"*Zhili-buili,*" said the blond woman above us. "You'll see what's what when you get a couple of kids."

Thwack...

"Without a man, who's going to take care of you?"

"Lenin," said the fat woman, and everyone laughed. She folded her giant arms across her breasts. "You'll see. Couple of kids, your man's out of work, you're coughing up cotton like half these sad sisters. Stand in the queues after a day on the factory line, then let's see about your *lya lya fa fa*. You'll be the one sobbin', 'Where's that Lenin now to take care of me and my brats?'" My interlocutor nodded sagely with her three chins. "Wait and see—a man's never there when you need him."

Laughter rose around me. Yes, they were right to laugh at me. Seventeen years old—who was I to lecture women about anything? No husband, no children. An *intelligentka,* I'd never worked a day in my life. The room started to spin. My neighbor and the girl with the braids caught me before I fainted, helped me stumble out the wooden door, laid me down on the bench, and threw a pail of cold water on me. "She'll be all right," the older one said.

I lay staring up at the wooden beams in the ceiling, thinking about the women in the steam and those washing at the taps. In ten years, fifteen, this would be me, no longer carefully tended and fed and ministered to by dentists and doctors, hairdressers and dancing masters. This woman washing herself had lived on bad bread, horsemeat, and fish soup. She lifted children with that back, walked miles on those arthritic feet. Women like her were invisible to men like my father, who never noticed who did his laundry and cooked his dinner. He never thought twice about who painstakingly stitched his suits, wove his scarves, fashioned his shoes, though he'd been so sure he knew what was best for them.

Soon enough my beauty would vanish. On Grivtsova Alley or someplace just like it, I would lose my looks, my health, everything I'd ever taken for granted. The realization shook me. How stupid I was. I was not from another planet, I was not a visitor here. This was also my fate, my future. My own curved back, my bruises and sores that would not heal, my sagging breasts, missing teeth, poverty. My suffering, unless the Bolsheviks were able to construct a just society—and how fast could they do it?

Oh, to give these women their beauty back. Or if not that, then something—nobility, some recognition of their struggle. I was a poet, that was something I could do. This woman had once been young, maybe even beautiful. Her disproportionately large hands spoke of years of hard labor. Were they not as dignified as my smooth ones? More. I loved the pleasure she took in soaping her gray hair in hot water, her eyes closed, savoring. What were all my opinions and ideals worth compared to this one woman, no longer young, washing her hair in a public *banya,* humming under her breath?

29 *Fait Accompli*

HOW STRANGE TO FIND myself in such a politically thrilling moment without any inside information or pressure from either Varvara or my father. I was free to decide for myself. The Transrational Interlocutors of the Terrestrial Now leaned Bolshevik, though Anton and Gigo declared themselves Anarcho-Khlebnikovist. In the upcoming elections, the SRs were the frontrunners, representing the interests of the peasants and the less programmatic socialists. But there were lists for everything and everyone. Mohammedans, the Jewish Bund, Old Believers, rural proprietors and landowners, a feminist League for Women's Equal Rights. There were cooperativists, Cossacks, Ukrainians, Germans, Bashkirs. Everyone had a list but the Theosophists. There was even a Kadet list, led by Paul Miliukov, back for another try at leading the country, along with

Terekhov and a few others I recognized, but I saw no mention of Dmitry Makarov, either as a Kadet delegate or as one of the arrestees.

"And what is your platform?" Zina demanded of the Anarcho-Khlebnikovists as she singed her split ends with the burning coal of her cigarette, adding the stench of human hair to the already smoky miasma. A blizzard had threatened all day, and this evening, its first tentative flakes fell past our window.

Gigo, seated cross-legged on the coveted divan, leafed through the pages of his tattered, three-hundred-page futurist novel in verse. "We of the Anarcho-Khlebnikovist Party oppose governments and zoos of any kind."

Anton steadied a walnut on the table and placed a chisel he'd taken from Sasha's bag into the crevice, as if he were performing surgery. "Down with all parliaments." He brought the hammer down on the chisel and neatly split the shell in two. Half went skittering off the table. "No congresses, zemstvos, or queues. No more choirs. No sing-alongs." Sasha picked the half walnut up off the floor and tossed it back to the editor. "Free the periodic table!" Anton said. "We demand free air. Free poverty for all." He extracted the meat with his pencil. "Vote list minus two."

"Free the feet of the women of the *banya*," I said from the stool where I sat posing for Sasha as he painted a cubist portrait of me onto the door. "Free their bunions, their fallen arches."

"Free the women of the Terrestrial Now," Sasha said, painting my nose in. "Free their lips and their adorable backsides. Free their freckles. Free the blondes, brunettes, and redheads. Free Vera Kholodnaya!"

Sitting at the table, Genya screwed an empty half shell into his eye socket like a monocle. Gigo's mother had sent the sack from Georgia, and walnuts had become our main source of nutrition. He screwed in a second shell. "In the land of the blind, a blind man shall rule."

"Free the alphabet from its unspeakable bondage," said Gigo from the divan. "Free the *ya*. *Ya* before *A*. The last shall be first."

At Genya's side, Zina burped and sighed, fist under ribs. "These walnuts give me gas. I hope to God whoever wins gets some food into the city. I'm inflating like a dirigible. One night I'm going to explode."

Only the Bolsheviks were surprised when the SRs won the election. No one else could have imagined it would turn out differently. Although we in Petrograd could fool ourselves into thinking we were an industrialized nation, the factory proletariat was a sprinkle of salt in the vast bowl of kasha that was Russia, a dollop of sour cream in that great vat of borscht. "The vanguard of the working class" could not carry the day in a country where most people still plowed behind a horse and wove their own clothes and bast shoes. In that Russia, *revolution* still meant "Land and Freedom," the SR slogan.

Though I could not vote, being only seventeen, I had my favorites. I liked the wide embrace of the SRs, their historical roots, but it was also true that they didn't have their eyes on the future. The bulk of the SRs were Defensists, wanting to fight the war to the end. They were old-fashioned populists of the last century, fighting old battles, while the Marxists were coolly working their program like mathematicians, organizing the proletariat and, even more important, the soldiers. They were the future.

Though they lost, the Bolsheviks made a good showing—they won a quarter of the vote throughout the country, and they proved overwhelmingly popular in the big cities, among the industrial workers, in the army, and in the fleet. What would happen now? Only the Bolsheviks would get us out of this war.

At dinnertime we descended on the Katzevs en masse. Dunya swooned at the sight of Sasha in the doorway with an armful of flowers shaped and painted from squares of *Izvestia* and *Pravda*, an adorable hint of blue paint clinging to his shaggy forelock. As for me, a different girl entered that apartment from the one who'd cringed with them under the tabletop the day the soldiers burst in. Different even from the girl I'd been when I'd returned from Maryino. Now I was a free woman, on my own, with my lover, coins from a street performance jingling in my pocket. My hair was rough, my clothes becoming worn from heavy use. I'd gone from windowsill pussycat to something of an alley cat.

Solomon Moiseivich greeted us from the divan, folding his *Novaya Zhizn*—and holding out his arms for an embrace. "So you've become a bohemian," he said, kissing me three times. He wore his Bukhara cap and a caftan. Now Sofia Yakovlevna came in from the kitchen, and I reveled in the unfeigned pleasure on her face. "I wondered where you'd been hiding yourself."

But Mina seemed less thrilled as she glanced up at us from her pile of homework. "Right on time," she said sardonically. "Could you smell dinner?"

"All the way from Grivtsova Alley," I said and pinched her upper arm. *Don't be like that.*

Meanwhile, Gigo bestowed a bag of walnuts on Sofia Yakovlevna. "With my compliments," he said. Genya handed her a loaf of bread we'd all pitched in to buy and followed her into the kitchen. She was like catnip to all the boys, with her soft bosom and kind round face. I helped Mina clear off the table—chemistry volumes, journals, notes in her small, neat hand—and felt a tiny pang of envy. Was I still jealous of her being at the university? I played with the feeling as you would toy with a slice of lemon, deciding whether it was too sour to eat. A little, I decided, but I wouldn't have traded places with her. I was a poet among poets now, living the revolution. I couldn't have stuffed myself back into that book bag, that lecture-hall seat.

I went back to the kitchen to see if I could help. Sofia Yakovlevna had Genya stirring the soup while she cut up more vegetables, doubling the recipe to accommodate the unexpected guests. Seeing me there, she caught me by the sleeve and pulled me to the sink, where she could talk under the cover of running water. They still had running water—imagine. "So are you happy, Marina?" she asked.

I turned to watch Genya solemnly stirring the soup as if the future of mankind depended upon it. "Very happy," I said.

Worry argued with hope across her face as she washed a dish, a knife. "Will you marry?"

"Marriage isn't revolutionary," I said.

She sighed and wiped her hands on a towel. I could tell she was about to say something, but she just shook her head and smiled.

Six Transrationalists and seven Katzevs gathered around the big table, passing bread and garlicky pickles as Sofia Yakovlevna ladled up the borscht. All here, all together, everyone I loved. Except for Seryozha. I'd been writing to him faithfully, telling him what was going on here, but all I had to go on was the name of the institution, the Bagration Military School, and the address in Moscow. Maybe they'd censored my letters. Maybe the postal system had broken down, but I never received a response. The papers said there'd been fighting in Moscow, where the anti-Bolshevik forces were more organized, but after a week, their cadets, too, surrendered, and now the city was coming around to the new way of life.

Looking around the table, I was amazed at how we'd

all grown up this year—Shusha, Dunya…Mina was wearing lipstick, her hair in a soignée chignon. Genya sat beside me, and Solomon Moiseivich beside him. They'd fallen into conversation about the elections. Genya was furious about the Bolshevik loss. He attributed it to the fact that the lists, drawn up months earlier by the Provisional Government, didn't properly represent the new coalition between leftist SRs and the Bolsheviks, which he was convinced would have won. But the Bolsheviks still didn't have the numbers. "They'll have to restage the election," he insisted. "We didn't get rid of landlords to be ruled by ignoramuses in bast shoes genuflecting to painted boards."

"The SRs got the majority," Mina's father said. "It's the will of the nation."

"The Bolsheviks have to reach the villages if they want to win in Russia," said Aunt Fanya.

"The hell with the villages. I'm sick of the villages. I'm so sick of them I could scream." Genya's deep-seated hatred of peasants, stemming from his childhood on the Volga, always caught me off guard. He was otherwise such a loving, enthusiastic man, so his hatreds seemed all the more shocking.

Zina, seated across the table, was quick to jump into the fray, pointing her spoon at Solomon Moiseivich. "The advanced proletariat is the revolutionary class," she said. I hated the way she spouted stock phrases, like a child reciting her lesson. I could take that behavior from Varvara—she'd actually read Lenin and

Plekhanov and Kropotkin, *Das Kapital* in German. Zina just memorized slogans.

"If it wasn't for the Petrograd worker, there wouldn't have been a revolution at all." Genya swept his arm in a gesture that barely missed his water glass. "The worker made this happen. Without the proletariat, the peasant would still be asleep in the haystack scratching at his lice."

Just the mention of lice made me itch. Gigo ignored all the fulminations. He was doing sleight-of-hand tricks with his napkin for Shusha.

"It's a peasant country," said Solomon Moiseivich thoughtfully. "You can't make a revolution without them."

"But who should lead?" Genya said, letting his heavy hand fall to the table, making our dishes jump. "It's got to be the most advanced. The head has to lead." He poked himself in the forehead, hard enough to drive a nail. "The revolution's the future, and there aren't any plows in it." He rested his arm across the back of my chair, and I saw how Mina blanched to see this familiar gesture. So each of us had something the other had missed.

Mina's father sipped his tea with an indulgent smile. "There will always be plows, *sinok*." *Little son.* "Someone has to bring in a crop. Unless you're going to eat Bolshevik handbills."

"Now there's a field of plenty," Mina said.

"I've lived out there." Genya's voice rising, his former good-fellow expression gone. "None of you have lived like that. The peasant doesn't care about social-ism. *Land and Freedom?* Once the peasant gets his land, he'll consider himself free, and the hell with you. Just you watch."

I waited for the echo of his voice to die down before I said, "You have to agree that the peasants *should* have the land. Without the soldiers, there would have been no revolution, and they're all peasants. God knows they've waited long enough."

He turned to me, hurt and surprised. "They only want to be the next landlord, don't you see?" He backed away from the table to give his gestures more room. "They all have capitalist aspirations. The work-ers are the only ones who will protect the revolution."

Sofia Yakovlevna watched me, and the expression on her face had nothing to do with the revolution and everything to do with my new life—to wit, Genya. *Is he always like this?*

"Whoever gets power will find a way to keep it," An-ton said from the foot of the table, where he perched on a footstool between Dunya and Shusha, enveloping them in a haze of cigarette smoke. "Bolshevik, Men-shevik, the Committee for the Preservation of Wigs—they'll set up a nice system of privilege for themselves and their friends."

"Finally, a man to make some sense," said Uncle Aaron, the old-time anarchist. "I'm with Mephistophe-les over there."

"The workers are no geniuses," Anton continued, dropping ashes into his soup. The younger Katzev girls watched, horrified and fascinated.

Dunya stole shy glances down the table at Sasha. He smiled at her, wiping his moustache on the back of his hand. Gigo pulled a walnut out of Shusha's ear, then a spoon out of his nose, making her laugh.

Now Genya couldn't sit still anymore, he was up and pacing behind Anton, who turned around to speak to him. "You're all mistaken if you think the worker is going to create a utopia," Anton said. "Once you have a concentration of power, you're screwed no matter who's in charge."

Uncle Aaron picked up the black flag of anarchism where he sat at the corner of the table. "The state's a flawed tool. But I have more confidence in the people than you do, my smoky friend."

"The people are a monster," said Anton. "Individually bad enough, but once there's a committee, you're sunk."

"I for one will take whoever clears the garbage." Sofia Yakovlevna surprised us by the sharpness of her tone. She ladled a bit more soup into her husband's bowl. "The SRs knew how to keep the streets clean." It was true. Municipal services had almost ceased since the Bolshevik takeover, and the city was rapidly becoming a rotting trash heap. Everyone prayed for a good heavy snow. "And we could use some police protection while they're at it. It's one thing to take the

Palais de Justice, but to fire the police? These Red Guards are hopeless. I'm afraid to leave the apartment."

The common sense of this was undebatable. It's what they talked about in the bathhouse as well—not the future but the present, the one outside the door. Where was that in the Bolshevik schema? Yet it was almost counterrevolutionary to mention it.

"They can only do so much," Zina explained. "If we wanted just clean streets and police, we could have kept the tsar."

Luckily for us, we lived in revolutionary times, which meant that the trash and the police would have to wait for bigger things. Jam tomorrow, as Alice would have said.

The Constituent Assembly walked into the Tauride Palace for the first time on an ice-covered January day. The snow glittered pink and lilac. We had turned out with thousands of others to watch the delegates arrive. I wondered if Father was here. I bet he was, hiding somewhere in the crowd. He wouldn't want to miss this historic moment, a freely elected democratic body to rule Russia. Genya was still angry about the Bolshevik loss. Like many of the spectators, he and Zina shouted, "Soviet power!" and "We demand new elections!" but I felt tears welling up, seeing the solemn representatives of the Constituent Assembly move into the palace, preparing to sit for the first time in history.

I hadn't paid much attention to the presence of the Red Guards that day. I assumed they were part of the grand occasion. But the next morning, I read on a wall poster that the Red Guards had taken over the first session of the Constituent Assembly and that it would remain closed thereafter. The workers' militia hadn't been there to protect the assembly but to close it down, lock it out. The Bolsheviks had never intended to give up power, whether the transition was legitimate or not.

Genya was ecstatic. "It would have just been the Provisional Government all over again—don't you see?" he argued. "Talk, talk, talk. The war's grinding us to dust, and the industrialists back running the country. It would only have been a matter of time until we had to get rid of them. No more kowtowing to retrograde classes. That's over."

I understood his argument but I couldn't share it, not deep down in my bourgeois heart. This was a fairly elected body. Genya and I weren't speaking by the time we drifted up to Znamenskaya Square, where speakers of all political stripes pleaded their causes, every lamppost resonating with hot oratory. Genya was the one who spotted Varvara exhorting a crowd from the base of the Alexander III statue. "Look. Your friend's moving up in the world."

I didn't want to talk to Varvara. I didn't even want to look at her, not after what she had done to me. It would have been one thing if my departure had been voluntary, but it was another to have my best friend rip my skin off for me and hand it back to me as if it were a cape.

"Only the workers can lead the workers!" she shouted. "We, the laboring classes, told the Constituent Assembly we *demand* it recognize the October Revolution, *our* revolution! And they refused!"

"Soviet power!" Genya shouted. "Down with the lackeys of the imperialists!"

Varvara saw me now, stumbled, but quickly recovered. "The majority of the Constituent Assembly *rejected* our demand for Soviet power, the highest democracy in the world. They refused to recognize our achievement—your achievement!"

"Down with the Bolshevik grab for power!" a solidly built man belted out. "The Constituent Assembly represents all of us!"

"Parliamentary democracy is a bourgeois throwback," she shot back. "It ignores the leadership role of the revolutionary working class!" She held her hand high. "The Bolshevik revolution represents the triumph of the working class."

"*Urah!*" shouted Genya along with other pro-Bolshevik elements of the crowd against the booing and furious heckling by Constituent Assembly advocates. Rhetoric flew back and forth. Varvara gave as good as she got, never folding, never tiring. I wondered where I would be now if she hadn't pushed me into my new life. She'd been the violent midwife of my personal revolution, forcing me to do the very thing I'd been afraid of, to stand up for what I believed in, out in the open. I'd been happy to go behind people's backs, but she forced me to take a side—exactly as the Bolsheviks had just done to the country.

They had flushed us out of our old cherished notions, our beloved dreams in sepia frames. Under the nose of the tsar and his bronze horse, Varvara argued that the Bolsheviks couldn't take the chance that the other parties would chip away what the worker had wrought. Yet I couldn't quite shake my regret that we never got the chance to see this thing, an elected assembly. To turn it over in our hands, marvel at it, and decide for ourselves what it was. To have February again, just for a little while—that's all I wanted. Maybe I would have come around to her point of view eventually. But everything had happened so fast. The assembly had sat for just one night, and now it was gone, and we would never know it for itself. Just as Varvara had done that October night in my parents' salon, the Bolsheviks had swept in and made up our minds for us. *Fait accompli.*

30 *Former People*

IT WAS A HARD WINTER. The only thing heating the flat was our own fevered talk. Our little tin stove was voracious, an idol, a Baal, a starving beast:

Gap-toothed, ravenous
Secret wolf, hushabye
For you we go a-hunting
For you we'll tear this town to shreds
Feed you its savory bones.

We tore down fences to slake its hunger, stole siding from abandoned houses, broke off slats from stairway banisters. We burned whatever we could pry loose, though it was considered a serious crime now. The Bolsheviks were rightly afraid that the freezing citizens would consume the city like termites. But stoves must eat. Petrograd became ever more dilapidated — windows broken, boarded up, traces of bullets on the walls. Rent became a thing of the past — only the bourgeoisie had to pay it — and that was a blessing, as we had few sources of income. Anton was our main provider of cash, through a stipend from *Okno*'s patroness, Galina Krestovskaya, an actress with poetic aspirations. Genya and Sasha made money hauling junk, unloading carts, plastering walls with newspaper broadsides. Gigo disappeared from time to time, returning with packets of cash, evasive about their source. I continued to sing for loose change — not only the revolutionary songs, although my repertoire was expanding. Often people just wanted to hear something beautiful or nostalgic. *Do not awaken my memories... you'll not return...my soul does cry...*

But it wasn't enough. I had to find some real work.

Factory work would be best, something with dignity that would confer proletarian credentials. But one needed a labor book to work, get housing, do anything now.

"Ask Varvara to help you," Genya said. "She knows people."

"I'm not talking to her." How she would love that, for me to come a-begging.

That morning, I walked up the icy, unshoveled street to our local district soviet on Kazanskaya Street, my scarf tight around my neck, my hat drawn down, taking small mincing steps and trying not to fall. My route sent me past the familiar sad array of "Former People"—the previously well to do, now outmoded, terrorized, standing against buildings, silently offering bits and pieces of their former lives—silver spoons, a lace-edged towel. A new organ of the government had recently been formed to fight the hydra of counterrevolution, sabotage, and speculation. The Extraordinary Commission, *Chrezvychaynaya Komissiya,* it was called. And it considered all private trade, even the necessary sale of petty personal goods, to be speculation, punishable with confiscation and arrest. In the spirit of the time, impatient and modern, it was known by its initials—*Che-Ka.* Cheka.

Despite the danger, a woman in a thin black coat held out something discreetly wrapped in paper. Her deadened face came to life as I passed. I supposed she smelled my own Formerness. Her voice was low and plaintive. "For God's sake, child. It's a brass clock. From Hamburg. A hundred rubles. Fifty."

I didn't have ten rubles, much less need of a clock. But that coat was too thin for the weather—she was blue as a Picasso. I tried to imagine my mother standing by a building in the shadows, trying to sell a clock, but I knew it was impossible, even if she were starving. I gave the woman the money from my pocket, around eighty kopeks. Most of the Formers had left by then, heading for the south, where there was more food and fewer Bolsheviks, or striking out for the West.

The Kazansky District Soviet, housed in an ugly building that was once a police station, gave the lie to the notion that the city had emptied out, however. There must have been a thousand souls packed inside, standing in queues that snaked down steamy, murky halls, then folded over and doubled back. Half of ambulatory Petrograd must have been there. It smelled of wet wood and wet coats and the ozone of terror.

"Labor books?" I asked a small woman wearing a man's greatcoat.

She pointed to the next floor up.

The Bolsheviks turned out to be as fond of bureaucracy as the tsarists had been. If only one could eat red tape. I struggled through the closely packed bodies and found the right queue on a back stairway. People stood with their hands in their pockets, silent, each wrapped in his or her own private worries. No one felt like commiserating. The man in front of me had a cold. He sneezed in threes. I grew sleepy from the heat, my feet and ankles swelling as we moved forward by centimeters. I dozed and thought of the spacious Krestovsky flat where we held our poetry evenings—specifically, of the butter cookies Galina Krestovskaya served. Her husband owned seven snack bars in Petrograd theaters. Their flat had heat and hot water and a working telephone. I could taste those cookies melting in my mouth, good as anything Vaula ever made. Where did they get the sugar, the flour? Money could buy almost anything, even now. Except Anton's respect. He was no more civil toward his patroness than he was toward anyone else, though she was supporting us all. His scorn only intrigued her. He didn't even publish her poems in the journal she bankrolled.

Passing open office doors, I listened as bourgeois petitioners pleaded with rough, barely literate soldier "clerks" and worker "secretaries" to solve this or that problem, or let them off the rent. "The water isn't even working!" The secretaries could barely write their own names. However, public service employees were still on strike, ever since the Bolshevik coup, so the local soviets had to find staff wherever they could. I considered joining the Bolsheviks—I could be working here instead of queuing like a penitent—but I wasn't nearly fanatical enough. The Bolsheviks were more than a political party, they were a religious order.

I'd made it up the stairs now, close enough to see

the front of the line, where a woman pleaded with the soldier-clerk, a weary-looking man with a big untrimmed moustache. "I *am* a proletarian," she insisted, though she wore some stuffed bird atop her ancient hat that clearly identified her as a Former.

"Birth certificate," the soldier said.

They needed a birth certificate?

"It's been lost," said the woman with a tremulous voice. "There was a house fire. My father was a carpenter. Mother—laundress."

"Next," the soldier said, indicating a woman two places in front of me.

I had to think of another story. I, too, had been planning on claiming proletarian origins, changing my name to Marina Moryeva. I'd practiced my story. *Born Harbin, China. Father, printer. Mother, seamstress.* Let them try to track that down.

"Please, Comrade." The woman with the bird hat would not move on. Now she started crying in earnest. "I have to work. No one's hiring us."

"Lady, look at all these people. Most of 'em worked all their lives. They've got skills. They haven't been lying around, living off our sweat. Now move along."

It was my turn. "Papers?" he asked, extending his hand, not looking at me.

I gave him my form but I didn't have any personal papers. They were all back on Furshtatskaya Street. My birth certificate, baptismal records, school transcripts. I didn't have a single one.

"My bag was stolen," I said. "On the tram. Please, what should I do?"

The soldier appeared to have some sort of indigestion, belching and thumping his chest with his fist. It was the bad bread we all ate. "Guess you'll have to write to China," he said with a smirk. "We're not handing out labor books like they're posies." Those small books, our very lifeline.

"But it's *China*."

"China," the comrade sighed. "That's a new one." He indicated the door with a disgusted thumb. "Next."

So it came to pass that on a bitter snowy January evening I swallowed my pride with a cup of barley soup and, together with Genya, crossed the Nikolaevsky Bridge over the frozen Neva to enter the broad, dark Lines of Vasilievsky Island—specifically, the Seventh Line, where Varvara had brought me to the illegal print shop that day. I knocked, and a pale suspicious face appeared in the doorway. Steel-rimmed glasses, pallid blue eyes. I asked for Varvara. "I don't know anyone by that name," he said.

Another man took the place of the first. "I'm looking for Varvara Razrushenskaya," I tried again. "I'm a friend of hers. We were distributing leaflets before the insurrection."

The second man squinted at me. "She's back in her mother's old flat," he said. "If you're her friend—you must know where it is."

"On the Sixteenth Line," I said.

The comrade nodded and closed the door.

Varvara's old building was more than a mile farther west. Half the streetlights were out on Bolshoy Prospect as we trudged and slipped along, trying not to break our necks. I was glad to have Genya by my side. I recognized the dark hulk of the brothel opposite Varvara's apartment house, but there were no women outside or in the windows. Was it the revolution or just the cold? Inside her building, the stairs had grown gap-toothed just like ours. It seemed strangely quiet after our noisy tenement. People here were hunched behind their doors over their scraps of food, listening for criminals or for the step of the Cheka making a raid. Our building was too poor for raids, so we'd escaped the worst of it. I stopped at her flat. I could hear voices inside. As soon as I knocked, they stopped talking. I knocked again. A familiar lean, sneering mug answered the door—the printer Kraskin—formerly Marmelzadt—smoking a crooked little cigar.

Varvara sat at the table, wearing a black sweater with a ragged collar, among six or seven comrades perched on stools and hunched on old tattered chairs, young men and women startled at the interruption. When I approached her, she stuck out her hand like a man. Her palm felt very dry. She nodded at Genya, and they, too, shook hands.

"Where's the countess?" I said, lowering the shawl

from my head but not taking off my coat—it was almost as cold in the flat as it was in the hall.

"Dead," Varvara said. She examined the ember on her hand-rolled cigarette. I couldn't tell whether her bluntness was to impress me or Kraskin, leaning against her chair back, or the cluster of comrades. *"Vot tak." Like that.* "She got into bed one day and turned her face to the wall. Said, 'I don't care to see any more of this.'" My infuriating friend considered me with a slightly amused, cruel expression, the same one that Kraskin wore. "So what brings you to this side of the river?"

"I've been looking for work," I said.

Kraskin's smirk toyed with his thin lips like a scrap of paper circling in dirty water. "Does this look like an employment agency?" he said.

"Excuse me, but I was talking to…her." *Friend* was out of the question.

Varvara leaned her chair back on its hind legs and planted her boots on the table. They were in terrible shape. "Try the telephone company. That's the place for nice bourgeois girls like you."

"As if you're not one," I snapped back. I didn't need her supercilious attitude. If I was going to claim proletarian status, change my biography, I needed industrial labor, not association with the anti-Bolshevik class. She owed me this. I wouldn't let her play with me to show off for Kraskin. I wondered what their relationship was. Though I couldn't really imagine her with a lover, he did seem to show up in too many places for them to be just comrades.

"Try the banks. The bourgeois workers are still on strike," she said.

"They'll show us, eh?" Genya laughed. "As if the Soviet's going to disappear without bank clerks and telephone operators."

"I don't want to be a bank clerk." I plucked the cigarette from Varvara's fingers and took a deep puff of the cheap *makhorka*. *Remember me?* I wanted to scream. "Find me a metal factory. A printworks. I'll make shoes, work in a tannery, weave."

"Bourgeois baby wants to play the proletarian," Kraskin mocked. "Oh what would Papa say?"

Genya clapped his hand on Kraskin's little bony shoulder. The top of the printer's head barely reached my lover's chin. "Hey, brother, who are you again? And why is this any of your business?"

"This isn't a game," Varvara stated flatly. "We can't fill these clerical jobs. And we can't take factory jobs from workers to flatter your revolutionary romanticism."

"Maybe I can be a robber," I said. "How's that for romantic?"

She let loose a great cloud of smoke above her head. "Better start soon, the field's getting crowded." It was true, more and more audacious criminal gangs were robbing apartment houses, bakeries, theaters — even in daylight. Krestovskaya's husband's snack bars were regular targets. Just the other day there had been an out-and-out gunfight in a theater between a gang and the Red Guards.

"I already went to the district soviet, but they wanted to see my papers."

"So?"

"I don't have any." I glared at her, not wanting to say, *You remember why, don't you?* "In any case, I need better ones." Ones that wouldn't scream *Class: bourgeois.* "You've got to help me."

Kraskin shook his head over his cigar. "Smolny'll love that."

Varvara turned on the sour-faced printer. "Why don't you show Genya what we're working on? He's a poet. Maybe he can make it sound better."

He took his arms off the back of her chair and touched his cap, ironically, and he and Genya drifted over to the group huddling by the stove and making notes on some pages. I sat down next to Varvara, shoulder to shoulder. She sighed, swung her booted feet to the floor, let her chair fall back to all four of its rickety legs. "All right. Get me your birth certificate, et cetera. I'll see what I can do. But it's going to be the telephone company, something like that. We need people on our side who can read and write, do sums. Unemployment's over the moon in the industrial sector. No materiel, no fuel. We need those jobs for the workers."

I could smell her scent, slightly sour, dirty hair plus

graphite and paper, apple cores. "I'm never going to forgive you, you know."

Her mouth twisted, trying to suppress a smile. "You can't play both sides. I just gave you a push. Don't be so sore. Look, if you're interested, he's still out there, making trouble, as you can imagine. He's on the Committee for the Salvation of the Fatherland and the Revolution as well as the Committee for the Defense of the Constituent Assembly. Tenacious, you have to give him that. But go back and get your papers. I'll see what I can do."

I had little choice but to return to Furshtatskaya Street and hope my papers were still there. They were like soap—essential, yet a part of life I'd never considered while I packed my pictures and poetry that night three months earlier. A whole world had passed away since I'd last walked down this broad avenue. The sidewalk had barely been cleared, the snow piled into high tunnels of icy white. So many things I hadn't known back then. What it was to be hungry, and tired, and bug-bitten, and restless for a moment of privacy. Looking down the block, I could easily see which apartments were still occupied and which had been abandoned—the exterior walls of the living flats showed dark, while the "dead" ones gleamed with silvery frost. So many dead buildings. Here was ours, still blue with white plasterwork, elegant even now, though I noticed the pipes of the little *bourgeoika* tin stoves dribbling smoke through some of the windows. Not enough coal or wood to stoke the big porcelain stoves anymore, not even up in this part of town.

I felt my way up the back stairs from the courtyard, tried the kitchen door. It swung open. The very path Varvara had taken that night in October. With all the robberies, I was amazed it was left unlocked. Frost grew thick on the windows of the large tiled kitchen. The stove, ice cold. All down the back hall, the doors to the servants' rooms stood open, revealing beds without mattresses, empty wardrobes. We'd read that the Red Guards had been carrying out a general confiscation of furniture and clothing from the bourgeoisie, to be re-distributed to the poor. So it had happened here, too. Feelings warred inside me. I was all for redistribution, yet I couldn't help feeling robbed.

My footsteps rang out in the empty rooms. I felt as though I'd entered my house in a dream. The cloak-room, where I had first kissed Kolya, looked so much larger with nothing in it—the Transrationalists could have lived there quite comfortably. In the main wing, the desolation was even more obvious. The foyer rug was missing, the marble-topped table lay on its side, too heavy to cart away. In the parlor, pieces of wood lit-tered the parquet, and empty frames of the art that nor-mally hung on the walls. The Repin portrait of Sery-ozha and the Vrubel were gone. A flush of anger re-turned.

I crept down to Father's office. Would my papers

still be there? The door gaped open revealing the oak file cabinet turned over, its drawers gone. The desk drawers, too, had been breached, broken open with some crude instrument, a hatchet or a crowbar. Yet the green-striped wallpaper was still the same, and, incredibly, photographs still hung on it. My brothers and I. Our Makarov grandparents. All of us at a picnic on the coast of Finland. Only one was missing—Volodya the cavalry officer on his sleek bay horse. Had Father removed it? Or had the Red Guards taken it as evidence of our family's allegiances? I took a photo of the three of us as children on the porch at Maryino, our legs hanging down, Volodya dark-skinned in a bathing costume, I in my braids and freckles, Seryozha with his floss-blond hair and enormous eyes.

The telephone still sat on the desk. I tried the receiver, depressed the cradle, and—mirabile dictu!—an operator came on the line. "Number, please."

"Sorry," I said, then hung up. Would that soon be me, my new Soviet life?

I turned to the big Russian stove in the corner of the room, and slid open a panel in the tile, revealing a metal-lined safe where we hid valuables and important documents, not so much out of fear of theft as fear of fire. I breathed a short prayer of gratitude—they were still there. Birth certificates, passports. My parents' elaborate wedding papers. My high school diploma and the letter of acceptance into the department of philology at Petrograd University. Only Father's documents were gone—passport, law degree, his first from Oxford, his MLitt, even his certificate from the Tenishev Gymnasium.

Surprisingly, stacks of ruble notes, gold coins, and Mother's jewelry—luminescent opals, Indian sapphires with their mysterious stars—were still intact. I took my own documents and a few rubles, stuffed them in my bag, slid the tile closed.

I knew I should go, but it had been three months since I'd seen these rooms. Who could have blamed me for nostalgia? The nursery was as it always had been, but dustier and ice cold. Here we had learned our letters, shared secrets, played endless games of *durak*. Here I had cast the wax that long-ago New Year's Eve. I knelt by the old rocking horse, pressed my nose to his, wrapped my arms around his wooden neck and horsehair mane. "I wish I could take you." The horse forgave me, he was filled with such love. Why hadn't some Red Guardsman taken him for his own children? "Be brave," I whispered to him.

My bedroom, by contrast, was a scene of devastation. Pictures askew, anything made of fabric gone: clothing, rugs, the bed just a skeleton of springs. But Seryozha's watercolor of the Finland shore still hung on the deep pink wall along with the poets' silhouettes he had so painstakingly cut with his fine-pointed scissors. I took them down and piled them on the bare bedsprings. My jewelry, long gone. The little drawer of the vanity table empty. But the photographs under the glass remained untouched. I pulled them out and stacked them on top of Seryozha's pieces.

Father's English bedroom had been even more thoroughly ransacked—clothing gone, wardrobe gaping. The dresser top lay bare of the beautiful toilet set that always rested there, the bone-handled brushes and combs for head and beard, tiny nail scissors, powders and pomades to tame his crinkly hair. Did I dare look into Mother's room?

I turned the door handle but found it locked. I knocked. "Hello?" Could she have lain down and turned her face to the wall? I began to beat the door with the heel of my hand. "Mama? It's Marina. Avdokia? Open up."

I heard the tiny click, the latch turning, like a sound from a grave. In the gap, Ginevra's frightened face. She pulled me inside, locked the door, and embraced me, patting me, touching my hair, my cheeks. "You're here...I can't believe it."

What a sight! Furniture had been squeezed into every last inch of space—a tumble of chests, chairs, and trunks like in an antiques shop. The nursery piano! They probably couldn't move the Bösendorfer. Three mismatched beds were lined up against the far wall. Mother, Avdokia, and *the English* had probably retreated to this bedroom so they could devote all the wood to one stove. In her ornate canopied bed, Mother sat propped up on pillows, her white hair a disordered nest. She was fumbling with something in her hands. At first I thought she was knitting, but there was nothing there. "Mama, where's Avdokia?" I was afraid to approach her.

"She'll be back. She's off selling a few things," Ginevra said. She hugged me suddenly, awkwardly. She was never very physical. "Oh, child." Her hand flew to her mouth, and her face withered like a cut bloom. She motioned for me to come out into the hallway. She was only twenty-eight, but she looked forty. Her lips trembled as she tried to speak.

"Is it Papa?"

She shook her head.

A great hand wrapped itself about my throat. *Volodya?*

She shook her head again and started to cry.

Seryozha. Oh God.

She told me that it had been in the battle for the Kremlin, the first week of the Bolshevik insurrection. Moscow had been more prepared to fight the takeover than we had been and the Provisional Government had pitted the cadets against the Red Guards and revolutionary soldiers. Thousands of them. Boys, defending the city against seasoned men.

"We had a letter." Her voice was as empty as the hallway, with all its staring doors. "Please, Marina, you're hurting me." I hadn't noticed that I was gripping her arm, digging my fingers in. I let her go. "Wait here," she said. "I'll show you." She scurried back into Mother's room, shutting the door behind her. I stood in the hallway, my mind a howling waste.

After a time, she emerged and held out an envelope to me, her back against the door, as if I might rush at her. *Bagration Military Academy.* Beautiful stationery, bearing the Romanov eagle. I pulled out one big, creamy sheet. I had never hated anything so much in this world.

Dearest Sir and Madam,

It grieves me to inform you of the death of your son, Sergei Dmitrievich Makarov, in the battle for the Kremlin, October 28, 1917. He fought hard and honorably, as befits a Russian soldier. You can be proud your son died heroically, in defense of the rightful Government. He was a fine soldier and a fine young man.

With my greatest sympathies,
Captain Yuri Borisovich Saratov

He'd been dead since October. I stared down at the page as if I expected the letters to rearrange themselves and spell something else. "Does Father know about this?"

She answered quietly, holding my hands. "Dmitry Ivanovich was going to give himself up for arrest, to go in with the ministers, but this changed his mind. He said he still had work to do."

This was how you saved Russia, Papa? "You could have at least sent word."

My governess sighed as if she could expel all the sorrow and guilt in one single breath. "No one was allowed to speak to you." Tears dripped from those watery English eyes. Her nose was red and runny. She blotted at herself with a wadded handkerchief.

My mouth felt full of the metallic bitterness of dirty kopeks.

I was alone now. Absolutely alone. What good was all our knowing, all our love, our secrets and shared memories? A fanged animal lodged in my throat. I tore at my neck, trying to let it out.

Ginevra caught at my hands. "Marina, don't...for pity's sake..."

I would find Father in whatever high-ceilinged drawing room he was in, talking so importantly about Russia's future, and I would kill him.

"Ginevra?" Mother appeared at the door, barefoot in a white nightgown—a frightened ghost. She saw me but gave no sign of recognition, only fear and stupefaction. The Englishwoman pushed between us.

"Come, Vera Borisovna. Let's go back to bed." She ushered my mother back into her room.

I was still standing in the hall when my governess returned to the door. "Don't go, Marina. Come talk to your mother." She faced the figure now sitting on the edge of the bed, the quilt around her shoulders. "Vera Borisovna! Look who's here. Look who's

come to see you." She waved me closer. I saw that
the last months had turned my mother into an old
woman. Her beauty hadn't disappeared, but her flesh
was thinned, her bones sharpened, her lips chapped
and pale. Her eyes, so much like Seryozha's, consumed her face. Ginevra tucked her back into bed,
drawing the bedclothes up around her, plumping her
pillows.

My family had disappeared—brother, mother, father. Here I thought their lives had continued without
me, but there was no home anymore. Not for any of us.

"Are you able to get some food for her?" I asked.

"Avdokia trades things. And Nikolai Shurov has been
a tremendous help."

Kolya was here? Kolya, taking care of her? "He's
been here?"

"He's saved our lives—you don't know," she went
on, tucking the lace-edged sheet over the edge of the
blanket. She was back to her resolute, tranquil demeanor. How could she have calmed down so fast? But
her tears had been for me. Seryozha had been dead for
months. She'd had time to get used to his death. His
death! She went on talking. "We can't get a thing out
of the banks, what with the teller strike. Nikolai sold
some of the paintings, and told us to hide the money in
the stove, her jewelry. Thank God he got to us before
the last sweep. They took everything." We watched
my mother, her hands fiddling again. I could see now
that she was working a tangle of thin necklaces, trying

to get them apart. "We've heard from Volodya. He's joined the Volunteer Army in the Don."

Seryozha was in the ground in Moscow. Volodya was fighting against the revolution. My lungs couldn't expand. They'd been frozen solid.

My mother looked up from the tangle of chains. "Where's Tulku?" I didn't know whether to laugh or cry. She still hadn't noticed I was here, but she wanted her little greyhound.

"Avdokia's taking him for a walk, dear," said the Englishwoman. She turned to me, whispered, "They shot Tulku during the first search, poor thing. He growled at one of the Red Guards and the man shot him the way you'd swat a fly. Frankly, it was just as well. We couldn't have kept feeding him."

Why was she talking to me about a dog? I had to get out of there while I could, while I still had the strength.

My mother turned to me, her eyes big and uncomprehending as a squid's. The heat was unbearable in here, the closeness, the lavender, their helplessness. My brother was gone. My sensitive, anxious brother who had never wanted to climb beyond the first branch of the maple that grew in the Tauride Gardens. Even then you'd have to hold him on. Killed defending the Kremlin. I pictured the dead in Znamenskaya Square, a blond head, the cap fallen off. I put the letter in the bag with Seryozha's pictures and my papers and left the flat before I turned to stone.

31 *The Twenty Towers of the Kremlin*

BIG FLAKES SIFTED ACROSS the windows. Down in the courtyard, a woman pumped water, and a crow picked disconsolately at some kind of rag. The same snow was falling in Moscow, deep, deep over his grave. Falling as it had in the snow globe music box Avdokia would wind for us, gnarled hands turning the key and shaking the encased wintry scene — St. Basil's, a troika rushing. Seryozha in his nightshirt, I in my flannel gown, Volodya pretending he was too old for such things but watching all the same. "That's you three," she would say, pointing to the horses pulling the troika. It had played "Dance of the Sugar Plum Fairy," little tinkling bells, over and over. Warm from our Sunday night baths, we would watch the snow fall together. Moscow seemed a magical place then, not a backdrop to murder.

Moscow.
> *Crow among cities*
>> *I curse your churches*
40 times 40
> *their funeral bells*
>> *I curse your Kremlin towers*
Spasskaya,
> *Blagoveshchenskaya*
>> *Borovitskaya . . .*

Blackhearted Rus
   You barrow,
   You sow.
      Devouring your piglets one by one.

How would I live in a world without Seryozha? A world surrounded by strangers, a world that could kill a little boy in his nightshirt? The sky grew dark. I prayed he hadn't been lying about being happy at the military academy. The snow swirled, a silent answer. *You are all erased. You live to be erased. No one will be remembered by anyone.* They hadn't bothered to tell me—I wasn't that hard to find!—but let me go on thinking he was alive. I'd laughed and run around town, spouting verses on bridges and singing on street corners, when he lay—where? I hadn't even asked. All I could picture was a sad mound of snow by the Kremlin wall, one of its twenty towers looming above.

The tiny music box played over and over in my mind as I remembered Seryozha manipulating his Pierrot and Columbine paper puppets, making them jump with a tug of the string. *Come with me; we'll live on the moon.* His little voice, playing both parts. *Yes, I've always wanted to live on the moon.*

Me, too, Seryozhenka. I'd like to live on the moon, somewhere cold and shining, with no humans at all—just us.

* * *

I could hear them, the racket in the hall, and in they came, talking all at once, shaking snow from hats and coats. Someone lit the lamp, dispelling the calming shadows, the gentle dark. Shouting, laughing. Something had outraged Genya, something about Red Guards. Now they saw me.

"Why were you sitting in the dark?" he asked me. He pretended to fall on me, a joke, caught himself at the last minute, one hand braced against the wall over my head. He leaned down to kiss me. I turned my face away. "Are you on strike like the Red Guards?" He tried the other side. "Fishing for more rations? Higher wages?" He righted himself. "What's with you? How'd the job search go?"

I stared out to the windows facing ours in the courtyard. People making dinner for their children with what little they had. Families. How fragile it all was.

"What's with her?" Zina asked.

Not looking at him, I handed Genya the letter, the paper that felt so much like skin. I could not say it. *Seryozha's dead*. A girl on the far side of the courtyard lounged in a window, looking back at me. Maybe it was me in a different life. I held my hand over my mouth to stop sobs if they started.

"It's her brother," Genya told the others.

"What happened?" Zina asked again.

"Killed. At the Kremlin. Back in November. Remember him, at the Cirque Moderne?"

"The blond one with the curls?" Zina asked.

"The father sent him to junker school. Bastard. Bastard!" Junkers—it's what they called the cadets.

Junker school. My father hadn't presented it that way, but that was exactly what it was. Officers in training. I held out my hand for the letter without turning to look at him. He pressed it into my palm. I folded it and put it back in my pocket. It was all I had of him now, that and a landscape or two, some silhouettes. Genya took my hands in his, rested his face against them. "Marina. I'll kill him. I'll go up there and rip his head off. To send that kid down there for nothing? What can I do, Marina? Just say the word."

"It happened three months ago." I didn't want his histrionics or his tears. I just wanted to be cold, to freeze solid here by the window. I wanted to disappear.

But now he was pacing, swatting at the air. "I wonder what your old man has to say about it now. 'Your son died heroically.' Boys against soldiers—what did they think would happen?"

"Sorry, Marina," Sasha said, touching me on the shoulder. "He was a sweet guy, an artist. I remember him. He was good, too."

"Like meat to dogs," Genya said.

Stop, for the love of God.

Anton stretched out on his cot. Supine, he began to roll a cigarette on a book on his chest. "This is exactly why governments should be abolished."

"Sorry, Marina," Gigo said, awkward as a hayseed at

a costume ball. He held out a half-eaten bar of chocolate to me, linty from his pocket, as if I were a child to be appeased with sweets.

Sasha blew the stove to life. The smell of sulfur, newsprint, varnish.

"I hope he's satisfied," Genya said, still pacing. He was too noisy. Could he not just sit down? "I'd like to ask him that to his face. 'Are you satisfied now, Dmitry Ivanovich? Are you proud of your son at last?'"

I finally let out a shriek. "For God's sake!"

"I'm sorry!" Genya flung himself to his knees at my feet, clutching at my skirt, his head in my lap. "I'm sorry, I'm sorry, I'm sorry. I'm such an oaf. Just an organ-grinder's monkey. Please tell me what to do. Please…anything, Marina. It's just too hideous. I can't stand it." He wept into my lap.

I ran my hands through his hair just to quiet him. It was absurd—I wanted him to hold me, say nothing, and just be very still. Oh, none of these poets knew the first thing about life.

The conversation went on around me. I counted towers.

Spasskaya,
Blagoveshchenskaya
Borovitskaya…

"Power will defend itself to the end," Anton was saying from his cot, where he was examining the hole in his sock.

Beklemishevskaya
       First Unnamed
              Second Unnamed
Secret Tower,
       Tsar's Tower
              Trinity . . .

That night, I dreamed of Moscow. Seryozha was a bell ringer, up in one of the towers of the Kremlin Wall, and they'd tied him into the belfry, hand, foot, and neck, stretched between them. I knew that when they rang the bells it would tear him to pieces.

Life went on. Arguments, fires made, meals eaten, visits to the toilet, hours in queues and trips to the district soviet. I managed to secure a labor book. *Origin: bourgeois.* I saw no point fighting it now. The air felt thick in my lungs, unbreathable, like the atmosphere on Venus. I went through my days, living as if within a *matrioshka* nesting doll. One Marina functioned, while deep inside, another Marina knelt in the snow by the Kremlin Wall, weeping atop a small grave. No one could join her there. They didn't know that Seryozha didn't like people touching him on the head. That his favorite color was cadmium yellow with a dash of red at its heart. That he was bitten by a spider at the age of five and became so sick and swollen that he almost died. He'd read that the Chinese kept crickets as pets and insisted on having one of his own. Avdokia got him a little basket with a lid, and Volodya hunted for three nights to catch one for him. My loneliness possessed a gravity I thought would crush me.

That Wednesday evening, we all trooped up to our poetry circle, held at the Krestovsky apartment on Sergievskaya Street, near the English embassy. Genya had something special to present. He was dying to show me, dropped numerous hints. He'd been working on it all week. Thank God it kept him busy. Mechanically, I combed my hair and got into my boots, my coat.

The bracing walk did me good. Everyone was bundled up, our breath freezing in midair. Galina Krestovskaya, so beautiful with her golden curls, met us at the door, kissed us in greeting. I always loved coming to this big overwarm apartment with its faux peasant furniture, the flowers and birds painted on the walls, the young poets gathered from all over the city to share their work and listen to the critique, especially from Anton. Seryozha would have loved this place. He would have approved of Galina—he was always attracted to beauty. She wore an embroidered Russian blouse that my brother might have designed himself.

Everybody was talking about a brand-new poem from Blok, "The Twelve," a poem about the revolution. No one had seen it yet, but a friend of the Krestovskys had acquired a copy, and we eagerly anticipated hearing it. Galina, the star of the Kommedia theater, read aloud proudly and with great revolutionary enthusiasm, checking periodically to see what Anton thought of her performance. Her husband, Krestovsky, rattled his newspaper from time to time in his leather armchair in the alcove, occasionally surveying the gathering with a doleful, proprietary squint. It was he who footed the bill for our journal, for the snacks and the fuel to heat this room for our meeting, and for Anton's editorial salary, which in turn paid for the Poverty Artel.

"The Twelve" took around fifteen minutes to read. Intricate and modern, it captured the music of the revolution, a Blok no one had ever heard before. In the poem, twelve Red Guards patrolled the streets of Petrograd in a snowstorm, streets familiar to us all, haunted and laced with deadly dramas. We recognized the rough men, the haggard bourgeoisie, the prostitutes, the hunger and cold. A prostitute, Katya, seduced by a tough, is shot by her Red Guard lover. The action was brutal and callous, yet Blok could not stop the music inside himself. What a singular moment, to hear the first recitations of a master's work, to stand aside from the dullness of my grief—no, not stand aside from it, because grief was in the poem, along with coarseness and beauty. A contradictory piece, it was on the side of the revolution and yet accepted it for the wild, violent, uncontainable thing it was, a time when people were going to suffer.

The dangerous, ragged quality of the poem took impulse, rage, murder, and remorse and drove onward,

onward into the snowstorm that blinded us all. It
ended, most astonishingly, with Christ marching unseen at the head of the column of the twelve, struggling
through the blizzard, into the unknown. *And in front of
the flag / invisible in the snow / walks one more man* . . .

I would have liked to just sit and absorb what we
had just heard, but the discussion began immediately.
What was Christ doing at the end of the poem? Was
Blok a modernist or still a symbolist? I accepted a pastry from a tray being passed by the Krestovskys' maid
and chewed it without savor. Though pastry was usually a treat, tonight it tasted like paper.

Genya, the priest's son, of course was outraged. "Do
we really need Christ to redeem the revolutionary
struggle?" he thundered. "He says *without crosses* —
what's the line? *Freedom, freedom . . . oh, oh, without a
cross*. But then here comes Jesus. If you need a justifi-
cation from the Beyond, you're not a revolutionary, no
matter how many Red Guards you stick in a poem."

At least Anton didn't judge the ending. He was at his
best at times like this, examining each of the twelve sections on a cool technical level. In the end, he decided it
wasn't a poem at all but a play. Still, he had no respect
for the self-questioning of the poem. He was interested
only in its bones, not in the mystery of its flight.

Once, a night like this would have brought me to
near ecstasy, but I was fed up with our opinions, our
judgments. Life was too deep and full of currents that
could snatch you off your raft and drag you under for

such theorizing. I thought of Blok's Christ, leading the men through the snowstorm that was inside them as well as outside. Was He here, invisible, leading all this as well? Had He been there at the Kremlin the day Seryozha had breathed his last? Perhaps so. Invisible, weeping for us all.

After chewing up Blok's magnificent poem we turned to our own. Genya stood to recite.

> *Abraham was shaving when he heard*
> *a voice*
> > *in his head.*
> *"Who's that?" he asked.*
> > *"You know," said the Lord.*
> > > *"You and me, Abe, we know the score.*
> *"I've got your number, brother*
> > *"And I'm calling it in . . ."*

So this was his answer to my brother's death? The poem he'd been so excited to share with me? My father as Abraham, my brother as Isaac, the bourgeois father sacrificing his artist son to the corrupt God of the past, an ancient but bloodthirsty deity? How proud of it he was, how thunderous his delivery, the way he stuck out his chin, as if daring God to strike him down.

Genya kept looking over at me to see what I thought of his gift. I rocked myself, praying it would soon be over. Seryozha wasn't a poem. He wasn't a symbol. He was just a boy full of dreams, bursting with talent and eccentricities and fears, who'd been sent away on a fool's errand. Father was certainly no Abraham, anointed by God and called to the ultimate sacrifice. He was just a pigheaded man steeped in vanity. Neither one of them was an abstraction.

I saw what Genya was trying to do—shape Seryozha into a martyr, a legend, a narrative that could be delivered on a street corner so people could imagine a cosmic battle between good and evil. It would play perfectly at the Haymarket. His fervor took over as he recited, and he was completely lost in his own roaring.

I had to leave. As I was slipping out, I ran into Oksana Linichuk, a student at the university, shaking snow from her scarf. I must have looked as shocked as I felt. "Are you okay?" she asked. "Isn't that Genya reading?"

I could not bring myself to answer. "I'm not feeling well. Maybe I'm coming down with something. If he asks, tell Genya I'll see him at home."

Out on Sergievskaya Street, I scurried from swirling streetlamp to streetlamp, aware of the danger, staying away from the dark doorways. I had entered the poem "The Twelve." The hunched shadow of a pedestrian entered the egg-shaped glow of the streetlight ahead, cutting a cave in the whirling snow, growing to nightmare size then disappearing. My eyelashes were freezing, I had to blink them warm again. Although the Krestovsky apartment lay in the heart of the diplomatic district, there was no such thing as a safe neighborhood now. Thieves robbed you just for your clothes and left you to freeze in the snow. I kept moving.

The shops were all dark, though it wasn't that late. I caught the streetcar toward home—everyone inside looked hunched and miserable. Down on Nevsky, the windows of Mina's building glowed behind curtains. Up there, on the fifth floor, lived people who actually knew Seryozha. Would understand what I had lost. Oh, to be known! On impulse, I jumped off the tram and raced to that familiar entrance, slipping and teetering on the ice.

In the cracked gilt mirror of the elevator, I saw my face—broken, smashed. My unfocused gaze was like my mother's as she lay in bed, trying to untangle the chains. I pushed back my scarf, combed my hair with my fingers, tried to pinch some color back into my pale cheeks.

Dunya answered my knock. I hardly recognized her—she'd cut her braids. "Marina! Are you alone?" She immediately peered into the hall behind me, hoping for a certain tall blond painter. How grown up she'd become. The hands of our clocks whirled like pinwheels these days. Soon she would be seventeen, eighteen, she would have lovers, children. Whereas my brother hadn't lived long enough for a first kiss.

I followed her into the parlor. In heaven, it would be just like this: Sofia Yakovlevna sewing at the table, Solomon Moiseivich on the divan in Bukhara cap and dressing gown, Aunt Fanya laying out a hand of solitaire, Shusha banging out Rachmaninoff on their old upright. Sofia Yakovlevna paused over her work when she saw me and half rose. "Marina!" Her smile was bright, then overcast with concern. "You didn't come alone, did you? On a night like this?"

I wanted to throw myself into their arms, but for my own selfish reasons I also wanted to savor the beautiful peace of their lives, the warmth they wove about them, before I brought my tragedy into their midst. "Mina's in her room," Dunya said. "I'll go get her." She disappeared down the hall.

"Where's your young man?" Papa Katzev asked, his eyes kind. "Your peppery comrades?"

"Up on Sergievskaya, thrashing Blok." I couldn't just blurt out *Seryozha's dead.*

"Give her a minute to catch her breath, Papa," his wife said. She knew something was wrong.

Dunya reappeared with Mina in tow. Now it was my turn to be shocked. Who was this vision before me in a dress of soft blue wool? Red lipstick emphasized her mouth, and someone had fashioned her stubbornly thick ash-blond hair into a pretty upsweep. The food shortages that had turned most of us scrawny had distilled her toward a new beauty. She wore dangling earrings and looked...horrified.

"Have I come at a bad time?"

"As a matter of fact, I was just going out. To a party." Her lovely skin bore a bit of rouge. Where were her spectacles?

"You look...beautiful."

She gave me a nervous, gelid grimace.

"Who is it? Someone I know?"

She paled, and her gray eyes slid from mine like butter on a hot pan. As clearly as if I were at one of my mother's séances—I knew. *Nikolai Shurov has been a tremendous help....* Who else could have worked such magic on dull, stodgy Mina Katzeva? She had probably been singing before the mirror, getting ready for her rendezvous with my lover. *My* lover. "You're seeing Kolya?"

Terrified, she mimed buttoning her lips, glancing at her mother sewing at the table, her father, her sisters. Although we were pretty safe with Shusha banging away at Rachmaninoff, she yelled, "Let me show you a new dress Mama made me," then gestured with her head down the hall.

I followed her to her room, past pictures of grandparents, great-grandparents, men with sidelocks and beards, women with suspicious faces, stern with disapproval at their dependable workhorse turned siren. I could hear Uncle Aaron singing behind the bathroom door. In Mina's bedroom, where I'd slept with her and her sisters during the first revolution, she pulled the door shut. The room smelled of some light perfume. She never wore perfume. There was the bottle, by her bed. Something he'd brought her, no doubt.

I didn't want her to lie to me now. She had to understand the situation. "Mina, listen to me. Seryozha's dead."

On her face—shock. But something else…her gaze dropped to her feet, then met mine again. Her tear-filled eyes drifted off to the right. She knew! *He had told her.* Her lids dropped again. She couldn't bear the anguish on my face. She shielded her guilt with a cupped hand.

I grabbed her, shook her. "How long have you known?"

"I was going to tell you, I swear, it's just that we haven't seen you…" Sniveling, she tried to wrench herself from my grip.

"I've been right here. Ten blocks away." Mina, my best, my oldest friend in the world, had kept Seryozha's death from me. No wonder she couldn't meet my eyes. I shoved her away.

Her face was a kaleidoscope, emotion replacing emotion—shame, fury, pity—like impatient people all trying to get through a door at the same time. "I would have told you when I saw you again. I thought I'd see you. But the longer I waited, the harder it got." Her little earrings flickered in the electric light.

"And you got to see Kolya." I saw it so clearly. She would have done anything to have him. Even this.

Her chin stuck out a little farther. "Yes. Yes, all right?" She rubbed her arms where I'd hurt her. "Do you have to have everything? Everything, everything! What about me? *Good old Mina. Here, hold my coat,*

Mina..." Her mouth twisted into a bitter smile. "But maybe I'm not so good. Maybe I deserve a life, too." The smile hovered, crumpled. She held her hand to her forehead and began sobbing in earnest, the ragged sobs of a child.

"Mina, I need to see Kolya." I tried to keep my voice low and soft. "Let me come with you tonight."

"No!" Startled, she wheeled away from me. "What will you tell Genya? Remember him? Your boyfriend?"

I thought of Genya, so sincere, so caring. But it was Kolya I needed. Only he would know how I felt. Only he could know what it was to lose Seryozha, only he could console me. To think that a few minutes ago, I was heading home to sit alone and watch snow fall. I'd been thrown a lifeline and I wasn't going to let it go. Not for her or Genya or God Almighty. "Tell me where you meet him."

Her crying had left blotchy patches on her lovely skin. Her hair was coming down. She sat down heavily on the edge of her bed, took off her earrings, and threw them at the pillow. One bounced onto the floor, skittered under Dunya's bed. "I'm sorry about Seryozha. Oh God, what a mess..." She keeled over sideways on the bed and wedged her hands between her knees, her tears dripping on the chenille bedspread.

"Where is he? I need to see him."

"In a mansion. On the English Embankment."

Poor Mina. My tearstained, disloyal old friend. I had

never guessed her envy was so great that she would go as far as to withhold news of my brother's death so that she could keep her rendezvous with Kolya. "How do you go?" I pressed her. "Will he come here?"

She shook her head. "He sends a cab. You go. It's you he wants anyway."

Was it wrong that this lifted my spirits? I needed him. There would be no explanations, no awkward embraces, no ridiculous metaphors or poetic histrionics. It was a time for raw feeling, something there was no room for in the crowded Poverty Artel. Mina might love him, but I would burn down everything to be with him again.

32 *The English Embankment*

THE COACHMAN WORE A frozen lily like a starfish in his buttonhole. Frost whitened the poor horse, its ribs a clattering xylophone. Crouching in his great cloak against the whirling snow, the coachman clapped the reins and we moved into the storm as into a poem, a legend. Frost soon coated my shawl in a glassy shroud, making it crack. My eyes narrowed to slits as we slid through the deserted streets down Horse Guards Boulevard and up past St. Isaac's, across the vast white whirling plain of Senate Square.

On the English Embankment, the cold grew even worse. The wind sweeping across the frozen river drove sharp needlelike grains of snow into my eyes, my lashes crusted with frost. How different from that first joyous sleigh ride with Kolya. On one side, the great houses of the English Embankment braced like aristocrats before a firing squad, while on the other, wind and darkness, the howling expanse of the frozen Neva. The sleigh came to rest right in the middle of the road—there was so little traffic these days that it made no difference where we stopped. The coachman, hunched in his seat, made no attempt to help me scramble out. As soon as I had my feet on the ground, the bearskin piled back in the sled, he whipped up the horse, leaving me alone in this white blowing world.

I stood alone before a two-story mansion that had lorded it over the snow-crusted Neva for a hundred years, a looming blur of darkness one shade lighter than the sky. I stumbled my way through the drifts to the enormous door. Padlocked. I pulled on the chain, but it was fastened tight. No light appeared in any of the windows. I pounded with the side of my fist, barely making a sound. The cold sucked the last strength from my body, the benefits of the fish-soup dinner and the pastry I'd eaten at the Krestovskys' gone by now. "Kolya!" I shouted up at the windows, my voice lost in the roar of the storm. "Kolya, let me in!"

Down the embankment, a door opened, a flickering light. A figure waved. I didn't have to see the face. I ran to him. I flew.

He caught me by the waist. "Hey, hey, easy there!"

He held the lamp high so it wouldn't be knocked out of his hands and laughed as I stepped through the door. He bolted it behind me. We were in the frozen pantry of a great house. I pushed the shawl from my hair as he walked ahead holding his lamp. "Kolya."

He turned back. The look on his face when he realized it wasn't Mina, the smile of mild anticipation vanishing, then he knew me. He bundled me into his arms, repeating my name like a prayer. So solid, so real, his smell of cigar and Floris Limes and that powerful indescribable honey. I began to cry. He kissed my hands, smoothed my hair, held me tightly enough to make me believe this was real.

"Let's go upstairs. I've got a fire." We fell into step as we always did, as we traced our frozen path through the dead kitchens and ghostly pantries, the service rooms of the mansion, and climbed the stairs into the frosty grandeur of its foyer. I was too overcome to speak. He kissed my hair, rested his temple against mine. I had forgotten the waves of pleasure in that simple touch. My grief had found its home. This was why I had come—the world be damned. I didn't care if it disappeared forever.

The flickering light created and erased reception rooms as we moved through the public areas of the abandoned villa—flashes of red silk wall covering stained and denuded of paintings. White pillars, a broken sofa, abused-looking chairs. He opened a small door I might not have noticed, flush as it was with the wall. Before us, the lantern revealed a small, high-ceilinged room papered in yellow and warmed by an open fire. Paintings and beveled mirrors still hung on chains from its picture rails, portraits in oval insets peered out like passengers from the portholes of a passing liner. The firelight licked at his face, the high cheekbones, the smiling eyes, but they weren't smiling now. He knew. He understood. Objects gleamed on a small gilded table—wine, biscuits on a painted plate. For Mina Katzeva. I couldn't bring myself to feel jealous. What I needed from Kolya went deeper than sex, deeper than passion.

He poured some wine into a glass of cut crystal and handed it to me.

I drank. Port, sweet, clinging to the glass. I hadn't had alcohol since the Winter Palace was taken. It went to my head, along with the heat of the open fire and Kolya's scent.

We settled on the settee, his arm around me. "I thought I'd never see you again. Poor Sir Garry." That was Seryozha's name in our circus, Sir Garry Pekingese. Sir Garry was a dog who would jump through a hoop covered with paper.

"Nobody told me. I went by the flat on Furshtatskaya to get my papers and Ginevra told me."

"Mina didn't tell you?" I shook my head slowly, threaded my fingers through his. He tipped his head back. "Christ."

"You could have told me yourself."

"I didn't want to disrupt your new life." Tears welled in his blue eyes. "I'm not the scum you believe me to be. She said you were in love with a poet, that you were beautiful together, to leave you alone. Do you love him?"

Did I love Genya? Of course I did. But here I was. When all was said and done, I'd run to this man without a backward glance. I would have to think about that—later.

"What a mess." His arm around my shoulder, mine around his waist, we leaned into one another like people sheltering in a blizzard. But the hard black just under my ribs that I'd been carrying since that day eased over an inch or two. Seryozha, my beautiful brother. Sir Garry Pekingese. He remembered us. That was why I had come. We sat like that for a long time as the fire hissed and snapped. He poured me another glass of wine.

Not the Madeira from the Winter Palace, but sweet and warm.

He sighed, leaned back against the rose velvet. "I saw your father," he said. "I think he's trying to get himself arrested."

"Good." I began to pace. There was a packet of Turkish cigarettes. Did Mina smoke now, too? I took one and smelled the sweet, fresh tobacco. Kolya lit it for me, steadying my hand in his. "Does he regret what he did?"

"I didn't ask him. Would you have expected me to?"

Funny, I had waited so long to be able just to *talk* to someone who knew everything, and now that I was here, I found I didn't have anything to say. Just sitting with him where I could smell him and count his eyelashes was enough. Mina had been lucky to have him even once in her life. And I realized it would always be this way with us. Time, distance, politics couldn't touch what we had together. Life and death would be our meat, our bread, part of what we were, not separate from us. To ever express what crackled between us would need all the poetry in my possession.

Out of the depths of my grief, desire sent up its bloom of fire, like kindling sheltered from the wind. It found my lips, my breasts —and now my mouth sought his, his hands found my thighs, our clothing falling away, buttons surrendering as we clutched each other on the small sofa. "There's a bed," he whispered. Yes, there would always be a bed.

He led me into a room with a high bed. I could well imagine a duchess in her nightdress there—the canopy, the satin pull cord, a view of the Neva behind the yellow drapes. There would always be a bed, and we would be in it, even if it was just a pile of hay. We hadn't made love since that last day on the Catherine Canal, when I'd still been a schoolgirl and the first revolution was only a rumble on the outskirts of Petrograd. Although the world had changed, we had not. We grappled, clutched, bit, groaned. Our bodies strained to become closer than physical bodies possibly could.

How chaste Genya's and my lovemaking was compared to this. Only with Kolya did I hear the true bass notes of ardor, the soar of its melodies. I couldn't even say what these last months with Genya had been. Ah Kolya, Kolya, my heaven and my hell. My match, my curse. My eternal love. There was nothing to stop us now.

We lay together, resting, his head on my breast, his smell all over me, his chestnut body hair in the firelight. He toyed with the bangle I never took off. Of course I hadn't. "You've lost weight," he said, tracing my ribs, my waist, my hips with their bones cradling my flat stomach.

"No food. We don't have money for the black market." I inhaled the gorgeous smoke from Turkey, wrapping it around my tongue.

He got up, sturdy, naked, and brought the plate of sweets in from the other room, treats he was going to feed to Mina, to stuff her with like a pigeon and then eat her up. I let him feed me crumbly, buttery white shortbread and cherry-filled chocolates. But the cherry reminded me of Father. "Poor Mina, having to miss this. Did you enjoy making love with her?"

"You can't always have caviar. Sometimes you settle for eggplant."

I pinched his nose, shook his face from side to side. "Look at you—you're not even sorry."

"I'm sorry for many things, *krasavitsa moya.*" *My*

beauty. "That it's been a year since I've seen you, that's very high on my list of regrets." He kissed my breast. "That Seryozha ended up where he had no business going—that I regret. Your father's stubbornness. He's a good man but he's a man of principle." He relit his half-smoked cigar, propping himself higher on the pillows. "Always dangerous. Your whole family's like that—principled. You believe in things, you Makarovs. It's dangerous business. Give me a Cossack bandit, a whore, a soldier with blood on his hands, but God save us from people who believe in things. You're the ones who will get us all killed." He toyed with my hair. "Look at you, look at those big brown eyes. You're more like him than you would believe."

"Don't tell me that."

He turned his head to avoid blowing smoke in my face. I never liked cigars before, but the smell was his, it completed him. I ran my hands through the curly hair of his chest, down to his soft resting sex, his sturdy legs. "Seryozha didn't believe in things. He just wanted to make art. And please Father."

"He believed in beauty. It's not the worst thing. You've got some of that yourself." He fed me more shortbread. "But God you're strong." He tipped my chin up to look into my eyes, and his blue ones darkened in the lamplight. "Luckily. Because there's no easy road for people like you, the believers in beauty. Seryozha tried to make it out there—you've got to hand it to him. I admire that."

"Are you proud of his heroism?" I thought of that hideous letter.

"Sometimes just living is heroism," he said.

I studied the small mole under his right eye, the peaked eyebrows that faded out into nothingness, his diamond-shaped face with its high oriental cheekbones, the upturned laughing eyes. So rare to see them serious like this.

"You still remember Sir Garry." I pressed my finger in the dip of his upper lip.

Seryozha couldn't have been more than four. We'd tried to get Mother's dog, Tulku the First, to do the hoop trick but he proved untrainable. Sir Garry was also assistant to the mysterious Esmerelda in her "feats of daring." He'd walk along very seriously, as beautiful as ever a child could be with his big gray eyes and blond curls, and hold a stick aloft for me to hang on to as I wobbled along a tightrope strung between pines two feet off the ground. How solemnly he took his responsibilities. I felt the tears swell. I held out my glass and Kolya filled it again. "*Mesdames et messieurs, Damen und Herren*...you do it."

"Ladies and gentlemen, *meine Damen und Herren, mesdames et messieurs,* coming to you direct from performances for the sultans of India and Azakazan, for your amazement and edification..." For half a second, he flashed that smile, which had gotten him out of a million scrapes and probably a million more to come. Kolya had been our ringmaster, wearing gum boots and

Father's old crumpled top hat, brandishing a whip of woven ribbons from our child's pony cart. "The lovely Esmerelda, from the emerald caves of Capri, performing for you feats of gravity-defying amazement."

"Vladimir the Cossack and his Horse of Marvels!" I imitated his ringmaster tone.

"That fat pony. It was always trying to bite me," Kolya said, toying with his cigar. "What was its name?"

"Carlyle."

"Dmitry Ivanovich's choice, no doubt. I was terrified of your father in those days. I was sure he'd catch on that I was in love with Vera Borisovna and challenge me to a duel." He traced the top curve of my breast, then the U of it. "I had my first orgasm thinking about her."

Only Kolya would admit to such a thing. I wondered how he liked her now—crazy, in her nightdress, trying to untangle that nest of fine chains.

"I lived for those summers," he said, his fingers in my cropped hair, my head tucked under his chin. I could hear his voice rumbling through his chest. "Listening to Vera Borisovna sing on the porch after dinner—do you remember?" He brushed his fingers against my abraded lips. "She would come and kiss Volodya good night. The windows all open, a gentle breeze, and her in her evening gown, her perfume..."

"Après l'Ondée."

"She'd kiss him, then she'd come over and kiss me,

too. On the forehead. I think it was the zenith of my young life."

I nuzzled his well-shaved cheek. His lime cologne. Who else would remember her as she had been, in her lilac dress, her bare shoulders, the laughter in the twilight? "Thanks for taking care of her. It was good of you."

Outside the wind whistled, shaking the outer windows, where in here, only the springs spoke, the crackle of the fire.

"I wish I could do more." He plumped the fat pillows, sat up higher. "I think the English girl might have better luck getting them out. They take care of their own, the English."

"I hope so. But Mother doesn't seem to care anymore. Seryozha's death was the last blow."

He stubbed out his cigar, drank off the port, and placed the empty glass on the bedside table. "Just as well," he said. "What's left, even if she does get out? No money, no skills. Maybe she could remarry...but if not, can you imagine Vera Borisovna in a bedsit in London, living off charity?"

"Father has friends in London. Surely they'd be of some help."

He kicked off the sheets, wiping the sweat from his face and revealing the red-gold glow of his body in the lamplight. "Oh, it would be fine at first. The distinguished guest, risking all to flee to the West. Embraces all around. But one week turns into six, then to ten, and they're wondering if she's ever going to leave. Hints about the family closing up house and traveling for a while. She gets the message, and so comes the ghostly drift from home to home, begging for a little space. 'No, don't trouble yourself, dear.' I think she knows that. If it were me, I'd rather starve to death in my own bed."

"I think that's what she's doing."

How callous we'd become, to talk calmly about Mother with such fatalism. If I left Russia with her, I could support her, save her from the fate Kolya had so vividly outlined. But I had turned down Father's offer of England. I had chosen to align my fate with Russia's.

Kolya pulled me to him, draping my leg over his hip. I tasted his port wine cigar breath as his lips brushed mine. "I've told Dmitry Ivanovich he ought to leave, for her sake."

"Let's not talk about him."

"But he's decided to defend Russia instead. Citizen Quixote." He pressed his hand to mine, palm to palm, and slowly our curled fingers interlocked like swans bowing their heads in the corps de ballet. "Poor devil."

"Don't you dare feel sorry for him."

"I feel sorry for every living soul right now."

We lay there for a while, mournfully, understanding our mutual weaknesses, not needing to speak. Seryozha was dead, the world was exploding, and what we had was our passion for each other, our mingled souls and histories. The fire cracked and popped.

Finally he brightened. "Wait!" He got up out of bed, padded out to the sitting room, his strong muscled buttocks and thighs bare in the firelight. "Remember this?" The gramophone by the settee, all set up for a night of love—with Mina. My anger flared like a sudden rash and died away just as quickly when the guitar, the voice of Carlos Gardel filled the lantern-flickering room. Mina didn't tango. He held out his arms for me to come join him. The song spoke to what was true about us—passion and danger, longing, rebellion, tenderness. I didn't have to know Spanish to understand what it was about.

Naked, we danced, slowly, separated only by the thickness of our bodies, our essential selves once again foiled from perfect fusion by bones and flesh, and yet still yearning.

Kolya opened the drapes. Outside, the dark winter dawn crawled toward us along the white brow of the Neva. He'd already dressed, was in his old army uniform—epaulets removed for safety's sake, officers being uninvited guests at the party of the revolution—and set a tray on the bed. Real coffee and good black bread, herring and sour cream. "Where are you going?"

"I've got business," he said. *Beezneez*—he used the English word. "I'll be back. Keep warm. Eat something."

"What business?" I sat up in bed. Out on the Neva,

one sledge toiled along, like an ant in a sugar bowl. "There's no business in Petrograd."

The corners of his eyes turned up like his nose. "That's when there's the most business." He kissed my lips, bruised from the nighttime of unaccustomed passion. Smoothed my hair. "Silly."

"Don't go." I clung to him.

He grabbed my haunch. For some reason my flesh always conformed to the shape of his hand. "You think I'm not coming back? With that waiting for me?"

I pulled him toward me. I was raw as a grated radish, but I still wanted more. My greed was unslakable. "Forget business."

"I'm not a girl," he said, kissing me again. "I can't loll around in bed all day dreaming and writing love poems. I've got things to do. But I'll be back. There's a pail of water by the washstand. Stay warm and think about me." He pushed me away gently, stood, buttoned his coat, sticking his fur hat on his head.

And he was gone.

I ate fatty herring, sour cream, and black bread. After the previous night, I felt drugged, so safe in this hidden place, the smell of my love all over me, the tattered splendor. I hadn't realized how tired I was. Tired of queues and district soviets and frozen potatoes, tired of the communal squalor of the Poverty Artel, tired of the daily terrors and having to be a grown-up every day, tired of thinking and fighting and waiting my turn, while the real me was left unknown. I sat on the fra-

grant bed and watched the snow fall outside the windows. I should go and tell Genya what had happened.
The knowledge tugged at me, but it seemed too far
away. As any child can tell you, you must not leave an
enchanted place or it will be lost to you forever. All that
will remain will be a ribbon or a slipper, an enameled
bracelet on your arm, the smell of honey and Floris
Limes in your hair.

33 *Speculation*

I KNEW WHAT *BEEZNEEZ* Kolya was conducting out
there. Every morning the citizens of Petrograd woke
to see blood in the snow where some speculator had
been shot by the Cheka overnight, caught hoarding or
dealing in contraband. Dressed in black leather, with
Mausers at their hips, bands of Chekists raided buildings all night long. Not the Poverty Artel—we were
too poor for hoarding—but in the front building,
when the electric lights came on after midnight,
everyone knew a raid was about to occur. And I'd
found a hidden space off the mansion's laundry room
piled high with barrels and boxes, rugs, art in frames.
It was strictly illegal—all art belonged to the people
now, their national heritage. Perhaps some of my parents' things, too.

Before the last of the sun's frosty light dropped
into the gulf, footsteps sounded on the bare parquet.

I hid behind the door, but it was Kolya, balancing two full bags, one on each arm. He unpacked them gleefully, like a child, showing me cheese, butter, potted meats, a dusty bottle of Napoleon cognac under a red wax seal.

"Manna, my dear. Hallelujah." He made the sign of the cross, priestlike, over a can of deviled ham.

"The Cheka has permission to shoot speculators on sight," I said.

He pinched my cheeks as one would a fussy child. "Lucky for me, their eyesight isn't too good." He pulled at a lock of my hair, let it fall. "I wish you hadn't cut it. I miss it long. Was it always this red?"

"Mother hated the red." I watched him open the brandy, breaking the seal, tucking it under his arm, pulling the cork. "She thought it was vulgar. When I was little, she used to have Avdokia rinse it with rosemary and walnut shells to try to darken it."

"Didn't want to be upstaged," he said. The cognac unstoppered, he went looking for the glasses. They were still by the bed where we'd left them the night before.

He sliced a fat piece of ham and held it out to me. I opened my mouth for him to feed it to me instead. I would have liked to be one of those dogs who can't eat if not fed by the master's hand. As I ate, I wondered what it would be like to live with him, to follow him out into his mysterious world. It would be like walking through the looking glass. What lay on the other side of his life? Abandoned houses, villages, woods, gypsy camps? Was it true that there were men who could not love the way a woman loved, completely, devotedly? Akhmatova wrote,

> *No, I will not drink wine with you—*
> *You're a naughty one.*
> *I know your ways—you'd kiss*
> *Any girl beneath any moon.*

I dreamed about fish swimming in dark currents under the frozen Neva. I was visited by the ghosts of the dead mansion, dressed in the fashion of the 1830s, watching us, watching me. I dreamed of Pierrot, Harlequin, and Columbine, and they became mixed together with Katya and the tough and the Red Guardsman from Blok's poem, all at a masked ball in an open square like the Field of Mars, in the swirling snow.

The next night Kolya didn't return though the hour grew late. I had no way to gauge the time once darkness came, but I imagined it was at least midnight and still no sign. I lit the lamps, waited. Paced. Imagined him dead. Shot, robbed, arrested. But no, surely he'd been delayed with one of his customers, some old gent who had opened a bottle of wine hidden for months in a dusty cellar, accompanied by treasured cigars. A school chum, someone from the university he stumbled across

on Nevsky Prospect. In a city like this, it could be anything. Arrest, interrogation.

Or a woman. The thing I should not have imagined
was impossible not to. The female body sang for him,
and, as they say, a great violinist can play any violin.
If I can't have caviar…but he did have it. Absurd to
think he could go from our bed, so thoroughly torn
and abused that I had to completely remake it each
morning, to someone else's. We already made love
four times a day. But what of his need for admiration,
for desire? It drove him before it like the wind. Yes, he
could be with some poor lovely Former he was "helping." Just *beezncez*.

"Are you even a soldier anymore?" I'd asked the
night before. His unit was down in the Ukraine—or
were they? The Ukraine's Rada, its parliament, had
just signed a separate peace with the Germans while the
Bolsheviks were still negotiating to end the war.

"It's uncertain," he said. "I'm still in touch with my
superiors." He arced his head from side to side, neither
yes nor no. "Let's say I'm a useful fellow."

Yes, I imagined he was. Sitting in someone's
parlor—desperate Former People struggling to maintain their dignity—examining their objets d'art, a
Fabergé egg, a jeweled dragonfly. They would speak
of old times, friends in common, parties they'd
attended—*Oh, you were there?*—pretending that
nothing so low as commerce was taking place. While
he eyed the dark-haired daughter, or the mistress of the

house . . . the oval portrait on the yellow wall followed me with her eyes. *You, too?*

Well, they couldn't eat their silver, their art. Wasn't I grateful for the money he had left hidden behind the tiles in my father's stove? What good were our Repin, our Bakst, Vrubel's portrait of my mother in such times? You could not stoke the tin stoves with them. You could not get passage to Finland with their beauty.

I drank wine and out of sheer perversity imagined every violent fate that might have met him, then became terrified that it had really happened, that my ugly thoughts might actually become reality. *Please bring him back,* I prayed. But he'd always flown back before, eager for me, shortly after dark. Was he tiring of me, my neediness, my unquenchable passion? My body ached for him.

He returned in the early hours of the morning, stinking of vodka, reeling like a circus clown. Sank down upon the settee and attempted to take his boots off, failed. He held one foot up for me to help him pull it off, but I ignored it. He let it fall with a thud. "The city's a ruin," he said, removing a cigar from inside his jacket and cutting off the tip, lighting it. He puffed blue smoke into the air. "I fell over a dead horse tonight. Almost broke my damned neck. A dead goddamn horse, right in the middle of Bolshaya Morskaya."

"Write to the mayor. Tell him dead horses are bad for *beezneez.*"

He stuck his cigar between his teeth and tried pulling

his boot off again. "Marina," he said cajolingly. "Marinoushka." Drunkenly, he held his leg up with both hands, wagged it at me. I pulled off the offending footwear and tossed it into the fireplace, watched him scramble on hands and knees for his burning sole. His soul. Who did he think I was? "What the devil's gotten into you?" he asked, retrieving the smoldering object, brushing off the ash and embers.

"I thought you'd been shot. Anything could have happened. I hate just sitting, wondering whether you're dead or alive."

"Then you should be happy." He grinned, teasing me, and touched my nose with a sooty forefinger. "So what's the temper? I've been out seeing which way the wind's blowing. Making my daily bread." One boot on, one boot off, he poured himself a small glass of vodka, lifted it to me, and drank.

I sniffed him, his face, his collar. His hands. No trace of perfume. Nothing but cigar and vodka, maybe herring. "And you were mugged by a distillery."

"An old friend of mine gave a little party." He fumbled with the other boot and finally got it off. "Seems that she'd invited a poet. A great big boor spouting Bolshevik nonsense. Drunk as a cobbler." He unbuttoned the top few buttons of his tunic as if it were choking him. "God I hate poets. They should all be long dead, leaving us their words but not their stink." He grinned. "Especially this one, this ox, walking on her couch with his dirty boots, bellowing some dreadful love poems about some girl or other, some tramp who didn't come home."

Oh God, wasn't there enough torment in this world? Genya, drunk, suffering...because of me. Kolya disgusted me, my own desire for him disgusted me, and yet—God!—*this* was me, not that brave, plucky girl so proud of heating water on a little stove.

"Stupid sap," he said, staring at his cigar. "In a state like that over some little whore."

"You bastard." I snatched the Havana out of his mouth and tried to throw it, but he grabbed my wrist and slapped me across the face so fast I barely knew he had done it.

I held my hand to my cheek. The burn of it. The surprise.

"Oh God," he said, realizing what he had done. "Marina."

I began to scramble for my clothes, my woolen hose, my boots. I could hardly see through my tears.

"Stop, stop," he took my boots from my hands, put them back on the floor. "Marina, oh God." He sank to his knees, lay his head on my thighs, his tears soaking me. "I'm jealous, I admit it. I loved seeing him suffer. A big handsome devil like that. A Bolshevik! Oh, he's going to go far in this new world of ours."

How drunk was he? He was crazy! "I'm here with you, Kolya! Can't you see that?"

"Yes, that's just what I thought. I wanted to tell him,

'I know where she is. She's with me.' Really work him up. Maybe he'd jump out the window."

I could hardly take a breath. "But you didn't."

"No. Of course not. A man like that could kill you with his bare hands." He walked to the table on his knees and poured more vodka into his glass, sat heavily on the floor. "But you'd been his. This admirable fellow, this poet...and who am I? What am I? So I went out and got drunk."

I sat down with him and rested my forehead against his. We two impossible people, in this impossible life.

"I do love you so, Marina," he said. He had never said that word before. It worked its way under my skin, through the cage of my ribs, under my breastplate. It buried itself inside me like a jewel sewn inside a smuggler.

The next morning, I woke to noise somewhere in the house. I had been here long enough to sense the change. Rattling, men's voices. Kolya came in, dressed and composed, a far different man from the one he'd shown me the night before. Nowhere could I see the vulnerability, the madness. This man was sober, efficient, all business. "We're clearing out," he said. "You've got to get dressed."

I rose, looking for my clothes. "Where are we going?"

"Not you. Me. My men."

"What men?" What was he talking about? I was with

him now. There was no way back, no second plan. "Your regiment's gone. They're in the Don, with the Volunteers."

He spoke softly, apologetically. "These are my own men, Marina."

"Why can't you take me, then? You have to. I don't care where we're going. You can't leave me again."

He knelt on the bed, pushed me back flat onto the quilt. "Go back to your poet," he whispered in my ear. "You're safe with him—though God knows I hope he doesn't drink often. It wasn't a pretty sight. Or go back to Vera Borisovna's. But you can't stay here and you can't come with me." Making me look into his eyes, see the seriousness there.

"I can't go anywhere. There is nowhere else. Please." I pressed my face into his tunic, my tears streaming into the wool of his jacket. "You have to take me."

He held me at arm's length. "It's too dangerous. But I swear to you I'll be back, no matter what." He wanted me to agree, but I wouldn't. "I adore you, Marina." Kissing my hands, my neck. "Ever since you were a bratty little girl—you threw a snowball at me at a sledding party. In the Tauride Gardens, remember?"

He'd been talking to Klavdia Rozanova, with her perfect blond braids and her ermine muff. I'd been trying to knock that snotty look off her stupid face. My aim was just bad.

He crushed me against him, my face buried into the fragrance of his chest, his clothing. "I'll be back. I swear I will be. Look." He fished something out of his pocket. A box, its velvet an ancient, rusty black. I wouldn't touch it, so he set it between us on the bed. Pushed it toward me. Against a dark blue satin lining—a bit pilled—lay a jeweled stickpin, a yellow stone surrounded by diamonds, the kind of thing a wealthy dandy might have worn in a silk lapel in the 1830s.

"If you ever need money, take this to the market on Kamenny Island. Ask for Arkady." He pinned it onto my camisole. "Don't take less then ten thousand. It's a canary diamond. Don't let anyone tell you it's topaz."

I hit him. In the chest, on the arms. "You liar! You were lying all the time. You knew you were going to do this!" Even when he was saying *I love you* last night he'd been intending to leave. "You bastard!"

He gathered me in and held me tight, too tight to hit him, and into my ear, he whispered, "Don't...we're in a hurry." He let me go and I rolled away from him.

Standing, straightening his uniform, he put a wad of notes on the table. "Hide that and get dressed."

I wasn't going to do anything he said ever again. "No." How could he just scrape me off like mud on his boots?

"Do it. We're about to have visitors—in black leather jackets." He picked up my dress and shoes and handed them to me. His tone told me he was very serious. Weeping, I struggled into my things. I wasn't going to be arrested for his speculation. I downed the

last of the wine in a gulp—I wasn't going to leave that
for the Chekists—and bundled the rest of the food into
my bag, the precious sugar, the ham.

He led me down the hall, down an icy back stairway,
through service rooms, and out into the courtyard
where men were covering three sledges with tarps.
Seven big furry black horses stamped in their traces,
two pairs and a troika. It was a shock to be out in daylight in the yard of a house where I'd just spent three
days without ever seeing its exterior. The men worked
quickly, grimly, without comment, rifles strapped on
their backs, beards coated with frost. Kolya kissed me
one last time, my darling traitor. I would not let
go—he had to pry me away. I watched helplessly as he
climbed onto the last cart, the collar of his heavy coat
turned up, and signaled the men to drive out. He waved
back at me once, an ironic salute, his kiss still bruising
my lips as the small convoy disappeared onto Galernaya Street, the ghost of his embrace still around me.

34 *Mother*

SOME INSECTS LIVE OUT their lifetimes in just a few
hours. Once, I thought that was terribly sad. But now I
could see how brilliant those hours might be, how radiant, how intense, flashing and beautiful. Each precious
second might contain the riches of months, compressed
within tiny hearts and wings, before time tore them

to pieces. I felt as though I had just lived out my few hours, that the rest of my life would contain just the papery remnants of those three days in the winter of 1918.

I leaned on the embankment on the Neva side in the gray morning, feeling brave one minute, sobbing the next, trying to figure out which window had been ours. Two old women emerged from the house next door. A princess, perhaps, and her lady companion or her sister, leaning on each other in their dark coats and decrepitude. They gave me a hard stare as they passed by. *A worker girl,* I could see them thinking. Or a lookout, preparing to signal some gang to come and rob their house in their absence. Perhaps they could smell my wildness. Had these women experienced three such days in their lives? Or even an hour?

I watched them, wiping my tears and wishing I had a handkerchief, when the roar of automobiles reverberated in the silence. It was either soldiers or the Cheka—no one else had gasoline. Here they came, two big cars sliding around the corner. I began to walk, the noise and danger pushing me away. I could hear their commotion as they ground to a stop before the yellow mansion I'd left not ten minutes ago. Our bed would still be warm. Part of me was relieved. He hadn't been lying, not about that. I tried not to watch over my shoulder as leather-clad figures piled out, unholstering their Mauser machine pistols, breaking into the house.

I concentrated on my footfalls in the snow, the frost on the elms, the grand panorama on both sides of the river. The Dutch modesty of the Menshikov Palace, the pompous Academy of Arts. And, farther away, the Cathedral of Saints Peter and Paul, with its steeple stabbing the breast of the sky. The needle of the Admiralty lifted in response, like a swordsman's salute.

I wandered on, not knowing where to go, what to do with myself. I couldn't go back to Genya...I kept seeing him at that party, half out of his mind with grief and rage, walking on the sofas, howling my name. Cursing it. I couldn't go to Mina's, either. My loneliness was absolute. From the golden dome of St. Isaac's, the saints stared down at me, the angels at the corners over the colonnade looking like rooftop snipers.

So it was Mother.

I pushed my way onto a crowded streetcar, squealing and groaning along like a giant unoiled hinge. The ill-tempered young woman driver stopped and started with an impatient roughness, hurling us all against one another. A young Red Guardsman climbing in the window began to shout and curse. "Kick 'em in the face!" a man next to the window advised, trying to help haul him in. Evidently someone outside was taking advantage of the guardsman's vulnerability to steal his boots. Once inside, in his stocking feet, the militiaman drew his pistol and began shooting out of the tram. He didn't seem to care whom he shot—he was just angry that his boots were gone. My ears rang with the percussion for the rest of the trip.

In the little park down the center of Furshtatskaya

Street, drifts lay in formless humps, horse high. The front door of the building was now boarded up. I passed through the courtyard entrance. But this time I climbed the main staircase, making no attempt to conceal my presence. The stairwell was lit only by the skylight. The brass riser bars, once meticulously polished, were black as iron and empty of the carpet they used to hold down, probably stolen for shoes. Soon people would steal the rods as well, make them into pipes and lighters.

The flat was unlocked. I walked in only to be met in the vestibule by a hard-faced woman with a blond braid who was carrying a long, skinny infant. She stopped and stared at me. "Who the devil are you?"

A ferret-faced woman in a green coat and kerchief joined her. "What you want, *devushka?* Rooms? Ask the *domkom*. Third floor."

Domkom. The house committee. The Poverty Artel's building had one, but it seemed that the new era had finally arrived on Furshtatskaya Street.

Looking in, I saw that the expanse of our salon had been partitioned with furniture, the visible side crammed with beds and a few of the antiques Mother had not been able to sequester into her room. The flat had been collectivized. The Bolsheviks had decreed that workers should be allowed to move into the big bourgeois flats in the center of Petrograd. Every citizen was entitled to nine square meters of living space. We at the Poverty Artel hadn't had to worry about it, since we were well over capacity by anyone's estimation, but the bourgeois Makarov flat of twelve rooms could have housed two score. So it seemed that the surplus space had finally been claimed. Clothes drip-dried on a line stretched across the width of the room. The once-shining parquet, across which I'd danced a tango with Kolya, was now black as tile in a train station.

I wanted to run shrieking through the room, tearing down laundry, tossing their sad belongings out the window. But they had a right to be here. They knew nothing of us and our tragedy. "Old lady Makarova still here?" I said with proletarian rudeness.

"Oh, the tsaritsa? She's still here." The ferret-faced woman nodded down the hall with a sharp chin and took the baby from the other woman.

I ducked past them to avoid any inquiries and strode down the broad hall, noting the padlock now on Father's study as I passed, a new American lock. Another had been bolted into the woodwork on Mother's door. The Americans seemed to be the only ones getting rich in revolutionary Petrograd.

I pressed my head against the wooden door panel and fought a sickening reeling feeling. Listening for noises within, I knocked. Was everybody gone? I knocked again—*Fais dodo*—and heard the lock release. The door opened. Avdokia! In her blue kerchief. When she saw me, she stuffed her hand against her mouth to stop herself from crying out, drew me into the warm room, closed the door and locked it. She held me, weeping.

She still smelled like yeast, though there was hardly any to be found in the city. "Oh, my lovey. Oh, my girl," she said, patting my back. "My Marinoushka, they said you'd been here. That they told you."

My mother stood in a daze at the window wearing my father's old dressing gown, her hair in a waist-length braid over her shoulder.

"Where's Ginevra?" I asked.

I could feel the thinness of Avdokia's shoulders. "Gone," she said.

"Back to England?"

Avdokia nodded. "The English were leaving. They said she had to go."

"Couldn't you have gone with her?"

Her eyes flicked to Mother. "We weren't ready for traveling."

"*Son français était exécrable.*" Mother gathered the thick robe closer around her.

As if the quality of the woman's French summed up her entire usefulness in the world.

"I'm glad you didn't leave," I said, pressing Avdokia's withered old hands to my cheek. "I'm glad you're still here."

We heard women quarreling in the hall. "You took that egg. You know you did, you stupid bitch. My kid saw you!"

"It's like that all the time now," Avdokia said, low. "Who took whose egg. Whose piece of meat from the soup pot. We have to hide everything. People wear all their clothes at once so they don't come home to an empty wardrobe."

"*Il est indigne de nous d'en parler,*" Mother said. *It's beneath us to talk of such things.*

"Come, sit down." Avdokia took me by the hand and led me to the table they'd dragged to the window, cleared a box off a chair. "It's wonderful to see you. It's a miracle." Avdokia's tears leaked out of her hooded eyes into the wrinkles of her face like irrigation channels in a field. "Are you hungry, sweetness? Have you eaten?"

I remembered the food, my bag from Kolya. I'd been carrying it all morning. "These are for you." I set the sack on the table.

She began to unpack it. "Oh, lovey, you shouldn't have…where did you get this? Potted liver! And sour cream! Verushka, look what Marina's brought!" Then she frowned. "You didn't…commit a sin?"

I had to laugh. Of course I had—many. But prostitution was not one of them. "I robbed a commissar coming out of Eliseev's. Is it all right? Have some." I opened the jar with the potted meat.

"No, no, no," she said, grabbing it from me, putting the lid back on. "We'll eat it later, for supper." She took the sack and slid it under her small bed. "You were always such a good child."

Mother gazed out at the yellow-white sky, heavy with the promise of more snow, the light glazing her eyes. She looked like a blind seer, glowing in an unearthly way in the light from the window. Even in that man's robe, with her hair dressed like some peasant's, she was strikingly beautiful. "An awful child. Disobedient, noisy."

"You were a darling," my nanny said.

"Craved attention. She'd do almost anything to get it. Once Balmont was visiting, and she burst in wearing dancing shoes and a tutu. Proceeded to make an absolute spectacle of herself."

Who was she talking to?

"Walking on her hands, her bottom in the air. I'll never forget it. I'm sure he never did, either."

I remembered Balmont applauding. He even quoted his poem, *"I asked of the scattering wind: How can I be young always?"*

"You shouldn't have given me dancing lessons if you didn't want me to dance," I said.

The weak sunlight cast a white halo around her. This woman Kolya had loved so intensely. Though her skin had softened and creased, her bone structure was still beautiful. Her hand, holding back the lace curtain, so fine, so vulnerable. "Her father's daughter," she said, examining the street from behind the lace curtain. "Always. I had nothing to do with it."

Avdokia snorted. "I was holding your hand the day she was born, Verushka, and I promise you, you were there."

I went to Mother's side at the window, rubbed frost from the glass. Outside, the leafless tree in the courtyard etched the sky. Children played in the heaps of uncleared drifts like processions of ants. "I'm moving back, Mama."

She spoke without looking at me, as if recalling a dream. "He still comes, sometimes, in disguise—a beard, a workman's coat. Stealing into his own house like a criminal." She pressed the thick collar of Father's robe against her neck. "No, you can't come here."

I leaned against the frozen windowpane, the wind knocked out of me. I had felt sure I'd be welcomed. "Mama, it's my home."

She massaged her temples. "Stop plaguing me! Go away!"

Avdokia had tears in her eyes. I took her arm. "Who padlocked Papa's office?" I asked her.

"It's a Red Guardsman and his wife," she said.

"*So-called* wife," Mother interjected.

"And a good thing, Verushka," countered the old lady. "In times like these, to have a Red Guardsman here. They're robbing whole houses, pillar to post."

"Who do you think does the robbing?" my mother asked.

"Did she get the money out of the stove?" I asked my old nanny quietly.

Avdokia said. "No, we didn't get it."

I turned away and extracted the wad of Kolya's rubles from my underwear. "Here." I held it out to my mother. "Something to tide you over until I can get into the study." A fat sheaf. There must have been a thousand rubles there.

"We don't need your filthy money," she said. "We'll do fine. Dmitry Ivanovich takes care of us. Now please leave. I'm not well. I have to lie down. Avdokia?"

I freed a narrow slice from the sheaf of bills and slipped the rest to Avdokia, who tucked it in her apron. What would we do without her sweet presence running through our lives, grounding our unrealistic family? Romantics, idealists, dangerous fools. At least Avdokia was there to tincture us with a measure of common sense.

"Come, Marinoushka," she said, pulling me away by the sleeve. "Leave now. Come back another day." At the door, she whispered, "You don't know what she's been through. First you, then Seryozhenka, God rest his soul. And your father, wanted by the Cheka. The searches! And Basya, that devil. They came from the Soviet and dragged my poor Verushka off to clean the cesspit at the lower school—and who do you think reported her? That chicken-legged witch! She's on the *domkom* now, fluffing herself up like a peacock. She has it out for us. Be careful."

The last shall be first. Basya, our put-upon maid, now on the all-powerful house committee, had evidently ratted Mother out to the district soviet as a nonworking bourgeois, subject to the new labor conscription levied on the Formers. I'd seen them under the supervision of the Red Guards ineffectually shoveling snow in their once-elegant shoes.

"I tried to get them to take me instead, but they wouldn't, the beasts. She didn't come back until eight that night." Tears welled in the droop of her eyelid. "After that she wouldn't speak for days. A son just in the grave, and now this!" She waved her hand in the direction of the salon and the sound of people arguing. "It's enough to drive anyone to murder."

"Stop talking to her," my mother called out. "She's with *them* now."

"She doesn't mean it," Avdokia murmured in my ear, helping me put my shawl over my cropped hair. "She doesn't know what she's saying." She turned back into the room. "You know it's not her fault, Verushka. It's the revolution."

"They've stolen her soul. Look at her." Her eyes filled with dread, as if the experience of cleaning the cesspit had branded them forever with a vision of hell. "They've all lost their souls, can't you see? There are no people, only things. Nothing inside but dust."

Perhaps I had indeed lost my soul. But I could only wish there was nothing inside me but dust as I gathered myself for the trudge back to the Poverty Artel and the reception I was likely to meet there.

35 *My Disgrace*

I HAD NO CHOICE but to return to Grivtsova Alley, through the uncleared snowy streets and the frosty fog.

Home to unbearable pain and disgrace. I felt more alone than I had on that night in October when Father sent me packing. On the tram, I rehearsed in my mind things I could say, but I only got as far as *Genya, forgive me*. When I got off at the bridge over the Catherine Canal, I slipped on a patch of ice and fell hard onto my knees. The metaphor wasn't lost on me.

Wet and bruised, I mounted the stairs to the Poverty Artel. Groping my way in the dimness, I came upon a man lying on the stairs, the stench of alcohol and urine rising from him. "Girl, girlie." He grabbed for my leg. "How's about a kiss?"

"Get off, you stinking drunk." I kicked myself free of him.

He laughed and began to sing as I continued my climb:

Create, O Lord, create for me,
For me a pretty young beauty . . .

Our splintered door had lost its number. I steeled myself and used my key, said a prayer, and opened it quickly. Only Anton was there, editing in the light from the window. I quietly closed the door and headed for the divan, crunching across the detritus of sunflower seeds that had built up in my absence.

"Decided to creep home, did you?" he said.

I sat on the edge of the divan. Much as I'd dreaded facing Genya, now I wished to God he was here and not Anton so I could get on with my execution. What was I going to tell him? I thought I'd never see him again. It had never occurred to me that I would have to face the damage I'd done to his good, sweet heart. I had expected to disappear into the magical rabbit hole with Kolya Shurov and end up in some crazy folk song. But now I'd come back here like a shipwrecked sailor, half drowned in my wet clothes, wave-battered on the very same beach from which I'd departed four days ago.

"We were just getting used to your absence. It was wonderful. Like getting rid of a cold sore. And suddenly it's back."

I lay down, wishing I could be as drunk as the man on the staircase, singing and pissing in my pants. I kicked off my boots and pulled the quilt up over me, coat, scarf, and all. "I missed you, too, Anton."

He leaned over from his cot and opened the door of the little stove, poking at its sad contents, letting the room fill with smoke until my eyes stung. I knew he wanted me to shout at him so he could abuse me more, but I had no strength for it. I turned to the wall. I could hear him rattling around, slamming the stove door, pulling back a chair. "The trouble with you is that you think his genius is going to rub off on you like paint. But poetry doesn't transfer that way."

A portly old gent with a grand set of moustaches gazed out from a tattered advertisement, appraising me with utter condescension. I would tell Genya everything, and throw myself on his mercy. I could sleep on the chairs. Move in with one of the girls from the *Okno* group. He could beat me. There was no point in trying to anticipate it.

"He doesn't love you." The creak of the chair, the crunch of shells. "He just thinks he does. If you cleared out, he'd get over you in a week." He was back on his feet, prowling.

I ran my fingertips over the newspapers and announcements that served as our wallpaper: society fashion circa 1904 and portraits of captains of industry peered out from between the Bolshevik proclamations that Genya and the boys stuck there. *To the Workers, Soldiers, and Peasants: The Provisional Government Is Deposed*...how excited we'd been that day, almost a year ago now. *Soldiers, Workers, Clerical Employees! The Destiny of the Revolution and Democratic Peace Is in Your Hands!* That "clerical employees" had made us howl. For weeks afterward, every time soldiers, peasants, and workers were mentioned, we had to add: *and clerical employees.* I touched the paper, trying to hold on to the echo of Genya's laughter.

The soviets must remain a revolver pointed at the head of the government to force the calling of the Constituent Assembly...gone, gone. All the missed opportunities. While on the other side of the wall, Marfa Petrovna scolded one of her children: "Give it to Anya. See how you like that!" followed by high-pitched shrieks.

I could hear the tapping rain of sunflower-seed shells. "You think you're some kind of new woman," Anton informed me. "But you're just a cheap trinket with your romantic nights, your sentimental notions of the 'suffering Russian people.'" He finally settled back in his chair, propped himself against the table with a corduroy knee. "Why do you have to torture him? Like a fly laying her eggs in a raw wound. How women love to see a man suffer. It makes him sing so beautifully. Sing, Genya, sing!"

I saw myself as Anton must see me—as La Belle Dame sans Merci, the villainess of a *kinofilm* melodrama, a figure from Poe. "And here I thought you were a futurist," I retorted. "All you're missing is the amontillado."

"There won't be people like you in the future." I heard the skritch of a match, smelled the stink of his *makhorka*. "I know where you've been. I can smell you from here."

Guiltily, I drew the quilt tighter around me. How could he smell anything through that tobacco? He was just trying to unnerve me. I could go to the *banya*, but my going would confirm his suspicions.

"Mina told him everything," he said.

Of course she did. Maybe she'd tried to make love to him herself. She was good with my old lovers.

"You could leave right now. I wouldn't say anything. He'd never know you'd been here. And we could all get on with our lives."

From outside, in the hall, we could hear the drunk singing, *"A fig tree stands on top of the hill / Right at the very top. / Create, O Lord, create for me, / For me a pretty young beauty...*"

More smoke. The clang of the stove. "You should have heard Genya talk when you first met. 'This girl Marina, wait till you meet her. She's a *genius,* an *angel.*'" He took a drag. "Well, I never met a woman who was either. This doesn't surprise me at all. Only that you'd have the nerve to come back."

A genius, an angel. It was a knife in my breast, right under the diamond stickpin.

I sat up and opened my notebook, began to write, intending to let a decent period go by before I ran off to the *banya* for a wash. But before I could go, we both heard Genya's heavy footsteps on the stairs, heavier than usual. I waited the way a horse waits with its broken leg. Anton watched the door. It banged back, bringing a fresh burst of icy air, and he staggered in. Green eyes fogged over, skin pale, unshaved, the wide mouth that loved to laugh stripped of its mirth. This was what I dreaded more than a beating, more than anything.

He was halfway to the table when he saw me. I watched him grapple with the fact of my return as a man grapples to catch a falling bowl. His eyes focused, his Adam's apple rose and fell in his strong neck, then he lowered his head like a bull in the last minutes of the corrida—exhausted, its thick neck impaled with picks.

I had done this to a man I loved. He stood, swaying, staring at me with such sadness I thought I would break from the weight of it. How naked he was, his pain, his love, his fear. This beautiful man, whom I had betrayed. He deserved better. Better than me. I hadn't known this about myself, just how selfish I was, how untrustworthy. Anything he could say about me would be true.

"Tell her to bugger off," Anton directed. "You can't let her come back."

"Go take a walk," Genya said, not turning his gaze from me.

"I'm busy," said Anton, pretending to read a manuscript.

"Am I asking you?" Genya took a step toward his friend, more menacingly than I could have imagined.

Anton sighed and threw the pages down. "Look. I've put up with this melodrama long enough, and so have you, brother, if you'd get your head out of your pants long enough to see it."

In one swift movement, Genya seized him in a headlock, marched him to the still-open door, and threw him into the hallway. Then he slammed the door and turned the lock. He turned back to me with those wounded green eyes.

The whole house could hear Anton pounding on the door. "Let me in! I'm freezing my nuts off!"

Genya grabbed Anton's coat and gloves and hat and threw them out into the hall, then slammed and rebolted the door.

My relief at Anton's absence was followed by the

stark realization that Genya and I were alone together. Bearlike, he swayed, just staring at me. Would he fall? Would he rush at me, strike me with those huge hands he was unconsciously flexing and opening? He was not a violent man, but I had driven him to the wall. I deserved it. I wrapped my coat closer hoping he wouldn't smell Kolya on me. I couldn't stand seeing in his face the harm I had done him. I wanted to reach out, to comfort him, even now. Though he stank of vodka, he didn't seem drunk so much as heavy with suffering.

"Where did you go?" he asked. *Mina told him everything.*

I tried to think of something I could tell him, but all I could see was Kolya's greedy face and naked body in the bed on the English Embankment. "Genya, I'm not who you think I am. I'm..." and my throat closed up on me. I always saw myself as a good person who occasionally did bad things, but I saw now, that was a misconception. "I'm not careful. I make a mess of everything. You should throw me out. I wouldn't blame you."

"Where did you go?" he roared. Bull nostrils flaring. "Who were you with? Tell me!"

I looked down at my hands. They didn't even look like mine. "I have a lover. I haven't seen him since I met you." I felt like my face was on fire. I wished I could just tear it off. "He came back. I was so wild after I left Sergievskaya, so low. And I heard he'd come back. He knew Seryozha. I wanted to see him. Not to make love to him, just to see him. Just to feel known, do you understand?"

"No, I don't," he choked with a sob. "You don't think I know you?"

I shook my head. "Forgive me. I've lost everything. My whole life. I thought it would make me feel better to see this man from the old days."

"And did it?"

Did it? "For a while." But now I'd ruined my life for it, for three days. *Go back to your poet.* Would a man who loves you send you back to your lover?

"You should have stayed with him."

"He left." The air felt like glass. Broken, sharp, unbearably bright. "He's a criminal. A speculator."

"And you went to him."

"Yes." I couldn't stand to look at him. It was like looking into the sun.

"Don't you care about me at all? What am I to you? Just this big buffoon you can lead around by the nose?" He had started to cry. "Was it that poem I wrote? I thought you'd like it."

Oh, if only lightning would strike me right now, so that I would not have to live through this moment.

He shuffled to the window, rolling his forehead on the cold glass. "Did you ever love me?" he asked. "Tell me the truth."

"Yes," I said, letting the quilt fall from my shoulders, glad there was something I could answer with absolute confidence.

"Do you love me now?"

"Yes." From the pain I was feeling, I knew I did love him, not incandescently, not feverishly, craving his skin, unable to think about anything else. Why must there be only one kind of love? There had to be better words, ten or fifteen, a hundred. Love was such a mixture of things, each love with its own flavor and spice. I wanted to both reassure him and warn him. For him I had love, tenderness, pity. Attraction and admiration, friendship and trust. As opposed to what I felt for Kolya—animal passion, ecstasy, history—and a spoonful of black hatred as well.

"Do you love this other man?"

I nodded, barely moving my head, just tucking my chin. I would not lie to him now.

He roared and turned over the table, lamp and papers crashing to the floor. He wanted to hit me, I knew it, but he couldn't do it, so he threw chairs and broke things instead. "No. You can't. It's not possible!" He picked up a chair and brought it down onto the table. It flew apart, leaving him with just the chair leg, with which he battered the overturned table until he fell to his knees, sobbing.

Was I just as Anton had described, some sort of succubus draining the life from this strong, beautiful man? "I went home to my mother's, but she won't forgive me. I had no choice. I'm sorry."

"You could find a brothel," he snapped. "I'm sure they'd be happy to have you."

Would that be my next stop?

"Am I not enough for you?" he said softly. "You think I'm a bad lover?"

Of all things. Pity brought me to him, put my hand on his shoulder. He knocked it away. I leaned my face against his shoulder, hoping he wouldn't hit me. Under my cheek, a great sob. He grabbed me and held me, kissing me, pushing me down on the floor, hands in my coat, needing to make love urgently, his desperate fingers. This body, this borderline, this rocky shore. He needed to erase Kolya from this body that had been his. He tore at my dress, planting his mouth on mine as if he needed the very air from my lungs. Ripped at my bloomers. Was this love? Was it hate? Was he weeping or was it I? We made violent love on the dirty wooden floor among the debris of chairs and sunflower-seed shells, clutching, weeping, until we were drained. "Don't leave me, Marina," he whispered.

I lay on the floor, half under him, shells embedded in my back, his smell of green and wood, my hair a tangle, his like ruffled shocks of wheat. What was the body, this bloody field of stones? So many battles fought here, so many good men lost.

36 *No Peace, No War*

ONCE AGAIN WE WALKED together, breathing our breaths into the frozen days, my head in its thick scarf coming up to his rough wool shoulder. In an unexpected way, we had become more of a couple than we had ever been — considerate, protective. We spoke in low, intimate tones. But we had lost the joy, the spontaneity. What was between us felt fragile, clear, and breakable as a ship in blown glass. We had entered the formality that leads husbands and wives to call each other by name and patronymic. Yet I learned that a strange kind of trust arises after betrayal that no one ever talks about, that comes with the knowledge that one's lover is willing to be hurt — to absorb pain, to carry it — for the sake of love. And that one was capable of hurting someone deeply. And that it was not the end. You can live that way, you can go on.

In Galina Krestovskaya's apartment, we pale young poets of Petrograd warmed our cracked, chilblained hands by the stove and prepared to invoke the Muse — while ignoring the lingering smells of a decent meal recently consumed. Where Seryozha's death had placed cotton in my ears and a fog before my eyes, my disgrace had stripped my senses bare, and again I heard, I saw.

Anton began. His poem investigated the possibility of the *ya*, the I, the ego. It was woven with clever half rhymes and strings of sound, unintelligible at first hearing. And yet its meaning bobbed along like a buoy in rough weather, sometimes above the line of waves, sometimes below. He'd said no more to me after his outburst, but his disdain for me and concern for Genya were always simmering under the surface.

Genya's new poems thundered more emphatically than ever, in inverse proportion to our careful silences with each other. The poem he recited urged the people to be men and not children, not to examine their leaders for feet of clay, for all feet were of clay. The revolution could not live in the sky, the poem said, only in the mess of blood and fire and earth. He challenged the reader to embrace the heat and the darkness and the smoke and let it transform him, let it temper him hard. It was his wish for himself.

For my part, I found a place to stand in the details of daily life. I returned to the precision of rhyme and meter. I found it soothing to sit on the divan, day after day, working out rhyme schemes, counting loping iambs and foot-dragging dactyls. I had never been so technically accurate. The two university students, Oksana and Petya, liked the repetition, the clarity, but Anton of course hated them. "All its energy is in chains," he complained. "Where's the *sound?*" But Seryozha's death was silent as an owl flying through snow. Kolya's departure was the nicker of horses, a swish of runners. And Genya and I — the sound of breath being held, the tinkling of icicles.

Sitting in the tobacco fug, discussing each poem in turn, I watched lovely Galina Krestovskaya drink in our words like claret, sometimes gasping or applauding a good line, at other times nodding as Anton analyzed us. We were her little geniuses, her personal nest of golden cockerels.

Krestovsky, in his usual leather-backed chair, a balding man in a coat and tie, big-nosed and bespectacled, read a Nat Pinkerton novel, a cigarette burning in his fingers. He was resigned to our presence as he had been to his wife's redecorating the flat in the fashionable primitive style of the Diaghilev set designers.

My poem centered on women pumping water in the courtyard of a Grivtsova Alley apartment building. Exhausted, complaining, they shared gossip as they stood in the frozen puddles, then carried their water upstairs, two, three stories, slipping on the icy steps. It was called "The New Ice Age," told in tightly patterned stanzas as intricate as a watch.

Oksana began the critique. She enjoyed the repetitions and tight metrical schemes, the rhymes. Zina burst in, her button eyes afire. "But it's counterrevolutionary. You're saying the Bolsheviks are incapable of keeping water going in the buildings, when you know it's the landlords who won't make repairs."

"Are we critiquing content?" Petya asked Anton.

"Of course the landlords won't make repairs," Krestovsky called out from his lair. "Nobody's paying rent. So who's going to fix your water? Jesus Christ?"

Galina cast her luminous eyes to the figured ceiling, embarrassed at her husband's unfashionable views.

"Well that's the bourgeoisie for you. Money for wars but not for water." Genya sat on the windowsill, his

dirty boots defiantly resting on the satin of the seat below. He'd become more Bolshevik in the last weeks,
more intentionally rude, as if he had to prove to himself
he wasn't going to be pushed around by bourgeois
morality, least of all his own.

"I'm depicting actual life," I argued. "As we're living
it. Should I pretend it's already paradise?"

Zina flushed even darker. "But you're saying life is
worse under the Bolsheviks." She looked pleadingly to
Genya to back her up. Before, Genya would have been
the first to chastise me, but now he let me be.

"I'm not 'saying' anything," I said, defending myself. "Are you suddenly a symbolist?" Hers was the
kind of criticism that often split our group into factions,
whether content should be criticized or not.

"Those women should be glad to be pumping water
in a Soviet Petrograd," said sixteen-year-old Arseny to
my left. "It's their water now."

Krestovsky burst out laughing from his chair in the
alcove, and I had to slap my hand over my mouth not
to join him. Did Arseny's mother fetch his water?

"But they're not glad," I said simply. "I want those
women to be able to look into the mirror of this poem
and recognize themselves." I rubbed at a blister on my
right hand, where I'd burned myself boiling water on
the primus stove. "Not some sentimentalized notion of
'the people.'"

"You could write about the landlords not fixing the
water," Zina said. "They'd still see themselves, but

it would also make a statement." Her eyes flicked to Genya, but he just leaned back against the window frame and gazed over his shoulder at Sergievskaya Street.

Oksana came to my rescue, her gray eyes huge and dark-circled under her fringe of frizzy blond hair. "Not every poem has to be instructive to be revolutionary. To depict the life of common people in the contemporary context is itself revolutionary. This is poetry, not advertising."

Zina stamped her small black boot on the Krestovskys' parquet. "There are no sidelines. Poetry is part of the fight."

"You're all missing the point. The *babas* and their water aren't the issue." From the piano bench, Anton broke in, wearing that supercilious expression. "It's the form that's the problem. You're trying to make a Red Guardsman waltz in hobnailed boots. *Da dum da dum da dum da dum.* The revolution is in the lines, or it isn't a revolution. The poem is timid. It's strangling in its corset."

I resented what he was saying, but he was right. I was seeking solace in iambs and anapests, clever rhymes. I had become reactionary, not in my politics, but in my poetics. The trouble was that I could not write energetic modern lines, because I had no energy. These controlled intricacies reflected exactly my spirit's limitations.

After the discussion, Sasha and other artists began to drift in — actors, students, dancers — knowing there would be snacks and perhaps liquor. Our hostess, graceful, blond, and green-eyed in a gypsy scarf, flitted from group to group, her bracelets jingling, happy to be at the center of such an advanced artistic coterie, while Krestovsky played chess with Anton.

I was speaking quietly with Oksana when two familiar faces entered the archway of the salon — Dunya Katzeva and her newly glamorous sister. What was Mina doing here? Dunya smiled at me, but she was searching for someone else, and her smile broadened when she saw him. I stepped behind Oksana and searched for Genya. Had he seen Mina come in? No, he was safely across the room, explaining something to Petya and little Arseny. I excused myself and threaded through the clusters of guests into the hall, but Anton's quick eye had caught my exit. Mina's arrival had not escaped him, either.

I ducked into a little sitting room, where Galina's maid sat mending clothes. Surveying myself in the etched mirror, I pushed back my untidy hair, wished I had some lipstick. Compared to Mina, I looked like a washerwoman.

"Nothing to steal, if that's what you're thinking," the maid said.

"I'm hiding from someone," I said.

She assessed me like a woman appraising a sack of frozen potatoes that would cost a week's wages, wondering how many were rotten. But finally she returned to her sewing.

We were in a pretty room—like the rest of the apartment, flavored with a folktale motif à la Nikolai Roerich. On the bookshelf stood photographs of Galina in various roles: a peasant girl in braids to her knees and an arched *kokoshnik;* a gypsy with golden curls; a moody portrait, her black velvet tam barely discernible from the dark background, the light questioning her heart-shaped face. Not as theatrical as the other photographs, showing her as lovely but allowing the flaws to remain, it had to be the work of Solomon Katzev.

What was Mina doing out there? Talking to Genya, stirring things up again? I paced back and forth, hoping she would leave, or—a soft knock on the door. The maid looked up, cursed under her breath. It opened slowly, and my old friend stood in the doorway. Like a hound, she'd chased me to ground. Would she tear me to pieces, or would I be able to get away?

"Why did you leave?" she asked.

"Isn't it evident? I don't want to talk to you." I'd backed myself into a corner.

The maid smirked over her mending.

"Do you mind giving us a moment?" my friend, my enemy, asked her.

"The street's right there," said the maid, stubborn as a rock. I wondered if I'd found Anton a wife.

I tried to push past Mina, make a break for the hall, but she grabbed my arm, her gaze a purpled gray like a river in storm. "Marina—listen to me."

I wrenched myself away. Out the window, wind swept the snow up into the blackness, where it peppered the glass like insects on a summer night. A whoop of laughter rang out from the party. Someone had started up the gramophone. A little bell rang. Sighing heavily, the maid folded her mending into the sewing basket and, with a stern cast of eye, left us.

Mina stood with her back against the door. I didn't recognize her, only those small hands, the little ring on her pinkie that her father had given her on her thirteenth birthday. "Are you going to avoid me for the rest of your life?"

I didn't want to talk about this, but she was giving me no choice. "You didn't have to tell him. Did you enjoy that?"

"What was I supposed to do? He came over looking for you. You didn't tell me what you wanted me to say." Her lips trembling, she started to cry. As her nose reddened, she started looking like her old self. "I said you were beside yourself with Seryozha's death, that you'd be back, to just be patient…"

She'd been sure I'd be back. Funny. She hadn't dreamed that I'd been ready to follow Kolya to the ends of the earth, that I'd already imagined myself traveling with him to the south, living among bandits behind the Denikin lines.

"Was that all you said?"

Her cheeks flamed in her white skin—that beautiful skin—her eyes looked bruised. "I didn't mean to tell him. I swear. He was just so torn up, and it was a terrible thing to do—you could have at least done your own lying."

"So you told him about Kolya. You thought that would make him feel better?"

"I was angry. You just do whatever you want and get away with it. It's always been that way." She was shouting now. "Take what you want, leave everything else a smoking wreck. Why should I lie for you? Don't do things you're ashamed of doing if you don't want to be found out."

I drifted over to the tiled stove, smoothed the warm tiles under my fingers as if I were smoothing out a sheet. How clean it was here, the neat household of Galina and Krestovsky. How messy I was by comparison, how incapable of conducting my life. "Is that what you came to tell me? Or to find out what happened with Kolya? How it all turned out?"

She flushed crimson again, suddenly very interested in the state of her shoes.

"He's gone back south, if you must know." I could feel my own tears starting, welling up from where they'd been hidden since that day on the English Embankment. "Told me to go back to my poet."

She sank onto one of the upholstered benches, let her coiffed head fall against the painted wall, closed her eyes, and wrapped her arms around herself. "I'm sorry. I just didn't know what else to do. I didn't tell him where you were, did I?" She put her hand on my sleeve.

"We're not who we used to be, fine, but can't we be friends anyway?"

Outside, a bout of gunfire. What could be happening—a confrontation between robbers and Chekists? Life was so precarious now. Mina had betrayed me twice, withholding the news of Seryozha's death and of my lover's arrival.

Her gray eyes pleaded. "I didn't go out of my way to hurt you, Marina. Or maybe I did, I don't know..."

Yet who did I have who knew me as Mina did? Genya and I were still together, despite my betrayal. Should I hold my friend to a higher standard than I had been held to? In any case, I needed a friend now, clay feet or not. As Genya said in his poem, nobody lived in the air.

Anton spotted us as we came back out to the party together and sauntered up, trickling smoke from his long nose. "Gotten your stories straight?"

"You're the poets," Mina said. "I'm only a humble scientist. It's not my job to make things up." She took my arm and led me past him. It made me laugh. She really was growing up. But then I saw that she was leading me straight over to the group around Genya. God, did we have to do this, too? They kissed cheeks in greeting and he reached out for my hand.

More gunfire. "What the hell is going on out there?" I asked. "Another revolution?"

Petya, his pilled sweater covered in pastry crumbs, ignored the blasts. They were obviously talking about the war negotiations at Brest-Litovsk, already a month old. "Lenin's right. We're going to have to give in sooner or later. Your man Trotsky can't stall forever."

"Oh, this again," Mina said.

The negotiations had bogged down into a stalemate. Trotsky, as commissar for foreign affairs, refused to agree to the German conditions. He insisted that Germany must not be allowed to annex Poland or Lithuania and that Russia would not pay it any reparations. Lenin wanted to accept German terms and get it over with.

"Lenin's a defeatist," Genya said in his big bass voice. "Trotsky's playing them like a fisherman. Wearing them out." He kissed me on the top of my head, wrapped his arm around me.

Mina sought my eyes. *See? You have Genya.*

"You watch, a few more weeks, the kaiser's going the same way as Nicky—right to the autocrats' zoo. We'll go visit and feed them peanuts through the bars."

It was what everyone was hoping for —a revolution in Germany. They were so close. Five hundred thousand metalworkers went on strike in Berlin at the end of January. A million German workers were demanding peace without annexations abroad and democracy at home. Surely it was only a matter of time before the kaiser toppled.

"We've shown the world just what this war is about," Zina said. "Reparations and annexations, for the Triple Entente as much as the Central Powers." Upon the ascension of the Bolsheviks, Trotsky had outraged our allies by publishing the tsar's secret treaties with France and England, revealing their plans to divide up the spoils of Europe when we won the war. "The German workers won't take much more of it. They're the ones paying with their blood and their labor."

Petya took Lenin's view. "You can't underestimate the Germans. They're not going to give in, workers or not. We're a wreck and everybody knows it. They can roll right in anytime they want to."

I noticed Dunya with Sasha over on the far side of the room, holding hands, laughing. She was wearing that soft, rust-colored woolen dress decorated with Seryozha's sunflowers. She saw me watching her, and her smile saddened. She touched the patch. I wondered if her parents knew she was here.

"You'd better pray we don't give in," Krestovsky called out from his leather chair, his fringed lamp. "If you thought the tsar was bad, just try the kaiser. Trotsky should never have published those treaties. We might have gotten the English back as allies, finished the war, come out ahead. Now look what a mess we're in."

"Those treaties proved that both sides are the same," Genya shouted over the heads of the others.

Across the drawing room, very straight and tall, wearing a black leather jacket with snow still clinging to her shoulders, stood a familiar form looking about—Varvara. After the way she had dismissed me that day on Vasilievsky Island, I had assumed I wouldn't be seeing her again. I couldn't imagine what Varvara would want, that she would willingly enter such a lavish establishment as the Krestovskys'. And where did she get that jacket? She looked just like a Cheka officer.

She saw me with Genya and Mina, grinned and hurried over to us, then took my hands in her cold, bony ones and kissed my cheeks. She glowed at Genya, grabbing him by the upper arms. Beamed at Mina. "You're all here. My God, I've been looking for you all over town." Her hair was wet. She was breathing hard. "I had to tell you. At four o'clock…there was a call to Smolny. From Brest." The poets drew closer— Krestovskaya, Anton, Sasha, and his friends. "The war is officially over!" She embraced me vigorously and kissed me three times.

"They accepted Trotsky's terms?" Oksana asked.

Krestovsky rose, threw his book onto his chair. "You're sure?"

"I was out at Smolny. We got the news this afternoon. By tomorrow it'll be in the papers. But I just had to let you know first." She took my hands again. "You've given up everything for this. I wanted you to know."

"Peace," said Galina Krestovskaya. "I can't even remember it."

Mir. Even the word sounded strange to my ears. Four long years of war. I thought of those hospitals, the soldiers' fetid dressings, the windows that wouldn't open, the wounds that wouldn't close. They would all go home and take up their plows. We might even have decent bread again. *And Kolya would come home.*

I shoved that thought away.

"What were the terms?" Krestovsky asked.

Varvara looked into the faces of the crowd that had assembled around her. Her voice changed when she spoke again. "Comrade Trotsky's decided that nothing would put an end to the German demands. Who did they think they were negotiating with, another imperialist state? 'No annexations,' he said. 'No indemnifications.' The German people want to end it, too. It's just the German General Staff—they can't accept that their world is finished. So Comrade Trotsky ended it. This afternoon, he walked out of the negotiations. *No war, no peace.*"

"What the devil does that mean?" Anton said.

"It means we're out of the war, but we agree to nothing," she said. "If the Germans dare to attack us, a peaceful Soviet Russia, their workers will rise up and they'll lose from the rear. They can't risk it—don't you see? Either way, they lose."

"Genius," Zina pronounced.

Krestovsky mopped his forehead with his handkerchief. "The Germans will never let it go at that."

"You can stop worrying about the Germans," Varvara said. I could smell her leather jacket as the room warmed it. "Nicky started it, but Leon Trotsky just put it to bed."

Genya moved to the center of the room. I could feel his excitement. "Here's to Comrade Trotsky! *Urah!*" This is how I liked to see him, that huge energy, freed of wounds, my sins forgotten. Perhaps more had ended than just the stalemate at Brest—perhaps ours had as well.

Gunfire splattered the night. So that's what we were hearing—celebration! The war had ended! We began to sing "La Marseillaise"—not the worker's version but the original. In a minute, Galina bustled in with her maid, the actress holding up two bottles of champagne, the maid bearing a tray with wine glasses. "After four long years, let's have a proper toast." She gave a bottle to her husband to open. He at first returned her enthusiasm with an expression of dismay when he saw the label, then resigned himself to her gesture of largesse. Opening the foil, becoming caught up in the fun as he popped the cork and filled the glasses. She began passing them around. "Does everyone have a glass?"

We all did.

Genya raised his. "To Comrade Trotsky. And the end of the war."

"Your lips to God's ear," Krestovsky added under his breath.

We drained our cups—heads back, necks bared. Genya snatched me up, hoisting me to his shoulder and marching me around as he led us in singing "The Internationale." I ducked the chandelier as we sang. Even Krestovsky sang: *So comrades come rally / And the last fight let us face: / The Internationale unites the human race.*

The festive mood strengthened with the second bottle of champagne. Krestovsky put a record on the gramophone and began a wobbly-kneed sailor's dance to "The Boundless Expanse of the Sea." Not bad considering his age and level of fitness. Genya and Sasha and Arseny joined him, arms linked across each other's shoulders, their vigorous steps endangering the fine furniture. Varvara put her arm around my waist and hugged me again. "I just had to come tell you. I read about Seryozha..."

Oh, please, God, let her not say anything more.

"I know you're still mad at me...please don't hate me anymore. I can't bear it. I'm sorry about that night, your papers. I was being a shit."

"I got them anyway. *Bourgeois.*"

She brushed a lock of my hair back that had come forward during my triumphal march on Genya's shoulder. "Let's start over. Can't we? *No war, no peace?*"

Could we ever start over? Did I want to? The sailor's dance ended and Petya took to the piano, launching into an American ragtime piece I didn't recognize. Genya was enthusiastic but not much of a foxtrotter, stepping on my toes. After a while Gigo cut in, and he was a beautiful dancer, a surprise. Anton and Varvara sat out the dancing, exchanging cynical quips no doubt, but Dunya and Sasha, Galina and Arseny took the floor. Oksana danced with Nikita Nikulin, a poet.

At one point, Petya began "Two Guitars," and Galina, draping herself with the piano shawl, her blond hair falling loose over her shoulders, began a gypsy dance. Faster, faster she twirled, her little heels stamping, the fringe flying as we clapped for her. "You dance ten times better than that," Varvara murmured under her breath.

"Hardly," I said.

We applauded madly when she was done, and she bowed her graceful thanks.

Then Krestovsky, flush with champagne, broke out the vodka, and Petya began "Dark Eyes," with all the flourishes. The sound of it hit me with nostalgic force.

"Marina, you dance." Varvara shoved me forward.

"Marina!" my fellow poets chorused encouragingly. "Marina!"

Genya watched me, that dear face finally without the cloud that had darkened it these last days. Oh, but not this song. *Ochi chornye / Ochi strastnye . . . Dark eyes, passionate eyes, / How I love you, how I fear you . . . / An unlucky hour, the hour I caught sight of you.* "Go on," he urged me.

I moved out onto the floor, leading with my shoulders, gypsy style, and danced it for Genya—our love, our grief, our beauty. Slowly at first, filling it with my passion as you fill a glove with your hand, then faster and faster, while down below in the street, people fired off guns for the wild music alone.

37 *Germans*

IGNORING VARVARA'S ADVICE TO stick to the banks and the telephone exchange, I landed a job at a small knitting factory a few minutes' walk from Grivtsova Alley. It paid barely enough to buy a shoelace, but the important thing was to be working now, to have a labor card entitling me to precious ration tickets for bread and soap and even new galoshes when it came around to my turn, if that day ever arrived. *He who does not work, does not eat,* the tickets said.

The factory was owned by a tubby man named Bobrov, whom the girls called Count Bobo. His wife, Tatiana Rodionovna, made us a hot lunch every day. I liked to think of it as a factory, because factory work carried a proletarian dignity with it, but the place was really just a poorly lit, poorly heated workroom with tables and benches where eleven girls knitted socks on tiny machines. Their leader, fifteen-year-old Olga, showed me how to wind the yarn around metal pins, then trip them one by one. Click, click, click, all day long. After a week, I'd picked up the cough they all had from breathing the woolen threads. At eighteen, I was by far the oldest. It was like having eleven little sisters. They buzzed with stories, mostly about the German advance.

Contrary to Trotsky's assumption that the Germans

would give up on us, not daring to foment revolution at home, they came east at terrifying speed. In the girls' tales, the Huns hacked off Red soldiers' limbs and fed them to pigs before the very eyes of the mutilated men, and any workers they caught in the invaded towns were stripped and tied to fences, splashed with water, and left to freeze or gutted and left for the wolves. I didn't dare ask them to shut up. A protest would just increase their gruesomeness. They loved it when they got to you and would attack like a school of small vicious fish.

Silently I spun the wool, winding it around the pins of the little machine, composing verses against the click and spin as the tube of socks or gloves emerged. Poems kept my mind off the blisters, the ache, and the cold. I thought of Avdokia's gnarled fingers and for the first time really understood how it was to live off the work of one's hands. It took hours to straighten my fingers at night. Genya rubbed them, warming them between his own, until the blood came back to them.

These days he and I had the divan to ourselves. Sasha and Gigo had moved into a place of their own, now that Sasha was working at the Zubov Art Institute. And Zina had begun sleeping elsewhere out of sheer disgust at Genya's taking me back. I slept each night in the crook of Genya's arm and dreamed of red wool snaking through my hands.

In a second courtyard
A dark workshop

Three sisters cast their shadows
The one who spins, the one who measures,
And—don't ask.
The one who cuts the bloodred wool.

Our hands are raw
Our backs grow bent
Do we know whose fate we thread?
The pulse of blood runs thick and thin
As the heavy tread advances.

In the bread queue after work, I stood with the others, holding my thirty-day ration card, stamping my feet, and listening to the latest. All the standers agreed that the government had signed the peace too late. Against a broken Russian army, the Germans advanced like the tide. What reason did they have to stop when town after town rolled onto its back? They would teach Red Petrograd a lesson, a parable for their own workers to read.

"The *Petrogradsky Echo* says the embassies are pulling out," said a girl wearing a homemade fur hat.

"Which embassies?" I asked her.

"All of them," said an intelligent-looking woman with a soft, lined face.

The SR paper, *Delo Naroda*—the *People's Cause*—reported that the Bolsheviks were shipping the treasury to Moscow, preparing to abandon the capital. How upset Father had been when Kerensky had suggested it! Now it was *Pravda* and *Izvestia* denying the rumors.

No one knew anything for sure, but everyone had a bit of information to share. The woman standing behind me, broad-hipped and gold-toothed, holding a heavily swaddled infant, spat and said, "Ericsson's being evacuated. They're sending them out to the Urals." The giant electronics plant. I well remembered marching with their workers in February. "My old man works there. But they won't let him bring us. Ain't that something?" She joggled the baby. Only the slits of its eyes showed. "Safe in the Urals while we're here in Petrograd about get run over by Willie's boys. What kind of a government is this, turning women and children into sitting ducks? He says the Ericssons are going to strike."

"How close you think they'll come?" asked the girl in the hat. "The Germans?"

"All my neighbors are leaving," said an old woman with a fierce Turkish nose and a coat patched like a quilt. "And if I had a place to go, you bet I'd be on my way."

"It's one way to solve the housing crisis," said the soft-faced *intelligentka*.

Everyone was talking about whether they should leave, whom they could stay with in the country, when the revolution in Europe would start, and whether it would be soon enough to save us.

A well-dressed man strode along the street past us—whistling.

"Look at that," said a woman with an acorn-size mole on her cheek, wearing tattered gloves. "Disgusting."

We glowered at him. The new cheerfulness of the bourgeoisie was a slap in the face of every working person. Far from fearing the German advance, they whistled in the streets as if it were a holiday, their shoes shined, hair combed, faces newly shaved. They were looking forward to liberation by the enemy and the end of the revolution. The irony: these were the people who had kept us in the war to begin with, and who had called the Bolsheviks traitors for wanting to negotiate peace.

The government had granted greater powers to the Cheka to suppress this new bourgeois threat. The woman with the mole on her cheek said they were going to start rounding up the bourgeoisie soon and sending them to camps in the north. "And good riddance, that's what I say. They're ready to stab us all in the back."

The Germans were on the move. The district soviets held mandatory classes in sanitation and first aid, checking your name against your housing registration and your labor book. You could lose your labor book if you failed to show up. So after a day's work, we all spent two hours in the evening learning how to staunch an arterial wound, and what to do in case of a gas attack.

Newspaper headlines screamed, THE SOCIALIST FA-THERLAND IS IN DANGER! We went to hear the Bolshe-viks address the crisis at the Alexandrinsky Theater, worked our way through the crowd pressing in and found a bit of standing room in the aisle under the loge. I climbed onto the base of a pilaster, balancing my-self against Genya, so I could see the stage. Behind us, holes remained unpatched on the imperial box where the Romanov eagles had been torn off. In a single year, two governments had been washed away, and now the workers' state itself was in jeopardy.

Someone from the city soviet, bearded and grim, spoke from the stage lit by cheap smoky oil lamps. You could see his breath in the cold theater despite the density of the crowd. "They've taken Dvinsk and Reval." Reval, the capital of Estonia, a little more than two hundred miles away. "They're executing everyone with rough hands, a union card," he continued, his face like a funeral. "If we can't stop them, they're going to be at the Narva Gate" — the entrance to Petrograd — "in a week, tops. It's up to us, Comrades."

No false cheer. I balanced on my perch against Genya, my arms around his neck, which was swathed in the scarf that I'd knitted for him on the sly at my bench. I felt a sudden love for us all, all of these people wedged in and on the brink together — pale, dirty faces with red, sleepless eyes — the starved, gaunt citizenry of Petrograd. Anton bit his nails. A sailor ground his cigarette out on the floor.

I thought about the revolutionary uprisings we'd studied those last months at school—Spartacus, Pugachev, the French Revolution, the Paris Commune. The sad truth—they'd all failed in one way or another. Would October go down in history as another failed experiment, just before entries about how Russia became part of a glorious German empire? I imagined grim Prussian troops crossing the Russian countryside right this minute, their carts and great gray horses, their cannons. Their presence darkened the snow, turned the sky to lead.

The comrade from the city soviet yielded the podium to Karl Radek, a frail, animated commissar with a high forehead, wild curly hair, and round glasses. Radek's gestures were quick and confident, and he called out in oddly Western-accented Russian, "Comrades, they're coming to crush your revolution!"

A roar from the crowd, like the roar of the ocean striking a wild shore.

He continued. "Even as Trotsky was negotiating, the snake Hoffmann was already giving orders to advance!"

"Bastards!" the soldiers shouted. "Swine!"

"What did we expect?" Anton said, rolling a cigarette, sticking it in his mouth. "Badminton?" He lit the match with his blackened thumbnail.

Radek raised his hand for silence. "But Comrades, even now, your German brothers are organizing!" Fiery faith burned in Radek's small intellectual body, his hand outstretched, his round glasses catching the light from the smoky lamps. "They're striking in factories from Hamburg to Munich! They want the war to end! Now it's up to us to show them how socialists fight. Shoulder to shoulder, for the workingman. For the future!"

Cheers from the soldiers and sailors, the workers, the women in head scarves, the children and old men. I could feel my energy returning, my hope.

I imagined myself with a rifle, marching with these comrades. I'd hunted at Maryino. I was a pretty good shot—though, truth be told, I'd always felt ashamed to see a pheasant's or duck's bright eye cloud over, the way its beauty vanished in an instant. But these Germans had to be stopped.

"We must defend our revolution!" Radek said. "Not just in Russia but in Poland, in Latvia, in Germany and France and America! Down with every capitalist master! To arms, Comrades!"

Shouts and cheers echoed the diminutive speaker. People pounded Radek on the back as he left the stage, probably on his way to another such meeting.

A haggard-looking Bolshevik, tall and bony, took the stage. "The German soldier—what is he? A conscript. He's tired, he's hungry. His brothers are rebelling at home. With our example, he may just lay down his arms and join us! That's what made our revolution here. You cannot pit a conscript army against free men and women, fighting their own cause!"

"Long live the revolution!" Genya shouted.

An old, white-bearded worker leaned out from the second balcony and in a surprisingly loud, clear voice shouted, "Is it true the Soviet's packing up and heading to Moscow?"

The hall erupted into furor. The perfect acoustics of the Alexandrinsky Theater—which would let an actress's sigh be heard in the third balcony—filled with cries of "Yes, what do you say to that?" "Bourgeois lies!" "It's the truth!" "Shut up!" "You shut up!"

The gaunt comrade onstage held out his hands to quiet the crowd. "I assure you, citizens of Petrograd, the Soviet has no intention of abandoning you! We will fight to the last man! Some vital portions of industry are being evacuated to keep them from the invaders, but the Soviet isn't going anywhere." He stopped, leaning forward and pressing his hands on the lectern. "Ask yourselves, where are these rumors coming from? The bourgeois press! To whose benefit is it to promote chaos and counterrevolutionary hopes? The bourgeoisie! Therefore, the Soviet has declared the bourgeois press suspended until further notice. The Cheka will be especially vigilant about resurgent counterrevolutionary activity at this crucial moment. This is a warning to the bourgeoisie!" He slammed his fist into his hand to punctuate each syllable. "Do not give aid to the enemy of socialism!"

"Round 'em up!" I heard here and there around the auditorium. "Up against the wall!" "Shoot 'em!"

This warning to the Former People worried me. I pictured Mother, mustered out of her cluttered room in the middle of the night, marched through the city streets in the snow, shoved onto a train, and taken away to a camp in the forest, or in the far north. But what could I do? It was true—some of the bourgeoisie *were* plotting for the arrival of the Germans. They couldn't wait to take back what had been wrested from them and recover their former privileges, their former arrogance. My mother was probably polishing the silver. But a camp?

The full moon had risen, and deep drifts of snow threw back a light so bright, it felt like a setting in a play. I tucked my arm tightly under Genya's. Anton walked on his other side, hands shoved deep in his pockets, his face like a thundercloud. We found the rest of the Transrational Interlocutors huddled around the Catherine statue, smoking and debating in the bitter cold. We all decided to retreat to Sasha's new room close by, just off the Fontanka.

Genya and I allowed ourselves to fall behind, not speaking, just contemplating the size and gravity of what was about to happen. The war was coming to our door. In a matter of days, tanks and troops would be marching right up this embankment. Our shadows traced a complex calligraphy on the snow as we walked.

"Come on, you two!" Zina called back at us. "It's no time for lovemaking!"

"We'll catch up," Genya shouted ahead.

Instead of following them, we walked out onto the Chernyshevsky Bridge to watch the moon, huge and coldly white, rising over an empty city, the frosted walls, the sky unsmudged by chimney smoke. Ice glistened on the chains of the bridge's towers as we leaned on the parapet, his familiar solidity in his thick, patched overcoat which we slept under at night. Our friends walked ahead of long shadows poured black against the white snow.

I studied the big handsome face rising above me, the crooked nose, the pugnacious chin. Everything good about Russia was in that face—which I had betrayed, which I had stamped into the mud. I leaned into him and turned to watch the moonbathed west. From somewhere out there, they were coming, with their tanks and bloodied bayonets.

"I'm going," he said. "I've decided. I'm going to sign on in the morning."

I could see the determination on his face, the defiance in his jaw, but there was something else there as well. Unhappiness. Did he think this was a way out? Getting himself killed by the Germans? "You don't have to. You heard...they'll be here soon enough," said I, who had just been imagining taking up arms and marching to the front myself. How ridiculous! "We'll take those defense classes at the district soviet. Two hours of compulsory firearms practice."

"No." His eyes looked dark in the moonlight. "We

have to stop them before they get here. There's no time for practice. I'm going."

I stroked his cheek, my gloves catching on his whiskers. Genya, a soldier? He was so tenderhearted that if he found a spider in the Artel he would take it out into the hall, cradling it inside a cup. "You couldn't kill a chicken if you were starving."

He grabbed my hand. "I'll do what I have to do. You think I'm afraid? I'm not afraid."

"I know you're not. But I think you're trying to get yourself killed." I pulled my scarf up around my mouth and nose, my eyes tearing in the cold, the tears freezing onto my eyelashes. "I thought we were all right. That we were past all this."

His eyes blazed, I could see the whites in the moonlight. "This isn't about us. Does everything with you have to be about love? There are Germans out there, real Germans. They're not thinking about love. They're thinking about crushing the revolution. You heard Radek. They have to be stopped."

But I knew, deep inside, this was not only about what Radek said.

He put his arm around me, heavy, warm even through all the layers of our coats. He peeled the scarf from my face and kissed my cold lips, rubbed his stubble against my cheeks. His smell of sweet straw. "Would you really want me not to go?" he whispered in my ear. "To let old men fight for me? Would you respect me more?" He searched my face, begging me to understand. Begging me not to.

I pushed him away. "Seryozha went down to Moscow to prove he was a man."

"I'm not Seryozha," he said, his face suddenly steely. "He was a wonderful boy, but *I* am a man. Can't you see? It's war. And I need to get out there before they're at the door. Our door, Marina."

My eyes stung, my cheeks burned, the hair in my nostrils froze. I gazed at his heroic face over the striped scarf—my beautiful boy, my sufferer. I embraced him, I buried my face in his coat collar, that poor ragged coat that was going to the front. I should have sold Kolya's diamond and bought a sheepskin for him. What was I keeping it for? Memories of that betrayer? But it was too late to repent, to act. There was no more time.

38 *A Wedding*

I THOUGHT WE WOULD go back to the Poverty Artel, but now that he had made his decision, Genya wanted to go on to Sasha's. On a backstreet near the train station, the place was already blue with smoke and ripe with unwashed bodies when we got there. It was a room of two windows, and an easel took up half the space. Someone had found some spirits, made with God knows what—in compliance with Bolshevik asceticism, all the vodka shops had closed long ago.

"You're looking rather sober, young sir," Anton said to Genya as we came in.

"We thought you'd never make it," said Zina, sharing the one chair with Oksana Linichuk.

"I'm going," Genya said, shoving himself between Anton and Petya on the bed, forcing them to make room for him. I stood by the door. Why did Genya want to distance himself from me like this? Was he ashamed of me now?

"Going where?" Petya asked.

"The defense of Petrograd." Genya took the jar from Sasha, who sat on a box with a girl from the art school, and drank deep. "You heard them tonight. They need us out there. I'm signing up in the morning. Who's coming with me?"

The poets on the bed and around the low-ceilinged room exchanged glances like children caught in a prank after the schoolmaster asks the guilty one to come forward.

"I'd rather shoot myself in the head," Anton said, his elbow on Arseny's shoulder. "The Bolsheviks couldn't organize their way out of an intersection. If it gets down to a fight, I'll take my chances with the anarchists or the SRs."

Gigo, on the floor, brushed back his shining black hair from his eyes. "Death and I are bound to meet, its dark wing cooling my fevered brow," he said, quoting his own poetry. "And who will weep for me?" Gigo's last woman had ditched him for a Red Guard, whose rations were better than a Georgian translator's. "I'll go, and you women will curse the day you missed loving me."

"I'm in," Sasha said.

This was too awful, the poets and artists of Petrograd ready to trot themselves out into the fields to be killed. "You're all crazy. We need you here. The district is organizing something," I said.

"*You* go to the district," Zina said. "I'm going to defend the revolution. Count me in, too."

"Anton's got a point," Nikita Nikulin said. "Look how the Bolsheviks have bollixed it up so far. 'No war, no peace?' That was a good idea."

"Well, they got it half right," Oksana said, low in my ear.

"Listen." Genya stood and opened his great arms in the small room as if he were spreading revolution single-handedly, as if it were grain he was casting to the whole world.

> *When the enemy comes*
> *Will you watch him*
> *crush the skull of your newborn*
> *against History's cold wall?*
> *Will you cower beneath blankets with*
> *your spines unstrung?*
> *There's not time for lint-pickers,*
> *boot-lickers, liquor-misters.*
> *Let's go!*

before History
     flicks you away like clots of snot.
Step out, lace those boots,
Pull up your tattered underwear.
    The train, Red Dawn,
       is waiting at the station.

Sasha removed a bottle that looked like some kind of artist's cleaning fluid from his trunk, mixed it with water from a pan on the stove, and poured the concoction into another jar that he passed around. Each of us proposed our own toast.

"To history," Gigo offered.

"To a little less history," Oksana replied.

My brothers and sisters, the Transrationalists—would we ever be together like this again? Everything was ending, just as we came to know it and count on it. The alcohol proved oily and chemical. I could feel it chewing the lining of my stomach. I did my best to match their gaiety, but couldn't stop thinking that Genya might be dead soon. Gigo, Sasha... I was drinking with ghosts.

"Marina, I thought you were the brave one," Zina taunted me. "Are you really going to stay behind, like an old housewife?"

"I wouldn't want to deprive you of your Joan of Arc moment," I said. I couldn't very well explain what was really going on—that Genya didn't want me there to be his comrade, his brother-in-arms. He was desperate for a woman who would wait for him, worry about him, imagine his suffering, as he had waited for me during those nights and days I'd been away with Kolya. He needed his dignity back and this was to be my penance. And I would do it. Damn what Zina thought of me.

On a paint-smeared guitar Sasha often used in his cubistic still lifes, Petya played an old song about a peasant girl longing for her soldier boy. We sang along and we all felt something irreparable taking place, that it might be our last time together before history shook us, took us, killed us, changed us. Now I understood why Genya had wanted to come here after our talk on the bridge—not just to recruit comrades for the fight but to all be together like this, to complete the circle.

Now he whispered in my ear, "Let's go."

In the Artel, at last alone, we lit the stove and fed everything flammable we could into its hungry small body so that for once we could remove our clothes, producing our precious bodies—bitten, God knows, but beautiful. His heavy arms and legs, his neck like the branch of an oak, his eyes, wounded, searching, clouded green like swamp water. I could see the hurt child inside, looking out through the man's eyes—*Do you love me? Do you care if I die?*

I couldn't help thinking about the men in the hospital beds, their mangled and mutilated forms under the dirty sheets. If he were wounded, I would care for him. I would spend the rest of my life tending that body, wiping his chest, his legs. I let my fingers follow the lines of his bones, the wide collarbones, the knobby forehead, the strong, crooked nose, the lids of his yearning eyes. Was he thinking of the reality facing him tomorrow? Grenades, German guns, the points of bayonets, the hardness and indifference of war?

"Just don't die," I whispered, tracing his lips.

He pressed his own hand over my mouth. I tried the edge of my teeth against the knuckles. He pulled me into him. "I'm not the kind that dies," he said into my hair. "Bullets can't penetrate my genius."

We held each other before the stove, my cheek nested against his chest, his noble, vulnerable heart beating in my ear, the meeting place of will and destiny. We walked together to the divan, where I sat and he pretended to fall on me, then caught himself at the last minute, our old game. That night we made love freely, not silencing ourselves, not sparing each another, groaning, shouting out. He came inside me rather than pulling out. There was no going back for us, for any of us.

Later, we lay resting, sweating, his semen seeping out onto the blanket under me, his hand caressing my neck, which always felt too thin in his hands, like the stem of a flower about to be snapped, worry closing in again. I could see its shadows creeping along his jaw and into his eyes, along his nose, which some boy back in Puchezh had smashed in a fight over a chestnut when he was ten. I felt it rise in myself as well.

"Marry me," he said.

Had I heard him right? "You're kidding." Genya had always loathed that bourgeois institution. He called it as outworn as whalebone.

But I could tell by his expression that mine had been the wrong answer.

"We're already married, remember? That night on the Petrovskaya Embankment?" I showed him the ring finger on my wedding hand. "You gave me Saturn."

He pushed his hair from his eyes. "Seriously. Will you?" He wanted something he could hang on to in the snow outside Narva or Glyadino. How could I say no to him now? Was it right? Was it wrong? There was nobody to ask.

In the morning, I packed Genya's few things—pencils, a notebook, a pair of Anton's socks. He had blessedly stayed over at Sasha's. I could always make Anton another pair of socks. I gave him all our food. I cut him a lock of my hair and tied it with thread, put it in the Mayakovsky, *A Cloud in Trousers*. We sat holding hands on the divan a good long while, breathing together. Our lives would never be the same after this hour. We would leave through that door and everything would change. Even I, a girl of eighteen, looked around that room, memorizing it, knowing I would forever remember it as our youth's paradise—this spindly table where we wrote our poems, the torn newspapers on the wall, the little sulky stove, this moldy divan where we slept, and how we held each other very tightly to keep from falling out.

As we sat, knee to knee, on quilts smelling of sex, I thought of all the men in history who had gone off to fight for homelands and cities, for fields and villages, and all the women who had seen them off, just like this. I had the strange feeling of not being myself but rather some woman who had existed for centuries and whom it was now my turn to embody. I dared not cry. I dared not say a word that might burden him in any way. I just prayed, sealing my will around his body. *Please, Holy Mother, let him return exactly as he leaves.*

Time to go. We stumbled down the icy stairs and out across the dark courtyard along a narrow trampled path through great hummocks of uncleared snow, and out toward the district soviet.

This early in the morning, its windows were the only lit ones on the street. Inside, it was already busy, the halls smelling of wet wood, with people lining up, wanting to know where to go, what to do. And here were our friends waiting—pale, bleary, and disheveled from the party the night before, Sasha and Petya and Gigo. Zina with her cigarette dangling like a street tough. Nikita, Oksana—with flowers! Red geraniums. Where in the world had she gotten them?

"Have a nice sleep?" Scowling Anton looked like he'd slept upright. "Glad someone did."

"We need you all next door at the registry," Genya said. "We're getting married."

Zina dropped her lit cigarette. Anton turned away, bent double in a coughing fit.

Our Red wedding took less than two minutes. It was nothing like the wedding I'd imagined as a girl, in the little wooden church in Novinka, full of fragrant roses. My dress would be old ivory, my *kokoshnik* a crown of pearls. Bees would buzz around a long table set up for the feast in Maryino's yard, under the larch tree. A sapphire on my ring. A honeymoon in the South Pacific.

At my revolutionary wedding, there was no incense, no rings, no priest. No candles, no crowns, no feast. No Mama and Papa, teary-eyed and proud, no Seryozha, lonely and possessive. No Volodya, joking, making the toast. No Kolya, drinking himself stupid, realizing he should have considered the possibility of losing me. No music, no games. No bread and salt, no bride's bath. No rebraiding of my hair—no hair to braid! No Mina or Varvara. A war instead of a honeymoon. A group of hungover poets as our guests and our two signatures on a form, with Anton as witness.

But Genya never let go of my hand. That part of the ceremony was not forgotten. Nor was the wedding bouquet—Oksana handed me her geraniums. Their petals scattered over the wood floor like confetti, dotting the grime with crimson.

Outside in the hall, a somber crowd waited to sign on for defense of the city. A woman with a sharp, hawkish face behind the counter hung up the telephone.

"They've taken Pskov," she said. Less than two hundred miles southwest of Petrograd. How fast could an army travel?

His insecurities of the night before left behind, Genya was now all energy and manly enthusiasm. He held up his hand to get the attention of the room, and in his great, rolling voice began to recite his rousing new poem. People at first recoiled from the sheer force of him. But as they listened, a change came over them. They stood up straighter, with pride and vitality where before there had just been terror. I could see the Soviet registrars taking note. Yes, they would certainly find a use for him—if he survived.

When he was done reciting, he told the man at the counter that he and his friends were ready to defend Petrograd—Genya, Gigo, Sasha, Nikita. And Zina right alongside the boys. He glanced back at me with a sly smile. After they'd put their names down, Genya came to the place where I stood by the wall with Oksana and Anton, and swept me up in a grand embrace, kissing me—but it was all wrong, like a show, playing to the crowd. I had to fight myself not to push him away. He really was leaving. But why did he feel it was necessary to erase our farewell back in the Poverty Artel—something vulnerable and tender, just between us—with this public display? We'd learned in school that a wedding always signaled the end of a comedy, but this suddenly felt like the first act of a tragedy.

39 *The Smolny Institute for Young Ladies*

RINGLESS, MY WEDDING GERANIUMS still in my arms, I
hung from a tram strap thinking *a married woman* in
time to the rhythm of wheels, lurching and screeching,
metal on metal in time with the beating of my heart. *A
married woman. A married woman.* The terrifying reality of what I'd done was beginning to sink in. My last
sight of Genya hung before me—disappearing with
his gang of friends, a backward wave, a smile. Outside
the streetcar window, a grim and silent work party with
shovels on their shoulders marched southwest, in the
direction of the invader. Stillness hung over the riders
this morning, no talking, no arguing. The whole city
crouched, listening, straining to hear the approach of
the German machine, metal on metal. And Genya, so
foolishly brave, heading straight into the guns.

We passed a butcher shop, windows soaped over,
the store abandoned. No meat in Petrograd unless it
was walking in front of a cart or skulking in an alley.
Even rats were in short supply. Another shop valiantly
tried to sell things people no longer needed—wigs,
medals from the imperial court, parasols. Had there
ever been anything so useless as a parasol? I looked
down at the homely geraniums in the crook of my
arm, molting scarlet petals onto my broken boots as
the streetcar jolted forward, throwing me against other

passengers. Oksana had grown these flowers, with their bitter green scent, on her windowsill, tending them all through this sullen winter. I loved her generosity. She'd deprived herself of their beauty to send the poets off to the front and inadvertently provided my wedding bouquet.

This spring there would be lilacs—if we made it to spring. Maybe I could take Mother to Maryino, get her out of town and away from the threat of the camps. The irony—how hard I'd worked to get back to Petrograd this summer! How hard would it be to get a ticket out again? I swayed on my strap, wedged between tense people in winter coats. Perhaps Maryino was already in ashes...but if I could get them out there, Avdokia still had ties in the village. I could make it worthwhile for the peasants to keep her and Mother. One trip to Kamenny Island, Kolya had said. A man called Arkady.

More and more soldiers crowded onto the tram as we moved up Suvorovsky Prospect toward Smolny. All around me, they argued about wages and striking, the talk that had so angered Genya, who felt they were taking advantage of the emergency to extort concessions. A well-fed gang they looked, too. Shirkers and opportunists.

A soldier with a broad pockmarked face came close. "Give us a kiss, sister."

"I'm married," I said, pulling away, or as much as I could in the crush.

"Me, too." He grinned. He smelled of the fennel seeds he was chewing with his front teeth. "Live it up."

Soldiers took advantage of the crowding to rub up on me. Rough hands shopping, testing me like a bin of vegetables. I held my bag tight under my arm, clung to my flowers, turned this way and that to avoid them, hoped no one would find the stickpin in the seam of my dress. There was no room to slap anybody, but I stepped on as many toes as I could on what was a very long ride.

By the time I saw the cupolas of the cathedral hovering over the complex that was once the Smolny Institute for Young Ladies, I felt as though I'd already fought a battle. The soldiers helped me out of the tram with exaggerated solicitousness, mocking *burzhui* manners. I briefly fantasized how they would do when the Germans arrived—then we'd see what the famed Petrograd garrison was worth. What were they doing here anyway, griping about wages when poets and painters were heading out to face the foe? Then I realized—I sounded exactly like my father.

I took a moment to gather myself before entering the seat of the Soviet. Crowds of people came and went freely from the grand old place. It was like watching the aperture of an anthill. Soldiers and workers, commissars and Chekists, the simple and the important, all converged on this one spot, the center of everything. Somewhere in the halls of these buildings, Lenin worked over a simple desk. Comrade Trotsky argued

over the next move in the war negotiations he'd mis-
handled so terribly. There was no shortage of guards.
A cannon stood before the main entrance, and machine
guns were trained from second-story windows, but I
climbed the steps and pushed my way inside. It was
a scrimmage, new arrivals struggling against people
shouldering shovels and guns on their way out. Soldiers loitered in the deafening hallways. Filing cabinets
narrowed the passages, framed pictures leaned in
stacks. Everything was in motion, toppling, everyone
pushing, shouting. I knew that Varvara worked for the
Petrograd Bolshevik Committee, but how to find my
way in such a labyrinth?

Eventually on the second floor I found the committee
offices, a long room filled with desks and people typing,
shouting into telephones, giving orders, waiting for help.
But even at the center of godless Smolny there were miracles, and there I found Varvara, standing behind a desk
in a gray-blue dress and that same black leather jacket,
pressing the receiver of a telephone to one ear, her palm
to the other, while a tall man continued to harangue her.
I swelled with pride despite myself, seeing her there,
knowing we lived in such times that an eighteen-year-old
girl could become a person of responsibility.

She hung up the phone and collapsed into a chair behind a mountain of papers, putting her hands over her
eyes. The tall man leaned over her. Didn't he notice
she wasn't listening? Finally, wearily, she dropped her
barricade and plowed through the papers before her,

finding something and giving it to him, pointing down the hall. As he departed, the people waiting moved closer, as if to begin their own entreaties.

Then she saw me. Her tired face brightened, and that one glance restored my hope that she might be willing to help me with my mother. People waiting for a scrap of Varvara's attention grumbled as I jumped the queue. "Comrade!" "Comrade, I've been here since nine." An older woman, wearing an old-fashioned shirtwaist and a skirt to her ankles, caught her by the sleeve. "What about these children's homes?"

"Yes, Comrade Letusheva. I'll attend to it. But I haven't had lunch and I'm about to faint." She hooked her arm through mine and steered me out of the office back into the teeming hall. "I'm so glad to see you, and with flowers, too," she said. "That lot in there, they still believe in St. Nick and the golden cockerel. Do I look like a magician? *What about this? What about that?* Well what about it? Didn't you hear? The Germans are coming!" We began to walk toward the stairs up which I'd just come.

I told her about my job at the knitting factory, showing off my scarred, stiff hands as my mother might have once shown off new rings. "So what are you doing here? Shirking already?" she teased.

"Genya left this morning. He's enlisted — for the defense."

She nodded approvingly. "We need every breathing soul. We'll even take poets."

I held up the flowers. "We got married."

Varvara nearly collided with a man carrying a filing cabinet on his back. "Whose idea was that? Yours?"

"His."

She sighed, rounding her eyes as if to say, *Well, what can you do about it now?* "At least it's not Shurov." That put me on my guard. I felt the hardness of the pin through my dress where I always wore it and feared her keenness. She always said she could see right through me. "They almost caught him, you know. A few weeks ago, right here in Petrograd. Speculating. He's part of a major ring. You don't still see him, do you?" Narrowing her eyes at me.

"Not since Furshtatskaya Street."

We entered the broad stairway and joined the steady movement of people rising and descending like some biblical curse, in our case heading hellward. As we went down, I asked the question I'd come here to resolve. "What do you hear about the internment of the bourgeoisie?" The farther down the tight spiral of stairway we moved, the more I smelled food. I could tell her silence was intentional as her black head bobbed in front of me. "Are they going to do it?"

She pulled me toward the wall. "If the bourgeoisie would stop trying to undermine the Soviet, readying bouquets for the arrival of the Germans, they wouldn't have to worry so much. But with people like your papa stepping up operations..." She glanced at the people passing us to make sure nobody was listening. "Your old man's been quite the busy boy."

Well, he wasn't preparing any bouquets. I could bet on that.

Others pressed into us to let yet another filing cabinet pass by. Varvara waited until they moved on before continuing. "Yes, he's been collecting funds for the Volunteer Army. Working against us any way he can. Still in the pocket of the English. If they start rounding up hostages, you can bet Vera Borisovna will be first on the list."

Hostages? "Would they really do that?"

"Of course." She nodded at some men coming up out of the basement. "We think he's still using your apartment, though it's been searched again and again."

How did she know so much about my parents? "Who? The Petrograd Committee?"

She shrugged in a way that didn't deny my worst suspicions. "For now."

Why would they care? But it wasn't the time to worry about what Varvara was doing. I had to concentrate. "Help me get her out of Petrograd."

She glared at me. People were shoving us, trying to get by. She pulled me into a corner at the next landing. "Listen," she hissed. "One: like I told those buggers upstairs, I'm not a magician. And two: she's our tie to your old man. No way we're going to send her out of town."

Then I knew. *We.* "You're not with the committee at all. You're working for the Cheka."

She gave me a black-eyed under-the-brow gaze that

told me I was the biggest fool who ever put on a coat. Searches in the middle of the night. Blood in the snow. Was this where her faith in the revolution had led her? But I had my mother to worry about.

"Don't let them arrest her, Varvara."

She began to descend again. More workers carrying boxes rose from the basement and everyone had to press themselves to the walls. Suddenly, a picture resolved in the developing tank. I'd been so intent on Mother's circumstances that I hadn't been paying attention. All this furniture, these files…the rumors were true: the Soviet was abandoning us. All their reassurances at the Alexandrinsky Theater had been a fraud. "You're leaving, aren't you? All those promises, they were just lies. Oh my God, it's all lies! You're moving to Moscow!"

Varvara shoved me into the wall, staring holes into me. "Don't make a scene or it'll be the worse for you," she said under her breath. If she hadn't been holding on to me so tightly, I might have fallen. The government was saving itself, leaving the rest of us alone and exposed to the German army. "All those speeches," I whispered. "You accused the Provisional Government of exactly this and now you're doing it—"

Varvara jerked me again. "Stop it. Do you think this is some kind of game? The game of Revolution?" Her fingers dug into my arm as she pressed her bony face right up to mine. "If the Germans take Petrograd—well, too bad for us. It's a disaster for you and me and the rest. But if the Soviet is taken, we lose the revolution. This isn't about Petrograd. We're preparing for the years to come. In the end, what happens to you and me doesn't matter one tiny bit. If they have to move to Moscow or Omsk or Novosibirsk to keep the revolution safe, then so be it. The important thing is that the Soviet survives." Her eyes glittered, inhuman. "Don't cry. Don't even breathe."

My lungs hurt. I clung to my flowers drizzling petals onto my boots. Listening to Varvara was like going up in a rocket ship. I felt dizzy, sick. It didn't matter to her what happened to us—to me or Genya or Vera Borisovna, any of us. From space, even Russia would look small. You couldn't distinguish one human from another from that height, hear their cries.

Finally, when she saw I wasn't going to scream, she let me go, then took me by the nape of the neck and shook me, but more gently, tenderly this time. "The Petrograd Committee isn't evacuating. Look, I'm sorry. But I can't have you falling apart in front of…" She nodded toward the busy comrades, rising and descending. "What do you say? Let's eat." As if nothing had happened, as if I hadn't understood something fundamental about our new rulers—that lying would become a way of life now. I thought of Genya's poem about the feet of clay. *Don't be such a child*, I could imagine him saying. *We all have to grow up now.*

In the basement, we entered an enormous, windowless dining hall, steaming, smoke-filled, lined with long tables and benches, vibrating with talk that was subdued but keyed up, underscored with anxiety. "Any party member can come and eat at any time," Varvara told me proudly. "Smolny works around the clock." A red-faced woman dripping sweat ladled me some fish soup. From a giant tureen, a young girl poured us tea into which Varvara dropped tiny saccharine tablets. Then she led us to the corner of a long table full of intense young people poring over some posters.

Once we were seated, Varvara at the end, she bowed her head toward me, speaking low. "You have to stop thinking in individualistic terms. No one matters now, except what we're doing for the revolution. It's not me, it's my ability to make decisions. It's not Genya, it's that he's fighting the Germans, that he writes with a revolutionary consciousness. The question is, what are you doing? You're an educated girl. You can write. You can speak to a crowd. What are you doing knitting socks? Join the party. You can't straddle the fence forever," she said. "You might even be of some help to your worthless mother."

The party, the party. She sounded like Zina, with that same zeal. The poets were on their way to defend a government that was fleeing for its life on a carpet of lies. But I could also see it through Varvara's eyes—they were saving the revolution. Oh, it was all so confusing. I couldn't sort out the politics. All I knew was that my mother couldn't be a hostage, couldn't be caught in the cogs as history played itself out.

"What's that going to do for my mother? I won't throw her to the dogs."

"You've been doing a pretty good job of it so far," she said, sopping a piece of claylike bread in the soup.

I leaned over my bowl, very close. "You owe me, Varvara." Yes, I still held it against her. I was no more over it than Genya was over what I'd done to him.

"I owe you nothing," Varvara said.

"I see." Fighting tears, I drank down the rest of my soup and stood, buttoning my coat, stuffing the bread into my pocket, picking up my threadbare flowers.

She grabbed my arm, pulled me back down to the bench. "Shut up and let me think." The two long wrinkles between her dark brows deepened. It was what she was best at. Tactics, strategy. "You're only looking at the next few days. Either the Germans arrive and she'll have it made, or they'll be turned back and we'll move on to other problems. But she really needs to get off her ass. Nonworking bourgeois are going the way of the dinosaurs. Give her your sock-knitting job when you join the party."

"You'll never give up, will you?"

She grinned her crooked grin. "Surely there's something she can do besides talk to spirits."

"She sings. Plays the piano."

"Maybe she could help organize a workers' chorus."

An idea about as likely as warm snow.

She snorted at her own optimism. "Well, for now just

get her out of there. As long as she's gone when the *domkom* comes calling, you'll be all right."

"It's Basya. The *domkom*. Remember her?" I said.

"Sure. I told you, you needed to watch her, didn't I?" Varvara stretched her long, lanky form. "Anyway, either this'll all blow over in a week, or else we'll be speaking German by Friday."

How could she be so calm when the Bolsheviks would take the bulk of the retribution—Varvara and her comrades, all these people around us? I drank the too-sweet tea, wrapping my hands around the warm tin cup. "You're not worried?"

"We'll go underground, like before," she said. "Lenin spent years underground. Nothing's going to stop us, Marina. Haven't you figured that out yet?" She shook me by the shoulder, affectionately. "Cheer up. Think of it this way—Avdokia can do your queuing, cook, run your bath. You'll be a regular little missy again." She spotted a thin man in a black leather coat. "Excuse me. I have to talk to someone." We picked up our dishes and took them to the service station on the far wall. "See you soon, Marina." She went to join the thin man, leaving me to my own chaotic thoughts. Vera Borisovna at the Poverty Artel? Thank God Genya wouldn't be home to see this.

40 *Saving Vera Borisovna*

IN THE KITCHEN OF the flat on Furshtatskaya, two women boiled laundry on the stove. They stared at me suspiciously as a third admitted me through the back entrance, glanced at the tattered geraniums I still carried. I couldn't get used to seeing strangers in our flat. *Their* flat. The hard-faced blonde in her forties, all lower face and flat eyes, recognized me, but her expression didn't soften at all. "Looking for the nuthouse again?"

"Who?" asked the ferret-faced woman.

"The tsaritsa."

I wondered how crazy my mother had really gone. I would have stayed to glean a little more information, but I didn't want to attract further attention to my visit, especially as I planned to get Mother out of here without raising any suspicions that she was leaving.

"Make yourself at home," the blonde said sarcastically as I walked past her. "Just walk on through."

"I'd have rung the doorbell but the butler's on vacation," I said. "Anyway, you got the front door all boarded up."

"Anybody coulda come in through there," said the big blonde. "Robbers." She poked at the boiling mass in her pot. "Ready for dinner?" She lifted a diaper on her wooden spoon.

"I don't think it's done enough," I said over my shoulder, and moved out into the service corridor.

All the doors were closed on this side of the flat—where Vaula and Basya had lived as well as Father's driver Ivo before the war; where we stored junk, unneeded furniture and prams, sleds and skis and old clothes. I wondered if people were living in those rooms now. Each was barely big enough for a bed and a nightstand, true, but that made them much easier to heat. I'd begun to see housing differently since living in the Poverty Artel. For a second I imagined inhabiting one of those tiny rooms myself. It wouldn't be so bad.

I passed through the cloakroom into the main hall, catching a peek through the pocket doors into our salon. An old man wearing felt slippers and a heavy coat, scarf, and cap sat smoking, studying a chess board. I slipped along the passage to Mother's room. The odds and ends of discarded things—sacks and tins, trash—lay along the walls. I could already hear the nursery piano—no more the big round notes of the Bösendorfer. I stared at her door with its lock crudely bolted into the splintered wood. The last thing I wanted to do was knock, after she'd been so emphatic that she never wanted to see me again. But it didn't matter what she wanted. She didn't understand the fate that was awaiting her. I knocked. The piano stopped, but I heard no footsteps. I knocked again, our personal knock, *Fais dodo*. She knew exactly who it was, but the piano began again. "Come on, open up, will ya?" Rudely, in case anyone was listening.

And sure enough, across the hall, the door of my old room opened a crack. An eye, watching. A single eye.

Finally the door opened. She was alone, and I saw how bad off she was. She no longer looked like an otherworldly creature, merely a terrified, starving, exhausted woman of forty-three. She let me in and locked the door behind me, shoving a chair up against it for good measure. I took down my scarf, fluffed my hair, my ears still ringing from cold. I longed for the days of my big white fur hat, though I would have been robbed of it within an hour. You could not keep a hat like that without fighting for it.

"You didn't see Avdokia, did you?" Mother asked. "She was supposed to be home by now." She sat down at the parquet table, very still, staring at her hands. Her stillness was mesmerizing. "I wish you hadn't come," she said finally.

"I wouldn't have," I said, perching on the edge of one of the many hoarded tables. "But I need you to pack up and come with me. Right now."

"Why? Has there been another revolution?"

"You're not safe here anymore."

She laughed. It was half a sob. "You're just figuring that out?"

"There's going to be a sweep. I don't want you to be here when they come."

She gazed at her hands, so thin and blue, like X-rays

of themselves, the backs dry and papery. Her wedding ring with its platinum filigree was so loose that it looked like it belonged to someone else. From the courtyard, the jingle of a sleigh's harness reached the windows. Somewhere back in the apartment, we could hear men in rough conversation, shouting, then laughing.

"They're talking about internment. Hostages." She would not look up. I wasn't sure she understood me. "Because of Father. Look, I want you to come stay with me—just a few nights, until we see what happens with the Germans. There are old labor camps in the north. Rumor has it they're going to send the bourgeoisie there."

She examined her hands as if they were a world, as if those knotted veins could lead her out of this trap. "You're bourgeois, too, as I recall," she said at last.

"Yes, but I'm not married to Dmitry Makarov."

Outside the window, the bare branches of the courtyard trees stood starkly black and white. She gazed out at them, her hands folded before her. The light flooded her weary face, her transparent blue eyes. "So I'm supposed to leave my home, just like that. Flee for my life. *Que viene el Coco.*" *Here comes the bogeyman.* "How do you like your Bolsheviks now? It was that horrible girl, I suppose. I knew she was trouble that first day. I should never have let you become friends."

"She was the one who told me to get you out of here," I said.

We could hear a woman at the front of the flat scolding someone, perhaps in my father's office, maybe the Red Guard's wife, *so-called*. Mother's blue eyes filled. "I think I've given up enough, don't you?" That brittle tone dissolved. "This room is all I have left. I have no one anymore, not Mitya, not Seryozha…Volodya… you. My parents gave us this flat as a wedding present."

"It's just for a couple of days," I said. "You can come back when it's blown over. You don't want to be a Cheka hostage." I heard my father's reasonable tones in my own voice as I spoke.

"If I leave, some illiterate coachman and his five children will move in and chop up the piano for firewood." She stood and stroked the keys of the banged-up nursery piano with her fingertips, the chipped yellowed ivory. She loved three things—spirituality, culture, and beauty. But her value now was as a hostage against my father's counterrevolutionary escapades. There was no time to waste.

"You won't lose your flat. We won't let them know you're going. You'll leave just like you were going out for the day—"

"Sneak out like a criminal," she said flatly. "I know what you're saying. I'm a criminal now. In my own country. In my own home."

I stood and came to her, took her hands, so cold and bony that they were hardly made of flesh. How was she going to get through the rest of this winter? "We need to go now."

She pulled away from me. "To stay with you and

your hooligan?" She found a handkerchief in her sleeve and wiped her nose.

"His name is Genya." I didn't know if it would help or not, but I added, "My husband."

"You *married* him?" Her expression went from peevish to horrified, as if she'd learned that I ate worms for tea. "Your *husband?*" And then she started to laugh, even as tears streamed. She stopped long enough to wipe them, then the laughter started again.

"He won't be there. He's gone to the front. He's volunteered for the defense of Petrograd."

She would not stop laughing.

"Think of the cesspits," I said. "You liked that? A labor camp would be ten times worse. And a Cheka prison? I don't even want to imagine it."

Her desperate hilarity died away. The eyes opened slowly, still wild but more focused. She was facing it.

"We'll leave separately. It'll attract less attention. I'll meet you down the block in fifteen minutes."

"But what should I bring?" She backed away from me, clutching her skirt. "What about Avdokia?"

Yes, what about Avdokia? I wondered briefly if it would be safer for her to stay here and keep the room, but I knew I would not be able to handle my mother on my own. "I'll go get her. Don't bring anything. Nobody can guess you're leaving. Just wear what you need. The warmer the better."

Her glance fluttered helplessly about the cluttered room. "I'm not a sheep! I need things..."

"A small bag if you have to. As though you're going on an errand. You're just going out for an hour. Visiting a friend." I went to the armoire, pulled out her sable hat and warmest coat, mink-lined. I sighed, stroking the fur. They were too beautiful. They would arouse attention on Grivtsova Alley. A black sealskin coat was better, though not so warm, and a hat of karakul lamb.

I stuffed a few things in a small carpetbag— underwear, a towel, her brush...just as though she were going out to sell some of her dish towels. "Do you know where Avdokia's gone?"

My mother shook her head. "She just goes."

My mother did not know where her bread came from. Even now. I scanned the map of the neighborhood in my mind, trying to imagine where an illegal market would be in this, the most bourgeois area in the city. There had to be one somewhere, because the Former People who couldn't get work couldn't get ration cards. They all depended on the black market. I guessed that the "market" was in Preobrazhenskaya Square. Large enough, not on the water, with several side streets down which people could scramble in case of trouble. "Look, put on a few pairs of underwear under your skirt. Put these dresses on." I tossed her two, both wool, the heaviest ones. "Take a few things in your pockets and the rest in the carpetbag. I'll wait for you at the Church of the Transfiguration. Fifteen minutes. I mean it."

"I hate this life," she said. "Why can't they just kill us and get it over with?"

I headed over to Preobrazhenskaya Square. Yes, I was right. The starving figures of our neighbors stood like shadows against the walls holding out wrapped bundles of their prized possessions while buyers, mostly peasants, bartered with frozen potatoes and other questionable foodstuffs—eggs, most likely rotten, bottles of oil that could be anything. And there was Avdokia, right under the great chains of the church enclosure, in heated negotiation with another peasant woman close to her own size and vintage. They made the deal, then Avdokia deposited a wrapped item the size of a plate into the other woman's arms, hefted a bag of potatoes off a sledge.

When she saw me her hard-mouthed, determined bargaining expression melted away. She would have crossed herself had she not had her arms full of potatoes. "Marinoushka, what are you doing here? This is no place for you. God in heaven!" She looked around for the Cheka, Red Guards. "Is everything all right?"

I embraced her and took the potatoes from her, explaining the situation. "God save us." She crossed herself as we walked.

"I need to get her out of there, but she's worried that if she leaves they'll take the flat. I don't think I can handle her by myself."

She came closer, so that I could see every crosshatch

of wrinkle, every hair in the mole on her bulbous nose. "If Basya tries anything with that flat, I'll pull her legs off and bury them under a birch tree. Whose flat does she think it is, Lenin's? She'd better not pull anything or when the Germans get here, she'll be the one paying the piper."

The expression on Anton's face when the three of us entered the room on Grivtsova Alley could not have been more horrified than if the entire German army had burst in. He stared at Avdokia and Mother as if they had one eye between them, as if we were Macbeth's crones and had come to rip off his dirty woolens and tear his flesh from his bones. "Oh, no," he said. "No, no, no."

I just continued with the introductions. It didn't matter what Anton thought, not now. "Anton, this is my mother, Vera Borisovna Makarova. And this is Avdokia...Fomanovna." I realized I'd never formally introduced Avdokia before. "This is Anton Mikhailovich Chernikov. Your host."

My mother's expression exactly mirrored Anton's. But unlike our editor and universal critic, her horror lay in the scene around her, of which his unkempt surliness was only a part. To see the Poverty Artel through her eyes was to remember it the first time I saw it. The teetering stacks of books, Anton with his feet on the table, the overflowing ashtrays, the sunflower-seed shells all over the floor, the dirty clothes and crumpled pages. The pathetic little stove. The smell. I was thankful at least that the chamber pot under the divan was empty. I hoped she would take comfort in Seryozha's watercolor painting and silhouettes, even if they were pinned to the old newspapers and handbills that served as our wallpaper.

When I was busy persuading Mother to come, I'd somehow failed to mention Anton.

She lingered at the door, clutching the handle of her little carpetbag. Avdokia stood by Mother's elbow, her wrinkled mouth drawn so tightly that it almost disappeared below her pulpy nose. How sordid it all must appear to them, as if I'd brought them to a tavern. I dropped the bag of potatoes on the table next to Anton's feet, hopefully sweetening the deal.

"Really, Makarova?" Anton drawled. "He's gone for four hours and you're already moving the family in? Even Granny over there?"

"It's just for a few days. Until things shake out."

He carefully, ostentatiously, removed his feet from the table and put them down on the dirty floor. "Am I suddenly running a boardinghouse for itinerant society women and their servants? Renting out corners for fifteen rubles a pop? Maybe there's some room under the stove. Why don't you look?"

"For God's sake, Anton. Varvara said they'd use her as a hostage."

He crushed out his butt on the floor under the leg of his chair. "Look, it was one thing for Kuriakin to flop here. Then one day you appear, like something the cat dragged in and forgot to eat. Did I throw you out? No. I lived with it, like the *sympatichniy chelovek* I am." That was a laugh. No one in the world would accuse him of being an agreeable chap. "But this? What's next, a priest? Maybe you want to start a cotillion. Or a charitable society."

It had been hard enough to get her here. I wasn't going to let Anton chase her off now. I came closer so I could keep my voice down. "Have a heart, Anton. If she ends up a hostage, or interned in some camp in the Arctic, would you feel comfortable in your soul that you chased her away?"

"Are you accusing me of having both a heart and a soul? Mercy!"

"I've heard quite enough," said Mother from the doorway. "Not another moment will I remain under this roof, I assure you, monsieur. Come, Avdokia, we'll put our counters on *noir* and see what becomes of us." My mother took the old lady's arm and turned back to the door.

But the bets would be on rouge, Mother. "Happy now?"

"Yes, I am completely comfortable, thank you." He was the one in charge—no Genya to mitigate his pettiness. He knew he was wrong, and it made him all the nastier.

My mother put her gloved hand on my wrist. *"Tu t'es trompé en tes amis." You have miscalculated your friends.* "Let's be on our way, Avdokia." She tried to grasp the knob but I wouldn't move away from the door.

"Anton, I'm talking to you. Just tell me this, how do you live with yourself every day?"

"You should know—you're always here, aren't you?" He wiped his gaze away to the window, as if the most interesting sight in the world were outside the dirty panes, gilded elephants loping by in midair, bearing howdahs of Turkish clowns. He was waiting for them to leave, for us all to go, so that he would not have to recognize what a beast he was being. But this was no joke, no matter of preference. Even now the Cheka might be searching from flat to flat in the Liteiny district for the possible—the likely—fifth column. Makarov would be a name high on the list.

Anton had been spoiling for this fight for a long time, and with Genya gone, he wasn't the only one who could speak plainly. "Listen, Anton. I fell in love with your friend. Is that a sin? Is it a capital offense? Someone loves him. And now you're going to punish me? Is that what this is all about?"

My mother was whiter than her own white hair. She took my mittened hand in her gloved ones. "For the love of God," she whispered hoarsely. "Not one more word. Death itself would be better."

"No, it wouldn't, Mother. Death would not be better than this." I snatched my hand from hers. I knew she didn't like it but this was my life now, this life that people were living, on top of each other, arguing, saying the cruelest things right out loud. You had to have the hide of a buffalo. I was trying to do the right thing. Why did everyone have to be so difficult? "Anton, could you please just let them stay? I thought you were a mutualist. I thought you believed in spontaneous organization."

Anton heaved himself up and skulked to his side of the room, pacing between his cot and the table, his arms folded tight across his chest. His black brow thundered over his long nose, his jaw set. Mother tried the door again, but I wouldn't let her open it. What would he say? "Anton?"

Finally, he flung himself back into his chair. "Oh for Christ's sake," he said. "Just keep them quiet and out of my hair."

My mother drew herself up in her glossy black coat. "I don't intend to host a party, monsieur."

I quickly showed Mother and my old nanny to our corner, the divan and the bookshelf. They could have the divan, and I would sleep on the chairs. I stripped the linens off the divan, shaking them out and folding them neatly so that Vera Borisovna could sit down without soiling her spirit with the unmentionable activity the quilts and blankets embodied. I could see the unspoken words written on her forehead: *Is this where you sleep with him? You and he, like beasts?*

I did my best to play host, pointing to our books, to Seryozha's art works, to the zinc water bucket by the stove, our few sticks of wood, our old iron primus, which had been outfitted to burn just about anything. It was like giving someone a tour of the inside of a drawer. *And over here are the pencils, and that's our eraser.* Mother plumped the pillows and Avdokia fished Our Lady of Tikhvin out of her bag, placing it on the bookshelf and positioning an oil lamp before it. I ignored Anton's stare. *Are you joking?*

After studying Seryozha's painting and his silhouettes for a time, Mother seated herself gingerly, folding her hands in her lap, as if she could stay like that, frightened and stubborn and straight-backed, until it was safe go home. I threw some wood scraps in the primus to boil water for barley tea.

At the table, Anton importantly riffled the pages of his French dictionary, filling the air with the sound of autumn leaves blown in a strong wind. He mumbled, *"Les Chabins chantent des airs à mourir / Aux Chabines marronnes."* He slammed the dictionary closed. "What the hell are *Chabins?* 'The somethings sing their songs of death to their maroon something women.' Apollinaire you whore's son, you big fat turd." He threw himself onto his cot. "I have a headache." The springs groaned. He began to play with his revolver, spinning the cylinder, opening it, looking in at the bullets in the chambers. I was used to this but I knew he was trying to terrify my mother. I didn't think the gun even worked. He liked to tell us that he'd played Russian roulette with it. He imagined himself a Verlaine.

"Mulatto," Vera Borisovna said suddenly, her voice

clear and still as a stone dropped in clear water. "*Chabin*. It's when one of the great-grandparents is a black. Like Pushkin." We all turned to stare at her. "One-eighth's part. And *marronnes* means 'chestnut.'"

Anton propped himself up on one elbow. "Really?"

"Although 'maroon' is picturesque. You might prefer it." She stopped. Then a slow smile trickled across her pale face. "Also it's 'dying.' Not 'death.' *Les Chabins chantent des airs à mourir*." Her beautiful accent. "The mulattos sing songs of dying to their chestnut—maroon—women."

Anton sat up on his bed, put his feet on the floor. "Listen, do you know anything about Apollinaire?"

"A follower of Mallarmé, I believe."

"Not a follower. A colleague," Anton corrected her.

Mallarmé was Mother's sort of poet, very World of Art, decadent, symbolist. All those fauns and night-blooming flowers, absinthe. I cringed to hear her speak of him with Anton. However, the miracle was that they were speaking at all. Anton could just as well have taken that revolver and shot her in the forehead.

"*A throw of the dice will never abolish chance,*" she recited. At least Mallarmé was a modernist.

Anton nodded excitedly. "Have you read Apollinaire?"

"Not that I know of," she said, brushing the knee of her coat.

Anton got up and went back to the table and began to read: "*A la fin tu es las de ce monde ancien / Bergère ô tour Eiffel le troupeau des ponts bêle ce matin…*" His accent was atrocious. While Mother was a graduate of the Catherine Institute—and knew Balmont and Gippius and Pierre Louÿs personally—Anton was a poor teacher's son from Orel. He was doing the best he could with a tattered copy of *Larousse*. I watched her anxiously for sneers, but aside from the slightest reshaping of the lips from time to time, she betrayed nothing. All those years of dinners and teas and dances and receptions, generations of good form, kept her from sabotaging herself on Grivtsova Alley. Her cool and interested demeanor during the recital of these cubistic poems with which Anton had been torturing us for months was a monument to her upbringing. She sat with closed eyes and listened, carefully, as if it were a séance and she was trying to elicit words from the Beyond. Could she actually understand the disjunctive, futuristic spirit of Apollinaire?

"I'd like to see your translation," said Vera Borisovna after he finished. Then she gave him the slight smile she was famous for. "That is, if you care to show it to me."

41 *The Defense of Petrograd*

OUTSIDE THE DISTRICT SOVIET, a crowd of grim citizens gathered in the icy Petrograd morning. This was it. The head of the *domkom* of our building, a hound-faced old man named Popov, had come around with the notifications: *Mandatory fortification work for all non-combatants.* I'd quickly introduced my mother and Av-dokia, "evacuated from Pskov." He shrugged, not caring where they were from or what they were doing there, and he left without encountering Anton, who lay hiding under his cot. Now I stood in the street before the familiar worn yellow facade as lean, stubble-faced Red Guards distributed shovels, picks, sledgehammers, and axes.

A registrar signed my labor book, and I took my shovel. "Go down to the Narva Gate," the guard said. "They'll show you where to set up shop."

Shouldering my spade like a rifle, I joined a brigade of other charcoal-eyed citizens—clerks, students, ordinary workers from the *artels* and small factories of the Kazansky district—heading southwest through the frigid morning fog. Others fell into step with us and exchanged rumors, scraps of news. "It's all about the railways now," a small, craggy worker said. "My brother-in-law said it's getting hot down around Rostov." Rostov-on-the-Don, in the Cossack-dominated southwest of the country, where Volodya and the Volunteers were fighting.

"Think the Germans'll use gas?" said a woman with deep lines under her eyes that ran diagonally across her cheeks like scars.

Everyone had the same fear of the terrible gas the kaiser's troops had been using on the battlefield. I well remembered the ruined men in the airless wards of the military hospital, their burned eyes, their burned lungs. A thin-faced man, a first-aid worker with his Red Cross armband, walked alongside our crew carrying a bucket full of rags in case of a gas attack. We would soak the rags in baking soda and water and breathe through them. We'd been told it was as good as a gas mask, but I sincerely doubted it. I just hoped it would be some protection, better than nothing.

"Just remember, they're hungrier than we are," said a woman with a falsely cheerful air, as if she were persuading herself. "They're all workers. They could come over to our side in a heartbeat."

We marched along the Obvodny Canal, the outer ring of the city, as packs of workers streamed out from the electrical station, the Triangle Works, and the mid-size shops—tanneries, textile and shoe factories, laundries. Some clapped us on the back encouragingly, lightening our mood, but dread returned, heavier than the shovels we carried—the old world was returning to claim its own, coming to crush our new lives under its murderous heel. There was no need to draft these girls, these hard, sober men. No need to bribe them or threaten them. We intended to defend our new nation. We had won it by revolution. It would be up to us to keep it.

It felt good to be one with the revolution again. Despite the cold and the prospect of hard labor and the oncoming Germans, it was a relief to leave Mother and the whole mess of my sticky life behind. I thought

about Genya as I marched along. We had a chance
for a new, clean kind of life now. How loathsome all
that drama had been, all that unnecessary pain. Kolya
now seemed so murky and musky, foul as an unventi-
lated room. I felt the press of the pin under my dress.
I should just throw it into the road and be done with
it. Yet I wasn't that girl anymore, the little *barynya* of
gestures and pronouncements. I would sell it and buy
Genya a sheepskin. Then we could walk together and
look clearly in the same direction. No more secrets, no
more holding back. Genya was right. This was where
my attention should have been all along—the bigger
battle, the grander fight. Marching west along the canal
in the gray mist with these workers felt almost holy.
This must be what Varvara felt every time she said the
word *Revolution*.

Strangely, it reminded me of the day I had my hair
bobbed on Vasilievsky Island. How light my head had
felt as my pounds of dark red locks fell to the tiled floor.
And what emerged in the mirror was myself, but clean,
modern, shorn of foolishness. I felt like that again, a
new woman emerging from a chrysalis of tresses and
tangles, no longer the dreamy girl of former life, the
one full of secrets and divisions, but rather someone I
had not yet met.

"Think they'll get this far?" asked a girl in a rough
wool scarf the color of sawdust, wiping her nose on the
back of her mitten.

"Either they will or they won't," I said, pleased at

how brave I sounded. "Think what happened to Napoleon."

The girl's mouth fell open. "You think we're going to burn the city?"

It hadn't even occurred to me that this might be a possibility—that we ourselves and not the Germans might leave the city in flames. Where would we go in deep winter? "No, but that's why we have to stop them. We've got to."

The city blocks grew spare, the houses poor and poorer, served by roads barely worth the name—unpaved, just tracks in the snow. Smoke showed from one house in ten. To think I'd been born in Petersburg, but had never been this far into the industrial outskirts of the city. Now we passed rickety houses with wooden fences all falling down, lonely and sad in the white mist, their snow-filled dooryard gardens within smoke-stack range of the giant factories. Red tips of willow bushes poked out from the drifts like the fingers of buried corpses. The city soviet was trying to get the workers to resettle in the big flats in the center of town, to literally bring them into the center, but the proletariat had been reluctant to move. Now I understood. If I was a worker, would I want to live in a big flat with ten strange families, miles and miles from work, just for the pleasure of the parquet and the tony address? That, too, was bourgeois thinking. It seemed the Bolsheviks weren't as proletarian as they professed to be.

The road underfoot turned perilously icy. A stooped

woman in a rusty brown shawl slipped and fell, and a girl in a quilted coat with the stuffing coming out at the seams stopped to pick her up. "You okay, Granny?"

"I'll 'Granny' you," said the woman, settling back on her feet, collecting her shovel, and rearranging her scarf. "Tell you one thing, I'll be happy when spring comes."

Hollow-eyed women with ragged children watched us march past. A few waved, but most just stared, mute as cattle. The branches of the willows trembled above the snow. A tall woman with steel-gray hair cut in a fringe across her face was complaining about the Bolsheviks. "They say vote for them, so you vote for 'em and what the hell do they do? Give themselves the cushy spots, best rations, all their damn committees, yak yak yak. Lording it over everyone like the new aristos. Then the first sign of trouble, they're packing up and leaving us to go to the devil."

"They're not," said the girl in the quilted coat, her breath a white cloud.

"The hell they're not," said a woman who looked too old to be carrying that pick she nevertheless carried with the ease of familiarity, shifting the tool to her other shoulder. "Takin' the food with 'em, too."

"We shoulda all gone SR," said the woman with the bangs. "They wouldn't pull this kinda stuff. Spiridonova for me. Those old SRs, they knew who to shoot, right, girls?"

I wondered if Varvara knew what the workers were

saying about the Bolsheviks. Did they know that the bourgeoisie wasn't their only problem? It scared me. If the workers weren't behind the Bolsheviks, then what?

"They're out, though," said a girl from the Netrobsky shoe factory whose broken boots had been repaired with rags. "The SRs are done for."

"Don't be so sure," said the gray-haired woman. "I heard they're setting up at the Horse Manège." The tsar's old stables, on the Moika. "If it's a fight, all hell'll break loose."

This was the first I'd heard that there might actually be separate SR forces, as Anton had intimated in Sasha's room. I wondered if they'd fight the Germans or take on the Bolsheviks in their weak moment. Worker against worker? I shifted my shovel to the other shoulder and tried to still my panic. I was going to dig trenches. The SRs and Bolsheviks would fight or they wouldn't, but the Germans were on their way, and they had to be stopped. I looked at the figures struggling through the mist along with me. We needed the Bolsheviks to keep us believing in the future. Despite Varvara's assertions about the survival of the revolution, people didn't understand abstractions. I saw, even more than before, the danger in the soviet exodus. Because these women wouldn't see in it preservation of the cause at all costs. They'd see desertion. And though I could understand Varvara in theory, I was only a person myself, and I, too, felt abandoned.

We reached the southwestern edge of the city, the

Narva Gate outlined in the fog. Beyond it open snow-
fields lay waiting—the approach to Petrograd across
which, at any time, we might hear the crunch and roll
of German soldiers, German cannons. I suddenly felt
weak, armed only with this shovel. Citizens of every
sort toiled in lines across the forehead of the snow. A
comrade in an army greatcoat directed us. "Right along
there, sisters. The Huns may think they'll be checking into the Astoria tonight, but seven feet closer to the
devil is where they'll be."

The trench in the snow was five feet deep, almost
over the heads of the women already down there, and
about seven feet across. I could see how it could slow
down an army that might not see it in the fog, or give
our men shelter if they fell back before the Germans.
The comrade lowered us into the trench. Inside,
flanked by the snow walls, I was flooded by memories
of the countless snow tunnels and caves I'd dug in the
Tauride Gardens as a child. So strong was the sensation
I had to put my shovel down, my foot on the blade,
and gasp for air, eyes stinging in the cold. That ice
world, furious snowball battles, fought like wars. Now
this silent reality.

"You okay?" asked the girl in the quilted coat, noticing I hadn't filled a single shovelful.

"Sure," I said, and started to dig. The snow was
heavy and compacted, thawed and refrozen. I scraped
at it to no avail while women all around me managed
shovelfuls, throwing the hard clumps up and over the

lip of the trench. A young blond woman marched up to me. "Not like that. Put your boot in it!"

I tried again, but she snatched the shovel away from me in disgust, catching me a blow on the cheek with the handle in the process. "Like this." Boot heavy on the blade, she thrust the shovel into the snow at an angle. It sliced off a hard white alp that she flung high over the crest of the trench. She shoved the spade back into my hands.

I flushed, my eyes watering, the skin of my face prickling in the frost as the girl with the broken boots watched from the corner of her eye and snickered. I burned with shame to have my uselessness so publicly exposed. But I told myself that humiliation was personal and the task at hand was anything but. Who cared if the girl from the shoe factory was amused by my dressing-down? I tried again, cutting downward through the snow with my foot rather than my body. The first strike broke through and filled the blade with a neat slice of frozen white. But when I flung it, most of it fell back into the trench. The girl laughed. "Oh, that's good. You'll have it all filled in by the time the Germans get here."

"Why don't you stand there yakking?" I said.

"Eat my dust, *devushka*," the girl said.

"Davai," I said. *Let's go.*

We fell into a rhythm, shoveling, breaking the snow, heaving it out of the trench, which began to deepen. Between shovel loads, we exchanged clipped conversation, part of the rhythm of the labor: "What's your name?" "Where do you work?" "Do you have a boyfriend?" The work made me feel strong and clean. Some women started a song—a haying song, of all things—and we all caught it up, men farther down the line responding, just as they would in the fields. I had never worked alongside others like this. It felt good to be just one of the many, our heartbeats in time, our arms, our lungs. You didn't have to be the best, it would have ruined the whole thing—not the best, not the worst, just a part of. The important thing was that the revolution survived.

As we moved along the trench in the blue-white fog, our breath forming ice on our scarves, I heard the women call out, "Here they come, those bastards!" "Hey, look lively!" "Watch out, honey, your slip is showing!" Having reached a shallower portion of the trench, I could now see over the lip. A party of people straggled along, prodded by Red Guards. Bourgeois, pitiful in their thin shoes. Had they had their boots confiscated? Had they sold them? Old men and slender-waisted women, their formerly fine coats and hats showing the wear of the revolutionary year. Rounded up for labor duty. They certainly hadn't volunteered. "That'll show 'em." *"Burzhui!"* My teammate, Alya, called out at top volume, "See how ya like wiping your own asses, and you can wipe mine as well!"

The woman with the steel-gray bangs yelled, "Pretend it's a road for the Germans!"

I could hardly bear to watch them struggle. Old men and fragile women who had never so much as handled a dishrag let alone a pick or a shovel were handed heavy tools and shoved toward the line. Just the weight of the implements was more than they could manage. I could well imagine their hunger, their weakness.

Then I recognized one of them—Lisa Pod-harzhevskaya, from the Tagantsev Academy. And her parents. Lisa wore a draggled fur hat that looked as though it had been dropped into a puddle and frozen. She was the class beauty, the haughty type. How ill they all looked, especially the father—miserable, struggling in the icy fog, their gloves too thin. I was selfishly grateful I had Mother stashed away on Grivtsova Alley.

Now the work seemed colder, sadder, the women not so nice.

"You're not feeling sorry for 'em, are you?" Alya asked.

"A little."

"Well, they weren't feeling so sorry for us, now were they? Like who was paying for those big flats and Sunday hats? You and me, girlie. So now they get a taste of their own medicine. It's good for 'em. Like a big dose of castor oil."

They don't feel the cold as you and I might, my mother would say when she'd send Basya off on some frivolous errand. I'd once heard Lisa's father opining about workers' demands for the eight-hour day. *They wouldn't know what to do with themselves. They'd just drink and beat their wives.*

But I couldn't stop thinking of the Podharzhevskys' misery, rounded up and marched across the city, rained upon with abuse. Not like me and my crew, who worked to save our own city, our own future. We were hungry, but our rations were lavish compared to those of the nonworking Formers. And tomorrow they might all be gone, put on a train, taken out of the city. Vanished into the mist.

I ducked down, hoping Lisa wouldn't see me, wouldn't recognize me among the other workers. I reserved my loathing for the Red Guards, sitting on boxes by little fires, taunting the conscripts instead of putting their own shoulders to the work. What were they doing here anyway? Why weren't they out there, trying to stop the Germans? Easier to torment scarecrows.

Now the father stopped to lean on his spade, clinging to it as if he might otherwise fall over. He had already been an old man when I first met Lisa. From behind him, a guard rose from his box and shoved him with the butt of his rifle between the shoulder blades. The old man lurched forward, throwing his arms wide, and fell. Our women laughed. "Hey, watch your step over there, *baryn*." "How do you like being on the other end of the foreman's stick now, boss?"

"It's just an old man," I said.

The woman with the steel-gray fringe called back to

me. "Believe me, when we was on the bottom, they pissed on us good and proper."

Ice weighted the tips of my eyelashes. I brushed it away angrily. "What's the good in making people suffer? What difference do they make now?"

"You don't keep feedin' a bad dog," said a woman in a brown shawl over her brown coat. "You take it out and shoot it."

I was losing ground with every word, and soon I would reveal myself to be as Former as the Podharzhevskys. The girl Alya already suspected it. "So *that's* what happened to Fluffy," I said. "Come to think of it, didn't they have meat at Dining Room 12 yesterday?"

The women laughed and went back to their work, but all the spirit and energy had gone out of me. I imagined Varvara's scorn. And Zina's, fighting at the front with Genya. I knew what they would say — that I was too soft to be a revolutionary, too muddleheaded, too individualistic. I hadn't read enough Marx, didn't understand the anonymous forces of economics and history. But I hoped pity would not prove a Former virtue, outmoded as parasols. Who would do battle against this inhumanity? I supposed that was why Blok put Christ at the head of the Twelve.

I hacked at the snow alongside Alya. I'd lost the flush of solidarity that had kept me warm. Now the work was just hard and my hands, arms, and back ached. Snow leaked in through my own broken boot. After some time, they fed us bread and tea, and we went back to it, the cold growing denser, clawing at our faces. They couldn't keep us out here much longer. I had really thought that the revolution would change people, change their very souls. *Romantic,* I could hear Varvara say.

Maybe they would change, when they had the time and security—this woman with the brown scarf, the girl with the stuffing coming out of her coat. Maybe when they could stop worrying about the Germans, when they had eaten their fill and really understood they were their own masters, they would have time for mercy as well as justice.

42 *The Lost Eden*

I RETURNED TO THE Poverty Artel after dark, to the incongruity of Mother and Anton sitting together at the table, their heads bowed as if over a missal. Mother coolly corrected his French, while Anton clutched his head and cursed. Over the old divan, a light burned in a red glass before the icon of the Virgin of Tikhvin. The place smelled of cabbage—a pot of soup kept warm for me on the little primus stove. I sank onto a chair, too tired even to take off my wet boots. Avdokia knelt to pull them off. *A regular little missy again,* Varvara had sneered. Yet the familiarity of Avdokia's care was so comforting...exactly why I shouldn't allow it. "No, please don't. I'm eighteen. I think I can pull off my own boots. Everybody has to pull off their own boots now," I said, louder, for Mother's sake.

"Marinoushka," Avdokia chided in her *chu-chu-chu* voice. "Give this old woman the pleasure of taking care of her baby." She got my boot off.

I wrestled the muddy thing out of her hand. "What did we fight a revolution for? So you can wait on me on your knees?"

She sighed, sat back on her heels. "You were always such a stubborn child. What should I do—sit by the fire and grow roots like a turnip?"

"We all have to change," I said. "This is exactly why people hate the bourgeoisie. An old woman on her knees, serving a perfectly healthy young person."

"People hate the bourgeoisie, period," my mother said from the table. "They'd rather see an old woman digging ditches. Or sweeping the streets."

Avdokia sighed, watching me struggle to take my other wet boot off with clumsy, frozen hands. She set a pair of my mother's embroidered lambskin slippers toes out in front of me, ready to be stepped into. The yeasty smell of this old woman, the velvety feel of her cheek, were as familiar as my own eyelids. She cupped my chin in her gnarled hand, rubbed her nose against mine. "The devil never tires of new ideas."

She straightened and brought me a bowl of hot cabbage soup. The bowl felt wonderful in my cold hands. She claimed my boots and cleaned them with a page of *Pravda*. Such levels of irony there. Mother watched me eat as Anton grappled with Apollinaire. "I don't like 'with shame you overhear,'" he said, but she wasn't listening. I saw curiosity, even respect, in her blue eyes. Who was this girl, her daughter? A married girl, a poet, capable of earning a living with her hands? I had lived her life for so long. Now she was having a taste of mine.

Avdokia set my boots by the door on a piece of newspaper and began to sweep the room. "Could you stop that?" Anton snapped. "Babushka. The place is fine."

"Pigs shouldn't live in a place this fine," she muttered, moving dangerously close to Anton's territory between table and cot, picking things off the floor, dusting them or stacking them, tucking his shoes under his bed.

"Leave those things alone!" He grabbed her armload of balled-up paper, pamphlets, dirty clothes. "Women. Can't you ever sit still? Just leave things as they are? I'll never find anything again."

Mother burst out in silvery laughter, and I had to join in. Anton could never find anything anyway. He spent half his day raking through his haystacks of poems and papers for the lost scrap of an idea. Now he was outnumbered. He cursed us all roundly, then grabbed his coat, cap, and revolver and stalked out, pausing in the door like an actor leaving the stage. "I'm going to go shoot someone now. Perhaps myself. If only the Germans would come and put me out of my misery."

Two days later, the Soviet voted to accept the German ultimatum. The deal the kaiser offered with his foot on our necks was far harsher than the one Lenin had wanted to sign in January—the one that ideologue Trotsky walked away from, proclaiming, "No war, no peace."

With the Germans on our doorstep, we had to accept it all. So much for our old demand of "no annexations." We would cede the Baltics and Poland to the Germans, the Transcaucasus to the Ottomans, and the Ukraine to a puppet government ruled by Berlin. Our borders shrank to the size of old Muscovy, like a heart inside the breast of a dying beast. As for "no indemnifications," the socialist state owed six billion marks to the kaiser. Not to mention the irony of forced demobilization. We had wanted all along to take apart the machine of war and bring our men home, yet forcible disarmament by a foreign power felt quite different. And more demoralizing still, the workers' state agreed to stop exporting revolution to the West. No propaganda, no assistance to foreign workers, a complete rout. Trotsky resigned rather than have to go to Brest to sign such an odious declaration.

Still, after four barbaric years of war—exhausted, beaten, truncated, and bankrupt—Russia was finally at peace.

Soon Genya would be home. I imagined him as I sat on my bench at the knitting factory, the pins falling in a clatter and the wool sliding through my fingers. I pictured him home alive, intact, his confidence restored. How I would rush into his arms and kiss him, never let him go. It was high time for Mother to leave the Poverty Artel now that the danger had passed. But it was Anton begging her to stay on another day, and another.

I would return to the flat after work to find her discussing the manuscript with him, cigarette in her hand—she'd started to smoke!—as Avdokia fried potatoes over the primus stove. Eight days earlier none of us would have believed any of it. She'd come to accept me as the woman I was. And I had begun to experience her anew as well, as an independent intellectual. Freed from her overcrowded room on Furshtatskaya Street, she'd been reborn. Her ability to tolerate Anton continued to astonish me. She treated him like a bad-tempered little dog whose outbursts were of no consequence.

That night I worked on three new poems—one about maroon women, one about socks, and a third about the boxed statues in the Summer Garden emerging in spring, not knowing all that had taken place while they'd slept. As I wrote, Anton explained to Mother why the futurist Khlebnikov was the only poet in Russia worth reading now, better than even Mayakovsky. He was just launching into a recitation of

"Bo-Beh-O-Bi Sang the Lips" when we heard scrabbling in the lock. Oh, Lord. I threw my pen down and
ran to the door. There stood my dear husband, filling
the doorway, dirty, exhausted, and grinning, his thick
overcoat snow-dusted and smelling of wood smoke. I
couldn't stop kissing him, touching him, his whiskery
cheeks, drinking in his smell of hay. In one piece.
Thank God he was here.

Zina and Gigo crowded in behind him. "Don't mind
us," she said, pushing past me.

Anton stood and embraced him, pounded him on the
back. "About time, young son. I was about to rent out
your corner."

He kissed me, hugged me in the crook of his arm,
laughing, so happy, before noticing Mother at the table,
and Avdokia with her mending on the divan. He took
in the neatly folded bedding, the washed floor, the
emptied ashtray, and stiffened in my arms. He'd never
met my mother, nor had she laid eyes on him except
from a second-floor window. I should not have let this
happen. Not like this, not now. I took a deep breath,
but the air in the room seemed to vanish. "Genya, this
is my mother, Vera Borisovna. Mother, my husband.
Gennady Yurievich Kuriakin."

She gave a nod—courteous, formal. But the light
had gone out in his face, as if he'd stepped into a
shadow. He pushed his cap to the back of his head,
stalked to the table, and slumped into my vacated chair.
Slow rage built in his face. He reached out and drank

from the cup of roasted-oat tea sitting before her, finishing it off in a single draught. She pulled away,
valiantly trying not to show her disgust.

"She's been helping Anton. With the Apollinaire," I
added quickly. "She came during the offensive. Just for
a few days. Varvara said they might take her hostage."

Gigo flopped onto the divan next to Avdokia and began to inspect her, clowning, fooling with her mending,
touching her scarf, examining her like a chimpanzee
would, as if he'd never seen an old woman before.

Genya took off his snow-brushed cap and tossed it
onto the table, ran his fingers through his hair. It was
cut short now, like a soldier's. "Enjoying our hospitality, Vera Borisovna?"

Her eyes flashed in panic. "We have been comfortable, thank you."

"How nice," he said. He wasn't a sarcastic man, it
didn't suit him.

I wished Anton would speak up. "Anton invited her
to stay on." But our Mephistopheles just leaned back in
his chair watching the scene unfold, head to one side,
thin fingers on the tabletop. He would never side with
anyone against Genya. Genya glowered at him, then
back at my mother. Zina picked up Mother's karakul
hat from a hook by the door, put it on her dirty hair,
and posed. "What do you think?" I hadn't missed her
little sharp-chinned face, her spiteful black eyes with
their dark circles. As I was sure she hadn't missed mine.
It had given her a chance to work her influence over

Genya, in case he might be persuaded to change his mind about me. She glittered with malice as she modeled, holding her hands at fashionable right angles. "Will it do?"

I snatched it off her head, hung it back on the hook. "Don't do that."

"Ooh, sensitive," she snickered.

Mother, still as an ice-encrusted statue atop the Winter Palace, watched Genya, now pacing, anger darkening his pale face as all the chill in her personality returned, freezing the warmth and charm. He opened the stove door, letting smoke into the room, poking it with the stair rod we'd stolen from the front building. His brows pressed on his deep-set eyes, and his wide mouth pinched at the corners. He was about to explode.

"Anton," I whispered, cutting my eyes toward Genya. *Say something*.

But Anton rolled a cigarette in a scrap of newspaper, breaking the tobacco off each end. Genya reached over and plucked it from his lips, stuck it between his own, lit a straw, and ignited the cigarette with its burning edge. The smell of smoke hung in the air like a warning. He slammed the stove door.

"Genya, can we talk? In the hall?" I asked him. If only I could get him away from his audience, take him in my arms, I knew I could explain. Surely he could understand the danger. His fury was being fed by the presence of spectators. This new swagger and sarcasm must be the spoils of war. Where was my tender Genya?

He crossed his arms, his jutting jaw telling me all as I moved close, speaking low in his ear. His green, fresh smell was the same as always. "So talk."

"They'll be gone tomorrow," I began. "Please. It's not a big deal."

He didn't meet my eyes. His face darkened even more. "I've been sleeping in ditches on the snow. I get back to my loving wife and it's Vera *Borisovna*. Not to mention the old nanny. You say it's not a big deal? Anton, what the hell were you thinking?"

Anton raised his hand. "Don't involve me in your domestic fiascos," he said, moving onto the cot, where he rolled himself another cigarette to replace the one in Genya's hand. Mother gazed down at the book of Khlebnikov poems she'd been discussing with Anton, knowing she'd been thrown to the wolves.

I still stood in front of him. "Genya, look at me."

But his attention was seized by something over my shoulder. "Oh, no. No, no, no." In one step, he swooped over and scooped up the Virgin of Tikhvin in his huge hand. He gazed down at it with such loathing I thought he might spit on it. He hated religion more than anything. It meant authority, superstition, tradition, ignorance, reaction, and irrationality all rolled into one.

I reached for it, but his smile chilled me as he pulled it away. Eyes narrowed at me, his brow like a ridge, he dropped it to the floor. Its silver frame made a tinny clatter. Gigo and Zina were watching him, fascinated. Then he lifted his enormous boot and crushed the small painted panel. I heard Avdokia's gasp. I felt as if he'd just crushed my own chest. He kicked the shattered thing against the wall, and the pieces came tumbling out of the frame. "What do you think you're doing?" he shouted. "Bringing something like that in here. You think this is a joke?"

Avdokia rushed in to salvage it, heedless of danger, gathering up the smashed remains, weeping and hissing curses at him. "Enemy Satan! Depart from us a hundred, a thousand versts..." And he did look, if not satanic, then like some elemental chthonic power coming up from the dark halls of the earth. "May he know every grief and woe..."

"Don't you curse me, old witch," he said and took a step toward her.

I picked up the stair rod and slashed through the air with it as if it were a saber. How I wanted to hit him with it, to beat it over his back until it broke. "Don't you go near her!" I shouted at him. "Who are you? Where's Genya? What did you do with him?"

I helped my weeping nanny stand, the broken pieces of the icon in her apron's skirt. Zina held her hand over her mouth, trying not to laugh. I brandished the rod in her direction and she stopped. My mother stood, picked up her carpetbag, and began numbly collecting her things. "We're leaving," she said. Outside the windows, the wind howled, the snow in the courtyard whirled but Mother and Avdokia put on their coats. Avdokia snatched her sewing basket away from Gigo. "I would not wish to spend a night under the same roof as you, monsieur," Mother said.

"You can't leave," I said. "Not in that storm. And it's late—the trams have stopped running."

"Did they think of that when they kicked you out?" Genya said to me, throwing himself into the chair. "Pitched you right to the curb in the middle of the night? Soldiers were shooting. Did they care? No. The question is, who are *you*, Marina? Revolutionary poet or..." He tipped his chin at my terrified mother.

"Didn't I tell you?" Zina piped up. "Right from the beginning, she came waltzing in with that fancy coat she used to wear—"

"Want me to part your hair for you?" I asked her. My mother was stuffing her things into her carpetbag. Gigo was pulling things out as she put them in, clowning around.

"She killed your brother. You forgive her for that?" Genya said. "Threw Seryozha to the dogs."

Mother stood up straight, her face so pale I thought she would faint.

"And now you're hiding her from proletarian justice, in my house!" He jumped up and crossed to the door in two long strides, opened it wide. Immediately the air from the icy hall emptied the warmth from the room. "Allow me!" He was playing it for theater, for Gigo and

Zina. "Too cold for you, Vera Borisovna? I'm sorry. But really, it's time to go."

Was I going mad? She and Avdokia were all the family I had left—couldn't he understand that? Couldn't he find one shred of pity? I grabbed Mother's hairbrush out of Gigo's hand and put it into her bag. "I'm leaving, too. I can't stay here with this impersonator. Let me know when Genya comes back."

He laughed, so painfully. "Oh, so it's my fault! How quickly we forget."

Mother and Avdokia stood with their coats on, waiting for me to get out of the way so they could make a run for it.

He turned away from us all, sat in his chair again, his arms folded. "Go on then." Daring me.

I grabbed my coat, my thick scarf, wriggled my feet into my boots, sobbing, hoping he would see what he was doing, beg me to stay as he had begged me to marry him only eight days ago. But as he sat at the table with his back to us, his shoulders like the fortification of a city, I knew he could not relent. "Anton?"

Anton lay on his cot, spinning the cylinder of his revolver, mortified at such naked displays of personal drama, looking like he was going to shoot someone — or himself. Gigo lay on the divan like an odalisque, while Zina had slipped into my vacated chair—ready to replace me. My home, my life. Why was this happening?

Yet I buttoned my coat, the wind roaring outside, and

inside my head. "Neither of us wants this," I said to him but he didn't turn around. It had all gone too far. "Anton, give me your gun." That made Genya glance over at me.

"What for?" Anton asked.

It would be a long trip across the city in the storm. Nobody was offering to walk us, and I wasn't about to ask. "For me," I said.

Mother waited by the door, tense as a cat, while Avdokia glared at Genya as if he were Beelzebub in a tattered coat.

Anton glanced questioningly at his brooding pal. "You really going to let her go? After all this crap I've been forced to listen to all this time?"

He actually understood how ridiculous Genya was being, but Genya wouldn't even return his gaze, just stared moodily into the stove.

"Oh, hell." Anton brought me the weapon. "If you need to fire it, you pull this back"—he showed me a catch at the butt end of the gun—"then fire. And if you do have to use it, keep firing, and don't stop until it's empty." He reluctantly handed it over, the metal warm from his playing with it, and the weight of it, the ugly greasiness, surprised and revolted me.

Anton was actually being nicer than Genya—the world had gone crazy! I stuffed the gun into my coat pocket. Genya still hadn't turned around. Mother looked frail and exhausted by my unseemly life in all its squalor. I wondered whether she would even stand the walk home. *Home?* Had I actually thought that? *This* was home, the Poverty Artel, the poets, Genya. I wiped my nose on the back of my hand. The cards had turned again. *Do you have to have everything?* I heard Mina saying. But I was leaving my husband with only the rustle of the clothes on my back and the howl of the storm for a farewell. We walked down the slick stairs of the Grivtsova tenement, and out into the night.

Part IV

Hyacinths

(Spring 1918)

43 *The Islands*

HE WHO DOES NOT work, does not eat.

The knitting factory closed shortly after the Soviet accepted the German terms—an event nothing short of apocalyptic. I arrived in the morning as I always did to find the rest of the girls standing in the courtyard like so many stunned oxen, the metal door rolled down and locked tight.

"Do you think he's been arrested?" a girl asked.

"That skunk, that fat *burzhui,*" said pug-nosed Olga, their ringleader, and gave the door an enormous kick. "He's moved down to Moscow like the rest of the rats." Though the danger of the German invasion was over, the Soviet had left anyway, sneaking out in the middle of the night like tenants behind on their rent.

The weight of what had happened hit me. "No war, no soldiers," I explained to my little comrades. "No army, no contracts. No money, no socks."

"Bastard," said Olga. "There's capitalism for you."

"We're leaving anyway," said one of the younger girls. "Mama's got sisters in Kiev. They say there's food down there."

We kissed each other goodbye like school chums before summer break, and left the courtyard in dejected groups of two and three.

Back at Furshtatskaya Street, I tried every trick I could think of to get into the Red Guard's room, but no such luck. His wife, *so-called*, was always in there, and she distrusted me from the start. There was no trace of Father's supposed support. I kept waiting for him to make an appearance, steeling myself for the explosion that was sure to follow, but he never surfaced. Perhaps he'd gone deeper underground. Or maybe Mother had been lying all along.

After the knitting factory closed, I haunted the labor exchange, but they were only looking for the most vital, skilled professionals—obstetrical nurses and engineers. Mostly I wandered around avoiding the apartment, stopping in at Wolf's and reading the poetry I couldn't afford to buy anymore. I wanted to know what poets were saying about the revolution, whether *Okno* had appeared and if I'd been included. And, yes, I was hoping to run into Genya. Rehearsing what I would say to him. Yet I could not bring myself to go to the Poverty Artel to beg him to rethink his actions, beg him to let us start over.

I drifted over to Znamenskaya Square, scene of so many rousing and traumatic events of the previous year. The train station was a kicked-over anthill. Half of Petrograd seemed to be trying to get on trains for the south or Moscow or back to the villages. A porter I talked to had been there for the evacuation of the Soviet. They'd had trains waiting on sidings a half mile out—that's why no one saw them. "I carried stuff out there all night," he said. "Desks, chairs, pictures. Bathtubs. Wives. Mistresses."

I stood under the clock, watching people rush by me like a run of salmon around a rock. I felt becalmed, invisible. A great migration out of the city was taking place and like a lone goose on a lake, I'd been left behind. The concourse, once a showpiece, had grown impossibly grimy, the floor black as if it had been painted, the stuccowork cast in high relief, each medallion picked out by a heavy coat of soot.

Suddenly, a woman with three small children tugged at my sleeve. "*Devushka,* can you help us?" The woman was young, pretty—well dressed, I noticed—but harried. Her hair was coming down. "I need to find my husband. Could you stay with the children and our bags?"

I was evidently still identifiable as bourgeois, a girl who would be trustworthy and sympathetic, a strong-looking girl who was nevertheless *one of us. Nasha.* I sat on their luggage, holding the baby—a novel experience as I'd never so much as touched one before. It was heavy and made mewling sounds, which fortunately never broke into out-and-out bawling. I jiggled it as the oldest child, a boy, told me all about trains, especially the one they were taking to Moscow, the Nikolaevsky Express. He didn't know that it was the very train upon which Anna Karenina met Vronsky, the train under which she'd thrown herself. "You never heard of Tolstoy?"

He shook his solemn head. "Papa works for the Commissariat." More desertion. I dandled the baby and couldn't help wondering what Genya's and my child would have looked like. I'd left all my things back at the Poverty Artel — my books, my brother's silhouettes. I imagined going back to retrieve them, seeing if there could be some reconciliation between us. But we were both so terribly stubborn. The little girl, around four, in a puff-sleeved coat and a little tam, sat next to me with her soft-bodied doll and amused herself by kissing it and shaking it ferociously by turns. How like life.

At last, the woman returned with the husband and their tickets. The man asked if I would accompany them to the platform to keep an eye on the children and the porter. I received a twenty-ruble tip for my efforts, and it gave me the idea to see if there was more work in it. I set myself up as a porter, babysitter, runner after lost items or people, and cleared nearly fifty rubles that day. And spent it all on a packet of meat on the way home. Sure that there was a new career in this for me, I returned to the station for several days running, but never made as much money again. However, I was propositioned by three pimps and threatened by a porter who thought I was taking business away from him.

I had to find work. I was grateful that I still had a

few more days on my monthly ration cards, but come March, those cod-liver pancakes would seem like a feast. There were only so many things Avdokia could sell in the shadows. I felt like a drunk pitched out into the street by the tavern keeper only to be run over by a cart. My brief marriage was over, the poets' circle closed against me. My revolutionary life had ended. There was nothing left but two old women and a flat full of furniture that nobody wanted except to chop up for firewood.

In the overstuffed boudoir, I ate a meager dinner with my mother and nanny—pancakes consisting of shredded frozen potatoes fried in a malodorous substance that was mostly cod-liver oil, all I could find on the black market. Mother was depressed, her friends the Gromitskys had had a visit from the Cheka the night before. "Everything confiscated. They only left them the clothes on their backs and the bed. Now, tell me, what does the worker need a Venetian mirror for? Dresses by Worth—can you imagine? Trotting around on some commissar's mistress, no doubt." I choked down the meal and thought of the future, my stomach bubbling like a cauldron. Mother pushed her plate away, unable to eat any more. She covered her mouth with the heel of her hand and looked away. All the brightness I'd seen in her at the Artel had faded. There was no reason for us to live like this when I had a diamond threaded into the seam of my slip. If this wasn't the time to sell it, what would be? When we

were peeling the paint off the walls with our fingernails
and eating it? Although the idea of walking all the way
up to the lawless outskirts of the city to sell such a valuable item was sobering. "Don't cry," I said, rinsing the
oily taste of cod liver out of my teeth with tea. "I think
I have a plan."

I woke at first light to find Avdokia already up, water
boiled, tea and kasha made, warm water in the
washstand—as if she had read my mind. Now that I'd
decided, I was impatient to get it over with. I washed
my face and hands cursorily, ate standing up, bundled
myself up in two wool dresses, and pulled Anton's gun
from the bureau drawer. My nanny's birdlike little eyes
caught the motion, though I kept my back to her.
"Marinoushka, what are you up to?" she whispered,
squinting at me, trying not to waken Mother, who'd
stayed up late reading *The Secret Doctrine* by Madame
Blavatsky.

I reached up under my clothes and unfastened the
diamond stickpin from my slip. I turned it so it caught
the lamplight. Canary sparks lit the room. The old
woman regarded me with alarm. "Where did you get
that?"

"Kolya. He told me about a market on Kamenny Island. Said if we ever needed money I should go up
there." I pinned the diamond back under my clothes,
donned my coat, tucked my shawl in tight, and put the
revolver in my pocket.

She crossed me and herself and pressed a piece of wood into my hand—the light wood, the torn edge. I guessed by feel what it was. "Be careful," she said, but she didn't say "Don't go," as she might have earlier. We had all changed, even the unchangeable Avdokia.

Preobrazhenskaya Square and its sad market emerged and dissolved in the milky fog. I followed the frozen Kanavka, the gold-touched rails of the Summer Garden. Inside those famous fences lay the paths where I'd walked with Genya so long ago. Now it lay in deep snow, the imperial statues shivering in their winter boxes, like vertical coffins. How we'd laughed as Diana had disapproved of our young love. The memory was a sharp pain in my side, as if I'd impaled myself on one of the railing's spear points. The Kanavka reminded me of the Mallarmé poem about a swan trapped in the ice, that small white agony. *Le vierge, le vivace et le bel aujourd'hui*...Would that be me, left behind, alone and abandoned, trapped in these beautiful ruins?

Damp clung to my face, crystallizing into ice as I emerged onto the Neva, the southern end of the Troitsky Bridge with its *style moderne* tramline down the center. As I crossed, threadbare people eyed me and each other with distrust, each of us locked into our own loneliness. The bridge seemed interminably long, as if it were telescoping outward as I walked. For a moment, I panicked, wondering if I had fallen into some weird pocket of reality. My mother and her spiritualist cronies believed that there were parallel planes to this world—other lives, other levels. What if I had entered one? Or perhaps I was caught on a bridge forever suspended between the two banks. I might become a legendary ghost, seen from time to time through the fog of a tram window.

With relief I saw the outline of the Peter and Paul Fortress emerging, its golden needle shrouded in white. Dostoyevsky had been imprisoned there, and the anarchist philosopher Kropotkin, even Trotsky himself, silver-tongued and foolishly believing his own propaganda. Now it held tsarist officers and Kadet ministers and a raft of speculators, whose ranks I was about to join.

A little ways on, the great wooden wreck of the Cirque Moderne loomed. Were they so long ago, those electrifying days when SRs and Bolsheviks and Mensheviks all mounted the same stage, part of the same movement? Now all I could think was how long it would take to burn in a small *bourgeoika* tin stove. People were destroying the city for firewood—fences, banisters, whole houses. The Bolsheviks had banned any but official cutting parties going out to the forests above the city, making criminals of us all.

My broken boot had rubbed a good-size blister into my left foot. No one strolled idly along the wide boulevard of Kamennoostrovsky Prospect anymore. Why would they? The shops were all closed. There was a time you might have walked halfway across the city just to meet someone for hot chocolate. Now you thought of your pitiful rations, your hoarded strength, your precious boot leather, like an old maid counting kopeks in a tea shop.

A man emerged from the fog, a small man with burning dark eyes, a dirty fur collar on his coat. "Hey, chicken," he said. "Sweetie pie."

I felt for Anton's gun in my pocket. I didn't know if I could really shoot someone. The man looked so sad, so desperate, his dark eyes glittering hot. He had a fever, maybe consumption, maybe the onset of typhus, which was beginning to spread in the city. I began to walk faster but he was following me. "Thirty rubles," he called out. "Queen of my dreams." Thirty rubles—it was a good price, when women would lift their skirts for half a loaf of bread. I walked faster. "Forty, princess of my heart," he said. "Please, sweetness, I'm dying." He grabbed my arm.

I pulled out the revolver and pointed it at the bridge of his nose, his great shining eyes. "Please," he whispered. "Shoot me. For God's sake, I can't live like this anymore."

Someday soon I might be as desperate as this man, as sick and crazy. I lowered the gun. "I heard something the other day," I told him, pocketing the gun. "Want to hear it?"

"Why not?" he said.

In the middle of the white fog, with no one else around, I began to recite a Blok poem for him, holding his sleeve as he was holding mine.

A girl was singing in the church's choir
of all the weary souls on foreign shores,
of all the vessels sailing ever farther,
of all who'd lost the joy they'd known before…

Blok understood this kind of despair, understood it very well, perhaps better than the two of us standing there. I let the man go, and he vanished into the fog.

Around midmorning, I crossed the last bridge into the park-swathed elegance of Kamenny Island, the old playground for affluent Petersburg. What absolute silence. Frost painted every contorted tree limb and traced the railings in white. Somewhere in the fog, the dachas of the upper nobility lay empty. Here the Soviet government planned a utopia of workers' clubs, hospitals, and old-age homes. But there was no trace of the new purpose, nor remainder of the old.

In places, the snow rose to my knees and higher. It was difficult to keep to the road. My nerves were tattered, like a sweater that moths had gotten into. If this trip ended in failure, I couldn't imagine how weary the return journey would be. Maybe I could find the man with typhus and go home with him. But no—I would find this Arkady somehow. Yet if I asked the wrong person now, I could find myself in a Cheka cell by nightfall. Who would tell Mother and Avdokia? I couldn't put them through that.

I found it hard to believe a market thrived up here.

All I could see was acre after acre of white parkland fading into the fog. There was no one to even ask the time of day. I came to a crossroads. If there was any semblance of a market, it would either have to be east, at the old Church of St. John the Baptist, or west, out near the Kamennoostrovsky Theater. Like everyone else in Petrograd, I was trying to spare my boots, and the church was closer. I bet on St. John.

I kept to the prospect as best I could, until finally the church's rosy brick bled through the mist like a watered pastel. In the little square, the shadowy shapes of human beings appeared, a small silent Kabuki of sinister figures with sleds at their feet, ropes in their gloved hands. I let my eyes run over the men with the sledges, looking for someone to approach. But who? How to choose? One man's solidity somehow reminded me of Kolya's men, and on impulse I approached him.

"I'm looking for Arkady," I said, my breath blending into the mist.

A bright pair of Kirghiz eyes stared out from under a fur hat. "The Archangel?"

"Sure," I said. "That's the one."

"Or the Antichrist?" He grinned, his leathery face breaking into jagged lines.

Was he playing with me? "It's pretty much the same, Uncle, now isn't it?"

He shifted from foot to foot, stamping to keep them warm. "Yes, it's all the same. Yes, you're right about that one."

"So where is he?" I tried again.

"You should pray," he said, and nodded with his bearded chin to the church. "God knows everything."

Arkady was in the church. I didn't like the idea. What happened out here would be visible at least to someone, but in that ancient darkness, I could disappear like Alice's rabbit. Yet I had come up here for a purpose—what else could I do? I was not about to leave now. The eyes of the men burned holes in my back as I approached the entrance.

Inside, the air was even colder, if that was possible. Dutch Gothic beams and pillars arched, high and gloomy, like the trees of an ancient forest. The church smelled of centuries of incense and damp. A couple of old women stood meekly before a tall bent priest and sang prayers in surprisingly lovely voices. A votive flame burned before the icon of St. John, stripped of its frame, which had no doubt been silver or gold. The flame wasn't from a candle but rather some sort of rancid fat in a jar. It smoked horribly. The iconostasis had also been stripped of its gold cladding but otherwise had been left miraculously intact. I crossed myself and bowed. *Mother of God, please let this Arkady be here, if not for my sake, then for my mother and Avdokia. And get me home safely.*

I felt I was being watched, that subtle pressure of another's gaze, but I didn't see anyone besides the old *babas* and the priest. Then I noticed that one of the side doors in the iconostasis was open, just a crack. Archangel Gabriel's door, Gabriel the Messenger, the Angel of Death in Exodus. I could see the slightest movement of someone watching from behind it, blocking the light. The Archangel? Or the Antichrist? I was no great believer, but my neck prickled as I walked toward that opening, hugging the shadows, giving the worshippers a wide berth, my hand on the butt of the heavy revolver. Nudging the door just a crack more, I held my breath and slipped inside the great altar screen.

Dark. Movement up high. Birds. I heard a step on the stone floor.

"Who are you?" A quick voice, a man's, low but not whispering.

"I'm looking for Arkady," I said. I could hear only breathing in the dark, a bit of thready wheeze. On the other side of the iconostasis, the pure high voices of the old women rose. "A friend sent me." As my eyes adjusted to the darkness, I saw the silhouette of a man and smelled...cooked meat. Now I knew I was in the right place, for who but speculators would have meat in our starving city?

"What friend?" came the voice.

"Nikolai Shurov," I said.

The scritch of a match revealed the profile of a man with a salt-and-pepper moustache and heavy black eyebrows. He lit a lantern and I could barely conceal my horror at the sight of the altar being used as a picnic table for the lamp and a greasy wad of papers that

smelled like sausage. It was like watching Genya trample the Virgin of Tikhvin, my luck breaking in a thousand pieces. "Are you Arkady?"

He stuck out his lower lip, shook his head. "What do
you have?"

My panic redoubled. "I'm only talking to Arkady," I
said, trying to sound tough, my voice strange against
the ringing crystal tones of the *babas*. I wondered if the
priest was in on it, too. "So who are you, anyway—St.
Peter at the gates?"

He waggled his finger in front of my nose. "You'd
better watch that mouth up here." He picked up the
lantern. "Come with me."

Every instinct shouted at me to turn around and flee
while I could. But it was too late for instinct. I followed
him through a door into the sacristy, smelling of ancient incense and dirty hair, and out the back of the
church into the snow.

44 *The Archangel*

I STAYED CLOSE BEHIND my surly guide and tried to
walk in his footprints, sinking into the snow, struggling
to keep up. I didn't trust him. He knew I possessed
something valuable. Why pay for it when he could rob
me and leave me up here to freeze? *Kolya, what have
you gotten me into?* I wanted to keen aloud like a terrified child, but instead I gripped the handle of Anton's

gun, hoping it worked, hoping there would be enough time to use it.

To my relief, we came upon a path of sorts, churned by many boots. I did my best to memorize the spot so I might find it again if I needed to flee. Now a long shedlike building coalesced in the fog. It must have been used to service one of the great dachas. A bundled man emerged from a small door. It closed behind him, and he marched off into the park. Soon my churlish Virgil pounded on its peeling gray wood, three long blows. A small bowlegged man let us in, his quick eyes taking my measure.

Servants' quarters—for gardeners, cooks—had been converted into a kind of barracks. Men sat in the makeshift clubhouse playing cards, smoking, and eating. I could smell their cooked meat, and it made me wolfish with hunger. They glanced at me in rough disinterest. I gave up clutching the pistol in my pocket lest it draw their attention. The black-browed man led me to a door, knocked, opened it, stepped aside like a butler—or a jailer—and waved me in.

On a threadbare divan with stuffing coming out of the arms lay a handsome man of around fifty, though it could be sixty—I wasn't much of a judge of old people. He was languid and long, with untrimmed pale hair and eyebrows, a long Swedish face with sloped nose and eyes of brightest blue, intent upon a web of string in his hands. I watched, fascinated by fingers that could move so deftly from cradle to diamonds to fish. "So?" he said, his voice dry, unimpressed.

"Shurov sent her," said the man with the black eyebrows.

"Interesting." His eyes flicked from my brown proletarian shawl to my wet and broken boots. "Leave her."

My guide closed the door behind him. I didn't know whether to stand or sit in one of the hard chairs dotting the room. I pushed the shawl off my head, let it lie on my shoulders. It was so warm here, bliss. I removed my dirty gloves, too, and rubbed my hands, wishing I could take my boots off and let them dry by the stove. My feet ached, and I wondered if they were frostbitten.

"Do you know who I am?" he asked.

"Arkady, I guess." I hoped I sounded nonchalant.

"I am Baron Arkady von Princip," he said, looking only at the shifting figures between his hands.

Von Princip. I had read all about him in the nonparty papers, him and his gang. Responsible for outrageous daylight robberies and armed assaults, gun battles with Red Guards, the lurid stuff of our knitting-factory fantasies. The girls followed the stories of his bold attacks as if they were the exploits of some folktale hero.

Arkady's clever hands turned the fox into a purse and then into a throne. "You have something for me?"

I turned my back, then unbuttoned my coat and the bodice beneath it to unpin the canary diamond. Warm from the heat of my body, it flashed in my hand. *Well, Kolya, farewell*…sentiment was history. I closed my dress and turned back to him, holding out the jewel in the palm of my hand the way you feed sugar to a horse so it doesn't bite your fingers. But he didn't reach for it, just transformed the string throne into a broom. "Very nice," he said, not even looking. "I won't ask how you came to receive such a fine offering from our young Shurov. I'm sure whatever you did for it, it was quite impressive."

I didn't think I could blush anymore. But there was no mistaking the hot tingle in my cheeks. I could see Arkady, lying there on the divan like a lizard that lived in the dark, was a man who enjoyed making people uncomfortable. He wore a tweed jacket and a knitted scarf and had a hole in his sock. Couldn't the prince of thieves afford a new one? I dropped my hand with the offered pin.

"It's odd, don't you agree? That you take this from Shurov and sell it to me?" he said. "Why didn't he just give you the money? Or is that too indecorous? Oh, youth. Tell me your name, girl."

I knew I should lie, but something perverse in me—pride?—refused to be cowed, even for my own sake. "Makarova," I said. "Marina Dmitrievna."

"Dmitry Makarov." He looked up at me now, arched one pale eyebrow.

"It's a common name," I said.

He regarded me wearily, as if he could see everything about me, who I was and where I came from and even what would happen to me after I left. The men in the hall were arguing, and Arkady cocked his head to listen. Evidently it was nothing that bothered him, for he went back to his string. "I know you didn't come here just to sell me that little trinket."

I tried to imagine what he was getting at. "Kolya said to ask for you. He said it was worth ten thousand."

The old man shook his head, a faint smile creasing his thin, bloodless lips. "You were curious. Who is this Arkady fellow? Perhaps you wanted to hear a bit more about the fate of your elusive friend Shurov." His strange gaze—you couldn't feel a human being behind it. It was more like a blue-eyed tiger's. "Perhaps your friend wanted us to meet. And this is your letter of introduction."

I shuddered. I swore to myself I'd tell Varvara about this whole headquarters of thieves as soon as I made it back to the Petersburg side of the Neva.

"Would you like to know where our friend is at this very moment?" he asked.

"He's in the south," I said, and my lips were as dry as a Crimean wind. "He had a load of art. Three sledges' worth."

Arkady reached with his teeth to pull a length of string and loop it over his curled thumbs. "What would you say if I told you he was here in Petrograd?"

My heart dropped like a statue from a palace rooftop. Breaking like shattered plaster on the stones of a public square.

The old man nodded. "You care for him a great deal. No, actually, I put him and his goods on a train to Finland six weeks ago. He was headed to Stockholm.

And from there, Paris—if he can make it through the lines."

Was this also a lie? Some sort of test? I sensed he was telling the truth now. Kolya *had* gone six weeks ago. But he'd promised he would never leave the country without me. I didn't want the languid von Princip to see me cry. I could feel him watching me, enjoying his little game. I bent down to brush an imaginary lump of snow from my broken boot, examined the sole, the awful crack. I pressed the bridge of my nose, pulled hard on my forelock.

Von Princip wove a string crown, held it at arm's length, and squinted one eye, crowning me with it. Then he pulled it off his fingers and swung his legs over the edge of the divan, sitting up. "What do you do for a living, Makarova? Teach dancing? Give French lessons to pharmacists?"

"I work in a factory," I said defiantly.

A smile broke slowly across his face, like a crack moving through glass. "Ah, the little proletarian. No need to get defensive. I'm quite fond of the Bolsheviks, you know. After all, they've made all this possible." He rose from the divan and went to his desk, started rooting in the drawer. "Before the revolution I was only a criminal. Now I'm a regular tycoon."

I imagined the possibilities of panic and scarcity. I knew why Kolya did it—for the excitement, the gambler's thrill. Some spectacular bit of cleverness, perhaps gulling the uninformed but also helping when he could, that's what he loved. More than the money. And what did this man love? "There's nothing shameful in working for a living," I said.

"Oh, Makarova," said Arkady. "You're no proletarian." He put his bony hand on my shoulder. I was surprised that it didn't repulse me. "You're an adventurer. Just like your little friend Shurov." His voice was dry, precise, raspy, insistent. "Politically. Personally. Probably sexually, too." He was watching me with a half smile. What was he looking for? Shame? Agreement? I hadn't lived with Anton all these months to be baited so easily. There was a knock on the door. Arkady didn't answer it. "You weren't born to run a lathe or whatever you do at your factory."

Adventurers. Was that what we were, Kolya and I? Perhaps. But I wasn't going to give him the satisfaction of labeling me. "Maybe I'm a good lathe operator. Maybe it's my ultimate dream. You don't know the first thing about me."

Arkady held up the diamond.

I opened my hand, not quite believing it wasn't still in my palm. He turned the pin in his fingers, letting the lamp shatter its spectrum into yellow shards. He closed his other fist over it, opened his hands, and the pin was gone. "Another girl would have brought someone. But not you. You're frightened, but your curiosity is stronger." Watching my face the way a boatman scans a shore. He was standing right next to me, and I could smell wormwood, dark and a bit antiseptic, and camphor, like the church. "Hiding this all those weeks." The pin was back in his fingers and he held it before my face. "It must have burned quite a hole in your slip, knowing you could have ten thousand rubles any time you liked. Biding your time. Consider this before you tell me you don't play games. You have a bit of the criminal in you, Makarova. More than a little, I would say. You like secrets. You like knowing more than most people."

"But I don't rob them."

"*Ostorozhno,*" he said, waving a finger in the air between us. *Careful.* "Remember, if you're alive, it's only by my pleasure. I could strangle you right now, throw you out in the snow, and no one would lift an eyebrow."

I nodded, a very tiny nod. Felt the weight of the gun in my pocket.

"Though at this moment, I prefer you alive." He pursed his lips in a coquette's moue, which on his gaunt face was laughably incongruous. "But I won't have my profession maligned. Without the criminal, how would people live? How much meat do you think would be sold in Petrograd? Or oil or grain? The Soviet can't keep it on the trains long enough." He stood next to the window in his socks, gazing out at the milky sky, the gaunt trees. "Every region takes its share, and poor Petrograd's the end of the line. As simple as that. Without us, the city would starve." He threaded the diamond stickpin through the lapel of his jacket and poured himself a glass of vodka from a tray on the table, poured another and held it out to me. Standing, he was tall and rather elegant in an untidy way. "Never underestimate the genius of crime. We find a way when there is no way."

I knew I shouldn't drink with him. It implied some kind of agreement. But to what was I agreeing? Hesitating a moment, I drank. The vodka burned my empty stomach.

"I'll give you five thousand plus a can of cooking oil, ten pounds of good wheat flour, four of meat. And some sugar."

My stomach rumbled. Not *vobla*, that bony fish, our "Soviet ham," but something that once walked on four legs…and wheat flour…sugar, when had anyone last seen that? And cooking oil. No more of those bizarre substitutes—cod-liver or castor oil or liquids that didn't seem to be oil at all. I wouldn't be able to find such an offer of real food again, even with ten thousand rubles in my pocket. By comparison, money was nothing, birdseed, a shake of salt, though that, too, was hard to find.

Arkady put on a pair of leather slippers and went out into the hall, leaving me in his makeshift salon. On a wide, ugly desk dating from the era of Nikolas I lay piles of ragged papers, lists of abbreviations, and numbers scribbled on the scraps. I held one up. The baron had very small handwriting, spiked, Gothic. All in a sort of code. I considered taking a sheet and folding it into my pocket as insurance against a rainy day, but I put it down again. I suspected this, too, might be some kind of test. I turned to the stove to warm my feet and hands.

The baron returned. He pressed a thick wad of banknotes into my hand, like a paper brick. "Here's the five." I didn't count it, only turned away and tucked the bills into my bodice, packing them around my ribs. When I turned back, he was studying me, unblinking, long fingers pressed to his lips. "I start to see what our friend saw in you, Makarova." He made that terrifying moue again, contorting his bony face in a whore's pout. "But don't mistake my affability for idiocy. I might have something for you in a day or two. I'll be in touch."

45 *The Errand*

NO WAY TO HAVE something in these hungry days without the world knowing about it and hating you for it. When Avdokia let me in, I smelled incense—Master Vsevolod must have been there. Even though Mother no longer had tea and mille-feuilles to offer him, I was pleased to discover that it was actually a friendship. I had assumed the worst about him—unfairly, as it turned out.

Avdokia crowed as I dropped my heavy prizes on the table, the meat, the oil, the flour, which I'd carried home most of the way on my back, fully prepared to shoot anyone who got near me. She sifted the silky flour between thumb and forefinger. "Wheat flour! Theotokos be praised."

Mother said nothing. She'd turned inward again since our ejection from Grivtsova Alley. The fight with Genya, the attack on the Virgin, the terrifying walk back to the flat through the storm had snuffed out her time with Anton like a lamp at bedtime. Avdokia volunteered to brave the kitchen to cook the meat. She would be better able to withstand the catty remarks of women trying to guess where that delicacy had come from than I would. Envy ran thick as cold oil in the collectivized flat. Mother buried herself in her Blavatsky, and I thought about Kolya and what he was doing with the frightening, intriguing man whose company I'd just left.

Later, as we ate our heavenly dinner, real wheat pancakes and fresh meat, my nanny and I plotted what to do with the money and the rest of the food. We decided we would first buy a small load of firewood. Avdokia knew a woman who knew a man in the Haymarket who had a source. "We'll trade for a bit of the flour." But how to get the wood back here? If only I had a little sled…just a board with wooden runners and a rope to pull it with.

Mother cried out when I broke apart a drawer of the chifforobe using my hands and feet. "That was a wedding gift from my grandmother," she sighed.

I didn't bother looking for tools. Even in the old

days, we never had any. We'd used other people
as our tools—plumbers and shoemakers and tinkers
and tailors, the *dvornik*. And now we were paying
for it. No awl, no hammer, no ax—we were little
better than cavemen. These days tools were rarer
than radium. Though nails were easy. Every bit of
wood came with some—all you had to do was burn
it. Everyone's *bourgeoika* stove was full of them.
Maybe I should look for a hatchet while we still had
the money.

I emptied the bullets from Anton's gun and used
the butt to hammer the runners to the bottom of the
drawer's face using nails from the stove. Soon I'd fashioned a crude sled, no worse than many I'd seen in
town. I punched two holes in the walnut slab and
threaded a drapery cord through for a strap.

"Barbarians." Mother turned away, unable to watch
the destruction of the beautiful armoire.

"Rich barbarians," I said. "And soon to be warm
ones."

In the morning, we measured flour into a sack that
Avdokia had sewed from a pair of Mother's underwear
and hung from my belt inside my coat, pulling on it
to make sure it wouldn't break loose under a pickpocket's hands. "Make sure the wood's not wet," Avdokia said. "And don't settle for less than a pood. You
should hardly be able to lift it."

"Marina, don't go." Mother was anxious again. She'd
started rubbing her knuckles, knitting her hands, as

she'd been doing after Seryozha's death. "Stay home today. There are dark entities around you."

That was all I needed to hear before going out on this little mission. I exchanged glances with Avdokia. She walked me to the door, made the sign of the cross over me. "God have mercy...maybe I should come with you. I'd make a better bargain."

"You stay with her."

With the gun snug in my pocket, I descended the stairs to Furshtatskaya Street. I felt like a character from Dumas in seven-league boots. So glad to be out of the flat and Mother's aura of doom. The air seemed suddenly warmer, the fog less icy. Perhaps it was just the good dinner last night and a breakfast of fresh eggs. I had oil, meat, and soap, flour to trade, money hidden behind the baseboards. No Genya, no Kolya, but I'd survived, and spring was coming soon. A sudden feeling of well-being seized me. I strode down the street like a bogatyr. Life would return. Maybe for me, too.

Now that I was eating regularly, I felt better than I had in a long time and the city seemed more beautiful to me. Occasionally sunshine broke out and glinted on the icicles, which loosened from the rooftops and dropped like spear points from the sky to burst on the pavement. You could be killed if you weren't careful. Yes, spring arrived with the retorts like gunfire from the Neva as the ice began to break. I was writing again, three, four poems a day, the straitjacket of my soul broken loose.

Strolling along Sergievskaya, not far from the Krestovskys', I was startled by an enormous form at the periphery of my vision. A huge horse—black, and shaggy. My first thought—*Kolya!* But no. In the high driver's seat was the wizened little man who'd kept the door at Arkady's barracks. Yet the horse was the same as those in the courtyard that day on the English Embankment, a giant black feather-footed beast, powerful, beautiful, and well-fed when all Petrograd horses were either bags of living bones or already wrapped in paper, being sold in dark stairwells. Who but criminals could feed horses like these now?

"He wants to see you," the little man said. He didn't open his mouth much when he talked, like people from the far north.

"What for?"

"You'll see soon enough."

There are points in one's life where it's possible to turn back, and we know them when they come, even when we don't choose to take that option. Man is a curious and stubborn creature, and I was possessed of both qualities in full. So instead of running for my life, I took a seat behind the little man, who whipped up the giant horse. It surged off—my God! It had the energy to trot when most of the humans around us barely had the strength to stand. We raced to the river, crossing at the Liteiny Bridge, clods of softening snow thumping against the front of the sled, the freshening wind splashing my face. Gaunt pedestrians watched us hungrily, wishing they could ride, wishing they were as fat as the horse, wishing they could carve the horse up with their little knives right there and then. We moved across like royalty. It had been so long since I'd ridden anything other than an overcrowded tram.

On the Vyborg side, we passed the great factories, empty now after the evacuations. Broken windows, sagging gates. Ericsson, Nobel, Arsenal—stinking belching brawny plants now silent as dead mammoths. The workers' tenements looked colder and shabbier than ever, the streets full of debris. Workers with no work had gone back to their villages. If one needed more proof that Petrograd was dying, the fact was laid bare up here. How would the Bolsheviks ever breathe life back into this devastation?

We sped on through the industrial belt and emerged in the countryside. The sky had brightened, the sun threatening to break through. I had never been so far out on the Vyborg side, had only seen it from train windows, and never in winter. The horse thundered through little-used lanes between open fields, and I remembered another sleigh ride, lilac light on the snow...it seemed like a dream now. Or maybe this was the dream. The sweet cast of the warming air on the weary, sodden drifts.

We pulled up before a greenhouse, the glass obscured by steam, green things growing inside. The little man got down from his high seat. Funny to see such a shrimp driving a sleigh—Petersburg coachmen were always large and well padded. I stroked the giant horse's beautiful haunch, warm and shaggy, savoring the sweaty, earthy smell, and followed the little bow-legged tough to the greenhouse. Its entry still boasted fancy woodwork from the age of Alexander III. We passed inside the double doors, outer and inner, entering the warmth of the hothouse and its staggering fragrance, lilacs and lilies. They still existed, the greenhouses of Petrograd. Down one long aisle, Arkady von Princip leaned over a flat of hyacinths, closing his eyes over the deep blue of the blooms and inhaling, just like a man preparing to sip a glass of cognac.

He didn't look up. "What do you know about hyacinths, Makarova?"

"Only the myth."

"Tell it to me," he said, moving on to other flats.

I searched my memory. "Hyacinth, a handsome boy who became an object of rivalry between two gods: Apollo, god of the sun, and Zephyr, the west wind. So the gods decided that they would throw the discus to determine who should win the boy. Hyacinth thought to impress Apollo by catching it, and Zephyr, in his jealousy, blew the discus so hard it killed the boy. In mourning, Apollo turned him into a flower."

"Apollo couldn't bear for the boy's soul to end in sad Hades," Arkady said, breaking off a hyacinth and sniffing it. "So he turned him into a flower that rises from a bulb buried most of the year, to live again in the spring, full of this unearthly scent. Quite a tribute. Ovid says that Apollo's tears are written upon the petals. *Ai.* See?" *Ai, alas.*

He held a bloom between his fingers, bending the petals back. I was aware of how he studied me, the intellect behind those reflective blue eyes. Like most women, I knew when a man found me attractive. He would pay a certain kind of attention that wasn't so much listening as taking in the sound of my voice, the shape of my profile, the turn of my lips. I was no great beauty. I had my red hair, my round dark eyes, my fat lips, but they were rough and cracked now, the skin peeling from winter's harshness. I'd once had a good figure but now was all bones—and who could tell anyway under all these clothes? I was no regal Lisa Podharzhevskaya, no Akhmatova. I hadn't the dignity, the mournful gravity. And yet, who was he looking at like that? He put his hand on my scarf and pushed it down, left his hand on my neck. I thought it would be rough, scaly, like lizard skin, but it was very smooth.

What was it I found so alluring about him? He smelled peculiar—like cold cellars, like decaying pines—yet I couldn't help wondering what it would be like to be with him. How would such a man—whose gangs were the terror of Petrograd—make love? He stroked my hair just once, then turned and perched against the row of seedling tables like some giant messy hawk, his white hair long as an English poet's.

"I have a job for you, Makarova. Think you can do something simple for me?"

What in the world did he need me for, with an army of criminals at his command? "How simple?" I asked.

"I want you to deliver a package for me," he said. "You'll need to be unarmed, I'm afraid. The customer is a bit *pugliviy*." *Skittish*. He held out his hand. I stared at it. "Your weapon, Makarova." How did he know? I didn't want to be disarmed by him, but like Russia, I was unable to reject his terms. I took out Anton's revolver and handed it over. "Will I get it back?"

"You're likely to blow your hand off with it," he said. "That would be most unfortunate." He put it into his own pocket. "Although you might want it to wave around in unsavory company someday. Gurin will drop you."

I was annoyed to have lost the gun and surprisingly disappointed to find myself summoned merely as a delivery girl suitable for reassuring a skittish customer. I'd thought for a moment his interest was personal. Humiliating, to have thought that a man desired you only to find he just wanted his laundry done. "What's in the package?"

"Don't think too much," he said, and put the hyacinth behind my ear.

The address was in Kolomna, at the western edge of the city, an area of dockworkers, foreigners, and drifters, where Pushkin's Bronze Horseman once chased the little clerk to his death and where the great poet Blok lived, in a gray six-story building on Ofitserskaya—

now Decembrist—Street. As a girl, I had often lingered across from that building, on the embankment of the Pryazhka, imagining that Alexander Alexandrovich would look out from his desk and, seeing a young auburn-haired girl, might stop and wonder, might write a poem about her. I wrote dozens of poems for him that I left on posts and in the knotholes of trees and around the doorway of his building, in hopes he might find them. Such a thing of the past, when girls dreamed of poets instead of meat pies.

I clambered out of the sleigh and Gurin tossed me a small package wrapped in newspaper. "Pryazhka Embankment, number fourteen," he said, then cracked the reins over the horse's furry back. The monster startled, backed up on its huge round haunches, then took off again at a thundering trot. I watched them leave with an increasingly hopeless feeling. I'd assumed that if anything went wrong, I could run back out to the sleigh or that little Gurin would come in, guns blazing. I hefted the bundle, squeezed it, wondering what it contained. A package the size of a loaf of bread, wrapped in *Petrogradskaya Pravda*, tied with string.

The front house on the Pryazhka was 16–18, and the next 8–10, so number 14 had to be in the courtyard. I steeled myself and walked through the passage into the large courtyard, where a man was defecating in the snow, his bare buttocks sad and vulnerable over the dirty hummocks. Not a reassuring sight. A sturdy wooden house painted a pale green, older than any building on the street, sat back in the yard. Perhaps it had once belonged to a sea captain or had been used as a tavern—it would be the right size, and close to the docks. This had to be number 14. It was cold this far back from the street, slushy and forgotten, the pale sunlight muted, the air smelling of the gulf and the wet wood of the wharves. All I could hear was ice cracking—like boys breaking walnuts—from the house's eaves, where the icicles reached almost to the ground.

I knocked on the old door.

A man opened it. He held a revolver trained at my heart. I would have dropped the package and run, but I couldn't move. He was sweating—he looked as nervous as I did. He nodded me inside and patted my coat pockets. The room was bare but for a small wooden table and a couple of mismatched chairs. It probably had once been a cozy room—low beamed ceilings, a broad tile stove. Home for a sea captain, yes, but now, like half the city, it was being used for other purposes. On second glance, the man—thin, balding, blue-eyed and bespectacled, with a prominent Adam's apple—wasn't so threatening, only *pugliviy*. A teacher of philology, maybe, or mathematics.

He shut the door and locked it. "Open the package," he told me, and his Adam's apple bobbed like a buoy. I tore off the wrappings. Passports. Ten of them at least. I spread them out on the table. New Soviet passports. And permissions for train passage, covered with

stamps and signatures. What a treasure. They looked
real, there in the dimness of the room, the light from
the courtyard filtering through the dirty windows.
Were they forgeries? Stolen? Had Arkady bribed
someone inside the government?

The terror slid away from the man's intellectual face.
He actually laughed, his sharp Adam's apple rising and
falling. Tucking the gun into his belt, he started opening them up. Photographs were already affixed: mostly
men, beardless, with workers' caps. A couple of
women. The documents were made out in black ink
and stamped in a rainbow of colors, with different
handwriting and printing in three languages—
Russian, French, and German. Laughter gave way to a
more solemn emotion as the man looked at one, then
another. "Forgive me," he said. "You don't know how
long we've been waiting. It was essential..." He took
a handkerchief from the pocket of his jacket under his
heavy coat and dabbed his eyes. "Thank God."

I heard a sound from upstairs, the scrape of a chair.
I missed the weight of Anton's gun in my pocket. The
ticking of a clock was loud as a hammer, but there was
no second sound. Now that I'd delivered the goods, I
was eager to be on my way. The man put the documents under his coat. Now would be the time to shoot
me. Who would ever find me here? My legs shook.
But he went to the cold stove and reached inside, into
the ashes, and brought out a sooty package about the
size of a cigar case, also wrapped in newspaper, this

showing the masthead *Znamya Truda*—the Banner of Labor, the SR paper. "Give your mysterious employer our profoundest appreciation. You're doing a tremendous service," the teacher said, vigorously shaking my hand. "You don't even know...for Mother Russia. For us all."

Who could he be? What was Arkady abetting here? People leaving the country who might still have the wherewithal to buy ten passports on the black market? Not SRs, but aristocrats who had waited too long to fly. Perhaps they had held out for the Germans, and now realized their mistake. The combination of crime and political intrigue was dangerous indeed.

I took the smaller package and put it in my pocket, and nodding once more, flew out the door. Ah, blessed sunshine! But when I peered out the Pryazhka passageway into the street, I saw a man in a leather coat smoking under one of the bare poplars, watching the building. Cheka! Or maybe not, but I wouldn't be around to discover the truth. I retreated through the archway and lost myself in the maze of slushy courtyards. There must be a second exit somewhere. I could have thrown the sooty little package into the snow——I couldn't imagine the penalty if the Cheka caught me with something like this, linked me to speculation and counter-revolution and Arkady. But I didn't dare throw it away. Arkady was the threat I believed more certain.

I found an opening onto Angliisky Prospect and walked away as quickly as I could, thinking that if

Gurin had circled around to the Pryazhka, he would have seen our friend in black leather and would know enough to look for me elsewhere. I hurried east toward Senate Square and tried not to look back, not to look around at all, just to move forward. I wasn't that girl delivering packages for the Archangel. I was a girl late to an exam, late to work at the telephone exchange, muttering under my breath, with the crabby face and irritated march of the tardy.

I made it all the way to Gorokhovaya Street, walking at that fast clip among the ghostly, dejected Petrograders and waiting for the sleigh to find me the way I used to wait for Kolya's messengers. But that was in the high expectation of love, not this dread, jumping when a man started out of a doorway, flinching when people crowded too close behind me. *Holy Theotokos, please let this end!* Finally the black horse came abreast of me, passed me, and the sleigh turned in at a courtyard. I followed them in. The enormous beast nickered and blew hot air from its nostrils, its feathery fetlocks wet to the knee.

"Couldn't you have picked me up back there?" I said, leaning on its shaggy neck. "I just crossed half the city on foot."

The little thief shrugged. "You were followed."

A different note of fear sounded inside me, dropping half an octave, deeper and more certain. That was why Arkady sent me, of course. I was more expendable than his men. More expendable to anyone except Mother and Avdokia waiting back at the flat. The little man handed me the sweat-stiffened reins and went out to stand by the arch, smoking, watching the street. The beast, so warm, smelling of that good tangy horse smell, nudged my shoulder, getting snot on my scarf. I buried my face in the fur of his neck, big as a felled tree trunk, salty and solid. I hoped nobody would eat him. He made me think of Volodya, and Carlyle, his bad-tempered pony, and Swallow, his cavalry steed. To think that Seryozha had finally learned to ride—or said he had. I stroked the velvety black nose, thinking of Volodya practicing Cossack mounts and picking up handkerchiefs from the wet grass at a gallop. What would he do now that the war was over? I tried to imagine him here, in the midst of this hunger, this poverty. Volodya with a Soviet future? Could he reconcile himself to a room in the servants' hall by the kitchen while a Red Guardsman lived in Father's study with his woman? It would be best if Volodya stayed in the Don or left the country and never returned. And what would he think of me now, this mess I'd made of my own life? At least this particular mess would be at an end as soon as I got this package back to its owner. Then I'd be done with Arkady von Princip. It was a bit too much adventure, even for an adventuress like me.

After a while, the little man got the horse and sleigh turned around. "Get in." We set off again. The fun of the ride out to the greenhouses on the Vyborg side was a distant memory. Now I felt more like a prisoner on

the way to the gallows. We sped along, not up toward
the river but along Nevsky to Znamenskaya Square,
turning in at the train station. Oh God, was I leaving?

46 *The Station*

CABS AND HANDCARTS, HORSES and automobiles jostled
at the entrance to the Nikolaevsky station. Gurin urged
the shying, snorting horse forward into the fray.
Wasn't Arkady afraid the horse would be noticed, recognized? It was flashy—people gave us fast looks as
they hurried into the arrivals hall. But either he didn't
care or he enjoyed letting people understand his reach,
his power. That he was not afraid. The driver turned
around in the coachman's seat. "Take the package and
go for a walk. In the main hall. Not too fast."

"Who am I meeting?" I asked, watching passersby,
aware that any of these people could be Cheka.

"Just take a walk. A nice little stroll." His mouth
hardly moved. Perhaps he'd been a ventriloquist in another life.

"Can't I just leave it with you?" I couldn't afford
to be arrested. This wasn't my business—speculation,
passports, buying and selling. I took the package and
held it out to him.

"Don't get ideas," he recommended.

I crammed the bloody thing back in my pocket and
straggled into the station.

If it had been crowded the week of my adventure as a girl porter, the station had since become a giant squatters' camp as people waited for trains—any trains, going anywhere, especially south to the Ukraine, where there was food. Tattered but elegant people shepherded leather trunks. Workers sat on broken cases tied with ropes. Peasants lugged their bundles while veterans and pickpockets and vagrants loitered—one great simmering stew of humanity under the vaulted ceilings and electroliers. The metallic scent of panic, soot, and trains stained the air.

My eye caught opportunities for work—people with children struggling with bags. A man accompanying a heavily made-up woman carted all their luggage while the woman carried a single hatbox and a little dog under her arm. That gave me a moment's laugh. I picked my way through the anxious crowd in the grand concourse, watching for—what? I had to stop myself from continually checking the little package in my pocket. The corners were starting to fray.

On a bench, a man reading *Krasnaya Gazeta* glanced up. Was he watching me? Or against that pillar, that soldier? Which would be my contact? Or were those men watchers from the other side, searching out speculation and counterrevolution? I wished my mother hadn't made that pronouncement about evil entities. I didn't believe in entities, but it was hard to brush her words off with a laugh right then.

Then a figure halfway across the hall caught my eye,

a head taller than anybody else. The patched greatcoat, the wide shoulders, the cap. I began to run, pushing past the gangs of hopeful travelers. He was heading for the platforms. "Genya!" I called, though how could he hear me over this din? I shoved and squeezed, pressing my hands together before me like an icebreaker. "Genya!"

He turned, searching the crowd. He couldn't have heard me, but something in him did hear, and he turned and saw me. Emotion passed over his face like clouds racing across the sun—shock, joy, hurt, longing. I struggled like a salmon to reach him, climbing over people's boxes and forcing my way through until I could touch him, cling to that smoky, wonderful coat, and he held me tight tight tight. I hadn't known how much I still loved him, how I'd missed him, the sheer relief of having his body back in my arms. "Genya, I've been crazy. I'm doing the maddest things."

He was wearing the scarf I'd knitted for him, gray and red. The taste of his mouth, the sweetness of his kiss, the smell of him. How had I let my infatuation with Kolya destroy us? How had we let that little religious trinket split us apart? "You've always been crazy," he whispered, kissing my eyes. "But I'm such a moron. I don't even remember what happened, do you?"

Zina emerged from the crowd, all dressed for traveling in her tam, holding her gloves officiously. I saw on her face her dismay at finding me resurrected. "Genya, we need to get on that train." Someone jostled her and she elbowed and cursed. Now I understood the first look on his face, that guilty surprise. They were leaving Petrograd. Together. He pulled away from me, abashed and ill equipped to deal with this two-woman problem.

"I'll meet you on the platform," he told her. "Go on ahead."

Zina's face condensed with irritation. It shrank like wool in water. "We have to grab seats when they open the doors or we'll be riding in the corridor all the way to Moscow."

"In a minute," he said firmly.

Clearly there was more she wanted to say, but the tone of his voice put an end to the argument, and she walked off reluctantly, looking back over her shoulder every few steps before the crowd swallowed her angry little face.

Moscow. I laughed. A sob really. He couldn't go to Moscow. People died in Moscow. They became someone else. I stroked his face, handsome and forlorn, the wide mouth, the crooked nose, the bony brow over those dear eyes. "You don't belong there. Don't go. I have no right to ask, but please stay. Let's try again."

His expression begged me to understand. He was being pulled in all directions. "Petrograd's done for—you can see it as well as I can."

"No." I burrowed into his coat. I wouldn't see.

"She's got friends down there, a film company. They

want us to write a *kinofilm*. We've got tickets, permits."
He pressed his cheek to my head, pulled my shawl
down, ran his fingers through my hair. "I've thought of
you so much. I do nothing but write and think of you.
I'm going mad."

"I should never have left that night. I should have
fought you, claw and knucklebone." I held on to him,
speaking fast and low. "It's horrible without you. You
can't imagine how I've missed you."

"Come to Moscow," he said. "The poetry cafés are
filled to bursting. Everything's alive down there. Petrograd's had it."

"And live with you and Zina?" I laughed but it was
more of a cry, a choke of despair.

His face closed up, like one of those trees whose
leaves shrink at the slightest touch. "Look, I have to
go."

"Genya, I love you," I said, still clutching his coat.

He grasped my gloved hand, tore off the glove and
kissed my palm. I could feel the tears on his face, his
scratchy beard. But then he gave it back to me, my
hand, my useless hand, and he was pushing through
the crowd toward the platforms. I couldn't breathe. I
needed air. I staggered back through the hall toward
the doors of the station and stood in the cold colonnade, sobbing like a child.

It was several minutes before I remembered Arkady
von Princip. I wiped my eyes with my handkerchief and
braced myself to go back in and finish the job, checking

the package in my pocket. My fingers touched nothing but cloth.

Impossible.

I checked the other pocket. I had put it in deep, hadn't I? I checked myself all over. My mind flew to the possibilities. *Don't think.* Pickpockets worked these halls like peasants picking cherries. *Don't.* I could not imagine the value of ten passports, visas, and railway permits. In these times? A million rubles? People died for a loaf of bread now. A hat, a pair of boots. Maybe I dropped it when I saw Genya, when I ran.

I shoved my way back into the hall. *Oh God, Theotokos preserve us.* It hadn't been that long. Who would notice a little package wrapped in newspaper? Who would stop in their hurrying to trains and pushing through the crowd to study the floor?

Anyone.

For an hour I searched, my tears blurring the view of the dirty floor littered with sunflower-seed hulls and cigarette butts, hairpins and sputum, a glove, a page fallen from a book, a baby's shoe, scraps of paper, but no package wrapped in *Znamya Truda*. I scanned the crowd, looking for suspicious people, people too interested in others, especially those without baggage, and—yes, a girl in a black coat, my own age. I saw her reaching into a man's coat. "Hey, you!" She looked up, startled, and the man clapped his hand over his pocket. She hurried away into the crowd. "Wait! Stop that girl!" I fought my way through the throng, following her hat, her pigtails, but I couldn't catch her. It was like a terrible dream where you run through mud or a flood. That figure, always moving away, always vanishing.

Light lingered on broad, quiet Furshtatskaya Street and the slushy melting snow as I returned to the flat. What was I going to do? I should go up to Kamenny Island and tell him, *I lost the package. Why did you ever send me? You who know so much, you should have known better.* But what was the point of trudging up all that way to deliver bad news? He would find me eventually. He would find me and kill me. I hated to go home, but what choice did I have? I vowed I would never leave the apartment ever again.

Everything looked worse—the dirty courtyard, the warming staircase that now stank of rotting fish and mold, the women in the kitchen drinking tea from Mother's Limoges coffee service at the table on which Vaula had once rolled out her huge sheets of pastry dough. They stared at me as if I had a goat balanced on my head. I was used to having to walk the gauntlet of barbed remarks, especially once we began cooking meat. But blessedly, nobody said a thing. Not even the hard-faced blonde spoke, or the tall gaunt one, nursing her baby at a flat pap. Even the Red Guardsman's woman, chopping a carrot, said nothing.

A strange smell permeated the hall as I walked back toward Mother's room, a floral scent unlikely but familiar. One of Mother's spiritualist friends? I knocked wearily on the door. Avdokia opened up quickly, glanced down the hall, and waved me in with great urgency. "Thank God," she said. *Slava Bogu.*

The wall of scent hit me. Mother stood near the table by the window, her hand over her mouth. She looked as if she'd seen her own death. A great heap of blue hyacinths buried the tabletop, their scent replacing all the air in the room. Hyacinths, each petal sighing its secret Greek sigh—*alas.*

47 *Kommunist*

THE SPRING RAINS BEGAN. I jumped at the slightest sound. A week went by, and still I didn't know how things stood with the Archangel. The flowers breathed their terrible message. *I know where you live,* they said. And, *You're alive only by my pleasure.* "Don't ask me anything," I said when Mother questioned me. I developed a throb in my temple, a flutter in my eyelid. My knitting-factory cough returned. We got rid of the sheaves of blooms, but there was no way to get rid of the scent. I smelled it in my hair, on my clothes, as if it were searching me out. Oh, how I would have loved to ask Kolya what he was thinking when told me to go to Kamenny Island and find that man. I felt like he'd slammed my fingers in a door. If he ever came back, I would ask him: *This is how you take care of a girl you love?*

I wrote a poem about the dreariness of spring, that which had been buried brought to light again. I wrote about lovers in a train station. I wrote about Ariadne, abandoned on Naxos by her lover Theseus. I wrote about a photo album with silver hasps sold on the streets of Petrograd. And I wrote about the tragedy of Hyacinth, the plaything of the gods.

I kept thinking of Arkady's fingers, so quick, so deft, touching the hyacinth petals, taking the diamond from my hand without my knowing it. If only I hadn't lost his merchandise...I was sure there had been something, some interest. I would have enjoyed getting to know a man like that, but now...there was only dread.

Every day I peered out to see if anyone was watching the house, and every day I saw someone who might or might not be one of Arkady's people. A woman walking a dog outside in the parkway kept glancing at our building. A man, his hat dripping with rain, stood in the lee of a still-leafless tree, smoking. But ultimately I saw no one who set my nerves on edge, and I simply had to get away from the apartment or go insane. I quickly left the courtyard passage and walked away under the umbrella I had borrowed from Mother. Oh, it had been so long! The air smelled like spring, like softened snow, and dirty puddles, and water dripping from the icicles.

As I walked out toward the Fontanka, I peered at passersby and listened for footsteps behind me, but all I saw were slow, hunched, miserable citizens, their faces turned to their damp, brooding thoughts. That's when

I noticed a figure crossing Liteiny. What was it that caught my eye? The gait, the pace. At a time when everyone had slowed to a wheezy shuffle, the brisk movement stood out—someone with somewhere to go. A tall girl in a black coat, moving like a hare through a forest, her umbrella rising to avoid those of other people. "Varvara!" I ran into the street, the hem of my wet coat slapping against my legs. A tram screeched as I raced in front of it. "Varvara!"

She turned. Her expression was grim, and her face looked puffy and swollen. She had a cut under one eye. But when she saw it was me, she broke into a grin. I embraced her with my free hand. We kissed cheeks three times. "Thank God, someone who doesn't want to beat my head in."

"Assuming a lot, aren't you?" I laughed.

She kept her arm around my shoulder and we resumed walking under overlapping umbrellas out to the Fontanka Embankment, then down, past the shabby facade of the Sheremetev Palace, where they said Akhmatova lived now.

"What happened to your face?"

"Strike at the Rechkin coach plant," she said, twisting her mouth into a bitter knot. "They have a country now, and all they do is scream about rations and galoshes." As if rations and galoshes were nothing. "They have to remember why we're doing this, what it's all for."

Still fighting for the revolution. "How'd it go?"

"Rough."

She'd gone in to face a factory full of striking workers to present the Bolshevik side. She was absolutely sure this was all going to be worth it—her certainty was bound to have inspired people. It was a kind of courage you had to admire. She had one goal, the establishment of the workers' state, and she would fight the workers themselves to give it to them. "Does it hurt?"

Varvara brushed the words away with an impatient swipe of the hand. "Think that's bad? Have you seen this?" She stopped and removed a newspaper from her pocket and unfolded it under cover of our umbrellas. *Kommunist,* it was called. A manifesto of some kind. The dense print was already smudged.

THE REVOLUTION IS AT A CROSSROADS... "What is it?"

She folded it and put it back in her pocket. "The Left Communists have resigned from the party. Bukharin, Kollontai, Radek, and Uritsky."

The fiery speakers of October. I recognized the name Uritsky, Varvara's boss.

The party was coming apart. Now what? They'd won the revolution, but the Titans were fighting in the heavens. I had been so busy thinking about my Arkady problem that I'd forgotten the wheel of revolution continued to spin, that the fate of Russia was still unfolding. "Resigned from the party? But why?"

"What else can they do? They can't agree to these peace terms—they end the revolution! German extortions, threats of Japanese occupation in the Far East, annexations... we're forbidden to propagandize in the West, forbidden to work against the Germans, right when we were on the brink of World Revolution. Lenin thinks it's buying us time, but it's not. It's selling out the world proletariat to save our skins! 'Saved the territory but killed the revolution,' as Bukharin put it." She still hoped that revolution would catch fire in the West and save us at any moment.

Reflexively, I glanced around to see if anyone was following us. A workingman smoking, cigarette in his cupped hand, looked out at the buildings across the Fontanka. A pair of men passed by, heads close together under umbrellas. I wanted to tell her about Arkady, but I wasn't sure how sympathetic she'd be. What was a gang of criminals compared with the fate of Russia?

"So who's behind *Kommunist*?" I said, lowering my umbrella to hide my face.

"The Petrograd Committee," she said. Then she, too, glanced around, as if she'd caught my suspicion. "Bukharin, Radek, and Uritsky. We needed a voice apart from Lenin. He used to be a revolutionary, but now he's just plugging the dikes like the little Dutch boy. Just another politician."

We. So she'd placed her bets on the schismatics, the true believers.

Out on the Fontanka, the ice was breaking, like a puzzle once solved, now coming apart.

I didn't like the way that worker was loitering. Who

would be standing in the rain without an umbrella just watching the ice floes drift? I had that strange prickling sensation. "Is there anywhere we can get off the street?"

She cut her eyes to the man, having seen him as well. *"Da, koneshno." Yes, of course.* "I've got a new place. It's not far."

The rain intensified, blowing first from the east, then from the west across the thawing Fontanka. She grabbed my arm and we began to run, splashing through the puddles, laughing, feeling like girls again as our umbrellas tugged against the wind and our skirts grew heavy with water. We crossed Nevsky where the bronze horses of the Anichkov Bridge fought their eternal tamers.

Her new place was just as she said, not far—on the Fontanka below Nevsky, a flat in a building designed in the heavy Russian style of the 1880s. We stopped to wring out our skirts, then ran up three cold flights to a subdivided flat whose inner hall was lined with numbered doors. I followed her into number 3/8, a room of two windows overlooking the river, with old flowered wallpaper in stripes, a bed in an alcove, papers everywhere, books, a typewriter. "My villa by the sea," she said, opening and closing her umbrella to shake off the water, then propping it by the door. I did the same.

I took a seat on a splintery chair, undid my wet scarf and fluffed my hair. The place stank of cold tobacco, mold, and soot from a leaky stove. She tossed *Kom-*

munist on the table, cleared off some of the papers and the typewriter, and went to start the little stove. I took off my gloves and rubbed my hands together, blew into them, opened her paper and read aloud from *Kommunist* about the "vertiginous decline of the Petersburg region," dangerous unemployment, the disruption of production, and the "declassing of the proletariat." "Peace has saved the territory, but the spirit of the Red capital has been sold away."

"Petrograd's a disaster." Varvara squatted and placed kindling in the stove from her modest woodpile. "You've got the seasoned Bolsheviks out in the villages trying to recruit illiterate bumpkins, leaving our factories full of whiners and snivelers, the most nonmilitant elements." *The declassing of the proletariat.* "So who jumps into the breach? Of course—petit bourgeois SRs. And anarchists, always happy to make a muddle of things." She blew on the fire, sending smoke and bits of ash into the room. "Sometimes I'd just like to shoot everyone. It's like driving a stupid ox that would rather freeze in the snow." Her eye drooped where she'd been hit.

It was probably a bad time to ask about Arkady.

"You're pacing like a nervous cat. What's going on?"

She could always see through me. I shrugged. She was being beaten up by striking workers for arguing on behalf of World Revolution while I was dabbling in petty crime, speculation, and possible counterrevolutionary activities. How could I begin to tell her about my problems involving Kolya, illegal flour and oil and meat, passports, and rendezvous up in the islands with Arkady von Princip? "It's un-Soviet..."

"Then don't tell me about it," she said. "There's nothing I can do anyway. My guy is on the outs, and I've got as much on my hands as I can possibly handle. Did Vera Borisovna survive the offensive all right?"

"Yes, but Genya came back and we broke up. I'm back on Furshtatskaya now."

At last she got the fire lit, stood and brushed her hands off. "You never learn." The fire was going but the stove leaked, made my eyes smart. She opened the *fortochka,* peered down. "Does it have something to do with the man by the embankment, with the cap?"

"Is he still there?" I shrank away from her.

"He followed us all the way down," she said.

Surely she would have some ideas if I could figure out how to couch it so it wouldn't look so bad. I wondered what her position was now that her boss had resigned. "Are you even at Smolny anymore?"

She shrugged, set out glasses for tea, lit the primus, set a pan of water to boil, then peeled an old carrot into the teapot. No actual tea anymore—you either got roasted barley or carrot peel. But any food preparation was uncharacteristically domestic for her. She seemed...hesitant. As if there was something more she wanted—but also didn't want— to tell me. That made two of us.

"Look again."

She took a peek out the window. "He's gone. Now

there's a woman, walking a little dog. It's not us, I don't think."

We eyed one another, sizing each other up like wrestlers. I realized that between my dubious commercial and romantic entanglements and her political engagement, we probably could never again be as completely open with each other as we'd once been. Our girlhood friendship had been transformed into a new thing, a sort of hungry, wary circling, a friendship not between girls but between women. Each would hold back a piece of herself that could not be shared.

As Varvara was in the middle of pouring boiling water into the teapot, we heard a key turn in the lock. She stopped, listening, and a slim woman entered. Shorter than either of us, she shook her umbrella and stuck it in the stand in the corner. Her little glasses were steamed from the rain. "Hello," she said, and smiled.

All the color had drained out of Varvara's face. "I didn't expect you back."

"We've been meeting all night," the woman said. "I'm about to drop." She regarded me with unabashed curiosity.

"Manya, this is Marina. I told you about her. We ran into each other on Liteiny." Now my friend noticed she was still holding the pan and poured the rest of the water into the teapot.

"Oh, yes! Marina the poet. Good to meet you." The woman offered her hand, and I shook it. Small, firm, still icy cold from the street.

"Good to meet you, too," I said. A roommate? A lover? The double bed. Varvara wouldn't look at me.

"I was just making tea. Want some?" she asked Manya. Pretending casualness, but I could see her nerves in her twitchy gestures.

Although Manya was the smaller of the two, she seemed the more self-possessed. She took off her hat and hung it on a hook, touched her dark, wavy coif, threaded with gray. "I think I'm just going to—" Then she noticed Varvara's beaten face. "What happened?"

"Rechkin," Varvara said, embarrassed at her attention. "It was a mess."

"You've got to take care of that. Oh, you're going to have a shiner in the morning. Sit down." The older woman moved about the flat efficiently, brisk and precise as a field nurse, getting iodine, wringing out a cloth in the washstand. She cleaned the cut on Varvara's face, then pressed the cloth to her eye and cheekbone and had her hold it there.

"She pretends to be so tough," Manya said. "Well, you're going to look like a brawler now." But she left her hand on Varvara's shoulder.

Not a roommate. Not a comrade. This woman with the white threads in her black hair was—Varvara's lover.

My friend watched me as she pressed the white cloth to her swollen face. She loved to shock people, but only when she'd done it on purpose. I didn't know who was more shocked now. Any response would seem hope-

lessly stupid, ridiculously backward. Other people had
their locked rooms, their secret corridors, and Varvara
had planned to keep this one to herself. The flash of her
black eyes, of being so revealed, dared me to judge her.

Now Manya bustled about pleasantly, finishing the
tea, setting our glasses in front of us, taking one for
herself and moving to the bed, where she set the glass
down and took her shoes off. "I wish I could join you.
There's so much I'd like to hear, but I can't keep my
eyes open." She took off her wet dress and hung it on
a peg. Her slip clung to her body. She had a nice figure for an older woman. How old was she? Thirty?
Younger than Mother, certainly. I wondered how two
women made love. But passion makes use of all
equipment——I knew that better than anyone.

We drank the carrot peel tea, which tasted primarily
of dirt. Varvara's eyes searched mine—for judgment?
Signs of disapproval? She looked so comical with that
cloth pressed to her face. I would not have thought
to take care of her as Manya had done. To me she
always seemed indestructible. I thought back on our
friendship—her kisses, her possessiveness. Her loyalty
and disloyalty. Unexpected emotions tumbled over me:
hurt, abandonment, jealousy. Jealousy? Really? Was I
was jealous of Manya, this woman who had taken possession of my friend? I'd come to expect the intensity of
Varvara's feelings. Now someone else would be the recipient of her enthusiasms and her rages, her crises and
triumphs.

I wondered if this was how she felt when I fell in love with Kolya. I heard Mina's voice in my head. *Do you have to have everything?* Did I? I wasn't sure. I felt her rocketing away from me as we sat there on either side of the small wobbly table.

Varvara and I spoke of this and that, but like actors in a new play, we were unable to settle into a rhythm. Cloth still pressed to her face, she talked about Manya's party work and how they'd met at the Smolny canteen. The travails of the Left Communists, the pressure the trade unions were putting on the party. Neither of us able to say what was really on our minds. After a polite interval, I said I had to leave and got back into my coat.

She walked me to the flat's outer door, took my hand. Hers was trembling, but she still couldn't say what she wanted to say.

"I know," I said.

She hugged me hard, kissed me three times, as if we were saying our last goodbyes. "There's an exit on Rubinshteyna. Be careful," she said. And I returned to the street, the rain.

48 *Never Say No*

AVDOKIA STOOD ROASTING OATS in a little iron pan while Mother sat deep in study of some occult tome. She pressed her slender fingertips to her lips in concentration, her fur-lined coat draped about her shoulders. I felt sad she'd returned to her Blavatsky and Ouspensky after she'd had such success helping Anton with Apollinaire. I supposed I'd imagined she might take up translation on her own, but instead she'd returned to unfurl her mania at full length, an iridescent banner of otherworldly faith.

"How were the Gromitskys?" I asked. She'd visited her friends today, also followers of Master Vsevolod.

"Packing," Mother said, turning the page. "They're going to China. Master has friends there."

Maybe she could go with them. I wondered about getting railway permissions. Maybe I should go, too. I didn't know how much longer I could bear this, listening for footsteps, bracing for a bullet. I drew up a chair before the *bourgeoika*, held my hands out to warm them. At least we had wood now, so I could take my wet coat off.

Rain pelted the windows, then subsided. I leafed through the new verses I'd written since leaving Grivtsova Alley. Ours was a time for short poems that could be finished in a single sitting before the political situation changed again. I imagined it would be years before a new great novel would come out of Russia. Life changed too quickly. I liked one about digging fortifications:

We handled our spades like rifles,
      our rifles like spades.
It was impossible to say

what we were digging—
        trenches
        foundations
                or acres of graves.
We ourselves didn't know.
        The times said dig, and we dug.

Perhaps with Genya and Zina gone, I could safely return to the Transrational Interlocutors. How I missed them, those lively Wednesday nights at the Krestovskys' in the company of the poets and painters. I had to do something. This waiting was driving me mad. Although I wasn't looking forward to admitting to Anton that I'd lost his revolver, perhaps he could use Mother's help. That would distract her from this obsessive research into the kabbalah and the Golden Dawn and give me somewhere to go besides this room.

Promptly at nine, the electric lights went out, and Avdokia lit the lamps. At ten, Mother uncoiled her silver coif before the dressing table, appraising herself in the mirror as Avdokia brushed her hair smooth. At ten after by the old travel clock on the dresser, there was a knock on the door—light, rattling, intimate—but it was far too late to be anyone we knew.

"Don't answer," Avdokia whispered. "For the love of God." She blew out the lamp nearest her, and Mother blew out the other one on the table.

"Makarova." Spoken with a teasing menace. A man's

voice with its dry rasp. We waited in the dark, afraid to move, afraid to breathe. The Antichrist had come himself, right into the heart of the city, where every Cheka officer in town was looking for him. Though if Varvara was right, there weren't many Chekists left—they'd all gone to Moscow. "Don't hide under the covers," the voice came again. "You insult my intelligence."

I lit the lamp. It was ridiculous to try to hide from him. I had set this in motion. It was up to me to finish it. Avdokia grabbed my sleeve as I went to unlock the door, shaking her head, begging me with her eyes, but I pried her loose.

The Archangel looked as unkempt as he had the last times I'd seen him, shabby in an ancient overcoat and crushed broad-brimmed hat, like a horse trader's, even as the wealth of starving Petrograd flowed into his hands. He glanced about, seemingly casually, but I knew he could read our lives in every chair and table—the mismatched beds, the superior quality of the armoire, the dresser missing one drawer, the chandelier, the smell of our dinner. "Good evening, ladies."

Avdokia crossed herself, her mouth silently moving in prayer. For once, her spells of protection weren't being invoked in vain. Mother rose from the dressing table, long hair to her waist shining silver like a priestess's. She gripped the back of the chair for support but nonetheless stood firm and straight. "Who are you, monsieur? What are you thinking, barging in on respectable people in the middle of the night?"

"Get your coat, Makarova," he said to me.

"Pardon, monsieur." Her voice trembled. "My daughter is most assuredly not going anywhere with you. What can you mean by this?"

"I'm taking your daughter, madame. You have nothing else I want or I'd take that too."

I was already putting my boots on, trying to appear calm and confident. "I'll be all right. I have a little unfinished business with this gentleman." I reassured myself with a glance toward Arkady, praying that what I said was true. He didn't seem angry, but I didn't know what his anger might look like. Avdokia was crossing herself furiously as I got my coat. It took forever to button it, my fingers were so stiff with fear. In a kind of terrified daze, I wrapped my shawl around my head, took an umbrella from the stand. He opened the door. Avdokia was weeping. I kissed her three times, told her not to worry, nodded at Mother, who nodded back. A whole lifetime in that nod. I had to remember all of it. It could be the last time I ever saw them.

Then Arkady and I walked down the hall.

I knew how a man must feel walking to his execution, although this was more confusing, because I didn't know if it was an execution or not. We came out onto dripping Furshtatskaya Street. I opened my umbrella, and we began to walk together, his hands in his pockets, rain spilling off the brim of his hat. He made no attempt to touch me or to hold on to me in any way. An odd semblance of a couple we must have made, ambling toward the Tauride Palace—the very route Father took to work in bygone days.

"Can I ask where you're taking me?"

"To dinner, of course."

That was a turn I'd never expected. I was intrigued, but I didn't want to give him the satisfaction. "What if I've eaten?"

He stopped. I couldn't see his face under the broad brim of his hat. "Never say no to me."

It was more than an order. It was an edict. A commandment. I gave no assent, but it seemed that a pronouncement from him required no agreement. We began walking again. We skirted the Tauride Gardens, fragrant in the wet darkness, the fresh earth and the rain. Where could he be taking me? His legs were very long, and he swung along soundlessly, gracefully, as if just out for a stroll, a man walking with a woman. He didn't touch me, although I felt he wanted to. Was this some twisted courtship? "Did you like my flowers?" he asked.

I searched for an adequate response. *I couldn't be in the flat with them. We put them in the hall, all the tenants had a little bouquet. I will never be able to smell a hyacinth again without terror.* I decided on the most neutral reply. "They were lovely."

He took my arm in his, and there it was again, to my shame, my strange attraction to him. The way his arm pressed my breast under my layers of clothing excited me.

On the other side of the Tauride Gardens, he led me down the steps to the ground floor of a six-story building, once extremely elegant, now a bit battered, and knocked on a door. A woman opened it partway, saw who it was, and for just a moment, shock and fear were plainly written on her face. Then she slapped a smile over it like a poster slapped onto a wall.

It was a restaurant, a private dining room, such as I'd heard rumors about but never actually seen. I thought they were a myth, the fantasy of a hungry populace. Seven tables occupied a small room, four of them in use by groups of men voluble with drink. The smell was dizzying. The woman took our coats and my dripping umbrella and led us to a table by the fire, replete with a tablecloth and napkins, glasses, cutlery. She offered menus, but Arkady waved them away. "You know what to bring," he told her.

He did not pull out my chair, so I sat down, smoothed the napkin across my lap. I couldn't imagine what the prices in a place like this might be. Thousands. Tens of thousands. Who could afford it? Well, from the look of the other patrons, the restaurant catered to criminals, foreigners, and the last *haut bourgeois* left in Petrograd.

Dishes began to arrive. Mushrooms in sour cream. *Solyanka,* a meat-rich fragrant soup. Blini and salad, smoked fish and vodka. Arkady ate little, just sat watching me. I tried to eat with indifference, though the florid rumbling of my stomach betrayed me. I drank more than I should have. I was letting myself become careless, noticing my own pretty gestures, my arm falling from the sleeve, the gleaming bangle adorning it. I felt like a performer, like an actress in the smallest theater of all, with an audience of one.

"That bracelet—is that from our old friend Shurov?" He leaned forward and clasped it in his supple hand, turned it to catch the light.

I forced myself not to protect it from his view, to act as if it were nothing. He would catch any slight movement. "It's from Bukhara."

"Give it to me."

I slid the bracelet from my wrist.

He turned it between his fingers, its inlay glowing in the soft light. I wanted to snatch it out of his hands. What right did he have to touch that bangle? "He has an eye, doesn't he?" He weighed it in his palm and put it in his jacket pocket. "What do you want most in the world, Makarova? If you could have anything. Anything at all."

The world, unshattered. Love. Books of my poems, read and reread. My brother, alive.

None of which Baron Arkady von Princip could offer. "The success of the revolution," I said.

He laughed out loud. He removed something from his pocket and slid it under his hand across the table. "Put your hand over mine."

A shock of electricity to touch his bare skin.

He put his other hand over mine, as in a child's game, pulled his lower hand away, and I felt what was underneath, a wallet, about the size of a cigarette case. He released my hand, and I lifted it.

On the crumbly dark red calfskin gleamed the Romanov double eagle embossed in gold.

"Open it," he said. "Discreetly."

I pulled it onto my lap, opened the clasp. And there, lying against the white satin of the wallet's lining, appeared a brooch the size of my palm. Four Romanov eagles in gold, perfect down to their beaks, talons, and the crowns between their double heads, each surmounted by a cross, interspersed by four rubies shaped like arch stones. The eagles were set in diamonds—their bodies, their individual wing feathers, the graduated stones around the rubies. And in the center, St. George on his horse trampled the dragon.

"It's the Order of Saint George. Catherine the Great gave it to her lady-in-waiting, Countess Alexandra Branitskaya. What do you think? Worth a couple of hours' trouble, wouldn't you say?" He lifted one pale eyebrow, gave the hint of a smile.

This is what was in my package at the train station, wrapped in *Znamya Truda*. This was the price of sanctuary for some high royal family. The wealth of Russia, falling directly into the hands of Arkady von Princip, bypassing its true owners, the Russian people. Crime would find a way—to serve itself.

But what a weight off my shoulders! It had not been stolen after all, it had been duly delivered. I started to cry. My sentence had been commuted. A last-minute stay. Now I could eat the rest of this beautiful dinner in peace.

I watched his face through my tears. All these weeks he had tormented me, left me in the dark. I gazed back into his long, bony face, the sunken cheeks, the wide mouth, the Swedish nose, and saw the pleasure there.

"I thought you understood when you saw the flowers."

I held out my hand with the wallet under it. He put his hand over it but didn't pull the wallet away, not immediately. This strange, strange being. His eyes searched me. Would I? Would I stay with him tonight? Yes, I thought. I just might.

It was a good house. There was still power, even after midnight, and the elevator worked. On the fourth floor, a man guarded a door—the bearded man from Kamenny Island with the bushy black eyebrows over his mistrustful eyes. Arkady said something and the man opened the door. I went in first. No one forced me. There was no knife, no gun.

The flat lay empty. Some broken-up furniture, an armoire facedown, a pile of garbage. He led me down the *enfilade* to a narrow room, beautifully furnished, where a tall stove on the short back wall pumped out a fair amount of heat. Wood was stacked next to it, enough to heat a *bourgeoika* for a month. The study, it must have been, of a home belonging to some Former family recently decamped. The gold-and-blue *style moderne* wallpaper showed them to have been a chic family, a touch artistic. Maybe we had known them. A daybed covered in a dark gold velvet sagged against one wall, with a wide-seated Louis XV chair drawn up alongside it.

Arkady closed the door, locked it. I didn't like the locked door, but there was no turning back now. He slumped into the Louis chair with his usual careless slouch. I was coming to recognize it by now. Keeping his blue eyes on me, casual as unfolding a napkin, he unbuttoned his fly and pulled himself out. His member was enormous, lying there against his thigh.

I didn't know whether to sit, where to look, whether to laugh or beat on the door. "Touch it," he said, in his rough, gravelly whisper. "Go on. You've been thinking about it all night."

Had I? Well, yes. I'd been thinking about him, imagining how it might be to be with such a man, to let him touch me, make love to me, but nothing so—bluntly to the point. Well, I was beginning to get the idea. It would be like this—outrageous, unpredictable, a game of nerves. First the terror, then an exquisite dinner... then, *Here's my cock.*

And it was certainly impressive—he was obviously proud of it. Even as I watched, it grew, rising like a baby's arm, or a devil's tail, from the worn trousers. How he savored my embarrassment. Well, what had I thought this would be about? Roses and aubades? "Come shake hands," he said. "Make friends with my little man."

Daring me. I reached out, but just as I brought my fingertips onto that monster, he made it jump, startling me and making me cry out. He laughed and clapped his hand over mine and began to stroke himself. "Oh, you have to be firmer with him. He's a real Cossack. You're not painting a pole, you know."

I gripped it like a pipe, like a wrench or a hammer, something you'd drive nails with, or split logs. "Yes, that's right, there. Oh, good," he groaned. "You like how big he is? Tell me, have you ever seen one this size? Your boyfriend Kolya doesn't even count. He has nothing—he's practically a woman. This is what a man looks like." He squeezed my hand around him, up and down. "Spit on it, please."

I spit on it, making our hands slide more easily. He moaned. "Yes. You're still a virgin as far as I'm concerned, Makarova. We'll make you forget all about him. I'll make you forget about all of them."

It was true that for size, Kolya was a child by comparison, but Kolya knew how to make love to a woman. So full of delight, and he knew how to bring that to you. He made love as if he were touching the world itself, the world made flesh in your body. Every word, every touch, every joke and caress. Arkady was just stimulating himself. Even in sex, he was lonely and controlling.

"Take that off," he said, nodding at my dress, letting my hand go. "All of it. I want to see you. I want to see what color your muff is, if your nipples are dark or light."

I was afraid but excited, too, to see where this would all go. I unbuttoned my dress, removed it slowly, while he ran his hand up and down that tumescent organ. My slip, dingy white, my boots. Perhaps I was the slut my father said I was, but I had to admit, this game aroused me. His voice was hypnotic, it went on and on. "Do you bruise easily, Makarova? I'm not the gentlest man. No—not the stockings. Leave them on."

Was he trying to scare me? Or was that part of the game? I didn't know that men his age even wanted to have sex anymore, that they had cocks like that, that I might be as nervous as a virgin—or in my case, even more so. I knew a sensible girl would leave now, would have fled after dinner. But I was not a sensible girl. I was every bit the adventurer he had seen in me that first day. So I did what he asked, and stood before him in my white freckled skin. No wonder he'd heated the room so thoroughly. I let him admire me. I knew I was beautiful. What would he think of me now? Would he really want to bruise this?

"Pale. I was thinking they were dark, because of the hair, but they're very pale, aren't they?" he said as he worked on himself. "You're not as small as you look. The fullness is mostly on the sides, under the arm." I saw he had to keep talking, that it was the talking that excited him. And it was arousing in a peculiar, unwholesome way. "I knew a girl like that when I was a boy, back in Estonia, a servant on our estate. Very pale skin, but her nipples were larger than yours. And dark. She had done something, I don't remember what. Stolen something, probably. They dragged her into the yard and stripped her to the waist and beat her. Three lashes. I'll always remember the sight of those welts rising on that white skin. Her breasts, swaying. It was my first erotic encounter." His voice was dark, the exciting memory lowering it to a whisper. "And your crimson hair. A shame you cut it. It should fall down your breasts—it would look like dried blood. Think you could take three lashes, Makarova?"

Did he have a whip hidden somewhere in the room? I forced myself to keep my eyes on his, not to glance about nervously. Was it just talk? If I screamed, people would hear me in the other apartments. Someone would break in. Or would they? I had heard women scream on Grivtsova Alley, had watched Genya pound on a door, threaten to kick it in. But he was a long way away.

"Come over here. Closer."

I imagined the young baron watching the girl being beaten, jerking at himself. Though it could be a story he'd made up for my benefit. My heart beat raggedly in my chest. No one knew where I was. I was entirely on my own. Was he going to hurt me like that, beat me or cut me? Or was all this just something to scare me with? I couldn't show him I was afraid. I felt the moment like a knife edge in my teeth. *Steady…*

I came over to his chair. He leaned into me and sniffed me like an animal, my belly, my plume of red hair. It was repulsive and exciting. I was appalled at how dirty I was—how much there was to smell. It had been so long since I'd taken a real lie-down bath. He ran his finger between my legs, and I trembled, repulsed and excited in equal measure. "Now open up for me." He sprawled back on the chair, like a man in the theater. "I want to see you. Put your foot up here." He patted the far arm of the chair.

I wanted him to see me. I was ashamed how aroused I was. Yet I didn't have to confess this to anyone. If I made love with him, who would know? My love life was no one's business—not Kolya's, Genya's, or anyone's. I wanted to play this out, hoping he was just exciting himself with his talk of lashes and blood. Very possibly he was making it up—I wouldn't put it past him. I lifted my foot up on the arm of the chair and spread myself so he could see me, the silky insides, the peaks and folds.

The way his eyes almost closed, like a man fighting sleep. Oh, he liked it all right. "It's so pale. The color of your nipples. I wonder if it will change." Still, he did not touch me, only himself. "Finger yourself for me. Yes. Just like I wasn't here."

I slowly drew my fingers along my folds, and his eyes narrowed. He wet his wide mouth with his tongue. It was disgusting and exciting. *Trollop. Jade.*

"You're so lonely," he began. "Your lover's in Paris, or God knows where, out banging the help. A maid—no, a little actress he found, in some cheap revue in the Place Pigalle." His low hypnotic voice painted the scene. "You're in your room. Your mother and the old *baba* have gone to sleep. Your little boyfriend's left you there all alone. You're a passionate girl, and you haven't had a man in a long time."

God knew that was true. Though I would never have dreamed of touching myself in the room with Mother and Avdokia. Between the two of them, they could chill desire in the most confirmed libertine. Yet this was the Archangel's fantasy, and I was prepared to go along, see where it took me.

"Your friends have all gone abroad, leaving you here, your beautiful youth fading away in that collectivized flat. Night after night, you sit with that dried-up grande dame. Who would blame you for touching yourself, trying for a little pleasure? At night you sometimes leave the shades open—yes you do. I've seen you."

I could imagine it, the shades open…though no one could see—we were on the second floor. I'd have to hang myself out the window. Easier to imagine a ground-floor window…

"Just in case someone comes along, some lonely man out walking. And there is someone. You've seen him in the street. He waits for you when you come home at night. He's waiting, he watches your windows. You feel him there, don't you?"

"Is it you?" I murmured. "Are you watching me, Arkady?"

He sighed heavily. "Your mother and that old *baba*

are snoring away, safely tucked up in their beds, and you stand at the window. You're naked, so lovely, so yearning. You touch yourself, and he watches you, and you move together, you and this stranger."

We moved together, there in the room, separate and yet together in this fantasy. I rubbed myself, tracing the slickness, letting his voice take me into the moment. It was an insistent, rumbling throaty whisper that I rode. I wanted him to keep talking, telling me the story of the man in the dark. My eyes were closed but I could hear him panting, slapping away at himself as I teased my body into orgasm. I buckled forward as the sweet waves of sensation moved through me.

Suddenly he was no longer sagging in the chair with a view of me. He was up on his feet, lifting me by the waist, and he shoved me, kneeling, onto the couch. I threw my arms up so I wouldn't hit the wall with my head, but my forehead struck as he jammed himself into me from behind. I twisted to find a position where he couldn't ram himself up painfully against my womb, but he kept moving me back so he could get it all in. "You're so little—who would have thought?"

But I wasn't that little. Genya and I made love and it wasn't like this. Arkady knew exactly what he was doing. He either wanted to hurt me or didn't care. I screamed.

"My big dick—is it too much for you?" he whispered in my ear, bent over me. He twisted my nipple, hard. "Yes, I'm hurting you?"

I gritted my teeth so I wouldn't cry out again, he seemed to enjoy that he was hurting me. I would not add to his pleasure in it. I held my arms before my head so I wouldn't knock myself out hitting the wall. "Get off…let me go."

He slapped my ass, hard, like a horse. "Tell me how it hurts. Tell me, or I'll keep it up all night. Tell me how you like my steel."

I braced my forehead against my arms. "Why are you doing this?" I choked out.

"So your boyfriend Kolya'll feel it when he fucks you," he said, close by my ear, petting my hair. "He'll know you've been fucked by a real man. How do you like fucking a real man?" He grabbed my hair and plowed all the way into me and a scream rose from my guts into the room and my head hit the wall again. Would he never stop? He twisted my nipple like he was trying to pull it off. "Tell me."

But I could not say it. I could only cry as he scoured me raw as a sandpapered plank. When would he come? What would make him finally stop? It wasn't the sound of my sobs—that was clear. Would he just keep going forever? I was dry as a piece of toast, and he kept going. I was cramping with pain. What a fool. This was what he really wanted. All that sexy talk was just one more thing he could take away from me.

"Does your Kolya have you like this? Do you feel him in your lungs, in your throat when he fucks you?"

Was that it, to erase Kolya from my body? Who was

the fool here? Only pleasure erased pleasure, Arkady. I must be bleeding now. He was never going to come.

Finally he pulled out and sagged onto the couch next to me, both of us puffing and panting, his pants around his ankles, his cock stark white like a radish. He needed a mare, a camel. He was puffing, stroking himself. I hoped he'd have a heart attack. "Put your finger up my ass, Makarova."

I'd never heard of such a thing.

"Do it," he said. He kicked his pants off and knelt there, pumping.

Trying not to look, I fingered the puckered orifice.

"Oh, for Christ's sake," he said. "Stick that thing in before I pop."

I pressed, just to the first knuckle. And he groaned, and I could feel him contracting around my digit, such an odd feeling. It must be the way a man felt inside me, the slick walls of muscle gripping him. Well, it was far better than what had preceded it. Finally he made a sound like he was having that infarction he richly deserved when he grabbed my head like a cabbage and forced it down onto him, spearing me in the mouth, up into my throat. I gagged as his hot, sour semen streamed into me. I couldn't breathe, even through my nose, and I struggled to pull away—pushed against his thighs, scratched at his chest, tried to find his face, bite down but my jaws were locked open. He held me and held me as he released into my throat, then finally he let me go.

I flung myself away from him, coughing and gasping,

sagged to the floor, spitting, tasting him, smelling him. I scrabbled back against the wall, as far from him as I could.

He picked up my slip from the floor, wiped himself and threw it to me. "You'll get used to me. That wasn't so bad now, was it?"

I wiped my finger on the Louis chair. My throat was as raw as my vagina now. I inched the slip over my head, covering the pale sore nipples that he found so exotic, the wet patches on my crumpled chemise. The sordid remains of adventure. "At least let me have my bracelet back."

Arkady stretched and yawned on the daybed and pulled his pants back on, though he left his cock out to air. He'd had a fine time. He looked ten years younger. "No, I have something else in mind for it." He took the enameled bangle from his pocket, twirled it on a long forefinger. "I'm going to bring your young Nikolai home for you. Your little mischief maker. You'd like that, wouldn't you? A little gift for your trouble?"

"Was that what this whole evening's been about? Kolya?" The romantic dinner, the brutal sex, everything? It had never been about me at all. I had been so sure there'd been an undercurrent of desire. But I was only a tool.

Arkady made that horrible moue. "Oh, Makarova. It doesn't diminish our love, does it?" He buttoned that monster back into his pants like an eel returning to its hole. "It just makes it more interesting."

"He won't come," I said defiantly. I reached out warily for my dress, dragged it toward where I sat, oozing onto the floorboards. Blood? Yes. *Bastard*. He was counting on Kolya's love for me, his loyalty. *I have your woman. Come back if you want her. Before I flog her, cut her in tiny pieces, and feed her to the geese.* And what would he do to Kolya if he returned? How perfectly I had played into Arkady's hands. "He'll never come back," I spat. "He doesn't love me like that."

"You should hope he does," Arkady said.

I dressed as quickly as I could, half doubled over from the cramping, imagining Kolya dashing into the trap. I prayed he would not. I could only imagine what Arkady might do to him. Yet a small part of myself, a selfish, vain part, could not help wishing he would come for me, would be willing to risk even death for me.

The tall, spectral man put on his coat and hat, and I put on my own, snatching it and moving away from him, still unwilling to get within arm's reach. The speed with which he had turned on me was indelibly imprinted on my body. Arkady von Princip was dangerous at all times, not only when he appeared to be. He started through the door, glancing over his shoulder. "Sorry. Didn't I mention? You're not going anywhere."

He closed the door and locked it behind him.

49 *Captivity*

I DREAMED THAT A crowd chased me through the streets of Petrograd. I turned and twisted to avoid their grasping, clutching hands, but there were too many. They got me down onto the ground in the filth of a market square and were peeling me with their knives as you'd peel summer fruit, starting with my face as I screamed and twisted and tried to get away. Finally, they got my skin off in one piece and someone ran away with it. And they left me there blinded and bloody, a hunk of living meat. How could I go around Petrograd without a skin? People were so hungry these days.

I awoke, curled in a hot room, still in my clothes, covered with sweat. *Thank God,* I thought. I still had my skin.

Then I remembered where I was and why. My head thundered and my throat was parched, but I grabbed my coat, stuffed my feet into my cracked boots, and flew to the door.

Locked.

I battered at it with my fists, yelled to anyone listening to let me out. I couldn't breathe. I pleaded to be set free, but no one came. The room stank of him, our sex, a miasma, disgusting and shameful.

The windows! I opened the drapes, but the windows wouldn't give. Locked. No, I saw the blocks hammered into the wide sill. A prison. And I'd walked in on my own. Thinking I had a new lover. What a fool. I pulled the chair from the desk to the window and climbed up onto the sill, dislodging a geranium growing there. Dirt all over the floor. The smell of my wedding. Down in the street, I could see the enviable people, walking by under battered umbrellas. Rain blackened the trees. Oh to be out there, wet, hungry but free.... I opened the *fortochka*, I would have cried out, but I was afraid men in the outer room might hear me, stop me. I tore a piece from my slip, waved it. No good, who would look up into the rain? "Help!" I called out. Louder. "Help!" Still no one. I listened to hear anyone coming. No.

I tried the escritoire in the bookcase, lined with drawers and cubbyholes. Nothing dangerous, no letter opener, no penknife, but here was a pen, and a bottle of ink. I found a small notepad and wrote in block letters, *HELP being held prisoner fourth floor COUNTERREV-OLUTIONARIES March 30, 1918. GET HELP.* Threw it out the window. Waved my white flag, now a wet rag. The sound of the rain erased my pleas.

The glass in the window was divided into squares, each too small for me to climb through but perhaps... I broke the first window, my coat over my hand. Listened. Nothing! I had to work quick. I broke out the second above it. Yes. The outer window opened, they had not thought to lock it. Now there just remained the matter of the crosspiece. Clinging to the wide wall of the recessed window, I lifted my foot in its boot—*Put your boot in it!*——and broke out the crosspiece. Waited for the sound of men running on the parquet outside the locked doors. I jumped down, dragged the Louis chair to the door and jammed it under the doorknob, then returned to my perch on the windowsill. Was I ready? I carefully brushed the glass away from the ledge. Holding on, I stuck my leg through, straddling the entire width of sill and window. Then ducked and got the rest of myself through. My head and shoulders, outside. My heart was pounding, my hands sweaty, the rain falling on my face.

But to my disappointment, there was no balcony, no ledge, no ornamentation one could balance upon. I waved my white flag. "Hey! Help!"

A child looked up. A child, across the street, tugged at his mother's coat, pointed to the girl climbing from the window. The mother stopped, put her umbrella back, saw me. Other people stopped on the sidewalk and watched. "Help me!" I shouted, weeping, holding on to the inner window frame, praying it wouldn't break. "They've got me locked in!"

But they just looked up dumbly. They thought I was a suicide.

"I NEED HELP!" I screamed.

Nobody moved. Then someone came running from this side of the building. Looked up, ran back in. "HELP ME!"

The drainspout. It ran down the building, past the next window. If I could stand, and make the big step to the next window, and then to the downspout, I just might be able to climb down. Or tie the curtains together and lower myself the four stories.... I heard the falling chair, but my position was too awkward to extricate myself quickly.

Suddenly, a heavy hand reached through the broken window and grabbed me by the hair, pulled me roughly inside, knocking me onto the floor. A blow to the face. It was the bearded man. "What do you think you're doing, huh? Trying to escape?" Another blow. Openhanded, but his hands were like blocks of wood. I curled myself into a ball around the geranium, the dirt.

"Hey, hey, take it easy." Another man, pockmarked, shoes wet. The one down in the street, the one who'd caught me.

"You take it easy, shithead." The bearded man. "Where were you? You were supposed to be on watch."

"I can't watch everything," said the other one. "She looks bad."

"Get some boards. Fix that." The bearded man bent over me, his gut straining his pants. "You. Stay away from those windows or I'll pitch you out. Head first. *Whee*..." He showed me with his hands, *flight,* and then *smack!,* brought his two hands together. "Shoulda helped you out the rest of the way, would have solved the woman problem right then and there." He turned to the other man. "I told him you can't mix women with business."

"You told him that," the other man said skeptically.

"In my way," said the bearded man.

My hair hurt, my face was bleeding, scratched where it had been pulled past the window frame. My cheek throbbed where he'd hit me. "I didn't choose to be here," I said.

"Shut up," said the bearded man, lifting his backhand, then thinking twice about it. "Stay out of my hair or I'll cut your throat just to get rid of you."

He waited for the other man to return with boards and a tool box, watched him board up the broken panes. My head still rang from the blows, I could feel the swelling coming on already.

"Could I have some water?" I asked.

"You get nothing, bitch," said the bearded man, and slammed the door, turned the lock hard.

At least the *fortochka* opened. I breathed the cold freshness of the rain. I could see the trees across the way in the Tauride Gardens, their black limbs studded with new buds. I wept like a child reaching my hand out to touch the rain, licking it off my palm. So close, those gardens, the trees I'd climbed as a child. That I made Seryozha climb, though he was afraid. I should have been more afraid, and he less. Among them lay the pond we pretended was Lake Svetloyar. Avdokia would tell us the story: *Zhili-buili, once upon a time, a prince built a city without walls on the banks of Lake Svetloyar....* Nothing seemed as precious now as the black pond that concealed the holy city, guarded forever against the Great Khan when it sank beneath the lake. *And upon the midnight, if you are pure at heart, if you are faithful, you can hear the bells of Kitezh ring out from beneath the waters.*

I waited all morning for someone to arrive with water or breakfast, a knout or a gun, but no one came. I examined the room's two dull landscapes and a portrait in a slightly cubist style. I took the latter off the wall and threw it against the door, enjoying its smash and screaming in frustration, waiting for the man to come back and hit me again, but the door remained shut.

Surely someone in the building must have heard me. But most likely Arkady had them all terrorized. He was probably paying off the house committee, too. It could even be that the residents felt safer with him around. And got electricity at night. I stood by the window, watching the rain and rehearsing my sins.

Was it raining in Moscow? I imagined Genya making his *kinofilms*. Genya whom I had let slip through my fingers—how had I not clung to him in the station, sworn not to let him go? If I ever got out of this room, I would go and live with him in Moscow—Zina, too. I didn't care anymore. A city in which Arkady von Princip drew breath was cursed down to its cobblestones.

Or I could go Maryino. I was no *barynya* anymore—I knew how to work. I could walk cows to pasture, cut rye, saw wood, make shoes. You could vanish like that. Safe under the waters.

I sat down in the blue empire chair and searched the

escritoire again to see if there was anything I could use, something I'd missed, but the little drawers and cubbies held nothing but old letters and ticket stubs. Not even a hat pin. I couldn't stop thinking about the way that man had *used* me, like a cow or a horse.

It all came back to Kolya. When I thought of him, my heart didn't jump as it had even the day before. This was his fault, in more ways than one. Not only had he given me the jewel and told me to see Arkady if I needed to sell it. No. He had introduced me to my own boundless passion, the possibilities of the flesh, had left me wide open to this kind of seduction. That's what made me want to retch with self-loathing. I tried to think back to our good times, the sleigh ride, snow on the Catherine Canal, but that cruel parody of love with Arkady had erased it.

I used the chamber pot. The pain made me grit my teeth. No paper to wipe with, only dusty copies of the old journal *Severny Vestnik* from the bookcase. I ripped out a sheet—a poem by Sologub—and gently blotted my torn flesh. No blood on the paper, that was good news. My vulva would be very well read. I started to laugh. Of course, love was the poem's subject.

Later in the day, I heard a key turn in the lock and my heart spun like a tumbler. But it was only the Kirghiz, impassive, wrinkles deeply etched, a basket in one hand, a pitcher in the other. He glanced at my battered face, the boarded-up window.

I ran to him, clutching his arm. "Get me out of here," I whispered. "I beg you. I'll give you four thousand rubles. You know I'm good for it."

He shook his head, grinned. His teeth were dark from tobacco, ground to stumps. "He likes you, little bird," he said. "Imagine what he'd do to someone he didn't like."

I slumped in the chair. "Will he ever let me go?"

The man shrugged, setting the basket on the desk, the pitcher alongside it. "The Archangel holds our fate in his hands."

In the basket, an egg. A loaf of good bread, a sausage. Like a love letter from a hangman.

The room measured ten paces by four. I spent the day pacing it off, or gazing out at the Tauride Gardens, and avoiding the daybed and the Louis chair. I knew their treachery. The chair stared back at me, blank as a babe. The hypocrisy of furniture. I sat at the escritoire and read all the family's correspondence. Old letters from Moscow and Tsarskoe Selo, a postcard of the harbor at Novorossisk, to the *Dearest Mustasovs, from Elena*…a stack of overdue bills. The *Dearest Mustasovs* were evidently behind on payments to the butcher, the florist, the stationer. Maybe they were relieved that the revolution wiped out all their debts. In fleeing they could leave those problems behind.

I closed my fist around a pen, imagining stabbing him in the neck with it. Did I have the nerve? The speed?

He was quick as an adder. And would avenge an attack without mercy.

Someone was playing the violin in another apartment. How crushing it was to know how little I mattered. Even if I died in this room, people would go on making dinner, taking children to the gardens, practicing the violin. How enviable they all seemed, unaware that in this room in their own building, a girl was being held prisoner.

No. Not unaware. They'd heard me. And decided to do nothing. Even on Grivtsova Alley someone would have come by now. Even the meekest of housewives would have knocked gently once the coast was clear. But here, as long as it wasn't their own problem, a human being's misery was something the neighbors could close their ears to, pretend it was a cat yowling.

I hated people. Who could go on living as if nothing was happening when something hideous unfolded just overhead, or in the next flat, working its way into their dreams? "I hate you!" I screamed. "I hate all of you!" I took the children's silhouettes and pitched them across the room, one by one—their little curls, their overbites—where they broke with a satisfying crash.

Light bled from the sky, abandoning the bare branches of the trees. Would he return? Maybe I wasn't that important. Maybe I was merely a hostage against Kolya's unlikely reappearance, no more. I switched on the electrolier. At least the electric lights worked. I picked up a book—Chekhov—read a page or two of "The Lady with the Lapdog," and then "The Black Monk," but they held no interest, these men and women, fathers and daughters, orchards and oceans.

I found some paper in the desk, ink still in the inkwell. They had departed quite recently. Maybe Arkady had threatened them. I looked down into the black soul of the ink. Maybe I should drink it. If it were the previous century, that's what I would do. *A ruined girl.* The idea sparked a sudden rage. Ruined for what? That murky melodrama. Better to throw it in his face, savor his pain. Before he caught me and killed me. Or handed me over to men rougher than he was. Anything could transpire in a room like this.

On a blank sheet, I wrote my name. *Marina Makarova.* My father's name. I crossed it out and wrote *Kuriakina.* But I'd not been *Kuriakina* long enough to even recognize the sight of it. Under it, I wrote the character *ya. I.* That was the only name that belonged to me. *Ya* was the city under the lake, the thing I could claim for myself. I would keep it well hidden. I, Marina. Like a pebble in the mouth in a desert.

He came on the night of the third day, waking me out of a hungry sleep. Light from the streetlamps blued the window and splashed the ceiling with rain. His hair caught some of that glow. He didn't look quite human in that unholy radiance. I eyed him sullenly from the daybed.

He passed his hand over the boarded window. "What did you think you were doing? Would you really have jumped?" He seemed fascinated. "We're on the fourth floor." His eyes shone for a second, transparent as a cat's, then disappeared into his inky silhouette. "I thought you'd want a little company," he said. "I've had an interesting night."

"Rape anyone?" I spat it out like a bad taste. I would not collaborate. I would not be seduced.

"Makarova." He placed his long hands over his heart, right where I would have stabbed him if I'd been able to find anything besides pens in the drawer. "We're having an affair."

"You're joking."

"Not at all." Silhouetted against the windows, still in fedora and coat, he was like something left over from a dream. "You wanted to know this man, this Arkady von Princip. So different from all those little schoolboys. You were intrigued—admit it. By my power. By the danger. You came up here of your own accord, took off your clothes for me. Don't pretend you don't remember."

Lord, I remembered. My body still reminded me. "And then what happened? I remember that, too."

"Oh, that," he said. "You can't play with me like you can with your little boyfriends. You're mine now. A man can't rape his own wife. It isn't possible."

I regarded his slow, languid movements as I would a snake's. I inched—imperceptibly I hoped—toward my boots, in case he became overconfident, in case I got the chance to bolt. "If she doesn't want him, what else would you call it? If he forces her."

"She's already his. She's already accepted him." He gazed out at the park, the tops of the trees. "She's already taken her clothes off and spread herself out for him. Like this city. Petrograd is mine. I own her. I'll do what I like with her. And I'll do the same with you." He turned back to me and I changed position on the bed, to conceal that I'd been reaching for my boots.

He took off his coat and hat and settled himself on the Louis chair. Only his face and hair stood out in the gloom. He crossed his long legs, fished his string from his pocket. The fingers moved quickly in the nets they were weaving. He seemed incredibly pleased with himself. "Ask me a question."

"If that's not rape, what is?"

He turned the figure in his hands. It was a woman, tangled in a web, her arms and legs outstretched. "Semantics. I own you now. I can starve you so that you'll lick my boots. I can flog you so that, believe me, you'll do anything I ask. If I get tired of you, I'll kill you. Who would stop me? No one. Who cares? One girl more or less in this terrible world—it wouldn't even make the papers." I could smell him from here—cold and astringent, like cellar dirt. "Girls are there to be used. It's how you're built, and anyone who can be used will be." His hair, a white nest. He threw his hat on the divan. "Are you looking for justice? Justice is a fiction. There's only power." He turned another figure—a crown. Then lowered his hands. "That's what attracted you to me. The freedom of unapologetic power. A smart girl in your situation would think of how to make it work for her. How to cozy up to me. Flattery is good, for a start. Tell me what a wonderful lover I am, how brilliant I am."

And he joined me on the couch.

> *Where were the proclamations about this?*
>> *Where were the decrees?*
>>> *Where were the posters*
>>> *handbills*
>>> *commentaries from*
>>> *Rykov and Bukharin?*

> *I should have known*
>> *more would come out of a Revolution*
>> *than steady progress*
>>> *toward a Workers' State.*

50 *The Minotaur*

I BECAME ACCUSTOMED TO things one should never become accustomed to. I struggled to remember precise details about the outside world. The clean, gummy smell of fir boughs at Christmastime. The loamy richness of the forest north of town, where we collected wild mushrooms in the fall—bright foxes, chanterelles. The felted *valenki* boots Avdokia stitched for us, with little animals embroidered across their toes, hedgehogs and leaping stags. The details helped keep me sane. I recited poems by the hour, speeches from Shakespeare, sang songs, danced. I was sure the men guarding the flat thought me stone-cold mad.

The baron came late at night, bearing food and drink, wanting to talk, wanting sex. He was never again as cruel as he'd been the first night, but I was at no risk of forgetting what he was capable of. Occasionally he was inward, gloomy and strange, which was even worse. Who could follow the Minotaur into the depths of his labyrinth? He drank the most on those moody nights. I hoped he might grow sloppy, giving me a chance at his keys, but he liked me to drink with him, and he held it better than I did. He never stayed the night. By dawn he was always gone. I imagined him having to return to his coffin.

As my despair deepened, my mind cleared. Voices flooded in, begging to speak through my pen—Persephone, captive queen in the halls of the Dark Lord. Ariadne in the labyrinth with her half brother the Minotaur. Vasilisa the Beautiful and her knowing doll. And the faithful women of Kitezh. Arkady, too, appeared on my pages despite my efforts, the source of dark mythologies.

And so we returned to robbers and thieves
Songs sung on the banks of rivers
Under the bright eyes of beasts

The electric light found me sleeping. Arkady entered, carrying a basin, a pitcher, and a towel. He rested the washbasin on his hip and closed the door behind him. I felt for the elbow of glass beneath my pillow, a shard from a broken picture frame. The time had come to treat an animal like an animal. My fingers found its bladelike edge. When he bent over me, I would slash his throat from ear to ear.

He placed the basin on the desk and poured in the water, the steam rising.

I swore I would not react, that I would wait, but the lovely sound of water...I had not had anything to drink all day. "We're going to have a little scrub down," he said, pulling something from his pocket. I could hear the paper tearing, could smell it from the daybed. *Levkoi* soap. My grandmother used to buy this soap in the Nevsky Passazh, said it reminded her of stock flowers that grew in the dooryard at Maryino. Arkady was about to drop the soap into the water.

I called out, "Wait!" And despite my vow, I stumbled to the desk and lapped hot water from the basin into my hand, drinking deep from my palm like a peasant.

"Oh, you're thirsty. How remiss of me," he said, like

a fop at a party who had forgotten a lady's lemonade. "Such a hectic day."

Suddenly he seized my other hand, my right, and squeezed it, hard. I screamed as the glass sliced through my palm, a pain so intense, so unexpected. He kept squeezing, his face a mere inch from my own, enjoying the pain, delighting in it. "You waited," he whispered into my ear as he held my hand there. "That was stupid. You should have done it right away. Only amateurs wait." Finally he let me go. My blood spilled out of my fist into the water, over the desktop, the chair. It was running down my arm. The shard of glass fell to the floor.

I keened over my damaged hand, holding my wrist. "Bastard. Whore's son. Motherfucker."

He grabbed my wrist and yanked me to the stove. I fought him with all my strength, shrieking and cursing, when I saw where he was dragging me but he was strong as a bear. Forcing me to kneel, he opened the stove door.

He pressed my palm to the hot metal.

I screamed so loudly that it should have been heard on every floor of the building, echoing onto the street and up into the pitiless sky. The black trees must have recoiled, the windows shattered for miles. He grabbed my hair and bent my head back. "Quiet."

At last he let me go. I sat on the floor, trembling with the shock, holding my hand by the wrist.

He crouched next to me, ran his bony fingers through

my hair. "You'll thank me tomorrow." All I could do was rock back and forth. "A nasty cut. Cauterization's best. Stitches become infected."

He picked me up under the arms and hauled me back to the daybed. I let him. I had not one ounce of fight left. He offered me some vodka from a flask he pulled from his pocket. I shook my head. I didn't want anything from him except his disappearance from the face of the earth. All my being was locked in the nine square inches of my right palm.

"Come on, Makarova, don't be stupid. There's no one here to applaud your martyrdom." He waved it under my nose.

I took the bottle and swallowed, once, twice. It burned my empty stomach, and it was a relief to feel pain somewhere besides my hand. I drank more.

He went to the door and spoke to someone. I held my wrist, my burned hand curled to my chest, as if it were a small wounded animal. Arkady returned and began unbuttoning my dress. This, too? Would I have to endure everything?

He pulled my boots off, removed my slip, my bloomers, even my hose without really touching me. As I stood naked in the hot room, he tenderly—like a nurse—began to wash me. Lathering the sweet soap on a cloth, wiping my shoulders, my arms, my breasts. The water was warm, the soap creamy. I closed my eyes, holding my wounded hand high above my head, and let him bathe me, concentrating on the sensations rising, an uncanny mixture of intense pain and pleasure.

He sang a lullaby under his breath as he washed me, something his nanny used to sing at bath time, no doubt. I didn't recognize it. Every so often, I'd take another sip from the flask.

As he washed me, he talked. He wanted to talk about childhood. "What were you like as a child, Makarova? Did you play when you were a little girl? Who did you play with?"

Play? What was he talking about? Everything had acquired a slight halo. My hand throbbed overhead.

"Those games in a circle. I see them sometimes. They all seem to know how to play them. Does someone teach them, or do they just know, like ants?"

Despite myself, despite everything, I laughed, dribbling vodka down my chin. "*Caraway, caraway, you can go any way*...they didn't play caraway in that castle of yours?"

"No, there was no playing," he said. He had me lean over the basin and poured water onto my head. *In the presence of mine enemies*...worked the soap through my hair. "I was raised a gentleman—that is, beaten regularly, my head held under water, left outside without clothes. I learned about power. Useful, but not much of a childhood."

I could smell him, antiseptic wormwood under the sweet soap. The vodka had gone to my head, my fear ebbing like the pain in my hand. It seemed like someone else's now. How lovingly he touched me, as if he hadn't just crushed my hand around a blade of glass. Rinsing my hair, my shoulders, my breasts and belly, the V of my cunt, as if my body were something beautiful and rare, not a sordid object he regularly used and forgot. How could one understand a man like this?

"You played as a girl, I know you did," he said. "Tell me what you did."

Poor monster. His fate, like the Minotaur's, had been cast before birth. "Was there nothing you loved as a boy? Nothing that you enjoyed?"

"I rode well. Shot, of course. I was good with horses and dogs. I raised wolfhounds." He ran his hand along my ribs. "My hounds—that was my great pleasure. You should have seen them, Makarova. There's nothing quite as beautiful as wolfhounds chasing a wolfpack across the moonlit snow."

I actually felt pity for the man. In another week, I would be as insane as he was. "My mother kept Italian greyhounds. The last one was named Tulku. But Red Guards shot him. He tried to bite one when they came to take her furniture."

"Bastards. Dogs are far superior to people. They're incapable of betrayal, for one thing."

The cloth moved around my neck. I bent forward to let him wash my back, losing myself in the warmth and the rough cloth on my skin. He washed between my legs, down my thighs. "Tell me," he said. "I want to know you as a child. I want to know everything. What did you play?"

I shook my head. I would sink beneath the lake, out of reach of the invader's hand. The bells sang under water. He could never reach me there. *If you are pure at heart...*

"You'll tell me eventually," he said. "I'm all there is now."

Something about that struck me hard as I stood there, dumb as a horse, with my fiery hand and my heavy tongue, being washed by this evil thing that had come out of the earth.

"I had a brother," I said. "We were like twins. We had our own world, our own language. We invented our own games. Fairy tales, secret signs. He was a terrific mimic. We wrote our own plays—"

"And where is he now, this prodigy?" Arkady asked.

"He was in Moscow. With the cadets." And now he was nowhere. I began to cry. I pressed my good hand to my eyes. All the fight had gone out of me. I needed someone to hold me, to pity me. Even him. Even him.

"Too bad," he sighed, patting my shoulder awkwardly. "Dying like that, for a lost cause—Holy Russia or whatever. I want to die with my eyes wide open, believing in nothing."

"I'm sure you'll get your wish," I said.

He took it in good spirits. Obviously my pain had put him in a cheerful mood. "Other brothers? Sisters?"

"My older brother fought with Brusilov. He's in the

Don with the Volunteers." As if it were a matter of pride. Even now. I pictured Volodya on his beautiful Orlov trotter, Swallow. My brother's shining hair and dark eyes, his cap just so, the horse polished like brown satin. Though I knew after years of war they were both roughened, it was how I liked to imagine him. Safe from all this squalor. What would he think of me now, my heroic brother—his sister a corrupt, corrupted, stinking piece of whoredom?

Suddenly my captor's hand fell away from me. "That's the connection, isn't it? The older brother, the school chum." He collapsed onto the empire chair. "Of course. So simple. Why hadn't I seen it before? Drinking bouts, shared whores. Typical Petersburg boyhood. Signed up together, I imagine. Oh, I should have guessed." Amazed at his own genius. His mind was like an elastic band that always snapped back to the same shape.

Angry as I was at Kolya, I trembled for him, to be the object of such a relentless obsession. And I knew, at that moment, that my lover would never return to Russia. He wouldn't dare. Once you'd escaped Arkady von Princip, you were best off staying very, very far away.

Arkady stood, came close, sniffed my neck. "Have you always been in love with him? Tell me. Were you the little girl admiring your brother's pal from behind the curtains? Letting him fondle you in the cloak-room?"

I was his prisoner, to do with what he liked, and still

he was jealous as a schoolboy. "That was a long time ago." But Tuesday was a long time ago, too.

"How old were you? Eighteen? Fourteen? Twelve?"

I felt a rush of perversity. It was like poking a snake, I couldn't resist. I was sick to death of him. "You want to know? You want to know about me and Kolya? Yes, I was twelve and fourteen and eighteen. Everything you're thinking and more. I was mad for him. I loved him more than any man alive."

He squeezed the washcloth out into the basin, rested it on the side. "You might rethink that position. He may not be alive very long. Speaking of men alive," he said, drying his hands on a towel, "guess who I ran into the other day?"

I did not give a damn.

"Our Dmitry Ivanovich. He's been in Vologda with the English." He shook out the towel and wrapped it around my shoulders.

I dried my hair with my good hand. Why did Arkady know my father's whereabouts? He'd been interested in him even that first day, on Kamenny Island. Arkady was capable of saying anything to torment me, but that bit about the English sounded true enough. My father, still not reconciled to the fact that the future belonged to others.

The Archangel picked up the bloody basin and rapped on the door. It opened, and he handed the washbowl through. Then the Kirghiz and a younger man came in, carrying a small table and baskets of food. The younger man, a big-headed blond, found it difficult to keep his eyes on the table and the foodstuffs instead of on his master's naked woman. I didn't bother to cover myself. I was a horse, a cow. Shame belonged only to human beings.

They set out the feast before the Louis chair and the room filled with the fragrance of cooked food, meat. My stomach welcomed it with audible gurgles, that traitor. I hated that I needed to eat, hated that I needed him, my master, this ghoul. The men left silently.

Arkady sat in the chair before the low table and peered into the basket, his forefinger lifting the checkered cloth. "Yes, the noble Dmitry Ivanovich, somewhat the worse for wear." He filled a plate—a small chicken, potatoes, mushrooms. I hadn't eaten since morning, just a roll and some tea. My stomach growled viciously. "His mistress was with him."

Hungry and burned as I was, I laughed. "You must be thinking of the wrong man." I drank from his water glass.

My captor began to eat. "Viktoria Karlinskaya. Didn't you know? It's been going on quite a while." He held out a piece of chicken to me on his fork. I reached with my good hand but he pulled it away. "No, open up."

Feeding me like a squirrel he wished to tame. But in the end my stomach was more insistent than my pride. I ate, bite by bite—chicken, warm bread, salad. "You're still wrong."

"She's an attractive woman," he continued. "Married

to an SR of some prominence. You people are so civilized. No pistols at dawn."

It was impossible. Ridiculous. Though my parents' marriage certainly wasn't the warmest, it went against everything I knew about Father. Arkady was playing with me. I concentrated on the sensation of his crushing my fist around the shard of glass. I wouldn't believe anything he said—even if he said the sun rose in the morning.

He pressed a piece of bread to my lips and I chewed it. "Ask me a question," he said.

"Why are you like this?" I asked.

"A person can't see what I've seen and not be affected by it," he said, and stroked my wet hair. "You won't be the same, either, after this is all over."

I was glad he thought it would be over. That was cause for hope.

A few nights later, he urged me to recite poems for him. I considered poets I thought he'd like. Pushkin? *Groan.* Lermontov? Better. I tried the symbolists, the acmeists. He pronounced Blok "dreary" and Akhmatova "a frigid bitch," but he adored the mocking, incendiary Tsvetaeva, especially the poem *"We shall not escape Hell, my passionate sisters..."* He had me recite it three times, savoring the lines,

> *...we sing songs of paradise*
> *around a campfire with thieves,*

we, the careless needlewomen
(all we sew splits at the seams!),
prancers, players on the panpipe,
the whole world's most rightful queens!

...in the jails and in our revels
we have given up the skies...

...on starry nights, we stroll among
the apple trees of paradise...

Yes, this was the place for Tsvetaeva. Akhmatova was too reserved, too mournful and ready to grieve. Tsvetaeva knew what it was to make mistakes out of passion, how to let the madness in, let it flare and dance. Arkady lay with his head on my bare breast. I was unfortunately getting used to all this. My captor, my enemy, my lover...the saddest man I ever met.

"Tell me one of yours," he said. "They say you write all the time."

I poured myself another vodka, knocked it back. "I burn them as I go."

"You don't expect me to believe that." He stood up and glanced around the room, pressing his long fingers to his mouth. He began searching. He tapped briefly on the open writing surface of the escritoire but didn't touch any of the drawers. He peered behind the ugly landscape painting, a hiding spot that wouldn't have occurred to me, then went straight to the bookcase and methodically began shaking out the books. I knew he would find them eventually. His delight was almost comical as the loose pages fluttered out from a volume of Turgenev's *A Hunter's Sketches* like so many gulls. He gathered them up from the floor and brought them to me, rustling them, and settled in for a show.

I sorted through them, all my characters. Persephone, tragic Pandora, Ariadne. The woman of Kitezh. Frankly, I'd never had a better audience, more intent, more focused.

> *Oh the squawking these days*
> *Women fight for bones*
> *Someone's being murdered*
> *In the building next door.*
> *And the bells of Kitezh*
> *Grow faint*
> *Once I heard them singing.*
> *But now it's only streetcar bells*
> *Except very late at night...*
> *Shhh!*
> *There?*
> *No.*
> *Only a late tram.*

I shared one I'd written in the voice of the sorcerer Koshchei the Deathless as he speaks to his soul, which lies hidden

inside a golden needle,
   inside an egg,
      inside a duck
         inside a hare,
            inside a chest of gold
               at the bottom of the sea.

In the poem, the soul's so very lonely that she wants to join with him again. But he will not give up his power for his soul, no matter how lonely they both are or how much misery it causes them.

"You really believe I have a soul hidden away somewhere, like a dog's buried bone?" He laughed, his head on my shoulder. "That I could just unlock the chest of gold, and my soul and I would be one again for all eternity? As I recall, Koshchei dies when he and his soul are reunited." He tipped the bottle back, then held it to my lips.

The vodka had ceased to burn, ceased to taste like anything. I drank and wiped my chin on the back of my hand. "Yes, but think of the suffering of keeping them apart. All this power, this greed," I said. "To what end?"

He was silent for a time. "What's the point in a soul if it kills you? Would you rather have life or a soul?"

"What's life without a soul?" I said. "It's not even life."

"So Russian." He laughed. "It's why I'm the new prince of Petrograd and you're a naked girl in a room."

*   *   *

Sometime around dawn, I must have passed out. A long, headachy sleep, with scraps of nightmares slicing this way and that.

I woke to full daylight, and flew from the couch as if it were on fire. What in the devil had he done to me while I slept? Poured candle wax between my shoulder blades? The pain was as bright as branding irons, phosphorescent. I raced to the mirror that hung between the windows and, twisting around, tried to see my back in the glass. Stretching, craning, my skin burning.

When I saw what he'd done, I clapped my hand over my mouth.

He'd incised into my back a fiery alphabet, a network of cuts, delicately inscribed, oozy red upon the white flesh. A poem. For me.

salA
devoleB
ton llahs eW
esoht raeH
slleB
niagA

And I knew, as surely as I'd known anything in my life, that I would never walk free of this nightmare.

51 *The Meeting*

THE KIRGHIZ FOUND ME in a state of shock, naked, my back a mass of bloody cuts. He stopped when he saw me, holding my breakfast in a bag. I looked at him over my shoulder, gazing into the intricacy of his hard-burnished wrinkles. He didn't flinch, he didn't soften. What those old eyes must have seen.

"You've got to get me out of here," I whispered hoarsely. "He's not going to stop. He's never going to stop, is he?"

I was searching for a shred of humanity. Yes, there it was—I could see the pity in his eyes. He put the bag on the desk and filled my pitcher with water from a pot. But what he said was, "If you don't like wolves, stay out of the woods."

Yet he came back later with bandages and iodine. Yes, Arkady's men would know how to treat knife wounds. They would have had numerous occasions to perfect their art. He cleaned and dressed my flesh, quickly and efficiently, and changed the dressings each day afterward. But the marks would never fade entirely. *Alas, Beloved, we shall not hear those bells again.* I heard voices in other rooms, people in the street, hail on the roof, the snapping of fire logs, but under it all was silence.

*   *   *

The twelfth night Arkady came early, in a brisk mood. He held up my laundered slip in his bony hands. "I thought we'd go out. Let's get you dressed, shall we? Would you like that?" His blue eyes were all concern.

He was going to take me out?

I stared at him blankly. Was there such a place as Out? Where one would be permitted to walk, dressed and booted, outside these walls? Not free, of course, but at least in the world? I hadn't dressed since the day he'd cut me. I couldn't bear anything pressing against my back.

He slipped the cotton lisle down past my head, pulled it gently over the bandages, tenderly even. As if cutting my flesh had been some necessary operation and he was my solicitous nurse. Yet I'd been so sure I'd never leave this room alive. I knew there was no way he was actually letting me go, that he was just expanding the walls of my prison to include the night and new air, but I'd take any scrap of it, anything, even a firing squad.

He helped me into my clothes, my coat and scarf, and turned the key in the lock. The door swung outward. It seemed impossible. Another room. Fresh air, cold compared to the hothouse I'd been living in. The shock of seeing the flat again. Men, just in the next room, playing cards amid rolls of rugs, racks of coats, objets d'art that hadn't been here when I'd arrived. They looked up and quickly back at the worn fans of spades and diamonds. All this time, they'd heard my screams, knew exactly what I'd endured, and not one of them had so much as lifted a finger. They were just so many dogs that showed their bellies to the leader, the most vicious of them all. I felt their eyes on my back as Arkady led me on. I wished I could burn the house down with all of them sealed into it. Then I would hear their screams while I played my own game of cards.

The other rooms of the *enfilade* swarmed with men, eating, carrying boxes and bags, flour and cans, even a live goat, its hard hooves clicking on the parquet. I felt like a long-lashed dairy cow being led to the milking shed before a pack of wolves, though none of them dared so much as glance at me. Queen of the Underworld with her Dark Lord.

We descended the small elevator to a long car waiting at the curb in the icy night, a Benz Söhne with a surrey top. Little Gurin sat at the wheel like a monkey in a leather cap, and next to him, burly in a thick coat, sat the bearded man with the heavy eyebrows, St. Peter. He glanced at me without curiosity from under his astrakhan hat. As usual, Arkady cut a poor figure in his old coat and crushed fedora. He clearly relished the masquerade, his power concealed inside his shabbiness. I wondered what he wanted. What was his game? I knew him well enough by then to know there was a reason for all this. He looked far too pleased with himself for my liking. I slid across the seat. It occurred to me to keep on going and I grabbed the door handle on the street side, but Arkady yanked me back by my coat collar. "Oh, don't leave us so soon, Makarova. You'll miss the fun. Won't she, Borya?"

The heavy-browed man turned and scratched his forehead under his hat with the thin barrel of his Mauser. Everyone had them now, it seemed—the Cheka and the criminals alike. You could tell the Mausers from the regular guns by the sound of their rapid fire, Petrograd's nightly lullaby.

I made the mistake of sitting back against the upholstery, and my unhealed wounds sent me jolting upright again. Gurin wrenched the car from the curb and I had to clutch Arkady to keep from falling backward. But I was *out*, that was the thing. I wanted to stick my head out the window as Tulku used to do, drink in the Tauride Gardens, the icy night. I couldn't imagine where it would end, but for the moment I was moving away from that prison.

"Smile." Arkady grinned like a corpse. "Breathe." He demonstrated deep breathing, theatrically throwing his head back, his arms wide on the seat as we careened through the pitch-dark town. "Ah, Petrograd. I love this city." At this hour, streets that would once have been teeming with pedestrians traveling to and from the theaters and restaurants were as deserted as those of a town emptied by plague. No one walked on the ice-glazed pavement, no lights appeared in the windows. Only when we crossed Nevsky at the train station did we see any signs of life.

The Benz Söhne slid on the frozen road, Gurin neatly avoiding all the potholes and detritus. The wind tore in through the car's open sides. I reluctantly accepted the bearskin rug over my lap and pulled it to my shoulders. I could still smell the bear. Arkady worked his hand under my skirt and warmed it between my legs as a man rests his hand on a dog's head, as if no one else were in the car. Yes, I had submitted, utterly, I was hollow as a gourd. Arkady's woman.

"Did you see the look on that blonde's face?" Arkady said to the heavy-browed Borya.

"She shouldn'ta held the goods in her corset," said the man with the Mauser. "That was her first mistake."

In a short time we were out of the city, heading south toward the Pulkovo Heights. The moon rose in the east like a voyeur peeping through a blind. A beautiful night in any other life, the road slick and shining, the smell of the surrounding fields. In the daytime, the Benz Söhne would have been sunk in mud to the running boards, but the temperature had dropped and set a fine crust on the land. Here and there, I could detect the trench lines we had dug against the German advance. That, too, seemed like years ago, those days working alongside the women, their camaraderie. What I wouldn't give for a friend.

The men talked about the job they'd pulled the night before, a theater robbery. I wondered if they had attacked one of Krestovsky's snack bars. Beautiful Galina and her pretensions to poetry. Did they still gather at the apartment on Sergievskaya? Or had all the poets gone their own ways, each scrambling for a livelihood and a bit of bad bread? Maybe it had been collectivized by now. Arkady kissed my neck, sniffing me as he massaged me under the bearskin. "We made the front page of the *Petrogradsky Echo*—third time this week. The new Cheka head, this Uritsky, vows to clean us off the face of the earth. Ironic, wouldn't you say, as there is officially no crime in Petrograd?" He snorted, "I'd like to see him try to get rid of me. I heard someone stole his hat right in the corridor at Smolny." Uritsky was Varvara's boss. He was the new chief of the Petrograd Cheka? I filed that piece of information away in a secret drawer in my head.

In the distance, the pale dome of the Pulkovo Observatory gleamed on the heights. Someone was working up there tonight, some quiet scientist for whom this madhouse on wheels would seem stranger than all nine moons of Jupiter.

We turned into a smaller lane, bumped and slid through a small forest of bare birches and thin evergreens, to a log dacha, smoke curling from its chimney. The men got out. If I ran now, how far would I get? To the observatory? I estimated I'd make it no farther than the dacha gate before I felt a bullet between my shoulder blades.

I climbed out of the back, Arkady taking my hand. My breath was full of frost. "You're going to like this," he said. And we all marched down the crunchy frozen path under the blistering stars to the old dacha.

A small group watched us enter, four men dressed in a variety of styles and a woman, full-lipped with thick reddish-blond hair. The room was rich with fragrant fir-smoke and tobacco. The mood was tense, as though a heated discussion had just ceased when we entered. They cast sharp glances at each other. *What have we gotten ourselves into?* I could almost hear them asking themselves.

Borya took up guard post near the door, Mauser at his hip, arms crossed, dashing my hopes of a quick bolt to freedom.

I squeezed myself into a corner, hoping to be ignored, wondering how I would be perceived by these people, a charcoal-eyed girl in my old coat and tattered gloves, my shawl and boots. I recognized a familiar scent married to the fir: cherry tobacco. *There.* By the mantelpiece, in a worker's black blouse and a full beard, his corduroy trousers stuck in his boots, Father had already seen me. He'd been smoking a clay pipe but it now hovered halfway to his chest as he stood, frozen in horror, taking in my wasted face, my bandaged hand, the company I kept.

Shame rose up in me like water in a fountain, filled me so quickly with its hot roaring substance that I felt I might be knocked off my feet. I wished I could melt into the floor like butter. Had Arkady planned this all

along? Of course he had. His blue eyes danced with
fun. If I'd had a knife—even the edge of a can—I
would have cut his throat.

And who might these other people be? The woman
in her modest black dress wasn't tall, but deep-
breasted, her bright hair in a tight chignon. The man
seated across from Arkady had soft brown hair and a
drooping moustache. He nervously fingered his workman's cap, resting on the table. Arkady tossed his own
disreputable hat beside it, letting his pale rat's nest
sprawl on his cadaverous head. I saw the fun he was
having at Father's expense. Arkady reached behind him
and pulled me to stand next to him, the way a man pulls
a woman to the roulette table for luck as he places his
chips on *rouge*. He was parading me before my father
like a trophy of war, like the cursed captives of Troy.

A man in an indeterminate army uniform without in-
signia settled on the arm of a chair, eyeing my captor
with distaste. The various comrades glanced anxiously
at Arkady and the heavily armed Borya stationed at
the door. Father struggled to maintain his composure,
lighting his pipe, emotion trembling just under his eyes.
Disgust? Grief? His reddish-brown hair and beard
were frosted with gray now. He had become old.

A small dark man in a black jacket next to the army
man assessed the situation. He had soulful, intelligent
Mediterranean eyes. A Greek maybe, or a Jew, or Armenian. The twitchy man with the long moustache—
he looked somehow familiar—spoke to Father over his

shoulder. "You said he'd come alone." What did Father have to do with any of these people?

"I never come alone," interrupted Arkady, as if oblivious to the other currents in the room. "I don't take a shit alone." He stretched his long legs. "When I piss, someone holds my dick."

The moustached man worked his jaw, swallowing his outrage. "So where's the money, Princip? We've been waiting for weeks. I don't think you have it."

I knew how much Arkady would dislike this fidgety, impatient man's purposely leaving off the honorific. The fellow could not guess how volatile the man seated across from him could be. But Arkady chose to ignore the slight — for now. "It'll be ready when you and your people are ready for us, Karlinsky."

If this was Karlinsky, then the voluptuous woman with the red-blond hair would be... my father's mistress. I felt less ashamed than I did a moment before. So I was Arkady's whore. Well, what of it? *What about your whore? Were you seeing her all along?* All that moralizing. She wasn't as beautiful as my mother, but she looked like she knew her way around a bedroom. But why had we come if Arkady wasn't prepared to do business? Surely not just to make me suffer or for a private joke. It had to have been to get the upper hand in some way.

The dark man spoke. "It should have been here already, Baron. That was our understanding. The timing is crucial." Slim and intense, he had a quality of speech, rapid and a bit garbled, like someone who spoke many languages but none of them quite natively. I guessed him to be from Odessa, a city famous for its gangsters. The woman glanced at Father, but he was gazing down at the fire as if he'd like to throw himself into it.

The man in uniform whispered something to the Odessan, who turned away from the rest of us to reply.

"It will be here," said Arkady. "In good time. Three hundred fifty thousand gold francs can't be sewn into someone's clothes."

All at once, the picture came into focus. This money wasn't moving on its own. Arkady must have sent Kolya to the West to sell the valuables of the Formers and return with the gold. But Kolya hadn't fulfilled his end of the deal. Ha! Of course he hadn't. Three hundred fifty thousand gold francs would buy a lot of women, a lot of wine, in Paris during a war. That was where I came in. *Ya*, hostage. And it was all for this—for some underground organization hatching a counterrevolutionary plot.

"The Czechs won't wait," said the small black-eyed man. "They're already moving."

The Czechs? I remembered reading about the Czech Legion in the papers. Tens of thousands of Allied troops stationed east of Moscow who had been trapped in Russia after the peace was signed. The government couldn't exactly march them out through Germany— it would violate the treaty. I thought it had been de- cided to send them out through the Pacific, via the

Trans-Siberian Railway, then sail them back to the West. But it seemed these people had something else in mind.

"It will be here in time," Arkady said languorously, stretching his long legs.

The Odessan spoke again to the man in the army uniform.

"But how can you be sure?" the man blurted out. In English. "Really, after all, the man is a criminal." Ah, of course. If Father was involved, the English wouldn't be too far behind.

"*The* criminal," Arkady corrected, in his own English.

The Englishman's face flushed in ugly patches, and his nostrils flared like a hound's scenting the wind. His accusing glance leaped at the Odessan. *Why didn't you tell me the bloody man could understand me?* "The Czechs are depending on us." His voice strained with the effort of trying not to shout. "So far as I can see, this has been just so much stalling and excuses. I think the money's long gone and this one has no intention of providing—"

"Our experiences with the baron have been entirely satisfactory," said the neat man with the black eyes.

"Excuse me, gentlemen," said Father. He'd been silent up to now, his forehead perspiring. He said it in Russian, sharply. "Due to the confidential nature of this meeting, I suggest that only essential personnel be present for the rest of this negotiation."

"We're all essential," the woman spoke up, insulted, eyes flashing. "Aren't we all at risk?"

"He means *my* personnel, Madame Karlinskaya," Arkady interrupted her, lazily looking over his shoulder at me, at Borya at the door, at Gurin cleaning his fingernails by the fireplace. "These are my most trusted staff, Dmitry Ivanovich." And to put a point on it, he kissed my hand. He might as well have put his hand up my skirt.

Father blanched white. His lips moved silently. He was fairly chewing on his beard. Finally he couldn't contain himself any longer. "I must insist. For security's sake."

"What's going on?" asked the Englishman in his native tongue.

The Odessan spoke low to the Englishman. Father wouldn't look at me, only at Arkady.

"You aren't accusing my people of being unreliable, are you, Dmitry Ivanovich?" Arkady said mildly. *Please God, make this not be happening.* "Maybe Borya here? Or Gurin? Or is it my lovely…companion?"

I could see the horror redouble in my father's face as he realized that Arkady knew exactly who I was. "That girl…" he spluttered. *Don't say it, Father. Don't.* "Is a Bolshevik spy."

My blood turned to metal.

The smile fell from Arkady's face. This was not how he imagined this game would play out, and he wasn't a man who liked being surprised. He couldn't really think I'd sought him out for the Bolsheviks, could he? That I was a plant? Not that I was in any position to go around telling secrets, locked in that room, but the idea that I had played him for a fool...not good. "Are you sure, Dmitry Ivanovich? Are you very sure?" In one swift motion, he rose and grabbed me by the scruff of the neck like a rabbit, dragged me to the fireplace to push my face inches from my father's. I could feel the fury in his grip. He would kill me. "This girl?"

I thought I would die. The anguish on my father's face. I once would have done anything to bask in his love. "I'm not," I pleaded. "I swear to you. He's holding me hostage." *Please, Father.*

Arkady pulled my hair, holding me to one side. "Is she or isn't she, Dmitry Ivanovich? Time's short. This is no light matter." He twisted my hair harder, hard enough to make my eyes water.

My father's voice was soft, thick. "God save me, yes."

"What are you waiting for? Get rid of her!" Karlinskaya shouted.

I could have screamed out *Papa!* But I didn't. Why didn't I? I wanted him to remember me just like this. I wanted him to remember that I didn't ruin him in front of all these people the way he had just ruined me.

The others were already packing up, grabbing their hats. "Nobody move," Arkady said. "Keep an eye on them," he told Borya, and hauled me out the door.

Outside, I slipped on the ice like a dog on a polished

floor as he pulled me to the middle of the yard and shoved me to my knees in the frosty dirt. "I should kill you right now. Give me one reason not to." He pulled out a revolver and pointed it at my head.

Were these to be my last minutes on earth? Was this frozen, rutted yard all of life there would ever be? I talked fast, trying to keep the tears from my voice. "How could I have imagined where you were taking me? How could I have planned this?"

"What did you tell them about me? Who did you tell?" He circled behind me. I tried to turn, but he grasped my hands and forced them behind my head.

"Nobody! If I was a spy, I'd have turned you in that first day on the islands. You'd be in the Peter and Paul Fortress by now."

"You're not convincing me." Suddenly, a hot liquid hit the top of my head, seeped down my neck and into my bandages. Urine trickled into my hair, my eyes, my mouth—hot and stinking in the cold.

"Who was I supposed to tell?" I screamed. "I am not a spy!" He came back to stand before me, but all I could see were his worn boots. "I once passed on his dinnertime conversations to a Bolshevik friend, and he found out. He threw me out of the house. Now he thinks I'm trying to get back at him. It's just an accident."

He yanked my head back by my hair. My eyes smarted. He looked like a furious ghost, like the king in *Hamlet*. "I don't believe you. He wouldn't have signed your death warrant for mere dinnertime conversation."

"He doesn't know you. What you might do..." But he didn't care to ask, either. The sight of his back turned as Arkady dragged me off—I would take that to my grave.

A man came running out of the dacha, Borya on his heels. "Von Princip!" the man shouted.

Arkady turned his head, a reflex, and it was all the opening I needed. I scrambled up and broke for the woods like a rabbit heading for its burrow. I plunged into the trees, weaving blindly among the shaggy trunks of spruce and pine. A bullet zipped past me like a giant wasp. Another zinged by. I was making my way by touch alone through the dark, stumbling over frozen hummocks. Bullets continued crashing into the trees, but there was no way Arkady could see me now, a black form in the darkness. Was he following me? I didn't stop to look.

How long did I run in those woods? Five minutes? Twenty? A year and a day? Terror stretches time—all of hell can exist in a moment. I had no idea where I was going except away from him.

The trees ended abruptly. Before me lay a field dappled with swaths of old snow, the moon like a policeman holding his searchlight aloft, raking the bare strips. The observatory glowed on the heights, its dome round among the trees. I stood, panting clouds of vapor into the icy air.

I had just this one chance. The Archangel would never grant another.

Part V

The Year One

(Spring 1918–Autumn 1918)

52 *The Observatory*

ZHILI-BUILI, ONCE UPON a time, five old people lived on a hill not so very far from the capital of Once-Had-Been. Their minds stalked through the corridors of the universe, galaxies without end. Every night the domes filled with the vast cotillion of the stars, the swirling waltz of the infinite. Comets streaked frozen tails past their five wrinkled foreheads, painting them with light. Constellations dotted their white hair and glazed their spectacles. Nebulae nested in their eyebrows. They knew where stars were born, and where they died, and why, and how. White giants studded their frail arms, yellow dwarfs gleamed in their lapels like diamond stickpins. They were the Five—*pyat'*.

The First studied the fingerprints of the stars, caught them coming and going.

The Second photographed their passports.

The Third pondered the possibilities of their planets.

The Fourth measured the distance to the end of the night.

And the Fifth, the *starushka,* she catalogued them, soup to nuts.

Like Chinese celestials, they lived above the wreckage of the world and quietly kept the heavens in their place. As with the city in the lake, the air around them chimed with the subtle music of contemplation, though here it was the music of genius, of Great Time and the secrets of creation, without boundaries or edicts.

Snow melted. Mud came and went. Leaves budded tender on the birches. The rains came, then the sun. The grass grew tall in a yard that must once have been a lawn of some majesty. The days lengthened, shortening their working hours, for they, like owls, saw better at night.

And what became of that other place? The capital of Once-Had-Been? They could see it when the day was clear. Twenty miles away, no more. But to them it was of less consequence than dust on the telescope's lens. Mausers and collectivized flats, the fate of the bourgeoisie, the crush in the train stations, *Kommunist* and holdups in snack bars, madmen with their strings. How much better to keep one's eyes on the sky.

The domes shone in the moonlight like the breasts of women. I had followed that gleam to the only unlocked doors in all of Russia, the doors to the house of the stars. I had to find a hole and jump down it. But this was no hole. It was the portal of heaven.

An Ancient stood at the top of the steel stairs under the vast central dome, gazing down through the eyepiece of a mighty telescope into the night sky, when the girl, the girl without a tongue, found her way in. Voiceless at the bottom of the stairs, she waited, still steaming from her run, a girl with great sad-clown eyes. Her ears rang from gunshot blasts. Finally he heard her heavy breathing, noticed her down there in the gloaming. He closed his notebook and descended, slow, majestic in velvet skullcap, unkempt white beard, coat and gloves. Time finally slowed. She could feel her heart, steadying. All around her, busts of famous astronomers gazed down from their circle in the dim hall.

The Ancient gestured for her to follow him down a cold marble corridor to a door. Inside a warm room nestled among rugs and furniture, even a straggly plant, glowed four more ancient faces, their spectacles flashing under the glaciers of furrowed brows.

"We have a guest," said the First.

The Second turned on his wheeled chair. He had a beard like a double ax and was holding a photographic slide and a magnifying glass between his fingers. "Oh Lord, what next?"

"Are you from the village?" asked the Third, the only clean-shaven one, wearing a knitted hat. He had a sprig of green in his hand, though it was too early for green. "Has something happened?"

The girl eyed the pattern in the rug, pomegranates and deer. Bukhara. So many lives she could have had.

"What do you want then?" asked the Fourth, frail and cantankerous, hunched in on himself, pencil in hand, a slide rule. "Speak up, girl!"

But the girl discovered that her voice had been taken

from her. She saw herself as if from a distance, very small. Small and insignificant, and what could she have to say that would make any difference? She had lost her tongue and felt no urge to find it. Better to be a stray cat, a donkey, nobody at all.

"You're frightening her," said the Fifth, the woman, who rose from her thick ledgers and approached her as one would a lost dog, slowly, speaking softly. She put her arm around the silent visitor. "Are you all right, *milaya*? What's happened? Can you tell us?"

The girl, the lost dog. She pulled off the bandage on her right hand and showed the Fifth the wide swath of cut and seared flesh. Her passport.

"Nikolai Gerasimovich?" the old woman called in a trembling voice.

The Third came close and studied the hand. "I can get some iodine on it, but it seems to be healing."

"What happened to you, *dorogaya moya?*" the *starushka* asked her, so kindly that the girl began to cry.

"She can't stay here, if that's what she's thinking," said the Fourth. "It's not a home for mental defectives."

"Speak for yourself, Valentin Vladimirovich," said the First, the starman with the velvet skullcap, stroking his long moustache contemplatively.

The girl, the mental defective, pulled the *starushka* out into the hall, struggled out of her coat. Her hands flew to the buttons of her dress. She had to show her, the woman had to see. The old one tried to move away, so the girl hurried, pulled the woolen fabric from her shoulder, tearing at the dressings.

When the old woman saw the bandages, the terrible poetry, she understood that whatever had happened to the girl, whatever had chased her to the observatory's heights, she could not be sent back down. The girl fell to her knees and kissed the *starushka*'s hand, kissed the hem of her rusty black dress, her laced boots. The girl wept wordlessly. Words had flown from her like birds fleeing a fire, an explosion. The old woman pulled the girl to her feet. "Don't worry, *devushka*. Nobody will send you away." The visitor, the mute, clung to her. With much patting and clucking, the old woman sat her down on a bench in the cold hall, lined with portraits of men with telescopes and astrolabes and compasses, then went back into the room, and closed the door. She heard their voices, discussing, arguing. Who was she? How could they feed her? Rations were bad enough as they were. But sitting there on the hard bench as before the headmistress's door, the girl vowed she would not be sent away. There was nowhere else in the world for her, not a square inch in the world of Once-Had-Been that would permit her feet to rest. Only in the stars, among these Ancients, this precious, silent island drifting above the world could she find safety.

The old woman returned, gestured for the girl to follow. Back in their warm study, the Second had prepared a small slate, as one would use for schoolchildren, upon which he'd written the alphabet. "Can you read?" he asked. He pointed to his eyes, then the slate. The girl didn't want to be dismissed as an idiot. She needed them. She had to be seen as useful. She was young, she was strong, she could read. She nodded.

"What's your name?"

She began to point to letters. *M*. The *starushka* smiled triumphantly. *A. R.* "Mar," said the old woman.

Impatient, the Fourth began to guess. "Maria." She shook her head. "Marta. Martina."

The Second chimed in over the slate. "Marina?"

God, no. Anyone but her.

"Marusya?" said the Fifth.

Marusya. It meant bitter. Yes, that was her name. She allowed them to baptize her like Achilles in the black waters of the Styx. Leaving only the heel. She wondered what that would prove to be. But for the rest, sealed in darkness, Marusya be her name.

Thus the girl, the visitor, the vagabond, scarred and renounced, stepped away from all that she had been. Left herself behind like a glove dropped in a train station. What she found was—silence. She wrapped it around herself like an Orenburg wedding-ring shawl. So light, so soft, so warm. Her life now could pass through a wedding ring.

Marusya woke early. Collected their firewood, breaking it from branches before she found a few precious tools still left in the shed—the empty pegs evidence of a larger store, vanished now. To the credit of the

thieves, or someone else's foresight, the departing gardeners or Red Guards hadn't stolen everything. A couple of spades and hoes hung scattered, a rusty saw, a
hatchet, an ax, a large hammer, and a wedge. Most important, the observatory's well was good and deep, the
water blessedly clean—it didn't have to be boiled to
drink! She could not imagine such luxury. She washed
their clothes, took their ration cards down to the village, and walked the mile back up, their food on her
back, bread and potatoes and herring, deflecting the
prying of the housewives with shrugs. She did
everything she could to justify her presence there, ate
as little as possible.

The place had been terribly neglected. The servants
and most of their colleagues had left after October's
battle on the Pulkovo Heights. The rest left when Bolshevik miracles failed to manifest themselves. The girl
swept and scrubbed, sewed underwear, darned socks,
boiled sheets, dragged bedding out to the yard, hung
the quilts and beat and beat them. The dust could have
spawned a new galaxy.

The days warmed, and one by one she seated the
Ancients outside in the new wildflowers and washed
and trimmed their hair and their beards to their
specifications—the First liked his in the style of the
tsar, of medium length and gently rounded at the bottom. The Second favored his double ax heads. The
Third liked his hair trimmed short, but shaved himself.
The Fourth was so ancient that his beard was spare and

wiry, like a goat's, but he would permit only half an inch of trimming. Soft old hair, light as dandelion floss in her fingers. The *starushka*, Ludmila Vasilievna, practically wept with pleasure as the girl washed her hair in the yard and combed it and let it dry in the sun, then brushed and braided it for her. Their mute servant cut their hornlike toenails with a pair of scissors the First Ancient kept in a leather case only slightly older than the moon. The girl saw many things they could have sold to make their lives more bearable, but it never occurred to them. In many ways, she felt these Ancients were her children, and she their young mother.

They gathered at moonrise like moths. The Third had made yellow dandelion wine they enjoyed before the evening meal. Marusya served them sorrel soup and spring onions and rationed bread and fed upon their learned conversations as they ate in measured bites, drank their thin soup. They spoke of colleagues in far-flung universities, at Freiburg and Berlin, at Greenwich and Cambridge, of discoveries in mathematics and physics and chemistry. They bemoaned the lack of contemporary publications. "When this is over," said the First, "we're going to be as antique as knee britches." They made jokes about former students. Marusya remained quiet, alert, unobtrusive, and as adoring as a good German shepherd. She would have killed for them, she would have laid down her life.

They explained to her over their yellow wine that there had been scores of astronomers and other staff members living here before the revolution, but alas—sighs all around—the younger people preferred life "down below," where they could continue their careers at the university. "Their wives and children hated the isolation," said the Second, Boris Osipovich, "when travel became difficult—"

"Impossible," said the Fourth, Valentin Vladimirovich, in his high, cracked, crabby voice. "Who could go back and forth five times a week? We used to have an automobile—remember that?"

"We had to choose," said the First, Aristarkh Apollonovich, the director of the observatory. "The university or this." He sipped his yellow wine, stroked his moustache. "Most chose to stay in Petrograd with their students and continue teaching. Only we *stariki* preferred our researches, though it wasn't the easiest choice."

"It was for me," said Ludmila Vasilievna. "It's too awful down there now."

Marusya nodded her agreement.

The girl fell into the rhythm of the observatory. She liked it best when Aristarkh Apollonovich permitted her to climb the metal stairs with him and gaze upon some spectacle of the cosmos. The double star in the constellation Ursa Major, which the great Arab astronomers called the Horse and Rider. The Moving Group of stars in the Big Dipper—her silent tongue ran over the shapes of their names: Alioth, Mizar, Merak, Phad, Megrez, Alcor—like a stable of Arabian stallions...all moving together toward Sagittarius. Which showed that this constellation was not, like most, a mere appearance—stars superimposed in the same sector of the sky—they were in fact related. A family, born together around three hundred million years ago. The girl so loved to hear numbers like that, to contemplate the vast age of the universe. It somehow made life on earth seem less desperate.

This old man had been at Pulkovo Observatory for years. His specialty, the fingerprints of the stars: spectra and motion. He trained the telescope on great Jupiter and the glowing rings of Saturn. "See those rings? They don't turn like a phonograph recording," he said, spreading his fingers and rotating his hand. "Each ring moves at a different rate. This indicates they're made of a flow of small objects. We discovered that here." He stroked the wing of his moustache in a way that made her realize it was he who had made the discovery. This very man, the First, who gave her a guided tour of the seas and mountains of the moon, who showed her rising Venus and red Mars.

Sometimes he told her of his wife, who had died, and his son and grandchildren, who lived in Brazil—a distance more than light-years away now.

Ludmila Vasilievna continued to be her favorite. She brushed the old woman's hair out every day and helped her into her bed after a long night's cataloguing of the stars. She massaged her old feet and hands, which tended to arthritis, and brought her a cup of chamomile tea so that she would sleep soundly through the morning.

But soon Marusya discovered that the Third Ancient, Nikolai Gerasimovich, was to be her main charge. He was the one who actually needed an assistant in his work. A physicist and chemist who specialized in the composition of atmospheres, he was a passionate astro-botanist. She had never heard of such a thing. What plants could there possibly be in space? "When we travel, it's not going to be a day trip to Novgorod, Marusya," he explained, interpreting her quizzical expression. "We'll have to take them with us. They'll help us breathe, and feed us, and filter the air. And when we land, we'll have to have something to start with, won't we?"

She almost wept. This learned man really thought they were going to the stars. It had never occurred to her how optimistic scientists were. He spoke as if he would be on those ships himself, heading out into the cosmos, though he must have known that he would likely not live to see even the return of hot water. She followed him around like a little dog as he gave elaborate instructions on how to tend his plants—if you could call them that. Most weren't even plants, just lichens and mosses and foul-smelling algae growing in washtubs.

Marusya could only imagine what a certain Petrograd speculator would say about this childlike fascination with mucky goo. "The Aztecs grew this very same algae centuries before Columbus," said Nikolai Gerasimovich. "It's the fastest-growing protein source on earth. They grew it on vast lakes, dried it in blocks, and ate it when food was scarce." He gave her a chip off a cake. "Try it." Without hesitating, she bit into it. It tasted like dirt and pond scum, but no worse than the dried deer pellets she'd eaten as a child, thinking them candies. She chewed and swallowed it nevertheless, not wanting to spit it out, since he was so proud of it. "Good?" She nodded. He laughed and ate some as well, chewing it up. "You'd do well to get used to it. We might have to eat this next winter if rations continue to erode and the garden proves insufficient. If only we had better laboratories... I'm working with simulations of various atmospheres—ammonia, sulfur. So much knowledge has been lost about the medicinal and nutritional value of substances we would never consider as food sources. Insects, for example."

She glanced over at his screen-covered terrariums hopping with beetles, and realized in horror that he was growing them as food. He laughed when he saw her face. "They're not bad, really. I learned to eat them in Java. They multiply at a wonderful rate in warmth and damp. The latter we already have, but the former..." He seemed positively nostalgic about entomological cuisine. Professor Nikolai Gerasimovich Pomogayush... Marusya wondered, if she had met him at a party in the capital of Once-Had-Been instead of at the Pulkovo Observatory, would she have thought him venerable or mad? "These insects, this algae, lichen, and fungus—this is most likely the fodder that will take us to the stars, my dear. Not asparagus and beef-steak."

To the stars, that was the important thing here. This was what they thought about day and night: what lay beyond. They wanted to catch the stars in their beds, know how they danced, what held them and what forced them to blow apart. Stars in their matrix——how hot, how cold, how far, how old. They wondered about the sense of it all, the physical laws that weren't opinion, that weren't voted upon. There were no commissars here.

Every so often, the Third asked about Marusya's past, what had brought her here that night in early spring. Whether she had ever spoken, if she had always been mute. But she simply ignored the questions. "You've had an education, though, haven't you? You understand what we say. Every word, I'd wager. What happened to you?" But a shrug was the only reply he would get for his trouble.

They were lucky to have Nikolai Gerasimovich. Unlike the more theoretical physicists and mathematicians, he understood the needs of poor earth-bound bodies. He showed her the seeds he'd saved—cucumber and carrot, dill, onion sets and beets and even some seed potatoes in sand. He proudly showed her where his currant bushes and raspberries grew—their green buds had already begun to swell. He was

the one who'd given Ludmila Vasilievna an herbal oint-
ment for Marusya's wounds. He showed her how to
plant seeds in flats indoors and keep them watered under glass.

Now her silence had become a shimmering sari. It
was both beautiful and comforting not to have to reply
to people when they spoke to her. It energized her, left
her with hands and actions alone. She would not have
to lie if she didn't speak, she would not have to explain
or confess. How simple life was that way. Everything
that was inside her stayed inside. Nothing spilled out.
She realized how much of herself she normally leaked
away, gave away to anyone and everyone. Now she listened, companionably, and worked. There was a poetry
in it.

When it grew warm enough, she took their seedlings
outside to bask in the lengthening days. Under the demanding eye of the Third, she dug the garden. It would
be a big one. She didn't like it when he tried to work
alongside her. What if he had a heart attack? A stroke?
She preferred it when he sat in the shade and explained
about the varying atmospheres on other planets while
she did the bulk of the digging.

Silence rinsed her bitter soul as clear as their well water, silence and starlight. The garden began to grow.
The observatory stood above the plain, untouched as
a holy city in a lake, and she lived safely at the secret
heart of her own Svetloyar, and cared for her five
beloveds.

53 *The Clinic in the Trees*

IN ANY EARTHLY IDYLL, time and events will inevitably
intrude, and so they did, in the form of a young astronomer and his family: a wife, a pretty but ill-looking
blonde, and two children, a girl of seven, a boy, maybe
five, his round head shaved against lice. The astronomer carried the boy to the house of the stars.
Marusya met them at the door. "I'm Mistropovich. Ro-
dion Karlovich," he said, hoisting his son higher on his
shoulder, that round head lolling. "I used to work here.
Are they still here—Aristarkh Apollonovich? Nikolai
Gerasimovich?"

The way the woman looked—dull-eyed—
frightened Marusya. She thought of the Five, the Ancients, how frail they were. She was afraid of these new
people. Not for herself but for her charges. Nothing
must harm them. Not these visitors. She felt as protective as any peasant nanny as she stood in the doorway,
barring their path.

"Please," he said. "Just tell Aristarkh Apollonovich
I'm here."

Reluctantly, Marusya stepped back and allowed them
to enter the great hall, showing them to a bench, indicating with her hand for them to wait there. "Water,"
the woman said, "for the love of God."

It was late in the day. The Five were already gathering in the salon for the evening's cordials. How could she tell them, *Beware, beware!* She went to Pomogayush, caught his sleeve. "What is it, Marusya? What's happened?"

She mimed the knock on the door. Showed the number four on her fingers. Their heights, small, medium and tall. And that two of them were ill—lines under their eyes for the dark circles. He rose with alacrity. "Somebody's here. Something's wrong." And the others followed him into the hall. She tried to slow the others, waving them off, tugging at Ludmila Vasilievna's sleeve, but they wouldn't heed her.

"Mistropovich!" the Third shouted. And then they were out of Marusya's hands, running to the strangers, embracing them, O Holy Theotokos! Bringing them into their parlor! The woman collapsed onto the sofa, the boy by her side. The gray-eyed daughter looked at Marusya curiously.

"I'm so sorry." The man was weeping. "I just didn't know where else to go." They patted him and made conciliatory sounds, even Marusya could see how they loved him. He took the elders to one side and explained something to them very quietly but she could see his panic, their solicitous concern.

"Of course you should have come, of course," said the First.

"We would have expected nothing less," said the Second.

"Marusya, bring them some water," said Ludmila Vasilievna.

The sick woman and her sick son terrified her. She wanted to throw them into the yard and bar the door, but she did what she was told and dashed to the kitchen to bring them their water.

The Third met her in the hall, as she was returning with a pitcher and glasses. "Marusya, listen to me. It's cholera. Do you understand what that is?"

Cholera! Why in God's name had they come here with it?

"There's an epidemic in Petrograd. They were lucky to get here."

The water. Cholera was transmitted in water. Sanitation in Petrograd had all but vanished. The plumbing was broken, people had been using the courtyards as latrines all winter, and then with the spring melt...oh God. The drinking water came right out of the canals, and water ran just inches below street level. Dead horses, garbage, no soap, people shitting everywhere, then pumping the same water. Everyone was in danger. The whole city could be infected by now. How many people—a thousand? Ten thousand? She did not want to think of the horror unfolding in the capital of Once-Had-Been. But what about the Five?

"They're all right for now. It's only contagious through contact with bodily fluids," said the Third. "Not breathing or touching them. Understand? It's the dehydration that kills them. They need water, and we will have to keep everything perfectly clean, especially our hands. Their wastes need to be sequestered— away from the water and the vegetable garden. God knows what must be going on down in the city. Are you ready for this?"

She nodded vigorously. She wanted them out of the observatory, silently begged with tugs and gestures for the Third to let her bring them out of doors. She led him to the spot where she often slept, in a pleasant grove of trees, away from the well, away from the garden. He concurred, and the rest agreed. They brought cots into the clearing. The husband washed and gave the boy water with salt, while Marusya helped the wife hold her cup, dipped the precious liquid between her chapped lips. "I'm so sorry," the father kept saying. "People are dying in the streets—you can't imagine. The hospitals are no better than giant latrines."

Each patient was assigned a bucket and a pillow. The husband dug a pit for their waste and lined it with pine boughs. He held the wife's hand, stroked the son's shaved head. "Don't be frightened of the girl. Her name is Marusya. She'll be your nurse while you're so sick."

"I don't like her," the little boy said. "Don't leave, Papa."

"I have to. I have work to do, and someone has to look after Katinka. But Mama's here, and Marusya will take care of you. She doesn't speak, but she can hear."

The boy started to cry, and the mother, who was also

weak, reached across from her cot and held his hand. "Where's my brave little boy?" And Marusya remembered another little boy, how scared he was whenever he was ill. She found it hard to be angry with these people for their illness. Now that they were in the pines and not in the observatory, she could find her pity again.

Within hours, their symptoms worsened. They trembled, they vomited. Marina would have been disgusted and helpless with pity, but Marusya stoically supported them to the pit, where they shat so loosely that it might have been urine. She wiped them on pages of a thick German astronomical journal, then washed her own hands in water she kept boiling over a fire pit the husband had dug and filled with wood. The wind was sweet in the pines, but she had never seen such sick people. She washed their hands and her own until they puckered. The Third Ancient brought a host of supplies to her clinic in the trees—a glass straw for each of them so dirty fingers wouldn't reinfect the water as they drank. He brought her a little bottle of chlorine to add to the patients' drinking water, just in case.

"This is food for you," he said, giving her a packet in paper. "Don't touch it with your hands, if you can avoid it. Just to be safe." He tucked a fork and a knife in her pocket, wrapped in a napkin, then gave her a rag and a stack of towels. "Don't touch anything with your hands. Wrap your hands when you use the pump."

Marusya kept the cauldron of water boiling day and

night. Carried pails of clean water back to their sad camp. Pomogayush brought salt and a clutch of desiccated sugar beets from last year's crop to mash into the water and help fight dehydration. He'd imagined they might take the beets to the stars, not to a makeshift clinic in the trees.

When the patients could no longer make it to the latrine, and all the sheets were soiled, and the oilcloth over the cots just too hard to keep clean, she made pallets of long grass and sweet ferns and fennel on the ground, and hour after hour sat next to them and forced warm, slightly sweet, slightly salty water into their dry mouths. She was stubborn as a donkey when they waved her away. She held the buckets under their mouths for them to vomit into, then forced more water into them. Marina would have become discouraged, but Marusya would not be dissuaded by their pleas, their vomiting, their moaning, their shitting themselves, or their shivering and sweating as they lay on the ferns and pine needles, which she periodically gathered and piled up for burning. The boy told her about the dog they had to leave behind, about his friend who got sick first, about how he was going to go up in a rocket ship. He wept and asked for Mama. She moved them close together so the woman could hold his hand, though she could not lift her own head. The father came to their hideous camp several times during the day. She made him wash and wash. He had to think of his girl. He had to think of the Five. His boy and his wife were in the hands of Fate now.

They shat into the grasses, and Marusya raked them and put down new. They shook in the warm summer air and vomited into their buckets, which she rinsed with boiling water and chlorine, then threw the contents into the woods. When they were done they lay on the straw and moaned so pitifully she wished she were deaf as well as mute. Often she couldn't decide which end to serve. Each time she gave them more salted water with mashed beet and tried not to think about the fate of the city. No medicines, no clean water, the sick dying by the thousands. And what would become of all those bodies? What of her mother, Avdokia, Anton, Mina and the Katzevs?

The nights were warm and brief. The crickets droned, mosquitoes bit. She dozed but did not sleep, watched over her patients like the moon. She didn't drink except with her own glass straw. She ate bread and the cucumbers she and the Third had grown, all with a fork and knife. She slept with her hands in her pockets for fear she would touch her mouth in her sleep, and dreamed of the wards and sickrooms of the capital of Once-Had-Been.

Three days she worked at them, three days of terrible struggle. She had no thoughts, only images. Sunlight through the trees. The explosive birth of stars. Her own hands, cutting grass with a sickle she'd found, sharpening it on a whetstone produced by the Third. The stars of the wildflowers she sprinkled on the grass between the woman and the boy so they could look across the flowers as they gazed into each other's faces.

On the fourth morning, the husband stood on the brink of the lawn, looking in at their stand of pines. The wife was sleeping, holding the dead boy's hand. Marusya stood by her own cot and waited. She had nothing to say. He came closer. She mimed "sleep" and pointed to his pretty wife.

"And him?" he whispered.

He'd been convulsing, become too weak to drink. The water just seeped out from between his lips. Then it was over.

Have you heard a man sob for love of a child? Have you seen his tears? She stood aside and let him crouch between them. He'd studied the stars, but everything he loved was lying right here on this earth.

The summer passed. The visitors stayed on, waiting to return to the capital of Once-Had-Been. The wife sat on the steps of the observatory as Marusya worked in the garden. Sometimes she sang, sad songs. She had the loveliest voice. The little girl helped pull weeds and told Marusya her nursery rhymes. The wind turned fresh, the days shortened. The husband tried to persuade the Five to return with him and his diminished family. There were classes to teach, students who would share their rations with their professors. The epidemic had surely passed. Marusya walked amid the rows of fattening cabbages, the potatoes not yet dug, the onions and ferny carrots, the cucumbers too numerous to count, the melons done. It was time to start pickling and hunting for mushrooms. What would she do if the Ancients left? Where would she go? She would have to stay on, alone.

The old woman, the Fifth, walked with Marusya along the verge of the woods, told her they had no intention of going back to the university. They had their work to do here. Perhaps now others would return to the observatory. It was safer up here, though it would be a hard winter. They sent the young family on their way, watched them walking away down the hill—the man, the woman, and the child in the autumn light. Marusya felt as old as the Five. It was such a danger to love people. Nobody ever told you about that.

54 *The Crows*

NOW IT WAS HARVEST time, the ripest time of the year, when the wheat on the plain grew golden and the sky was the cornflower of heaven. It was then that their heaven grew dark with an invasion of dirty, glossy crows, wings studded with lice. They landed clumsily upon this island, crumpling the maps of stars, jabbing their beaks into the corners, chasing the Ancients like furies.

What were they looking for? Weapons? Hoarded food? The Grand Duke Michael?

Counterrevolution.

Blood.

They inspected the labor cards, interrogated the Five, collected their research in messy handfuls. They had no idea what they were doing. One of them struck Aristarkh Apollonovich—a man with a crater on the moon that bore his name—in the face when he tried to interfere. Of course they found the girl Marusya. No labor card. No papers. No name. It was not permitted to have no name. To those who occupied the leather jackets, having no name was not a personal matter. It indicated an attempt to circumvent the state. In this, the revolution was no better than what had come before.

"Who are you?" asked a hollow-cheeked thug.

"She doesn't speak," Ludmila Vasilievna said. "There's something wrong with her."

The astronomer knew much about the stars, but she knew little about men. It was a terrible thing to tell a tough with a pistol and Chekist arrogance that someone could not speak. That person would become a challenge, like a virgin who must be tested and tested again.

The local political police were looking to make an arrest. In the end they took three, calling them spies: Aristarkh Apollonovich, Nikolai Gerasimovich, and sad-eyed Boris Osipovich along with a couple of boxes of papers whose value they could not begin to imagine. And Marusya, who had no papers at all. They took them down the hill in a wagon, leaving fragile Valentin

Vladimirovich behind, and Ludmila Vasilievna, who they thought was the housekeeper. "Water the garden," Nikolai Gerasimovich called out over his shoulder. "Pick the cucumbers and get them into salt. And water the algae if you can."

Aristarkh Apollonovich sat in the wagon with great dignity as Nikolai Gerasimovich rubbed his face, worrying about his plants, his work. Boris Osipovich winced at every jolting of the wagon down the hot, dusty road. Crows flew by overhead. The grain was ripening. Marusya sat very still next to Aristarkh Apollonovich. "They've searched before but they've never been so aggressive," he said in a low voice. "I'm afraid something's happened. We should have paid more attention. We forget about the outside world to our peril." Such galaxies inside these three weathered heads jouncing down the road behind a mismatched pair of horses. What light would be lost if they were snuffed out.

Three of the crudest Chekists Marusya had ever seen brought them to a house in the village. They prodded the Ancients out. "Not you," said one with a low brutish brow, and shoved Marusya back into the wagon. She watched as the astronomers disappeared through a door around which stock flowers grew, pink and white. *Levkoi*. Nikolai Gerasimovich turned and waved sadly, and Marusya waved back, holding her skirt down with the other hand where her guard was trying to lift it with the barrel of his pistol. He was probably the village hooligan before the Cheka recruited him.

They unloaded Marusya at what looked like it had once been a small store. Inside, the brutish tough and another rural thug set to their business. "Who are you? Where are your papers? Where are you from?" They pulled her hair. They twisted her arm. "What's your name? Say something!" One of them waved a revolver in her face. It wasn't a Mauser, just some old and battered thing left over from the war before last. She could smell the cleaning oil. "Say something!" Beetle-Brow slapped her while the one with hollow cheeks smoked a cigarette. "We know you can talk, so stop pretending." Her hair, bunched in his fist, as he screamed into her throbbing face and threatened her with his fist, huge as Jupiter rising. "What's your name?!"

Her name.

Her name.

My name.

A curse.

A name.

Bitter was my name.

He punched me in the stomach. Bastard! I doubled over, gasping for breath. His knee to my back, he forced me to the floor and lifted my head by the hair. "You're going to tell me, aren't you? Who're you working for? The British?" Knocked my forehead against the wooden planks. My brains swirled. He kicked me as I curled around myself, got me in the ribs. He had just lifted my skirt over my head and ripped down my bloomers when someone came in with heavier boots—had he heard me scream? Or maybe it was just luck. "Vovka, you pig fucker. Put it away. The commissar's here." Beetle-Brow rose, kicked me again—in the ass, angry to be denied his final payoff, and left me with my unintentional savior.

I rolled over on my back, trying to breathe through my bleeding nose, my aching ribs. Had he broken one? *Vovka, I will remember you. Someday I will return the favor.* The one with the hollow cheeks returned, yanked me to my feet by one arm, my bloomers falling around my knees, opened a trapdoor in the floor revealing a steep wooden stairway, and pushed me down it. I would have fallen all the way but I caught the rail in time. The door dropped shut above me.

The place must have been the cellar of a grocery store or maybe a vodka shop—low ceiling, dirt floor. Light came through a dirty window up at street level framing the proletarian footwear and bast shoes of passersby. Three other women already sat on the benches. I recognized two of them, a plump woman who worked in the bakery where Marusya collected the Ancients' bread and an old *baba* I'd seen in the village. A third, a younger woman in a summer dress, sat hunched in the corner quietly weeping, holding herself around the waist. I was grateful that Ludmila Vasilievna had been spared this.

"Got you, too, did they? Poor unlucky girl," clucked the bakery woman, helping me over to the bench, supporting me as I sat. I wondered why she was here. Speculating? Shorting the customers, as people complained to one another in the queue? I lowered myself to the bench. Every movement was excruciating. I sat half curled, wrapping myself in what was left of my silence. I kicked off my torn bloomers, there was nothing to be done with them. The woman used the corners of her apron to wipe my face, the blood from my nose. "Those Makushkins. Pig thieves. If your pig is missing you can count on it that a Makushkin's behind it. And now they've got a license."

"Someone shot the big boss," said the old *baba* from the other bench, working her toothless gums. "We're in for it now."

Which big boss? Some rural commissar? Lenin? Could someone have shot Lenin? I was dying to ask but I couldn't suddenly reveal myself as capable of speech or they'd think me a spy indeed. I kept my head tilted back, trying to stop the blood from flowing. I could taste the salty thickness down my throat.

"To think, I voted for them," said the baker, spitting on the dirt floor. Her eyes were very blue. "Lord have mercy on us." Both women crossed themselves.

The third woman moaned and whimpered. Young and pretty, her hair coming out of its braid, she sat with her arms across her belly, rocking herself, and I suspected worse had happened to her than the kicks and blows I'd suffered. Probably the fate I had been about to receive before the commissar showed up. I'd been lucky, despite my throbbing eye and aching ribs—I'd only lost my underwear. And what of the Ancients? Would they beat Aristarkh Apollonovich, the man who'd discovered the composition of Saturn's rings? Torture Nikolai Gerasimovich?

In the afternoon, the trapdoor opened and the other pig thief, Hollow Cheeks, called down for me. "You. Red." I climbed the steep steps as I would the stairs to a gallows. Across the dusty road, in the village tavern, a moustached man in tinted spectacles sat at a plank table that smelled of old beer. The commissar. He wasn't from around here. He was neat and looked intelligent and efficient. Papers lay piled before him. The pig thief shoved me forward. There was nowhere to sit.

The commissar regarded me wearily. Would he notice the city cut of my clothes, worn as they were? "How did you come to stay at the observatory, *devushka*? Who brought you there?"

I just stared at his lips, that moustache. I, Marina, had no trouble cringing at the sight of the Chekist and at the hollow-checked pig thief behind me, but Marusya had no idea what they wanted. I clung to the last shreds of her, a poor girl bewildered by such an important man, not understanding any of this.

"We can make things very unpleasant," said the commissar. "Why do you have no papers? Where are you from?"

Marusya's silence soured on my tongue. Her raiment was already in shreds. She was half naked. It would be every bit as easy to kill a silent girl as a verbal one. *Merde.* I had to end this charade. But how? People so disliked being mocked. I gripped the edge of the table and leaned forward, opened my mouth as if trying to give birth to speech. Or vomit. The commissar instinctively sat back. "I...I..."

He leaned forward to catch my revelation, as if expecting miracles. Suddenly I wanted to laugh at the way he was watching me. But he would not have taken it well.

"Pe...Pe...Pe..."

"What's she trying to say?" he asked Hollow Cheeks.

"She's an idiot," Hollow Cheeks said.

"Pe...te...te..."

"Petrushka? Petrovka?" The commissar tried to help me along.

I shook my head. "Pe..." I stuttered more forcefully. "Pe Pe PePe..." My eyes were full of realistic tears. And I pointed, jabbing my finger. North.

"Petrograd! You're from Petrograd!" The commissar slapped the poor gouged plank of a table like a man who guesses the clue in charades. "She's from Petrograd!" he told the pig thieves. "Do you write? Can. You. Write?" he repeated, enunciating each word, miming a hand, writing.

I just let the tears stream, thinking of the Second

and his slate, and my throbbing eye, and my painful ribs, and what could possibly save me. The precious Five—whatever I did, I must not be forced to implicate them. These people had to leave the stars alone. They must not be allowed to wipe their Cheka asses on the sky.

I nodded.

The commissar took a piece of paper and a pencil that looked like it had been sharpened with an ax and set it before me. I knelt to write. How wrong I was to think I could hide myself away out here in my silence, in my absolute service. I'd confused the observatory with the city in the lake. Alas…it was true, after all—I would not hear those bells again, not on this earth. Tucking my tongue into the corner of my mouth, I wrote my SOS, my message in a bottle. Hoping the handwriting would suggest that of a simply educated rural housekeeper, I wrote the words— *Varvara Razrushenskaya.*

"Is this your name?" he asked.

I shook my head violently, tapped on the name several times, and after it added the fatal acronym, the black crow wings.

Cheka.

He looked at the paper for the longest time, lost in thought. He'd been so happy to have solved the first puzzle…would he understand? Or would I be delivered into the hands of the pig thieves again? Maybe pressured into saying something about the Five? He took off his glasses and rubbed them on his handkerchief. His eyes were without any light or emotion. Outside the high window, a maple tree was losing its leaves, bright scraps floating through the afternoon air. A single leaf hovered impossibly in midair, twirling and twirling, glowing, lit from behind. A small flame of hope that my message was understood. He put the paper in his pocket and nodded at Hollow Cheeks to take me away.

55 *Red Terror*

I WAS SUMMONED FROM that dirt-floored cellar at dawn. A shabby Chekist I recognized from the observatory search marched me to a police van waiting in the unpaved road. A dull rain was falling and the air smelled of ozone as it hit the dusty earth. Guards opened the back doors. The van was packed tight with prisoners. I couldn't imagine there being room for any more bodies. "The tram's not made of rubber," a man in the back shouted out, and a few laughed. It's what we said when the trams were full in Petrograd. I tried to keep my skirt down as the guards shoved me in, my drawers having been turned to rags by the pig thief. Before the doors clanged shut, I could see that all the prisoners had been beaten in one way or another. A fleeting impression of black eyes, bloody noses, cuts, and contusions. But no Ancients. I didn't know whether that was a good thing or not.

"Where are you from?" I asked the bulk next to me, a man who smelled of coarse wool and tobacco. It felt so strange to speak after my long summer of silence. It felt dangerous, like a vow I was breaking.

"Tsarskoe Selo," he said.

"Detskoe Selo," someone nearby corrected him in the close, thick, fear-tinged darkness. Ah yes, the re-naming of the world. The tsar's village had become "children's village," in preparation no doubt for its re-purposing as a site for orphanages and schools.

The prisoners smoked and talked as we rattled along. There were no guards back here and I was dying to know if the rumor was true. "They say someone shot the big boss—which one?" I asked.

"She doesn't know?" another voice said.

"Someone tried to kill Lenin," said the man in the wool jacket at my side. "A woman."

"Botched it, too," said a higher-voiced man, and there was a flash of a match, a cigarette, a narrow face, a shock of blond hair.

My head reeled. What would happen if Lenin died? What would happen to the revolution?

"They assassinated the head of the Petrograd Cheka, too," said my neighbor. "Deader than dead. Some stu-dent shot him in Palace Square."

Uritsky! Varvara's boss.

"I wish the woman had been so lucky," said the

smoker over his bright coal. "Now they think there's a giant counterrevolutionary conspiracy. They're rounding up everyone with a pulse. It's been going on for weeks."

I could not imagine what was happening in the kingdom of Once-Had-Been, but I was afraid I was about to find out. The van swayed over the ruts in the road. At times the wheels spun in the mud. "Are they taking us to Petrograd?"

"They're taking us nowhere!" A woman's voice rang out from the back of the van, urgent, edged with hysteria. "Don't you see? They're going to stop somewhere and shoot us all!"

"Why would they bother putting us in a van for that?" argued the smoker. "They could have just shot us back there and saved the gasoline."

My neighbor predicted they were taking us to Petrograd. "Most of these are hostages," he said to me under the rumble of the engine. "Families of White officers. What use is a dead hostage?"

"White?" I had an image of men bled white, shuffling through the snow.

"White Army. Where've you been living, *devushka,* a henhouse?" My companion made a scornful sound. "The counterrevolutionaries. They're massing in Siberia and down in the Don." Volodya and his Volunteers. "Country's dividing up like a red-and-white cow, with the English in the north getting ready to milk us dry."

It was all making horrible sense now, the commissar's questions, everything that had been said in the dacha the night of my death. Father, Karlinsky, the British. *He's in Vologda with the English.* Invasion, counterrevolution, money for the Czech Legion. "What's happened with the Czechs?"

"That's how it started. A clash on the Trans-Siberian. Trotsky tried to disarm them and it backfired. Instead of going east, the Czechs came west and took every town on the line. The counterrevolutionaries rushed out of the woodwork to join them." The van careened and threw my neighbor right onto me. I shrieked and pushed him off. "Sorry, sorry." He scrambled to right himself. "Forgive me. I wasn't taking advantage." I immediately judged him to be ten years older than I'd first imagined. It was a relief to realize that the "victim sign" on my forehead wasn't visible in the dark.

"Why do they toy with us?" wailed the woman. "Why can't they just deliver the coup de grâce?"

"Akh, would you shut up?" someone called out.

"I'll ask them to stop if you want, lady," said the smoker. "If you want them to shoot you, I'm sure they'll oblige."

Despite what my neighbor said, I, too, kept waiting for the van to halt. To be rousted out into a field, told to turn our backs...a couple of times we slowed, and the woman shrieked and sobbed. It was terrible—panic was contagious. I couldn't help thinking of having escaped Arkady von Princip only to have my short stupid life ended by a Cheka bullet, my head exploding like a watermelon fallen from a cart. Sinking in the field to my knees, then toppling over, my naked ass exposed to the wind. No poems, no children, no memories. Left to the crows.

But the van continued sliding and bumping along the road.

Finally we all felt the change from mud to solid, pot-holed paved street. "The city," my neighbor called to the smoker. "That's ten rubles, Goncharov."

Now the prisoners spoke in short whispers as we listened for the change in pitch and timbre of the tires, trying to guess our location. When we crossed the first bridge it was clear—the difference between the bridge pavers and the roadway. *"Obvodny,"* three people said at once. Yes, the smell of the tannery. So this had to be Moskovsky Prospect. If there was another bridge in a few minutes, it would be the Fontanka, and it would mean we were heading into the heart of the city. My longing for Petrograd bloomed inside me. Crazy, to feel hope—it could be far worse here than with the rural Cheka. And yet better to be at home than on some railway siding in Karelia.

After a few more minutes, there could be no doubt as to where we were headed. If I could have seen through the black, shuddering walls of the van, I knew I would behold the wide Fontanka with its wet pavements, its stately buildings on each side admiring themselves in the water. And all around us would be Petrograd—girls walking to appointments, old bony nags clattering along, Formers selling spoons, workers carrying boxes. The state dining rooms would be dispensing tea with saccharine and watery soup. There would be bread queues and poets and, somewhere, a certain madman. Yet I felt such yearning love for every unseen facade and yard, every canal and stone. Would I ever set eyes upon them again?

A turn, and we all toppled to the left. The sound of gates banged back. Close reverberation off stone walls told me that the truck rumbled through a passageway. Then we stopped with a jerk that sent us all tumbling, and the van's back doors opened with a bang. I squinted against the comparative brightness of the day, though it was still raining. I climbed out with the others, gazing up at this building, most likely Gorokhovaya 2, once the home of the Okhrana, the tsar's secret police. How easily the revolution had donned the master's slippers, taken up his pipe. A few steps from here, St. Isaac's Cathedral lifted its golden dome, and the *Bronze Horseman* scanned the Neva. I held my face to the sky, let water fall on my eyelids.

Guards immediately separated us with shouts and shoves. They marched me and the other woman, younger than I'd imagined—a schoolteacher most likely—to a communal holding cell on the second story that must have once been a refectory or classroom. Every spare inch of floor space was occupied with women and beds and bundles, prisoners weeping on cots or sitting stonily on the old boards, gazing at nothing. A group shouted over some slight. It was a waiting room in the train station to some hellish destination. The schoolteacher clung to me. We gingerly picked our way through the bodies and found a place to sit on the floor between two bunks.

A woman on the bed above us gave me a kick between the shoulder blades with her thick-soled men's boots. I was grateful for Nikolai Gerasimovich's ointments, my wounds had healed perfectly. My assailant's face was a fist of rock, and her ears stuck out like honey jars. "Got any food? Any chocolate?" she asked.

My training as a mute held me in good stead. I considered biting her calf in response but didn't relish having my teeth kicked out.

"We don't have anything," the teacher said.

On the other cot above us, a woman wailed, her head in her hands. "I don't understand. I didn't do anything! What about my children? They're alone in the flat!"

An older woman sitting next to her patted her shoulder. "The neighbors will take them."

"They killed my husband," she said, weeping. "Because he wore a hat. A hat! His cousin sent it to him from Bremen. They called him bourgeois and chased him down the street!"

Things in Petrograd were worse than I could ever have imagined. I'd forgotten the difference a month could make in revolutionary times, and I'd been gone for four.

"It's a reign of terror, that's what it is," said a thin, sour-looking woman propped up against the wall. "They've let loose the hounds of hell. The Bolsheviks are whipping them up— 'You've always hated them, your boss, your landlord? Here's your chance to get even. Go in, Ivan, settle your scores!'"

The widow told us, "My neighbors turned me in! I knew them. I shared my firewood with them. How could people be so cruel?"

Every so often the door opened and one or another of our keepers called someone's name. "Novik!" "Rostova!" Once a woman pretended she didn't know it was her turn, and the guard came in, hit her with his stick like she was an animal to be driven, and dragged her out, her head bleeding. We winced at each ugly blow as if we ourselves were being beaten.

"Yes, a reign of terror," the sour-faced woman continued. "What's next, the guillotine? The oubliette?"

The widow keened. My companion was starting to cry.

I thought of Vera Borisovna. Some part of me actually hoped she'd succumbed during the cholera epidemic and did not have to endure this. I could well picture our neighbors: the blonde with the dirty braid, stirring diapers on the stove; the ferret-faced woman; Basya leading the pack of Furies...cholera would be kind in comparison.

With the English in the north and the Czechs along the Trans-Siberian, five thousand miles of Russia were in the hands of the counterrevolution. No wonder they were arresting us all. Although I was sure Father had slipped the net. Sensibly disguised, adequately funded, without address, he was a moving target, whereas Mother was stuck in full view. I could see him colluding with reactionaries, foreigners, the devil himself, anyone who would get rid of the Bolsheviks. Poor suffering Petrograd. It was supposed to be the new, just society, and now it was a bloodbath. Civil war. My country, coming apart.

In this bedlam, one group of women comported themselves very differently from the rest. They sat soberly and spoke not only among themselves but also to those listening nearby. "Who are they?" I asked an older woman who'd been here since we arrived, sitting at the foot of a cot reading a tattered book through half-glasses.

She looked up from her reading. "Politicals," she said. "Left SRs. They've been outlawed." So the Bolsheviks had turned on their own revolutionary brothers. How calm those women were. I drew strength just looking at them. Dignity calls to dignity the way pettiness and panic stir the same in the human heart. Though they had tried to overthrow the Bolsheviks and failed, they shed no tears.

I wanted to be close to them, but I was sure the cell was crawling with Cheka spies. I told my companion from Tsarskoe Selo to hold on to my patch of floor, that I'd be right back, and I inched my way along until I could hear them.

"We aren't trying to overthrow the Bolsheviks," an older woman with cropped gray hair calmly lectured other women nearby. "We just want a change in policy. They've got to stop making concessions to the Germans. Lenin is a traitor to the revolution. He's betrayed the workers of the world for a separate peace."

Women were purposely looking elsewhere, trying not to seem as though they were listening. My scalp prickled. Such daring, to say something like that while in a Cheka cell.

"The Bolsheviks better start listening to the workers or we'll make them listen," said a flat-faced girl with an upturned nose and small Tatar eyes.

A tremulous woman in black with the sagging cheeks of the formerly fat hissed, "Damn all of you. You shoot the man and you can't even do a decent job of it."

"I have the statement of Fanya Kaplan," said another of the Left SRs, a very tall blond girl with deep-set green eyes. She dug a paper out of her pocket and began to read. "*My name is Fanya Kaplan. Today I shot at Lenin. I did it on my own. I will not say from whom I obtained my revolver. I will give no details. I had resolved to kill Lenin long ago. I consider him a traitor to the Revolution. I was exiled to Akatui for participating in an assassination attempt against a tsarist official in Kiev. I spent eleven years at hard labor. After the Revolution, I was freed. I favored the Constituent Assembly and am still for it.*"

The words hung in the air.

"They tortured her. Made her drink hot wax," said the tall blonde, folding the paper back into her pocket.

A silent wail rose inside me. Would I face torture? Hot wax? I thought of what I had already suffered in the room on Tauride Street. I kept thinking of hot wax in my throat—it would burn and choke you at the very same time. The talk moved on to the recent execution of Uritsky's assassin.

"Good riddance," said the formerly fat woman who had criticized Fanya Kaplan's poor marksmanship.

"Unfortunately for us, Uritsky was relatively moderate," said the Left SR with the gray hair. "He was firmly opposed to the death penalty—the one man in Petrograd holding back the flood. And that idiot Kannegisser had to go and shoot him. Of all targets. It wasn't even politically motivated."

When I learned the name of his assassin, the hair stood up on my arms. I knew the Kannegissers, a publishing family. Their salon had been home ground for the entire progressive bourgeoisie. It was where my parents had met so many of their famous friends. It couldn't have been the father. But I remembered a son, Lyonya—a slight young man, pale and excitable, a little younger than Volodya.

"Was it the son? A poet?" I asked quietly.

"Yes, the son," she said. "Leonid. A cadet at the

Mikhailovskaya Artillery Academy." The woman's old face seemed to glow, the soft creases burnished in the light from the tall, frosted windows embedded in wire. "The cadets devised an uprising at the time of the German invasion." When I was out digging trenches. "The Bolsheviks shot a few of the boys as an example to the others. One was evidently a friend of this Kannegisser. He skulked around for a long time, thinking of how to get his revenge. He observed that Uritsky crossed Palace Square every day on his way to the General Staff Building. Shot him on his way to work."

And what he had unleashed. Russia, the great home of unintended consequences.

We were all in the same kettle now: politicals, criminals, students, grandmothers, widows, hostages, and the accidental victims of Fate. All of us used the same slop bucket. We braved cholera and typhoid together with each cup of water. The Third Ancient would have been fascinated with our bread. It certainly wasn't taking us to Neptune—we'd be lucky if it took us to Tuesday. I had much time to listen and think. I clung to the hope that Avdokia had gotten Mother out of the flat before the arrests began.

We'd been there five days when the teacher from Tsarskoe Selo was called. She collapsed into shrieks and tears. The guard had to come in and drag her out. She wasn't a hostage—she was just an educated woman, and in the village where she taught, she was the closest thing they could find to a bourgeois. They'd discovered her copy of *Aesop's Fables* in Greek and decided it was code, that she was a spy. I was haunted by the thought that if she could disappear for a book of Greek, what would the village Cheka make of astronomical calculations?

Lines looped and snaked in my head, images swirled. A silhouette in a doorway beckoned us into the Future. What would it be—a camp? Torture? Another prison? I was nobody special, but the liquidation of an entire class was going on, and I was no proletarian regardless of whether I'd sewed a few socks. Schoolmistress, piano tuner, proofreader, poet—it didn't matter now. All guilty.

I lay on the dirty floor at night, wrapped in my coat, listening to the rain and the coughing and weeping and snores of eighty women, wondering if tonight would be the night the guards banged back the door and called the name I had given them—Maria Mardukovna Morskaya. If I died as Maria, Mother would never know what had become of me. Genya...I could not bear to think of dying in this place without a friend, without my name. Though I would see Seryozha again, on the other side. The dead were our Kitezh. They carried our love, our most precious moments, concealed beneath the waters. They were the city that could not be taken, like the secret roots of trees.

The woman on the cot above my patch of floor, the one who'd kicked me, leaned over and whispered, "The guard, Vanka, the fat one—he's giving out chocolates for a fuck. Real chocolate."

I had had enough of her. "And how much do you get if I fuck him, Grandma?"

"Half," she said.

Amid a group of new arrivals, a familiar face appeared. A face I would never forget. The thick red-blond hair, wet with rain, the shapely build inside her shapeless coat. A wave of nausea swept over me. I bowed my head, pulled my kerchief lower on my brow. Did the politicals—the estranged left wing of her own party—recognize Karlinskaya? She certainly didn't cross the cell to join them, embrace them as long-lost sisters. I could still see her in that room, watching Arkady drag me from the dacha. Hear her yell, "Get rid of her!" It was all I could do not to shove my way over, grab her by the collar and shout, "So, do you still think I'm a Bolshevik spy?" But she would never believe me. I imagined slapping her and slapping her.

She thought I was dead, shot back at the dacha, and I was better off leaving it at that. I could always hope a Left SR would kill her in her sleep. The SRs had begun as terrorists and some of that always remained. I watched her as she found a place on a cot and sat with her back to the room. Her graceful form, her heavy hair, created a kind of halo around her. My father had stroked that hair. She had spilled it across his face as she leaned above him when they made love. While he was supposed to be at Kadet meetings. It made me sick to contemplate my father as just another carnal man—and a liar to boot. I wondered if they'd arrested him when they got her.

Each day, rousted from sleep, we queued to use the slop bucket and receive our terrible rations. Nowhere to wash. The stench, the weeping, the bravery and despair. Were there eighty of us? One hundred now? More? We were taken out in groups to walk about in the yard in the rain. Ah, just to breathe the fresh air, though the clotted sky was only a small square wedged between the high walls. Women sidled up to speak to me—the tearful widow, the old chocolate pimp, others—but I kept to myself. They never aired the Left SRs at the same time as the rest. I waited to hear my name called: Morskaya, prisoner V367. But day after day, as others went to interrogation and returned beaten and bloody, mute, or pretending nothing had happened, or disappeared altogether like the schoolteacher, I was never taken out. The waiting was slowly crushing me. Some days I wished they'd just call me and get it over with.

The women whispered the names of prisons among themselves. Kresty, the Crosses; Peter and Paul; camps in the north, about which we'd heard rumors since the war. Or there was that much shorter trip, which I could not stop thinking about—out to the courtyard.

There were no firing squads anymore. It would be only a single bullet to the head. "Saving ammunition," the woman with the jug-ears joked grimly. We listened for that single shot, even in our sleep.

Still no one came for me. Not for Morskaya, or for Marusya, or Makarova. I suspected the commissar had not bothered to solve the puzzle—too many bodies to process, too many fates to decide. To judge from this cell, the Cheka had its bloody hands full. They seemed to have arrested every third person in Petrograd. And what was I but just a loose piece of dirt that happened to be lying on the floor when the big broom came through?

56 *Up or Down*

THE AUTUMN RAINS GREW heavy, and many of the women declined the opportunity to march around the small courtyard for exercise, but I always went. I would take any opportunity to leave that cell. Outside, I lifted my face to the weeping sky. *Please, God, reach down and pluck me from this life.* Upon my return, the cell always seemed smaller, as if they'd moved the walls in just a foot or two while I was away. The presence of Karlinskaya sent up a stink I could sense even in sleep. I'd been here two weeks now. Perhaps they'd lost my paperwork, sent the files to Moscow.

I'd been trying to remember Genya's poem about

Abraham and Isaac when finally the fat guard called out through the bars, "Morskaya, V367."

He led me to a different door from the one we came and left by to go to the prison yard. This one was solid metal, and we passed through it into an unfamiliar part of the building. Yellow walls, low ceilings, shouts, the brutal clang of doors. He brought me to a stairway and I studied the broken tile while he jawed with another guard. Which way would I go? Up could mean interrogation, but it could also mean freedom. Down could only mean one thing.

Like a soul on the scales of heaven, I waited.

Another man arrived. A vigorous, short, athletic blond in black leather. "Morskaya?" The fat guard stepped back and the blond shoved me ahead of him.

Down.

The smell of wet walls and mold, and a dirty animal odor, increased as we descended. A slaughterhouse stench. He walked me down the dim hall. Muffled voices came from behind thick doors. A rising shriek snaked from the base of my spine and coiled around my heart, squeezing my throat in its knot. We passed yellow walls the color of old teeth. Black sticky floors sucked at our shoes. Bare bulbs buzzed overhead. The rest of the country was plunged in darkness, but the Cheka would have its electricity.

From behind a metal door, a gunshot reverberated like a crack of lightning in the closed-off space. Panic was a bird crashing into walls, my heart within my rib cage. The smell, the tile, the promise of pain. I felt as though someone was pressing a wet pillow to my face. I stumbled. The Chekist hauled me along. "Don't pass out yet. Plenty of time for that."

A heavy door swung outward, and two Chekists dragged a man's body out in front of us. He'd gone into that room alive. To think I had scorned the schoolteacher's terror. I melted into a hysteria all my own when I saw the dead man's bare feet. And there were his boots, tucked under the arm of the taller man. It was hard to both drag the body and keep the boots from falling.

The Chekist shoved me inside.

The room was windowless, tiny. Black oilcloth lined the walls. A drain in the middle of the floor pooled with blood. A sound—a howl, a moan, a wail all in one—emerged from me like an animal's from a cage. Now I, who'd been silent for so long, was suddenly chattery as a mockingbird. "This is all a mistake. You have the wrong person. I need to see Varvara Razrushenskaya. She's Cheka, she worked for Uritsky. She knows me. She can vouch for me. Please call her!" I started to beg but then I remembered what Arkady once told me about men like him, that tears make them cruel. *We hate weakness. It inspires us to violence*, he'd said. I certainly didn't need to inspire this man. I had to get a grip on myself.

"Save your breath." He shoved me against the oilcloth. I sank to my knees in the still-warm blood. Again

that wail. Was this to be my end—this? Unknown, un-
sung, my only crime to have been alive at the same
time Lenin was shot. I pictured the Left SR women up
in the cell. They'd started a hunger strike before they
disappeared, one by one. How weak I was compared
to them. Because I was alone. I had no comrades, no
friends. This man wouldn't even have to pull my hair.

The stocky Chekist stood over me. He smelled like
pork fat. "All a mistake, *da?* Let's start with your
name."

The letters were like doorknobs in my mouth. My
mouth so parched. My throat. A paper mouth. A paper
tongue. "Makarova. Marina."

"What?" He bent over and yelled into my ear.

I was afraid to look. His boots were very good.

"Makarova," I said again. "Marina Dmitrievna." I
fought the luxury of weeping. I had to think, to hear.

"Address?"

"Pulkovo Observatory." Name, province, district,
village. Name province district . . .

He kicked me in the side of the head. I saw constellations. Cygnus, flying across the Milky Way, Deneb
in its tail, a comet of bright red. "Last registered? And
don't waste my time."

I gave him Grivtsova Alley.

"Why were you arrested?"

Didn't he know? My tears and my snot and the blood
all ran together. Yet my big ears were twitching. I hid
the perception like stolen cash into a loose sleeve, the

possibility that he knew less than I'd imagined. "There was a raid. On the observatory," I whispered. "I hadn't any papers."

"Where were they? Did you destroy them? To hide your class origins?" His waxy jaw seemed so firm, seen from below. If he were a fish, how easy he would be to land. He towered over me. The thought came: *How he must hate being small.*

"I was attacked. They were stolen." On my knees, a holy petitioner, in the blood of the Lamb. Paint the doorposts so the Angel of Death will pass over. The Angel of Death—I thought I'd already met him, but perhaps not.

My blond captor shuffled through papers in a file he'd tucked under his arm. "You are from Petrograd. What were you doing in Pulkovo?" He stood so close I could smell his boot blacking.

"A place to hide, Comrade," I said to his footwear.

"From whom?"

How could I explain in such a way that my story wouldn't trip over itself? "I'd been kidnapped. I escaped."

"Why? Are you wealthy?"

"No. It was... of a sexual nature."

His long nostrils flared. I imagined the pupils of his pale green eyes widening and narrowing like a lizard's as he scented the air. "Did the observatory personnel knowingly hide you?"

The Five, oh God. "No. They took pity on me. They

didn't know. To them, I was just a misplaced person. I wasn't quite right in the head."

"They recognized a fellow bourgeois..."

That word, that word again! What did it mean? Words like bits of cheap currency. It meant everything, it meant nothing. Like saying "yellow." Yellow yellow yellow yellow.

But the drain awaited.

"I'm a worker. I do factory work."

"Which factory?" He squinted a pale eye.

"A knitting workshop. In the Moskovsky district. Bobrov's," I said. Would it help? There was no Bobrov's anymore.

"You have no labor book." He forced me to look up. This same horrible sensation, on my knees, a man yanking me by my hair. If I lived, I would never allow a man to touch me this way. I would shave my head for the rest of my life. "You are a bourgeois parasite!" he shouted into my face. "Selling yourself! Debasing our socialist revolution!"

"I was raised bourgeois but I'm a worker now. Look at my hands." I spread them out, bloody but coarse from boiling laundry and scrubbing floors, calloused from digging and hoeing. Was it illegal now even to live?

"You can put a deer into harness but it doesn't make it a horse. What are they really doing up there at the observatory? Were they sending signals to the British? Answer me!" He released my hair and unholstered his gun. I could smell the oiled leather, the metal.

I couldn't stop my useless tears. The bitterness of my situation was a poison in my throat, the hopelessness of it all. I would end here, in this filthy basement. "Please—I'm telling you the truth. I swear on my mother's head." Though my mother had probably already been here, perhaps in this very cell, kneeling in someone else's death.

"How well do you know Razrushenskaya?" he asked.

The question caught me up short. He was like a horse that had suddenly turned, trying to unseat me. In that one question, he gave me more than he'd intended. Was Varvara in trouble? What if she was on the outs, under investigation herself? The authors of *Kommunist* opposed the main body of power. Uritsky had been one of them. Could it have been they who shot him, and not Lyonya Kannegisser? I felt sick—it had never occurred to me that Varvara might be vulnerable. "We were in school together, that's all." Furiously backpedaling.

"Did you know she was *dvoryanstvo?*" *Nobility.*

Oh God, help me get out of here without incriminating her. "When I knew her, she lived in a tenement on Vasilievsky Island. She was a party member, even in school. Organizing among the women in the textile factories. Working an underground press."

"Did you ever see her with members of the nobility?"

"She was a Bolshevik!" Was my friend in a cell somewhere in this building herself? Waiting for the tap on the shoulder, the shout from the guards?

"Did she ever take money from members of the nobility?"

"Absolutely not."

"Is she a member of any counterrevolutionary groups?"

The devil tickled me and despite myself I laughed. He grabbed the back of my head and smashed my forehead into the floor. Into the blood. Blood everywhere. My hands, my face covered with it. Fresh. Warm. Rivers of blood. Oceans of blood. I saw it, like a vision. Russia. Washing into the drain. I could not stop screaming. He kicked me to shut me up but the screams kept coming out. The blood, which had once been inside another person, coated me, drenched me in its viscous red.

The door opened. Even the dank smell from the hall was fresher than the iron smell of the blood and the rot of the drain.

A woman's boots. Long and narrow. "I'll take this, Comrade." He left without saying another word.

Weeping, I crawled to the boots, clung to them.

A bony hand pulled me to my feet.

I threw myself around her neck, forgetting that I was covered in blood, forgetting everything but love for this tall, leather-clad girl, my savior. Bloodying her neck, her cheeks, kissing her, clutching her as a drowning man clutches a plank of wood.

She shoved me away roughly, embarrassed.

"He asked about you," I whispered, the words tumbling over each other. "Your family. Your social origins. Asked if I knew you were *dvoryanstvo,* how we met. I didn't tell him anything."

"Berzhins, that treacherous scum. He knew you were my prisoner. Thought he'd get a head start on you, see if he could find something. He'll get his soon enough."

My prisoner. She had known I was here all along. "He could have killed me. Why didn't you come for me, if you knew I was here?"

"Don't you interrogate *me,*" she shouted. "You can't imagine what's going on now, so just shut up and do what I tell you." Like a cop, she hauled me out of the room and toward the stairs by my bruised upper arm.

Eighteen years old, and my school chum held my life in the palm of her hand. And the lives of how many others? Yes—who was I to interrogate her? I didn't even own a pair of drawers.

As we ascended the tile stairs, she kept a close grip on me under the armpit, the practiced hold of a prison guard. I couldn't help asking myself how many times she'd been down to that cellar. Had she held a gun to somebody's head there? Pulled the skin from his flesh? I felt the blood drying on my face. My hands were sticky with it, and the cold whistled up my skirt as we climbed to the third story, then down a long hall painted the dingy yellow that was the palette of Russian officialdom. Prisoners waited along the walls, pale-faced, like patients outside a hospital ward. Would the news be bad, or worse? They blanched when they saw me drenched in blood and looked the other way. Varvara opened a door and shoved me inside.

It was an office like any other—small, high-ceilinged, painted a dirty green, with a chair rail that ran around the room. A portrait of Lenin hung on the wall along with one of a gaunt man with a pointed beard. Heavy mesh on the windows, in case one thought to jump. Outside, charcoal clouds boiled in the early October sky. *"Sadis'*, " Varvara ordered. *Sit.*

I took the straight-backed chair before a small, scarred table. No calendar in here, no clock. The smell of graphite and wet wood tinged the cold air with a special despair. My body felt not quite my own, my head semidetached, as the English would say.

How much she had changed since spring. She was every inch the Chekist now, in creaking leather, the square body of her machine pistol menacing at her belt. Her expression perfectly echoed that of the grim, pointy-bearded man on the wall. Yet somewhere in there was still the girl who loved puns and puzzles, who stole sugar from the bowl with a grin. She disliked tenors and squeaky chairs and had not been pleased with the broom she got on St. Basil's Eve.

So this was what it meant. A broom indeed. Still standing, she spread my dossier before her like a choir book and leafed through the hymns, her mouth sliced into a deeper-than-customary scowl. Patches of red broke out on her bony cheeks. "I can't believe you used my name. What the devil did you think would happen?" She read aloud: *"One unidentified person, aka Maria Mardukovna Morskaya, arrested Pulkovo Observatory, twenty-third September. Without papers. Confessed to passing secrets to the English. Named Cheka commissar Varvara Razrushenskaya in confession."*

I hadn't realized it would sound like that. "You're a commissar?"

"No—I'm the Little Humpbacked Horse. You were passing secrets to the English?"

"No! I never confessed to anything. It's all made up! A commissar with a little moustache interrogated me and threw me onto a truck for Petrograd. I only used your name..." I didn't know it would get her in trouble. "It was all I could think of. But I swear I never named you as part of a confession. I swear to God, Varvara."

"And you were in Pulkovo doing exactly what?" The squeak of her leather jacket, that smell would forever after remind me of this day. She had an extra skin now, and I had none. "Everybody said you were dead. No news, nothing. And then, when they arrest you, you think of me? Not a word for months, and suddenly, you drag me into it?" She leaned forward, and I couldn't believe the hatred in her eyes. She had looked upon me in many ways—grudging admiration, sneering superiority, even sisterly scorn—but never with loathing. Pure disgust. "Thought I'd come to the rescue? 'Oh,

Varvara will clean it up. Varvara will make it all go away.' That's not going to happen this time. Everything's different now." She puffed her cheeks out and exhaled, like a swimmer emerging from under water.

And I felt myself sinking, my head going under the waves.

"What were you doing at Pulkovo?"

How could I tell her the way I'd careened through the winter like a drunk on a frozen pond? I didn't want to lie to her. She always knew, and she was my one chance. But I didn't know how to tell her the truth—how much of it to tell, how not to sound like the adventurer Arkady had labeled me.

At last she sat, threw her cap on the table, and scooted her chair in, her black frizzy hair standing up like a madman's. She took out some paper, dipped her pen in the ink pot. How far we'd come from those days leafleting outside factories together, talking to women in tenement courtyards. I would have mentioned it, but the rage in her eyes told me we'd gone beyond friendship. From her point of view I was simply a liability now, a hot coal of which she was only too eager to rid herself. "Start at the beginning."

The beginning? I sorted through my life since then, the way you sort photographs before placing them in an album, deciding which pieces fit and which don't and in what order. In the next room, an interrogator was badgering someone. I was distracted by the incessant stream of his hectoring accusations. Outside, the

hoofbeats of a cabman's nag clattered down Gorokhovaya Street. "I'm losing patience, Marina." Her pen
was about to drip on her papers. She tapped it on the
ink pot.

I suddenly saw myself—I was exactly like this city,
with its classical facades and labyrinths of dirty courtyards behind them as I unfolded my story, beginning
with Seryozha's death and Kolya's return, the house on
the English Embankment. I held nothing back, watching her face, her jealousy at my passion for Kolya—
how she hated him. Well, she'd wanted to hear the
whole thing. I had no other cards to play.

"You know what he was doing here, don't you?" she
asked. "Speculating under cover of army provisioning.
The man's complete scum. I can't believe you'd go to
him when you had a man like Genya. You're really a
piece of work."

Something heavy dropped in the next room, startling
me—but not her. What was she accustomed to that
that sound was just an ordinary workday?

She liked it better when I told her how Kolya left
me. My return to Genya. Our marriage and its implo-
sion. The move back to Furshtatskaya. I noticed she'd
stopped taking notes.

I got to the part about Arkady. The islands, St. John
the Baptist, the barracks. Then her pen flew, blotting
the cheap paper. The hothouse on the Vyborg side. The
trip to Kolomna, the passports and the station.

She rubbed her temples with thumbs and forefingers.

"And you never thought to tell anyone? You never thought how this was harming the revolution?"

"I tried to tell you, remember? When I came to your place? You'd just been roughed up by the strikers…" I trailed off. Maybe she didn't want to be reminded of that. "I wanted to tell you, but Manya was there. I couldn't. Compared with what you were doing, it sounded so unbelievably squalid."

Varvara placed her palms on the edge of the table as if she were bracing herself, her head lowered. The interrogator in the next room started up his questioning again. My head ached where I'd been kicked.

I had to steel myself to tell her the rest. My visit from Arkady, the private dining room, the Order of Saint George. My residence in the room with the striped wallpaper. I spared her nothing. After a time she stopped writing again. She looked like she was going to be sick. She got up and paced the room, pausing often to look out through the mesh as if she'd like to fly into the sky. I got to the poem he'd cut into my back. I stood and unbuttoned my dress, slipped the fabric from my shoulders so she could see for herself the truth of my words. His poem had healed into perfect lines, pink but less three-dimensional.

She stood behind me. Suddenly her arms were around me, her lips kissing my shoulder. "I'll kill him," she whispered into my ear. "You'd like that, wouldn't you? I'll find him. I'll fill him so full of lead it would take twelve men to carry his coffin."

I embraced those leather-clad arms around my waist, leaned my head back against her. We had each had our own revolution. I thought that any given moment in time was not a point but a city tunneled through with parallel passageways. People could be marching overhead and underfoot, all around you, sharing exactly the same real estate, and you could miss each other entirely.

Finally I bent down and pulled my dress up.

Pale and shaken, she sat opposite me, her eyes now shining and bright with pity. Then we recognized each other, no longer interrogator and prisoner, but two friends in a terrible position. "How'd you get away?"

I was nearly done. One last bomb. I described leaving the flat. The road to Pulkovo, the observatory in the distance. "I watched it up there, glowing in the moonlight, and thought that the only happy people in the world were the ones up there on those heights."

She took my hand, the scarred one. "The people who come after us, they're the ones who will be happy. It's not for us."

"But I want to be happy myself," I said. "Is that bourgeois of me?"

"Painfully individualistic." She laughed mournfully.

I described the final chapter, the dacha in the woods. But I was no longer the innocent, the idealist I'd been last October, when I'd played at spying, running off to place my notes in Plato's *Republic*. Now I knew the harm that could be done. But how to do the least and still get out of here? I carefully laid out the scene: Karlinsky and his wife, the small dark man, the Englishman in army uniform. And Father—how could I tell the tale without him?

She let go of my hand and began taking furious notes. To the pen's dry music, I related as much as I could remember. That they were waiting for money—three hundred fifty thousand gold francs—and it had been delayed. But I left out the name of the person bringing the gold. Even now, after all that had happened, I would not give him up.

It began to rain outside. She was still writing as I got to the tale's end—my father's betrayal, my run to the observatory, my service as Marusya. My arrest along with the three celestials. "You've got to help them. They're just scientists. They didn't even know Lenin'd been shot."

She bristled again. "Don't tell me what to do. I don't care about your damn scientists. I need something better than this if I'm going to save your sorry ass." She batted at the page. "Not to mention my own. Give me something I can use, Marina."

She took me back through my story, asking questions, demanding specifics, every inch the professional. "The meeting. Who was calling the shots, would you say? Von Princip?"

I saw I'd been focused on the wrong things. I'd been able to think about nothing but Father, how he was involved, and his horrible mistress, how he saw me, and whether I would ever escape. But it was the Englishman and the Odessan who had been at the center of things that night.

"The Englishman. Describe him."

"Well built, sharp nose, dimpled chin. Blond. Six feet tall." I could see him in his insignialess uniform, hear his clipped manner of speech.

Her eyebrows were like two dark goats colliding. "No one you'd seen with your old man? From the consulate, maybe?"

"I hadn't seen him before, but he spoke like a military man. He didn't trust Arkady."

She snorted. "And what about the other one?"

"Short, slender, black-haired. Well dressed, clean-shaven. Smoked continuously. Maybe a Jew or a Greek, Turk, Armenian—who knows? I thought of him as the Odessan. He spoke fast, but not clearly—like he had marbles in his mouth." *It should have been here already, Baron. That was our understanding.* "He and the Englishman were the link to the Czechs."

She groaned and leaned back in her seat. "If only you'd come to me then...didn't you have any sense of what you were sitting on? What they were about to unleash? Instead you go bury yourself at Pulkovo Observatory. Could you really have forgotten your allegiance to the revolution?"

How could she ask such a question? "If you knew Arkady, you'd know why. He's not just going to forget about me. I bet he has Chekists on the payroll. Otherwise, how could he have operated so long?"

She got up and paced. "There's got to be something. If you want me to save you—think!" My stomach rumbled, but she ignored it. "Tell me, did the Englishman have a name? Who would meet the Czechs? Who was their contact?"

I ran my hand over the rough table, wondering how many people had confessed to how many crimes sitting just here. Who was innocent? Most, I imagined. I could hear their whispers in the wood... *You have to believe me.* Who had named others, men and women forever lost. I thought about Karlinskaya in that cell on the second floor. I kept testing it, like a bad tooth. Karlinskaya would know all kinds of things—the identity of the Englishman, and perhaps the Odessan. Karlinskaya, my father's mistress, the woman who ordered with such coldness that I be led out—she must have known it would be to my death. She might even now be conspiring with foreign powers to overthrow the revolution.

"There's something. I can see it on your face." Varvara grabbed my arm. "Marina, don't even think of holding anything back from me." Her gaze drilled into my forehead. "I see through you like a gauze curtain. What?" She pulled me across the desk so that we were nose to nose. I could smell the fish she'd had for lunch. "I could get someone to sweat it out of you," she growled. "Don't play with me. You've implicated me at a very bad time. You owe me. You can save us both. Tell me, and don't leave anything out."

"What are you going to do, make me drink hot wax? Like Fanya Kaplan?"

At the name, Varvara's skin turned gray. She let go of my arm. "Marina," she said in a slightly softer tone. "Do not mention Lenin's assassin. Give me something I can use. Give me some reason to save you." She ended in a whisper. Almost pleading. Her emotion wasn't a tactic.

"It's about someone who was there that night," I said. "But what will you do to them if I tell you?"

"Who is it?" She was all alertness now. "If it's a traitor to Soviet Russia, if it's someone conspiring with the English to overthrow us, why would you want to protect them? Have your politics changed so much? It's civil war!"

"Those Chekists at Pulkovo thought the astronomical charts were British code."

"Everybody's on edge. What do you expect?" She was shouting again. She sounded just like the interrogator next door. "The English are at Murmansk. Reactionaries have a dictatorship in Siberia, a separate government, supported by your father and those goddamn Czechs! And you should see some of those Siberian psychopaths if you think we're rotten. You've been away a long time. So if you know something, this is not the time to keep it back. Give me a name and where I can find this person and I swear you'll walk out of here free as a bird."

I was exhausted. How long had I been in this room?

All around me I could feel the grim machinery of Gorokhovaya 2 turning, turning, a factory stamping out molds, the waiting forms stuffed with human beings. We, the prisoners, were what was being processed. But what product demanded such tons of flesh? Where was this all going? For the happiness of some future people who were somehow more valuable than the people sitting in the cell downstairs or out there in the hall?

But I had a key in my molar. It ached there. It would unlock the door.

What are you waiting for? Get rid of her!

At the observatory, the Ancients should have been gathering for their yellow wine right about now. Later, Ludmila Vasilievna would make her calculations while Aristarkh Apollonovich would mount the metal staircase to the big telescope, to observe the young stars in the Moving Group. Should be. Could be. Were not. Were in a Cheka cell. While Varvara, across the table, was caught in her own dark nebula.

They had made Fanya Kaplan drink hot wax. They had shot the man downstairs. Those were not metaphors. And yet *Get rid of her!* still rang in my ears.

A Bolshevik spy. Here I was again. "Promise me they'll leave the observatory alone and let the astronomers go. They're only thinking of Alpha Centauri up there."

"I'm sure you're right," Varvara said. "I'll write the order myself. I'll do it today. *There's to be no in-*

terference with the state work of the observatory. Now who is it?"

There are some things that shouldn't be said, words that bring states into being. "Viktoria Karlinskaya. She's in the cell with me."

"Karlinsky's wife?" She sat up very straight. "We have her? We have Viktoria Karlinskaya?" She threw back her head and laughed. "Oh Marina! You just said the 'Open sesame'!" All the worry fell from her face. She rose, tugging down the sleeves of her jacket, squaring the hem.

I couldn't share in her excitement. I didn't care about her embrace. My bitterness outshone my relief as she called a guard to take me back to my cell. I knew I was wrong to give Karlinskaya up. But in the end, we were all swimming in the same infected waters— Karlinskaya and I, Varvara, Berzhins, Father and his conspirators. This terrible place, this was also the revolution. The blood from that basement room still staining my hands and face, I had named her. I was not separate from this. They would not let you be separate.

57 *Rubinshteyna Street*

AND SO I SOLD Karlinskaya. Sold her for the good of the revolution. Sold her for vengeance. Sold her for love, for friendship, for freedom—my motivations as snarled as a mat of hair. Something to ponder in the deep hours of the night as water ate away at the roots of the sleeping city. The following afternoon, the fat guard called me from the cell. Varvara was waiting for me in the hallway. She already looked better—cleaner, rested, authoritative, as though she'd gotten a transfusion. She gripped my arm but it was only for show, the pressure light.

"I have to get away," I said, low, as we walked to the stairs. "Help me get to Maryino."

"There is no 'away,'" she said, our feet clattering on the dirty stairs. "It's civil war. It's going to be worse in the countryside than here. With us it's almost over. Hold on." She stopped in the stairwell, glancing around, and surreptitiously pressed a key into my palm, closed my fingers over it. She smiled, touched my cheek with the back of her hand, the way a mother checks a child's temperature. Her tenderness alarmed me. "You remember the way?"

I hefted the key in my hand. "What'll Manya say?"

"Manya's at the front with the troops." We finished our descent, prisoner and Chekist once more. She nodded to a guard who opened a door into a sort of reception area with worn counters and dirty floors. Wary pale clerks eyed us as ordinary citizens stood in line with bundles for prisoners.

"He won't let me go, Varvara. He'll find me and kill me."

"Trust me—he's got his hands full. He doesn't even

remember your name." She opened the door. Outside it was raining. "We'll get him. When all this is over."

I walked free into the cold rain with all of my worldly goods—the coat on my back, the boots on my feet. I had vowed never to return to Petrograd, but there I was at the corner of Admiralteisky and Gorokhovaya, the smell of blood still in my nostrils, knowing that I'd set wheels in motion I'd never be able to still.

Keeping my head down, I fled to Varvara's flat, on Rubinshteyna Street just across the Chernyshevsky Bridge. The key in the lock, a drab hallway, an inner door to a joyless room. I remembered the faded striped wallpaper, the typewriter. But I could still see black oilcloth, blood, a drain. After locking the door and checking it to be sure I took off my boots and stretched out on the mushy bed like overrisen dough. Yet what luxury after two weeks on the floor of a Cheka holding cell. Blood still caked my clothes and hair from yesterday's interrogation—I smelled like an animal. I should light the stove and wash, but I couldn't force myself to rise.

I fell asleep as one plunges into a black lake, the water closing over my head.

I didn't know where I was when I awoke in the cold, dark room. I turned on the bedside lamp and tried to breathe. Safe—for the time being. I got up and moved to her little *bourgeoika* stove in my stockinged feet, eyed her meager ration of firewood and stack of newspapers:

Izvestia, Petrogradskaya Pravda. Krasnaya Gazeta, that bloodthirsty rag. I began to twist up a *Pravda* for kindling, then stopped and registered what I was seeing in my hands. In a box on the front page was a list of executed prisoners. I sat on the floor and read. Shock after shock as I recognized names: hostages, landlords, generals, publishers, and revolutionaries alike, all bundled together and canceled like stacks of old checks.

Dukavoy, Ippolit Sergeevich, Counterrevolutionary. My father's chess partner.

Gershon, Pavel Semyonovich, Counterrevolutionary. Pavlik, my old boyfriend. His beautiful green eyes. He was only eighteen, like me. I could still picture us walking together with the food for both schools in the early morning. His face when Genya stole me out of the Cirque Moderne. Dead. And here was *Semyon,* and *Julia…* my God, they got the whole family. Execution, moving through the population like cholera.

And *Krestovsky, Andrei Kirillovich, Speculator.* The type blurred with my tears. I searched for his wife, the beautiful Galina, but it seemed she'd been spared, at least that day. Perhaps she'd only been sent to a camp. Poor Krestovsky. I could still see him uncorking that champagne, doing the sailor's dance. What had he done besides feed a raft of theatergoers, support a flock of poets?

I couldn't read on. I wadded the paper up and threw it in the stove. Was this the revolution we'd dreamed of? Our glistening future? If the cellar of Gorokhovaya

2 hadn't drowned my last hope, this list had. And each issue had more. Hundreds, thousands of names, the liquidation of a class. Yet even as I wept there in the cold, I still had to light the fire, to twist their names into kindling. *Forgive me.* I searched each paper for *Makarov, Dmitry Ivanovich.* Or *Makarova, Vera Borisovna,* but found neither. With the names of the dead I boiled water, washed the blood off myself, and set my clothes to soak.

Dressed in someone's robe—Manya's most likely, I couldn't imagine Varvara even owning such a thing—I poked around the flat. There was nothing personal. Clothes on a hook, some hose, a photograph of Marx torn from a journal, a handbill from the Military Revolutionary Committee—a souvenir from the day they took Petrograd. But the anarchist Peter Kropotkin's cheery Father Frost face no longer presided as it had in her room on Vasilievsky Island. Neither did I see Delacroix's *Liberty.* I cleared the table and moved the typewriter to the floor, adding to it a pile of manuscript pages. They were a political analysis: "A Commentary on Comrade Bukharin's *Anarchy and Scientific Communism*" by Varvara Razrushenskaya.

Her stern black bookshelf tolerated no fiction or verse, only big dictionaries, and volumes on economics, politics, and history. But I recognized a small sliver of aqua blue, a title traced in gold, tucked in between two volumes of Marx. I slid it out from its hiding place.

She'd kept it through everything. I traced my fingers over the cloth cover, remembering how Father and I had discussed colors. I'd been torn between the lighter blue and something more dignified. In the end the beauty had won out. I turned the soft, creamy pages—and they blurred as I thought of him, the pain I would always feel when I touched that volume, the memory of what had been.

Something fell out and fluttered to the floor. A pressed sprig of white lilac. I picked it up, sniffed. Dusty, but I could still detect the lingering scent of that long-ago night, St. Basil's Eve, 1916, when we had cast the wax and seen our futures. Varvara had pressed one of my mother's lilacs into the pages. So unlike her to be that sentimental.

I thought of how she'd kissed my shoulder, how she'd embraced me.

My inscription,

For Varvara,
And you'll say you knew me once,
All my love, Marina

That kiss on my shoulder, that embrace. *Manya's at the front.* Her fingertips on my incised back.

Of course I knew she had feelings for me. But I'd never expected to have to live at her mercy.

Now I was burdened with a new set of problems. I saw that I was never going to be my own woman, I simply had traded Arkady and the Cheka for Varvara. Oh, what I would give to just be free, alone, without compromises or betrayals, beholden to no one. Out in the open. A caravan, a campfire, stars in their stately progress overhead. I was tired of rooms.

Varvara returned after dark, talking, laughing, full of news. She spread her meager rations on the table—bread and a few dried herrings. I could only imagine what the Formers were eating if this was the Cheka's fare. She ceremonially divided it up onto two chipped plates.

"I wanted you to know they let the astronomers go today."

They were free. A weight lifted from my chest. At least I'd done something good. Then I asked the question that had been haunting me from the start. "What about Mother? Is she a hostage?"

"We never had her." She wiped her mouth, took a sip of tea. "She disappeared when all this broke out. Maybe she's clairvoyant after all, eh? Or else she's learned a thing or two from last time. When we stopped by, both she and the old lady had already flown the coop. Feel better?" She chucked me under the chin as you do a sulky child.

"And Karlinskaya?" I knew I shouldn't ask.

She sighed. "You're worried about that bitch? She sang like a bird, if you want to know. She saw what was up the minute we called her in."

"Did you..." I swallowed past an imaginary bolus of wax. "Torture her?"

"I never torture anyone," she said, and held my hand in both of hers. "I simply give them choices. Karlinskaya believes in the revolution. It wasn't hard to convince her to help us. I let her go this afternoon. She's off to work for us now. You've done the revolution a service."

Which of us would be the Bolshevik spy now? I thought bitterly. "Do you swear?"

"On Marx's beard. Whatever else you think of me, I'm no liar." She let that hang in the air, with its unspoken rebuke. "We knew most of it already, thanks to you. I told her I'd put her on a train to Samara if she told me what I wanted to know, and she was ready to oblige. She's not the hard-liner you'd have thought. A practical woman, I'd say. More so than you."

As we ate, Varvara delineated the conspiracy they'd partially uncovered at the time of Lenin's assassination attempt, which my information further revealed. It seemed that a British diplomat had been caught bribing the Latvian Rifles—Lenin's personal guard—to kill both Lenin and Trotsky. Dzerzhinsky, the Torquemada of the national Cheka—he of the gaunt face and the pointed beard in the portrait in Varvara's office—had been on the hunt for others involved. Evidently Karlinsky was the conduit.

She went to her bag, pulled out a photograph, and put it by my plate. "Look familiar?"

It showed a dark-haired man with round, sad eyes and drooping moustache in an old-fashioned high white collar and soft tie. It was him, the Odessan, years ago. I nodded.

"Konstantin. Recruited by the British in 1903 in the Pacific before the Japanese war. The one in the uniform you described is a naval attaché, Commander Fielding Brown. Your meeting was preparation for the invasion of Russia by the English—and the Czech uprising on the Trans-Siberian. The plan was to meet up with the Czechs and eventually the Whites under Denikin, to attack Moscow. Karlinskaya confirmed what we knew. Added a few details."

"And Father?"

She picked a fish bone out of her mouth and set it on the rim of her plate. "He's in Samara, with Komuch."

A new acronym, no doubt. "Translation, please."

"The Committee of Members of the Constituent Assembly—the old Kerensky gang mostly, plus some other assorted malcontents like your old man. For some reason, Karlinskaya stayed behind in Petrograd. She said it was because she'd "been ill," but later admitted she'd been knocked up and needed an abortion. Quite a woman. We picked her up in a random sweep. No idea who she was. Berzhins almost wept—you should have seen his face."

So Arkady hadn't been lying. I could have had another sister or brother. Thank God she'd put an end to that.

She sat back in her chair, propped her knee against the oilcloth. "We did find out how they got the gold in for the Czechs. In case you were wondering."

I forced myself to meet her gaze. She would notice if I looked away. She would notice anyway, but I had to try. "How?"

She spun her spoon around. "Surprise, surprise. Your old pal Shurov. Neck deep in it. A strange coincidence, don't you think? Want to change your story?"

I tried to imagine how an innocent person would react. Exasperated. "I can't imagine anyone, let alone Arkady, trusting him with a load of gold."

She stared at me another moment, then gathered up the dishes. Nobody washed them anymore—we licked them clean. "And you didn't know anything about it."

I shook my head, a piece of herring bone stuck in my teeth.

"He never contacted you? Do you know where he is now?" Her black eyebrows arched to disbelieving peaks. She set the dishes on the windowsill.

"Is the interrogation still on?"

I could hear the rain gargling in the drainpipe outside. "Your father, Arkady, Shurov. Konstantin and Commander Brown? You swear you had no part in it?" Her nail-bitten hand suddenly grasped my forearm. "If you're playing me for a fool, I'll shoot you myself." Her eyes glared like sun on metal. It hurt to look back into them. "Think before you answer."

"I gave you Karlinskaya, didn't I?" She loved me but

I had no doubt she would shoot me if she thought I had turned against the revolution. She would shoot me to prove to herself that she valued the revolution over her personal feelings, even love. "I told you everything."

She drew her face even closer. Her hair smelled of smoke. "Tell me about Shurov." Was this politics or jealousy?

I gazed right into her black, frightening eyes. "I haven't seen him since the last day on Galernaya. I don't know where he is or what he's doing." The absolute almost truth.

"Too many coincidences. I don't like it." Varvara pursed her lips so hard, her wide mouth nearly disappeared.

"After what he did, setting me up with von Princip? You think I'd forgive him for that?" She was making me angry all over again.

She sighed and lowered herself back into her seat. "All right. We won't speak of it again." She lit the primus with a twist of paper, set the kettle on to boil. I tried not to cough. That bone was sticking in my throat. She prepared the tea, with something that looked like real tea. A sad celebration. The smell uncoiled in the room. We waited for it to brew and rearranged our faces.

She rolled a cigarette and put her stockinged foot up on the table. Her heel had a huge hole in it. "I didn't get a chance to tell you. There are going to be massive celebrations for the October anniversary," she said. "In

honor of Year One. The futurists are knocking themselves out. They're preparing theatricals, parades, puppet shows. They're redesigning Palace Square. You
should do something with them."

"Funny, I don't feel much like celebrating." Just as
I watched our dreams fall under the horses, they were
staging a parade. There was no bread, but it seems
there would be circuses. Still, hope was as real as bread
and more easily constructed from papier-mâché, wire,
and broadsides.

"*This* will be over soon," she said, meaning Red Terror, "and then it will be Petrograd's chance to live a
little—remind people what it's all about. The Commissariat of Enlightenment's somehow twisted the
money out of Moscow. There's a ton of work. You
should write a poem for the celebrations—it'll reinforce your revolutionary credentials. I'm sure there'll
be readings. Some of your poets must still be around."

But you had to have a soul to write, and I wasn't sure
I had one anymore. Maybe it was with Arkady's now,
inside an egg inside a duck inside a hare, at the bottom of
the sea.

Varvara's rations didn't include enough firewood to
warm the room past nine. We lay together under a pile
of blankets. She held her manuscript on her knees, cor-
recting pages. I had nothing to read, didn't dare open
a newspaper to hear the shrieking of the dead. Instead
I was writing a poem—about the Year One—on the

back of a discarded page. She smelled of smoke and pencil lead. "You know, I've missed you, you idiot." She rubbed my shoulder awkwardly. "It was hell to see you in that room. That's not how I like to see you."

And how do you like to see me? I resisted asking the question, which would sound flirtatious. I could not shake the image of her in the interrogation room, her expert hand under my armpit leading me out of the cellar, her working in that hellish place every day. She was writing about it even now, urging people to have less heart so they could get through this insanity.

She brushed a hair from my cheek. Smiled.

I fought the impulse to push her hand away.

"I'm so glad you're here," she said.

To this rangy, dangerous girl I owed my life, and that of the astronomers, and probably Mother's, too, indirectly. She and Avdokia would have waited for the Cheka like geese on a pond if not for Varvara's lesson of last winter: when you smell trouble, make yourself scarce.

"I worried about you every day." So close in my ear. She put her papers down, her arm across my shoulders. "I thought you were dead. I went looking for you. Anton said you were with your mother, but by then she was gone. Couldn't you have sent me a note? Things could have turned out so differently..." She plucked at the ends of my hair, traced my nose, my lips.

I turned over the page I'd been working on. "I needed to disappear. For my own sanity."

"All those months, I thought...then they said someone had been arrested in Pulkovo and had mentioned
my name."

She brought her face close, studied me, kissed my
temple hesitantly. She shivered. Her eyes searched
mine. *Would I?* That drain, the blood. Another room of
the nightmare. Her body's pungent smell, a higher acid
smell than a man's. Even if I'd been a lesbian I wouldn't
have been excited by her. I'd rather have made love to
Manya. But I pitied her, and I owed her my life. I knew
how long she had been carrying this burden. I knew
what it was to love hopelessly.

"Please?" she whispered.

I couldn't see what it mattered now, after those
twisted nights with Arkady. I leaned across her to turn
off the lamp.

"No," she said. "Leave it on. I want to see you. I want
to know this is real."

Timidly, she began to make love to me. Her nervous
hands explored my breasts, tentatively caressed my
hips. How little experience she must have had. I was
sure Manya had been her first. It was unreal having
my old friend embrace me and feeling her growing
excitement, the catch in her breath, the sensation of
soft breasts against my own instead of a man's hard
chest. Her awkward touch, her keenness, was unbearable. There wasn't even any vodka to make things any
easier. She had no gift for lovemaking.

I showed her how. *Kiss my throat,* running my fingers

down it. Offering her the nape of my neck. *Kiss my neck, bite it.* Using my hand over hers to cup my breast. *Like this.* My body warming now. I imagined Kolya watching us, sitting open-legged in a chair, his breath speeding up. I ran her hand up my haunch, over my hip, down my thigh. *Here. Here.* She kissed my mouth, my breast—not biting or twisting the nipple—my belly, and buried her face between my legs. I hoped I wouldn't have to reciprocate. But how Kolya would adore this. It was easier, imagining him here as our third.

I moved her with my thighs and hands to a better sensation. What I would give for his clever cock now, his hands, his mouth. Thinking about his pleasure, my gleeful fox. Would I ever see him again?

She did not let me go until she felt the arch and ripple of my climax. Then, face smelling of me, she wrapped her legs around mine and rocked herself to completion. I'd never thought of doing that. "Marina, Marina...I've always loved you," she whispered, nestling her chin on my shoulder, her tears dripping on my skin. "Did you know?"

I nodded. Yes, of course I knew. For that reason, the power in our friendship had always tilted a bit in my direction. What I hadn't foreseen was the day I would lose my sense of what I'd never do, of what was impossible. Nothing was impossible and anything could happen. In the right situation, you could sleep with your best friend, you could turn over your father's mistress to the drain.

"I'm so happy. You can't know." Finally, she turned off the lamp and settled under the blankets to sleep, her leg flung across me.

I tried to get some sleep myself, but her leg was heavy and I was hot and the sheets reeked of her. I pretended to stretch and turn over, out from under that leg, but she moved again to press her breasts against my back, and wrap herself firmly around me.

58 *Alice in the Year One*

Alice in the Year One

I slept just fine
       on your floor.
              Like a baby.
Who doesn't love concrete?

    It makes you stand up straight,
          But what to do with a spine
          in the current condition.

  You ask for a poem
       for the Year One.

  I greet it!
      Da zdravstvuite!

Excuse me, Comrades.
> *I seem to have lost my drawers.*
>> *Like many of you, I was born*
naked.
> *I thought the Revolution*
>> *would solve that problem.*
> *But it continues, despite the edicts.*

Sorry, I forgot. You wanted a poem.

> *A celebration.*
>> *Urah!*

"Hey, you, devushka,
> *with the fire in your hair.*
>> *Tell me, where does the Future sleep at*
night?
Can you see it from here?"

Yesterday, your silhouette
> *In the doorway of a lighted room.*

> *"Come into the Future," you said.*

I peered in,
> *But it was just another room.*

No, my sister,
> *It won't do.*

See that ceiling?
   Rooms in the Future
     must have no ceilings
   They block out the stars.

  Down with ceilings!

Who cares if it rains?
   But Comrade, we need more skies.
   Tell Narkomprod.
     The sky rations ran out before
   eight a.m.
   And I was almost to the head of the queue.

  We demand more sky!

Second of all—no walls.
   Things happen behind them
     And not only the blah blah of the
   neighbors.

Walls hold you
   too tight
     like an overbearing nurse.
I don't mind being naked in public.
   That's a poet's job,
     To be naked for all of you.
But I don't care for swaddling.

And don't let's forget—beds.
*   That fluffy stuff—it's strictly passé.*
What good are whispered words on the pillow?
What good are dreams?
They keep us asleep
*   make us reluctant*
*   to get up and take our places*
*   on the assembly line of the Future.*
*   Also pillows have lice.*

Down with snuggling!
*   Waiting for kisses!*
*   The next page of the fairy tale!*

In the Future we'll all sleep standing up
*   like horses in a stall.*
*   It's far more comradely, wouldn't you say?*

*   "Are you coming or not?" you said.*
*   "I'm getting tired of holding the door."*

*   "Of course," I said, sniffing the air.*
*   There was no quarreling with the Future*
*   even if it was only the next hour's*
*   room.*

*   A party was raging*
*   There was nowhere to sit.*
*   Tomorrow played with his Mauser,*

Sprawling on the couch.
All the guests had telescopes
trained on their feet.

Well, there was still next Tuesday
And the year twenty fifty.
I went out for a smoke
But the door had disappeared.
The floor wet with broken eggs.

and the only way out was through.

I wrapped my head in the fringed shawl that lay on
the bed and gazed in the small mirror over the washbasin. I'd been hoping to disguise myself, but my face
only seemed framed and highlighted, even when I
pulled the wool low over my eyes. I wadded some
paper and stuffed it up against my gums, then took
some soot from the *bourgeoika* and rubbed it around my
eyes, hollowing my cheeks, darkening my eyebrows. In
the wavy mirror over the sink, there I was as an old
woman, as if I had gone straight from this day to the
edge of the grave, missing my life entirely.

A relief to be out on the drizzly, quiet streets of the
city once more, the Fontanka wide and green, still flowing below the powdered pastels of the buildings across
the way. Ah, to be out from under that cracked ceiling,
away from those striped walls and Varvara. Down with

rooms! A man stood on the Chernyshevsky Bridge, staring down into the water, smoking pensively. I could remember standing just here with Genya the last night before he went out for the defense of the city and came back to explode my life.

Nevsky Prospect was shockingly deserted. Broken and boarded-up windows, block after block. Signs had either been torn down, or stood in sad advertisement for shops long since closed. Whole sections of the wooden street pavers were broken, missing. We were going to celebrate the Year One here in this ruin? Yet I'd missed this place as a soldier misses his leg, like a broken-off piece of my heart. Or perhaps I was a broken-off piece of the city's heart, and it was Petrograd's great longing for one of its children that I felt. As I rambled—or, rather, hobbled—I felt as if I were walking along the lines of my own hand, the coils of my own brain, the veins of my own body. I knew every building, every bridge, my short life inseparable from these facades and railings.

An old woman, I walked unnoticed and undisturbed along the rippling canals, the mist holding the promise of more rain, veiling the buildings' faces. I walked all the way to Palace Square and saw that Varvara was right. The scaffolding of some great project was being built, preparations for the celebration in this next room of the dream. One blond broad-shouldered man way up on the planks at the General Staff Building arch caught my eye. *Sasha!* I almost called out, but then remembered who I was supposed to be, this hunched old woman—I thought of her as Marfa Petrovna—and shrank back under my shawl. Seeing him made me four times lonelier for my former life.

I wandered for half the day, trundling around in my hagdom, drinking in the sights, this beloved and heart-breaking city. At the corner of Liteiny and Nevsky, the doors of the building swung in easily. A good or bad omen? The old sign for Katzev Studio, gold lettering on black glass, still hung on the elevator cage, though the machine itself crouched uselessly like a miserable, toothless lion in a small-town zoo. I was happy to note that the iron balusters were still intact—cleverly eluding the fate of the wooden ones.

I climbed to the fifth floor slowly, clinging to that solid railing. At the top stood the shiny black door, a bit pocked and peeling now, with its familiar brass plaque under the bell. Did they still have electricity? I pushed the bell and miraculously, deep inside, heard the familiar buzz.

I felt myself inspected via peephole, then heard the clicks as several locks were released. The door opened. Sofia Yakovlevna, thin, wrapped in a gray shawl, blinked at me. We could have been sisters. Her face listed to one side, as if she had had a stroke. "Yes?" She didn't have her glasses on, thank God, but her appearance troubled me.

"Good day," I rasped. "Is Mina Solomonovna in?"

"She's in the darkroom." Her voice was uncertain,

her brow a puzzle of wrinkles. My face was familiar to her, I could tell, but she couldn't place me. "Are you expecting photographs?"

"Yes. Yes I am." This woman had known me since childhood. How could she be so easily fooled by a bit of paper and stove grime, a hoarse tone? Being dead would feel just like this, walking about as people you've known look through you. I could tell she was wondering why I wasn't taking my scarf off.

"Don't trouble yourself, dear. I think I know the way," I said as Shusha walked in from the back of the house, wearing her school uniform. Her eyes flew open, then her mouth. I touched the side of my nose—*careful*—and she clamped her mouth shut again. "Maybe this girl will escort me." I took Shusha's arm.

We bundled ourselves back to the studio, which was cold but clearly still in use—the green velvet backdrop, the chair for the sitter, the big camera on its tripod. Shusha's grimy school uniform was too short for her. She'd defied all odds by growing. "Marina, what's going on? Are you in trouble?" She seemed excited by the possibility, as if it were all one romantic adventure.

I wagged my head noncommittally.

"Papa died this summer." Her brown eyes glistened. "He was sick all spring."

I had been so caught up in my own bad news...that wonderful man. I had to catch my breath. "I'm so sorry. How are you getting along?"

"Bad. Mama's had it the worst. And Mina, she had to leave school to take over the business."

Poor Mina! I could imagine how devastated she must have been. She loved the university, her chemistry courses. She was no artist. If only Seryozha were still here… "Was it cholera?"

"No, it was his stomach."

"Vechnaya pamyat', " I said, even though they were Jewish. *Eternal memory.* How warm he'd been, sweeping us all up in his familial embrace. I could see him sitting on the divan in his caftan and cap, one leg propped up from the gout. How kind he'd been to Seryozha—only a year ago. The Katzev apartment had always been our sanctuary, but without their father, it felt cut adrift, a raft instead of a mountain. Now he and Seryozha could walk together, could take photographs for eternity.

The red light over the darkroom door was on. "It's crazy. The studio's busier than ever now," Shusha told me. "Even Lunacharsky came for a portrait." The head of the Commissariat of Enlightenment, in charge of all Russia's educational and cultural affairs. It was a coup for any enterprise, but especially theirs. We entered the light-baffling turnstile into the darkroom, warm and reeking. Mina stood over the sinks, washing prints. Red flashed on her glasses. Her hair was tucked up into a scarf. "Mina, this lady asked to see you," Shusha said.

My old friend glanced up, frowned at this strange creature her sister had brought in. "Can I help you?"

I peeled back my shawl, spit out the paper from my mouth into my palm. The expression on her red-washed face echoed that of her sister the moment before. "Marina." No smile, no arms flung around my neck. "You're alive."

"Don't go spreading it around." I smiled, trying to make a joke of it.

She looked older than the last time I'd seen her, thinner, a bit worn, a professional. Taking her father's place had changed her—whether for good or ill it was hard to know. She glanced darkly at Shusha. "Don't you have some homework to do?"

"I'm going." Shusha kissed me, quickly. "I have to go to class anyway. See you, Auntie." She started for the turnstile, but I grabbed her by the arm.

"Don't tell anyone you saw me."

"Who am I going to tell?"

"Anybody."

She mimed a lock across her lips and disappeared through the revolving door.

Then Mina and I were alone, silent but for the sound of the water in the sinks. They still had water, at least. Mina's bespectacled eyes examined me, evaluating, then turned back to her work. "So?"

Not at all the welcome I'd imagined. "I'm sorry about your father. I loved him. Seryozha worshipped him."

"I know." She sighed and lined up a plate in an easel, her movements deft in the glow of the red safelight. She slid in a sheet of paper behind it, exposed the print, then slid it into the first bath, poking at it with tongs. We watched the image consolidate itself. A group of patient, weary faces over open books. Workingmen, adolescents, old women. "The Liteiny District Soviet Literacy Class," she said. "There are so many clubs and organizations now. Everyone wants a place in the new world. And they all want it recorded for posterity." She fished the print out of the developer and plunged it into the stop bath, wiping a lock of hair back with her forearm. I tucked it into her kerchief for her. She worked quickly, efficiently, intelligence in every motion she made. "I know why you're here. Kolya said you'd gotten yourself into some kind of rotten mess."

He was back? And had come looking for me? With Arkady right here, waiting for him? "When was that?"

Mina poked at the print contemplatively. Extracted it and slipped it into the fixer, checked the thermometer, poured off a little water from a small tank heater into the tray, checked the thermometer again. "The last time? Back in August. Maybe July. I'm not exactly sure. I've got my hands full these days, as you can see."

She put another sheet of paper behind the easel, started again, revealing a face very pale and grim, then plunging back into red.

"Shusha told me. I'm sorry about the university."

"Nothing to be done." Her mouth turned down even more sharply.

"Nothing more from Kolya since August?"

"Don't I have anything better to do than keep track of your love life?" she snapped, poking irritably at the print in the bath. "You've been gone since April. Do you think our lives just stop when you're away? That we freeze into place, only to reanimate when you next appear? I've been here all along, trying to keep a roof over everybody's head. It's not a thrill a minute, narrow escapes and bold adventure, but it's the way real people live. We just keep living."

I struggled not to show how her words appalled me. She thought I'd died, and now that I hadn't, she wasn't even happy about it. I tried to see myself as she saw me. The self I saw reflected in her eyes, in her fury, was not me as I was today, but as I had been as a spoiled girl. It was like looking at a star, the light it emitted a million years ago finally reaching our eyes. But you could not talk people out of their impressions of you; only time could change them. I could tell her about the room on Tauride Street, but she could say that that, too, was my fault. I could tell her about the observatory, and cholera, and Gorokhovaya 2. "We've all suffered, Mina."

She slid in yet another sheet of paper. "Maybe so. But I have my own life now. It's not my choice but it's a good life. I don't chase after whirlwinds. I don't have time for your dramas. I'm engaged to be married, thank you for asking. I'm trying to live my life in a rational manner."

Engaged? Our little student? "Mina! Engaged to who?"

She finished counting and extinguished the light. "A medical student. You don't know him. Roman Ippolit. We got engaged when Papa was sick."

"I'm so happy for you." I reached to embrace her.

"Don't." She shrugged me off with a shoulder. I thought about her coming to find me, our reconciliation. "You don't really care, so don't pretend." She pulled the exposed paper and put it in the first bath. "You only came here to find Kolya." I could see she was seething. At least this time he hadn't given her a whirl, no great big dollop of coo to butter her up. "He showed up here back in May, looking for you. As if it were life or death. Really, you're two of a kind, you know that? You deserve each other. I don't know who's more melodramatic, you or him."

"And you told him..."

"I said no one had seen you. But I'll admit, Papa was so sick, I didn't pay a lot of attention."

Her father had died, and I had not been there. That's why she was so angry.

She pulled the photo out of the developer and into the stop bath. "'Maybe she's dead,' I said, half joking. And he started to cry."

Kolya!

"'I'd know if she was dead,' he said. 'And she's not.'" Her mouth got very small, and wrenched to the left as she rubbed her nose on her shoulder. I held my hand out and let her rub it on my palm. In the red light, I couldn't see her eyes behind her glasses.

"He looked around for you, but then he had to get out of town. He said things were 'too hot' for him. Needless to say I didn't ask what he'd gotten himself into."

She printed another plate on the glass easel. Lights on, lights off. She had a rhythm to her work. It was pleasant to watch people who were good at their work, even if they resented it. Into the trays went more faces, more clubs. Hopeful new citizens of the Soviet utopia. I plucked one out of the last bath and clipped it to the line for her. The faces on the slick sheet pleaded from their borders, *Remember us. We, too, have been here.* Ordinary people who probably had never before had a likeness committed to a photographic image. This, too, was the revolution. I had to remember that.

"He asked me if there was anything I needed," she said. "I told him I needed silver to coat my papers. The Cheka took mine on a raid, even though I had an order from Lunacharsky himself. And film, if he could ever get some. I was back to using glass plates. When I have film, I can do more work in the street. Cover events and so on. The world isn't going to come and sit in the studio and pose anymore."

I wanted her to talk about how he looked, if he'd indicated where he was going. But her father was dead, and she was still angry at me for my past sins. "I hope he brought you the film."

"He did. And flour and soap. Silver. Platinum salts. All kinds of things. Up to his old tricks, but I'm not complaining. That was June. I saw him once again in August, and that was it."

I helped her hang the prints as she pulled them out of the fixative. "Tell me about Roman Ippolit."

She laughed, hoarsely. "What do you want, Marina? I never see you unless you want something. What kind of trouble are you in? That ridiculous costume—it's not Maslenitsa, is it?" The butter festival, our pre-Lenten carnival week.

"I got involved with some bad people. Disappearing's harder than you think."

With all the prints drying on the line, she washed her hands, dried them on a towel, picked up a stack of finished shots. I followed her out into the studio. It was colder but at least we could breathe. She turned on a lamp at the long table and began organizing prints into piles and sliding them into envelopes. "I can't have you here, if that's what you're hoping for. Things are hard enough as it is. The Cheka comes two nights a week."

I saw where I rated on her table of ranks—somewhere between cholera and a ricocheting bullet. She wouldn't let me endanger her family, no matter what kind of trouble I was in. "It's okay. I have a place," I said. "I'm staying with Varvara."

She wrote something on one of the pink envelopes. "Be careful with Varvara," she said. "She's not the person you used to know. She's in the Cheka now."

"She got me out of the cellar at Gorokhovaya 2. Took me in. I have to trust her." I looked through a stack of prints and stopped at a big group—youthful faces posed in a pyramid.

"The so-called Third University," she sniffed. "The new privileged class." It was a recent innovation: the children of workers were allowed in without qualification. Studying while the brilliant Mina Solomonovna herself could not. "They get twice the bread ration as real students. Nice, eh?" she said bitterly. "While our professors were dropping like flies. Some teach over there for the bread."

She took the Third University picture out of my hands, stacked it with two more and put it in its envelope. "Don't trust anybody." It gave me the chills, the way she said it. It was so unlike her.

"Not even you?"

She sighed, took off her glasses, wiped her face on her forearm. I took her glasses, polished them on the tail of her kerchief, then put them back on her nose, delicately threading the earpieces, first one, then the other, over her small ears. Her eyes were deep with some emotion. Was it kindness leaking out? Was it regret? In that instant, she looked very much her father's daughter. She smiled a half smile. "What are you doing for work?"

I hadn't thought of it but of course I would need to get some kind of work. I couldn't go on eating half of Varvara's rations. She was so rigorously honest that she wouldn't take advantage of her rank to get more than she was strictly entitled to.

"Look, I've got more work than I can handle," Mina said. "As you can see. Especially with the October celebrations coming up. I can't pay you much, but you'll get rations...and nobody's going to come looking for you in a darkroom." She took a scrap of notepaper and wadded it up, handed it back to me. I crammed it against my gums. "Come back tomorrow. I'll set you to spotting negatives until your eyes bleed."

59 *The Eye*

I HAD TO FIND a better disguise than Marfa Petrovna. Marfa was too cumbersome with her wadded teeth and sooty face, her limp. Varvara stood by as I chopped my hair off with a pair of blunt scissors, peering into the small mirror above the basin. I turned to examine the profile, left and right. I looked like a boy of fifteen. "Not bad, eh?" I said.

She came up behind me, ruffled my hair— proprietary, like all lovers—kissed my neck, rested her chin on my shoulder, and gazed at the two of us in the mirror. "You have to do something about that red. And these." She weighed my breasts in her hands. "I can get you something from the infirmary, bandages or something. In the meantime..." She went to her wardrobe and pulled out a red kerchief dotted with small white flowers. Nothing I could ever imagine her wearing—it must have been Manya's. I wrapped it around my breasts, pulled it tight, shrugged back into my dress, examined the profile. Not bad. But the hair. The red. He'd spot me at a hundred paces.

Mina, the chemist, solved that problem in the darkroom, staining my cropped hair black with something toxic she cooked up out of her bottles and jars. The smell of sulfur and ammonia lingered in my hair for days. But the inky black held fast.

For suitable attire, I went out behind Haymarket Square and speculated, trading a precious egg, a hunk of sausage, and some firewood—courtesy of Cheka rations—with a Former for a pair of woolen pants, a student's jacket, and a boy's cloth cap. One look into the woman's eyes and I saw a dead son performing this last service for the family. Such sorrow, everywhere.

The clothes fit me well enough. I hoped it hadn't been typhus. I tried not to think I might die because of my disguise. I sewed some crude drawers from a pillowcase with a needle and thread Varvara had to borrow from a neighbor, and she wound my breasts with a bandage she'd secured for me from the stores of the Cheka. It bore brown stains, which reminded me of Viktoria Karlinskaya. My soul would never be free of that invisible stain.

Now I looked for all the world like a beardless boy, bright-eyed and black-haired, too young for the army in this new civil war, which was gathering up the last youths and even middle-aged men into its sack like pickers stripping the last apples of an orchard. I practiced walking like a boy, chin up, kicking out my heels as if my male parts were in the way, elbows akimbo, thumbs tucked in my belt. Varvara shrieked with laughter. "Not so swaggery. You look like you're going to start singing Puccini."

I tried a more bashful boy, slouching, hands in pockets, shoulders a little hunched, rubbing my nose, my chin where I had no beard yet. I practiced walking on the balls of my feet to straighten out my feminine sway. I would have scuffed my shoes but boot leather was more precious than eggs.

"That's better. I believe that," she said, sitting on the bed, her knees tucked under her chin. I could see the schoolgirl in her at times like this. "What's your name, *mal'chik?*"

"Misha," I replied, but my voice came out high, too girlish. I tried again lower, less clear. "Misha." Ending downward. My jaw flexed, a little defensive. Boys were on edge, it seemed. "Who wants to know, shitbrain?"

She jumped up, held me close. Kissed me three times.

It felt different to walk about the city as a boy. I hadn't thought of that. When you were a boy, nobody gave you a second thought. People might shove me and shoulder me aside, but they never looked in my face. That first day I headed up to Nevsky passing scores of citizens, and not one even glanced at me. I tried staring right into their faces to see if I could make them. Their eyes slid over me as if my skin were buttered. Just a boy. Nobody worth paying attention to. How strange. How remarkable. How free.

I presented myself at the studio every morning at eight. Misha, the new assistant, was eager, hungry. Sofia Yakovlevna embraced him as she had once embraced another boy . . . a more sensitive, more beautiful boy, better in every way. "Misha, are you hungry?" "Misha, could you thread this needle? My glasses aren't strong enough."

Shusha and Dunya saw through me like a window. Dunya understood that I was in trouble, but to Shusha it was just a wonderful big joke. She made eyes at me, blew kisses, pinched my rump. Her mother told her not to torment me — I was there to work.

Eventually, I even met the fiancé, Roman Ippolit, the medical student. Opinionated, with a square jaw and short, straight, bristly hair, he enjoyed giving Misha the benefit of his vast manly knowledge of the world. Especially its filth and decay. "Misha, the thing you need to know about third-stage syphilis . . ." He liked to tell me dirty jokes when Mina left the darkroom, about Lenin and his wife, Krupskaya. He was awfully sure of Misha's politics, yet in his own way he was as much a dialectical materialist as Varvara. No God, no poetry, no grace. Only arrogance and a sort of advanced crudity. I could not imagine the lover Roman Ippolit would be. Even Varvara the Chekist was capable of passion and tenderness. All I could think was that Mina must have made a rational decision to find a man she couldn't possibly love. That way she would not care if she lost him, wouldn't have to waste any time dreaming about him or replaying his touch in her mind. She was a practical girl. Her thwarted love for Kolya seemed to have soured her on the whole enterprise.

I started out, as promised, spotting negatives, scanning for the places where the emulsion's bubbles had formed white dots and painting them out with a fine-tipped brush. Eventually I graduated to the darkroom. We would develop plates she'd shot that day, and I learned to print them, then recoat them for the next series. And as promised, my eyes grew bloodshot with the effort of scanning the hectares of negatives for those white dots and feathering in the darkness.

But soon, she required help with the photography side of things and asked me to accompany her on jobs in the city, to haul her equipment, to help her with crowd control, to organize unruly schoolchildren or factory committees.

Printing was the best part. I loved the moment when the paper went into the developing bath. When something that was apparently blank revealed its true nature. I felt like all of revolutionary Petrograd was passing under my hands. The Dinamo factory's chess club, the workers' committee of the Vyshinsky printing plant. Portraits of artists and journalists, bureaucrats and Soviet young ladies. How complex this world was. Was it dying, or was it being born? Both at the same time. How could I reconcile this with the cellar of

Gorokhovaya 2? For every hopeful face, a name on a list. Eventually I stopped thinking about it, lost myself in shape and grade and density, the elegant process of the work. At times I felt Seryozha watching over my shoulder, and I talked to him. He didn't always approve of Mina's portraits. *Her father had a better sense of people's inner character.* But I was only the assistant, and after swimming in that acidic murk night after night, I felt I should be developing gills. I usually came home just as Varvara was waking up and getting ready for work, which suited me fine, relieving me at least of that masquerade, but left her restless and longing.

Mina told me to be ready at ten that morning. We had an assignment. She handed me the camera and tripod and together we descended to the street, just as we'd once descended with her father, so long ago, it might as well have been another century. As we walked up Nevsky, she told me she was worried that Dunya was still spending time with Sasha Orlovsky and wanted to marry him when she got out of school. It sounded all right to me. Evidently Sasha had a job now, teaching painting at the Free Educational Workshops—the old Higher Art Academy. "She's too young," said Mina.

But the time belonged to the young. As we walked in the cold drizzle, I thought of Sasha, and Anton, of *Okno* and our Wednesday nights, Genya in Moscow, poor dead Krestovsky with his newspaper, his wife dancing with the piano shawl. It wasn't until we were shoving our way onto the tram at Sadovaya that I asked Mina where we were headed.

"The new mothers' home on Kamenny Island," she said, slipping between two door-clingers.

Halfway on, halfway off, carrying the camera and the tripod, I almost fell backward. I would have, but the woman behind me was too forceful and crammed me on before I could change my mind. "Watch your step, *mal'chik*. Live another day."

I stood pressed up next to Mina, the tripod shuddering between us, and lowered my cap over my eyes. The boarded-up windows of Gostinny Dvor peered at the street like a blind man behind smoked lenses. My skin crawled as the tram came onto Palace Embankment and started over the Troitsky Bridge. I could almost see myself out the window in the fog, marching up to Kamenny Island to sell that pin. *Ask for Arkady.* Maybe I was still there, on a parallel stream. *Marina, don't go,* I tried to tell her. *Turn around now. Throw that cursed pin to the goddess Neva.*

As if it had heard me, the tram jerked to a stop. A collective moan went up. "It's broken again." "Every day." "Enough whining!" But nobody got off.

It was a sign. "Mina," I whispered, "I'm thinking maybe I shouldn't—" But then the car started up with a jerk that threw us into others and them into us and caused a chain reaction of elbowing and shoving, curses and grumbled relief. Soon we were over the bridge, right alongside the Peter and Paul Fortress. I held my breath as we passed, averting my eyes. Who was imprisoned in the Troubetskoy Bastion today? Anyone I knew?

It turned out that the mothers' home was installed in a dacha that had once belonged to the Danish ambassador—a famous spot in Petersburg's old society. The big trees, leafless in October, were still black from yesterday's rain. I, for one, was glad for the somberness of the day. I felt less conspicuous in the flat dull light. We started by photographing the nursing sisters, whom we arranged in four rows on the dacha's steps. Some of the nurses were as slovenly as the ones I remembered from the Anglo-Russian hospital, others somewhat more appealing.

I set the camera on the tripod for Mina, locked it down and inserted the big lens, put the cloth over my head to look at the subjects upside down on the ground glass. The grid made it more abstract. You could see the composition purely. If only life had something like that—a grid overlay to help you check your composition. You could square the edges, make sure it was straight. Perhaps that was why people were devoted to Marx or religion. But people like me always had to work freehand. It was our blessing and our curse.

Mina came to check the solidity of my handiwork, then went under the cloth to examine the shot. "Bring them in on the left," she said, motioning with her left hand. "Third row—make sure I can see all the faces."

Oh, the winks and pats from the maternity nurses as I tried to move them closer together.

"Hey, sweet face, got a girlfriend?" They squeezed and pinched me like a suckling pig. I hoped no one would notice my lack of male equipment.

"Squeeze in tighter, Comrades. That's right— tighten your corsets, girls," Misha directed.

How they laughed and flirted. Women loved little Misha. I could have had half of them. The young men were all out of town vacationing with the Red Army, and it seems they were sorely missed.

We took pictures of the mothers in the ambassador's dining room, sitting at his long wooden table, attended by the same stoic servants who had once served state dinners to the great and powerful. I was surprised they had stayed on, but then again, where would they have gone after a lifetime of service? Now they passed plates to poor women who'd just given birth, the women grateful but a little confused. What did this splendor have to do with their travails? Soon they'd be back in their smoky rooms with their squalling babies and other kids, the old man and the cold and *vobla* soup for dinner, and outside, the queues. We photographed their skinny blue babies, too, bundled up like cigars on a cart, scrunching up their wizened little faces. Clearly the Bolsheviks were serious about trying to keep alive what proletarian babies there were. Considering the epidemic level of malnutrition in Petrograd, each one was a miracle. I myself hadn't had a period since last winter. But life wanted to assert itself even in the least promising places. One of these poor things could have been mine. How lucky I'd been in that regard, in my otherwise ill-fated life.

After our day's work and a special treat—a meal of milk and kasha with a few members of the home's staff committee—we began the long walk out of the parkland back toward the tram. I was lugging the heavy camera and tripod, and Mina was carrying the wooden case with the film, when through the icy drizzle, which had started up again, we passed a form in a belted coat with a skirt and a curly astrakhan hat. I lowered the brim of my cap practically to my nose. Luckily for me Mina noticed nothing, and continued jabbering away about the director of the mothers' home and how insulting he'd been when he realized it was us and not Solomon Katzev himself who'd come to photograph his nurses. "The nerve of that man," she was saying. "If someone hates women, what's he doing running a mothers' home?"

I glanced back. Lot's wife. The flash of the Kirghiz's gaze over his shoulder told me he had seen me, all right. Seen me, recognized me, knew it all. My mouth went dry. How long would it be before Arkady knew I was back in Petrograd, masquerading as a boy, working for a photographer? It would be only a matter of time before he tracked me down. It was clear we were going to the tram. Perhaps someone would join us right there as we waited, and the rain would wash my blood down

Kamennoostrovsky Prospect. Or they would drag me away, and I would pass once more through the iconostasis, never to be heard from again. Back into the Archangel's hands, to be nailed to the barn door like the skin of a fox.

What to do? I could drop everything and run. But Mina…there was Mina to think of, her mother, her sisters.

"Wait here," I said, then tipped the tripod up, leaned the camera against her.

"What—are you crazy?" But she grabbed the camera before it fell. "Misha!"

"Akim!" I called out, his name jumping to my lips.

He stopped but did not turn. He was waiting for me. He lit his long pipe as I approached, squinting at me as if I were the wind and he was staring into my sting. I felt myself being weighed on an antique scale in his mind, but what I was being weighed against I couldn't tell. This man had seen my abasement, but he had also nursed me. *If you don't like wolves, stay out of the woods.* Now it was too late and the woods were everywhere.

We stood before the iron gates of the old Rybashkov dacha, glistening with wet iron flowers. Was this Arkady's new citadel? "Hello, Akim. How is it"—I nodded in the direction of the Church of St. John the Baptist—"these days?"

"He has not forgotten you," said the Kirghiz. "The girl from Kitezh, he calls you. 'I didn't kill her?' And

I say, 'No, Archangel. You let her fly away. Blessed are the merciful.'"

He'd kidnapped me, raped me, crooned to me, fed me, burned me, humiliated me...but the Kirghiz was saying that those bullets hadn't missed me from any stroke of good luck. In the end, he had let me live. I let that knowledge sink in.

"Why are you back in this place?" he asked. "You should have flown fast and far. You should have disappeared from the face of the earth."

"I was arrested. They brought me back. Please don't tell him you saw me. I beg you."

Behind us in the road, Mina stood unhappily, holding the camera. "Misha, let's go!" The days were growing short now, the light beginning to fade, and we had another sitting back at the studio.

I put my hand on his sleeve. "I beg you, do this for me."

"Things have changed since your time," he said over his pipe. The dark eyes glittered. What was he trying to tell me?

My lips were bone dry. "How have they changed?"

"The Archangel...is not himself now."

I shuddered to think. How could he be more mad? Yes, this man—not a good man, but better than many—was trying to tell me that Arkady wasn't even partially sane anymore. He tilted his head toward Mina, shuffling her feet and looking anxiously at the tram stop. "Your friend is waiting. Take care, little hawk.

There are bigger hawks than you. Their wings will darken the sky."

He wouldn't tell. Though it didn't mean I wouldn't be found. But today, this hour, I had my reprieve. I kissed his leathery cheek. "I'm gone."

60 *The October Celebrations*

SUDDENLY THE ANCIENT DRY-ROT empires began to collapse like a row of sand castles: Germany, Austria, the Ottomans. In Vienna, mass strikes and meetings capped the headlines. A red flag topped Munich's city hall. The kaiser teetered on his throne, clutching at the tattered brocade. After four long years, the war had at last ground itself to dust. It looked like the World Revolution had really begun—and thus our salvation. Rescue for isolated Russia, rescue for starving Petrograd. Although we had turned our backs on the workers of the world in signing the German peace, they had not forgotten us.

Now Petrograd rinsed the carnage of Red Terror from its streets and unrolled its futurist bunting, its agitprop carnival tent. The city's artists labored around the clock to prepare for the October celebrations— October, though our calendar had changed over in January, finally catching up with the rest of the world, producing the amusing phenomenon of the anniversary of the 25th of October being celebrated on the 7th of November. Why not? It was all part of our looking-glass world, where girls became boys and society ladies became beggars, and the newly literate took their places in the lecture halls at the university while the learned ate library paste. The streets and bridges took new names, and every construction worker from Narva to Vyborg set to sawing, hammering, and painting new facades for our venerable buildings, transforming the peeling and exhausted remnants of the Past into the palaces and monuments of the Future, at least for a few days.

I walked home in darkness through the metamorphosed city. Though I came and went at all hours, I was never molested. A woman on Nevsky, a furtive blonde in a ratty fur, offered her affections to Misha. "*Mal'chik*, come visit Paradise." She was a Former, older than me, perhaps someone who'd once attended the Tagantsev Academy. Was that really what she thought whores said?

"Thanks, Citizen. I get it for free." Misha was impudent. What people will accept from a boy continued to astonish and delight me. "No hard feelings—I'll tell my dad you're down here."

"Brat!" she called after me. "I hope they beat you!"

I turned around and blew her a kiss.

I loved walking these dark streets. I'd never imagined the sheer freedom of the male sex. How remarkable it felt to go where I wished at any hour, ignored and unmolested. If I hadn't been thinking of hawks far bigger than myself, and Varvara at home with her dreams of togetherness, I would have been perfectly content.

Working for Mina had whetted my appetite for my city like a knife on stone. I exulted in the cold mists, the smell of the sea, the sound of my boots resonating off the facades, the lapping of water in the canals. This wall, with its richly layered surfaces of announcements and proclamations. How beautiful! And this glorious puddle reflecting the lamplight—like an opening in the world, a tear, revealing a brighter, hidden life right beneath our feet. I was in ecstasy in the rain and the first peppering of ice, the way moisture drew halos around lamps and the few glowing windows. I wanted to eat Petrograd whole, like a boiled egg—pop it into my mouth all at once. Thank God I was finally out of rooms—Mother's, Father's, Arkady's, Varvara's, and those belonging to the state—while Mina worried only that the weather boded poorly for tomorrow's celebrations.

Down on the Neva, the ships would already be coming in from the gulf. We'd gotten copies of their schedules: *Cruisers south of the Nikolaevsky Bridge, destroyers between Nikolaevsky and Liteiny.* But now I stood before the black entrance to our building on the Fontanka as a man in a worn cap and sheepskin sidled up to me from the shadows. "I have meat," he hissed.

"How much?" I couldn't help asking, though I hadn't two kopeks to my name.

"Fifty per pound. I've got two."

Fifty rubles for a pound of God knew what. "Was it dead before you cut it up?" said I. "Or did you ride it first?"

The man's brutish eyes retreated into his puffy face in the hazy light from the streetlamp. "Get out of here, you little son of a whore, before it's you." He pulled out a folded knife, the blade flashed into place, and my impudence fell away like a suicide. I stood motionless as the man faded back into the darkness. I was wrong about being a boy. Misha was no better prepared than I.

I ran up the stairs to Varvara's flat, two at a time. I'd hoped she was asleep, but she'd waited for me, propped up in the mushy bed reading one of her political tomes, taking notes. The room was cold and stank of damp. She'd put some bread and a bit of sausage out, which I ate, feeling ungrateful for all she did for me. I tried not to taste the mold. It grew everywhere—the blankets, the rugs, the walls, our coats, the bread. I couldn't help longing for snow, the cleanness of winter, the crisp dry whiteness of it.

"How'd it go at the studio? You ready for tomorrow?" She set her book aside, dropped her dark head onto the pillow, yawned and stretched.

The bread was dark, sour, more sawdust than wheat. "She's plotting our schedule like it's a military maneuver."

I didn't ask about her day. *Did you kill anyone? Investigate any of our old friends?* I washed my face and brushed my teeth, trying not to imagine her striding into some poor family's room—their terror, the baby crying, the crash of furniture, the wife stifling her tears as her few scraps of silver were confiscated, the husband beaten. Varvara might be miles more professional than her colleagues, but she was essentially a violent person, and the Cheka gave her absolute liberty to exercise that trait. I once asked her why she couldn't stay a party organizer. "The party needs educated people in the Cheka," she'd said. "It shouldn't just be sadists and goons. They asked us to volunteer, and I did."

Her Red star was rising, shooting upward like a rocket. At nineteen, she was already a commissar. She was ambitious, always had to be first, best in everything. I remember how angry she used to get when I beat her in chess. In many ways she was a very poor Communist. She drew the covers up to her neck, kicking her feet like a child. "Come on, it's nice and warm under here."

I peeled off my boots and hung my coat on a peg, climbed into bed to undress under the covers. The springs bucked and squeaked with our combined weight, sloppy as an ungirthed saddle. But it was warm. I wondered if she skimped on the heat on purpose. I took off my shirt and let her help me unbind my breasts—such a relief. Misha converted to Marina again. Varvara ran her fingers over my compressed skin, the angry red marks, kissed my neck, and turned off the light. As a lover she was so unlike her normal certain, direct, unapologetic self. She needed me and was abashed by her own passion. Her hands on my skin were rough and dry as a washerwoman's, her breath slightly bitter. She had no sense of rhythm or humor and her gracelessness was worthy of pity. If I ever chose a woman for a lover, it would be someone like Galina Krestovskaya, flirtatious and lively and sensuous. But when someone pulled you from a Cheka cell, you said thank you. As she kissed me, I never forgot that she was also capable of shooting me in the head. The tiger purred for now. If I didn't cross her, this would be the safest place in Petrograd.

"I wish we could be together tomorrow," she whispered, fingering my nipples, though the flesh was sensitive after being bound all day.

"I'll see you in all your triumph," I said. She would accompany Comrade Ravich, the pro-Cheka commissar of the interior for the northern region, to the unveiling of Marx's statue in front of Smolny. Ravich was another woman who—after years of underground activity—had risen to an unheard-of position of leadership. Varvara adored her. Mina and I would photograph the events, and all the bigwigs would be there—the leadership of the whole Petrograd Oblast, called the Northern Commune. "Maybe I should put Zinoviev"—the Petrograd party boss—"between Ravich and Lilina and watch him sweat," I joked. Mina had heard that Ravich was Zinoviev's mistress and that his wife, Zlata Lilina, head of the women's department, would also be there.

"That's not funny," Varvara said, resting her sharp chin on my shoulder. "The people look to us as examples. Comrade Zinoviev of all people should be more rigorous."

"They're Bolsheviks. It doesn't mean they're saints," I said.

"We ask people to sacrifice. We should sacrifice as well," she replied, outlining the letters of Arkady's love poem incised in my back. She couldn't stop touching them, tracing them, then smoothing the skin over, as one smoothed down a new sheet of paper. Yet there they stayed. "We've heard von Princip's men are abandoning him like rats," she whispered in my ear. *The Archangel...is not himself now.* "When we get him, would you like to shoot him yourself?"

I burrowed into the old quilts. Yes, I think I would. I would do it just to make sure it was done. I knew he wouldn't plead. He would look me right in the eye as I did it.

"We're close." Her breath was warm, her frizzy hair against my temple, arm around my waist. "I'll save him for you. An anniversary present."

What strange days. I turned onto my back. Though I wanted him dead, I wouldn't want her to do it. I could never tell anyone that. Who would understand? But I felt him so strongly—his brilliance, his driving insanity, his loneliness. He'd revealed himself to me, a soul weirder and more trapped than anyone's. I wanted his soul and his dark self to meet.

She traced the line of my brow, my eyes, my lips. "Think, one year ago we were standing in your father's hall."

Yes, my unholy shame, my father's fury, and her glee at having ruined my family in a single stroke. Ah, the things we'd done for the sound of the word—*Revolution*. I'd been hypnotized by it. We all had. But I'd pictured change, not terror. I had imagined that the bourgeoisie would mend their ways. Not that one day they would literally be crushed—people I knew. People of goodwill who had nevertheless lived at the expense of others.

"To think I almost didn't find you again." She buried her face in my short, chemical-smelling hair. "I still want to cry when I think of you in that cell, covered with blood." Pressing herself to me. Her long body, her breasts, loose and surprisingly large, her wide hard hips, her knee between my legs. Kissing my breasts, my navel, wanting to taste me, wanting to bring me off. She wanted me the way I'd wanted Kolya. How cruel life was. Poor Varvara could not raise my pulse on her own. She came back up, holding me like I was some treasure from a sunken ship. Oh those wasted kisses. My deceitful self. I took over, touching her the way I touched myself, until the sighs came, the catch in the breath. I bit her, slapped her, pulled her hair. She loved it. I held her wrists together and pressed myself onto her, my thigh between hers, hers between mine and we brought ourselves off together.

I fell into a dead sleep, only to be awakened by a sharp, hard percussion. Were we under attack? Were the Germans here?

Varvara leaped out of bed and ran to the window, flung it wide. "It's the fortress!" The guns went off, *Boom! Boom!* I threw on my shirt and joined her, barefoot on the cold boards. *Three, four, five…* her arm around my shoulder, mine at her waist. Twenty-five cannon shots from the Peter and Paul Fortress announcing that the first anniversary of the revolution had arrived.

The celebration uncoiled like the spring of an enormous clock, an endless conveyor belt of intricately meshed gears—what Enlightenment Commissar Lunacharsky called the Revolutionary Carnival. Streets bulged with crowds, battalions of workers marched past, arm in arm, singing "The Internationale," and "Dubinushka," and "The Worker's Marseillaise." Each district provided its own section of the ongoing procession, complete with banners, marching band, and orators as it wound through the city ten abreast. Every bridge had become a work of art, replacing the old railings and ironwork with the colors and forms of the Future. It was hard to hate these goings on, so long had it been since I'd detected any sign of hope anywhere.

Mina and I worked together like right and left hand to capture this moment on film. By midday, like a surgical nurse, I could anticipate where she would want the tripod erected, what the frame should hold. I could get the camera onto the subject, have it ready to go within a minute, and stand sentry to make sure nobody got in the way of the lens or jostled her while she hunched under the cloth. I kept a stern eye on the film case so that it didn't walk off by itself.

She'd calculated her film stores, planned her shots, mapped out the day's schedule for maximum economy of motion with a precision that would have made Brusilov himself proud. She refused to be inveigled by serendipitous tableaux—empty shop windows enlivened with posters: BRUSH YOUR TEETH DAILY! Middle-aged women under the banner of the TSIGANY TOBACCO WORKS, marching arm in arm, eight abreast, smoking! She wouldn't waste the film she'd been allocated on such trivial moments. Sadly, she hadn't her father's eye. Worthy subjects were limited to speakers at assorted district soviets, artfully decorated squares, and elaborate factory banners—PUBLIC WINE DEPOT NO. 2, OKTOBRSKAYA FABRIKA METALWORKERS.

At noon we moved over to Smolny, where we photographed the momentous unveiling of a statue of Marx on his plinth. He gazed over the heads of the gathered commissars, looking toward Insurrection Square and the train station, hand resting inside his coat as though he were checking for his tickets.

Up by the inner circle of party brass in the autumn drizzle, Varvara quietly stood beside Comrade Ravich. How solemn my friend looked! It was supposed to be a celebration. *Loosen up, Varvara!* Ravich, tall and striking in a soft velvet hat, stood well away from Comrade Zinoviev, who was more youthful up close than he came across in pictures, with wild, thick hair that every caricaturist had drawn at some time or other. So this was the man responsible for the madness of Red Terror. He hadn't even wanted to go forward with the October Revolution at the time. I could have shot him easily if I'd been armed, though I sensed the Cheka presence was thick in the crowd, especially around the many dignitaries who'd come up from Moscow for the celebration. Nonetheless, their desertion remained a sore spot in every Petrograder's heart.

Luckily, there was no question of arranging them for a photograph. These were the leaders of Red October—you didn't tell them how to pose. All I had to do was make sure they stayed in the frame. Ravich, skeptical, with soft hat shading dark eyes, stood to the left, and a handsome man next to her, and a fat one, looking like he had a hot *pirozhok* in each pocket. My guess: the commissar for provisions. Zlata Lilina looked small and fragile compared to her rival, though none of those old comrades could be very fragile given what they'd gone through to arrive at this day. Zinoviev stood next to her, and behind them Lunacharsky stood upright and proud, his bald pate gleaming with the success of his Revolutionary Carnival. This was his day, shepherd of Russian Culture, single-handedly fighting to keep monuments intact and artists alive. He beamed like a proud Scottie bitch over her pups.

After the photographs, the speeches began. Zinoviev stepped up to the dais to announce news even better than yesterday's. "Today, we've learned, the kaiser has abdicated. The Germans are out of the war!" The cheers rebounded above the packed crowd. "The triumph of the German working class is inevitable," he thundered, his dark frizz bobbing, and I remembered his other role as head of the Third International, the spear point of World Revolution. "In Vienna, in Budapest, in Prague, Soviets of Workers' and Soldiers' Deputies are taking their places. A red flag flies today over Berlin! Can the same flag over Paris be far off?"

After the applause died away, a dignitary from Sovnarkom joked with the men around him. "You heard that in a year's time, there'll be just five kings left? The king of clubs, the king of hearts, the king of diamonds, the king of spades…and the king of England."

No kings. No empires. I needed a moment just to absorb all this, but Mina was already taking down the camera. "Hurry up," she said. "We're due at Uritsky Square in half an hour." I admired how quickly she absorbed the latest nomenclature. Palace Square had been renamed for Comrade Uritsky as the place of his martyrdom. We packed up our gear and flew down to the palace to photograph the speakers at the Alexander Column.

In the square, constructivist paintings had transformed the grand autocratic buildings into a spectacular vision, a city of the Future. The Alexander Column was a geometric blossom, while all around the circumference of the plaza, murals forty feet high proclaimed the new realities. FACTORIES FOR THE WORKERS. LAND FOR THE LABORER. HE WHO WAS NOTHING WILL BE EVERYTHING. In the midst of the crowd, agitprop groups on flatbeds enacted melodramas and acrobatic feats for the throngs, slapstick comedy with a revolutionary flair. How I longed to be up there with them. This was the fun we had not seen since the days of the Provisional Government. Lunacharsky had been right. The people needed this. They loved it.

I could hear Anton in my head, the dour ass: *It's not art, it's just advertising*. But the players were wonderful and I laughed right along with the crowds to see the agile clowns juggle colored balls, demonstrating how the kaiser and the Entente had juggled our world. Mina for once agreed on the importance of capturing this scene.

By early twilight, the crowds began to turn toward the theaters for free concerts and plays. Thousands of workers streamed through the doors. Those not lucky enough to have tickets moved toward the Neva to watch the fleet preparing for the evening's spectacular. I wanted to see it all, disappear into the crowd like a fish into the sea.

"That's it." Mina yawned, stretched, cracked her neck left and right. "Thank God. My head is ready to explode. Big day tomorrow." She took off her glasses and rubbed her eyes.

"Let's go see the ships." I didn't want to miss them. I was as eager as a child.

"I've seen ships. We've lost our light. I can't shoot in the dark, and I need to get off my feet. Let's go." She picked up the film box and turned for home.

"Old lady. Who cares about your feet? This is history!"

"This"——she lifted the box with our exposures from the day—"is history. And *I* care about my feet. We have a big day tomorrow, remember?"

I shook her by the shoulder, trying to loosen her up. "Come on, Mina. Sailors! Fireworks! You can't go home now."

"Don't tell me what to do!" she snapped, shrugging me off. "Do whatever you want to do, *Misha,* like you always do. But get this stuff back to the studio first."

How she enjoyed ordering me around. *He Who Was Nothing Will Be Everything.* I shouldered my waltzing lady and we pushed our way back to Liteiny, with the entire Red city shoving in the other direction.

Back at the Katzev flat, Sofia Yakovlevna was waiting, the samovar steamed. I could smell dinner cooking. Nostalgia gripped me as we carried the equipment back into the studio, dropped the big camera and its tripod, the wooden case. But the noise from the crowds, the pipes and whistles, called me. I had to go—it was a physical yearning. "Give me a camera," I said. "Let me see what I can do."

"You must be joking. I'm not going to give you a camera."

"Your old Kodak? I bet you still have it." A little box camera with bellows her father had given to her on her thirteenth birthday. She'd only used it one or two times to please him—never dreaming that some-day she would support her entire family with a camera.

"I don't know if it even works. And the film's easily four years old. You'd have to use a very long exposure in the dark. I don't think you'd get anything."

"Let me try," I said. "What would you lose?"

She dropped into the studio prop chair, a plump tufted armchair from the 1890s. "A camera?"

"I'll fight them to the death for it, as the devil is my witness. And if I'm lucky, you'll have photos like no-body else's."

She sighed, but she pushed herself out of the chair and into the darkroom.

The little leather-cased Kodak sat on a high shelf next to a magazine of film, under a coating of dust. She wiped it off, slowly, then loaded it for me. She ex-plained about the aperture and the exposure, blah blah. "The tripod's there—no, the little one. But don't you lose that camera. I swear, Marina, I'll drown you in the developing tank."

61 *Hooligans*

OVER THE NEVA'S CROWDED shores, a shining dark rolled out like a bolt of silk taffeta, no longer recognizable as our poor Soviet night, homely as a darned sock. This was something we'd dreamed after going to bed hungry. A dream of ships transformed into floating cities of light, strands glittering between smokestacks and masts like spiderwebs in new grass, the black water transformed to lightning. Such sound! Cheering, whistles blowing, pipes and rattles, bouncing off the tsarist facades like kopeks off a taut sheet. The ships' searchlights wrote their angular signatures across the sky, sweeping over crowds so dense they looked like fields of dusky wheat. Mina was right—no way could I capture this with chemicals and celluloid. Yet I would try, if only to prove her wrong.

What would have been the perfect vantage point—Liteiny Bridge—was now impassable. I'd have to sprout wings and fly to it. I worked my way instead down to the Nikolaevsky Bridge and crossed it inch by inch, using my tripod like a sorcerer's staff to part the woolly masses, those worn and hungry faces full of light. Hard to begrudge such pleasure. Everyone smiled at me, even as I shoved. When was the last time we'd seen such smiles?

An hour of determined force brought me onto the

Strelka, the tip of Vasilievsky Island, wedged between the Bolshaya Neva and the Malaya Neva, with its view into the heart of the river. Before me lay the grand jewel of Petersburg cracked open like a walnut—the Winter Palace, the Admiralty with its constructivist flags and spire, the Peter and Paul Fortress, prison and palace. All lit up, no rationing tonight. But the mansions on the English Embankment turned their blind eyes to the fete, resentful, lost in the past. I thought of that long-ago summer night—or was it only last year?—when I walked here with Genya in the small flame of new love, our heads full of revolution. Well, we had gotten our wish. I never suspected how it would unfold—you changed the world, but then the world came back and changed you.

I saw that people had climbed the bases of the Rostral Columns, those red granite lighthouses, each guarded by gargantuan statues representing the four great Russian rivers, and studded with the prows of bronze boats that in Viking days would have been those of captured ships, lit with signal fires. If I could get up there, I'd have a clear shot over the heads of the crowd. I wriggled and pushed my way through a mass growing denser by the moment until I'd reached the muscular statue of the Dnieper—or was it the Volga? Resting the unwieldy tripod on its giant lap the way a cripple holds his crutch on a tram, I scaled the bronze river god to the granite pedestal upon which the column stood. A sturdy man above me gave me a last hand up. Others made room. Looking down on the tripod, I saw that bringing it had been a mistake. Well, Mina had said, "Don't you lose that camera." She said nothing about the stand.

And it was worth the struggle. From up here I could see the breathtaking vista, fortress on the left, palace on the right, and half the Baltic fleet floating in the middle. I felt like a prince overlooking his birthright. My city had not died. I felt pride and an overwhelming nostalgia in my tightly bound breast.

Then a small shower of something fell on my head. Sunflower-seed hulls. I peered up and, in the lowest projecting prow, saw human arms twenty feet above the crowd. Another spray of sunflower hulls. Someone had climbed up to one of the symbolic bronze boats —every Petersburg child's fantasy.

I had to be up there. And only now, in the chaos of Bolshevik rule and the complete absence of police, would such a thing ever be possible. I shouted up into the darkness. "Hey, Comrade! Sunflower spitter!"

A boy leaned over the side and spit some seeds into my face.

I brushed them off. "Hey, brother! I need to come up. I'm taking pictures for *Pravda*." I held out the camera. I felt like the golden perch in the stories, bargaining with the old man.

His head disappeared into the darkness.

"Come on, have a heart!" I shouted up. "For Lenin!"

There was really no need —I had a perfectly decent

view from here—but I yearned to be higher above all
the world, as I once needed to climb all the way to the
treetops.

Then the sturdy man next to me elbowed me and
pointed.

A rope had descended from the ship.

I was not nearly as strong as I'd once been, but I
tucked my camera into my jacket, grabbed the rope,
and wound it around my leg like that circus girl I'd
once imagined myself to be, and pulled myself up, a
foot at a time, until unseen arms hauled me up the rest
of the way, bracing the rope against the side of the hull
like fishermen pulling in a full catch. *Don't let go,* I
thought as I slowly twirled on the rope, the pounding
of my heart drowning out the din from below. Hands
dragged me in over the lip, and I squeezed in between
two boys, hooligans Misha's age, flashing grins.

One thumped my shoulder, face full of freckles.
"Good man, *Pravda*. Vanya thought you were gonna
chicken out."

"You really takin' pichurs for *Pravda*?" said the other
one, with a nasal voice, a smashed nose.

"Lenin's going to give you a prize, personally," I
said.

All along the Neva, the embankments were so thick
with human beings they looked like they'd grown fur.
It was colder up here, the wind sharp. My nose ran, my
head throbbed, but I wouldn't have traded places with
a king.

I pulled my cap down over my bruised brow, where I'd struck it on the way in.

"I'm Misha," I said.

"Yura," said the first one, and we shook. "We always come up here."

"I always wanted to," I said. "Willya look at that?"

Gazing out at our city, shining, twinned in the black water, I ached for all the exiles who would never return to this. I wiped my nose on my sleeve—it was un-Misha-like to cry. My terrible, my beautiful land.

I got to work, opening the bellows of the Kodak, resting it on the cold bronze lip of the boat, the strap secure around my neck. I sighted with one eye, although it would be pure luck if I got anything at all—the viewfinder was nearly invisible in the dark. I framed my shot as best I could. It was so different from the ground glass of the huge camera, where the image was clear and bright behind the grid and the whole thing rested on a stable tripod so you could leave the lens open for ten minutes if you needed to. All I could do now was point at the lights, open the shutter, and hold my breath.

"At first Vanya didn't want you up here," said Yura.

"But we figured, *Pravda*? Might be worth somethin'." Vanya's nose had been smashed almost flat—or maybe he'd been born that way. "Got any booze?"

I shook my head.

"Smokes?"

"Nah. No caviar neither." I should have packed some

kind of offering, but I'd never been a photographer before.

"Then what're you good for?" He lit a *makhorka*,
the foulest I'd ever smelled. He must have picked up
butt ends off the street and rerolled them. He handed it
to Yura, who handed it to me. My eyes watered but I
would not cough and disgrace myself.

Perched there above the glittering scene, I felt like a
hero, like I could eat the entire glorious night and drink
the river dry. Even Marina wouldn't have risked coming up here with two hooligans. But I was just a boy,
smoking a horrific cigarette and drinking in the sights
as if I were Peter the Great.

Over the river, a mechanical roar even louder
than the crowd drowned out the voices, the whistles, everything—and a hydroplane flew past our
nest, right at eye level. Then another. The boys
stood and shouted, waving their arms. Vanya almost
fell out of the boat. I balanced the Kodak on the
boat rail and tried to follow their flight—their
delicate gleaming wings—upriver, over the ships.
They went as far as the bend toward the Okhta side,
and then circled back. The crowd roared like waves
on the ocean.

"Better get it if yer gonna get it," Yura said.

I got the picture as they raced past. At least I hoped I
got something.

Now searchlights from the destroyers combed the
night, raking the mobs. A rocket went up from one of

the ships and exploded into a fiery rose, and the noise reverberated off the river and the buildings. Fireworks responded from other light-bedecked battleships. We cheered at each glittering explosion and laughed at the percussions. My comrades' tough-boy faces filled with equal parts fear and delight, like the children they were. I turned the Kodak onto them, and they posed for me like sailors, their caps on backward.

All this firepower reminded the boys of the civil war, and they began to talk about the Red Army, recounting its victories. Budyonny, Stalin—these were the names they mentioned with awe. "Didja see the Kronstadt sailors last week?" said Yura.

"What about 'em?" his friend asked.

"Had a rally on Nevsky is what. Think they're gonna get rid of the Bolshies. They ain't afraid of nothin'."

The Kronstadt sailors were protesting against the government? Varvara had said nothing about this. Why? It was a serious thing.

"Anybody get shot?" asked thin-faced Vanya, sniffling in the wind.

"Nah. But they marched over to the Mariinsky and stole the band. It was hilarious. Took 'em down to the river to get the dockworkers to walk out." He leaned back with his *makhorka* like a man in a hammock, eyes full of fireworks.

"I'd rather be in the army than the navy." Vanya filled his mouth with sunflower seeds. "Stuck on a floating tub? Not me. I don't even like fish." He chewed and spat the shells down on the crowd below. "What about you, *Pravda*? You gonna join up?"

"Maybe," I said. "Maybe the cavalry." I thought of Volodya, fighting against boys just like these. Trotsky had called for a universal draft—he wanted to build a three-million-man army. "I like horses."

"I'd rather be in an armored division," Yura said, wiping his nose on his hand.

The fireworks flowered like seasons and the air grew thick with smoke. I wondered whether we'd have enough gunpowder left to fight the Whites.

But eventually it ended. If getting into the boat had been a risk, a dare, a leap of faith, getting down was a moment to savor. Vanya made a sort of lasso and tied it to the prow. The two boys slid down neatly as alpinists, and though I didn't have their strength, I followed as smartly as a fairy-tale prince down a maiden's braid.

To my surprise, the stocky man handed me the tripod after I'd clambered down to the Volga statue. "World's going to be different for you boys," he said. I shook his hand. *For us girls, too, Comrade.*

Vanya shook the rope free and it tumbled down into his arms. "Hey, you're pretty good," he said, twining it into figure eights, hand and elbow, tucking it under his coat. "Ever think of makin' some money like that?" It took me a moment to understand what he was saying. Thieves. My new pals were young second-story men. I didn't dare ask if they knew the Archangel.

The crowds began to move off the embankments,

and we wandered over to Nikolaevsky Square, where someone said there'd be an outdoor movie. They were playing *Tillie's Punctured Romance,* with Charlie Chaplin and Mabel Normand. In the shadow of the Xenia Institute, to be anointed the "Palace of Labor" in the morning, we shared a bottle with some other hooligans and picked up a group of factory girls out for a good time. A girl with a little pert nose kept touching me, clutching my arm. Yura glared. Obviously she was *his* choice. I leaned against the wall as my girl chattered about her friends, and who said what at their Okhta mill, and did I like her kerchief, and what did I think about Charlie Chaplin? It never occurred to me how dull girls were, how tedious our minutiae. I pretended to read a poster affixed to the wall over her head, and then suddenly began to read in earnest:

THE POETS, ARTISTS, DIRECTORS, AND ACTORS

OF THE

COMMUNAL THEATER OF THE FUTURE

WILL CELEBRATE THE ANNIVERSARY OF THE

OCTOBER REVOLUTION

WITH REVOLUTIONARY SPECTACLE

ARCHI

PEL   AGO

MINIATURE THEATER, LITEINY PROSPECT

10:00 P.M.

KURIAKIN — TOMALIN — SHCHAPOLNIKOV — OS

"What time do you think it is?" I asked the little girl with the pert nose.

"Who cares? No work tomorrow, lambie," she said, kissing me.

I glanced around for someone who might have a watch, but it was a solidly proletarian crowd. I gave my new sweetheart a squeeze, saluted my comrades, and began pushing through the crush toward Liteiny.

62 *The Miniature Theater*

THE THEATER CROUCHED IN a cellar hard by the Muruzi House, where the art collector Tripov used to live, though surely no longer. The tattered placards gave evidence that the cabaret was ferociously clinging to life in the new revolutionary climate. Like séances, cabarets were stained with bourgeois tar—too inclined to the ribald and satirical—but not completely done with. I would have imagined that after Red Terror, they'd have boarded up the doors, but the company seemed to have fellow-traveled its way through the Year One. A group of ticketless clamorers beset the chipped black doors and stairs and I thought of the Stray Dog all those lifetimes ago. Tonight I approached importantly, shoving my way through with my tripod and Kodak. "I'm from *Pravda*," I announced to the ticket man, a small *intelligent* in a necktie and frayed white collar. "Have they gone on yet?"

He eyed me skeptically. In honor of the anniversary, free tickets had been issued by the thousands to tobacco girls and metalworkers' boys, to literacy classes and orphanages, and—who knows?—possibly even Soviet newborns. A boy with a small camera—who was to say he wasn't from *Pravda*?

"We're documenting the Revolutionary Carnival. Lunacharsky himself ordered it." I waved the name before his unimpressed nose like a pass.

Other people crowded in behind me. He had to make a decision. "*Nu, khorosho*. Just don't block anyone's view." And he parted the curtain.

I descended into the tiny nightclub, packed with unwashed bodies, muggy with cheap tobacco. I—or rather Misha—pushed to a spot by a post and set up Mina's ridiculous camera on its spindly tripod. There I could shoot—or pretend to—past the shoulder of a woman in a hat with crushed feathers. Onstage, very young and energetic actors wound themselves into the crossbeams of an ultrastylized set, the scaffolding casting strong diagonal shadows on the wall. A few geometric shapes in bright colors, an abstract backdrop, and some ropes completed the mise-en-scène. It brought to mind a cross between a construction site, an amusement park, and a gallows—a nice metaphor for the place where we found ourselves on the anniversary of the revolution.

People coughed extravagantly, and the man next to me shoved me, almost toppling the camera. I elbowed him back. "Watch it, Pops. I'm with *Pravda*." Someone jarred me from behind. A small group of workers burst into sudden laughter. I was thankful it wasn't a real assignment. I could never get a decent shot in a crowd like this.

On the upper deck of the stage, a boy in a yarn wig and a swallowtail coat swaggered with an open umbrella like a parasol, arm in arm with a girl in a constructivist version of a satin evening gown, looking a bit like a starfish when her arms were extended. Laughter and shouts all around as the boy balanced on two chairs and recited in a pompous voice:

> *Of course, we must have a Revolution.*
> *Of course!*
> *In the Future*
> *in the Future.*
> *Someday, if they trust us*
> *If they let us educate them properly*
> *Teaching them French philosophy,*
> *all the things they'll need*
> *to help them when*
> *in the Future*
> *We give them their Revolution.*

A roar of indignation suffused the house. Now a second boy, in a dinner jacket with a giant belly and a monocle, international currency signs scrawled on the waistcoat, exhorted in a deeper voice:

In the Future
        The distant Future.
        Give me a bit of a head start,
            Will you, old chap?

I gathered that this was a ship, or a shipwreck, and all these people were stranded on a boat or island together. I was jealous. Genya and his friends were having fun down in Moscow, clowning for the revolution, while I was binding my breasts, taking orders from Mina, and sleeping with Varvara every night, jumping at shadows. Now, the banker pulled out a guitar, and the girl in the satin evening gown delivered a song in a high clear voice pronouncing the need for order—a place for everyone and everyone in his place.

God's in heaven,
        fish swim the seven seas,
        and everybody knows the worker's place
                is to serve the bourgeoisie.
To make things nice,
        to make it easy
            I don't know what the trouble is
                God save the bourgeoisie.

The crowd stamped and booed as the girl patted her coiffed hair. I longed to be alive again. I should have been one of these actors or writers in the Communal Theater of the Future. If I'd gone to Moscow I would

have been, if I hadn't been too proud to share Genya
with Zina. And where was he? Hovering in the wings,
whispering to his actors? Making last-minute changes?

No...there! In the audience, crouching so as not to
be seen. Grimy-faced, in costume. Even in the dark,
he glowed—the size of him, the bones of his face,
the breadth of his shoulders in a worker's coveralls. I
would talk to him after the show. I would tell him, *I
changed my mind. I can't live here anymore with Varvara
and Mina. They're sucking the life out of me. I'm dying.*
Surely I still meant something to him.

Now the Proletarians emerged from their hiding
spots and stormed the stage, the Workers begrimed
in greasepaint, the Sailors sporting striped jerseys.
Genya, the lead worker, led the way. He planted himself onstage like an explorer planting a flag upon a rock,
threw back his head, and roared:

> *What is this world where good men toil
>   While the greedy spit on us from above...*

At home in his element like a fish in the Kapsha. Now
I saw Zina as one of the Sailors, her face full of pride,
a member of the elect. Her eyes never left Genya—so
devoted, so doggishly loyal. I'd been a poor wife by
comparison. He mounted the stairs, followed by the
crew, as the Aristocrats and Capitalists shrank at his approach. He absorbed the light—more arresting, more
confident than ever. But I saw he'd lost his humility,

his bit of clumsiness. Was that something Moscow had done for him? How we were all changing.

"Hey, *mal'chik*, long time no see," came a voice in my ear. I instinctively turned but it came again, "Don't look. Watch the play." A voice not deep but rich like short fur, it moved down from my ear to grip my heart. Tumbling... was the floor tipping? I felt myself falling, the theater folding in like the set with its strange angles. *Oh let me just be, just for a second. Let me believe that it's true.* I closed my eyes. Could I smell him under the fug of a hundred cigarettes, his honey scent in the cramp of the room? Yes, I could. I trembled, all my strength gone.

"I knew you'd be here. It was my last hope."

I had to force myself to attend to the antics onstage—this mummery, this puppet show, Genya spouting while the professor in the swallowtail coat tried to fend him off with the umbrella. To think I'd just been beating myself up, wishing I'd left with him that day at the station. If I had, I wouldn't have been here to be found. "How did you know?" I whispered back, counting on the noisiness of the crowd to cover our conversation.

"Tell 'em, Ivan," the woman in front of me shouted.

"It was my last guess," Kolya said. "I've been looking for months."

I peered into the viewfinder to give myself something, anything to do besides crush him to me and kiss him so long and so hard we'd both faint from lack of air. Through the camera, Genya was just a blur standing on the stairs like a Soviet colossus, the embodiment of Proletarian Virtue. "I never thought you'd come back."

"Get 'em, Comrades. Don't let 'em piss on you!" "Watch the stairs, Ivan! It's a long way down!"

"You really thought I'd leave you to that lunatic?" He was standing so close that I worried what people would think. *A man and a boy*. Though maybe we were brothers.

Yes, that was exactly what I'd thought. That he'd save his own skin. Now I was ashamed. "What about Shurovistan, population one?" I chanced a sideways glance. He'd grown a beard and wore a rough cap, a shabby jacket, and a turtleneck sweater. He looked like an intellectual worker, a printer or typesetter, like Kraskin. He even lit a *papirosa*. So much for his beloved cigars. His blue eyes were transparent in the stage-light reflection.

"I'm an ass. I could drown myself in the Fontanka," he said.

"Why don't you?" a man from behind us called out. "I'm trying to watch this nonsense."

We had to get out of there. With Kolya around, it would be easy to put two and two together. "I've gotten my shots," I said loudly, collapsing my tripod. "What do you say let's get out of here, find ourselves some girls?"

He clapped his hand on my shoulder. "Lead on, brother."

I began to shove my way toward the door to a chorus of "Watch it!" and "Hey, 'scuse you!" Glancing once more at the stage, I could have sworn Genya saw me leaving. For a moment, he paused mid-speech and looked right at me. Impossible—no way he could see in the dark with the lights in his eyes. Even if he could, how would he have recognized me? Still it gave me a shock. Too late, too late, it had already been too late even at the Cirque Moderne, even at the Stray Dog. I'd already belonged to Kolya Shurov. My heart pulsed to the syllables of his name.

Out on Liteiny, celebrants caroused in the novelty of nighttime illumination. It was as if the promised Future had finally blossomed, a weird flower that would only last a night. And by my side, my one and only love. We fell into perfect step, as we always did, but we couldn't risk touching—it would be obvious. He'd taken quite a risk to come for me. But if I did not kiss him soon, I would explode. I needed his hands on me, his mouth.

"This getup suits you," he said, pretending to inspect a building. "I never liked boys, but maybe I should rethink my stance."

I didn't even want to discuss it. "We should get off the street. Where are you staying?"

Suddenly he snaked his arm around my waist and swept me into a dark courtyard entrance, pressed me to the wall. Our lips flew together, bodies locked tight. Everything in me rose up to seal myself into the moment, into this man, his fragrant body, his strength. He searched for my breasts under my student's tunic and found them bound, kneaded my hips, my unboyish ass. If I'd died, I would never have felt *this* again, this flame coursing through me, like a trench full of gasoline set on fire. It was worth having lived to this hour. It was worth everything, no matter what it had cost me or would.

He spoke quickly between kisses. "I swear I never meant to hurt you. I didn't foresee, I swear to Almighty God." He pressed his cheek to mine in the darkness. "My darling girl or boy or whatever you are." My magician, my life. "I knew you were alive, I knew it in my bones."

So many things he didn't know: Arkady, my father, Marusya, *Varvara*. But their hold on me had broken, and there was only this shape in my arms now. "Don't cry," he said, kissing my tears. "We're here. We're here now."

How long did we kiss in the shadows? When Kolya and I touched, the night held its breath. My cap fell in the mud, the camera clattered to the ground. Would I make love with him against the slimy wall of the courtyard like a desperate whore?

He unbuttoned my tunic, bit my neck. "Can't we go to your place?" Still trying to get the bandages loose.

"I'm at Varvara's."

He laughed, despairingly. "Well, that's out."

He didn't know the half of it.

"I've got an idea." He backed away, smoothed down my tunic, hoisted his trousers, settled himself.

Shaking with undischarged passion, I scooped up my wet cap and slapped it against my leg. He picked up the camera and tripod, hoisted them onto his shoulder. We straightened ourselves and walked back into the street like friends who'd just shared a piss. I could smell his honey all over me. It was madness. We blended in with the other revelers. I thought briefly of Mina, asleep, rehearsing her plans for tomorrow. How could two friends be so impossibly different? She loved that sensible life, but at my core lived something hot and red that could not be contained and put to bed at nine. She could no more understand the forces that moved me than I could find delight in a closely planned timetable.

And Varvara... I couldn't think of how she'd react when she realized I'd slipped her noose, when she saw my little fox footprints disappearing in the snow. Right now, only joy welled up in me, knowing I wouldn't return to her bed tonight or any other night. It increased the danger—not only would Arkady be looking for me, but so would a deadly spurned Chekist. Scylla and Charybdis. I felt my disguise falling from me. Where was my boy's walk? Couldn't anybody tell we were lovers? Could they not see the steady pulse of attraction, the light in our eyes, feel the surge of current between us? He began to whistle "The Internationale."

Common sense would have me go back to the Miniature Theater and try to burrow myself into the Communal Theater of the Future. But common sense slept in the bed with Mina, and I was myself again, a careless needlewoman among the apple trees of Paradise. How wonderful it felt not to disguise my true nature. Though I had learned many lessons since that day on the English Embankment, in the end I was not such a good student. I was still here, and night beckoned, shimmering before us with all its fragrant promise.

Part VI

The Bright Foxes

(November 1918)

63 *Golovins and Naryshkins*

OF ALL THE PLACES in Petrograd he could have taken me, my love led me straight into the brutal environs of my Arkady captivity   a building right across from the Tauride Palace. Even being in this neighborhood terrified me. We entered a dignified house that nevertheless sported a number of broken windows, then raced up the ravaged stairs to the second floor. He knocked a pattern on a door: one, two, three — pause — fourfive. *Ochi chor-nye* — the song's first syllables. Two taps back. Three taps from Kolya and we heard the scrabbling at the lock. The door opened to the length of a chain. A blue eye surveyed us from elbow height. Quickly, the chain fell, and a tiny old woman resembling a white mouse stood before us, holding her shawl close around her throat. She checked over our shoulders for loiterers, and satisfied, bundled us in.

She scolded Kolya as he propped the tripod and camera against the wall of the vestibule, stacked with firewood. "Oh Nikolai Stepanovich! You gave us such a start! Who in the world could be knocking at this hour? I asked myself. God save us, it's never good news anymore. And this ruse, this joke . . . " She cocked her head, presumably to indicate the world outside. "Patting themselves on the back with their bloody hands. The first year of hell—I can't wait to celebrate the second! And who is this?" She eyed me suspiciously.

"Elizaveta Vladimirovna, may I present my friend Mikhail Bogdanovich . . . Orlov."

Oh, was I to be an Orlov now? From hooligan to high nobility in a single night? Misha was to be the great-grandson of the adventurer who'd risen to favor as a lover of the future Catherine the Great. Orlov had served Russia by eliminating her feeble husband so she could rise to power. Later, she'd cast him aside for Potemkin but named the jewel he'd given her the Orlov diamond, which until recently had rested in the imperial scepter. I assumed now it lay in the hands of the people, or perhaps it had been put to work funding the forces of reaction.

The old lady noticeably warmed, satisfied I was *nash*, one of ours. She received her formal three kisses from Kolya, pressed my hand, and led us into a parlor that must have once held many fusty objects but now was sadly denuded, probably for the better, though there were still chairs and a proud, ugly tufted divan with carved mahogany legs. At a table sat three old people of decidedly aristocratic demeanor: playing cards, gambling—but for what?

"Well, come and kiss me," commanded another old woman, this one flabby and overdressed, reaching out her hand to Kolya. I guessed she had once been round as a Volga apple but in the food shortage had melted like beeswax. Her gray hair was coiffed as elaborately as it had been in the 1880s.

"Dear Emilia Ivanovna." Kolya kissed her and shook the men's hands—everyone wanted to touch him. His young man's touch was more precious than gold. "Viktor Sergeevich. Pavel Alexandrovich. You're looking hale." Were they his relatives? He'd certainly spent enough time with us, and we never thought he had any family to speak of other than his profligate father.

Nervous glances were sent in my direction. Our hostess reassured them by introducing me. The others visibly relaxed when they heard my famous name. "Welcome to our 'commune,' dear boy."

Kolya explained, "Elizaveta Vladimirovna was very clever. When she heard the Bolsheviks were going to collectivize the apartment—"

The old woman interrupted with an impatient hand on his arm. "I said, well, I'm certainly not going to share my flat with a bunch of thieves and Bolsheviks, so-called workers who never worked a day in their lives! So I called our dearest friends, the Naryshkins and the Golovins, and suggested we throw in our lot together."

"Best idea anybody's had in a long time," said the man with a terrifying sweep of whiskers, Viktor Sergeevich. A Naryshkin! Or a Golovin...both families known for their ultraconservative politics. I was a

Golovin, too, on Mother's side, though I didn't recognize him. I thought better of mentioning it. I remembered visiting my Golovin relatives in luxurious old flats just like this one. So this was how the aristocrats were celebrating the Year One—sitting behind their locked doors, slandering the workers, and hoping for the restoration of the tsar. A lamp flickered before the icon in the far corner of the room. I could only imagine what Genya would say if he could see this.

"Aglaya!" the mouselike old lady called out.

A servant with a nervous demeanor and eyebrows like an untrimmed hedge appeared through a second doorway. *A back hall.* Ever since my imprisonment with the Archangel, I'd become conscious of exits. "Aglaya, pour Nikolai Stepanovich and Mikhail Bogdanovich some tea!" The old lady sat down heavily in an armchair.

"What tea?" said the poor servant.

"This tea." Kolya produced a brown-wrapped package from his pocket, which stopped all conversation. I wondered how many packets he carried for just such occasions. I'd like to see what else he had in that magician's coat.

Aglaya curtsied and bustled to make the tea.

The oldsters insisted we sit with them and partake of the tea and some stale biscuits, though it was the last thing I wanted to do—sit politely and chat to a commune of rheumy-eyed *baryny* with Kolya tantalizingly within reach. But he seemed to enjoy tormenting me.

He launched into a long explanation of how he'd gone to school with Misha's older brother, and had run into me in the audience of an advanced revolutionary play. "You know the type," he said. "Poetry that doesn't rhyme. Sets so modern you can't tell them from the scaffolding."

"It's the same all over the city," said the melted grande dame. "You should see the Palace Square." *Uritsky,* I itched to say.

"We keep trying to get our permissions to travel," said the white mouse, adjusting her shawl. "But it's fifty thousand rubles. Each. Which is worth about five hundred in real money, but when you don't have it, it might as well be a million."

"I assume you've been to the station," said the other old man, Pavel Alexandrovich, bald with a few streaks of white hair combed over the dome. "Like the entrance to an abattoir. I think I'd prefer the Roman solution. If only they'd left me my sword."

White Whiskers sipped his tea and closed his eyes in ecstasy. "Oh, real tea. And sugar, too. Thank you, boy. What a wonder."

Kolya faked a big yawn and stood. "I hate troubling you for a bed, Elizaveta Vladimirovna, but I've been traveling since Kharkov, day before yesterday. I just got in when I ran into this one. He's in from Tsarskoe Selo—"

"*Detskoe* Selo," I corrected him.

Harrumphs all around.

"He wanted to see what the proletariat was doing with its dictatorship. We're all in."

The bald man shuffled the cards. "And what is your impression of Piter now, boy?" Our name for Petersburg. "Unrecognizable, isn't it?"

"Hard to say," said Misha. "But really, people must do something here besides parade in the streets."

The aristos thought that was quite funny. "No, they don't," said Elizaveta Vladimirovna. "Not one blessed thing. Protest, parade, and send in the Cheka to torment law-abiding people."

Kolya yawned again.

"Oh, don't let me keep you young people up," said our hostess, clapping her little bony paws together. Then, maddeningly, she continued talking. "But Nikolai Stepanovich, in the morning you promise you will tell us about your travels. Ever since they stopped publishing the *Petrogradsky Echo,* we know nothing about what's going on except the self-congratulatory columns in *Pravda.* How are our brave boys in the south? Will this be over soon?"

Over soon, meaning a White victory. "I wouldn't start hanging out double eagles quite yet," Kolya said.

Elizaveta Vladimirovna lit a kerosene lamp and led us through the huge flat to a room by the kitchen, apologizing profusely for the meager accommodations but explaining that all the good rooms were occupied now. The one she showed us, a maid's room, was packed with odds and ends waiting to be sold off. Sleds and skis, tables and lamps. But we unburied the narrow bed and found its thin mattress rolled on top of the springs. "One of you could use that, and the other could perhaps——"

"We'll figure something out," Kolya interrupted her, trying to push her out of the room. "Thank you from the bottom of my heart."

"Aglaya will bring you blankets and sheets." The old lady kept talking, craning her neck back into the room. "She's just next door if you need her. Here's a candle." She dug in her pocket and produced a short stub. "I wish we had something else, but the world——"

"After a week on the road, traveling on top of trains, believe me this is paradise," said Kolya, lighting the candle off the lantern wick. "Good night, dear. May God bless you a thousand times." He finally got her out and closed the door behind her, stuck the candle into a chipped china candleholder on the windowsill, and surveyed our love nest. Certainly we had made love in better surroundings, but we unrolled the mattress eagerly, and were just sitting down when a knock broke us apart—the maid, bearing sheets and two quilts they had given up for our comfort. I was touched, as the old would suffer so much more from the cold than we would tonight.

Finally we were alone.

The scuffle of flying clothes I'd presumed would ensue turned into a sudden awkwardness, an uncertainty.

I think Kolya was ashamed of what a mess this had all turned out to be, and for my part, I couldn't avoid a moment of remembered pain from the last time I'd seen him, when he'd left me to fend for myself, sent me back to Genya. If it hadn't been for Arkady, he probably wouldn't have come back at all. In the dark entranceway I hadn't been able to get enough of him, now I couldn't look at him. Instead, I pressed my forehead to his, like a good horse. I remembered this.

He knew enough not to speak, not to move. He put his arm around me and we sat for a lifetime. Continents drifted and collided as we just drank in the presence of the other. How lucky we were to have found each other again, in this world like a river in a spring flood that was carrying away horses, trees, villages, whole cities.

"Marina, dearest, I'm so sorry—" he said, but I stopped his words, planting my fingers against his mobile mouth. He didn't have to say anything, I was already his. I just needed time to remember him again.

My fingers moved through the curly beard, marveling at the texture, until he couldn't stand it anymore and turned my hand over to kiss the palm. And the hand came to life, as in a magic act where a piece of paper suddenly becomes a dove and flies away when the magician softly blows on it. Tenderly, he removed my cap, my coat. I trembled uncontrollably. "Are you cold?" he whispered.

I shook my head.

He gently arranged my short black hair with his

fingertips, ruffling it, then smoothing it, tickling the sideburns. He stroked my brows, my eyelids, my lips. His fingers when I kissed them tasted of smoke and leather. He slowly unbuttoned my student's tunic, beginning at the high neck, coming across the chest, down to the waist, and slid the brown fabric off my shoulders, then the undershirt, to reveal the tight bindings around my breasts and torso, my maiden's armor.

He unpinned the fastenings and began the unwinding. I held my arms over my head until he had finished. He ran his warm hands gently over my breasts, which always surprised me a bit as they sprung loose—so accustomed was I to being Misha. The other hand stroked my back, then stopped. His expression turned to puzzlement. He turned my shoulders so he could see what his hands had sensed.

Yes, my love. I'm afraid this isn't going to be as simple as you'd hoped.

"He did this to you?"

I turned so he couldn't stare at it, or perhaps I wanted to witness his reaction. His face painted with pity and shame, his hand across his mouth. In the silence, I could hear the old people chattering in the distant parlor. This was the moment Arkady had planned, ensuring that Kolya could never again look at me or touch me without knowledge that he had been there, had left his mark. The devil Kolya himself had summoned. Would it diminish me for him? "He could have shot me, Kolya."

"I'm not grateful," he said. "I'm afraid I haven't graduated to sainthood yet."

The lines across his forehead—one, two three—like waves coming in low and even on the Finland shore. Plus the strong double line between his brows. I took his hands. "It was another lifetime. I don't care about that now."

He knit our fingers together like we were praying, pressing our knuckles to his lips. "Forgive me. I should never have started all this. I should have left you alone." And he began to weep. "I'm a bad man, Marina—you don't even know. If you stay with me, you'll only have grief. If I had half a heart, I should leave you right now and let you have your life back."

Of all the things I expected when we'd gotten away from the waxworks in the living room, I never expected this. I stroked his cropped hair, pressed my temple to his. "You can't, though, any more than I can. So stop thinking like that. I'm responsible, too. I sold the diamond—and it kept us going for a good long time. Getting involved with Arkady—that was my mistake, and I paid for it, and it's done." Though it was hardly done, I had stopped blaming Kolya for it.

"I should have seen it coming. I should have been there. I thought I was keeping you safe. My God, what a fool!" He struck himself in the forehead with our clenched hands.

"Stop it." I jerked my hands away.

"Forgive me, I was such an idiot, such a fool." He

slid to his knees by the bed, where some maid had worn a bare patch through the oilcloth with her praying, pressing his cheek to my knees in Misha's rough trousers. "Can you ever forgive me, Marina?"

"Two idiots. Who's here to do the forgiving?" Kolya with a conscience? I kissed his sweet, agonized face. My God, what now? Would Kitezh rise from the lake?

"I'll make it up to you. I swear I will," he whispered.

I held out my foot, still clad in a boot. "Pull," I said.

My smile reached him at last. The sorrow and shame on his elfin face retreated, the way a wet pavement dried in the sunshine. He just wasn't made for regret.

Suddenly my boots were off, then my trousers, replaced by magical hands and gifted mouth. This is why I'd survived. I wrapped my thighs around him, knowing again that this was my church, my redemption. It wasn't the same act as I'd been enduring with Varvara, not even like Genya's loving efforts. As we rolled on that narrow bed, I knew *this* was why one needed a body, why it was worth all the pain, the hunger and harm it was prey to, why the angels envied us.

I felt sorry for the maid, Aglaya, in the room next door, to have to listen to such pleasure. I did my best to stifle my cries, and made Kolya stuff my coat behind the iron bed frame so it wouldn't crash into the wall like a bull kicking its pen to pieces. Luckily the other inhabitants were elderly and hard of hearing. If they could have heard us at all, what a scandal! I imagined Aglaya mortified in her straight little bed, praying under her breath. But at least she'd never have the nerve to relate to her mistress the horrors she'd endured—that those boys had fucked like lions in the desert, all night long.

64 *Vikzhel*

I WOKE TO THE sight of Kolya dressing in the tender morning light. It fell on his shoulders, caressing the light hairs, the freckles. Even that milky scrap of sun wanted him, wanted to run its tongue along his arms, his squared-off chest with its fan of hair, that narrowed waist, leaner than it had ever been. He bent down to kiss me. "Go back to sleep. I've got a few things to do."

I pulled him to me, rubbing the crown of my head against him, like a cat in a patch of grass. "No, stay here."

"I can't. I've got some business." He pressed his lips to my brow. "I'll be back, don't worry."

I groped for the binding cloth that had fallen to the floor, sat up, and began wrapping myself into it—second nature, compressing myself into my armor. "No. I'm coming with you."

He grabbed my wrists, shoved me back on the pillows, and lay on me, holding me there, a delicious captivity. *"Nyet,"* he whispered and kissed my nose.

Hurt feelings were a pain Misha wasn't used to experiencing. I was so unused to being a girl. Compared to all the other pain, this one, Marina's, was almost nostalgic. Only Kolya could hurt me this way. I tried to buck him off. "I didn't come here for you to tie me to a post whenever you want. Leave if you don't want me. You'll never see me again."

He kissed my eyes, my mouth. "Don't be melodramatic. I'll be back by noon. We'll go celebrate the workers' state." He let me go, then worked his head through the neck of his sweater.

I went back to binding my breasts, pulling the cloth tight, as if it were my resolve. After last night, Misha's rigid masculine form seemed intolerable. My body had returned to the feminine and resisted confinement.

"You're not listening," he said.

"No, I'm not." I slipped on my trousers and shoved my feet into my poor socks, my broken boots. What I would give for a pair of socks like the ones we used to make at Count Bobo's.

The exasperation painting his quick, restless face settled into resignation. He helped me on with my shirt, delicately, as if it were an evening cape. I buttoned my tunic as he dug my coat out from where we'd wadded it behind the headboard. "You're being ridiculous, you know."

"We're going to do some *beezneez*." I crammed my cap on my head. "So? Let's go."

We slipped from the flat, snores arising from every room. I grabbed Mina's tripod on the way. Even last night with the hooligans seemed weeks ago.

Outside, we could hear distant noise, though

Shpalernaya Street was quiet. The Tauride Palace with
its columns and its dome—the seat of the Duma, the
home of the Constituent Assembly—lay silent. Whatever happened now, a new chapter was beginning in my
life. We crossed through the garden—the open park-
ways where as a child I'd thrown that snowball at Kolya
in a fit of precocious jealousy, and which I watched with
such yearning through the window of my prison. The
sky stretched fresh, a pale blue, scrubbed and starched
as Vaula's aprons.

Proletarian families on holiday were filling Znamenskaya Square, now called Insurrection, their normally
drooping heads held high, and why not? The World
Revolution was at hand. At last it might be safe to look
beyond cold and hunger to a new day. I felt a twinge of
guilt for abandoning Mina to all those speeches. But I
was with Kolya now, and we had business to attend to.
At my side, he stretched and sighed, speaking to me as
men do, facing front. "So wonderful to be back. I never
thought I'd see it again. What a day. And you!"

I felt it, too, but I didn't like being down here at the
station, out in the open with Kolya, even disguised.
This was prime territory for the Archangel and his
men. "Shouldn't we walk farther apart?"

"You were the one who wanted to come along," he
said. "Getting nervous?"

He bought *pirozhky* from a street vendor, and we
walked through the crowd, watching the revolutionary
circus of holidaymakers, modernist constructions,

agitprop players. "What a farce. I hope they like what they're getting." He finished his pie, brushed his coat off, and tipped his head toward the pillared entrance to the station. "Follow me."

Happy as I was, the sudden realization that my life was completely in Kolya's unpredictable hands whistled through me like a wind through a too-light jacket. I did not want to go back into that station.

"Cold feet?"

"*Davai,*" I said.

The darkness of the terminal after the morning light left me temporarily blinded. Suddenly I felt the sly inquiry of a pickpocket's fingers. I twisted to catch sight of my assailant, a girl of around twelve, and made a half second's contact with her blue eyes gazing back at me, round and hard as quartz. Then she stuck out her tongue, a little girl again, and laughed before diving back into the crowd. The orphans of the revolution, left behind by starving families or by cholera or typhus or just lost in the madness, wandered the streets in gangs. Sometimes the girls worked as prostitutes. The boys scraped together a living as thieves, lookouts, or second-story men, like my hooligan friends from the Rostral Column. The station was lousy with them—the very reason people had been so happy to employ me as a porter and watcher of luggage.

"Still have your bankroll, Misha?" Kolya asked.

"Call me Count Orlov." But I did still have Mina's Kodak tucked under my arm.

All around us was the unmistakable station smell of stale coal, discouragement, fear, electricity, and unwashed bodies. People sat on their bundles, watched for thieves, or else stared off longingly toward the end of the tracks from which they hoped help would come. Trains ran seldom now, and the soldiers took priority—the new Red Army, a million men under arms preparing to escort the World Revolution to the ball. What was in their heads, these anxious escapees—images of the south? Of food? The lands east of the Urals, where the Whites ruled? Some were heading to villages, others just hoping for a corner of a room in Moscow and a job sweeping a government office. I took out Mina's camera and snapped a picture, then followed Kolya through the human reef, at once thanking God for the unbelievable good fortune of having found him again, and praying for the wits with which to withstand it.

We inched our way through the bundles and the unhappy pacers, and back into the light and air at the end of the platform. Kolya jumped down onto the tracks. Instinctively he held up his hand to steady my descent, but that wouldn't do for Misha. I leaped down and followed his jaunty saunter out onto the cinders and into the vast train yards behind the station.

I had often seen these yards, of course, these rusted cars, but only from a train window. I'd always dismissed them as a mere unsightly jumble to be endured before the onset of green countryside. But as we crunched on foot through a wilderness of snaking iron, cross ties and coal stations, signals and ruined trains, the tracks separating and coming together like a frozen quadrille, I realized it was a world unto itself. Huts for the signalmen, water towers. Kolya raised his hand to the workingmen. He was known here, or else he made it seem so. "All right, you're my brother," Kolya said. "Mikhail Bogdanovich Mikhailov. My mother's second husband's brat."

"Brother." I threw an arm around his broad shoulder in what I hoped was a comradely way. "I could eat you up," I whispered in his ear.

"Eyes are everywhere," he said.

I dropped my arm. "So, Brother Kolya, you have a plan?"

He picked up a rock and threw it, hitting the side of a train car with a satisfying clang. "Stick with me, Misha, we'll go to the top of the Himalayas and have conferences with the Buddha himself."

That I doubted. But for the first time, we would truly be together. Not just meetings after school, brief, passionate rendezvous. I would be with him when we awoke and when we went to sleep. I would know where he went, what he did, who he saw. He was mine now, this clever, impossible man, all of him, delight and danger and even mundanity, if there was any. We marched a mile or more down the sidings, and there, lurching and swaying like a lumbering pachyderm, a train grumbled toward us, heading for the station at such a rate that you could have jumped off and jumped back on again without having to catch your breath.

And people were jumping, hundreds of people with sacks on their backs, struggling under the weight of bulging loads. Bagmen, the villains of Soviet propaganda, the rats in the food distribution system. Opportunists, profiteers taking advantage of the brutal hunger of Petrograd. It was they who were breaking the backs of the soviets, siphoning off much of the food that should have been coming into the Petrocommune warehouses for direct free distribution to the people. But it wasn't so easy to judge them—there were regular people here, too, workers who'd had to leave their factories to go out into the countryside to forage. I even saw office workers with their suitcases. It didn't matter if you had ration cards; there wasn't always food to fulfill them. And this was why. The flip side of the Revolutionary Carnival was scarcity and the means, any means, to alleviate it. Everywhere you saw the signs, even printed on our ration cards: HE WHO STANDS FOR THE FREE MARKET OPPOSES THE FREEDOM OF THE PEOPLE.

Watching the bagmen disappearing into the wayside trees, I heard Arkady in my mind: *Never underestimate the genius of crime. We find a way when there is no way.*

And this was the world I was joining. This shadow world.

I knew this had been going on all along, but I'd never seen it so starkly—the sheer numbers. No one met anyone else's eyes. Now I could understand what a flood this traffic represented—the Cheka could only stop the smallest part of it. The rest got through. But surely Kolya must have something better in mind—he hadn't come all this way to introduce me to this hideous hand-to-mouth trade.

I waited for him to say something, but he just kept walking, his hands in his pockets. I could see why he hadn't wanted me to come. If I hadn't seen this, this murky world of speculation and profiteering he lived in, I'd have gone on thinking of him as the clever fellow, gone on delighting in his trickery. Was I ready for this?

Now smaller stationlets appeared, other platforms, other sights, signal posts and coaling stations. We arrived at a small wooden shack, some sort of train official's. Kolya knocked on the Dutch door. A slight man in his forties opened the upper half. He sported a patchy beard and hair cut straight across his forehead, as though he'd done it in the mirror that morning. He saw us and paled.

"Comrade Vorchenko." Kolya grinned. The man stepped back, clearly less than excited to see my fox, who nevertheless took the liberty of opening the lower door and walking in. I followed him. Kolya shut both doors and locked them.

"I knew it was going to be a bad day," said the little man. "The moment I woke up. Who's the puppy?"

"My kid brother." Kolya pulled up a stool that sat under a counter by the closed door. "We find ourselves in need of a bit of Vikzhel help, Vorchik."

Vikzhel, the railwaymen's union. They were the masters of Russian transport and, since last October, the sole arbiter of the Russian rails. They'd been essential to the victories of February and October by keeping troops from entering the city and putting down the nascent revolutions. So this was Kolya's secret: he was hooked into the railway network. My lover, my devil, lounged, easy, one leg on the ground, the other displaying the sole of a worn boot. Leave it to Kolya to know the secret doors of possibility in a world where nothing seemed possible. *Vikzhel.* Every other union was in trouble, the Bolsheviks draining them of their independent power. What did workers need unions for, Varvara said, if the whole country belonged to them already? Whenever there was a strike, the workers were accused of being declassed, their unions vilified. But the Bolsheviks could do nothing against Vikzhel. Nothing moved in the country without the railway union's consent.

Of course. How else would Kolya have been able to move about the country so freely? Yet it obviously wasn't out of friendship. The small man kept his distance and the lines on his face seemed deeper than when he'd first seen us. I hated that we represented trouble to someone. "It's not so easy now," he said. "As I'm sure you must have heard, this new Railway Cheka is applying a lot of pressure."

Kolya's smile disappeared. It was shocking, the speed at which his affable demeanor changed and the laughing blue eyes turned steely. This was a face I didn't know, a hard man's face. Then, as fast as it had left, the smile returned, and with it the likable, winning, persuasive Kolya. "Vorchenko, clearly your memory's better than that. Haven't I done Vikzhel a favor or two? A certain stationmaster specifically?"

The man blanched white as a mushroom. "Aren't you tired of sucking the scum off the bottom of the world, Shurov? And now you're dragging your kid brother into it? Very nice. Nice family business." But all his fight seemed to have gone out of him and he sank into a chair behind a squat, ugly desk.

Dust motes floated in the light from the dirty window. I yearned to be out of this hut and in the freshness of the morning, but clearly Kolya was not leaving until he had extracted whatever concession he was pressing for. He brought his steepled fingers to his lips. "The thing about scum is that there's always plenty of it."

The man sighed.

"How soon can we get out of here?" Kolya asked.

The man listlessly flicked through a tattered log on the desk. "This one's heading for Vilna. It'll be out of here in about four hours. Say, fifteen hundred hours."

"How about the Moscow train?"

"Half midnight. But security will be tight, a lot of bigwigs on it, going back to their big fat Bolshevik tit in the Kremlin after the parades. It's up to you."

"What else?" Kolya asked, looking at the raveling cuff of his corduroy jacket.

"Tomorrow morning there's a milk run to Vologda. Four a.m."

Vologda. Tikhvin was on that line.

"Track?" he asked casually.

"Eight. Nobody gives a damn about Vologda. Or take Vilna and be damned with you."

I tried to look indifferent, picking at the raw wood that sided the stationmaster's hut. But inside, my heart was thrashing about like a big fish in a small net. We were leaving Petrograd. And tonight—or in the small hours of the morning. I hardly heard the rest of their conversation. Kolya and I, leaving the rest of the world behind. Was the fish leaping with joy or terror—or something more primitive, an indistinguishable emotion that just thrashed with the electricity of change? I'd been waiting for this moment my whole life. What if I hadn't accompanied him this morning, if I'd been a good girl and done what he asked? Would he have even told me he was leaving? Would he have feigned some excuse and jumped on the train by himself, not wanting me to see the true nature of his business?

I was ready to come with him. What was left for me here? Mina, Varvara...Arkady. Yet I felt like a traitor. This was my Petersburg, my home. Vilna meant Poland and a run for the West. If we went west, we might never return. Vologda? Maybe he was trying to get to the Urals, to the White-controlled territories of

Siberia. It terrified me that with Kolya I could well end up on the wrong side of this war. Why could no choice ever be clear and simple in life, just one single good thing without a shadow?

I watched him pull a packet from his magician's coat and throw it onto the desk. "Here. Thought you'd like something better to smoke than back issues of *Delo Naroda*."

Vorchenko didn't find that particularly funny. The *People's Cause,* the SR paper, had long been banned by the Bolsheviks. Vikzhel had supported the SRs. The stationmaster pulled out from the shag tobacco a fat roll of bills, pocketed the money, and stuck the tobacco into his pipe. Kolya reached out to light it, and I noticed how Vorchenko flinched, then flushed when he saw what it was—just a lighter made out of stolen pipe fittings, which were the biggest industry in Petrograd at the moment. Sheepish, he let Kolya light his pipe. We sat for a moment as the Vikzhel man puffed away, his former irritation giving way to a more resigned posture now that our business had been conducted.

"Fighting's died down around Samara," the man said.

"Komuch didn't put up much of a fight." My father's friends, the Committee of Members of the Constituent Assembly. Suddenly my big ears were open.

The man leaned back in his seat. "Now they've thrown their lot in with Kolchak. To hell with them." Admiral Kolchak, with his tall fur hat and his Cossack coat, was the charismatic dictator of the Siberian Whites. So the moderate government at Samara, the last hope of the liberals, had come under the wing of the reactionary Siberian dictatorship. Varvara had said all along it would happen.

"What do they say about the Ukraine?" Kolya asked. Yes, the south, where so many of my classmates' families had gone, and Kolya's aristocrats were attempting to go, where there was food. The Germans were done—we'd heard that yesterday—so what would happen with their occupation of the Ukraine?

The man exhaled the sweet Turkish tobacco. "With the German surrender? It's going to be a free-for-all. Why don't you go wallow in the mud before the Reds arrive?" He leaned back in his seat, making the chair creak.

"What about the Don?" Misha blurted out. It was a marvel to talk to someone with access to real news. We civilians got all our news filtered through the pages of *Pravda,* but Vikzhel had the telegraph. Vikzhel took the nation's pulse, had its nervous system right under its fingertips.

"Pretty heavy down there," said Vorchenko. "Krasnov's a puffed-up idiot, but Denikin's no fool." General Denikin—Volodya's general. "They're already at each other's throats. My bet's on Denikin coming out on top. If I was a betting man."

"If?" Kolya snorted. He rose from his stool, stretched. Evidently we were done here. He betrayed no indication of our plans. "Hungry, Misha?" He punched me playfully in the shoulder. He made no attempt to shake the stationmaster's hand, just unlocked the door. "See you around, Vorchik."

"Don't fall off any trains, Shurov."

We didn't return to the terminal. Instead we crossed over the tracks and tramped east through little wayside woods and stubbly fields. The crows gleaned the leftover rye and the boggy lowlands bristled with reeds. I was feeling melancholy despite myself. I couldn't shake the way Kolya looked when he was threatening—yes, threatening—the Vikzhel man.

He bumped my shoulder with his. "Was it so bad? You shouldn't have come. What I do—it's not pretty. If you want a shining example of revolutionary idealism, stick with Varvara. This is the real world."

"That's the real world, too. I've been in that cellar, thank you."

He slung his arm around my shoulder. "We'll be together, I promise you that. The way you always wanted it to be. But I'm not a prince with a golden feather."

I wanted him to hold me tenderly, but that was out of the question. Instead I threw a comradely arm over his, and we bumped along under the blue flag of the sky. He started whistling "Mephistopheles's Song of the Flea," making me laugh. He always did know how to cheer me up.

"So tell me, Mephistopheles," I said, trying to hook my foot around his ankle as we walked to see if I could trip him. "What's your plan? And stop trying to be mysterious."

"All in good time, brother Misha," he said. "You shall know all." He gave a magician's fan of the fingers, pulled a coin from the air, made it disappear. "That is, unless you want to go home to your Cheka girlfriend." He succeeded in hooking his foot around mine while I wasn't paying attention, and suddenly I found myself sitting on my ass in the dirt. "Goodness, watch your step!" Laughing, he offered me his hand and pulled me back to my feet. "We'll just have to see how the winds blow."

I dusted off the seat of my pants. "Just like that? Flip a coin?"

"The great world's spinning, and we're about to jump on," he said. "Make up your mind. Want this or not?" How I loved that clever face, smiling slyly, the thin top lip, the full bottom one. Suddenly I didn't care who saw me or what they thought. I threw my arms around him—this maddening man, this infuriating beast.

65 *Apprentice Mikhailov*

IT WAS LATE AT night when we returned to the station, though what a difference! As we entered, we could hear the scream of a train coming in. The sagging forms of the dispossessed, dispirited, and depressed

rose fully animated, grabbed their earthly possessions and loved ones, and pressed to the edge of the
platform as the old train came staggering into its
berth like a dowager queen, black and stately, grimy
as a kettle. The tension of the crowd stretched to
the breaking point. A terrible sight—citizens straining toward the train, preparing to fight their way to
Moscow or heaven itself. I shrank back, hoping I
would not have to join them. I had been through a lot
but didn't think I had what it took to claw my way
onto a train like an animal, assuring my own place at
the expense of God knows who. That old gentleman
with the square-cut beard? This young couple with
their brood of sick-looking children?

Soldiers beat back the crowd with the sides of their
rifles so that arriving passengers could alight, pushing
their way out. Who in the world would be arriving in
starving Petrograd now, when everyone in the city was
trying to leave? Kolya stood with me against a pillar off
to one side of the hall, smoking, his arm loose around
my shoulder, so I could feel that solidity and warmth as
we took in the monstrous scene.

"Is this our train?" What would happen when they
let the departing passengers loose? How could he be so
calm? "There's going to be a riot. They'll never get
half of them on. How can they stand it?"

He checked his watch. He must have been the last
man in Petrograd who still owned one. "They'll get on.
They've had three days to get ready for this," he said,

watching as if it were proof of something. "Sit on your bags for three days, you'll do what you have to."

Then the crowd surged forward to strain itself into the doors of the cars. It was hideous. A man shoved ahead of a woman, causing her to drop her bundle and almost lose her grip on her infant. Others behind her stepped on her things as they pushed past her. She wept, begging for help, but there was no way anyone could lean over in that stampede. People grabbed at each other, trying to get in front, passing children and bags overhead, hand to hand. Men separated from their families fought to rejoin them. I struggled not to cry—Misha wiped angrily at his tears with the back of his sleeve. I saw a boy of ten dash off with a bundle, someone's precious things that could never be replaced, but no one gave chase, no one had a choice but to keep on struggling, trying for a few feet of standing room on this horrible train. Suddenly my tunic, coat, and hat were unbearably warm, and my unwashed skin prickled. I swore I could smell my own fear above the reek of the hall.

After a time, the train swallowed its load of human urgency, the doors closed, and now the passengers themselves forced people away who tried to climb in through the windows.

"Davai." He led me past the despairing would-be travelers, sleepy orphans returning to their rags, their refuge for the night, and led me once more down off the end of the platform and out into the yards. Why had

he wanted me to see this if we weren't getting on? To show me, *Here is your Soviet utopia. So much for all your ideals?*

Dotted along the tracks, fires burned in barrels around which the railway men gathered, hands extended, bundled in their quilted jackets. By their flickering light, we found a group chucking wood up into the locomotive being fueled for the trip. My God, we were running our trains on wood now? Had we run out of coal along with food? Poor Russia! The reality of the war writ large—coal was supplied by the mines of the Don and Siberia, and both were behind White lines now.

Indicating for me to wait behind in the darkness, Kolya approached a group in the phantasmagorical firelight. He spoke to a short, barrel-shaped greatcoated man standing with the loaders. They shook hands. Overhead, the darkness was both cold and bright, the stars shimmering high and untouchable in the vast smear of the Milky Way. I wondered if my Ancients were still alive, peacefully conducting their work down at Pulkovo. Right now, Aristarkh Apollonovich would be gazing up at his nebulae while we were going to get on a rust-bucket train headed for the ass end of nowhere.

A bottle passed from Kolya to the man by the fire barrel. Where did he stash all these things? His tea, his tobacco, and now, magically, a bottle of vodka? I swore he hadn't had it on him this afternoon, and I'd brushed up against him all day. It had been a sweet day, too, I thought as I stepped from foot to foot in the cold, waiting for a sign to approach. It had been the closest we'd ever come to just being a normal pair of lovers strolling along together—though we could of course not hold hands or kiss. We'd walked along the Neva, admiring the decorations on the Admiralty, the bold new constructivist flags, and watched the performances. At a Punch-and-Judy booth, I spotted Mina's sister Shusha standing with some other girls, laughing at the old stories. I left Kolya behind and approached, plucked at her sleeve.

Her friends giggled when they saw this older boy approaching their school friend. "Misha!" Shusha grinned, then her smile faded into alarm. "Where've you been? Mina was cursing you to the seventh generation this morning—"

"Something came up." I pulled her to one side, out of earshot of her comrades. "I had to lie low."

"She's going to kill you. She made Dunya do it, so now Dunya's mad—she had a date with Sasha. Mina said she's never going to lift a finger for you even if you were dying." Her bright brown eyes flashing with the drama of it all.

I took the Kodak camera from around my neck and strapped it over hers, handed her the tripod. "Give these to her, tell her sorry. There are some amazing shots on that roll, if they come out." I hoped it would redeem me, but I doubted it.

"Give them to her yourself." Shusha took off the camera, held it out to me. "I just saw her—she's in Palace Square. You can catch up to her."

"I can't. I'm leaving," I said.

"Leaving Petrograd?" Her attitude changed, suddenly solemn, genuinely alarmed. She loved me. And I realized this was real, what I was planning. I was leaving. Everyone I loved and everything I knew. She dropped her voice. "Why? What's happened? Are you really on the run?"

I felt my lips quivering. I was about to break down. I gave her a hug. "Give your mama a kiss for me, and tell Mina not to hate me. You be good." I tugged at her dark braid.

It was possible I would never see her again. The enormity of what I was doing threatened to engulf me. Not to see Mina marry that idiot, or Dunya...I would never know what happened to Mother, to Father...Mother, not Father, I corrected myself. The children burst into laughter at the puppet show, and when Shusha turned back for a moment, I took advantage of her distraction to fade into the crowd. I soon rejoined Kolya, who grinned and clapped me on the shoulder, but the flavor of that last exchange and the jerking, quarrelsome puppets had unnerved me.

In the cold train yard, I felt those tears coming again. What was I doing? The men were drinking together. A railwayman on the ground rapped the side of a tender and threw the almost-empty bottle up to another man who finished it off then threw it gaily onto the rails, where the glass broke with a merry crash.

At last, Kolya gestured for me to join him. I breathed deeply, trying to pull myself together before I approached him and the squat man in the greatcoat, with a face like a wall. The man took one look at me—"So this is our new stoker?"—threw his head back and laughed. Then surprisingly, he burst into song. *"Ven ʒhon khenry vas a little bebby..."* He squeezed my skinny bicep with a hand like an iron claw.

Kolya shook me by my neck the way you'd pick up a rabbit. "I know he doesn't look like much, but he's a good boy. He won't give you any trouble."

The man nodded to the tender. "Go on up then, kid. Give 'em a hand."

I glanced at Kolya, who indicated with his chin the second tender of the rusty locomotive they were loading. He was sending me up there alone?

"I'll be up in a while." He slapped a pair of stiff, filthy leather gloves into my hands. "You'll need these."

"Where are you going?"

"Comrade Olinsky and I have a little *beeʒneeʒ.*" A world of meaning lived inside his smile. "I'll be there before the train leaves."

Olinsky shouted up to the men in the wagon, and a giant glove lowered itself to me. I clambered onto a monster iron wheel and let the gloved hand pull me up into the car. When I landed, three sets of eyes regarded me with disgust, as a fisherman looks at a monkfish

when he thought he had a halibut. Surely if the bottle hadn't preceded me they would have thrown me back.

Their captain, a talkative dark man with a thick Georgian moustache and an accent to match, put me to work catching and stacking wood. Split wood came flying thick and fast from the ground into the car, and a man balanced on the load, catching logs and stacking them. He hauled me up on top and I tried to emulate him while attempting not to fall and break my ankle on the loose wood. I caught more wood with my chest and ribs than with my arms. In fifteen minutes, I felt as if I'd been beaten. "You're really running this can on wood?"

"Just in case, kid. We thought you were a veteran."

The men laughed and began to sing *chastushki* as we loaded—about all sorts of filthy things, whores and unquenchable lust, erections that would not cease but grew larger than the man. There were political ones, too, making fun not only of the tsar but of Lenin and Dzerzhinsky as well. They were afraid of nothing, these Vikzhel men. "Hey, little girl," my partner called out, throwing a chunk of wood at me. "At least amuse us, you useless little cunt."

I caught the block and placed it on the pile, then struck a poet's pose, foot up on a log, as I scraped my thoughts together.

They say there's not one shred of coal
From Tula to Donbass

Instead the trains run regularly
On birchwood chunks and Vikzhel gas.

Har har har. Oh they loved it. They even stopped throwing wood at me so hard. Encouraged, I continued.

Vikzhel men they love their pipes
Warm outhouses and ugly wives
Vikzhel men jerk off at night
Their daughters have to sleep with knives.

Admitting my uselessness, I managed to keep them entertained until we'd filled the wagon. I hadn't known Misha was such a shirker. So unlike Marina, who would work until her fingers bled, always trying to prove herself, her value, her intelligence, her stamina, prove herself willing and capable, a real comrade. But Misha was a natural anarchist, traveling on charm, a wastrel and hooligan desiring only to seize the color and avoid the dreariness of life.

Finally Kolya returned with Olinsky, I could spot his jaunty stride painted in the light from the fire barrels at a hundred yards. The two of them climbed into the cab of the locomotive. The Georgian waved me forward, and the others left. Now it was the four of us: engineer, fireman, and two unauthorized passengers, and a tight squeeze it was indeed. Most of the space was occupied by the monstrous cast-iron cylinder of a boiler,

a remnant from the reign of Catherine the Great. I wouldn't be surprised if it had run on her ex-lovers at some point.

As the Georgian stoked— with coal, thank God— he urged me to sing some of my better *chastushki* to the newcomers. I was shy, but he remembered the first lines—I could not help but complete them. I could see Kolya adored the masquerade. Olinsky, who proved to be the engineer, chuckled but spoke little, his attention absorbed in checking dials, turning cranks, and pulling levers on the side of the big boiler. Slowly the pressure mounted, steam building. You could feel it, like an immense winding spring. He released the steam with an enormous rush, then let it build back up again, twice, three times, and finally we slowly backed into the station, the tenders behind us, until, with a clang and a jolt, we met the waiting train. My excitement surged ahead of all waiting fears. We were finally going to be off on our adventure. Kolya's secret grin flashed, just for me.

Olinsky checked his own watch. "Tea, anyone? The samovar's hot."

"Company's here," said Kolya, nodding out the window.

Black leather jackets signaled the arrival of the Railway Cheka. Six of them. They boarded the train, disappearing inside the crowded cars. This would take a while, if they planned to inspect the contents and travelers on this densely packed train. Surely they would find us. But Kolya was sunny and cool as a September morning. Olinsky siphoned off some of the boiling water from the engine into a pot. Kolya added tea to the mix and I tried to hold my cup steady so I wouldn't betray my nerves. A sudden bang made me jump—a blow to the sheet metal of the cab. The Georgian opened the door and a tall, leather-jacketed man climbed up, letting in a rush of cold air behind him. "Well, Comrades? Let's see some papers."

Runnels of sweat trickled down my neck. I was afraid to even blink. The engineer handed over his clipboard covered with curled, greasy papers—records of settings and inspections. The Cheka man, tall and graceless, with a knobbly nose under his leather cap, looked through them perfunctorily and thrust them back at the engineer. "Labor books." He wiggled his fingers, as though tickling the chin of a billy goat.

Oh God. My labor book was for some girl named Marina. I watched as Olinsky and the Georgian pulled theirs out and handed them to—or, rather, tossed them with purposeful insolence at—the Cheka man. They bounced off his chest and fell to the floor of the cab. "Pick them up," said the Chekist.

"Kiss my ass," said the engineer.

Kolya produced two from his coat and scooped the two from the floor into the Chekist's hands.

"What are these clowns doing here?" He pointed at me and Kolya as he inspected the labor books. Specifically, me. "You. How old are you?"

I could feel sweat rolling down between my shoulder blades, my breasts pushing at the bandage. My heart thumped as loud as the engine. "Eighteen, Comrade." Misha tried to keep his voice deep.

He was looking at one of the books. "*Fif*teen," he said. "*Apprentice engineer*. What a load of crap. You Vikzhel bastards. Featherbedding. How about you, Shorty? What's your excuse?" he asked Kolya. Narrowing his eyes as if he recognized him. "Haven't I seen you somewhere?"

I felt my guts rumbling, hoped my bowels wouldn't let go. To have come so close only to have Kolya fall into Cheka hands...all for nothing. What would I do if they arrested him? Head cast on this train, I supposed.

"Yeah, I was visiting your mother," Kolya said.

The Georgian laughed.

"Shut up," said the Cheka man. "What are you doing on this train?" He went back to examining Kolya's labor book in the light of the kerosene lamp. "Mechanic Rubashkov."

"I'm going to Vologda. There's a train they don't know how to fix. The English left it behind, a little gift to the Soviet people. Only they wrecked it first."

"Why do you have"—he looked at my labor book again—"Mikhailov's documents?"

"He's my brother. Half brother. He was going off with a whore earlier. I didn't want him to lose anything while he was out getting the clap."

"Prostitution is a filthy remnant of bourgeois culture," the Cheka man warned Misha gravely. "There is no place for prostitution in our soviet society."

I nodded. I didn't have to fake the terror I felt. "She's just a regular girl," Misha protested. "My brother envies my luck with women."

"Are we done?" said Olinsky. "I have a train to run."

But Knobbly Nose was still eyeing our labor books. "You will move at the convenience of the Petrograd Railway Cheka, Engineer Olinsky."

He handed us back our documents but gave Kolya an icy, close-range examination before letting him take his book back.

Then he clambered down from the cab and the engineer slammed the door shut.

The visit took the steam out of our boilers. No one said anything after that, or even exchanged a glance. We all knew what was happening back there on the train as the Cheka searched among the terrified passengers. Finally Olinsky produced a deck of tattered cards, and we played a few quiet rounds of *durak* as we waited for the all clear. The Cheka operatives removed half a dozen people from the train, marching them through the now empty station toward their own painful future. Each one of us imagined the day when this might be our fate.

66 *A Peasant Wife*

OVERHEAD, CLOUDS FANNED OUT into a giant winged angel, while around us stubbly fields still showed patches of brown through an expanse of snow. Thank God the road had frozen over or the wagon would have bogged down ten miles outside the railway town of Cherepovets. I swayed on the seat next to Kolya, feeling queasy as we alternated between dense pine forest and open land under the mesmerizing sky. This land had a dream life of its own—the drama of the sky, the forlorn, harvested fields, the distant lines of trees. Bare birches rattled their knucklebones as we passed by. Every once in a while a single man on horseback or in a wagon waved a short salute. Sometimes we overtook a group of recruits or a man driving cattle with a willow switch. I thought of Annoushka as we silently passed ruined manor houses two stories high, the roofs caved in, surrounded by a few blighted fruit trees. I couldn't help wondering how Maryino had fared.

Kolya clucked and snapped the reins of the dappled gray as the road unspooled from between its ears. I hadn't felt well for a week, spending most of my time with my head resting on his lap, looking up at his curly beard and the puffs of steam coming out of his nostrils or at birds crossing the big churning sky—ducks, cranes—flying south. The travel had proved harder than anything I'd imagined. Well, what had I pictured, that we'd be sipping sherry and appraising jewels and precious art? The reality was, we were making a map of remote villages, woods and fields, fording gelid streams not quite frozen over, sleeping in peasant izbas if we were lucky and in the straw with their animals if we weren't.

In the beginning, our greed for one another drove us like a fire. How miraculous just to kiss openly! I was a woman again, dressed in *sarafan*, blouse, and woolen kerchief bought in Cherepovets along with a jacket and a sheepskin, complete down to felt boots and red beads around my neck—Kolya's peasant wife. How luxurious it had been to lie naked next to him in an inn and have him slip a ring on my finger. "With this ring, I thee wed." It was a joke and not a joke. I had waited so long to be with this man, to really know him for the very first time. All his mysteries about to be revealed.

We boarded the Volga ferry in Cherepovets with a big gray horse and a large wagon and arm in arm, rapturously watched the shore fall away. I'd never had such a sense of high adventure, Kolya and me, husband and wife, the red cord of our fates braided like our laced fingers on the railing as we stood on that deck, gazing out at a river so wide it could have been an ocean.

We traveled south as far as Rybinsk, awash with sailors and flats of lumber, Volga boatmen, fishermen and their wives. This was a world I'd only read about—a world Genya knew, full of barrel makers and the smell of planed wood. Riding along in our wagon, we sang and played tricks on each other, sometimes we made love in the back because we were unable to wait for nightfall.

Our first successes astonished me. In village after wretched village, peasants opened their cellars to us, led us to springhouses, dug up pits in which their hoarded grain had been stashed. Grain, potatoes, even butter and cheese. I was shocked. It was just as the Bolsheviks had said—peasants were holding back, hiding their surpluses in the woods and under the floors of their wooden cabins. Genya used to say that the Russian peasant, once he had his land, was done with his revolution. But our peasant hosts complained that the fixed price the Soviet provisioning brigades offered was impossibly low. They knew the cities were starving, and they cared to a point. They all had relatives in the cities, in the factories. But they didn't know what would happen come spring. They had to think of the future.

"What do the Bolsheviks know about our lives?" our first host had said. "Why should we sacrifice when they offer us nothing in return?" The peasants needed scythes and plows, machine parts, nails, but the factories were dead. Half the workers were out self-provisioning, being pressed into the food brigades terrorizing the countryside, seizing the grain of the so-called kulaks, the better-off peasants who hired others, who often made money in trade as well as by farming.

"What's a kulak?" our host had railed. "I hire someone to replace my boys in the army, and suddenly I'm a kulak and my grain's good for seizure? I supported the revolution! I gave up grain when the workers first came along—I don't want anybody to starve. But when these so-called Kombedy come along"—the Committees of the Village Poor—"telling *us* how much *we* can keep? When they've done nothing, these village termites? What does Lenin know about crops? And how much seed you need come spring? The devil with them, that's what we say, and their nine poods per person." A pood, about thirty pounds, was the allowable holdback per person for the year.

But soon we'd seen what happened to villages that were discovered to be holding back more. We drove through one that had been burned to the ground. It was a new kind of civil war—not Red versus White but town versus country, peasant versus worker, the poor versus the poor. Waged over not politics but grain. I remember when I'd begged Varvara to send me to Maryino during Red Terror. *It's going to be worse in the countryside than here. With us it's almost over.*

She thought it was all the fault of the speculator, people like Kolya and the peasants who sold to him. If only the peasant would sense his historic role as the ally of the proletarian, she used to fulminate. If only the Cheka could eliminate the speculators, then the Petrocommune stores would have food, the workers could get back to work, the peasants could get the factory items they wanted, and Russia would move ahead into the future.

I used to think I knew what people should do, that I had a good sense of right and wrong. But since I'd been out here with Kolya, I saw the true tragedy—that everyone was right from his own point of view, everyone was suffering and needy. The workers didn't want to be in those brigades, but once they'd grimly accepted their duty, they transformed themselves into men who could perform those tasks—in exactly the way armies turned peasant boys into killers. All I knew now was that what we were doing was dangerous indeed, that I was not well, and that I was homesick for Petrograd.

I leaned against Kolya as we rode through a pine forest, mile after mile, the wall of trees and a strip of sky. It made me nauseated, the regularity of the trunks, the way they passed. I couldn't even look at them. I worried about returning to the city. It would be so easy for Arkady to find us, especially if Kolya had all this grain to sell—surely we'd be traced. But Kolya insisted it had to be Petrograd, to bring the most money. "Then we can get on a ship and go anywhere," he said. "Where shall we go?"

"Argentina," I said. "Spain."

"Not Paris?"

"Too wet. Take me somewhere hot and dry. With

mosaics and a little fountain in the courtyard. And guitars. I'll dance with a black mantilla, and I'll break
men's hearts."

"They'll die in droves for this redheaded Carmen."
He leaned over and kissed me. A few weeks ago, our
kisses would have caught fire, and we would have made
love right here. But now I was so tired that it was hard
to believe there was even a place called Spain, somewhere the sun was hot and the little burros climbed
the rocky hills, and great cathedrals rose like pastry,
with pigeons bursting into the sky. My body ached,
and an unnamed foreboding, heavy and thick, sat on
my stomach, the sense of something coming. I remembered my mother's nervousness just before the revolution broke. She'd been like a cat sensing a storm. I
lay down again with my head on Kolya's thigh, curled
up on the wagon's seat, the hard wood biting into my
bones. How much longer could we go on? I slept and
dreamed of grain, bags of grain heaped on a wagon
over our heads, coming loose and crushing us.

Kolya woke me, shaking me gently by the shoulder. I
sat up to see gentle columns of white smoke rising from
a copse of trees. Chimney smoke, thank God. The eerie
red sun was already low on the horizon as we drove
into an enclave of izbas, nicely maintained and well
spaced, the gates and fences in good shape. A fairly
prosperous village, it had done well without a landlord. The inhabitants we saw did not melt away into the

yards, but watched us curiously. We pulled up in front of a proud house with four windows to the street—red windows, as they were called under the tsar. *Krasniy, krasiviy*—red meant beautiful, because they had glass in them. The peasants had once been taxed on every window and on the chimney, too, so this was an announcement to the world: we can afford light and fresh air. Many of the poorer huts we'd visited had been little better than smokehouses.

Our horse stopped, snorting plumes of vapor into the cold air. Kolya handed me the sweat-smelling reins, leaped lightly from the wagon, and walked off whistling *In the meadow stands a little birch tree*. The gray threw back his head, making his bridle jingle. He couldn't wait to be unhitched. Dogs barked as Kolya knocked on the small door next to the gates protecting the yard from the street. *"Privet!"* he called out. He wore a patched sheepskin over his jacket, his pants in his boots. With his little cap and homemade pipe, he looked like something you'd put in a wheat field to frighten the crows.

I sighed and stretched. I couldn't wait to get out of this cursed wagon. My back hurt, my hips ached. I felt a hundred years old and stupid as the feeble-minded boy peeking at me from around the corner of a neighboring house. To think I'd once been a poet. Had placed word next to word just for the thrill of it, the burr of *zh* and the arch-throated *ya*. But the miles had reduced me to an ache and a

queasiness, a certain melancholy, an animal's desire
for warmth and a moment's safety.

The small door opened and a woman poked her head
out, a beauty with a blue kerchief over her blond hair,
pink cheeks, and upturned wide-spaced eyes. A big dog
came out in front of her and sniffed at Kolya, then
barked at the horse. I had not seen a beautiful peasant
woman on this trip. I watched her take us in, the wagon,
Kolya's deferential stance. She was suspicious but also
curious, a tiny girl in a little kerchief clinging to her
skirt, and a bit more belly than that short jacket could
conceal.

They spoke for a while, then she leaned over and said
something to the tot, who went trotting back into the
yard. Kolya waved for me. He helped the woman open
the big gates and I drove the horse in. "You can put the
horse in the stable, *devushka*," the woman called up to
me. "You'll see where." And Kolya followed her into
the izba.

"Put the horse in the stable," I grumbled as I began
to unhitch him. "You can water and feed him, too, if
you like. And would you mind fetching some more water while you're at it?" Now that I was a peasant wife,
all the work was left for me. It had been a joke at first, a
delicious imposture. But now I was getting tired of it.

I was still unhitching the horse when she brought out
the two pails on a yoke. "To water the horse. The well's
across the road." She wasn't that much older than me,
maybe twenty-five, but she was already the mistress of

the house. She set the pails down on the porch and went back inside. "The well's across the road," I imitated her to the horse. He swiveled his ears intelligently. He was sweaty, he'd done his part, too.

I put him into their barn, dark and close after all the fresh air and light, heady with rich smells—urine, animals, and straw. A cow lowed, and her calf replied. Cow and calf meant milk. Goats bleated, hoping to be fed—more milk and meat. In the dim light, I made out a manger and a watering trough. Their own horse must be out with the husband. I led our big gray in. A pig grunted, and I heard the higher notes of piglets. Around my feet, chickens made their crackling, irritable racket, filling the air with down, and the rooster wandered around in the doorway crowing, trying to peck at me. Eggs, milk, bacon...a prosperous family. They would have grain as well. I wondered where they stored it.

I made myself laugh. I was starting to think like a thief.

I scooped out some oats from our wagon for the horse. I gave it to him first in handfuls, to enjoy the softness of his nose as he ate from my hand. "We'll be out of this soon, Comrade," I said, petting his steamy neck, listening to him chew. Then I put the feed bag on his bridle and went to fetch the water in the reddening dusk.

Two women stood chatting at the well, their pails already full. I greeted them politely and lowered the well bucket on its chain. The splash came quickly—that was good, I wouldn't have to haul it up so far. I groaned and huffed as I cranked the handle.

"You ought to watch your man with that one," one of the women said, a sturdy peasant of around forty. "She's a witch, you know."

The other one said, "She might turn him into a pig, or a duck."

"A duck would be easier to train," I said, and they laughed.

"She flies around at night," the second woman said.

"She dances in the woods," said the first one.

"May God protect us," I said, crossing myself piously, feeling sorry for the woman for having gossips like this as neighbors. The world always envies the beautiful and the rare.

I squatted down like a strong man at the circus and lifted the buckets straight up, the yoke across my already aching shoulders. I'd filled the pails too full, and the water splashed as I tottered through the smaller door of their gate, banging one end of the yoke so water drenched my soft boots. I was so tired I didn't even care. I filled the horse's trough, barely visible now in the warm darkness of the barn, and left him with the other animals, eager to be inside and sitting down.

Oh the warmth and the smell of cooking! Herbs and tea and smoke and meat—and people. Kolya already occupied the place of honor—the bench in the red corner—where a boy of around five sat at his elbow and gazed up at him, fascinated, as if my lover were a seven-league prince or a hut on chicken legs. An old man with a spade-shaped beard sat on the other side, and an old woman sat by herself at the end of the bench, mumbling. A cradle hung from the ceiling and I could see a baby sitting up in it, like a man in a boat.

The mistress stood at the stove, stirring something into a big earthenware pot. How on earth could she be so lovely, even from the back, with her figure concealed under padded clothes and her hair hidden by a kerchief? I imagined the woman's braids under the flowered kerchief, two great ropes of gold wound crownlike around her head. Her breasts and hips were full, her belly—she was bursting with life. No wonder Kolya was trying so hard to be charming. I envied the self-confidence of her face, the bold eyes, the little upturned nose, the firm chin and wide bones. I could feel her pleasure at the unexpected company.

I was more interested in the food. The smells! The place was crammed full of produce as a storehouse, the season of preserving having just passed. Fragrant herbs and ropes of dried fruit and mushrooms hung from the ceiling, and jars of pickles and sacks of vegetables were tucked everywhere, along the shelves and under the benches, their earthy breath adding to the smell of dinner and the dog and wet clothes and the tea in the samovar.

On the bare, scrubbed table sat a crock of milk and a bowl of salted cucumbers, a loaf of black bread and a bowl of *smetana*—sour cream. Kolya drank milk and *smetana*-slathered bread, telling a story about the bandits we'd encountered on the road, how he scared them off with his gun and they turned into magpies and flew away. The woman laughed, showing her even pearly teeth, and the melody of her laughter turned Kolya rosy and garrulous. How that man loved an audience, especially if it was a beautiful woman.

The tantalizing aromas issuing from the oven distracted me from my jealousy, and the sight of that bread, the milk. Since we'd been on the road, there had been so much lovely food, and I was as hungry as a bear in spring. Sometimes Kolya would buy me a chicken or some eggs or shoot a grouse and cook it out in the open for me. We'd devour it in the wagon. Now my stomach growled, while the rest of me politely pretended not to notice the savory bounty. As a good peasant wife, I could not ask for it myself.

"Please, have some bread," the woman finally invited me. "The milk's from the goat. I'd just finished milking when you came. Ilyosha, give her a cup." The five-year-old got up and brought me a tin cup, then tucked himself back in next to Kolya. Big-eyed and sharp-chinned, he had long eyelashes just like Seryozha's. He looked afraid to blink lest the visitor disappear on him. And I remembered so vividly how my brother would become obsessed by people, just like this. I poured myself warm milk, sweet and grassy. The bread was fresh and smelled of coriander. I slathered the thick sour cream on top. "God bless you and your household," I said.

"You are most welcome," she said.

"So you're from Danilov," the old man cut in on our womanly exchange. A real old-time patriarch, chewing his toothless gums in his untidy beard. "Pack of thieves, if you ask me. I bought a horse there once — this was back in the seventies. Remember that horse, Faina? Had the wheezes. Didn't last the winter."

"In the seventies?" our hostess snorted. "How old do you think I am?" It must be the husband's father — clearly no love lost there.

Kolya lit his pipe. "I remember that horse," he said. "A noble beast. The noblest."

Faina laughed out loud. I was sure she'd never seen such charm in her life. She lowered her eyes to her pots. She had the big fork out and was moving earthenware jars inside the oven, but whenever she looked up, there was hunger and pleasure in those eyes. She barely noticed I was there. The old granny next to me played with a little doll, dancing it on the table. She smelled sharp and, I hated to say, urinous. My envy for the good wife melted away. The village wives were all against her, she had nobody but these old people for company, three children to take care of, and a husband she kept nervously watching for out the windows. How could I begrudge her the fun we'd brought, the relief from boredom and labor?

The little boy at Kolya's elbow wanted to know more about the bandits. "How many were there?"

"Hundreds," Kolya said. "But nothing like the ones in the Caucasus. I was stationed there during the war." And he began to tell a twisted tale about having been kidnapped by bandits in the mountains and the time he spent at their campfires. He described their women, who were all beautiful gypsy girls, and the wild tribesmen, their high hats and curved Circassian swords, the tale working up to a bet on a horse race. The adventures were strongly reminiscent of Lermontov and Pushkin, but luckily our hostess hadn't read these venerable authors.

She brought me a pail of potatoes and set a short knife and a pan down in front of me. And so I began to peel, making myself useful just as I'd done at every stop on this journey, while my man sat in the place of honor under the icon and held forth, amusing everyone. I didn't really mind working, it was warm and pleasant here. But there was no hiding from the fact that a woman was worth exactly nothing but labor. This beauty and I counted the same—a pair of hands, a womb to endlessly produce, breasts to suckle the young, feet to drag and carry and plant themselves in the dirt.

As I listened to Kolya—he was really outdoing himself tonight—the pan filled with my peelings, probably slated for the pigs. To think people in Petrograd clung to life on such peelings. The Third Ancient could make a passable cake from them. One thing you could say about a revolution, we all discovered hidden talents.

The shelf over Kolya's head lovingly displayed the family treasures: a lacquered cup, a daguerreotype of two stiff people—maybe these two old people when they were young—two small paraffin lamps, and a black clock, stopped permanently at 2:50. And of course the icon in its silver frame, the red lamp dancing before it—the Virgin posed before a strip of water, and behind that, the shining towers of a white city. Peeling my potatoes, I wondered if this tidy izba, this warm kitchen, was a taste of faithful Kitezh, timeless and far from Marxist ideology and ration cards and modernity's nightmares. I could feel the peasant woman studying me as well. I sat up straighter, tried to look less dejected. Was she envying me my clever man? Or perhaps curious about my relative youth and my freedom to travel the roads of Russia.

Meanwhile, the baby's whimpering had become a wail. "*Tishe, tishe*, Lenochka," she said from the stove. "Don't I have enough to do? Pick her up for me, *devushka*."

Inside the wooden tub hanging from ropes, the baby looked at me with sodden eyes, blond as the other children and flushed, her curls all sweated through. My first thought was for myself. Was she ill? I couldn't afford to get sick now—I was already tired and achy all over—but how could I refuse? Keeping my head as far away from the infant as possible, I lifted the hot, heavy

body from the boatlike contraption. The child immediately began to scream. I didn't know what to do. I'd
never picked up a baby before, and she knew it. Frankly
I had about as much maternal instinct as a turtle that
lays its eggs on the shore and leaves them there for the
snakes and weasels. In that, Vera Borisovna and I had
much in common.

The baby shrieked and arched her back and held out
her arms to the woman at the stove as if I were about to
eat her.

Faina swept down and picked up the pail of potatoes
that I'd almost finished with, peeled the last ones with a
few sure strokes, and chopped them into the pot, wiping hair from her face with the back of her hand. "The
first ones were so easy, but this one, *ai*. You don't have
children?"

"Not yet," Kolya said. "But we're going to have tons
of them. At least ten."

Funny.

Holding the ailing infant on my lap, I bounced her,
tried to amuse her with my fingers. I'd have her almost
quiet, then she'd break out wailing again. Nervously,
I thought of the boy who'd died of cholera. But children got sick all the time. It didn't mean they were
dying. "Check her diaper," said the mother as the baby
screamed. She took something away from the tiny girl
holding her skirt and smacked her hand. "Not for you."
That one, too, started to cry.

"Can't you keep them quiet?" said the patriarch in

that high cracked voice of age. "Always someone crying. None of my children were allowed to cry like
that."

"Who asked you, old man?" snapped Faina. "At least
these will grow up and be of some use someday, unlike
you."

I steeled myself and raised the baby's shirt, loosened
the cloth bound around its waist and peeked inside. A
stench rose that made me gag. Oh, why couldn't I be
Kolya right now, happily sitting over on the bench doing magic tricks for the little boy? "It's dirty."

"There's a pail for the dirty one right here, a clean
one on the shelf over your head."

I didn't want to admit that I knew less about diapers
than I knew about the birth of stars. I lay the child
on the bench, but it immediately started to roll and
the diaper came off and the shit flowed like lava, all
over everything, the child screaming as if I were mur-
dering it. I looked at Kolya, who was enjoying it all
immensely.

"Oh the devil take it. You are useless, aren't you?
God help you when you have one of your own," she
said and moved quickly to take the infant from me.
"Stir those pots."

I held up my messy hands.

We heard the jingle of a harness, the gate scraping
open. *Gospodi bozhe moi.*" Panic had entered in her
voice. "Here." She had already removed the soiled diaper and held it out to me, folded in a neat packet. "Put

it in that pail, wash it out, dump the water in the yard. I could use some more water, too, while you're out there." Of course — I had been waiting for that one.

We could hear the horse as it was led around to the stable. I could feel the temper of the house change, everyone's urgency and unease.

Quickly I tipped some boiling water from the stove into the water in the enamel pail and dropped the dirty diaper in it. By the door, I washed the green muck off as best I could. I'd just opened the back door to throw the contents into the yard when the master of the house appeared at the bottom of the steps. He was a shrewd-looking peasant, taller than average, with matted hair cut straight across his ears and a squared-off beard. I bowed my head, a mere woman beneath the notice of the head of the household, perhaps of the whole village. He moved past me and into the house. "Whose horse is that? Who are these people?"

I was happy to take the pails and the yoke and leave Kolya to do the explaining. It was what he did best anyway.

When I returned, the husband was seated in the red corner, with Kolya next to him and another curly-headed blond child, a boy of around six, who had displaced his younger brother. Four children? Kolya and the peasant were talking easily, a bottle of vodka between them. But now the wife was suddenly dumb as a doorpost, tending to her pots like someone not wanting to be noticed, the infant propped on her hip. I couldn't help but admire the clean, neatly folded diaper now wrapped expertly around the baby's legs. "Can you put her back?" She held her out to me.

I was happy to put Lenochka back in her cradle and rock her gently by the ropes as the husband and Kolya talked about early oats and the rye harvest, how many acres under what crop, a lawsuit about a nearby forest of walnut and oak. I must have fallen asleep in the warmth and the pleasant scents because I was wakened by the sound of a big earthenware pot being dropped onto the table with a bang, a pot I probably couldn't have picked up empty. Steam rose from a rich stew fragrant with mushrooms and potatoes. A second crock held *shchi*, a cabbage soup. Faina's husband was served first, then my husband and the grandfather, followed by the children and finally, the women. The food was better than we'd seen in most of the villages. I ate in a dream, sitting at the table's foot with the crazy grandmother and the toddler girl, who was fascinated by my red beads.

Ivan Ivanych, Faina's husband, spoke with authority about the doings of the village. He was probably one of their headmen. He was older than his wife by at least ten years, and gray threads already ran in his hair and beard. I wondered if he had married her as a child or whether there had been a wife before her. But these children were certainly all hers—they were as alike as ducklings. Marx said that power lies with whoever controls the means of production. Clearly she was the means, and he was the owner. A certain stiffening of her posture when she spoke to him, the way she forced herself to look at him, told me she despised and feared him. And I noticed her effort now not to pay too close attention to the guest of honor.

Kolya was also careful to keep his regard evenly divided among his audience.

"So what's going on in Danilov, boy?" Ivanych asked, helping himself to the stew pot with his decorated spoon.

Danilov was a district center about a four-day walk from here. Kolya always picked our "hometown" carefully, far enough from where we were staying to make it unlikely that people could question him too pointedly about acquaintances, but close enough to be plausible.

"The new draft, brother," Kolya said, leaning toward our host, peasant man to peasant man, as if they were the only ones in the room. "Trotsky wants three million men under arms."

The one thing I'd learned out here was that distance was time. The distance from a muddy village like this to anyplace with a newspaper and a telegraph could be a week, a month.

"We just got done with a war. Why the devil do they have to start a new one?" the old patriarch chimed in, eager to still be part of the masculine court.

"Do you support the Reds?" asked Ivanych, plucking at his beard as if searching for something. "You think they're going to last?"

"That's the question, brother, that's the question," said Kolya. He toyed with his empty glass. I could tell he would have liked to pour another, but it wasn't done in a peasant home, to serve your own drinks. "Kolchak's just declared himself dictator of Russia." The White admiral with whom my father's faction had recently joined. "All the other generals have sworn loyalty to him."

"To the devil with them all." At last Ivanych refilled the men's glasses. "If they think we're going to give up the land, they better think again." They drank off the round in a single draught. "So what's your trade, boy? Why aren't you with your own people, getting ready for winter?"

Kolya began to tell our story. I had heard this act before in many an izba, but it was still magical, a tale as good as Afanasyev, in which he was the enterprising son of a poor widowed mother. With his new bride, he had left their town for the sake of his older brother, a worker in a factory in Petrograd—or Moscow—who had been crippled in an accident or in the war. He explained how badly he needed to buy enough food to see his brother's family through the winter, as well as the old lady back in Danilov/Kostroma/Cherepovets/Rybinsk.

"There isn't a morsel of food left in Petrograd," Kolya concluded. So the brother was in Petrograd this time.

"The last shall be first," said the peasant.

"They're fighting over who's last, then, brother."

Our host snorted. "So tell me, why should I sell to you? Maybe someone comes along and offers me twice as much." He fingered his beard as if he expected to find a small animal in it.

Kolya leaned on his elbow as if he were a student working out a difficult theorem. He pulled on his ear, bit his lip, looking like he was about to fail the exam. I tried not to smile, knowing that when Kolya put on the ermines of pure innocence, he would be picking your pocket clean. "Well, that's true." He opened his blue eyes wide. "Only, you know, it's this million-man army they're raising..."

"What about it?" Our host's bushy eyebrows knitted together over his skeptical eyes.

"Well, you know, I was in the war, in a provisioning unit. The Southwestern Army. And I can tell you, when they say an army marches on its stomach, they're not joking. They don't bargain with you, and you won't see any handfuls of gold."

Now the headman was quiet. The little sons' eyes shifted from their father to this handsome red-bearded man next to him, learning, absorbing. Faina, too, was watching.

Ivanych considered, rolling the empty glass in his hand. "We've already had the Yaroslavl workers. Twice." It obviously had not been a pleasant encounter.

"And they're the workers," Kolya said. "Soldiers are another story."

Now it was the peasant nodding. He poured vodka all around, even for Faina and me and the granny, so we could toast. "To Russia," then to luck, then to the harvest. We drank, and I thought of this suffering land, bored full of mouse holes, the mice scurrying in before the storm.

67 *The Bathhouse Devil*

AFTER THE RICH SUPPER, the family treated us to a bath in the village *banya*. My stomach purring with the good meal, vodka pulsing in my veins, my clever lover at hand, my aching carcass free for the time being from that infernal wagon. And now a bath! What more could a mortal ask for?

We crossed ourselves as we descended into the log-and-earthen hut by a pond not quite iced over, glazed by sharp moonlight. Kolya, comically humble and visibly drunk now, gestured and wished us a good bath, loud enough that Bannik would be satisfied, as if he were actually afraid of the little bathhouse devil. Oh, I remembered Avdokia's stories about Bannik, what he had done to this or that relative of hers in the village when his rules were disobeyed or when some naughty young girls tried out some magic spell that went terribly awry. We never used the Maryino bathhouse. Father didn't believe in it. *We have indoor plumbing, damn it all. We're not savages.* I thought of him as we ducked

under the low entrance to the log shed—first the headman, then Kolya, then the patriarch, followed by Faina
and myself. Where was Father now? In what godforsaken hut in Perm or boardinghouse in Omsk did he sit
with his reason and his outrage, now hopelessly aligned
with reactionary forces in Siberia?

In the anteroom, under the log beams, we stripped
off our patchy clothes and modestly entered into the
steam, redolent of fragrant pine. Faina teased me about
my short hair, that I made a very pretty boy. I made
excuses, saying that I'd had scarlet fever earlier this
year. Ivanych threw water on the hot stones and disappeared in a fine mist. It was lovely here, the pine
perfume satisfying something in me so primal I hadn't
known it existed. It had taken a revolution to bring me
here. Compared to this close, dark, scented lodge, the
banya on Kazanskaya Street was a sewer illustrated by
Daumier.

I eyed Faina with her big belly painted red-gold in
the stove light. I wondered if she would give birth
here—I had heard that village women did, the reason
why proper relations with Bannik were essential. I
caught Kolya glancing at her ripe figure, her round
haunches and luxurious *poitrine*, her blond braids. Did
he want her? I was thin and ragged now, and my inky
cropped hair could not have been terribly picturesque.
My toenails looked like rawhide. I rubbed balls of dead
skin off my feet, wondering if Kolya had tired of his
boyish lover. Did he miss the women in Paris, per-

fumed and tantalizing? Was a woman like this more enticing?

Ivanych, drunk, held forth about the goings-on of the village, who had it in for whom, and assuring us that no one in the village council put up with the Kombedy and its finger-pointing. Then he moved on to the former landlord, Kachanovsky, who'd cut a stand of timber that belonged to him, Ivanych, and he'd taken that devil to court and won. It was the great triumph of his life. I couldn't help but notice his body, which was very white and surprisingly well built. He was younger than he'd appeared in his clothes. I tried not to look at the grandfather, sunken chest and little potbelly, his sparse nest of pubic hair. Instead I sank into the clouds of fine steam as one would sink into a lover's arms. Ivanych threw more water on the stones, and Faina beat him with the birch twigs she'd been soaking in a wooden pail.

The peasant was evaluating me as well. He seemed to approve of me, nodding. I actually thought he was going to say something kind. Instead he turned to Kolya and said, "You flog her good and proper, I see."

Kolya had to tear his eyes off Faina's breasts in order to respond. "Every Sunday," he replied. "That way she knows what day of the week it is."

Ivanych nodded again, wiping sweat down his wiry arms. His eyes were very pale under the dark brows. "Only one way to remind them who the man is, eh, boy?"

With a shock, I realized that this ignorant sot had seen my scars and assumed Kolya had been their source. Probably couldn't write his own name, yet he had no trouble reading the signs of violence on a woman's body. I waited for Kolya to stand up to him, to admit he was joking, that he'd never do such a thing, but my lover just grinned, drunk and too interested in the grain we were buying off this peasant to disagree. "She's a tough one." He swished the flail in the bucket, then switched his own back. "She looks sweet but she's the very devil. Her parents didn't tell me about that. They were just happy to get her off their hands."

And they laughed together. Hee hee hee.

Though I knew it was a charade and he didn't believe a single word he was saying, I wanted to kill him. I thought of those women in the bathhouse on Kazan-skaya Street, of Arkady's peasant woman. *Think you could take three lashes?* Whose fault was it that I bore these scars? Or had he forgotten? I knew he would say it was just part of the masquerade, but he was going too far now. He was way over the line.

"Show them a strong hand," Ivanych continued. "Or before you know it, they're ruling the roost and *you're* sitting on the eggs." He drained his vodka and handed it to Faina to refill, as if she were stupid as a cow and hadn't understood what he'd been saying.

When she turned to pour, by the glow of the flames I saw her pale skin crisscrossed with the uneven scars of lashings, one over the next. Ivanych beat her with a whip, as though she were a criminal or a serf. To do such a thing to a beautiful woman. To any woman. I hoped Kolya saw it and understood that these were not just empty phrases, not things one said as admission to some men's club in the hinterlands. His joke was her nightmare. No wonder she stiffened when her husband came home, no wonder she sat so silently. I tried to catch Kolya's eye, but he was having too much fun playing the rural idiot. He only saw her breasts with their egg-size nipples, her white haunches, her lovely face. And at that moment, I hated him.

She wouldn't look at me now, not at me or Kolya as she gave her husband his glass. Her eyes were cast down for shame, knowing what we'd seen.

"Yes, you have to beat the devil out of them," her husband continued, tiresomely. "They have to learn respect."

"A kiss might do the same," I said bluntly, surprised at the clarity of my own voice in the shadowy bath. "Violence wins fear, not respect."

Kolya laughed all the louder. He was really soused. I was on my own. So be it.

"You've been living in town too long, *devushka*," Ivanych said, waving his finger at me. "Come live out here. We'll get rid of some of those modern ideas."

I sat up straighter, didn't try to conceal the fury I felt like coals burning in my heart. He was threatening *me?* This illiterate bastard? And Kolya was going to let him? There was a gun in the pocket of Kolya's coat not eight feet away. I imagined holding it to Ivanych's fore-head. *Still want to beat me, Uncle?*

"Let me switch you," Faina said quickly, changing seats, and began to lash me with the birch flail, slicing through the steam and making the room even hotter. I cringed with every lash. Soon I felt faint with the heat. How far we were from civilization in this hut, as if we'd gone not only miles but years. So I was my father's daughter after all. So much for my Princess Natasha peasant dance.

"I have to go out." I rose from the bench, stumbled for the door.

"Yes," Faina said, taking my arm. "Let's go for a plunge." We ran out into the cold night, dashed bare-foot across the boards laid over the pond's lip, then crashed into the water. The shock, the intense pleasure, made me forget for an instant everything but the body and the night and the glow of Faina's white shoulders bobbing in the water next to me. How wonderful to be out of that hut, away from that man. I could feel the steam rising from me in the icy water. She floated be-side me, a white mountain.

"My scars—that's from something else," I said. "He's never raised a hand to me."

"May you never know," the pale form replied.

"You could leave," I said. "Come with us."

"You're very young," she said, swimming away.

I pedaled in the dark water. I knew it was cold but still didn't feel it.

She surfaced close by me, sputtered, wiped the water from her face, steadying herself with one hand on my shoulder. "Take my advice. Don't have children," she said. "They stake you like a cow so the wolves can eat you alive, until there's nothing you can do but pray for death."

"Maybe he'll get in an accident," I said, imagining plausible ways such a man could lose his life.

"Then we'd all die. There's no way out." A splash, and I felt the touch of a snowflake fall against my face. She continued, "When I was a girl, an old woman gave me a pillow of herbs. She said, 'Sleep on this, *devushka*, you won't get a child.' And I laughed at her. 'Why would I want that?' I said. 'Every woman wants children.' I didn't know what she was telling me." She caught her breath, there in the dark. "Some days I want to kill them all, myself as well, just bring it to an end." She swam to the edge and climbed out, a huge, full-bodied white blur in the dark, wringing out her long braids.

I followed her. I wished I had a word of comfort for her, but all I could do was loop my cold wet arm around her neck and press my forehead to hers. She was weeping, silently, as she must weep at night not to wake the children. This was the benightedness the Bolsheviks were trying to end. But could they get here fast enough to save this woman? It made me sick to think how Kolya laughed when Ivanych talked about beatings. Faina was caught in a terrible net just like the one

Arkady used to wind between his fingers. How could
I bear to go back in and see that man and hear Kolya's
coarse jokes? I wished we could leave this second, flee
this house as one would flee a massacre.

When we bedded down that night in the straw, Kolya
put his drunken arms around me, but I pushed him
away.

"Oh, don't be like that. Look, you've got your feathers all ruffled." He tried to kiss me, to make it up to me,
but I turned over. He kissed my shoulder instead, murmuring in my ear. "What is it? The *banya?*"

"What do you think?"

"That was just talk, *milaya.* You know it's how men
talk. He's got to think I'm just like him."

"Why don't you beat me and really show him? Did
you see her back?" I still saw it, crisscrossed like a
slave's.

"Oh, my little poetess. You take everything too much
to heart." He rolled onto his back. "In a week, with
any luck, we'll be back in Petrograd, having a laugh.
You'll forget all about this. It's their problem." He
shook me gently, trying to shake loose my determination not to forgive him. I only stiffened. "Come on, *ma
petite.* Where's your sense of humor?"

My sense of humor, where could it have possibly
gone? "I think I left it in the hut there. Why don't you
go look for it?" I could smell the vodka on his breath,
you could have set fire to it.

"Look at us. Who would have imagined, five years ago, we would end up like this, having a fight in some godforsaken barn?" He tickled my ear with a piece of straw. I knocked his hand away. "Marina, this is life," he sighed. "I can't edit it for you. We'll be back in Cherepovets in three days. I'm doing great with this guy." He shook me gently. "Come on. Look, some peasant beats his wife. It's going to make headlines all over Russia? I mean, where have you been living—in a candy box?"

Yes, I knew this happened, I'd seen it on women's flesh, but I'd never seen it written so starkly on a woman's body besides my own. That beauty, who wanted to die. I hated what I was seeing in Kolya now: he wanted what he wanted and the plight of others left him cold. "Just leave me alone. I'm tired. I want to go to sleep."

I could feel his restlessness in the dark, the crumpling of straw as he tried to find a comfortable position, an irritable rustling against the contented clucking of the chickens, the nickering of the horses. I was tired and fell asleep easily. At some point I heard the barn door open and shut again.

A light fine snow drifted down on us as Ivanych loaded his grain into the wagon inside the barn, out of sight of the neighbors, and Kolya put the bright gold coins into his hand, French francs with their cockerels. The horse tossed his head, eager to be off. Six poods of grain, more than two hundred pounds. He'd thrown in a flat of eggs and two rounds of cheese besides. Faina wouldn't meet my eye. Was she ashamed of her confidences? That I understood the extent of her plight?

We climbed up into the wagon, and Ivanych opened the barn door and the gates. His wife came out to watch us leave, hiding behind the manner we had seen at the beginning—abrupt, formal, indifferent. But before she shut the gates, she hurried up, thrust a jar of jam into my hands, and gave me the saddest smile I'd ever seen. Then she shot Kolya the strangest look. Her cheeks were flushed and her eyes held such a hunger, such longing, her lips slightly parted, as if for a kiss. And his expression...the way his eyes held hers. A secret communication. What in God's name did they have to keep secret? Kolya shook the reins and the gray headed off.

68 *A Delightful Man*

THE HORSE PULLED US through the sifting snow. It built up on his wide rump, traced the arch of the shaft bow over his shaggy neck. Next to me on the bench, Kolya lounged cheerfully, humming "All Along the Volga." I felt queasy and our departure nagged at me, the glance Faina and Kolya had exchanged. I rolled the jar between my mittened hands. Something had happened between them last night. Their brief exchange was too familiar, unspoken but urgent. On either side of us, pine forest closed in. No distance to pull back, no horizon line, no relief from the pressure, only two vanishing points, one ahead and one behind. He noticed me examining him and smiled. "Stupid *muzhik* really thought he'd put one over on us. We could have walked away with the floor and he'd have been lying in the straw, congratulating himself." He grinned at his own cleverness, the fox's triumph over a folktale goose.

That look, her eyes, the barn door closing. The jam. Her smile for me—almost an apology. No, not almost. A real apology. Yes, that was right, Kolya had left Ivanych the floor. The floor would have been too hard to steal. But a ripe, sad wife was as easy as eggs in an unguarded henhouse.

"Where did you go last night, when you went out?"

"To Prince Yusupov's," he said. "He was hosting a ball. Why?" Such a display of innocence.

I knew a sophisticated woman would tuck it under her wing the way a swan tucks its head. Akhmatova would not make a scene. She'd say, *Women have experienced such things since love began.* She'd be casual, shrug off her pain with words so exact they would be like lancets. They would drain the wound, and she would go on.

But I was not that girl. My suffering wasn't picturesque, it was hot and deep as an inflamed wound. I hadn't thought twice when he went outside last night—but the longer I thought about the way Faina looked at him, the more sure I was. He'd met her somewhere, maybe in the bathhouse or in a shed, and they'd consummated what began in the izba, that electrical storm.

To think he'd returned across a continent for me! Through a war! Had braved Arkady von Princip for my sake. How could he have done all that, then sneaked off with a peasant woman six months along? Of course she was beautiful, but my God! And for her part, what if she'd been caught? Kolya could drive away, but Ivanych might beat her to death.

The snow drifted down, frosting our coats and scarves, the horse's heavy clip-clop. Soon we'd need a sledge. But how could I go on? Still he prattled, his bad conscience filling the air with noise, pouring words into the gap between us, like a stream plunging into a chasm. Who cared about his stories, his daring escapes and colorful encounters in exotic places, the Russian d'Artagnan and Ali Baba rolled into one? I knew him for what he was now. An ordinary man, a bit frightened, full of bluster.

My stomach lurched as the wagon swayed and slid in the ruts. The jam sat heavy in my lap. I wanted to smash the jar into his face, to crush his head with it like an egg. I tried to hate her, her doll's face, her red cheeks, the wide-set eyes—but I couldn't. I didn't blame her. A woman like that, in this hinterland, wouldn't have many chances to enjoy a man like Kolya. No village Romeo could ever compare.

But Kolya! To bring me all the way out here, then go

with her? I tried not to imagine their grappling. They did it in the bathhouse, I was sure of it. It would still have been warm. I knew how sweetly he would have spoken to her, said things no one had ever told her before. He would know just how to soothe her anxiety, get her out of her clothes, his lips to her round breasts, his clever touch. How she would groan as he brought her off, maybe for the first time in her life.

The horse stumbled on a patch of ice and we jolted together. "Steady!" He laughed. "He had a little too much to drink last night with the cows." I wanted to wipe the little smirk from his face. So pleased with himself. He had stolen her under the very nose of the violent husband. *Serves him right,* he was probably thinking. And then filling my ears with talk talk talk. Would he never be quiet?

I was tired of his cleverness. I felt like the illusionist's assistant, having rolled the strings and fastened the pulleys, seen the doves stuffed into his pockets. How many other women had he had since those days on the Catherine Canal? He might have had me in the afternoon and gone with another woman in the evening. I thought I might vomit. I thought of all the women we'd seen on this trip alone, wives and daughters, nieces and wards. I'd seen the flashing eyes of girls unused to gallantry, and Kolya was as tuned to feminine desire as a stationmaster to the ticking of the wireless.

My face burned, and bile welled up in my chest. What a child I'd been. Though I'd known what he was,

I thought I was the exception, that I possessed some unique attraction. But everyone had something special, didn't they, if only the glamour of novelty? I'd really thought that his struggle to return to me proved his love, proved that I was essential to him. What a fool.

I remembered a woman I hadn't thought of for years, the vinegar-voiced wife of a writer in my parents' set. Everyone loved him. *That delightful man,* they said. Always a smile, candy for the kiddies, compliments for everyone from grandmothers to housemaids. And I used to wonder, *How could such a delightful man be married to such a sour-faced bitch?*

I'd always assumed it was money. But now I understood that perhaps she hadn't always been so tart. Perhaps she'd once been a clever, gay young thing herself, smarter, jollier than the rest, someone to whom he'd returned again and again, someone he might have pursued across a landscape like a roe deer, until she fell to his bow.

Now I imagined having such a man for a husband, having to endure the humiliation, the shame, the knowledge that he might pursue any kind of prey, though he'd seemingly already caught what he wanted—or wanted at the time. There was always more room in his game bag. And he intended to fill it, and keep filling it. Playing the delightful man wasn't a pastime. The game was the man, the man was the game.

At last, Kolya picked up on my mood. "God I'm so

tired of Russia." He sighed, slapping the snow off his cap. "I don't care if I never see another pine tree as long as I live. I can't wait for Spain — Jerez, Valencia." He exaggerated the foreign sounds. "Those perfumed nights."

I would not listen. I had to stopper my ears to resist the sweet singing of the sirens. I would not wreck upon those rocks again. I would not become the sour wife, drinking my pint of vinegar with my morning meal.

I studied the dizzying motion of the passing trees, like a book's pages flying past us. A book that I would never read. "I'm not going anywhere with you." *You'd kiss any girl, beneath any moon.*

He stared at me as if I'd grown a second head.

"You're disgusting. You slept with her. Don't bother to lie." The horse nodded rhythmically, its fuzzy ears collecting snow.

He laughed then, eyes wide with amazement that I could have such a thought, bearing his innocence aloft like a regimental flag. "Oh, little Marinochka," he purred, dropping his chin into a pose of gentle disappointment, his voice dripping honey. "Is that what this is all about? All this pouting?" He tried to touch my chin, as one wags a child's, to tease it, but I knocked his hand away.

"I could kill you. I'll cut your throat while you're sleeping."

"You can't be serious. You're jealous of a barefoot peasant with four kids?" His pointed eyebrows were

clownishly skeptical. As if this were an impossible in-
terspecies mating, like a man and a giraffe. "I'm sure
she signs her name with an X."

A wave of nausea came over me. "I'm sure you didn't
ask her to sign her name."

The idea of myself in Petrograd with him as he did
his speculating, undermining the struggle of the
people—for what? A better man would just admit it.
If he had gotten on his knees and begged my forgiveness—*She was sad. She doesn't have much in her life.
Think of that beauty going to waste. It broke my heart that
that pig was the only one who would ever touch her. How
could I refuse her?*—I might have forgiven him. But not
this. Whom did he think he was lying to?

So many years I had clung to this dream. Since childhood. *If only we could be together*, I'd thought. Well,
now we were.

"I'm not going on with you. I can't even look at
you."

"You want to go back to Five Huts?" He made an ex-
travagant show of turning back to examine the misty
road, the boughs of the frosty trees practically touching
the wagon, the hummocks of frosty dirt. "Or are you
getting out right here?" He pulled the horse to a halt in
the silent forest and turned all the force of his personality onto me. "I didn't sleep with her, Marina. I swear to
you. You're being completely unreasonable."

I gazed into that face. Snow gathered on his cap,
on that ridiculous beard. I felt like clawing my own

guts out. How stupid could I be? You couldn't expect
the fox to change its ways. Either you loved it or you
didn't. And I loved it, God help me. But I didn't have
the fortitude for this. I would not become pinch-faced
Alla Fyodorovna, feeling my love cut out of me with a
dull knife every day. I hadn't the depth for Akhmatov-
ian calm, my great soul expanding like a velvet purse. I
would shrivel into some sort of vicious reptile. We had
to part. Nausea overtook me, and I vomited off the side
of the wagon.

"You're tired and upset. Lie down in the back," he
said. "We'll be in Cherepovets in a few days, we'll load
the train, be back in Petrograd by Thursday. After that
we'll go anywhere you want. We never have to do this
again." He gave me a sip from the canteen of hot tea.
Suddenly, I saw that he, too, was tired, the skin pressing into his cheekbones. His uptilted eyes looked lined.
Funny, I always thought of him as a force of nature, as
little capable of tiring as the Neva.

I climbed into the back, taking the extra sheepskin, and
burrowed into the straw. I couldn't go back to
Petrograd—I'd burned every bridge there. For Kolya.
The bitter irony did not escape me. No, I would only go
as far as Tikhvin, get off the train and make my way to
Maryino, if it still stood. I would see if it was possible to
make a life there. It was my last refuge, a place I belonged.

In truth, I didn't believe I'd make it as far as Cherepovets, I felt so wretched. But I had to get to that train.

I had to be rid of him. After three days of hard travel, we finally entered the yards of the good-size town with our horse and laden wagon. I was once again presenting myself in the guise of Misha, my women's clothing back in my bag. And so it had come to this. I was learning that if a person did nothing at all, the world continued to turn, and eventually time passed and the day arrived when you found yourself in an impossible moment of separation.

Up to then I didn't quite believe that I would go through with it, that I would split with my one and false love, but I could already feel myself moving away from him, like being on a ship, pulling from the dock, watching him standing on the shore. I would never again love anyone the way I loved this man, the twist of his mobile mouth, the slant of his eyes, the curls in his reddish-brown hair. My magician.

"I'll go with you as far as Tikhvin, and then I'm getting off," I told him, looking forward as we sat side by side on the wagon seat. "I don't want to be with you anymore."

"One more chance," he said. "I beg you. I'll be a saint, a blind eunuch. Don't do this to me. To us! God, I'm sorry. I'm sorry. Listen to me, Marina."

It was the admission I'd been waiting for, but it didn't feel the way I thought it would. It was too late. I felt cold in my bones, cold and clear in a way I didn't think I was capable of. If one must cut off one's own right hand, it was better to do it quickly, then sear it with an iron and plunge it into icy water. My bones were cracking like the ice when it was only just thick enough to walk upon. My heart, cracking.

He leaned on his knees and wept, while all around us in the train yard, men continued to work, ignoring this sobbing man as if it were an everyday occurrence in Cherepovets, and maybe it was. The horse switched his tail.

A man neared us with the studied nonchalance of conspiracy. He took the horse's bridle. "You Rubashkov?"

"You've got work to do," I said.

I stayed with the load while they went off and returned with two grim men pushing handcarts. They unloaded the grain quickly—our precious, tainted cargo—and took it to a passenger car marked PETROGRAD. Then they opened a panel at one end and quickly filled it with our bags. Kolya closed it up, and I could see him passing something into the hands of the men, who faded back into the station. I returned the wagon to the livery stable and collected a third of what we'd paid for the horse and wagon, then returned to find Kolya squatting on his heels, watching the car from the scrubby woods. We watched and waited, and said nothing.

The Vologda train arrived in the afternoon. It picked up our car from the siding, and we followed it into the station. The platform swarmed with desperate people heading into starving Petrograd—bag people like us, workers returning from self-provisioning, hungry locals. When people are desperate, they seek motion, even if it is in the wrong direction. I was keenly aware that we were endangering everyone on the train crew with our contraband. If the Railway Cheka found that compartment, that load of grain, they would know it hadn't been smuggled by just one person. They searched the trains constantly, as did the local authorities.

We didn't speak. The engineer and fireman kidded us, making their crude jokes, thinking it was a men's-only locomotive. Kolya had his gloves off—he was biting his nails. It was like being in a funeral car. We watched dark fields passing. It stopped snowing, and the moon reappeared, revealing sleeping villages. "Come back to Petrograd, then do what you want. I won't stop you," he said low, in my ear.

"I am doing what I want." I wasn't going to point out that he had already done what he wanted and would continue doing it, no matter what he said, no matter how many tears he shed. The muscular music of the wheels, the roar of the engine, sang us their sad lullaby.

Babayevo. Podborovye. We bought tea and buns from *babas* on the platform. The tea tasted like dishwater, the bun was dust in my mouth. Every breath was a heartache.

"There's no sense to this," he whispered, gazing out at the dark arches of a station. We stood shoulder to shoulder but didn't touch. "We can just go on. People do. People forgive, they change."

He was so serious. I'd never heard him like this. My anger had evaporated, leaving behind only sorrow, pure and deep. "No, they don't."

The journey was agonizing, the train rusty. At times we moved at a walking pace. We were searched three times, once by Cheka, twice by others. Kolya watched the car with the grain, but so far so good. Before dawn we pulled into the station at Tikhvin. I climbed down from the locomotive, using the coupling rods as steps. He followed me, held me fast by my upper arms. Even now, my lips hungered for his. I could feel them trembling. They didn't understand why they couldn't have him.

"Wait for me," he pleaded. "I'll make it up to you. You're all I have, Marina. If I thought I was losing you forever, I'd kill myself, I swear." His blue eyes for once held no teasing, only a desperation that distilled that of the world around us. We couldn't embrace, so we stood awkwardly like abashed brothers.

"Good luck, Kolya," I said, and picked up my bundle: cheese and bread, a sausage, the jar of jam, tobacco and six matches, the money he'd pressed on me that I knew enough to accept. I had kept my sheepskin and my women's clothes. Kolya slid his pistol out from his pocket and put it in mine.

"You'll need it." Although I was leaving him, I didn't want to see him killed in his dirty dealings with the Petrograd underworld.

He attempted a smile. "In a few days I can buy myself a howitzer."

I left him there in the hazy darkness and the hissing steam. He would have followed me, but he couldn't leave the grain.

69 *The North*

I WALKED THROUGH TIKHVIN station, flanked by the arches my child self once imagined belonged to a palace. I could see her there through the thin veil of time—my mother in a huge hat, a mountain of luggage, her dog on a lead. Seryozha clutching his easel, Volodya bursting with joy to be heading to the country, Avdokia haggling with the porter. Now there was only the urgency of getting away. I emerged in the town square, dark and quiet in the early morning, and the gravity of what I had done hit me like a train. I felt my heart ripping like a piece of cloth.

And how exactly was I to make this journey to Maryino? On foot, with winter heavy in the sky? Kolya had warned me that it was beyond my capabilities, had outlined a tale of disaster, but all I could think of was getting away from the sight of his foxy, treacherous face.

I hadn't considered how this moment would feel. I was more alone than I'd ever been in my life, without companion or guide, lover or friend. My lungs hurt in the frost. I reminded myself that I was also free. No tormentor, no locked doors, no enemies, no traps. And I knew this place. I'd been here many times before. But now that I saw the town again, I realized it was like a person you thought you knew—a baker or doorman you saw every day, but who, meeting him in the street, you realized you never knew at all. This Tikhvin square gave me back that same kind of blank stare.

I couldn't just stand in one place. I was Misha again, Misha the hooligan, and what self-respecting Russian boy would exhibit such sniveling, such cowardice? *Buck up*, Misha said to Marina. *Stick with me and the devil take him, that lying son of a bitch. We don't need him. We'll do fine, you'll see.* Nothing for it but to go on and see if I could follow my own harebrained plan.

Walking through the town, I could see how much it had changed. Everything seemed sadder. The boarded-up shops, broken windows, fallen roof slates, like an old man curled in on himself, waiting to be beaten. I passed the ancient inn where we used to spend the night. The front door was boarded and nailed. Although it could simply be that nobody used the front doors anymore. Puddles had iced over during the night. The town was pulling in its chin for the winter, stiffening up, collar raised.

Ahead rose the towers of the ancient monastery, showing the same impervious face it had displayed for five centuries, the high white walls gray in the dull dawn, and behind them rose the domes and the famous bell tower with its unmistakable steeples like a comb with five tines. The monastery was a fortress, protecting its miracle-working icon that I knew so well, having slept under its tender image in every place we'd lived, the same icon Genya had crushed in a fit of proletarian rage. I was glad the original lay safe within those forbidding walls. I only wished they would ring the carillon and break the crow-filled silence, but it was the wrong time, and I had to get going.

And so I began to walk north, to my one remaining home, with its happy memories of childhood, of summer days and my family as it was. When I reached Maryino, I could rest and sort the great trunk of my losses. Even if the peasants had taken over the big house, I was sure Grigorii and Annoushka would let me have the old maid's room, or space in the stable. They could put me to work and enjoy their revenge.

My feet fell into a rhythm only they knew, unique to my own body, and the fresh cold air settled my nausea. Suddenly I was glad to be alone, to move to my own meter and accent, iambic tetrameter. It struck me how people either rushed you along, like Varvara and Genya or Father, or were maddeningly slow, like Mina and Mother. Only Kolya and I could ever walk together—even at the end, our steps matched stride for stride. But that was over. No point in thinking about it. Like Whitman, I would sing the song of myself—my own footsteps, the length of my stride, the strength of my back, the vapor I exhaled. I had food in my sack and somewhere to go.

I walked for three days, catching rides with peasants when I could, enjoying the changing terrain and the various opinions of my escorts. One peasant thought the next snowstorm would hold off a few more days, but the river was freezing. And the crows were thick this fall, he said, the woolly caterpillars fat—all signs of a harsh winter. I thought the opposite, out of politeness. But I also enjoyed the easy silences as a boy among men. Women liked to keep up a steady, reassuring sound of chat. One of the things women probably found so attractive about Kolya was that he could never shut up. He was compelled to conversation by some tension of his innermost nature, compelled to charm and entertain. Words forced themselves from his breast like songs from a nightingale.

It was pretty country. The lines of uncut trees plumed in windbreak crests on the hilltops, the subtle verticals of the trunks distinct in the clouds of bare branches. Below, rolling fields lay plump under a dusting of snow. And in the villages, I was the one who sat in the red corner, bringing news of the world and entertaining after dinner, weaving pictures in string and narrating the tale of Maria Morevna and Koshchei the Deathless and Prince Ivan. "*Zhili-buili*, once upon a time, there was a king with only one son..."

I wondered what would happen to these stories now,

when there were no more princes or queens. In thirty years, I might come into an izba like this one and no one would have heard of Maria Morevna or Vasilisa the Beautiful, only the Brave Bolshevik and Ivan the Kronstadt Sailor. What happened to old stories after the world changed? Would they all just go underground, like Bannik, to be whispered about in dark bathhouses?

No one to whom I spoke knew our village, but on the morning of the second day some peasants steered me to the hut of a woodcutter who was supposed to know the whole district. "Which Novinka?" he'd asked. "Near Alekhovshchina or the one to the west?"

I hadn't thought of the name of that village in years. "Alekhovshchina."

"Look here." He drew me a rough map on a bit of brown paper his wife had saved from a package, his nails like horn, striated and yellow and broken from work. On the wrinkled surface, he traced the road and the river it followed, noted where I should cross. I took his pencil and wrote the names next to the *x*'s on the map: Vinogora, Bol Kokovichi. He watched me with undisguised awe, as if I were swallowing a sword.

"Look at him, Alya," he said to his wife. "Writing away like the devil himself. Good boy." He thumped my back so hard I thought I'd break a vertebra. "The road's not bad but this stretch in here"—he indicated the long stretch before Alekhovshchina—"that's some forest. I should tell you you won't see a soul from sunup to sundown. Some good hunting there. Too bad you don't have a gun."

I shrugged. My revolver wasn't something I wanted to advertise. He folded the map and handed it to me. "So what's in Novinka you're in such a hurry to get to, hey boy?"

I put the map in the pocket of Misha's jacket, next to my heart along with the matches. "No hurry. My sister married a man from Novinka. Just paying her a visit, that's all."

It must be hard to be a woodcutter and be so outgoing. It was as if he'd saved up his breath to let it loose in a torrent this morning. "Girl trouble, am I right? A little visit out of harm's way?" He grabbed my shoulder with the strength of a man who wielded a thirty-pound ax half his life. "I don't blame you. Don't wait until you're old and ugly like me." His wife laughed. We stood and shook hands, and he kissed me three times. "Keep your eyes open, son." He winked. "Novinka's no bigger than a freckle on your face. Walk too fast, you'll miss it."

As the woodcutter had said, the road to Bol Kokovichi followed the river, skirting mixed forest and open fields. It was definitely colder than the day before—below freezing, the trees glittering with frost—but I was well rested, and the map gave me heart. I was glad to see there would be a regularity of villages every few miles until I reached that forest.

My luck was holding. If anything the sky was higher than it had been. I fell into step with myself, the aches and stiffening of yesterday's walk at first almost ridiculously painful, but gradually my body warmed as the day went on. Pain subsided into a generalized ache that I could ignore in the rhythm of my tramp. Crows complained over the snowy, stubble-topped fields.

I grew confident about my choice and my abilities. It felt good to know that I could trust my instincts, responsible to no one but myself. The world wasn't nearly as frightening as I'd been led to believe. And I was

> *not anyone's lover,*
> *   nobody's wife,*
> *not boy nor girl*
> *not daughter, nor friend.*
> *Just myself here*
> *   mocking the crows.*
> *Eighteen years old and full of why not.*

But toward the end of the day, weariness came over me like a fog. In one village, I asked a woman where I might be able to spend the night. She said, "With your own people," and slammed the door in my face. I had to approach five different souls before I found shelter with a sour but greedy old couple. They took my money and let me sleep in their shed. Later I discovered they'd locked me in. I went crazy—I couldn't stand being locked up anymore. I pounded and yelled, and the old woman shrieked back through the door that they'd let me out in the morning, but they had chickens to protect. "Unless you want to sleep outdoors, you better stop that racket." Luckily I was tired and soon slept. But my hopes of getting an early start in the morning were dashed—I felt sick and the oldsters took forever to pull themselves out of their rural torpor and open the door. The old witch thrust a crust of bread at me, and a boiled egg in the shell, which made me want to vomit. I warmed my hands with it and headed out toward Alekhovshchina.

Soon I found myself in the forest the woodcutter had described. The road deteriorated into a dismal wagon path through the lines of tall pines. The going was hard—branches and even tree trunks had fallen across the road and been left there. The ruts were deep and the darkness of the day and the closeness of the path sucked out my spirit like a chimney drawing smoke. After a few hours, my weariness deepened to pure misery. I stumbled along, a quarter mile at a time. I felt like I'd fallen into a nightmare, shuffling along through a forest without end. A line from a Longfellow poem my father liked haunted me: *This is the forest primeval...*

I concentrated on hating. I hated the endless identical trees, leaving only a strip of white sky overhead. I cursed those old people for the late start. I cursed Kolya and his endless seduction. I cursed the day I kissed him in the cloakroom at my parents' New Year's Eve party.

I cursed the peasants and the speculators and God and the devil, cursed the revolution and the year 1918. I grew sweaty, then chilled. I felt weak and stupid. After a while I stopped cursing, stopped making a sound, and just stumbled along, without thought, moving out of inertia—not walking so much as falling forward.

To make matters worse, the snow that everyone had been waiting for began to fall. Now a sick, dull panic rose. No "Song of Myself" now, just the dawning realization that I might not make it to Alekhovshchina. The snow fell faster, big flakes whirling with an updraft. It gave me vertigo. Within minutes, up and down became confused, and all that whiteness made me seasick. I dropped a pinecone, just to see it fall. The sky gave no clue as to the time—it could have been noon or two or four. I stopped to rest and drink a bit of boiled water from my bottle. I'd felt sick when I left the shed that morning, and now I just wanted to lie down on the road and curl into a ball like a hedgehog. I looked back at my own footprints, filling with snow. Was it too far to go back to those horrible old people?

I should have been there by now. Surely I was well past the halfway mark. I had to press on, see if I could make Alekhovshchina before nightfall. I just had to. No one in this world had any idea where I was, and no one would ever come looking. I lurched blindly from rut to rut. The snow was sticking to the ground, my cheeks were freezing, and my nose felt like a piece of metal stuck into my face. I wrapped my woman's woolen scarf over my sheepskin and up all the way to my eyes, though breathing through the wool made it wet, and then that froze, too.

I was a fool. I should have emptied my pockets in Tikhvin, found a wagon, paid someone to take me. I was a stupid girl wearing the clothes and bravado of a boy. I stumbled along, watching the white end of the forest road for the shape of rooftops and chimneys. Just beyond those trees, I told myself. *About a day's walk,* he'd said. Damn that woodcutter. And damn me for trusting him. I would never get out of this forest. I could not stop shaking, though it was unclear whether it was from the cold or my exhausted state.

Finally I could walk no more. I stood in the center of a vast white world, between two endless walls of trees, and I was done. I was going to die here. I had come to the end of my luck. Even if Alekhovshchina was just beyond that clump of trees, I could not have made it. I imagined next summer, the woodcutter coming across my half-decayed body. *Guess he never made Novinka, poor donkey.* Maybe he wasn't even a real woodcutter. Maybe he was some kind of devil, sending me off on a fool's adventure. Well, I had supplied the fool. Death was watching now, sharpening his knives. I could feel his breath on my neck. I thought of Seryozha, dead in the snow in Moscow. *I'll see you soon, little brother.* I stood there like an old horse, my head down, snow building up on my sheepskin.

For some reason, I thought of Volodya. Down in the

Don with his men. Snow on the broad shoulders of his
overcoat. He would understand this. Soldiers marched
past exhaustion, out in all weather. Volodya always
liked that sort of thing. The forts he used to build at
Maryino — lean-tos, in which he imagined himself kidnapped by Indians or in Alaska with Jack London,
hunting with bow and arrow, sledding with huskies.
I could see that lean-to, its lichen-covered sticks,
smelling of damp earth, its Volodyan mystery. Big boys
and their forts.

A shelter.

I could build a shelter.

I didn't know how, but if I wanted to live, that's what
I had to do. I needed to stop reeling with panic, and
take some action before dark caught me and the cold
cracked my bones. I couldn't just stand here and cry,
like an infant expecting someone's large hands to come
out of the sky and pick me up, pat my back, say, *There,
there*.

I had to do something. Or at least try.

I mustered the energy to shuffle off the road into the
trees. Before I did, I broke a branch and laid it as a
crosspiece astraddle two narrow pines standing side by
side at the road's edge like children waiting for their
nanny outside a sweet shop. I would look for that, and
turn left when I came out. If I came out. *Holy Mother,
don't let me die.* I went along, marking my way at eye
level every five feet or so by breaking a branch and
leaving it hanging like an arm. I must not become lost.

The idea was as dreadful as freezing to death. Worse than dying. I would go mad. I was already halfway there.

I crashed through the close-spaced trees, and the snowy boughs snapped back, lashing my face. I could barely see, and didn't know quite what I was looking for until I saw a fallen pine snagged in the branches of another—the triangular shape of shelter. A frail hope kindled within me. If only I could summon the energy...I began to collect sticks and branches, fallen wood, everything I could see that I could move. My hands were clumsy with cold, my eyes watered and ice formed on the lash tips. My feet were frozen in my boots. How I wished I still had my long hair to cover my poor ears. I wrapped the scarf tighter around my head with hands that felt like bear paws. Luckily there was a good deal of fallen wood. Clumsily, I dragged lumber into a heap, resting with my hands on my knees, head down, gasping, before I began again.

I chose the straightest branches and leaned them at intervals against the fallen tree, awkwardly pressing them into the ground with my boot. The wind was quiet here in the trees, but every movement was hard. It was as if I were trying to build a hut on Jupiter. Now that I was building, though, slow and difficult as it was, I felt determination harden within me, pushing despair aside an inch or two so I could breathe.

Who are you kidding? This isn't going to save you. Why bother?

"I'm not listening," I said out loud. I knew it was the voice of death. Grimly I labored on. It was the hardest work I'd ever done, but every stick I pushed into the ground increased the possibility of surviving. I wrestled with a longish branch, trying to break it across my knee. I finally propped it in the snow and broke it with my boot, laying it on the growing skeleton of my hut. How I wished for a bit of cord, remembering how Volodya had lashed his shelter together, but I had not expected to become an Arctic explorer on this journey.

Now I had sticks on both sides of the center pole, low at the foot and higher at the top, the whole thing reminiscent of the spine and ribs of a fish on a plate. Not a very impressive structure, but night was the only thing on my mind. I broke boughs from limb after limb, layered them onto the skeleton until I'd got it fairly covered. I set aside boughs of springy fir for my bed—I couldn't lie on frozen ground, it would leech out every bit of heat from my body in the night. Sticks to weigh down the boughs, boughs to fill in between the sticks. Toward the end, I was throwing anything and everything onto my construction.

I crawled inside to claw away the frozen leaves and snow, tossing the debris backward like a dog digging out a badger, then stuffed in the springy fir boughs, as many as I could cram inside, matting them down with my knees as I went. I lay on this green bed to see how it would be to spend the night there. It was dark and cold and smelled of must and sweet, aromatic evergreens.

I crawled back out and added another layer of boughs for good measure, even scooping frosty armloads of leaves and ferns and decomposing wood to seal over the whole mess like frosting on a cake. When I was done, it looked less like Volodya's forts than like a rural brush pile waiting for a match. Did I really think this pile of twigs would keep me from freezing? *I built my house of sticks, I built my house with leaves. And then the wolf he huffed, the wolf he puffed...*

The sweat I'd worked up was beginning to freeze. I had to get a fire going. Wearily, I collected dead boughs from the underbranches of the pines. They seemed reasonably dry, though my frozen fingers could barely manipulate them. I was getting fuddled, my mind icing over like my gloves.

I piled up the kindling and stood, trying to remember what to do next, as snow fell onto my camp and the wind roared overhead in the pines. I dug out a spot a foot or two from the lean-to with the heel of my boot and made a little pile of kindling there, tenting it with sticks. It still didn't look right. *Rocks.* I needed to circle it with rocks. At least that's what Volodya did. *Merde.* I stomped around, irrationally furious that I had one more damned thing to do, kicked out some rocks, carried them to my pathetic pile of twigs, and laid them in a circle.

That was it, I could do no more.

I took out my matches from my jacket pocket, removing my gloves, and knelt to this rude altar. Saying a short prayer to the Virgin and one to Prometheus, I struck a match. It broke and flew off into the snow. Shit. Shitshitshit. How had Kolya managed to give me such lousy matches? And now I only had five. There could be no more mistakes. The second match I dropped twice just trying to hold it. It took all my effort to keep it between my blue fingers. My mind knew what it was doing, but my hands wouldn't cooperate. My teeth were chattering hard enough to break one, and my hand was shaking so badly I had to stop, put the matches back in my pocket and stick my poor paws under my armpits to warm them. I rubbed them together and tried again, struck the match on the rock, gently, once, twice. It lit. I put it to the kindling, but it guttered out.

I started to cry. I didn't even bother wiping my tears. I had to do this, crying or not.

I needed something I could count on to burn. I thought of the paper I carried. My Vikzhel documents, ruble notes, what good would any of them be to me if I were dead? Though if I lived…then I remembered—the map! It was as if the sun had broken through the snowstorm. I fumbled it out from my coat pocket and, trembling, shredded it and tucked it into the tiny pile of kindling, trying not to knock the whole thing over with my circus-bear hands. Gently, I lit the third match and holding one hand in the other to stabilize my grip, touched the corners of the paper, shielding it between my palms and my body. *Please, God, let there be light*. I barely breathed. Live or die.

The ecstasy, to see flame lacing through the tiny twigs! As though I had given birth to a fire child. I fed it tenderly, a bird feeding its nestling, an inch of dried twig at a time. Once or twice, I did so clumsily and watched in horror as it guttered, shrank, threatening to die. I breathed on it as if it were the flame of life itself. The relief as the heavenly streaks of red and orange crept back. Carefully I fed it slightly larger, finger-size twigs, trying not to topple the cone of sticks, which was starting to glow. I braced a couple of flat pieces of bark against the small tepee and—heaven!—they, too, began to smolder, and with a bit of breath, ignite.

Only then did I dare put my gloves back on, and I forced myself to use the last daylight to collect firewood, reluctant to move away from my fire child, to leave it to the wind, which was getting worse. I'd cleared just about all the easy wood already, and had to move in wider circles. I worked as quickly as I could, piling my gleanings alongside the fire, to shelter it. Finally, as the light faded, I sat down on the mat of fir boughs under my lean-to, my women's clothes wrapped around my legs where the sheepskin wasn't long enough to cover them. The fire fed busily before me, the stones warming and reflecting the heat. I hadn't understood their function before. And it occurred to me that I just might survive this. An hour or two ago, I was ready to die. Who would have guessed I had it in me?

Night fell like a blanket over a birdcage. One moment it was light and the next, the darkness was complete but for the glow of the fire. The trees, growing so close together, protected me from the worst of the wind, but the pines groaned overhead like ship masts, and my fire seemed very small in a very large world. In its flickering, the trees appeared to dance, which elevated my uneasiness where I huddled in my sheepskin. Yet I was warm, I had this fire, I had food, I wasn't dead yet.

An owl began to hoot—if it was an owl, in the middle of a snowstorm. It should have been huddled in the hollow of some tree. Every hair on my body stood out sharp as a pine needle. Owls were omens of death. I didn't believe in omens, but out here, with nothing but forest for miles in any direction, it was hard not to read messages into the slightest event.

Suddenly a giant shape swept over me. I ducked and screamed, almost tumbling into the fire. It disappeared between the tree trunks. How could an owl that size—wings perhaps three feet across—fly between such closely spaced trunks? Was it real? Had I imagined it?

I listened with every bit of my skin and ears, I listened with my very toenails. I thought of wolves. Could they smell me even in a snowstorm? The sausage in my sack, the cheese? Wolves are afraid of people, I reassured myself. Wolves avoid men unless they're sick or starving, and it was too early in the season for wolves to be starving. Not like us poor humans. Wolves weren't on rations, there was no speculation in the forest, only animals living their own secret lives. Life all around me. I felt the animals just out of range of the fire, among the crazy shadows.

Thank God for this fire, the fingering flame—red and beautiful. I took off my gloves and dried them on the rocks. I stuck my boots out toward the fire, warming the leather while I gnawed tiny bites out of the sausage, frozen hard, and bits of cheese, spoonfuls of viscid jam. The snow fell like a curtain outside the small dome of light. How grateful I was that something had moved me to come into the forest and build this shelter, that something had helped me. It had to be—it wasn't the kind of thing I could have done on my own. Maybe it was Seryozha, watching over me from the other side. Or the Virgin of Tikhvin. The fire snapped, and I watched the sparks uneasily as they rose into the dark, worried that they would drift into my brush pile and burn secretly, bursting into flame as I slept. But burning alive was not the worst fate I could imagine, not right now. Anything to feel warm.

Something was stinking. My boot was on fire. God! I jumped up and I stamped it out in the deepening snow. My boots were so poor to begin with—there was barely any sole left. I didn't want to imagine what I had done to them in my carelessness. I huddled miserably back under the lean-to, cold again, keeping my boots a respectful distance from the fire this time and putting off the moment I would have to leave it and crawl into the brush-pile coffin.

Gazing into the firelight, I tried to think of something to look forward to. But the place where my dreams nested lay empty. The one thing I'd always dreamed of—marrying Kolya Shurov, being with him for life—had been extinguished. A dream concealed like a jewel you discovered to be a useless piece of glass. This was all I had—this hundred-something pounds of bone and gristle and poorly functioning organs sitting on twigs under a pathetic lean-to in the middle of a forest in a snowstorm. I felt as hollow and collapsed as an old sack and so weary I could have slept sitting up.

I was loath to abandon my beautiful child, but I was running out of firewood and the storm was gathering strength. I had to sleep. Carefully, I urinated on the other side of the fire—the last thing I wanted to do was let my pants down, but it would be impossible once I'd sealed myself into my burrow. Finally I crawled inside the brush pile, inching backward so my head would be at the tallest spot, carefully trying not to displace the fir boughs. I brought the food sack in after me. It was probably the wrong thing to do, but I was damned if I was going to leave it out to feed the animals. Finally, I pulled the mat of boughs in after me to stop up the small entryway.

Lying in the darkness atop the aromatic pile, I

wrapped my woolen scarf all around my head, covering my eyes, and waited for sleep. The fir boughs had been a stroke of genius, thick enough to keep me off the icy ground, something I could be thankful for. I turned, ever so gently, onto my side, hands plunged in their gloves under my armpits—at least the gloves were dry and hadn't burned. I couldn't draw my knees up more than a few inches without touching the side of the burrow, so I lay shivering and miserable and colder than I could ever imagine being. I tried to breathe slowly, intentionally. Master Vsevolod said there were yogis who breathed through their skins alone, who could stop their heartbeats for half an hour at a time. They could be buried alive for three days, then dug up, and they would sit up smiling. My mother would listen, her blue eyes shining, rapt at such nonsense, while Seryozha imitated him behind his back. Now I wished I had learned a few of those esoteric arts, instead of making fun of them with my brother.

I fixed my mind on things that were hot. A crock of soup. A train's boiler. The sun on the lavender fields— the very smell of sunshine. A candle burning in the nursery. I saw a line of camels crossing bleached dunes, heading to Bukhara. I imagined the city's square blazing at midday, the wavering lines of heat, its giant tower like a rook in chess. I saw my uncle Vadim lying out on rocks in California wearing nothing but a loincloth. I walked the long allée at Maryino in the summertime, the sun pouring onto the red valerian and

Queen Anne's lace. I climbed with Seryozha into the stifling hot attic, the smell of cedar chests and old wedding dresses.

Seryozha. At least one person I hadn't disappointed.

From my grave, I could hear the roar of the storm, but muffled. *Idyosh, na menya pokhozhii*... Tsvetaeva's great poem, the poet speaking to a casual cemetery visitor from under the earth. *Passerby, stop! Read — my name was Marina.* But there wouldn't be any passersby here. None who could read, anyway. Only a red fox, perhaps, with his sensitive nose, sniffing at this pile, smelling the sausage, knowing something strange was buried here. I prayed the animals would not try to dig me out. I had to hope the storm would do for them what it had done for me — send them to their burrows for shelter.

My exhaustion was absolute, but I was shivering too hard for sleep. How long would this night last under these leaves? Without even knowing it, I began to recite "Winter Evening": *Darkness spreads across the sky, / whirlwinds whip the snow around; / first the storm cries like a child, / then it bellows like a hound.* I might be buried in a brush heap in the middle of a nightmare, but I still had this. I had forgotten. I had been so busy throwing Pushkin from the ship of modernity, I had forgotten that he was in my bones, my hair, my fingernails. I was made of Pushkin, as was every educated person who spoke the Russian tongue. I knew reams of his lines. Oceans of them. Now I had to beg his pardon.

Alexander Sergeevich, forgive me! Help me. Keep me warm, blessed companion.

Memories came back to me of reciting these classic verses in my Makarov grandmother's stuffy parlor, her potted palms and cutwork lace, the rustle of her black taffeta dress. She would give me a silver ruble for a recitation, but only if I didn't make a single mistake. "Not so Wagnerian," she would correct me. "This isn't opera, child. You must think it, and then breathe it out, like an intelligent person, not a trained monkey." She was the one who gave me poetry. Not my mother at all. My father's family. Distant and conventional though they were.

This poem—once I'd learned it, I'd recite it in the nursery for Seryozha as we sat by the window, watching the snow as it fell. Those nights we'd listen to Avdokia tell her stories about growing up in Novinka with its peasant cottages, just like in the poem, as if she'd lived in Pushkin's time.

And so I passed the night, shivering and whispering Pushkin to myself like a nun saying her rosary as the storm roiled outside my burrow. Like bells sounding out the liturgical hours were these bells of meter and rhyme. I remembered all of "The Gypsies." Aleko, who wanted freedom for himself but not for Zemfira, his gypsy love. I always thought I would be a Zemfira, but now I saw I was Aleko, trying on a foreign life but unable to sustain it.

After "The Gypsies," huge parts of *Eugene Onegin*

came pouring from my lips, lips that had been born to speak them. There with me in that cold retreat came maddening Onegin, with his Byronic pose, and naive, book-mesmerized Tatiana and her dangerous love for him. I recited her famous letter, the dearest verse in the Russian language, as she admitted her passion, baring her heart to his cynical eye: *Ya k vam pishu — chevo zhe bole? I write to you — what more to say?* Oh, to someday create lines a hundredth, a thousandth as immortal as these! I vowed to the close darkness and to the storm and the branches and the heavens above that if I lived through this night I would dedicate myself to poetry alone and leave passion to those better able to withstand its fury.

Part VII

The Ionians

(November 1918–Spring 1919)

70 *Novinka*

I AWOKE TO BLACK and the scent of evergreens. I couldn't believe I'd slept but I must have. In the darkness, the shelter actually seemed warmer — like a bear's den. I had lived through the night. *Thank you,* I prayed to the brush pile. Was it morning? There was no way to tell. I didn't want to emerge too early, like a misguided crocus, to find it was still night, or be caught in the blizzard. But I didn't hear anything, and after a few minutes I reached for a stick, and thrust it between the layers of boughs sealing off the mouth of the lean-to, working my arm through the brush until I felt snow. Carefully, I turned over onto my belly — and, yes, through a patch of snow I could see a faint glow — daylight.

I clawed my way out like a chicken from an egg and burst into the world so violently that parts of the shelter collapsed. It was a bitter morning, but the gray light was as good as rainbows in the falling snow. Oh praises, oh glory and hosanna, the wind had stopped blowing! Bless Pushkin, Seryozha, the Virgin, and anyone else who had joined me in that grave through that long night.

I took care of my needs and stood looking at my shelter with the fondness with which one gazes at one's own mother. It had saved me. I would never ever doubt that I had survived for a reason. That there were forces that wanted me to live. I began to follow my clues back to the road—broken branches, the twin pines—and turned left at the road to Alekhovshchina. My boots, having been burned, were worse than before, but I was alive in them.

Alekhovshchina proved to be a large village half a day's walk from where I'd buried myself. No way could I ever have reached it in time. Gratitude swelled within me. I had made the right decision. I wasn't as foolish as I thought I was. A printer and his wife gave me a bite of supper, and their neighbor, a wizened crone, treated my frostbite with a stinking poultice. She wouldn't tell me what was in it—chicken dung?—and kept laughing whenever she looked at me. I had a feeling she could see right through my Misha disguise. The old printer hinted that if I wanted to stay on, he could use a smart boy with good eyes, quick hands. But Novinka was only an hour or two farther, and Misha had places to go. Maryino had taken on a mythic significance for me by now. It was Kitezh, it was the kingdom beyond the seas seven times seven.

I found the road and soon began to recognize landmarks. A huge wide spruce. A fence with decorative piercings. Dusk fell, but already I could see the lit windows of the village, smell its dinners cooking in huts covered by the snowstorm.

As I entered its single lane, I was pleased to find it was no longer the vaguely threatening place I remembered. I eyed its small brood of izbas with the clear, slightly appraising eye of a salesman. I easily imagined its poverty, its worries, its petty rivalries, brutalities, and simple joys, which brought back thoughts of Kolya, and then his rural mistress, whose good jam I had just eaten. What was she doing now, that village seductress? No doubt still dreaming of the clever stranger she'd had in the bathhouse, the sweet words he'd poured into her ear. Probably she was feeling worse than before, when she hadn't known how sweet a man's love could be.

The hamlet was quiet, peaceful. I stopped an old peasant heading toward one of the poorer huts. "Excuse me, Grandpa, but does Lyuda, Olya's daughter, still live here? She was going to marry the blacksmith, last time I heard." The old man eyed me, alarmed. Did he recognize this boy covered with snow and wrapped in a sheepskin as the little *barynya* from up at the manor house?

"They're having a meeting," he spat. "Meetings. And nobody gets a speck of work done. Only talk talk talk." His thin jowls flapped, his mouth sunken in. "You could lift the whole village on that hot air."

"Where are they meeting, Granddad?"

"At the blacksmith's, boy. At the blacksmith's," he

drawled, disgusted with my ignorance. "Where else would they be?" He tramped into his windowless hut and slammed the door.

I poked around until I heard voices—a group arguing and a woman's voice, high and assertive, cutting through the others. The smell of smoke led me to lit windows. Through the fogged and dirty glass, I could see ten or twelve peasants deep in discussion. I strained to see if there were any leather jackets in attendance and was happy to detect only kerchiefs and caps. Even so, I didn't want to announce my presence, so I waited in the lee of a cabin—by the woodpile, stacked to the eaves for winter—and watched the doorway.

So the revolution had come to Novinka. I imagined what my grandfather would have said of such a meeting, of Soviet rule in general. My Golovin grandfather, who still spoke of "our peasants"—as did my mother, truth be told, in unguarded moments. People we had once owned. Human beings. *Our village. Our land. Our country.*

My nose burned with frostbite from the night before. I could smell the old *baba*'s poultice—resinous, sharp, suspiciously fishy, even in the cold. At last the peasants emerged from their meeting, talking as they went out, like people coming out of church. A few lingered in a cluster to talk in the doorway. *Hurry up!* I stamped my feet to keep them awake. Finally the peasants dribbled off into the night, leaving a single woman to lock up.

I wasn't sure. The braid was gone, but the movements were still hers, quick and decisive. I came closer, crossing the dark lane. The woman stepped out from the cover of the porch.

"Lyuda," I whispered.

She stopped, lifted her hand to her forehead to shield her eyes from the sifting flakes. "Who's that?"

I couldn't exactly shout out my name. Who knew what the situation in the village was these days? But I imagined whatever attention I might draw here wouldn't be all that welcoming. "So you married the blacksmith." I called it out softly, continuing to approach—slowly, as one would approach a dog in the road. Darkness had fallen. Nobody seeing us could tell who it was. She stepped forward. "Who are you?"

"They say there was once a cow from Novinka…"

And now it came, the sharp intake of her breath. She rushed forward into the snow to grab me by the arm, pull me back into the cover of the blacksmith's shop. She embraced me, glancing around, back over her shoulder. "Shh." Unlocking the door, heavily pad-locked with an American Yale lock. *"Buistro!" Hurry!* We slipped inside. She lit a kerosene lamp, pulled off her head scarf.

Lyuda had changed and yet not changed. Her hair was short now, though not as short as mine, and her wide-boned face had become quite arresting. She tucked her hair behind a well-formed small ear. "I didn't recognize you in that getup. Who are you sup-posed to be, the phantom woodcutter?"

I looked down at my sheepskin, my trousers stuck in my boots. I took off the scarf and knocked the snow off my cap. "Safer for traveling."

"What—did you walk all the way from Petrograd?" I recognized the warmth of her smile, the gap between her front two teeth. "Look at you—what a mess! Well, anyway, it's good to see you. Been a long time."

Tears sprang to my eyes at her words of kindness, surprising me. She couldn't have imagined how long it had been since anybody who knew me had welcomed me anywhere. I shrugged my Misha shrug. "Going to Maryino. You know, just wanted to know the lay of the land. You're looking good. How're things here? Mind if I sit down?" I'd been standing too long, four days too long, and the black potbellied stove was still hot from the meeting. No shortage of firewood here. I sat down on a stump that they'd been using as a stool, took off my boot and rubbed my frostbitten toes. They hurt like the very devil. "So you didn't go to Petrograd after all."

"As you see." She smiled, trying to conceal an obvious pride, an air of superiority even.

"And it's been okay? The blacksmith?"

"I'm on the committee now. He doesn't dare get out of line. I'd throw him out on his ear."

This was what Faina had needed. Soviet Power. Lyuda was going to live a very different life from the peasant wives of the last generation. I looked around the shop. It was nice here, warm. Harnesses hung from the walls, chains and traces and all sorts of tools for refashioning them—tools! Better than any bank account. Huge hammers, an anvil—black and evil-looking—and the fire pit. Lyuda draped her scarf over the back of a chair by the stove, around which were arrayed a collection of mismatched stools and crates from the meeting. She'd grown into a solid, capable-looking young woman. I could only imagine what she thought of this scarecrow who stood before her.

I put my foot back in the boot and unsheathed the other one, held it out to the fire. I hoped it didn't stink too badly. "What's going on at Maryino?" I asked as casually as I could.

She put a kettle on the stove, using her skirt as a potholder. "Nobody goes out there," she said. "All sorts of strange things going on. We don't bother them and they don't bother us."

"Strange how?"

She gave me a look that was pure Lyuda, a bit impish, more than a bit stubborn. "You'll have to see for yourself."

"Is Mother there?"

"We don't know a thing about it," she said, running her hand along a piece of harness, stroking the worn leather. "And that's the way it's got to be. Understand?" She leveled her gaze at me.

I didn't. But I felt that my mother was there, maybe even my father. Was that what she was telling me?

The committee was protecting them. She was protecting them.

"Are you in the party now?"

She nodded, once, emphatically. "Since last September." She set up two glasses for tea, glasses that had clearly been used earlier by members of the committee. "Everything's changed. Novinka's joined the modern world, if you can believe it. What we think matters. Even what the cow thinks. We sent a representative to Tikhvin this fall, after the harvest…you don't have any tea on you, do you?" I should have brought a gift, but it hadn't occurred to me. And even if it had, what could I have brought? Fir boughs? Lyuda sighed and put some sort of leaves in the brown teapot. "What good are the bourgeoisie if you're poorer than us?" she said to the teapot. She poured the boiling water into the pot. "Only guess who the representative was."

"The cow?"

"Idiot." She tucked her hair behind her ear again, pleased with herself, and for good reason. She had done well, a barefoot village girl becoming the representative of the local committee, voting in regional meetings at Tikhvin. And all this had happened not in a generation, but in a mere two years. I was proud of her, proud of all of us. This was what the revolution had been for. Not the glacial changes my father had envisioned, so incremental that they never would have happened—the bourgeoisie would have made sure of that. "We haven't bothered them out there," she continued. "We're not Alekhovshchina. They're really going for the prize, lording it over everyone, those stick-up-the-ass bastards. We don't need Alekhovshchina around here, telling us what to do. I guess we can wipe our asses all by ourselves. But they're not all that safe there at Maryino. Tell them that. It's only a matter of time."

My refuge, which I hadn't yet seen, was already in jeopardy—like a house that begins to crumble just as soon as you carry your bags in.

71 *Maryino*

IN THE MORNING, LYUDA brought me a bowl of hot kasha and sent me off before the blacksmith arose. But first, she agreed to sell me a chicken and some grain to feed it with. I kept it warm under my coat as I walked along. I could feel it fluttering there, its heartbeat, as I made my way through virgin snow that reached to the tops of my boots and above. It was slow going but I didn't care. I was so close to Maryino I could smell it. Although I had to follow fences to stay on the road, I knew where I was. I couldn't get lost, and my excitement urged me onward. Eventually dawn emerged weakly from under the night's heavy cloak. It would not brighten to much more than twilight on a day like this.

I tried to steel myself for the worst. I'd seen ruined

manor houses, their broad roofs caved in, their steps buckled, trees all cut down, doors and windows boarded up. But that wasn't what Lyuda was intimating. It was something else. And if it was livable...I would find a way to live there. I was sure, now, after my night in the forest, that there was a reason for my life. I'd never doubt it again. The chicken curled quiet and warm under my sheepskin next to my heart. She was a good layer, Lyuda had said. I was just glad for the company.

The shape of the land became more familiar. That peculiar formation of trees, a fallen pine, that copse. That ridge like a bristly pig's back, falling off toward the unseen river. I recognized it all. Only the heaviness of the snow kept me from running. Here, the very turn of the river where the house nestled beyond the line of trees. The squawk of crows in the birches and the occasional movement of the chicken accompanied my ragged breathing as I plunged through the accumulated inches like a short-legged dog.

A white plume of smoke rose from the trees through the quiet veil of falling snow—chimney smoke. The house was alive. Joyfully, I crept closer, tramping through the allée of bare lindens. At last the house came into view. Maryino! Its gingerbread woodwork still white against the black wood, the windows intact, the roof. But in the yard, there was too much light. I realized that the enormous larch had been cut down. A hatchet rested in the reddish stump amid shards of wood. Firewood lay stacked against the house all down its right side. So much fuel—enough for a whole winter if carefully shepherded. Dear house! It knew me, too. It was not fooled by my youth's disguise. I hadn't changed so very much after all. It was like Odysseus's dog, Argos, who recognized his master after twenty years.

And yet who would have had the strength to cut such a tree, I wondered, and move all that wood? I shrank back against the cover of some little pines to watch and wait. Perhaps Mother and Avdokia had a man living with them, or someone from the village. But it might be someone else—squatters, deserters. The double windows had been hung, windows I'd never actually seen in place, only stored in the shed. The steps had been swept as well, and paths dug out from the house to the outbuildings and into the woods. The industry was clear, and recent. So tidy that I couldn't imagine it was deserters. It had to be peasants, though this was tidy even for them. A Cheka outpost? No—Lyuda would have told me. She wouldn't have let me walk into something like that.

Perhaps it was my father come back after Red Terror, waiting things out for another try at Petrograd. I thought of the conspirators assembled in the dacha at Pulkovo. But I couldn't imagine them digging paths. They would have tried to be as inconspicuous as possible.

I crouched in the trees. The chicken's warm flutter-

ing under my coat felt like my heart held gently outside
my body. I'd traveled so long, all this way, but had no
plan, only the destination.

A woman in a patchwork quilted coat emerged
from the kitchen door and walked away toward a
shed, a basket over her arm. She moved gracefully, as
if she were being watched. Like a dancer onstage. No,
this wasn't my father and his cronies. Then a man
emerged from the same door, a handsome young one
in a black beard and, like the girl, in thick padded
coat that looked like it was quilted from rags, and a
strange patchwork hat with a point on the top. He
picked out some wood from the pile, carried it down
the stairs to the stump, and proceeded to split it for
kindling. He was precise and unhurried, like a woodcutter in a fairy tale. It all seemed so...enchanted.
He stopped for a moment as if sensing something. I
hunched down with my chicken. Could he smell me
in the snow? Was it that frostbite medicine, which
smelled like dead herring? He listened, then went
back to his work. He didn't work like a laborer. I
couldn't describe it, but it was as if he were playing a
role onstage: the Woodcutter.

The woman came back from the shed like a maiden
in a processional. What in the devil was going on
here? Who were these people? Some sort of stranded
theater troupe? Had I stumbled into the world of my
childhood fantasies? I sidled along through the trees
toward that shed. As I got close, I could hear squawk-

ing and crowing inside, and my chicken started to rustle and claw me. In the house, dogs barked. I opened the shed door a crack. A chicken coop, nicely appointed, lined with wood chips and shavings. Twenty fat hens flapped their wings and a tall black rooster ran at me, trying to fight me.

I latched the coop and backed away, looking for the best place to hide. Then suddenly two huge dogs appeared on the porch. They hurled themselves down the steps, racing toward me. I opened the chicken coop and closed myself inside moments before the dogs crashed into the door, their weight heaving the boards. They continued barking and growling while the rooster attacked me from within. I gave him a good kick while keeping my shoulder to the door, praying someone would rescue me. Had I been through all this only to be mauled by dogs?

"Bonya. Buyan," a man's voice clearly articulated. The growling and scratching stopped immediately. "Come out, thief."

I cracked open the coop door. "I'm not a thief."

"Don't try my patience. Show yourself."

I opened the door and slid out. The dogs sat on either side of a broad-chested, moustached man wearing a long sheepskin coat, Mongolian style, and an astrakhan hat. Behind him stood a motley array of young people, all in the strange colorful dress I'd seen before. The older man appeared to be unarmed, but I kept one hand up, the other pressing my chicken under my coat. "I'm not a thief. This is my chicken. I came with it. I bought it in Novinka. I have grain for it, too."

He tilted his head at a dark-haired girl who'd come to his side. She had an eyebrow that grew together in the middle, like a gypsy's, and she had a gypsy's confident stare. She approached me and I pulled the white chicken from the warmth beneath my coat. It began to flap and struggle as soon as it was exposed to the light and the cold. She took it from me by its feet.

"And the sack," said the man, and she took that as well.

She brought my belongings to him, and he began to go through them, keeping one eye on me. The others watched from the porch, as if there were to be a horse race or a public hanging. "Who are you people?"

The man's eyes, black and slightly popped, like glass eyes in a case, ran over my face and form. He was dark, with a bull's neck and a shaved head, a long moustache, and a ring in his ear. He continued examining the contents of my bag. He produced the jar of jam, which he opened and sniffed, tasted; then the small bundle of grain, which he rolled between his fingers. Then my women's clothes, my peasant's dress, which he fingered, then lifted to his nostrils. It was obscene. I knew then that he knew Misha was really a woman. He would call my bluff, as they said in poker. But he didn't. He just stuffed it all back in the bag, threw it at my feet.

Now he walked a circle around me, hands behind his back, as if I was a bit of statuary someone had deposited in his yard. Pulled off my cap and dropped it at my feet in the snow. "Who are you?" he asked in perfect Russian.

"Misha," I said. "What about you, Pops?"

He glowered at my insolence. "How did you find your way here? Don't lie to me."

"I'm from here. I knew the way." I didn't want to say how. For all he knew I was the son—or daughter—of a servant. "I was living in Petrograd, but it's a bad time in the city. I decided to come back."

His face betrayed nothing. He came closer, sniffed my hair. He looked like the strong man in a circus, and he smelled of something. Incense? Saddle leather? "You've been in the village. What do they say about us?"

"They didn't say anything. Only that your business was your own." I didn't look at him. I kept my eyes fixed ahead, like a good soldier.

"Until it's not," he said. He kept walking, his gait that of a military man, commanding. Perhaps he was a deserter, a noncommissioned officer hiding out, hoping to avoid the new draft. But who were these others? I counted six of them, four young women, including the gypsy, plus the young man who'd been chopping kindling and an older one in wire spectacles, his hair a wild bush—an *intelligent* if ever I'd seen one. Behind them, I could see what they could not—myself as a child, peering out from the lilac bushes beside the kitchen door, sticking out my tongue, and the ghost of my Golovin grandmother standing on the porch, preparing to summon her coachman to escort these strange people off the land.

"Go back to the village," he told me. "Tell them monsters are living here." He made a terrible grimace, and the others laughed. "With three legs and four heads. We'll come and eat their children if they're not good. Go on. Pick up your things and go." He turned back to the house.

I picked up my bag. "My chicken," I called after him.

He gave the order like a king expecting to be obeyed. "Give it its chicken back."

The dark-haired girl handed me the white chicken, which I put back under my coat. That was it? He was sending me away? Returning me like a flat of bad eggs? "I walked all the way from Tikhvin. I slept in the forest. And now you're going to shoo me away like some stray dog?"

"Isn't that what you are?" he asked.

"I belong here."

His people waited like children, not sure what was going to happen. Obviously few people said no to this man, this sergeant or corporal or whatever he'd been at the front.

"Suit yourself." He turned and mounted the porch steps as if rising to a dais, and his entourage followed him like little ducks. They all went inside, and left me standing in the yard.

Snow fell softly on my cheeks, like the lightest touch of hands.

Well, I wouldn't leave. I would stand here until they gave in, until someone took pity. I had foisted myself on the most hard-hearted of peasants, I would not be turned away now. Because I had no other ideas. I had reached the end of my resources. I walked out to a place where they could all see me—the larch stump, which was as wide as a table. I sat on it and watched the house, glancing up at the windows, wondering who was watching me. Nothing mattered but to be here, to spend the night under this roof again. I was home and here I would stay. I would simply outlast them. For the first time, I understood that the secret of resistance wasn't heroism but simple pigheaded balk. There was no question of a fight—I didn't have the strength—but I would shame him, if nothing else.

I toyed with the hatchet, slicing off shards of wood into smaller and smaller bits. I breathed great clouds of steam, my legs crossed, like a homeowner relaxing in his yard, smoking a cigarette. Yes, I was home. I knew that ownership was a thing of the past, but nevertheless, in some gut-level way, this was mine. The frosted gingerbread of the old-fashioned house, built by my great-grandfather for his bride, the allée, the aspens and forest, the river. How funny that it took a revolution for me to care, to feel its deep roots entwined with my own. Yet the larch had been cut down, as our family had been cut down. So which was the metaphor?

So many evenings on that broad porch. White nights and fireflies, our songs and plays. The tables and chairs set out in the yard for lunches and dinners with visitors. Lying on the musty cushions of the wicker chaise reading *Oliver Twist* and *Le Comte de Monte-Cristo* on drizzly summer afternoons. Wordsworth and Keats... *Bright star, would I were steadfast as thou art*... The requisite nap in the white-curtained nursery, the silence of those hot hours. Yes, the house knew me. If it were a puppy it would leap up and lick my face. It was these strange people who didn't belong. Someone inside played the flute, a mournful, quarter-tone Eastern melody, bizarre yet pleasant on the frosty air.

I balled up some snow, packed it tight and threw it against the front door. It plashed with a satisfying splat, the dry new snow bursting against the glass and the wood. It was getting colder, but I would not leave. I wondered what time it was, but the sky was still a uniform yellow-gray.

In a little while, a lovely doe-eyed girl with a finely drawn face and motley coat came out, and, holding her head high, she marched up to me and put something on the stump. Steaming—a potato. She gave me a single strong look, as if to say, *Don't lose hope,* then marched back to the house, slim and straight as a birch tree. I cradled the potato in my frozen hands, let it warm me, pressed it to my face. I had a friend here. And a potato. I was rich indeed.

I waited until the potato had cooled before I ate it. The snow built up on my sleeves. I didn't brush it off, in hopes it would stir greater pity. I fed the chicken little bits of grain from my sack, its head peeping out the V of my coat. My ears were freezing under the poor cap, but I didn't want to wrap my head in the scarf. I wanted them to see me, this poor boy they were leaving out in the snow. I wanted to pluck their hearts. I'd already won one of them over—how difficult could the rest be?

The front door banged back, and in the opening stood a tiny, bowlegged figure in a blue head scarf. "Merciful Virgin, you're alive! Marinoushka!" She broke into a tottering half run, holding the railing, side-stepping down the porch stairs, running to me, clutching at me, kissing my hands in their dirty gloves, holding my face, crushing me to her. The chicken clawed at my stomach. I pulled it out, set it free. How I had missed her! And when I lifted her, how heavy she was for such a tiny woman—she weighed as much as a barrel of wheat. "Avdokia, you're so fat!"

She laughed as she wept, touching my short hair. "You look just like blessed Seryozha," she said, "may he rest in peace. Oh, my child. Look at you. Oh, sweet lovey. I can't believe…we thought…we were sure…"

They must have thought I was dead. Murdered. How awful. I hadn't thought about them, what they might have been going through. I had only thought of my own torment. I felt like Theseus, who, upon coming home from Crete, had forgotten to change his sails from black to white, causing his father's suicide. The hell they must have lived, all these months. As I had when I heard of Seryozha's fate. "Shh. I'm here now. It's all right. It's going to be all right. And you're here. You're safe!" I twirled her around, her chubby hunched little body. "What's going on around here? The boss told me to clear off, but I'm not going to."

She petted me, kissed me again. "Yes, well, since when did you listen to anyone?"

"How is Mother?" I asked.

"*Ai*...don't ask," she said. "Let's get you inside. Have something to eat." She wiped her eyes on her apron. "And catch that chicken! We're not above eating. Even on the astral plane, you should see them put it away."

I lunged for the chicken, but it ran from me. Right up to Avdokia, who caught it. We walked to the chicken coop and she tossed my pullet in—the only white one—the others eyeing it with suspicion.

Warmth. That's what I noticed when we entered through the kitchen. How warm it was! The fine young woman, my savior, ground flour in a mill clamped onto the table. Something boiled on the stove in an enormous cauldron. Cabbage. The girl smiled shyly with her eyes but said nothing. The cabinets still showed their painted birds. We left our wet boots by the door, donned felt slippers, and retreated into Lyuda's and Olya's old room behind the kitchen.

The bright painted bed that they'd shared, mother and daughter, was gone. The room held only a crude cot covered with a quilt made from the same rags the young people had been wearing. But the stove! Even this room was merry with heat. Avdokia's shawl hung on a peg, and in the red corner hung a hand-colored print—a cheap reproduction of the Virgin of Tikhvin. Home. I was home.

I sat on the bed. The wildly varied quilt was made of velvet and charmeuse and wool. Dark colors, city colors, interlaced with squares of vivid cloth that would have done well at a village fair. Avdokia lowered herself down next to me, slow and heavy, stiff with age. The rigors of the previous year had left their mark on her ancient body, despite her well-fed look. "How's Mother?" I asked.

A great shuddering sigh went through her.

A torn space opened inside me. "Alive?"

"Oh, yes, yes, she's alive, God bless us," Avdokia said, yet her hesitation was confusing. "Oh, how can I begin to tell you, Marinoushka, what our lives have come to?" She gazed down at our interlocked fingers, mine hard, weathered but strong and young, straight-fingered, hers twisted as the roots of an old olive tree. "It's such a long story, my pet, my dove." She tucked a strand of my hair behind my ear. "A strange story, stranger than I can say."

"I want to see her," I said.

"A moment, sweetness, and listen to me." Patting me as she had when I was a child headstrong with some urgent idea, she wetted her thin lips, obviously trying to find the way to begin. But her aged brain could not find the end of the string. "Let me tell the story, so you understand. She's alive, but not the same. Poor Verushka, strong and weak in all the wrong ways. This year, when you disappeared, when that devil, when he..." The tears started again. That cursed night when Arkady arrived. "Well, it was just too much for her. For her mind. After everything—your father, and poor Seryozha, the flat...you don't know what we've been through." She spoke to our hands, stroking mine rhythmically as she would pet a small dog. "We searched for you. Even went to the district soviet for all the good it did. Like telling a hedgehog to fly."

Behind the kitchen door, soft voices, then a harsher one. A clatter of dishes. And from somewhere else, the unlikely Eastern sound of some stringed instrument. She leaned closer. "Well, after that, she took to her bed, not talking, or worse, talking to people who weren't even there. Like you. And Seryozha. 'They're gone, sweetheart,' I'd tell her. 'Gone to heaven.' But she said no, you were playing tricks on her, like you used to when you were young. Other times, she'd scream that the Cheka were coming, that they were going to burn the house down. She'd claw at the wallpaper until I had to wrap her fists, swaddle her in the blankets." She took a shuddering breath. I put my arm around her. "The neighbors complained. The whole house was against us. You remember what it was like. It only got worse." I could see their faces, the tired suspicious women and their hard husbands living in our flat. "I was half out of my mind. So I did the only thing I could think of—I called Vsevolod." Master Vsevolod, with his stink of incense and his boneless white hands. She lowered her voice to a whisper. "And he brought in that one." She nodded at the door, her face pale as cake flour. "You know, the devil waits for an invitation. Forgive me, child. I didn't know what else to do."

Past her face, out the frosted window, snow built up along the limbs of the old apple tree, quite bare now. In the spring, I would see it full of sweet white flowers—if I were still here. "No, you did the right thing," I said. Her pale, ancient face twisted with guilt, her small, tortured mouth. What did she have to be sorry for? It was I who needed forgiveness.

"Well, this one knows a good thing when he sees it. Vsevolod must have told him." She was whispering hard now. "So gifted, he called her, a seer. Of course she could see her dead children. 'No one ever dies…they just live happily in the land behind the sunrise'—anything he could think of." Her face darkened with rage. "Yes, and suddenly rivers will swim upstream and the dead sit up in their graves and ask for tea with two lumps of sugar. *Ai*, the lies he told her! You'd have thought the very walls would cover their ears and run away. But I kept my mouth shut, God forgive me." She crossed herself. "We needed him, *mi-laya*. We were being evicted. We would have been on the streets and not a soul would have lifted a finger to save us. This one had a circle living in a big dacha on Aptekarsky Island."

What wasn't happening up on the islands?

"That devil talks to her once—once!—and suddenly she's out of bed, ordering me to pack, when before she wouldn't get out of bed to save her own life. 'Prophetess…'" She snorted, wiped the tears tracing the riverbeds of her wrinkles. "Of course he had eyes, he could see. The flat. The furniture. He asked her about the photograph of Maryino. I saw exactly what was on his mind. Maybe I'm a prophetess myself, eh?" She chuckled despite herself. "Oh, you'll see, they're a regular pack of idiots. My poor lamb could never resist a grand role. Anything you put in her head becomes real. So now she's gifted. She's reading the future in the ice, in a bowl of soup. Such imagination. Like mother, like children."

I was stung that my nanny thought I was anything like Vera Borisovna.

She grinned a toothless grin and patted my knee. "All of you. Not a streak of sense in the whole family. So there we were on Aptekarsky. The Laboratory, they called it. The lunatic asylum, if you ask me. God preserve us." She spat. "All Vsevolod's people were there—the Gromitskys, the Kovelovs. Living cheek by jowl with people right off the street." She lowered her voice again. "He loves that—you'll see. Plagues them, stirs them up, sets them against each other. Your mother notices nothing."

I tried to imagine a commune full of bourgeois spiritualists and beggars, orchestrated by the man who sicced his dogs on me. And my mother prophesying while Avdokia cursed every soul. I rested my head on her shoulder. I was at the end of my strength, bone-weary, not just in my body but in spirit as well. What I wanted was right here—the familiar smell of her dress, the birds painted on the kitchen cabinets. This was why I had come. "Don't let him send me away," I said.

"No, sweetness. I have a few tricks up my own sleeve." She smiled and kissed me, petted me as if I were six. "But stay out of his way. Remember, we need these people more than they need us."

"I'll be as silent as a whore's conscience."

She rose and looked into my eyes, one of her pale brows arched in skepticism. "*Chu chu chu.* Just don't stir them up. Stay here until I can talk to him, see what I can do. Whatever happens, don't react. It's lucky the earth is still solid under our feet and doesn't go flying up into the sky."

She left me there in the small bare room. I lay drowsing on the cot, listening through the stout walls of the old house to voices, muffled laughter, the sounds of a hammer, the clatter of pots. Out the window, I watched one of their ragged number go past with that same gliding walk. Further on, a boy and a girl I hadn't seen before shoveled snow, making a soothing chop and hiss. Soft footsteps in felt boots shushed in and out of the kitchen. I smelled pungent sour cabbage, and bread baking. After a while, my nanny brought me back a bowl of soup and a piece of black bread. Gradually the noises settled, doors stopped opening and closing. I was happy to just fall asleep in Avdokia's bed. I was home.

72 *The Master*

I SLEPT ON FOR two days, rising only to use the chamber pot, eat, and fall asleep again. I dreamed I was in my lean-to in the woods, but I discovered a set of stairs that led down to an entire underground house. How had I missed them? It was warm and a young man who seemed to know me lived there. We'd gone to school together. He fed me and we talked about Lermontov. In another dream, there was a bathhouse in a goat pen, and a fire-spotting tower on the rooftop of the house on Furshtatskaya. I was aware of Avdokia going to bed and getting up, but still I dreamed on.

On the third day, I awoke to gray light, a snowy day, her empty bed. I waited to see if she would return, but when she didn't, I got up and cracked the door. The kitchen was empty, scrubbed and clean as an English doctor's office. Two loaves of bread cooled on the hearth. Wherever did they get the flour? Certainly a bunch of ragged intellectuals couldn't have brought in a harvest—it was impossible. How long had they been here? Since May? June? I could hear the scrape of wooden dishes in the back parlor and a sonorous voice. Their leader must be holding forth. A younger man spoke, then, deferential. Their master again. I knew Avdokia had warned me to stay out of sight, but everyone was occupied, and I itched to see what was going on in the other rooms. I crept down the hall, the back parlor smelling of sawdust and linseed oil, turpentine. A workroom. I imagined this mad gang carving strange totemic symbols—Lord knew for what purpose.

Whatever they were doing in the back parlor, the front one lay virtually empty but for the unfamiliar Bukhara carpets that had replaced our cheerful Finnish ones. My grandfather's wonderfully hideous Alexander III chair also remained. I remembered him sitting in it reading, an embroidered cap on his head, his legs stretched out on a stool. Strange paintings now hung along the walls in dark blues and purples featuring snowcapped mountains, veiled women, and deer. No evidence of the sofas and wicker armchairs in which we'd lounged and told stories and played games. No striped shades and cutwork curtains on the bare windows. The izbas of Novinka must be well decorated these days, rich with candlesticks and clocks and pictures of our Golovin ancestors.

Well, candlesticks could go to the devil. Let the peasants use them in good health. They'd left the house intact, that was the important thing. Oddly enough, they'd also spared the upright piano. It was amazing they hadn't stripped it for the wire. And the carved wooden stairs had been left unmolested. I ran my hand along the heavy wooden banister. How I'd loved sliding down this as a child, imagining daring escapes. But another Marina couldn't help but calculate how many weeks such a piece of wood could serve a Petrograd *bourgeoika*.

Upstairs, it was all the same as ever—the red-painted hall, the moldings carved from silvery birch. Capacious, with windows at each end and the strong scent of cedar wood. I crept to the door of Mother's room. She'd never been an early riser, and she took over my grandmother's room after her death, as it was the farthest from the kitchen, with its smells and morning bustle. I pressed my ear to the door. Had Avdokia told her that I'd come home?

I noticed a musky smell—leathery and resinous. The olive-eyed leader was standing right at my elbow. I jumped. How was it that I hadn't heard him? He was too solid a man to have climbed the carpetless stairs without my hearing, yet here he was, his shining bald head, dressed in a sheepskin vest. He took my wrist, not hard but in a way that prevented resistance, and pulled me from the door. "I thought I told you to leave," he said, his brow wrinkled in long folds, his voice controlled but commanding.

I stood as straight as I could, my arm clamped in his grip, fear lying thick in my throat. "I'm Marina Dmitrievna Makarova and this is my house."

I had to hand it to him, he didn't show a scrap of surprise. I would not want to have played cards against him. *Stay out of his way. We need these people more than they need us.*

"Ask her if you like," I said. "If you don't believe me."

"Stay here." As if I were one of his dogs. He knocked twice and, giving me one last searing glance, slipped inside, allowing me a quick glimpse into the room's interior—dim, the air full of incense—and the very quickest impression of a woman in a long veil, like the pictures downstairs in the empty room.

I pressed my ear to the wood. I heard him, low, and Avdokia, too, in short humble replies, more pauses than speech. My mother remained completely silent. "I know but she can't help it," I heard Avdokia say. Were they arguing my case before my mother as before a judge? Why did he have any say at all? Whose house was this, anyway? I tried the door, but it was locked.

At last I heard the key turn and jumped back. It was Avdokia. She said nothing but her cheeks blazed in sharp little slashes. She jerked her head to the stairs and I followed her. She was furious, though I couldn't tell whether it was at me or him, and we marched wordlessly downstairs and all the way back to the room behind the kitchen.

I did my best to stay "out of the way," but I grew restless by the afternoon. I grabbed my coat and boots and slipped outside to prowl among the neatly shoveled paths and snowbound trees. A girl was laying new wood shavings in the henhouse. The tall bushy-haired *intelligent* was shoveling a path, and another girl threw a panful of water out the kitchen door. I approached the handsome boy with the black beard, who was chopping wood using the larch stump as a block. *"Privet,"* I said.

He wouldn't even look at me. Had their master told them to avoid speaking to me?

I wandered off to try the girl at the henhouse. "How's my chicken doing? The white one." She, too, ignored me and a red rooster flew at me with his claws out. "Quit it!" I batted him away and she glared at me, closed the coop's door.

When they had safely gathered in the back parlor for their communal dinner, I attempted a second unannounced visit to the inner sanctum, slipping silently up the bare wooden stairs—only to find one of the patchwork people stationed before the door. It was the bespectacled *intelligent,* cross-legged on a mat on the bare boards, reading a small, fat book. He must have sensed me standing there before him but refused to look up. I cleared my throat. He slightly resembled Blok, but with a sharper, more pinched face—none of the original's grace and nobility. "I'd like to see her."

"Ukashin said the Mother must not be disturbed."

Ukashin. The first time anyone had said his name. "I'm her daughter."

A parade of emotions rolled past his face as he eyed

Misha, complex as clouds rushing over a field. Surprise, interest, hesitation, a note of fear? Judgment, then dismissal. "Ask Ukashin. It's not up to me."

"Why can't I see her?" I demanded of Avdokia when she returned to her room with a bowl of soup for me.

"Please, Marinoushka." She patted my head as though I were three years old, smoothing my ruffled feathers. "I'm doing my best, but—oh, you don't know. Don't make trouble with them."

"This is ridiculous. She's my mother. Am I to be a prisoner in my own house?" I dipped into the soup she'd brought, cabbage and potato. If there was one thing I had learned from Arkady about men, it was that you should never cower before a man with a whip. It just made him want to use it all the more. "I'm not going to be intimidated by some self-styled fakir, some roadside Houdini."

She glanced up and her face grew tight again.

I followed her gaze to find the man standing right behind me in the doorway, in his shaggy long coat and astrakhan hat, ready for the outdoors.

"Walk with me," Ukashin commanded.

I took one more spoonful and left Avdokia silently praying, to don my coat and boots and follow him outside. Snow was falling in light, crisp flakes. We walked silently together down a newly shoveled path—he clearly liked to keep his followers busy. I liked the feeling of the snow gently tumbling against my lips. I felt

alive again. The dogs, hounds with gray fur that grew in no particular direction, bolted by us to roll in the snow and chase one another, barking. It occurred to me to wonder how he fed such big dogs. Did his acolytes disappear every so often?

The man walked his slightly military walk—hands behind his back. He was vigorous and broad-shouldered, with the eyes of a bull, a wide moustache. Attractive? I had to say yes. A certain magnetism...a definite presence. I estimated his age to be around forty—a good fifteen years older than anyone here except Avdokia, Vera Borisovna, and the *intelligent* who'd shooed me away from my mother's door. Everyone else seemed not much older than me.

He spoke to me with a slight lilt, a slight purr. "Don't worry about the Mother. We are taking very good care of her."

Our steps crunched in the packed snow. I'd spent a night under this snow, had wrapped it about me like an eiderdown. I was not some cowering bourgeoise. "*My* mother, you mean." I felt Avdokia's reproof even as I said it, though she was safely back at the house. *Don't!*

He nodded, not as one agreeing but rather as a man nods when he's trying to gather his own thoughts and only hears your voice, not the sense of your words. My father did this, distracted, thinking of some essay he was writing. "I'm sure this is all quite strange to you," he said. "But the woman you knew as your mother no longer exists."

I picked up a gloveful of snow and packed it into a ball, heaved it at a tree. It smashed with a satisfying burst. "Who's upstairs, then? The first Mrs. Rochester?"

The man didn't appear to have read Brontë. "Let's say she no longer exists on this plane." As one might say, "She's gone to Odessa."

I was unable to stifle my impatience. "What plane does she exist on then?"

"You couldn't begin to understand."

We'd walked out of sight of the house with its fresh icing of snow and smoking chimneys, toward the aspen grove, white bark patterned with black in its wintery calligraphy. When I was young I imagined these marks were codes, secret messages from the fairy world. Perhaps I, too, was a prophetess.

"What do you know about aspen?" he asked.

I brushed snow from my cheeks, my eyelashes, blew icy vapor from my lungs. The insides of my nose, the corners of my eyes, told me it was fifteen degrees and dropping. "I'm no botanist, Comrade."

He took out a pouch of tobacco and rolled a cigarette, lit it. He smoked as if we had all the time in the world to stroll around on a cold day, taking the air like a couple of boulevardiers. My frostbitten nose burned. I was glad enough to be out of doors, however. The foul tobacco he smoked would have been unbearable in close quarters.

"The secret of the aspen," he said, gesturing with the

twisted butt of his *makhorka,* "is that it's all one tree. All connected, under the earth. All one." He cast his popped black eyes at me, the liquid eyes of an intelligent animal, a dog or a horse. I felt unnerved each time they met mine. Now he waited, snow accumulating on the curly lamb of his hat. I would not fall under his spell, though I felt his gaze urging me to do so. I knew a hypnotist when I saw one. "Sorry. I was never very good at riddles."

His powerful form gave the impression of a man who would not suffer insolence, wouldn't hesitate to deliver a blow. But instead he just smiled, superior, a swami pitying the crude materialist. "What you see here—us, my students, your mother, all of us—we're one tree. You understand? All one body, all one breath."

I tried to breathe though my mouth, shallowly, so I wouldn't take in any more of his stinking tobacco than I had to.

The master ran his gaze over the white tree trunks, as if they were troops standing at attention. "Think of us as strings on a harp or a great piano, all in tune. Our fields harmonize. We amplify each other. We create a complex vibration." In a surprisingly delicate gesture, he brought together the stout fingers of his hand, framed in the shaggy coat sleeve.

I puffed out a lungful of frost. "The peaceable kingdom."

Two definite vertical lines formed between his dark brows. "We're creating power." Watching the woods, as if expecting someone to arrive. "Of a kind normally experienced only by adepts in the most remote corners of the earth. But to do it, we must be in absolute accord."

"And I'm out of tune—is that what you're trying to tell me?" I wished he'd just get on with it. Or put out that cigarette. I was feeling very unwell. Snow was building up on my coat and cap and scarf. I saw why we'd come out here to have this chat—so I wouldn't pollute the purity of their vibrational field.

"If only you'd come to us back in Petrograd, you could have stayed on as long as you liked," he said, watching his mongrel dogs as they wound through the trees, sniffing and marking. "We had all the room in the world. But we don't have the luxury of hangers-on here."

I flushed with outrage. "This is my house! I'm the one who belongs here. You're the hangers-on, not me." I was feeling so sick that I thought I might vomit right in front of him. A nice sign of strength. "I don't care what you think."

He put his hand on my shoulder. A heavy, broad hand, like a bear's paw. All at once, I experienced a sensation of heat in my shoulder, then in my whole body. The nausea lifted. He released me and walked on. How did he do that? He stopped again and regarded me, and once more I felt the sensation of heat, of well-being, in my face, in my chest, my stomach. "I don't think. I *feel*. I *feel* you, Marina Dmitrievna. Your energy. It's very disruptive. The question is, what do you have to offer besides your ignorance and confusion? Tell me why we need you. Convince me."

I was actually hot, here in the falling snow. I could see the steam rising off my coat. What was he doing to me? "I'm not planning to be a burden. I'm a good worker. I'll do my share."

"But the work's all been done." One dog trotted up, its tongue lolling, steam rising from its mouth, and he patted it, sliding its furry ear between his ungloved fingers. "We could have used you back in the spring, when we arrived. Building the smokehouse, fishing, putting in the garden. We could have used the extra hands. But now? A poor time to show up with your cup and spoon, calling us hangers-on."

I could see that had been rude of me. I saw myself from their point of view, someone's spoiled daughter, appearing and demanding to be fed. I couldn't imagine they'd brought in much of a harvest, especially if they'd really grown their own rye, but certainly they'd gardened and built the smokehouse, which must be hanging with the fish they'd caught. And what did I have on my side? Inherited property, sullen, passive resistance, and the complete absence of other ideas.

He squinted against the smoke, foul as a burning carpet. "The father, can't you go to him?"

"My father? He's in the east, at Omsk with Kolchak. I'm not going there."

The man sighed, gazing at me like a schoolmaster regarding the stupidest girl in the class. "No. The father...of your...inconvenience." He dropped his eyes toward my midsection.

My what?

Again, that gaze, back at my face.

What was this man trying to insinuate?

The father.

No. That wasn't possible. I hadn't had a menstrual period in more than a year now. I could hang a coat on my hip bones.

Yet I'd certainly felt sick for some time.

Well, who hadn't? The food we ate, or what substituted for food...

Though I'd been eating well enough recently...since Kolya and I had left Petrograd and turned to the largesse of the countryside.

No. It was ridiculous. Kolya was fanatically careful, nursing his supply of *preservativy* as if they were relics of the True Cross.

And yet—perhaps prophylactics had not been intended for such heavy use. There was no way to know how old they were.

I felt the weird sensation of a heavy liquid being poured onto my head from a great height.

"Yes, that man," said the fakir. The dogs ran off, barking.

We watched them go. I was grateful for the distraction. "You've got it wrong, brother," I said, in my most

Misha voice. Hooligans didn't get knocked up. I was a boy. A boy!

"Have I?" He breathed out a cloud of his smoke, and I had to back away. In my head, the hurricane roared. My stomach lurched and I vomited into the snow as he watched with amusement.

I'd never conceived with Genya, though I wouldn't have minded. The last time we made love was right before he went out for the defense of Petrograd in March—I could have had his baby already. Thank God I hadn't with Arkady, I would have known by now. No, other than the filigreed love letter he had cut on my back, it was only in my darkened spirit that he'd left his impression. But between Kolya and me, there had always been such a strong charge of nature. My body wanted Kolya, ached for him. Such a stupid beast—it didn't know we were through. I imagined my reddest inner chamber, like a velvet-lined boudoir all prepared for this small guest.

Ukashin lifted his face, listening to the song of his dogs baying a higher, more excited note. I had to get away and think. He knew too much, noticed too much, and I had learned a few things, one of them being that men who knew things about you were people to be avoided. It was flattering to be understood but dangerous. A good man didn't need to be intriguing. This one, drawing on his tobacco, squinting against the smoke, looked like a rug merchant waiting for a client to make up his mind. I could see him in a fez in a coffee house sucking a hookah, the patience of centuries behind him.

What if I really was pregnant? Only the single most disastrous thing that could befall me right now, being so far from Petrograd. The city at least had hospitals and a modern attitude toward women.

I counted the months since the October celebration—November, December, January...July. A summer baby, if this was true and not some game he was playing. I glanced again at the broad shoulders in the shaggy coat. But I knew he was right. I could feel it. *Bozhe moi.* I was frankly terrified. What did I know about children? *Didn't every woman want a child?* Just as Russia was about to be torn apart like an old dress, what could I hope for here—to give birth in a bathhouse? Or roll in herbs in hopes of a miscarriage? In Petrograd I could have an abortion in a modern mothers' hospital. Unless a certain thief found me first. Then I wouldn't have to worry about my future.

An abortion...was that what I wanted?

Yet how could I have a baby? I couldn't even diaper Faina's brat. Any child with me as a mother would be in sorry shape indeed. And with Kolya Shurov, that womanizer, as a father? My own mother hadn't had a shred of maternal instinct, but at least she had a responsible husband and the comforts of home, the protection of money, servants, food on the table. A child of mine would be tossed into this world with nothing, dragged behind me like a goat behind a cart.

Somewhere in the aspens, we heard the bay of the dogs. He threw the cigarette into the snow. "They're onto a deer. Get your gun."

I'd forgotten Kolya's gun. How on earth did he know? No time to wonder. I pulled my glove off with my teeth, dropped it to the snow. The headman placed his warm hand on my shoulder as my bare fingers found the butt, the trigger. In a great crash, a young stag bounded out of the brush, leaping ten feet or more as the dogs bounded after it. "Shoot it."

Smoothly, with shocking grace, I extended the weapon, closed one eye, sighted ahead of the leaping deer.

"Now," he said.

The blast echoed. The stag dropped to its knees, then over onto its side in the snow, and was still. It was nothing short of a miracle. I'd killed it with a pistol I'd never fired, at forty feet. It was impossible, yet it had happened.

Amazed, I gazed at the pistol in my hand, but it was as plain and heavy and dumb as ever. The bull-necked man let go of my shoulder. Suddenly I was cold again.

The rest of the scene unfolded in slowed-down time. The dogs catching up with the beast. The master calling them off. Their wavering in the snow halfway between the stag and where we stood. On second call, they came racing toward us, tails all awag. "You see?" As if we had been having an argument and the deer was the proof of his point. "It's better when you don't think so much," he said. "Let doubt fall away, let confusion fall away. This is the true path. *Davai.* Let's see what you brought for our table."

We walked out into the snow toward the fallen creature. It lay there, real as a rug, one leg doubled under itself, its dainty cloven hooves, its rack of antlers, three points on each, its soft brown eye turning glassy. A second eye just above the first one showed where the bullet entered.

"You can give life, you can take it." He handed me the hilt of a deadly looking knife, its blade slightly curved.

I watched myself, under his instruction, slitting open the body of the stag I had killed, beginning at the genitals and slicing all the way to the throat. "Don't nick the organs," he said. "Steady..."

I placed my fingers inside. Hot. Wet. I guided the knife carefully, keeping the point away from the guts. The belly steamed in the frost, and with the steam rose a strong smell that should have been disgusting but wasn't. This was us—the heat, the beast's life, locked into this meat. My life and this life I might possibly be carrying. Fresh blood stained the snow bright red.

"Lung." He pointed. "Heart. Liver. Kidney." The white lung, the red heart, purplish liver, blue kidney, the heavy red coils of the intestine. The machinery of the body. It was clean and intricate, and the man kept his hand on my shoulder, pointing out what needed to be done. I cut the membranes, scooped out pounds of slick, warm animal guts, laid them out in the snow. I was careful to pinch off the bladder, to get the entire intestinal tract. The dogs crept closer, on their stomachs, whining, until they were within ten feet of the steaming mass, but he stopped them with a single gesture, one blunt finger pointing. Then he knelt and took the bloody knife himself, sliced off a strip of the liver and held it out on the blade. "For the hunter."

Raw? He expected me to eat it raw? I had avoided squeamishness so far, but this piece of bloody meat?

"This is your kill. Life and death. Eat."

He was waiting. I took it into my mouth. Hot flesh. I chewed. It was milder than I expected, even a little sweet, easy to eat. I was hungry. The protein sat better than I would have imagined, and I felt the vigor of the deer entering my own blood. He ate a piece himself, then cut two more and threw them to the dogs.

One of the followers ran up the shoveled path—a tall, silent boy I hadn't seen yet, his eyes a light brown, wearing a quilted hat pointed like a medieval helmet. How had he known to come? Did the man have a silent dog whistle?

"Ilya, bring a basin, a pail, and some burlap squares," the master ordered. "And a rope." The boy nodded, his earnest face knobbly like the knuckles of a hand. Prior to this moment, none of them would look at me directly, but before the boy ran back, he eyed me admiringly, even enviously. I wiped the sweat from my forehead with the back of my bloody hand.

Ukashin picked out some of the inferior pieces of offal and threw them to the dogs, who attacked them in a great outpouring of growls. "While we're waiting," he said, "find yourself a tree with a long sturdy branch."

In a kind of trance, I found a suitable tree, a tall fir whose lowest branches he deemed adequate.

The boy soon returned with squares of burlap, a basin, and a pail in which rested a coiled rope, a small saw, and a hatchet. The burly headman indicated the organs spread out on the ground. "Take these to Katrina in the kitchen." The boy filled the basin with them and carried them back to the house with the pride of Salome bearing the head of John the Baptist.

I thought I understood then what Ukashin would have me do—hang the deer in the tree, cold and safe, out of reach of winter's animals. Using the hatchet for a weight, I threw the rope up and over the outstretched limb. It proved a dangerous choice, as I barely avoided catching the ax head in my skull on the way down. He had a good laugh at that one.

Next, we braced the stag's legs apart, my instructor showing me where to cut holes in the hind legs to lace the rope through.

"Now pull it up," he told me.

I took hold of the rope and hauled. The deer was too heavy.

"Oh, come. This is your kill. Pull it up!"

I put all the strength of my arms and legs into pulling

it up, but it was hopeless. Yet I kept trying. I had to show him I wasn't the little *barynya* expecting to be fed and cared for, that I would throw myself into whatever work he gave me, uncomplaining, to the point of the absurd. He let me struggle a good long time, too, hooting as I failed again and again, before he finally bent down himself and lifted the deer straight up in his arms, neat as a prince lifting a swan in a pas de deux. I shortened the rope, and the deer's head swung two feet off the ground.

"We'll want the hide, too," he said.

There would be no shortcuts, evidently. Perhaps I would have to chew the sinews into cord, like the red Indians of my brother's Zane Grey novels. So be it. Despite the bloody liver, I was feeling strangely well. And I found I enjoyed the man's company. I liked his blunt solidity, his cheerfulness. It surprised me. I had been so prepared to dislike him, with all his mystical nonsense, but I had to admit that it felt good to be with someone who knew what he was doing, possessed the sort of understanding that inspired trust. Though I realized I had to be on guard against it. *Alas, Beloved...*

He showed me where to cut, around the hind legs at the thighs, a seam to free the hide from the flesh. Then I pulled the skin down, scraping and cutting the whitish membranes wherever they held fast, until I had the creature's coarse gray-dun coat down around its neck and upper legs like a sweater pulled over a child's head but not yet freed from its arms.

Stripped of its skin, hanging there, head down, legs splayed, the carcass looked terribly, touchingly human. Vulnerable and so light compared to the presence and power of the live stag—the heartbreakingly narrow legs, the slender waist, the narrow rack of ribs. I felt a shiver of recognition. It was like working on my own flayed body.

"Yes," he said. "This is you. And you will eat it and continue to live. And when you die, something will eat you. Look at it." He spun the deer on its rope. "Small isn't it, to contain so much life? A dead man's very similar. Imagine a battlefield full of dead men. A village. Walking into a village and seeing every man, woman, and child like this."

A deserter. I'd been right.

I cut the hide away from the neck and the forelegs and set it in the snow. It steamed on the ground as the perfect hexagons of snowflakes drifted down over us, dusting the blue trees, soon to cover the pink blood seeping down into the white. Blood dripped from the hanging carcass into the bucket. I was tired but happy with my work, looking forward to going back to Avdokia's room to sleep, to ponder what to do about *the inconvenience*. I held the knife out to Ukashin, but he raised his hands, as if it were red hot. "What, you think you're done?"

What more was there to do?

"You have to butcher it before it freezes. Start with those." He indicated two strips of meat on the inside of the deer, to either side of its backbone. "Reach in and pull."

How easily they came free, surprising me. A long strip of meat, nice as anything served at the Astoria Hotel. He laid out a burlap square and I set the fillets onto it. Now I understood. And as tired as I was, I saw he was right. If the unbutchered deer froze, we'd never be able to pull the meat free. We'd have to chop the flesh from the bone with an ax.

Now the work grew hard—severing the legs, the neck, the spine. I fought against the queasy sense of having murdered a person, and now tormenting its savaged body. It brought me back to the basement of Gorokhovaya 2. The dispassion with which one body could torture another. This strange thing, life, built upon such a fragile bit of flesh.

I worked like a medical student, separating the meat along its natural lines of musculature. One flesh-being dissecting another. I thought of the cat we once dissected in physiology class at the Tagantsev Academy—or rather that Mina dissected. I'd cringed and hung back. I didn't want to see a cat all open like that. Back when there still were cats. But I wasn't a girl in the academy anymore. I had nursed the dying, I had cleaned their shit. Perhaps I wasn't the chaos I'd imagined.

As I worked I had the sense of myself as someone I hadn't really met yet, someone silent and deep, patient and strong—not like Marusya, whose storms were as violent as the ones on the sun—but whole and quiet under the chaos of my apparent self. Perhaps it wasn't I who was chaotic. It was life itself. Existence was the whirlwind. I had just been too light to keep from being blown around in it. Now I felt a density forming within myself as I quartered this beast, hacking off great pieces and wrapping them in burlap, cutting out the pielike brains and folding them into the deerskin. "We'll tan the hide with them," Ukashin explained. "Make you a new pair of shoes." He threw the head to the dogs like a boy throwing a ball to his scrappy chums. One grabbed it by an antler and ran off through the trees, the other in pursuit.

Shoes would be nice, but I understood that he meant more than shoes. He was inviting me to stay on, to become part of his community. I felt the falling snow caress my cheeks and nose, and thought of the spark of life that might be embedded within me, growing, cells dividing, a child. Our child! I stood there, my hand throbbing from the hard work. There were worse places to face such a future. Here I had a roof, Mother and Avdokia, a place I could live, work, and time to figure out my next step.

73 *The Fire Child*

I DREAMED OF THE night forest. Cold, black, and starless, the snow coming down. I had to gather wood for a fire, but in the dark, I could only assemble the smallest pile. I squatted as I lit those poor shreds with matches, but the wind kept blowing them out. I was about to give up when I discovered a beautiful lighter in my pocket. I vaguely remembered it, someone had given it to me. It lit right away, and I let the flame lick the sticks of kindling.

A fire was born in the dark. Warm, though when I passed my hand through it, it didn't burn me. I picked the flame out of its nest and held it in my cupped hand. And I realized—this was my child. I felt it warming my face, like a kiss. It knew me. I passed it gently from hand to hand, marveling. I had to be careful—it was just a small flame, tender and bright. I always thought I would have a human child, not a handful of fire, but I understood, as it pushed the inky darkness away, that of course I would have a fire child. When I held it too close, it began to scorch my coat. I needed something to put it in—a lantern, a tin box, something to keep it from the wind. I held it as close as I could and fed it tiny scraps of wood, and to my delight, it consumed them. But how to keep it safe? I couldn't put it down, certainly not in a pocket. How would I sleep? I had to ready myself with one hand.

When I awoke, the sun was already up—a dull December day, as much of a day as we were going to get. I immediately looked at my hand. Empty. Sniffed it. Could I still smell smoke? Maybe...the flame was deep inside me now, and I was the lantern. Yes, this was true, wasn't it? Oh, but my neck ached, my shoulder, and my hand, which had butchered an entire deer the day before. I massaged it, tried to flex it open. It was swollen, painful. The room smelled of Avdokia—yeast and a slight tinge of lavender. I'd wanted to tell her about the fire child.

There was a slight knock on the door, and a girl's face poked in, framed by smooth hair of silky brown, a girl like flowing water. I recognized her, my savior, the one who had brought me the potato when I was staging my sit-down protest. "Are you awake?" she asked quietly. "I've come to take you for the bath."

"Where's Avdokia?"

"With the Mother." She held out my Misha clothes, but I could barely move my right shoulder, and my hand was cramped like a crone's. She helped me dress, don my boots, my coat.

In the kitchen, redolent of kasha, two girls in patchwork *sarafany* glanced up from their work—the fierce black-haired girl who'd taken my chicken and a spectacular blonde grinding grain. The dark one squinted with suspicion, and the blonde avoided my eyes as if the sight of me might turn her to stone. My Ariadne steered me out the back door into the yard. Outside, patchwork people shoveled paths as fast as the snow could fall. They too studiously ignored us as we passed them. Was I still persona non grata? I would have thought that last night's venison stew would have convinced them I was worthy of adoption. We followed the cleared path past some new, solid-looking wooden outbuildings I hadn't seen before, but she led me on until we reached Baba Yaga's hut—Maryino's ruined bathhouse.

Blue smoke rose from the chimney. I fought the urge to rub my eyes. What magic was this? Our spellbound playhouse, with its rotten porch and caved-in roof. Today it sparkled like fresh snow, the window frames newly painted, the panes washed, the roof and the porch rebuilt.

She swung open the door, silent on newly blacked and oiled hinges, and we entered, ducking under the heavy lintel. The smell of fresh-cut birch met me— walls, floor, all neatly scrubbed and clean. It was already warm—alive again, this *banya* built by my great-grandfather. This was no sooty bathhouse like the one in Faina's village. Ours had separate rooms for changing, soaking, and steam, and a cast-iron double stove with bright nickel-plated ornaments of scallops and scrolls.

"A good bath to you," I said loud enough for Bannik to hear as I hung up my coat and hat on a hook by the door. I felt like I'd arrived at a clearing in the forest where the animals spoke and sorcerers plotted and witches sat ready with their tests. You had to treat the local spirits with respect.

In the anteroom, with its little table and glass window, some bread and dried apple had been laid out for my breakfast. I ate quickly, then disposed of my boots, my hopeless socks. Such ugly feet I'd acquired since my first bathhouse visit, on Kazanskaya Street—calloused, red and bruised, still painful despite the old woman's stinking frostbite poultice in Alekhovshchina. Off came my student's trousers, my black Russian blouse, my homemade drawers—all Misha's impedimenta. The girl gathered them up and left them by the door. After I'd eaten, she offered me a glass of tea—mushroomy-scented and dark. "What is it?" I sniffed the liquid suspiciously.

She shrugged her small, fine-boned shoulders. "Something we drink."

So I drank it, sitting there naked and louse-infested, flea-bitten, and probably pregnant at the little table. The girl shed her own garments—the short jacket, the patchwork *sarafan* in blues and greens, the coarse linen blouse—and emerged lithe and smooth as a mermaid, her neat small head perched atop a long neck like a flower on its stem.

The tea, its earthy, musty taste and smell, lifted my tiredness without really waking me, gave me the strange sense that we had been thinned into two dimensions, as if we were painted on an urn. *Heard melodies are sweet, but those unheard / Are sweeter; therefore, ye soft pipes, play on.* Eternal Keats. I imagined Genya, thinking of me. I held the fire baby in my palm. He was its father as much as Kolya. We were still married, still had that tie. As I gazed at the girl, I kept hearing *Swan Lake*'s "Dance of the Little Swans." That magical tune wound through my head like a refrain in a music box.

I tossed down the rest of this murky tea and weight-
lessly followed the girl into the washroom, where she
opened a spigot and a sweet rush of hot water surged
into her crude wooden bucket. Steam coiled and
plumed in the air. She poured water over my head,
my shoulders, and I was in ecstasy. Thanks to the tea,
I could turn my head freely again, and my hand and
shoulder had stopped aching. She produced a comb and
a thick bar of soap with which she soaped my dirty
black locks. In Petrograd you could get a *funt* of potatoes for such a bar. Then she carefully combed through
my sudsy hair, and I realized she was crushing lice between her fingernails without a word or a comment.
What discretion, what tenderness. If I was drawn to
women, this would be the kind of girl I would want. I
imagined how envious Kolya would be if he could see
me now, with her soaping my hair, massaging my scalp,
pouring the water through.

Daylight peered through the steamy window of the
mist-filled room, sweet with the resinous scent of the
logs, the frostbitten sun pressing its face to the glass,
envying our coziness. My toes tingled in the hot water.
Such a cruel, primal difference between those who had
fuel and water and those who didn't. I remembered all
those miserable buckets of water I had milked from the
pump on Grivtsova Alley and lugged up a thousand
steps to boil on our tiny stove.

Laughter roiled around inside me as the girl massaged my knotted shoulders, my right arm, my hand,

like a page tending his knight after a battle. She expertly kneaded my horrible feet, unflinching. I turned so she could wash my back. The shame I normally felt was absent. My scars felt like a warrior's scars to me now rather than a slave's lashes, the mark of campaigns survived. And her tenderness was a revelation. This is what Arkady could never imagine. Simple human charity. Who had ever simply cared for Caliban, wanting nothing in return, a touch without fear? Who said I would never hear those bells again? Here, in the bosom of this strange community, I heard them chime.

After I'd been soaped and rinsed to impossible cleanliness, we moved into the steam, the fiery heart of the *banya*. Outside the window, the masses of snow in the dark branches of the firs blurred like memories dimly recalled. I ran my hand along the great logs that comprised the walls and could see the trees they had been, their heads in the sun, creaking in the wind. Logs that might have been masts of great ships. The girl threw a dipper of water on the stove, spawning a satisfying hiss and cloud. I stretched on the newly planed bench, imagining my great-grandmother and my great-grandfather here, felt caps protecting their tender ears, sipping tea with compote, listening to the gossip of provincial uncles and aunts. My mother and her brother, petted and praised, the most beautiful children in Petersburg.

"Are you allowed to speak to me?" I asked the girl.

She nodded but dropped her eyes, the lashes so long they grazed her cheeks.

"What's your name?"

"Natalya," she confessed softly.

"I keep thinking I've seen you before. Did you go to the Tagantsev Academy?"

She laughed, a bright tinkly laugh, and small dimples pierced her cheeks.

"Did you work at Smolny? In the canteen?" Now I just wanted to tease her, see those dimples. Little bells shimmered in the air. "At the Stray Dog then? Dancing on a mirror?"

"Perhaps at the Mariinsky?" she said shyly.

Of course. The tulle, the little tiara. The song in my head, "Dance of the Little Swans." The thin strength of her high flat chest, the knobby arched feet. The way she had massaged me so expertly. "You left the Mariinsky for this?" I was astonished. No one had more privileges than the dancers at the Mariinsky, except maybe the Kronstadt sailors. "I heard you got category 1 rations." Who would give up such a thing? Rations were dearer than gold.

Her expression grew stern, or as stern as she could manage with that sweet face. "There's more to life than rations."

"More than category 1 rations?" Maybe she really was a swan, and not a person at all.

"You're still walking in your sleep. You won't even know until you wake." She took birch flails from a nail on the wall and put them in a bucket, released hot water onto them.

I lay back, feeling the sweat bead on my body, pooling between my breasts, dripping down my ribs and filling my navel. Maybe it was the tea, but now I could clearly see that my breasts were noticeably swollen, my nipples dark as saddle leather. How had I missed that? My aching hips had seemed like a product of hard travel, and that infernal nausea...the fact of my new condition should have been evident to me, but I'd been moving too much, too fast to notice. Blown about in the wind.

Such an odd thing, to live in a body. This portable shell, this suit of meat and bone. Just the same as the one I'd dismantled the day before. I looked at my skin, flushed in the heat, my sweat, my navel, my knees. It didn't belong to me, not really. We were only using these bodies. They belonged to nature, lived their own lives, had purposes separate from our own. So who was the "I" within this body? A mere passenger? Hostage? Fellow traveler? Especially the female body, with its surprises and indignities. How much easier it was for a man to be a rationalist. As a woman, I might consider myself solely as my will, the sum of my talents and failures, my experiences and dreams, a poet, a rebel, the maker of my own destiny. But in fact I was a consciousness riding on the train of my body. An oblivious passenger, heading along rails I never put there. What was this female body? A prison? Or could it come to

be a home with its own strange logic? I sensed that
the Master and I could have an interesting conversation
about this.

"Tell me about the Master," I said. "Where's he
from? Was he in the war?"

I could see her wariness, but also her eagerness to
talk about him. "His name in the world is Taras
Ukashin," she began. "But no one knows where he's
from. If you ask, he just teases you." She stopped, uncertain if she'd said too much already. I waited, too,
hoping her desire to confide would win out. "Sometimes he says Bukhara. Or Kars. Or Alma-Ata. He
never gives the same answer twice." She lifted the birch
flails out of the hot water, tested their pliancy, plunged
them back into the bucket. "Master says it doesn't matter where you're from—you should create yourself
anew every dawn."

I liked how she said it, *in the world*. As opposed to
what? Was this not the world? "When I shot the deer,
he put his hand on my shoulder, and I stopped feeling
sick. A warmth came through his hands. He was the
one who shot the deer, wasn't he? I never could have
done it myself."

"It's our energetics," she said, swishing the flails.
"You'll learn. He's studied with holy men all over the
earth. Yogis and monks. He says we are the link between higher and lower. You'll see. There's nothing he
can't do."

This little deer was in love with him—I saw it in

her pleasure just speaking about him and I could understand his appeal, his combination of solidity and mystery, his competence. I also knew how flattering it was to think that someone could awaken things unknown to you. Flattering and dangerous.

"He's too funny. He's not off in a trance, like some holy man on a mountain." Not that I would have mistaken him for one. "He's the most down-to-earth person you'll ever meet. He never says he has powers. He just says he's a searcher, like all of us."

She handed me one of the flails and took one herself, stroking it like a child's hair. "But higher energies come through him. He's trying to find the way to transform us so we can do the same. That's what the Practice is. That's why there were so many dancers at the Laboratory. The energetics come through the body. The body is the link, not the mind."

Her lips, small and pale, parted as if for higher knowledge, or some other kind of kiss. The mushroom tea was making her glow. I felt my mockery oozing away with my sweat, along with my aches and my disbelief. "You were there at the Laboratory?"

Her gaze turned to the window, the steam transformed to trickles of water, as if the panes were weeping. She sighed. "Master says all things have to end. There's nothing eternal but the present."

The soaked, flexible bunch of birch twigs fanned in my hand, and I swore the little dried leaves were coming back to life. I felt fertile, like a goddess. We took turns whipping each other with the switches, making the room even hotter as we swatted the steam down from the ceiling to where we sat on the newly planed benches, so hot I could hardly breathe. "Tell me about the dacha. Avdokia said my mother was there."

Her green eyes widened, they glittered with excitement. "So it's true? She really is your mother?"

Why the breathlessness, the wonder? "Of course. Why do you ask?"

She came closer to me on the bench. "What was it like? Growing up with her?" Then she remembered her place, searched my face nervously. "You don't mind my asking, do you? Master says women should be more curious about the mysteries of the universe, and less about what people ate for dinner."

Master evidently said a lot of things. "She was a fashionable housewife," I replied, rubbing dead skin off the tops of my feet. "An aesthete. Hairdresser in the Nevsky Passazh, hats from Madame Landis, gowns by Worth and Poiret…"

"Hats and gowns—that's just the role," she said. "That's not who a person is." She eyed me hungrily. "What about her, elementally?"

Elementally? That was a new one. "Mostly air, I'd say, maybe a little water. Foggy. Like Petersburg in the fog. Like the Moika at dusk. Like Vrubel. If she were a poem, she'd be Blok. She was part of a spiritualist circle. Séances and so on. She liked art." The girl nodded as if I were revealing great secrets. "We went to the ballet. We probably saw you there. My brother wanted to design for the stage, like Benois."

"You have a brother?" As if it were impossible that my mother managed to push out more than one of us.

"Actually, two," I said. "One's in the Don with Denikin. The other one, the artist, died." More than a year I'd been living without Seryozha in the world. I felt guilty, even through the tea, like I'd left him behind, so much had I changed, so much had the world changed. I wondered how he would feel about my pregnancy. For someone so childlike, he didn't care much for actual children. And he would have been disgusted to think of my body growing coarse and heavy, my belly like a watermelon. But he worshipped Kolya. I could imagine a life in which Kolya and I were still together and Seryozha lived nearby. I would have the baby, and we could see one another every day.

"I'm sorry," Natalya said. "I shouldn't have pried." Then she straightened. "But Master says we shouldn't apologize. 'Act from the genuine impulse and stand by your actions.'"

"It's fine. We spent a lot of time here when we were small." I rested my head back against the logs. My lips, my hands, my toes tingled from the tea.

"It's just so hard for me to imagine her with children. A regular family life." How my mother must have changed so that this girl couldn't envision her as a normal woman with children and a husband. She edged closer. "Did she have visions back then?"

What was my mother up to here? Though she'd always been somewhat clairvoyant. "She liked to guess who was on the telephone before she answered it," I said. "Once, it rang and she said, 'Pavel Popov is dead,' before she picked up the receiver. It was one of my father's friends, calling to say that a mutual friend had died."

The girl's lips parted, rapturous. "At the dacha, a woman, Veronika Konstantinova, accused Ilya of stealing a locket from her room. We went to Mother, and she said it had fallen behind the dresser. And when we pulled it away from the wall, it was right where she said it would be."

Not exactly word from the Beyond. Something anybody might have thought of. How unpleasant, though, to hear a stranger describe her as "Mother." She was *my* mother. My mother the seer. I laughed, remembering her complaining about having turkey when there was no meat in Petrograd.

Natalya's eyes shone as she toyed with her birch flail. "She was the reason we came here." She dropped her voice in case someone might be eavesdropping from the Beyond. "She saw a tide of blood lapping up through the drains of Petrograd, flooding the city. She wouldn't let the Master rest until he promised we'd move out to her estate. 'Before the snow melts.' She was adamant about it. That's why we left. It happened, didn't it? The tide of blood."

I didn't want to reinforce this nonsense, but it was

true. "There was cholera in the spring. All the bacteria from people shitting in the courtyards. It went into the water."

"The drains," she whispered. "You see?"

But it wasn't the first time Petersburg had experienced the consequences of its shallow water table, and the lack of sanitation had been evident in every courtyard. Any doctor could have predicted cholera in the spring. Perhaps Mother had overheard it somewhere. But perhaps it was Red Terror she had seen. *Those* drains. "In the fall, someone tried to assassinate Lenin. The Cheka rounded up hundreds of bourgeois people, people from the intelligentsia— maybe thousands, who knows?—and shot them all. There were lists of the executed every day." Maybe it was coincidence, an intensification of her normal anxiety about the revolution, but the timing was uncanny. I certainly hadn't seen it coming, building over our heads like a great black storm. Then again, I was never one for predicting the obvious. Case in point: Kolya.

The girl's countenance was grave, fully imagining the horror they had so narrowly escaped. "Master didn't want to leave—we were doing such important work at the Laboratory. But she made us go. She'd start screaming in the night. You could hear it all over the dacha."

"Will they ever let me see her?" I asked Natalya. "He was very upset when I tried."

"You must prepare," she said. "Even we don't see her

that often. She has other duties. She's not of this world, Marina."

I thought of her discussing hats with Madame Landis. She was very much of the world back then. "Is he like that, too? Visions and whatnot?" I still felt Ukashin's knowing black eyes on me, the warmth of his touch.

A little dreamy smile replaced her earlier alarm. "Oh, no. He's very human," she said, swishing the birch twigs. The fragrance released into the steam, green and fresh and ropy. "Very elemental. It's the Mother who has the visions. Her guides show her everything. She's probably watching us right now." I imagined my mother's horror, forced to view this girl combing out my lice, or to see my pregnant body without benefit of cloth or modesty. *Can you see me, Mother? I'm going to have your bastard grandchild.* Her guides would be covering her eyes.

"The Master's purpose is to connect the higher realms with this one. We have the most contact with him." She shifted on the bench, tucking a long bony foot under her, straightening her spine. I wondered how much contact that was. I thought of the Master and my mother—like notes in a chord, higher and low. "The Mother deals with the higher realms exclusively."

"Except when she's finding lost lockets."

Her high smooth brow developed a small wrinkle. "Are you always like this?"

"Like what?"

"Making jokes."

Here I was, disrupting the harp again. I would have to be more careful. I liked it here, and I didn't want the headman to send me off. At least not until I could talk to my mother, find out what was really going on. "No," I said. "I'm just a little nervous. I hadn't expected any of this."

"Master says that it will take time." She switched at me with the birch flail, a sensation both painful and delicious. "To let you get used to us. Not to talk to you too much. But"—her dimples appeared again—"you don't mind, do you?"

Sweet girl. Although I didn't know if I could bear a whole winter of *Master says*. I could understand how Varvara felt, talking to me all those years ago—was it only three? *Papa says, Papa says. Can't you think for yourself?* The girl threw more water on the stones, and I thought about that woman up in the house. Where was the Vera Borisovna who'd sat at our table in the Poverty Artel translating Apollinaire and playing American poker? I'd never felt closer to her than I did then. Though inexplicably it was Anton who drew her out. She liked men. Women envied her, but men vied to outshine one another in her presence—which was why her soirees were always so successful. And now she was trapped in that room all day long, doing God knew what. "When will he let me see her?"

"You'll see her," the girl reassured me. "Sometimes she comes out to watch the Practice or see our hand-work. If she wants you, she'll call for you. Don't worry, she knows you're here. If she sees something you need to hear, you'll be brought to her. But she watches everything. It's not so important that you see her, it's that she sees you."

But she hadn't called for me.

When we couldn't stand the heat anymore, we ran outside, steaming, into the frigid air and hurled ourselves naked into the snow. The contrast was delicious. It felt superhuman to roll in the snow without feeling cold. The winter sun peered like a red eyeball through the icy layer of sky while I stood steaming and immortal, watching the snow melt around me.

If I stayed, perhaps I would learn their secrets.

But for now, it didn't take long for the true temperature to send us back into the embrace of the *banya* for another round of steam, though I declined more of that tea. I would have to keep my wits about me.

When we passed through for the last time, I noticed that fresh clothes had been hung on pegs in the anteroom—a blouse, a brightly patchworked *sarafan,* and a short quilted jacket. The ensemble would certainly provide more room for my possible *inconvenience,* if it went that far. But my Misha clothes were gone. "What happened to my things? My coat?"

"They're being washed," she said. "We'll put the coat in the smokehouse for a few days to kill the vermin."

A sensible move, but I felt disoriented as Natalya

helped me into these odd archaic-feeling garments. The blouse was embroidered, everything clean and smelling of the iron. But now I had nothing. No coat, no normal clothes. And Ukashin had my weapon, which had been in the coat pocket. I felt vulnerable in a way I hadn't felt before, vulnerable and tended to at the same time. I would have to sniff my way across this terrain very carefully, like a little fox crossing a river, testing the ice.

74 *The Ionians*

IN THE LANTERN-LIT front parlor, cross-legged on the carpets facing my grandfather's empty chair, the patch-work disciples sat deep in meditation. My benefactress leaned in next to me. "Breathe in the chaos of the world. Breathe out order." The smoke from their billowing incense burned my lungs, seared my nostrils. Her command made no sense. Why would anybody want to breathe the chaos of the world into her own body? I already held far too much of that particular substance. What if this was real, and I was absorbing the gigantic trash heap of the world, its suffering, its waste, its hunger, its rage?

"Wouldn't it be better to inhale order and exhale chaos?" I whispered.

She raised her lashes to regard me, as if from a long way off, her eyes dreamy water-green. A smile for my ignorance, my lack of spirituality, played about her petal-pink lips. "But it's how we heal the world."

I tried not to smirk, but somehow I doubted that this small group of Petrograd nincompoops could staunch human misery by sitting on a carpet in a candlelit room, breathing. I decided my lungs weren't up to such heavy planetary responsibilities. Instead I breathed in their order and breathed out my own chaos, hoping no one would notice, the way people throw trash out their windows into the courtyards.

There was no clock in sight. Was it midnight? Two in the morning? My God, how long could a person breathe in and out, even if you thought you were saving the world! Bored, I amused myself by examining my new coreligionists in the cult of whatever this was, Ukashinism. Here they all were, the entire community, ten of them, not counting the absent Master, my mother, and the unregenerate Avdokia, no doubt cursing them all from behind the closed door of the servants' room. Five men and five women, each more beautiful than the last, except for the gangly, bespectacled intellectual. Most appealing, I decided, was the long-lashed, dark-bearded, romantic-looking youth who chopped their wood. If I were looking for a conquest I would start there. His lashes flickered as he concentrated. Or the boy with firm broad shoulders and heroic dark eyebrows that met in the middle. The gypsy girl's fierce beauty begged for gold around her neck and dangling from those ears. The blonde from the kitchen this morning could have lit up the room all by herself—Helen of Troy was their scullery maid. All wore multicolored homemade clothing, vaguely folkloric, and not a one was older than twenty-two except the storklike *intelligent,* a decade older and decidedly uncomfortable with the long sitting. He rocked from side to side, occasionally uncrossing his legs.

Light formed a dome around the candles, polishing these youthful faces into a Vermeer-like serenity, licking at their closed eyelids. The tallow smoked and sweated, and the chunk of incense in its blackened pot wove complex patterns in the air.

The gypsy struck a small gong.

"Think of exhaling long strands of light," Natalya whispered from within her trance, gesturing with an impossibly graceful arm to evoke strands emerging from her lovely mouth.

I did my best, imagining producing long glowing threads from my lungs. I imagined wrapping the light around myself, then sending it snaking down the hall to tickle Avdokia's ear. How sad she'd been to watch me move from her room to the sort of women's dormitory or nunnery that had been set up in the old nursery. *You're with them now?*

I'd sent her a quick wink as they removed me. *Don't worry, it's still me.*

I gathered my strands, wove a glowing sling, and laid my baby in it. I threw a brilliant fine Orenburg shawl of light around Maryino, in glowing protection against the predations of the outside world. I tried not to think of Lyuda's warning in Novinka's blacksmith shop. *They're not all that safe there.* Watching the reflection of candles in the sparkling-clean windows, I wondered about the civil war unfolding somewhere in the night. How lucky I'd been to find my old nanny and my mother here. I would get through the winter with them, out of harm's way. I had been truly, undeservedly fortunate so far. I hoped my luck would hold.

At last the pocket doors slid open with a bang, and the Master entered as if to a fanfare of trumpets. In unison, the students rose, folded their hands—fist below, flat palm above—and bowed to him. I imitated them as best I could, even to the degree of kowtow, and remained in the bow as he bowed in return and settled into my grandfather's chair. I could feel Dyedushka's fury. I was surprised his chair didn't burst into flames. Finally we straightened and returned to our patch of carpet.

Wearing a Mongolian robe and Persian slippers that turned up slightly at the toes, he looked less like a mystic than a lost member of the Marco Polo expedition. The devil was tickling me ferociously. I fought it, strangling it in my throat. I had to get used to this. Ukashin lifted his hand and the others watched him hungrily, as if he were going to ascend bodily through the ceiling. "The devis have brought to us a traveler," he said, gesturing toward me like a sultan in a ballet, "who has come to us after a long and hard journey."

They turned to me at last, these lovely faces that had purposely avoided meeting my eyes even at the simple meals I'd begun to take with them. "Welcome!" "Welcome, traveler." "Glad you've come." Their unpracticed smiles and the warmth of their greetings shocked me.

I certainly didn't want to become another string in their cosmic harp, yet it hadn't occurred to me how it would feel to be welcomed anywhere at this point. Except for Natalya, no one had done more than move over on a bench for me. Now they all seemed quite human, eager to accept a new member to their circle. I reminded myself that this was a ritual greeting, not just for me but for anybody anointed by their leader. But it felt personal. Whoever I was—boy, girl, pregnant or not—I was welcome to share their meager rations of bread and all the incense I could inhale.

"The Mother herself called this traveler," said Ukashin from his throne, where he sat with one leg tucked up underneath him, his skull gleaming in the candlelight. He looked into each face, making sure he had been understood. How reverently they returned his gaze, how solemnly, like little children being warned not to touch the stove. "Introduce yourselves."

He nodded at Helen of Troy. In a throaty, resonant alto, she replied, "Katrina. Ionian."

"And you?"

The lean, bony-faced boy who had brought the butchering materials. "Ilya. Ionian." He had a shockingly deep voice that would be an asset to any men's choir.

"We don't use patronymics or family names," Ukashin explained to me. "It's of no importance 'who' you were. Only 'what' you are. We will be your family now."

I tried to memorize the names. *Katrina. Ilya. Bogdan*—lithe, with the heroic eyebrows. *Lilya,* a nervous girl from the henhouse with a pointed nose. *Natalya. Gleb,* quiet, like a Swiss shepherd. *Anna,* a motherly brown-eyed blonde who ran the workroom. *Andrei,* the *intelligent. Pasha,* the adorable dark-bearded woodcutter. And *Magda,* the gypsy, who sat at the Master's right hand.

"And you? Who are you, traveler?" He indicated me, both hands pressed together like a spear.

Something in me was loath to say it. I was prepared to go along with their nonsense, to work hard, keep quiet, and not ridicule their faith or his authority, but why must there be one more persona, one more disguise of self? One more set of rules? If I wanted to join something, I would have joined the Bolshevik Party. Couldn't I just be Marina Marinovna Marinovskaya, daughter of myself? Or, like Odysseus, No Man?

The Master was waiting. I felt the force of his presence, the weight of his will, waiting, demanding that I submit, while I struggled with my own natural inclination ever to meet force with resistance. But I had to be realistic now. I was alone and pregnant and friendless.

I'd burned every bridge, cut every tie. Of what importance could this be, another name to add to my list? *Marusya, Misha, Kuriakina, Makarova* were no more representative of my essential self than *Ionian*. I was not a mother's or a father's or a husband's or a lover's or the man in the moon's. I belonged to the Future alone. However, if I was to live, it would be because I'd accepted a berth here. The dead are forever nameless, while the living have to declare themselves sooner or later. We have to be *this* and not that.

I cleared my voice and christened myself. "Marina. Ionian."

What weird ritual could possibly have been missing that night? We intoned syllables—*ho hee hu ha*—vocalizing on the in-breath as well as the out-breath. We gathered the breath in our arms, then flung it up into the sky as if flinging confetti, lowering our hands back to the earth as the small glowing scraps rained back down upon us. My head buzzed. Ukashin drummed on a wide flat drum, and we moved to his varying tempos like so many life-size marionettes. The *intelligent*, winded from his exertions, finally removed himself to sit at the piano at the back of the room and accompany our exercises with long staccato themes cribbed from Stravinsky.

Our gestures gradually became larger poses, with much use of flexed hands and feet. We began using one another's bodies as counterweights, like acrobats, leaning upon each other, balancing in strange postures. What joy! The boy with the heroic eyebrows, Bogdan, partnered me with a sureness that could only belong to a dancer. *That's why there were so many dancers at the Laboratory.* I stepped on his thigh and stretched out into space. He held me aloft, and I wished I could have stood on his hands. I could feel strength returning to my body, the energy I'd once had, which my recent life had sapped from me. Then the tempo changed, became more fluid. They stopped their balancing, and ringed the carpet, grasping hands, creating a perfect circle.

"Marina Ionian, come sit by me," Ukashin commanded.

Disappointed, I went and sat on the floor by his chair like a chastised child, as they reformed their circle. Suddenly they bowed their heads, chins on chests, arms at their sides, as if they had all gone to sleep or fallen under a spell. Then slowly they began to turn, their arms coming up along their bodies, crossing on their chests. They twirled faster, and their arms rose and spread, as if lighter than the surrounding air. Then one hand floated up, one hand sank down, and they spun, their heads tilted to the side, eyes closed, as if dreaming. How beautiful! Perfectly tuned. Yes, now I saw it.

After several minutes, the circle began to move, each person still spinning within the slow, stately procession. It reminded me of the motion of planets around an invisible sun. So synchronized was their spinning that they maintained their distances, their perfect circle, even while rotating around their own individual axes. I had no idea how they did it. Their eyes were closed!

"Don't watch," Ukashin said above me. *"Feel."*

I felt their energy like a gas or a liquid filling the room. Whatever they were doing with their bodies, they were creating something absolutely real. Ukashin put his hand on my shoulder, its warmth suffusing me. "Can you see yourself there?"

I nodded, despite my pledge not to believe in anything, not to be sucked in by this dark-eyed mystic with his bald head and his bull's neck.

"You have to stop throwing yourself into things," he said. "You must wait and enter properly. All your life, you've been like a wild animal who finds itself inside a house—a panicked horse, slipping and knocking into everything, disrupting the bric-a-brac." He smiled and squeezed my shoulder. "Likely to break a leg."

He was right. Such a familiar sensation, crashing into things, causing my own chaos. But tonight I sat, my legs tucked under me, and *felt*. I took in their beauty, their peace, their dreamlike engagement as around and around they went, let it enter me. I wanted it. It was as if the room had lifted from its moorings, had risen out of this world to enter another state altogether. I was embarrassed even to be thinking in such terms. That was for my mother and her spiritualist crowd—*another dimension*. But the longer I watched, the more strongly I felt energy rising inside me, up my spine, and lighting my mind like a lamp.

"Now tell me, what do you *feel*, Marina Ionian?" said Ukashin in a low voice.

The energy in the room was so strong that I found it hard to speak. "Peaceful. Awake."

"And what do you *see?*"

Such beauty. A glow filled the room, and it seemed so much brighter than it had been before they'd started spinning. To think something like this could happen in a place where we had once lain on couches reading Dickens. "Radiance."

"Very good. I think you'll be happy with us, Marina Ionian."

I imagined they could do this for days and never have to stop to eat or drink or sleep.

"One hand receives blessings from spirit. Information, order, energy. The other hand gives it to the earth. We're the link—that's what we were made for. We hold together the light and the dark. Material and immaterial. Thus the human."

But there was no darkness in this room, only light, and this feeling of rising.

"Religion makes the mistake of forswearing darkness, forswearing the body," he continued. "But to forswear darkness is the worst thing. That's inviting it to approach from the unguarded door and run rampant. We're going to see worse in these times than we've seen so far. Each side trying to hold the light exclusively will create its own darkness. We're lucky we came to this place."

Trying to hold the light exclusively...yes. I had lived with Varvara, with Father. I knew what people who had no doubts about their rightness could do. We had been ruled by tsars who believed that God himself had put the scepter into their hands, and look where that had gotten us. "But they call you Master. Don't you worry about that?"

A mischievous smile was only half disguised by his big moustache. "Oh, I can be as wrong as I can be right. I'm no saint. Darkness only becomes evil when it falls out of connection with the light." He gestured to the spinning acolytes, his hand like that of a sorcerer who had created these creatures out of the air. "What you see is the Process, the power that turns the universe. Think how the earth turns from dark to light to dark to light. If it was stopped, even by the triumph of the light, the world would end. Everything flying off into space, and then—gone. Brahma awakens from his dream."

Though I had sworn I would keep a certain distance, I could not help yearning to experience what I was seeing. To have found such pure beauty hidden in the midst of want and terror and material hopes, classes at war, the convulsions of a new nation—it was a miracle. It wouldn't be hard to believe that the Ionians were holding the world together themselves, and that this room was an energetic anchor that went all the way to the center of the earth.

I could only imagine how Varvara would explode if

she could hear me. *How does this produce more food to feed the people? How does this provide justice?* To her, these beautiful, glowing faces would be just a handful of delusional young throwbacks who should be working for the betterment of the nation — creating posters about public health, taking classes on Plekhanov and Marx. *How is spinning around going to solve the problems of the socialist republic?*

But I understood with startling binocular vision how it was both absolutely irrelevant, and yet in some strange way more relevant than the latest decision of Comrade Lenin and his Central Committee. I saw how, like poetry, the inner life was both more and less important than the clash of armies. Perhaps this was why I had come to Maryino, what had propelled me through the blizzard — the need to find a clearing in the greater blizzard. Just to feel myself alive, to *be*. And now that I had that little flame to consider, I didn't want to go careening about the country like a ricocheting bullet. Maybe I needed to know where I was on the very largest scale of things. So that I could become the still point for this creature spinning inside me.

75 *Dreams*

IF THE FRONT PARLOR served as their sacred Practice space, the back parlor housed everything else: workshop, art studio, dining room and, no doubt, medical center. Half-finished chairs teetered, basted patchwork clothes lay atop mountains of rags. A painting lurked under a spotted cloth, while amateurish clay bowls dried on a plank. The big room smelled of clay and raw wood, turpentine. As we sat down for breakfast at the long, raw pine table, the chair at its head stood empty. Even vacant, it vibrated with the Master's vitality, wafting his traces of clove and sandalwood. Natalya slid down on the bench for me, yawning, heavy-headed from sleep. I stepped over, steadying myself on her shoulder, slipping into the spot between her and Bogdan, my new friends. Outside the windows, the late winter dawn blued the sky. It was good to have friends again. I'd missed that.

"I brought something for you, Marina Ionian," said Andrei the *intelligent,* seated at the foot of the table. He passed two books up the table to me. He'd not spoken to me since warding me off from Mother's room, and now he brought gifts? They were the first books I'd seen here. One, small and fat, was bound in royal-blue cloth, the other, slender, was clad in worn burgundy calfskin. The disciples handed them to me with oddly guilty expressions. The first was called *The Structure of Reality* by A. A. Petrovin, the second was *The Evolution of Man* by N. D. Tomashevsky. I opened the first. Charts and diagrams, complex spirals and starlike radii punctuated thick unbroken paragraphs that went on for pages.

The *intelligent*'s blue eyes shone behind his spectacles. "It's the mathematical basis of Ionia. It lays out the structure of multidimensional reality."

The slightly humorous dismay on the faces of the other disciples reminded me of a classroom of children steeling themselves for a teacher's lecture on comportment. "Are you familiar with the term *déjà vu?* That peculiar feeling of familiarity, that you have been here before, that we have had exactly this conversation sometime in the past?" He pointed quickly to one of the Ionians. "Gleb scratching his head just so and the snow on the trees just in those same clumps. All of it so familiar. But where does this feeling come from? Such a common phenomenon, throughout all cultures, all time. But what is it? Is it a message from the Beyond?"

Avdokia staggered in bearing an enormous towel-wrapped crock, which she dropped onto the table with a bang. When she opened the lid, a grippingly nostalgic fragrance filled the room. Not quite déjà vu, but close. Oatmeal. While everyone else in Russia ate kasha, we Makarovs always ate oatmeal. It was the English tradition. If the English ate shaving cream with their bacon and eggs, we would have, too. My old nanny flashed me a semaphore of horror when she spotted me on the bench listening to the man's earnest explanations, the books at my elbow, wearing my patchwork *sarafan* and white head scarf. I could hear her thinking, *Holy Theotokos, protect us.* Her big nose and chin came together across the thin line of her lips. *Don't trust them an inch.* Flicked her eyes over to the gypsy. *Especially that one.*

But even Magda could not dampen my mood this morning, nor could this storky *intelligent.* The regularity of the group's routines and the intensity of the evening Practice made me feel better than I'd felt in a long time. The morning sickness had gone. I tried to pay attention to Andrei's lecture, to illustrate my dedication as a new Ionian, while bowls were passed and filled.

"Such things aren't mysteries," he said, his voice full of gravitas. "Or only insofar as we fail to understand their inherent structure." He pointed his spoon at me. "We understand that fevers aren't caused by demons. We know you don't get rid of them by waving dead cats over your head." He ate, and a bit of glutinous porridge appended itself to his bottom lip, where it wobbled precariously. It took everything I had not to stare at that lump of cereal rising and falling and instead gaze into his impassioned blue eyes behind his spectacles.

The others either ate in resigned silence or suppressed giggles, heads lowered to avoid catching his eye. Bogdan cast quick sympathetic glances toward me. Manipulating his long pianist's fingers, the schoolmaster went on to explain how the universe was constructed—as a series of folds, like a Japanese paper flower. "What appears to be a linear phenomenon, when seen from the next level up, is actually folded space-time." He certainly didn't make himself popular by monopolizing the conversation, but perhaps on the next level up he was scintillating. "So a phenomenon which appears to move from A to B to C can actually be A and B and C simultaneously. See?"

I nodded politely. I figured I could catch up when I read the books. But now he'd moved from paper flowers to soap bubbles collecting around a soap bubble inside a soap bubble. Interlocking spheres. "Everything is happening inside the same moment, or what appears to be a moment linearly, in this dimension. But there is no linear time in the dimensions above. So in déjà vu, you've accidentally jumped to the next level and glimpsed one of the infinite parallel realities. The question is how to prolong that instant, how to investigate it."

Suddenly the Ionians straightened from their slumped positions of polite boredom. The sleepiness in the air vanished. The Master had arrived.

They rose as one and waited until he had settled himself into his chair, a figure both formidable and whimsical in Russian blouse, shaggy vest, striped velvet trousers, and house slippers. All he lacked were bandoliers and a curved dagger at his belt. "Good morning, children. Has Dyadya Andrei donned his professor's hat?"

Laughter, so far suppressed, rushed out like wind through chimes. Andrei's lecture came to an abrupt end, his face gone pale.

"Such weighty matters, Andrei." Ukashin frowned,

though we could see he was teasing. There was a smile under his moustache. "Too much theory first thing in the morning. Less thinking, more dancing, eh?" He ran his hand over his gleaming head—he must have just shaved it—and gazed down the table directly at me. "Is life to be lived, do you think, Marina Ionian? Or contemplated, with the thumb in the mouth?" He reached out and shook the boy Ilya's shoulder. "You don't just read an opera score, do you? You sing!" The tall boy with his prominent Adam's apple grinned. I could feel the pleasure he took in being singled out.

"You don't admire a pattern for a coat, do you?" he asked brown-eyed Anna. "'Oh, what a lovely pattern. Look at that clever design!' No. You make the coat and go for a walk." Bestowing his smile on her. She absorbed his charm with an indulgent smile of her own, like a fond mother.

"But surely you must agree, Taras, that understanding must come first," interjected the gawky professor.

"Must I agree?" He watched the flaxen-haired goddess Katrina fill a bowl for him, set it before him. The glance that passed between them—so intimate…was there more here than I had suspected? I smelled sex in the air, though maybe I was just overly sensitive after Kolya's night with the village temptress. Natalya had told me that separate relationships between the community's men and women were strictly forbidden. But maybe the Master was the exception. "Katrina Ionian," he asked the blond girl, "what do you think?"

She just laughed. "I'd rather eat."

"Exactly," concluded the master, tucking into his breakfast. "We would all rather eat."

"But surely—" Andrei tried again.

"But surely—" Ukashin echoed him, his mouth full, imitating his disciple's fish-gulping-air expression, detonating another round of giggles as the *intelligent* sat trying to collect himself. Where did this unprovoked cruelty come from? Was it for my benefit, or did he always do it?

"But surely, what do we have if we don't have our reason, if we don't examine these things—" the *intelligent* spluttered.

"What do we have, Professor?" Ukashin prodded him. "No doubt you will tell us."

The poor man was on the verge of tears. "A travesty," he replied. "A puppet show."

Ukashin held out his arms, hands dangling at the wrists, and began to jerk like a puppet, his dark eyes wide and unfocused, as the other man sat, straight-backed and stone-faced. The success of the depiction seemed to encourage the Master. He rose and began to wheel about, unsteady on his feet, jumping and collapsing. He moved to my side to examine one of my new books with an expression both studious and ridiculous—quite a performance.

It shocked me, after the peace and beauty of our exercises, to see such heartlessness. The *intelligent* was a bore, true, but he didn't deserve to be belittled. How

Ukashin delighted in the man's humiliation, how deftly he turned the others against him. His advocacy for darkness along with the light was certainly in evidence. No one said a word in Andrei's defense. The *intelligent* rose, trembling, glancing from face to unsympathetic face. I put my hand on the books and smiled. *I'll read them.* He nodded, but that stricken expression was terrible to behold. He turned and left us to his tormentor.

Ukashin was in a fine mood after that, like a man who has just vandalized a shop and walks away with expensive goods in his arms. As he ate, he asked for people's dreams, as if nothing had happened. They were all eager to share. Bogdan dreamed of food—whitefish soup and caviar, asparagus with hollandaise. "Tonight don't forget to take some sacks with you and bring some back," Ukashin said. "We could use some caviar around here."

Anna had dreamed of sewing a shroud, but no one would tell her whom it was for. She was afraid. She didn't want to finish it. I tried not to interpret—it was awfully personal for Ukashin to ask everyone to share their dreams in a group. The woodcutter, Pasha, dreamed they were all back at the Laboratory and the Cheka was coming. Everyone stood against the walls and became the walls, so that when the Chekists broke in, the place was empty.

"Yes, we will learn to do this," said the Master. "People are fools. They look, but they don't *see*."

Gleb, the furniture maker, with his bland face and

colorless hair, shared a dream about a village girl he'd come across, washing clothes in the river. He watched her from the trees—her breasts, thinly clad in her slip, her skirts tucked up around her, her long hair covered with a kerchief. She saw him and called him to her, teasing him. It was excruciating to have to listen to him describe how this village girl had him make love to her there on the banks of the river. He blushed and stammered, but still he kept on talking. It was agonizing to watch.

"Is she here?" Ukashin asked.

Gleb nodded, swallowed.

"Who was it?"

"K-K-Katrina Ionian."

Katrina listened, barely flinching, keeping her head cocked slightly to one side, as if she were listening to a tram driver call out stops, and none of the stops was hers. But down the table, Pasha's eyes flashed, and his lips turned down within the nest of his dark beard. Such intrigue! It seemed that the ban on sex could not quite eradicate the passions in young healthy people. Ukashin gazed at Gleb from under his emphatic eyebrows. "Yes." He nodded as if this were important information. "I see." As if he were unaware of the havoc he was stirring up. That devil. "We'll do something with that."

The night before, I'd dreamed I was a fox in autumn, the forest swirling with falling leaves. Ukashin's dogs were hunting me—they'd picked up my scent. I'd doubled back along branches and crawled under logs, every trick I had, but I was getting tired. I wasn't going to make it. He would get me one way or another. I certainly wasn't going to turn a dream like that over to this fakir. But my face must have revealed my resistance, for he turned to me immediately. "And what did you dream, Marina Ionian?"

I shrugged, laughed apologetically—*stupid, useless me*—glancing around the table. "Sorry—I'm a heavy sleeper. I never remember them."

He gave an exasperated sigh. His broad shoulders sagged with disappointment, but I suspected that, too, was an act.

"I wish I did remember. I envy all of you, having these nightly adventures."

He leveled onto me the force of his gaze, that heavy bull's face with the plum-dark eyes, but in turn I became a lump of clay. All he could do was harden me. He moved on to more pliable targets. Magda, the gypsy, leaped to share. In her dream, an enormous black horse flew into the window of the women's dormitory while the rest of us slept. It took her on its back, and they flew out over deserted villages and empty fields. "The world had ended," she said. "Everybody was gone, it was just me and the horse and all the land."

You didn't have to be an alienist to understand what that was about. Ukashin nodded as she spoke, but he was watching me, fingering his broad moustache.

*   *   *

Ukashin choreographed dances and exercises around our dreams. I actually felt a little left out, but I continued being unable to remember. The less he knew about what transpired in my psychic life, the better. Especially because he often figured in my dream life, and the way he did had to be kept absolutely to myself. The whole place was awash in repressed sexuality. But all romance had to be focused on Ionia as a whole—and especially on our admiration for and fascination with our charismatic Master. Andrei continued to improvise mystical compositions at the piano, while Ukashin took care to compliment him, at least for a while. During the Practice, they achieved some sort of rapprochement that nevertheless failed to prevent periodic jibes and mockery during the daytime hours.

One night we entered Magda's dream of the flying horse, imagining riding the terrifying beast out the windows on a star-filled night, carried by the Master's rumbling, rich voice, which became the horse, racing and plunging. What a feeling—the huge glossy horse beneath me, icy wind in my ears. What ecstasy to ride thus, over the sleeping world.

"No, not sleeping, my children," the Master told us. "Deserted. The snowy fields have returned to rest. The roofs in the villages—fallen in. No lights, no hearth fires. We fly for how long? A year, a moment, eternity? From now on, this is how it will be, just you and the horse and the wind. You are the master, a god, but absolutely alone. The world has ended, but you were spared because you were airborne. You're now past the end of the world. There are only the other dimensions now." Achingly alone, all but for the diabolical horse.

It felt just as it had when Seryozha died. All gone. Mother, Father, Volodya, Kolya. There was no one. The terror of that, the searing grief. But one small thought glimmered, like one small star. The baby. I would not be the only one who survived the end of the world. The horse plunged on while the flame rocked in the lantern.

Afterward, when I was leaving with the others to ascend to the dormitory, Magda stopped me on the stairs. "He wants to see you. Wait in his *kabinyet*." His office. Her nostrils flared with jealousy, her flashing eyes reduced to suspicious half-moons.

I imagined it was a privilege to be called by the Master to his *kabinyet* in the middle of the night, but I would have traded places with her in a second. His was the room at the head of the stairs that had once been Grandfather's study. I knocked, but no one replied. He must still be with the others. I saw that Mother's door lay unguarded—maybe I could slip across. But no—Magda lingered on the stairs, watching. Always someone watching. One couldn't take a breath that wasn't measured and reported. When would I see her? I wanted to tell her about her grandchild, about Kolya and Petrograd, and find out for myself if she was a captive or a voluntary recluse.

Now, under the scrutiny of glowering Magda, I had no choice but enter Ukashin's study. Inside, his two smelly dogs lifted their heads, but they went back to sleep on the carpets that completely obscured the room's wide floorboards, as if it were a Turkish seraglio. A portable campaign desk rested where Grandfather's huge pigeonhole desk had always stood. It must have been something when the peasants claimed it. I hoped they all got hernias trying to carry it down the stairs. He used to let me open its myriad small drawers, each holding a different wonder: medals, postcards, pastilles for us children. Matchboxes, receipts, and letters. The desk had a secret drawer that looked just like all the others, but it was really only half as deep. Behind it lay a concealed second drawer that held just one lock of hair, a dusty dark brown tied in a thin, sea-green satin ribbon. It had been given to him by the great Swedish soprano Jenny Lind. He would hold it and sing quietly her famous "Casta diva" from *Norma*.

In its stead, the campaign desk seemed provisional, its edges studded with cigarette burns, its surface filled with mystic clutter—statuettes of Buddhas and fat goddesses, a curved letter opener with an Egyptian god on the handle.

Amazingly, in their cases above the windows, Grandfather's books had survived the expropriation. I ran my hands along the beautiful gilded spines, pulled down his copy of *War and Peace*. I kissed its binding as if it were Dyedushka's own soft, wrinkled face, still hearing *Norma* in my head. Dyedushka and Tolstoy, born the same year. I imagined them together in a garden somewhere, in the shade of green trees, talking and drinking tea. That whole generation, gone. Now my parents' fading away, too, and soon, mine. All the children, going down before the scythe like waves of corn. Though Andrei would say it only appeared to be so from the limited viewpoint of life in the third dimension. As if that could make me feel any better. What did it matter what this life looked like from higher dimensions? We humans were stuck to this one like flies in sorghum.

Yet there was still this. I sat at the Master's desk and turned the thin, handsome pages of the thick book. It was all here—memory, the Russian language, Tolstoy's art—connecting us all, me and Grandfather and Mother and my child to come. The glory of this life, the earthy third level.

The dogs stirred, and then large warm hands enveloped my head on either side, so firmly that I could not jump. The carpets had silenced his footsteps, so I hadn't heard him come in. I could see him in the window's reflection, the bulk of him, his shiny shaved head, the wide moustache standing away from his face. "What's in this head of yours, Marina Ionian, I wonder?" he murmured, low but clear. "If we peeled all this away, what would we find?"

"Mattress stuffing," I replied. The suggestion of any-one peeling my flesh made me shudder.

"Haven't I given you what you wanted, what you needed?" he said quietly into my ear. "Family, shelter, a place to rest?" I could feel his voice in my bones, though he touched me only with his hands. He could crush my skull like an egg. His hands smelled of clove and incense and a bit of dog.

I tried not to struggle or show any panic. I would remain as composed as my mother, my grand-mother.

"You swore you wanted to join us. You declared yourself Ionian. But you insist on holding yourself apart." I started to protest but he stopped me before the first denial escaped my lips. "Don't. I'm stating a fact, not entering into a dialogue."

Yes, it was a fact. He dropped his hands and I corkscrewed my neck, as if he'd had me in a headlock. This room was too small for the two of us. I felt as though I were inside a boxing ring.

"What am I to do with you?" He moved away. "If it wasn't for the child, I would send you out to sleep with the chickens." He leaned over to pet his dog.

I rose, carefully, on the pretext of putting the book away. "I'm tired—do you mind? I'd like to go to bed now. Was that what you wanted to tell me?"

"The thing is, what will you tell me?" He turned around, and the way he searched my face, I felt like a horse, a dog—my eyes unable to meet his. "Who are you, Marina? Why have you come to us? What do you want from us?"

I forced myself to return his gaze. His bulging eyes glistened like polished stone, so dark I couldn't differentiate the pupil from the iris. "It's no mystery. I came home and you were here. That's all." I tried not to swallow, but the tightness in my throat commanded it. "I don't want anything. Just to get along." If only he would let me talk to my mother.

He collapsed into his desk chair, rubbed the top of his bald head again as if to clear his thoughts. "I like you, Marina. You keep me awake, like a faceful of cold water. Maybe that's why you came—to be the pebble in my shoe." He kept staring at me. "But I forgot. You're so tired. Lie down and rest." He gestured, open-palmed, to the carpeted corner farthest from the windows, where a pallet lay covered with a sheepskin. "Go ahead. You're exhausted. You can hardly keep your eyes open."

And suddenly I was exhausted. And that pallet looked so welcoming, with fluffy curls of the sheepskin, after the long day, the late night, the emotional strain. Or was it a hypnotist's trick? A lecher's ruse? "Is this a proposition?"

He picked up one of his little statuettes. "Don't make assumptions. Sleep, Marina."

Waves of drowsiness crashed over me. "This isn't really necessary," I said, trying to stave off my exhaustion. "You don't have to go through all this. I'm obviously not a virgin." I slipped off my felted footgear and climbed in under the sheepskin, fully clothed. Ah, it was so soft, so warm...

"Sleep. We'll talk in the morning." He turned on the desk lamp, pulled down a volume from Grandfather's library, and began to read.

I tried to stay awake, concentrating on the hardness of the floor through the mat, the same floor where I'd played when Grandfather wrote his letters. *Casta diva, che inargenti*...Running my fingers through the long, shaggy tufts of the sheepskin, lamplight flickering. My boat soon drifted from the dock.

I dreamed I was back in Petrograd. I had my son with me. My son! We were on Grivtsova Alley. He was a beautiful child, a solemn little boy with eyes like black olives, about seven years old. And there was something I had to do—deliver a book, a very important book. The child had to come with me, I couldn't leave him. So I tucked the book under my arm, got the boy into a jacket that was too big for him—Genya's?—and wrapped my old scarf around my head.

How poor the city was now. Dark and broken in the moonlight, the pavement half submerged, water everywhere. I was sad that my son had to see it this way. He would never know what it had been like when it was the imperial capital. But the book was the thing, something momentous about it, utterly precious. And I was the only one who could deliver it. People had died for this book. It was up to me to preserve it.

I walked as fast as I could holding my son by the hand. His legs were so short, he stumbled as we dodged piles of soggy furniture, signs, clocks, trams lying on their sides. As we turned a corner, I sensed we were being pursued, and I caught just a glimpse of a face under a broad-brimmed hat before it melted into the shadows.

We took shelter on the portico of Kazan Cathedral with its forest of columns, the church in ruins now, and I saw that it was not a man at all who pursued us but a wolf. A white wolf with pale eyes. I ran across Nevsky, pulling the child, splashing into the first lit store, the old Granitsky flower shop. I bolted the door, doused the lights. My poor little boy was soaked to the bone. What if he caught a chill? There were no doctors anymore—it would be entirely my fault. I held him under my coat to warm him. All around us, the unearthly scent of the hothouse flowers. The quarrelsome shopgirl said there was a customer at the door. *Don't open the door!* I screamed.

Strong hands shook me, pulling me from the dream like a child from the womb, still surrounded by the scent of cold flowers. "Marina. Wake up."

I fought to sleep's surface.

"Tell me. If you tell me, you'll never have this dream again. I swear."

So I told him. The boy, the church, the wolf.

76 *Krasniy, Krasiviy, Krov'*

A RASHY DAWN ALREADY filled the windows when I woke again to find Ukashin still in his folding chair, writing in a notebook at his portable desk. Had he been awake all night? His dogs lay curled up with me, their rough hair so much like the sheepskin's long tufts that I'd been unable to tell the difference. They sighed and stretched as I propped myself on my elbow.

He turned, leaning back in his seat, regarding me with his pen in hand. "How do you feel, Marina Ionian?"

I nodded. I'd slept quite well, as he had said I would. Gone was the ruined city, the broken church, the wolf, the man in the hat. The water, the boy in Genya's coat. "Fair. And you?"

How smug he looked. Delighted, as if we'd made the most wonderful love. But it wasn't my body he'd wanted at all. It was the thing I'd withheld from him—my dreams. He had me sleep in his study so he could seize what he wanted like a little bird rising from the wheat. Well, now he had it. What would he give me in exchange? Safety? Could he repair the city? Could he bring the wolf to heel? He closed the book he'd been reading. "I've been meditating on you. Your situation. Your *Trud*."

The word meant "work," "labor," but here the sense

was deeper. *Trud*, I knew, accelerated your spiritual development in some way very personal to each individual. Each acolyte at Ionia had his or her own *Trud*—couturier, chef, carpenter, chemist, teacher. I was the sole exception. I'd been waiting for my assignment, but I hadn't realized that it would depend upon my dreams. But of course. First you had to give him a window into your soul. Then the *Trud* would conform to the landscape of your psyche. I couldn't help but be intrigued. What would he give me? What did he see my soul lacking? He lit one of his disgusting cigarettes, crossed his legs, and gazed out at the day, presumably at the disciples clearing paths, before regarding me with the full attention of those dark eyes. I waited for my morning nausea, but it didn't come.

"You," he announced, "shall be our hunter."

Krasniy, red. *Krasiviy*, beautiful. *Krov'*, blood. Nothing exists without blood. Before the red of politics, before the red of art, blood was the first red, primeval. It was to be my trade.

My first assignment was to strip the parlor of its telephone wire. My father's precious telephone. How upset he would be to see me pulling it out, his necessary connection to the modern world. It had taken him years to have that line put in. Whenever he was in residence, the telephone saw more of him than we did. Strangely appropriate that my first labor required me to remove it. We were oddly progressing into a timeless past, and that long-ago future world of telephones and automobiles could not have imagined this one, with hand-dipped candles and homemade furniture.

Outside, the day had dropped its garments of mist and cleared to a brilliance we rarely saw at Christmastime, the sky a Byzantine blue, crushed lapis. From the workroom, I could see Ukashin's dogs race across the sparkling snow. I envied those who'd gone out to work clearing paths, cutting wood, even tending the henhouse. After I'd pulled the wire, Ukashin had me sit at the plank table in the workroom and laboriously strip the rubber casing from the copper. My hands bled. Alongside me, Gleb the woodworker planed a birch log, and Anna the couturier sang softly while she quilted rags onto a backing. In the corner, Bogdan heated something on the primus stove—glue?—and the stink of it threatened to reengage my morning sickness. Except for Anna's lovely voice, we worked in silence.

But they all watched enviously when the Master sat next to me on the bench and cut off a length of wire with his pocketknife. "Observe, Marina Ionian." He transformed his hand into a sniffing animal, its finger-snout testing the air. "Citizen Rabbit, on a brisk winter day." The rabbit, sniffing, finally stuck its head into the wire loop he'd fashioned. "*Okh!* Too bad." Ukashin pulled the loose end, and the noose closed around his wrist. "Unlucky rabbit. Unlucky for him, but for us—rabbit stew. Thank you, Good Citizen."

He loosened the loop from his arm and placed it before me on the table. The others studied it with intense interest. Anything the Master did or said was a subject of utter fascination to them. "You have some string, some cord?" he asked Anna, who immediately produced a length of rough cord from a shelf nearby. She handed it to him on both palms, as she would have handed over her own dress or her firstborn child if he had wanted it. She had woven it herself out of some kind of plant fiber.

He tied the copper telephone-wire loop onto the cord, kinking the wire to keep it in the knot, then waved the trap in front of my face. "Come, let's try it out on some real rabbits." Rising, he put his warm hand on my shoulder. I felt the others' longing for just such a touch.

The kitchen windows had steamed over, the air dense with the fragrance of cabbage soup. Katrina and Avdokia glanced up from their work—the one curious, the other alarmed to see me in the company of the Master. On the closed porch, Ukashin donned his greatcoat and astrakhan hat, and I put on my coat, which had been returned to me, smoked clean. With a flourish, he reached inside his own coat and produced my gun, handed it to me. And I understood that in sharing my dream, I had passed a test. Returning my revolver was a mark of his faith in me. I bundled myself into scarf and mittens, and Ukashin handed me a pair of ancient snowshoes. They must have been lurking in the attic for decades, for we never came to Maryino in wintertime. They'd been fitted out with new lacings—perhaps from the deer I had killed.

"Doubles?" I asked, showing my backhand.

He chuckled. I was glad he appreciated my sense of humor—nobody else around here had much of one. The dogs barked and jumped on us as we walked out into the sparkling white of the hard frost. He stopped on the steps and lashed my feet into the snowshoes, then applied a set of larger, newer ones constructed from bent willow, bast, and deer hide to his own felted boots. With these items secure, we stepped out onto the crusted snow, shadowed blue, pink, lilac, and green—and headed toward the glittering lindens at the estate's entrance.

It was extremely cold and clear, windless, dazzling. What a day! Ukashin took off across the pristine meadow at the same speed with which he would have walked across a room, but I straggled behind him, gasping for breath. There were skis on the porch, and I wondered why I couldn't have used them. But he hadn't given me time to suggest it, and now he was too far ahead.

Finally, he stopped. "Today you are the rabbit." He gestured all around us. "Where are you hiding, Citizen?"

I interrogated the sparkling meadow, the depth of the dark pines, the allée of big lindens with their smoky cloud of bare branches, the dense copse of aspens, the smudge of undergrowth at its verge, bilberry and blackberry and little firs. I pointed to where the under-growth was thickest, among the red willow twigs and blackberry bushes. "There."

His heavy face nodded once under his astrakhan hat. *"Molodets." Excellent.* "Citizen Rabbit can't afford to be caught in the open. He wants to be in the deep un-derbrush, where Chairman Wolf and Commissar Fox can't follow him. Come." We approached the aspens and began skirting the wood, the edges where trees had once been cut and berry bushes flourished. He pointed to a thin trail of trampled snow. I would have missed it, but Ukashin's keen eyes missed nothing. I clearly had a long way to go if I was to be a hunter in any-thing but his imagination. He squatted on his haunches and parted the brush like opening a book. A tunnel, a tiny trail in the snow. He pointed to a long double foot-print and a small one. A rabbit, bounding — I could see it. "Now find the narrowest part of this trail." I hung back. It looked impassable to me. "Go on."

I fought my way through the twigs and low branches that caught at my sheepskin, my scarf, my face. But sure enough, the tunnel narrowed further in a U of snow between two close trees. "Over here," I called out.

Silently he followed me in. We squatted on our haunches, low, reading the trail, but my legs weren't as strong as his. They wobbled, they burned.

"Citizen Rabbit, how tall are you?" He positioned the loop of wire a foot in the air. "Like this?" He had such a knack for creating fun, excitement out of the most ordinary thing. Without that talent, he never could have kept his little band of followers as enthralled as we were. Little wonder the others envied me, able to spend this kind of time with him all by myself.

I lowered his hand six inches.

"Now find a branch. Maybe a sapling, like this." He formed a gap about an inch in diameter with his ungloved thumb and forefinger. "Take the saw." He handed me the hacksaw from the workroom.

I found an aspen sapling that would serve us.

"Cut it at an angle."

After I'd done it, almost cutting my hand in the process, he lashed it with some of the cord Anna had given us, then jammed the sharpened end into the snow. I watched him tie off the knot, trying to see how he did it, but my nose was running unstoppably, and my head ached. It was so cold I could barely focus. He took twigs and used them to steady the snare over the little trail. "That's one. You find the next one."

We circled around the back of those bushes, deeper into the wood, and where small firs had begun to grow among the thousand-headed aspen, I found another rabbit trail. I'd never noticed them before, much trampled among the twigs and trees, exactly the kind of terrain one avoided when walking in a forest. "Mouse," he said, and pointed. Tiny splayed toes and the line of a tail in the snow. "Weasel"—five-toed prints, wider than they were long. "Deer are like hearts in the snow," he said. "Get us another deer, Marina, and you'll be queen of Ionia."

He knew so many things. So unlike Father, who knew how to be witty and withering and give speeches after dinner. Ukashin was more interested in the how of things than the why. This world was not a mystery to him, not a disappointing thing to be transcended, as it was to my mother and Andrei. I could well believe that he'd spent years traveling in the remotest areas of the world, learning the skills of the simple people as well as studying with their holy men. He liked secrets of all kinds. As did I.

He showed me another kind of trap, which used a notched stick and a sapling's natural spring. When an animal was snared, as he demonstrated, the stick fell away and the tree sprang upward, carrying the trapped animal with it, breaking its neck. "Now you do it." He had me set the trap, and I laughed with the glee of a small child as it sprang free. "You'll do well, Marina."

It had been so long since I'd done anything right, I felt like the sun had come out. Perhaps this — Ionia, my *Trud* — would work out after all.

Without Ukashin, trapping day after day was not so much fun. But I stuck to it and I learned. My bare hands bungled the knots when I attempted to tie them gloveless in the cold, so I learned to tie my nooses ahead of time and carry the prepared traps with me in my game bag. I immediately added Misha's trousers under my skirts and his shirt under my linen blouse for extra warmth, and borrowed a quilted hat to wear under my scarf. Warmer, I could stay out for hours learning my territory, discovering game trails, sketching unfamiliar tracks, and generally *feeling* my way into my new role. I sat with Ukashin at breakfast as he identified the animal tracks I'd seen. Snowshoe-shaped marks—squirrel. Pine marten with its delicate toes. Fox—doglike but smaller than his hairy hounds. "If you see Commissar Fox," he said, "you have my permission to waste a bullet."

My first successes brought me the respect of my fellow Ionians. Yet it took a while to get used to seeing the dead in traps, stiff and miserable-looking creatures resembling executed prisoners hanging from gallows—their blank eyes, their curled front legs. *Tried and found guilty of counterrevolution and speculation. The sentence, death.*

I skinned them quickly, trying not to notice just how much they looked like newborn infants as I pulled them from their pelts, the naked wet torsos delivered from bloody fur. I had to remember how sweet the meat would taste. The baby inside me cried out for it. Life and death, *krasniy, krasiviy, krov'*. I brought the pelts to Bogdan, whom the Master had taught to tan them. Soon squirrel and rabbit-fur collars, earmuffs, and mittens appeared in the Ionian wardrobe. These small deaths warmed us in countless ways.

The longer I worked outside, the better I liked it and

the less the cold bothered me. I was becoming a harder woman than I'd been—a paradox, as motherhood to me had always implied a fleshy and vulnerable femininity. And I was becoming acquainted with Maryino in an entirely new way, these familiar woods and meadows in their winter disguise. The silence refreshed me after the hothouse currents of workroom and dormitory, the secret enmities and collusions, the spying and the dramas. Here, despite the cold and the physical demands, I could find the peace and privacy I craved.

One day as I returned to the house after making my rounds, I glimpsed a flash of red against the white. The fox! Traveling merrily across the crusty drifts, probably returning from sniffing around our henhouse. It stopped for a moment and regarded me conspiratorially before trotting away on its fine black legs. I felt such a rush of pleasure, watching it pad along the hard-packed snow. It was only after it was gone that I remembered Ukashin telling me to waste a bullet if I saw it.

Normally I didn't let myself think about Kolya. I pushed him away from my consciousness like pushing an unwanted guest out the door. Yet why didn't I shoot the fox? I thrilled at the sight of the clever red creature, so much like Kolya himself that it made me laugh. Cocking a snook at me in my prehistoric snowshoes, my patchwork and sheepskin and rabbit-fur mitts. I remembered Kolya breezing through the kitchen, grabbing one of Annoushka's fresh sweet rolls on the run, and when she protested, holding it in his mouth and growling at her. Or dreaming away in a hammock, smoking one of Father's pipes. The creature reminded me of Kolya, and I loved it as I loved that impossible man. I knew then that I would never be free of him. This fox would be my secret. Although I was happy enough with Ionia, to have a place among them—and a place to get away from them—still one needed one's secrets or one could hardly be called human.

The weather grew foggy, and gloom set in— monotonous, melancholy weather. Christmas came and went without mention. The Master, like all true revolutionaries, had a calendar of his own, complete with events we could look forward to. We celebrated a Day of the Earth Devi and a Fast of Jericho. There were new dances to learn and long mystical hours when Ukashin led us to higher levels of existence, full of transparent fiery beings.

But the child was a clock in my body whose face I could not see. I needed to know the date. I kept my own calendar in my notebook, playing with the dates in brief poems. The word at the end of the second line gave me the month, and the one at the end of the last line was the day. *Dekabr'*, December: deliver, decide, derail, detail; *Yanvar'*, January—yearn, yeast, year. For the numerals—*odin, dva, tree, chetiri, piat'*: ordinary, drainpipe, tyranny, chinstrap, poultry. For the teens and twenties, two words. Fourteen, *chetirnadsat'*: constant nullity, clever notion. Twenty-two, *dvadsat'-dva*: devil's deal. Dying day. I wrote a poem in honor of each passing day. Poets are the spies of the world, and every poem is a code.

The year 1919 arrived without fanfare. No wax to be cast, no wishes made, no tangos. I looked back at the snow-wrapped house like gingerbread covered in white icing, nestled in its yard among the new outbuildings, and thought of that St. Basil's Eve so long ago, the smell of pine and goose and winter lilacs, Après l'Ondée and kisses among the snow-perfumed furs. Only three years ago—had a person ever changed as much as I had? Or a country?

I had no idea whether Admiral Kolchak had broken through the Urals or what had become of the Ukraine or what was happening with the Volunteers under Denikin. Was Red Russia completely surrounded? Had we surrendered? Were the English in Petrograd? Out here, who would have told us? If what the Ionians believed was true, Mother would know. But if she hadn't wanted to know these things when she lived in Petrograd, why would she pay attention now? How I itched to broach that door with its five inset panels. I tried to manage it periodically, even now, but one couldn't be more closely observed if one were an invalid's goldfish. And I was lucky to be here, lucky for the respite from the world's convulsions. If I could make it to July, I'd have a baby to bring home to Kolya, or I could travel elsewhere, I could make up my mind, or perhaps the world would make up my mind for me.

In February, I turned nineteen. Only Avdokia knew—and conceivably Mother, though she'd made no effort to contact me. Avdokia, my angel, my savior, continued to take care of me, even more so once she learned about the baby. There was always more in my bowl at dinnertime than was strictly my share. The meat on my tongue, warm and necessary, was the product of my own dark handiwork. What a drive for life lay inside all this killing, feeding the life growing inside me. Though the whole program of Ionia was intended to quiet the body, my own was becoming more greedy, more desirous. There were times I thought I'd go mad with desire, for Bogdan, or Pasha. Even Ukashin started to look appealing. I almost succeeded in inveigling Bogdan down to the Practice hall in the middle of the night, full of energy from our evening's exertions. But in the end he wouldn't. He leaned against the wall, his fingers stroking a thick eyebrow. "Try to understand, Marina. It's not the Laboratory anymore. Only us, you understand?" He left me there with my frustration like a pot of soup boiling over, the smell of scorch following me around in the air.

I missed Kolya, growling with a sweet roll in his teeth.

The suffocating closeness made me want to flee or start a fistfight. You could die from a thousand tiny cuts: hurt feelings, revenge, petty jealousy, jostling for favor. Who sat closer to Ukashin at dinner, whose dreams were chosen for a dance and whose overlooked. Whose question was considered seriously and whose mocked. You never knew. The safest thing was to lie low and not care too much. He liked keeping everyone guessing. Natalya was up, Katrina was down, Magda always on the lookout for a moment to attack. Bogdan the favorite, then it was Gleb.

I began taking refuge in the bathhouse after my trapping was done, to pass a private hour writing, dreaming, and just staying out of the house as much as I could. Natalya, mistress of the bathhouse, took to leaving small bundles of wood for me by the anteroom stove. These winter poems captured my sense of the life going on within the seemingly silent frozen landscape and the hidden life of the human heart. I wrote a poem about the animals in their dens, dreaming of their vague and shifting memories of spring. Only when the sun had lowered almost to setting did I venture home with a rabbit or two in my game bag and a new poem in my book.

It was when I was coming back in the sifting white of the afternoon after one such session that I again caught a glimpse of red through the trees. I hadn't seen my ruddy friend for some time, and the sight cheered me more than a hundred rabbits. I marveled at how close he was letting me come, as if he was waiting for me. I left the path to edge even closer. Then I realized—he was too still. *Bozhe moi,* he had walked into one of my snares. One of my earliest traps, which I never checked anymore because it was so close to the house. Suspended in the little trap, all four legs on the ground, was one long frozen board of Reynard, his black nose lowered in shame. This clever fellow, caught in a snare just large enough for his head. I could see how he'd worn his neck hair bare trying to free himself from the wire, spinning around and around, trying to attack his enemy but unable to fight, unable to flee.

I knelt next to him, tears freezing to my face, stroking his pretty coat. "What were you doing here? This wasn't for you." The misery on that pointy face devastated me. Ukashin said that a fox could smell a mouse under three feet of snow, that he could run along the tops of logs and sniff out every danger, using his bushy tail to brush away his own scent. He wasn't supposed to die! He was supposed to live and laugh at all of us as he stole our hens away.

The snow came down harder as I opened the noose, sliding my knife down the wire, freeing the fox. He was horribly light for his size, so thin, nothing but bone and fur. Nothing edible. His death was for nothing, taking that bit of light and joy from the world.

I returned to the house, threw my sad harvest of rabbit, hare, and fox onto the kitchen table, and though it was forbidden, went into Avdokia's room, where I lay down on her bed, coat and all, and buried my nose in her quilt, inhaling her smell of yeast.

Magda eventually found me and shoved me out into the kitchen. Katrina Ionian stirred something on the stove, reluctant to witness our warden manhandling me. If I had not gotten my feet under me, surely she would have dragged me in by my hair. The furry pile of dead animals was right where I'd left it, the rabbits and the fox, waiting for me to skin them and cut them up. "You think you're better than us? That you deserve special favors because you're the Mother's daughter? I *see* you." She pointed at her eye and then at me in a strangely menacing gesture, as if she would cast a spell on me. "Now get to work."

I picked up my knife and turned dully to my kill.

I skinned the hare and pulled it from its coat, still a moment that disgusted me. Opened its belly and pulled out the entrails, cut off its head, cut it into sections. The rabbit was smaller and, even worse, more infantlike as I drew it out of its skin. The fox lolled on the other side of the table, all the joy and mischief gone—from me as well. This wasn't a prize, this *Trud*. I was the hangman, whom everyone respected but no one wanted to invite to the christening. I started to gut the rabbit only to discover a clutch of babies in its womb. I felt sick. I set down the knife, wiped my hands on a dishcloth, put on someone else's quilted hat, and went back out into the snow.

I leaned against the house, taking great breaths of cold air in the twilight, shivering in jags, but I could not force myself to go back inside. That fox had been a messenger for me. I felt the noose around my own neck, the wire cutting into me. If I had been trying to ignore the message, the rabbit was the confirmation. What was I going to do?

The porch door opened. Footsteps on the stairs. A dirty dog jumping on me. I kneed the beast aside. "Marina," the Master said. "You can't stay out here forever."

"I can't do this anymore. Ilya wants to do the hunting. Give it to him."

"Let's go inside," he said.

I was shivering, but I would not go back in.

A patient hunter himself, he lit one of his cigarettes and smoked it, threw a stick for his dogs. When he was done smoking, he took my elbow. I didn't want to but it was too cold to resist. I let him lead me back into the house, into the warm kitchen. The hare was gone, the half-butchered rabbit. Either he or Katrina had finished my work for me. Only the fox remained. The girls had vanished, though the pot of borscht on the stove was fragrantly bubbling.

If I stayed here, I would end up as dead as that fox. That's what it was telling me. As dead as the rabbits. If not in body, then in spirit. Gutted. The snare hadn't been built for me, yet I was already caught in it. I *saw*.

The Master ran his fingers along the guard hair of

the fox's red tail—my secret rebel—its tragic pointed nose. He picked up the animal and draped it over my shoulder, the way a man gives a woman a fur scarf, placing it on her neck to see the color against her face.

"Please don't," I said, turning away.

"You are the hunter, Marina. This is your *Trud*. I didn't make this up. It came to you in a dream. It's for your good, not ours."

I trembled, the way a horse shudders to rid itself of a fly. I wished he would take the fox off me. "Why? Ilya wants to do it. You took it away from him. Give it back to him."

"But you are the one who is hunted. You must become the hunter," he said, stroking the dead creature lying on my shoulder. "You must think like a hunter, Marina. Lie in wait, read the tracks. Notice where the trail narrows, when you're being led to the noose." He took the fox off my body, held it out to me. "You pity this fox? He was not supposed to die—is that what you think? But he was a greedy, foolish thing. He wasn't paying attention. A ridiculous little person."

Yes. Careless, ridiculous, greedy. And so easily— dead.

"He dropped his guard. But you must not follow suit." Ukashin took my bloody hand in his. He studied my face, his dark eyes urgent. "You are the hunter, Marina Ionian. Say it."

My mouth was so dry. "I am the hunter." The fox thought it was clever, but it had been foolish and had paid the price. I could not fall prey to my own vanity. I must not think myself too clever. That was a fox's snare, its downfall. Maybe Ukashin's, too. "Again." His dark eyes very serious. "Say it."

"I am the hunter." I could feel my trembling ebb. He laid his arm across my shoulder, let his strength flood into me. I bent my head, leaning on my hands against the table. Either I was the hunter or I was the prey. There was no third option.

77 *The Feast of the Golden Egg*

IN LATE FEBRUARY, UKASHIN announced the Great Feast of the Golden Egg, to celebrate the birth of the fifth world. We'd had fasts before, but a feast? Now? We had months to go before we could plant anything, and months after that before reaping. Did we really have the larder for it? The idea reminded me of the story about a legendary city in the mountains of Georgia under siege by the Tatars. Desperate, almost out of food, the citizens decide to gorge themselves with their very last stores in clear view of the enemy. It broke the siege, the Tatars figuring that it was pointless to besiege a city with unlimited resources. Perhaps this was Ukashin's way of reassuring us that there would always be bounty — if we only believed.

I asked Natalya if she really thought we had enough food for a feast. "Master says worry creates a field which itself pushes away that which you desire. If we all stay in harmony across the dimensions, there will always be enough. Someday he's going to teach us how to absorb energy right through the skin, like the trees and the grass do. There are masters in Tibet who taught it to him."

So they believed, and there was no quarreling with it.

And how could I help falling into the spirit of the Great Feast of the Golden Egg along with the others? First we threw ourselves into a frenzy of cleaning—washed all the clothes, scrubbed the house from the doorstep to the bathroom ceiling, mucked out the workroom, aired the bedding, swept the floors, beat the rugs, cleaned the windows. We were two weeks in preparing, and I think that was the point, to give us something to look forward to, something to focus on, something besides the length of the winter and the scantiness of our means, the frustration caused by Ukashin's prohibition on "special friendships" within the blissful collective.

"Marina Ionian." Ukashin stopped me on the porch as I was putting my gear on to check my traps. "I'd appreciate your composing some verses for the holiday. Everyone's making an offering, and I would like this to be yours."

I thought of those young Communists in the canteen at Smolny, creating slogans for public health propaganda posters. So now I was to do agitprop for the Golden Egg. A commission—well, I could see by the

look in his popped black eyes that there would be no
getting out of it. Yet perhaps I could turn this to my advantage. "All right. But I need a place to work without
disturbance. Could I use your *kabinyet?* The energy is
very creative there, and no one would bother me."

The Master lifted one of his pointed eyebrows,
mocking me, knowing it was low-level extortion.
Maybe I could slip out and see if Mother's room was
unguarded. "For an hour. Before dinner."

I sat at his desk, taking the opportunity to look through
his papers. He had an atlas of central Asia, an ethnogra-
phy of Siberian shamans, and *The Way of the Pilgrim*,
plus the Vedas and crumbling little books in alphabets I
didn't recognize. All his small amulets, a jewel-handled
dagger that would bring a nice chunk of money even in
the lowest village in Russia. Powders and herbs tied in
little bags. A trunk, much traveled and securely locked.
No bed, only the pallet and a pile of sheepskins on the
carpet.

Across the hall, Andrei sat reading in front of
Mother's room, his back against her door. What was
she doing in there, month after month? She must be
mad by now.

Yet how pleasant it was to sit in a room by myself. I
put my feet up on the rung of the campaign desk and
felt like a king. I turned my attention to the Cosmic
Egg. I knew what the Master wanted—some sort of
faux-mystic rubaiyat full of "wherefores," but even in

contemplating it, my mind became a cart stuck up to its axles in mud. After trying to push myself out a few times, I gave up and leaned on a wheel, smoking. I would have to leave the cart mired there and walk away.

Yet the Egg, the Egg! Painted, shining, like a glorious Easter egg. Pagan, primordial. Not the relatively long succession of God-days of Genesis, but Creation as a hatching, pecking its way through the shell. All of existence. Imagine that bellyache. Hard enough to be pregnant with one little human. Imagine the fluttering, the pushing and shoving, the straining, having all creation inside you, waiting to be born.

And why would there be this expanding potential when before there was sweet, dark Nothing?

The Egg rolled onto the stage
Alone.

There, I had a start.

No one in the house.
          No audience, ushers, snacks at
   intermission.
          No intermission.
                    No Time.
      In darkness, resplendent, gold.

Now the question.

"Why am I here, if I may be so bold?
Why need a One?"

The hall made no reply.

Then deep inside the Cosmic Egg
Its guts
                began to seethe
                        with a nascent Universe.

Heartburn. How its back ached!

With Time, and Space, matter,
        At the heart of Nothing.

    "Cut it out," said the Egg. "I'm trying to
    sleep!"
But Eros stirred the pot.

Of course! How else did the world come into being?
Desire. Something wanted something. How did anything happen here?

    And Things started taking shape
            In that close darkness
        Like crystals growing in a cave.

Oh, the things of this world!

Spinning stars of the Milky Way,
    Romanian bonds and Latvian blondes
      The velvet antlers of springtime gods,
    The ticking sheets of racetrack odds.

The Egg tossed, sleepless and terrified.

    Things were waiting to be born!

    Doorknobs, drains, and philosophes,
     Pipes and prisons,
   barbershops,
    Samovars, love notes,
      Dostoyevsky
  Iambs and Macbeth,
  The sword of Orion
    The Rock of Gibraltar
  The Caspian Sea and
   Africa's Horn
Catherine the Great and Terrible Ivan and
   The Brazen Horse and Horseman.

   How it ached and bulged and cried
   Its mystic precincts wrapped so tight
   About the awkward baby!

I was positive that this was not what my client had ordered, but I felt the rush, the joy, of saying something quite true and equally unexpected. I had not lost the most essential part of myself. More than any lover, any scheme, this moment, my own creation.

> *At last, a tiny*
>   *C*
>   *R*
>   *A*
> *C*
>   *K*
> *appeared*
>   *no bigger than a sigh*

> *Come out! said Desire. Davai, davai!*

> *And like a Siberian prison break,*
>   *Like a bomb in an underground vault*
>   *Creation*
>   *B L A S T E D*

>   *O U T*

>   *!!!*

> *And out rushed oceans*
>   *Himalayas*
>   *Krakatoas,*
>   *warring nations,*
>   *Oedipus and Elementals,*
> *Principles and heavy metals.*

The wise
    the slow
        the cruel
            the dreary,

All dimensions   every city
Rushing, crushing, spinning away

Rocketing red and fiery across the dazzled brow
        of Nothingness

Till Nothing itself became a memory.

But that couldn't be all, not in a universe quickened by desire. Things just didn't keep spinning out and out. They settled down, they found relationships, they invented work and machines and childbirth.

And to this day
    each form, each face
Bears a bit of eggy trace

And by the fire
        late at night
    Each,
    (fingering
    a shattered shard of the Primordial Egg)

falls silent,
dozy, dreaming of
that sweet embrace.

Bright jars of bilberry jelly appeared from the cellar, and giant squashes. Berries in syrup. Bogdan produced a large crock of wine. There was much disappearing behind closed doors in groups of three and four and six, the sounds of rehearsals. I composed my poem and spied on Mother's room. Perhaps she would emerge for the feast.

The fatted calf was slaughtered—or, in our case, chickens, three of them, big and plump, and I was the executioner, untouchable. *I am Kali, Bringer of Death.* Lilya couldn't bear to do it herself. I borrowed the ax from Pasha and chopped them on the larch stump, threw the heads to the ever-hopeful dog Bonya. We plucked, we roasted. Ilya brought sprats and salmon from the smokehouse. My own miniature Egg was not to be denied—I nicked a sprat and wolfed it down right there in the kitchen, head and all, the oily deliciousness bringing tears to my eyes. I licked my fingers and silently dared Katrina, who stared, horrified, to say something about it.

The celebration began at sundown. I spent the afternoon braiding the girls' long tresses alongside Anna, who showed me intricate variations as the acolytes took turns sitting on a stool in front of us. My own hair had grown out a bit from Misha's inky crop and Anna trimmed it every week to remove the black ends from my fox-red locks. For the feast, she plaited me a crown, threaded it through with green cord.

Amid the bustle and laughter, I saw how much we needed this, saw the wisdom of this extravagance. We'd missed Christmas and New Year's and Epiphany. No birthday or name day had been acknowledged. This would be all of them rolled into one. I touched my crown and wondered how I looked. There were no mirrors at Ionia. Ukashin felt they were especially harmful to women, that they pulled our souls out of our bodies and left them floating between dimensions, and I wondered if that wasn't true enough, though I would have liked to have seen my own face that day. I felt the neat crown, my bones, the arch of my brow, my lips, soft. Did I have circles under my eyes? Was I still attractive? Would Kolya want me if we met again? Me with his child in my arms.

We watched the last low, red rays of the winter sun descend, turning the snow to blood. Anna, once the principal alto of the Mikhailovsky Theater, began to sing "Along the Quiet River." From the hall, Ilya joined her, and then Katrina's soprano—my God, the Mikhailovsky Theater really lost some talent when these three left Petrograd. The other girls took up the song, and the men.

There is no sound on earth as beautiful as the harmony that can arise from a group of people who sing together day in and day out. Floating on a current of song, we descended in a procession in that lilting, gliding step I'd finally mastered—male, female, male—down to the front parlor, where the rugs had been rolled up and the long plank table had miraculously appeared. We never ate in this room, preferring not to sully it with such third-dimension activities. But here it was, the table, covered with patterned quilts and decorated with colored eggs and pine boughs. Already enthroned at the table's head, looking like something out of *One Thousand and One Nights,* was our master, while at the table's foot, his regular chair from the back parlor was draped in a blue cloth. Could it be that Mother was coming down at last?

We circled the table seven times—once for each of the seven dimensions—to finally stop at our places, marked by elegant place cards painted by Lilya. Ukashin filled a goblet from a big crock of wine and we passed it from hand to hand around the table. Bogdan beamed with pride as he handed it to me—herbal, sharp, and green. Under normal circumstances I would have drunk deep, but the smell was abhorrent in my current condition, and I was happy to pass it on. The baby was more enthralled by the marvelous smells emerging from the kitchen. *Hurry up!* it shrieked as the elaborate toasts unfurled, to the heavens and the earths and the devis and guardians, the Mother. *Hurry up and bring out that rabbit stew! I want bread! Roasted chicken!*

The open seat awaited.

Avdokia stood in the doorway, and with each toast, a new unspoken comment radiated out from her eyebrows and her big nose, her mouth growing smaller with disapproval. *Idiots. Swindler.* I knew she was afraid. *What will we all eat come spring?* Yes, it was foolhardy to have a feast, my sweet old dear. Yes, it was insane. But we were not driving this train, she and I. We had not laid the rails.

At last she and Katrina began bringing in food. Oh glorious! Ruby borscht and big round loaves of bread. Pickles and smoked sprats followed by russet chickens in nests of potatoes, eggs dyed golden with onion skins and red with beets. Who could begrudge such bounty? We gorged, we drank. Calories pumped through my body, as intoxicating as wine, the baby floating in that heavenly sap of my blood. We sang old children's songs. Ukashin told a funny story about the Laboratory, and suddenly they all began to open up, trying to top one another with stories about the strange characters they had left behind, encounters between socialites and beggars, a man who kept a lizard in his mouth. Ukashin laughed and told jokes and drank right along with his disciples. Even Andrei drank, though it seemed to make him all the more melancholy. But for the rest, how they needed a night like this, of revelry, of bounty. Healthy young people couldn't live on oatmeal and the fourth dimension forever. All that vitality and beauty and smoky desire needed to have its day.

After the meal, the offerings began. Natalya and

Bogdan presented an original pas de deux to the accompaniment of Andrei's piano. It was about the love affair between the moon and the sun. I recognized bits of Ukashin's energy-accumulating choreography grafted onto modernist stylings from the Diaghilev ballet—*The Firebird* particularly. Oh, such grace in our midst! Natalya's lithe legs dabbed and fluttered like the legs of an egret through a marsh, and her turns and arabesques were kissed with moonlit delicacy. Bogdan's robust sun courted her with flashy leaps and turns. That such artistry, such ability, should dwell among us seemed unthinkable, like watching Karsavina dancing on the tiny stage at the Stray Dog. He lifted her on his shoulder and carried her away, careful to avoid the beams.

Then brown-eyed Anna rose and began to sing—of all things—the mezzo's great "Habanera" from *Carmen*. Miraculous—the gentle girl who sewed our rags and patches strutted around the table, transformed into the sultry Spanish seductress, while Ilya, Katrina, and Lilya played the other parts. Flush with food and wine, framed by those bright faces, Ukashin looked like a crow among songbirds, his plummy eyes slightly glazed. Was he drunk? Who could tell? The man had the energy and strength of four. There wasn't that much wine—it had just gone to everyone's heads.

When the "Habanera" finished and its performers rejoined the group, water and wine were passed around again. Ukashin rapped the table. "Marina Ionian, you think we have forgotten you?" He swept an expansive gesture in my direction, almost knocking over his big goblet.

All these lovely faces. My friends. Maybe this wasn't a mistake after all, this feast, this place, my having landed here, even with my doubtful heart. At that moment, I felt such love for these exceptional people, their sweetness, their dedication. Taking pleasure in one another's unlikely company. I rose and recited my poem.

The Egg rolled onto the stage
Alone.
No one in the house…

Moving my gaze from face to face, as each imagined the Egg's emergence. Was it a prison break? Or an expulsion from paradise? Ukashin remained unreadable, like a match behind a hand on a battlefield. He was wondering, I could tell, if I was sincere or mocking him. But there was no mockery in my poem. I had found the place where I could write without lying. I'd left that cart behind where it belonged.

And by the fire
        late at night
    Each,
    (fingering
    a shattered shard of the Primordial Egg)
      falls silent,

dozy, dreaming of
that sweet embrace.

The company was silent as the poem, which, like a thick, fatty yolk, dripped from their faces. Still dreaming around the fire, fingering their own bit of the cosmic shell, perhaps remembering their own mothers, their own homes, which they'd abandoned to follow the Master. They turned to Ukashin, waiting to see if it was all right to approve of me.

Slowly, a smile appeared on his complex face. I could see him congratulating himself on his own wisdom, having gradually led me into harness like a skittish horse. And now that the others saw it was good, they felt free to applaud and embrace me.

It was an evening full of wine, more singing, skits and monologues—it reminded me of long summer nights here when I was a child. Four of the girls sang in close harmony. Boys did Cossack dances with knives in each hand. Magda danced a real gypsy dance, with much flashing of teeth and shaking of shoulders, claiming her rights as the authentic Carmen. Even Ukashin made an offering, an athletic Circassian dance. He was at least forty but as energetic as a twenty-year-old, doing the spins and leaps and even walking on his hands! *Urah!* The windows dripped with steam. I spun and clapped and whistled with the others. But the chair at the foot of the table remained empty. I wondered if Mother could hear this up in her lair, if the sound of our gaiety reached the fifth dimension, or if she'd had to place a wet cloth across her brow and cotton wool in her ears.

Between dances, the Master fell into the seat next to mine, clapped me on the shoulder. "We've had a theorist and a prophet, and now we have our bard!" He kissed me on both cheeks. "We must talk. We need more of this. Maybe you'll write us some songs…and an invocation."

At one point I caught a glimpse of Pasha and Katrina disappearing together into the hall. Did the Master notice? But he was drunk, busy dancing with Natalya. Yes, a real carnival was taking place, and Ukashin was allowing it. This must have been what the Laboratory was like before the spartan life of Ionia. Andrei had fallen asleep at the table. Gleb and Ilya were arm wrestling. This was the time I could have had Bogdan if I wanted to, but it came to me—there was no one guarding Mother's door. I would never again have a chance like this. I practiced invisibility, blending with the woodwork as I slid out of the room and glided up the stairs.

78 *The Mother*

FIVE INSET PANELS MARKED her door like the spine of a forbidden book, and the scent of an oily incense emanated from the other side. I knocked softly, *Fais dodo.*

The wooden knob turned freely, warm as flesh in my hand. A cloud of incense spilled out like smoke from a badly ventilated stove. I stepped inside and closed the door behind me.

In the otherwise lightless room a small comma of flame burned in blue glass at eye level, farther away than was possible given the dimensions of a space I knew as well as I knew my own body. Maybe it was the effect of a darkness like the inside of a jewelry box upholstered in smoke and black velvet, but I was afraid to take a step, as if I might fall down into limitless space.

"Mother?"

Behind the flame, I could just make out two icons with overlarge Byzantine eyes, weirdly animated, as if they weren't painted but lived within their frames in two dimensions. The darkness was impenetrable but for that small blue flame and those saints.

Then came a clicking sound like the turning of a handful of pebbles from near the flame. It made me aware of the uncanny quiet of the room. I couldn't hear the party directly below us, perhaps because of the heavy carpet under my feet. It made me dizzy, standing still.

A shadow slipped between me and the flame. A ghost, a spirit. I remained perfectly still, like a rabbit eluding a hawk, which sees only movement. Colored patches appeared in the air, and my scalp tingled, the tips of my fingers went cold. *Click, click.*

"Mama?"

The elongated form discouraged my approach. My mother was not a tall woman. *What if it was not her at all?* Perhaps that was why they'd kept me away from her all this time. But it had to be Vera Borisovna. Avdokia wouldn't have lied about that.

The very air shimmered and swirled, alive as a Viennese ballroom. Was there a drug in the oily incense? I wouldn't have put that past Ukashin. And here I'd imagined my mother up here with a blanket over her knees, reading Madame Blavatsky.

"Mama?" I whispered.

She didn't turn but stepped aside so the two accusatory icon faces could observe me. I had the strangest feeling that she was watching me through their eyes, as one might spy on other restaurant patrons through a well-placed mirror. *Click, click* went the stones. "It's Marina, Mama."

"Approach." The clear high voice came from very far away, the words formed as if she'd had to push them through thick cloth.

With one foot, I felt my way ahead. "I've been here for months. They won't let me see you."

Her hands appeared, white in the darkness, pushing something around atop an inlaid table that I remembered being in the upstairs hall. Her forearms rested on the dark wood. I saw she was arranging tumbled stones—clear, pointed, smooth—some glowed amber, others red, blue, pale cloudy jade. Yes it was my mother, luminous but indefinite, like the underpainting

of a portrait. "Did you know I was here?" She hadn't
seen me since the night Arkady came to claim me.
"Why don't you say something?" I reached out and
pulled back the hood draped over her head. Her hair
tumbled down, loose, white, wild like a stormy sea.

She continued to swirl the stones on the tabletop.

"Will you stop doing that?" With a sweep of my
hand I sent the stones flying. They bounced and scattered, some hitting the wall. "Look at me! You haven't
seen me for almost a year! Don't you care that I'm
here?"

She lifted her blue eyes to me then, wide and transparent as tumbled quartz. "I see you. I've seen you all
along."

What was she talking about?

"In the snow. In the tower. In the forest and the
storm. Come. Marina. Come home." She lifted her
hand to the room's corner. I followed her gesture.
"Stop there," she whispered. "It's too far. *Marina!*"
Her voice rose in urgency. "Heed me!"

And I knew. She was seeing me in my desperate walk
through the forest. Right now. In a parallel time. It was
her voice I'd heard telling me to stop and take shelter.

"Why did you call me here if you didn't want to see
me?"

She shook her head, and from her throat emerged
bubbling laughter—like the water in a springhouse,
cool and clear. Was she mad? Or was this a private
joke? "Mother—"

Those clear, translucent eyes were on me again. "Don't mistake me for the one who was. What you remember is a bit of golden shell. The egg has vanished."

How had she heard that? The hair stood up all over my body. Where was my mother? I wanted to shriek. What have you done with her? The woman who loved hats and parties, who'd translated Apollinaire head-to-head with Anton, who loved white lilacs and risqué Pierre Louÿs novels. This Vera Borisovna wasn't even looking at me. Rather, she scanned me, as if I were a landscape painting too large to take in at a glance.

Then the thought came to me with the force of a blow—this was who she'd always been. Yes. Now I *saw* her, the mystic who'd always been waiting. I saw her the way you finally see the stones at the bottom of a pool when you stop wading and the water stills and clarifies around your feet. She'd only been playing the role of mother. It was that other person, the spoiled housewife, the glamorous society fixture, who'd been the impostor. She had stepped out of that suit and now stood revealed.

She settled her hood back over her hair. She had what she'd always wanted. No children, no husband, no earthly cares. It wasn't luxury she'd sought—it had never been about that, not beauty, not art. It was transcendence she was after. Ukashin gave her that psychic space, protection, freedom. And what did he get in return? Money, this estate, a mystical figurehead to awe the faithful?

"What about Father?"

She gestured circles with her hands, as if clearing a window or washing a horse. "So much motion. So much red. Your father has that as well."

Yes, I had that red. It bubbled up now, clouding my aura. She had been posing all those years as my mother, as a devoted wife. I found myself suddenly furious with her. "So you do remember him," I said. "Your husband? All those years, was that nothing?" Why was I defending him? As if he were still Papa, and not the politician who betrayed me though it meant my death.

"Some realities are tangential." She shrugged. "It's no one's fault."

Her detachment made me want to slap her. "I saw him, you know. Back in April. He's in league with the counterrevolution, plotting away. He exposed me as Red. Thought I was a spy. I was almost killed."

"White becomes red, red becomes white." Her voice, far away again. "Seryozha's here." She glanced up, the way you notice someone entering a room—in that same corner, where there was no one. "Can't you see?" She held her hand out to my right, where I saw nothing. "He watches you. He misses you. He's been trying to communicate with you." She nodded into the nothingness. "Yes, I know."

I gazed into the dark spot where her focus was trained. I smelled gunpowder. My hair felt electrified. Was it possible she could see my brother between the worlds? What if all this Ionian nonsense was true—

energetics and folds in space-time? Ukashin said there was no death, only transition.

"Don't look. *Feel* him."

I closed my eyes and tried, but couldn't sense anything more. I passed my hands through the space but it was neither cold nor warm, gave no whisper or rustle. I would have given anything to believe he was here, reaching out to me. *Seryozha!* But I didn't need a visitation to know that my brother was near me. He would always be near me. But oh, to see his face again—his slightly pointed ears, the way he read while biting his nails abstractedly, the way he mimicked Papa scolding him.

"How old is he?" I asked, my eyes still closed.

"A small boy. Though sometimes he comes as an old man. It depends."

This was crazy. I opened my eyes. "He'll never be an old man. He'll always be sixteen."

"In some of the streams he dies young, in others he lives to be an old man, or a soldier, even a priest."

That made me smile. I could only imagine how my sharp, attentive brother would imitate her now, mocking her mystic face. "And what about me? What do you see for me, Mama?"

That glowing spiritual expression dropped away. She lowered her gaze.

I stepped on one of the oracular stones, slipped, caught myself, picked it up. Smooth and hard. I wanted to throw it at her. Not even a word about the baby?

"Go now." She looked away from me, chin against her shoulder—that profile, still as beautiful as when Vrubel painted it.

What did she see that made her lower her eyes? I felt as if the ceiling were coming down on me. "Tell me." I grabbed her by the arm, pulled her so she had to face me.

Her eyes looked wild, as if she were in a snare, cornered and fighting for a way out. "The strong must suffer everything, everything! Don't you understand?" She struggled to break free of my grip, but though she may have been a prophetess she wasn't much of a wrestler. "I can't be upset. Let me go! Ukashin!" she called out. Her voice was shrill enough to carry downstairs. "Taras! Andrei!"

"Don't scream, please." I let her go, holding both hands up in surrender. "For God's sake, Mother."

She only became more agitated. "Ukashin!"

I had to stop her screaming. I couldn't believe my own mother was afraid of me. It was a nightmare. "Please, I'm not hurting you!" I reached out, but she shrieked again before I could touch her, shrinking from me as though I held a hot torch, a live viper. "Ukashin!"

"I'll stay away," I said, backing up until I hit something that clattered—her vanity table. "I'm way over here." *Please, Seryozha, help me. You were always her favorite. Come and deal with this. I was never good with her.*

The door opened and light from the hall fell across

the carpet. The Master staggered in, stinking of sweat and wine. How huge he looked outlined against the light from the hall, like a genie released from a bottle, filling the doorway. "What's going on in here?"

My mother cringed before her icons. "She's been tormenting me."

He lowered his great bull's head as if he would charge me. "I see."

"I just wanted to talk to her." I still clutched that clear piece of tumbled quartz.

"Forgive us, Mother." He crossed the room and yanked me out by the arm, shoved me into the hall, and closed off the Mother's world behind us.

I stood in the hallway holding my wrenched shoulder, hot tears shamelessly streaming, gulping air that hadn't been stained with that acrid smoke. I wished to God I had never opened that door. I'd been operating under the illusion that I was special, that I could walk a tightrope between worlds, a privileged character, the Daughter. But I was not special in any way. No father, no mother... now I was truly here, fully in the hands of this cosmic bully and his mad priestess. There would be no other future.

79 *Andrei Ionian*

MY PUNISHMENT WAS TAILOR-MADE to fit the crime. The night after my transgression, the Master stopped me in the hall. "Andrei needs to learn about hunting. Take him with you in the morning." And turned away. There would be no argument. How appropriate to consign me to Andrei Ionian, depriving me of the one thing I needed after that encounter with my mother: solitude. I needed time to think, to make some plans. Now I would have the professor dogging my days with his steady stream of philosophy and gangly obliviousness.

The following morning, I got him onto a pair of homemade skis, and soon we left the house behind, smoke trickling from its chimneys, the dark wood of the outbuildings slowly diminishing to train-set size, like toys dusted in soap flakes. I needed to sort out my thoughts about my place at Ionia, my responsibility to the baby, and the way Mother had looked at me like someone examining a stamp through a magnifying glass. The way she'd shrieked for Ukashin. But Andrei could not be still. The very air around him crackled with anxiety. For someone who extolled the virtues of the present moment, could Andrei be any less present?

He launched into a lecture about his favorite subject, simultaneous incarnation, the proposition that we live many lives at once in parallel streams of space-time. This was what my mother had been talking about—seeing Seryozha at four, Seryozha as an old man, a soldier, a dog, a dancing master. I only wished it were true. Then I might be back before the revolution, living with my child and my clever husband, hosting

Wednesday at-homes in turban and pantaloons, smoking a little cigar and writing my decadent poetry, instead of stranded in this mystical commune, trapping small animals in the bitter cold. But Andrei wasn't content with imagining it: he wanted it to literally be so. Mathematically provable.

Well, who was I to criticize? My job was to show him hunting, and that's what I would do. I pulled my scarf over my nose and mouth and kept moving.

"You see, it's all our perspective." It was the Ionian catechism—things that appeared separated on the third dimension were simultaneous when seen from the fourth, more so from the fifth, and so on. He panted to keep up with me, his breath a plume of vapor, but the flow of information never stopped. "You have to look at the position which encompasses the highest point of view."

He was so desperate that I understand. I *saw* that for an intellectual like him, the need to be understood was a trap. Once caught, he just kept tightening the noose around himself. He would be better off just admiring the beauty of his system for his own sake. I couldn't help wondering, what was my own trap? Reflexive hope? The yearning for peace? No, those held no allure. Passion. And the need to see what happened. One's strength, overdone, was one's weakness.

As I waited for him to catch his breath—a painful sight, hands on his knees, gasping—it occurred to me that this reassignment must be Andrei's punishment as well as mine. But what had been his crime? Not keeping me from Mother's room? On the icy, misted air, I could hear the rooster bragging how he'd made the sun rise. I hiked on, trying to get away from the tide of nervous chatter, which resumed as soon as he could speak.

I stopped on top of a rise, alone for a short moment. Overhead in an ancient apple tree, ravens cawed and clicked their strange squirrel sounds and dropped twigs on my head. I no longer saw them as harbingers of doom, but welcomed them as clever companions whose language I could almost decipher. I stroked the apple tree's trunk, its spiraled bark like a shirt wrung out by a beefy washerwoman. Its deformation probably had saved it from many a woodsman's ax. It looked like a claw, an old man's hand. *What do you have to tell me, Tree?*

Endure, it said.

I used to ride here with Volodya, the two of us on his bad-tempered pony. He'd put me in front and let me hold the reins, tall grass brushing our bare feet. We'd stop to let Carlyle eat the fallen apples, the fruit small and hard. In those days when you looked back at the house, you would always hear music, Mother playing her piano, Olya singing while she hung the wash in the summer sun.

Now all that was gone. Just me and the tiny passenger. What kind of a life was I facing? What did Mother mean, *the strong must suffer everything?*

Andrei finally managed the hill, his skis splayed in a

gawky V. His scarf, tied across his nose and mouth, had grown thick with frost. But still he talked on, about the folds of space-time: "So you're you now, but also you at eight walking with your mother, going to fetch some sweets. And eighty, leaning on your daughter's arm."

"But we still have to live here and now," I said. "I don't see why this is so important to you."

"It's essential. Vital! If we could figure out the mathematics of the parallel streams, we would be seen as magicians. Time travel, jumping between alternate lives would become a reality. Seeing the intention of the entire structure. That's what we should be studying, not whirling around with our eyes closed." He took out a handkerchief and blew his nose vigorously. The crows cawed in response.

But I liked the whirling. Opening the vortex, we called it. It was my favorite thing at Ionia. It made you less hungry, more peaceful, and the room held that beautiful energy. We got along better afterward. "What about the sacred spiral? I would have thought you'd approve."

"We should be examining the layers of existence. It's a different order of magnitude."

"But it's right out of that book you gave me, *The Structure of Reality*." The spiral was the gateway to higher dimensions. What could he object to in its embodiment?

"You're dancing it. It's not the same as engaging here." He knocked on his forehead. "You can draw a motor, too, but it won't take you to Moscow." He sighed, whacked a tree trunk with a crude ski pole. "But nobody cares. It's too much mental work. I've failed here if you can't see how it matters." I could see I'd offended him.

We started down the hill toward the aspen copse, the trees all talking to each other, their roots entwined. "I wrote a poem about parallel time streams," I said. He seemed so bitter that no one cared about his cosmic theories, I thought it might cheer him. "Want to hear it?"

"Go on."

> On the pond,
>   a girl
> etches figures in the ice.
> Redheaded as an oriole
> She poses, arabesque.
>
> Across the park,
> a woman
> stands on a fourth floor window ledge,
>   Caught between freedom and despair
>   Her falling hat frees crimson hair
>
> Passing below,
> the crone
>   seems to recall some still-life story
>   of her own, but when?
>   She catches the hat,

Midair.
>   *It's just her size.*

Racing ahead,
>   *the flameheaded tot*
giggles, naughtily.
Glancing back at Gran,
>   *trips and tumbles*

A creaking tram arrives
They board and vanish, life after life.

He said nothing at first, the crunch of snow under his skis. "Yes, but don't you want to know why? It's the manifestation of a universal truth, not just inspiration for a poet's reveries. Such a bright girl, too. I'd had such high hopes for you."

How tedious he was. He fell in love with patterns, ignoring the very things worth living for — the body in motion, the beauty of these frosty woods, a line of verse. Every bit the spaceman that Varvara was. Who was he to have hopes for me anyway? "I'm a disappointment to many. You'll have to queue, I'm afraid."

We reached the logged stretch, overgrown with blackberries and willows, their bare red twigs sticking up from the snow like the fingers of a frozen traveler. Andrei panted and coughed. I was tempted to send him off into the bush ahead of me, like a beater, to flush the game. I wanted to sneak up behind him and scream, "Wolf!" I knew exactly why Ukashin used him as a scapegoat and court jester. He was so wretchedly earnest. *Too much air*, Ukashin would say, *too little earth*. Though didn't we all suffer from the same complaint? Truly, which of us Ionians wasn't too much air, too little earth? It was lucky any of us had a roof over our heads. Without Ukashin, Ionia would have starved long ago.

"Hold up!" Andrei was caught. He tried to free himself and toppled over like a rootless aspen.

I tried not to laugh. I was tempted to suggest maybe he could leap over into a parallel time-space stream where he was graceful and useful and quiet. But it wasn't his fault, he really was helpless, and one didn't add to the suffering of others, even if they were annoying. I went back to help him, got him out of the snow, set his ski out for him to step into, and strapped him back onto the raw birch plank. I even set his hat back on his head and handed him my bottle of tea wrapped in birch bark.

After that he fell silent for a while. Perhaps he was finally noticing the beauty of the woods, the finely etched branches of maple and birch, the little berries the animals would come again and again to eat. The first trap of the day lay empty, also the second. I had to keep setting new traps in wider circles, I even crossed the river now. It took longer, but we needed the meat. I still could hear Natalya reassuring me that groceries would manifest themselves if we didn't repress them with our fears.

Andrei was wearying, forcing himself forward into the heavy snow. I stopped at a favorite spot with a view of the river and the low round ball of the sun, always near the horizon in these winter months. He stood next to me, gulping the frigid air, taking in the mesmerizing display of black marks on the white birches, vivid against the white sky, like the masterful strokes of a Chinese brush.

"You know, we've met before, Marina."

"We have?" I squinted at him. Tall, storky, in his quilted coat, squirrel-skin gloves, and felted hat. Emaciated, his lips blue. "When was that?"

"At a party. You wore a rust-colored dress and danced a tango with a young officer. You were laughing. I never see you laugh like that here."

He'd been there, that New Year's Eve, the night we cast the wax. He had seen me with Kolya...how was that possible?

Master Vsevolod. Andrei must have been one of Mother's table-rappers. Of course. "I've been here three months and you're just telling me this now?"

"We don't speak of the personal," he said, slightly mocking. "The past is irrelevant." He sighed. "But your mother and I were once great friends."

I wanted to hear more about my mother, but we needed to get going if I had any hope of crossing to my other traps and getting back before the weather turned ugly. Already the belly of the sky hung low and fat and was turning the yellow-green of impending snow. We were going to be in for it.

We made our way down to the frozen-over river and took off across the crisp whiteness of the open snow, stopping in the middle to listen to the muffled gurgle. There is no greater pleasure, any Russian will tell you, than standing on a frozen lake or river and contemplating hidden currents under the snow. I thought perhaps I should try ice fishing. Overhead, an osprey circled. The eagles didn't leave in the winter. I couldn't imagine the fortitude to last out these brutal winters in a nest of twigs. Even Andrei stopped talking to hear the river's quiet music.

On the other side, where once little boys had watched me swim naked, not understanding their own excitement, we stopped for our lunch. A good spot, though cold as the heavy clouds descended. We sat on a fallen fir. The white birches were scarred where deer had chewed on them. I shared our luncheon of dried perch and black bread, a red egg left over from the feast—a love offering from Avdokia. I peeled it and ate half—yolk, too—and gave the other half to Andrei. He gnawed the bread with his eyeteeth. It was not quite as tough as rock, but getting there. The fish was full of bones, but nice and salty. I forced myself to eat it flake by flake, careful not to drop any with my freezing hands.

"So you were one of Vsevolod's…circle," I finished,

not wanting to insult him. "My brother used to do a great imitation of him." I attempted it, the hunchy obsequiousness, the flabby lips, rubbing his hands.

"He was a kind man, though," Andrei said. "He didn't deserve the treatment he got from Taras, and me." He balled up the paper from the fish and threw it into the woods.

"Was this at the Laboratory?"

He looked impossibly sad. "We should get going," he said.

We finished the tea, and I led him off into the pines that grew tall on this side of the river, giving off a jammy smell. My first trap bore fruit.

"Oh look, you got one!"

Citizen Rabbit, condemned for crimes unknown. I slid the tip of my knife to find the precious wire buried in its neck, worked the noose open. In better times I would have cut it, but in better times I wouldn't be doing this at all. I dropped the dead weight of my catch into my game bag, then showed Andrei how to reset the little snare, steadying it with twigs over the game trail. He watched me with the same bemused curiosity I'd had in the days when I watched Mina dissecting things in the biology lab at the Tagantsev Academy—interest without any intention of trying it myself. I would make Andrei set the next one. I stood, straightening my legs, rubbing the circulation back into them.

The next trap also paid off—a large hare had been

caught around its neck and foreleg. I could *feel* its struggle before it finally froze to death. In the spring, I planned to catch rabbits alive and breed them. That way we would have fresh meat next winter without expending all this energy on hunting—though it had been designed for my psychospiritual advancement and not just as a way to feed the tribe. Then I caught myself. *Next winter.* As if I would still be here. Not a chance. Certainly the civil war would be over by then. Things would start to improve and there would be food in the city. My child would grow up there. I would not be fooling with rabbits by then.

I made Andrei reset the trap, bend the sapling down to the ground, lacing it into the notched twig. *Set them well,* Ukashin had said. *Even a rabbit will avoid a snare if he's been caught once and fought his way free. Only a person is stupid enough to be caught twice.*

The *intelligent* bashed himself in the face a couple of times, but eventually reset the trap. He beamed with his accomplishment.

"When I think of the man I was," he said, "I want to shake him. So confident, so naive. It took the revolution to awaken us from our dream of life. Perhaps that was its true purpose."

"The revolution's purpose was to free the worker, to feed the poor, not to awaken the bourgeoisie. If we could have fed the people, given them hope, we wouldn't have needed the Bolsheviks to be our alarm clock."

He blew into his thin long hands, rubbed them and

put his gloves back on. "Nevertheless, it *was* a liberation," he said, picking up his ski poles. "You were never yourself back then. You were the Good Husband, the Publisher, the Dutiful Wife. Even you. Rebellious Daughter? Daddy's Girl? Girl of the Season? The revolution made short work of all of that. It exploded all the roles."

"You think we're free now? Or are the new roles just less obvious?" I had been the Rebellious Daughter, also the Good Girl, and yes, Daddy's Favorite. And now I was the Mystical Orphan, the Haphazard Acolyte, the Husbandless Mother-to-Be. Kali, Bringer of Death. It hardly seemed an improvement.

"I've refused to take on any new roles," he said. I could see his energy had returned with his meal. "For the first time in my life, I am just a man. Only a man feels, only a man lives. A Publisher can't feel hungry, but I feel my hunger. What does a Good Husband feel? Nothing. He's a construct. *I* feel. Everything drops away but what's meaningful. Noumenon. *Ding an sich.* A rebirth."

I looked at us both, in our rags and patches. *Ding an sich.* The thing in itself. Kant in the woods. Platonists in sheepskins and quilted jackets. It made me laugh.

He couldn't really think this was freedom. Under one role there was always another. But I didn't have time for this house of mirrors. I had traps to check before the snow. "Tell me about my mother. Does she ever come out of that room?"

"She used to come out for Practice." He skied along in my wake, bumping the backs of my snowshoes with his tips. "She'd visit the workroom...we often played the piano together. She has such beautiful technique. So sensitive. She sometimes plays my own compositions. Occasionally she invites me to her room for tea."

I liked the idea that they were friends, that she had someone to talk to besides Ukashin. "Do you ever talk about Petrograd, the old days?"

"We never talk about personal things. We speak of the work, her experiences on the astral." He paused, remembering her, then his face darkened. "But Taras doesn't like us interfering with her. He wants to be her sole contact. As you've seen."

"But you're the one guarding her door."

How sad he looked. "She can't be disturbed. Changes are going on now. I'm no longer privy to the discussions." The bitterness around his small mouth. "There's a new darkness around us, haven't you noticed? No one talks about it. Have they said anything to you?"

Me? I was the lowest on the ladder of initiation. "No one talks to me," I said. "But I've felt it, yes. I thought it was the war...the violence. Red versus White. It's probably reverberating all over the world, even onto the higher dimensions."

"That's not how it works," he said. "The disturbance is above, and manifests on this level. Energy goes from higher to lower. The war is a disturbance in the higher dimensions, materializing in the third. That's your mother's work, to keep it from coming through."

I didn't like the idea of war in the higher dimensions. I liked my higher dimensions abstract and orderly and beneficent if possible. This was spooky, like devils in the bathhouse, witches curdling the milk. "I thought you were a scientist."

"There are all sorts of beings on every dimension, Marina."

We moved through the pines. Traveling on this side was easier, as some of the trees had been cut, though cover for small game wasn't quite as good. I saw something in the snow that made my heart leap. Split-hoof tracks, pretty as name-day roses. I crouched down to study them. Here were the small tracks of a mouse, and oval prints with small forward toes—marten or sable. A crow strutting. And, queen of my dreams, those delicate hoofprints of deer. Recent, too. Nothing else had degraded their edges. They were imprinted on top, firmly as a rubber stamp.

I rubbed my nose with my mitten, trying to warm it, pulled my scarf up again. If I got a deer, Ukashin would be appeased, and I would be taken off the punishment list, brought back into the breast of Ionia, forgiven my trespasses. I could feel my day brightening.

Andrei hung over my shoulder like a man reading another's newspaper. "What do you see?"

I pointed. "Deer tracks. Here, and here."

I scanned the trees, and *there*, between trunks, something large and gray moved silently. I yanked my glove off with my teeth and took the pistol from my pocket, held my other hand out to silence Andrei. As quietly as I could, I began to approach in the creaking snow. I had to get closer. There was no way to kill anything from this distance. As I moved, I was already thinking how I would get a deer home, whether I would have to hoist it into a tree, and with what. As I neared, I heard a crash. The *intelligent* had caught his ski and fallen into a clump of evergreens. The big shape vanished.

Damn, Andrei! Could he be any clumsier? I could have had a clear shot in another few feet. In my mind I'd already killed that deer, was already tasting a bit of its raw liver. That stag had lasted us a month. I plunged ahead to try to find the animal, leaving Andrei to sort himself out. Or he could just sit there in the snow for all I cared.

I moved in the direction where I'd last seen it, watching for tracks. *There* and *there.* Bounding. But I was no match for a running deer. I followed the prints for a few minutes anyway, in hopes it might calm down and stop to browse. Finally, I had to admit I'd lost it. Damn him! Why did Ukashin think this was such a good idea, to cripple me in my hunting? He should be thinking of the rest of the Ionians, not my transgression. And now I was in an area of the forest where I'd never been before, and the clouds were descending. I thought of Andrei back there. My charge, my albatross. My anger said *leave him there,* but remorse ticked like a clock. Even if he'd managed to right himself, he would probably fall in a tree hole and break a leg. The snow would be coming soon, and he would be completely lost without me. I had to get him home.

I released the deer in my mind. How sad it was to watch it spring away. Frustrated and furious, I turned to follow my big ugly tracks back to where I'd left the *intelligent*. The Ionians constantly preached the necessity of misery to help you awaken, but as far as I could see, suffering never made anybody better. It just made us petty and irritable and selfish. We got better despite our suffering, not because of it.

I found Andrei exactly where I'd left him, sitting in the snow, his arms wrapped around his legs, resting his forehead against his knees.

"I lost the deer," I said.

"I'm useless," he said. "Just leave me here."

"You can't sit here. You'll freeze. Get up."

"I don't care anymore," he said. "I'm done."

"Come on." I pulled him up, dusted him off, and we started home. I could tell that Andrei was tired. He dropped farther and farther behind. I wished I had another meal on me to perk him up.

As we moved back to the place where it was easiest to cross the river, I recognized a configuration of rocks where I'd set another trap. I tramped over to check it, watching for my ward. Yes! The trap had been sprung. But when I approached to collect my bounty, I found nothing hanging from the cord. Indeed the noose itself was gone, snapped clean, and the snow beneath lay trampled and bloody. Whatever I'd caught, it had barely been dead when the thief arrived, as the blood had flowed, not yet frozen. Although most of the tracks were trampled, one was clear as a signature. It sent a shiver through me. A doglike track, bigger than those of Ukashin's hairy hounds. A new arrival. But how long ago? Days? Hours? The print was clean—no mouse tracks or twigs or snow around it.

"Did you find something?" Andrei asked, coming up behind me.

I stood, kicking the kinks from my legs. My nose was running, and my cheeks stung in the cold. "No," I said. I didn't want to frighten him. The talk of darkness brewing already had me on edge, and the sky was heavy with coming snow. I still pictured that deer drifting through the icy mist, but the rabbit and big hare would have to be enough for tonight. I could not afford to tarry.

As we set off again, I had to admit I was grateful for Andrei's company and regretted that I'd contemplated abandoning him earlier. I would not want to be alone in the woods with the owner of that track. What was it the Kirghiz had said? *If you don't like wolves, stay out of the woods.* The two of us would present a more formidable prospect to a predator than myself alone.

"Sorry I ruined your hunting," he said. "I can't seem to do anything right these days."

If he was looking for consolation, he wasn't going

to find it with me. I thought I saw movement about a hundred meters off. It might have been my overwound imagination, but I could have sworn I saw a ghostly form weaving its way through the pines. I took my pistol out. It must have scented us, maybe back when we'd eaten our lunch. Perhaps it had even followed me when I was tracking the deer. Oh God. Ukashin might have given me hunting as my *Trud*, but that thing out there in the trees, *that* was a hunter.

I blinked to clear my eyes, my skin prickling. An icy fog gathered in pockets along the ground. Andrei's breath was short in my ear.

There—another flicker of motion. Or was it? If I hadn't seen the print in the snow, I might have convinced myself I was imagining it all. I turned slowly, trying to see through the trees and the deepening mist. I could *feel* it stalking us, as it had through the moonlit arcade of my dream.

"The deer again?" he said.

I didn't want to say the word. I might not believe in much, but I believed in the power of naming. "Maybe. But it's getting late. I don't think there'll be anything else today." What time was it? The light was unreadable, the mist blotting out shadows. Another hour at best. We had to get back across the river.

My heartbeat pounded in my ears as we moved through the bank of fog. I tried to hurry Andrei without alarming him, but he snagged his ski tip on a buried root and fell again. He was tiring. Something flew over our heads, silent until it was right on us. I ducked, held on to my hat. Owl. All the hunters were out today. It was as if this forest wanted us, had set its own snares.

We needed to make some noise, make ourselves seem loud, robust, confident. *It* knew we were here. We needed to impress it with our vigor. Well, that was something Andrei could do as easily as breathing— make noise. I asked him in a bright voice how he came to follow Ukashin.

I had not expected the reaction. He stopped. He even stopped panting. His bird face with its little spectacles, its red nose, its vulnerable mouth agape. "I don't *follow* Ukashin. Is that what you think?"

Well, he'd spent every day since I'd arrived doing the worst of our tasks, taking out the ashes from the stoves, washing the chamber pots, sitting before Mother's door, all while absorbing great shovelfuls of Ukashin-ian humiliation and spooling out reels of Ionian philosophy. "But you were at the Laboratory."

"You think I trotted after him like a little dog? Begging for his attention? That I'm just another of his sheep?"

Obviously I had stepped on one of Andrei Ionian's sore spots. "No, no," I said. "I was just asking. Really." *Keep moving.* I scanned the trees around us, the mist, trying not to picture the predator taking Andrei's skinny intellectual neck in its teeth. But Andrei wasn't with me. He was still where he'd stopped, as if he'd been hit by lightning. "I founded Ionia," he said. "I invented it. It's mine. Not his. Mine."

He thrust his face up toward the white sky, exposing that bony throat, as if begging God to witness his suffering. "You don't know anything. You think I'm just some clown. Andrei the fool. Useless, ridiculous Andrei, with his stupid books, his boring lectures. Can't even ski without falling down."

"You ski fine. Come on—it's snowing." The tall pines creaked. It was spooky, and I could see the first big feathery flakes, felt the kiss of one on my cheek.

"Just the village fool. *Dance, Andrei, dance!*" Strapped into his skis, he imitated the paws-up clumsiness of a dancing bear.

My hands were freezing, but I couldn't shoot with mittens on. "Please—let's go. Why don't you tell me about inventing Ionia as we go?"

"Don't patronize me." But at least that got him going. "You don't care about what he did. You're as besotted as the others. You're up to your neck in it. You don't care if it's a system or a moment's whim as long as it's Taras dishing it out."

No one had ever mentioned Andrei as the founder of Ionia. Avdokia said Vsevolod brought Ukashin to Furshtatskaya, not the two of them. "So tell me," I said, hoping I could console him. He was having some kind of breakdown. "Nobody talks about how it started."

I smiled to encourage him, all the while thinking: *You must be the hunter. Think like a hunter.* If I was truly a hunter I would double back and try to kill that beast. Even if I only succeeded in wounding it or scaring it, it would avoid us. But I had Andrei to think about. I couldn't leave him now, and I couldn't take him with me.

"I wrote the book. I gave it to you when you first got here." *The Structure of Reality* by A. A. Petrovin. Why had I not guessed? "You see? I had the idea years before I ever laid eyes on Taras Ukashin. Vera Borisovna could tell you. Vsevolod—" But then he remembered, the Ionians had abandoned Vsevolod and the others at the Petrograd dacha, left them in the lurch. Everyone who could have vouched for him had already been betrayed. "Taras could tell you—"

"Maybe I should ask him."

That got me a laugh, a single bitter *Ha!* "Yes, you do that."

Here was the river. Thank God. The snow coming down in thick, fat flakes now. It had already started to obliterate our footprints. I scanned for that thing, tracking us. It could be circling; it could be ten feet behind. "Hurry, please." I unstrapped my snowshoes and climbed down the short face of the riverbank, strapped myself back in. "Hand me your skis, Andrei," I said. But rushing him only made him clumsier, and he was more interested in his tale than in our pressing need to get away from this place.

"Maybe I am the fool. I was dazzled by him myself." He'd bent over to loosen his ski, in the process dropping his glove, his pole. "He came to my office, wanted to talk about my book. We talked until six in the morning." Finally he got a ski off and handed it down to me, but the cold was getting to him, and his hands trembled. "He wanted to know all about my work. And in return he told me about his travels. Egypt, China! Where hadn't the man been? He studied with Sufis and Tantric Buddhists. Secret practices no one had ever recorded."

I eyed the far shore longingly. Would we ever get there? His breath came short as he bent over the straps of his remaining ski. "He wanted to get his knowledge out into the world. I told him about my dream to create a society of brothers conducting research into the very shape of reality."

Would I have to climb up there and get that other ski? "Really, we need to go."

He ignored my urging. "You don't know what it is to be alone your whole life, Marina, and then meet someone like that. We became the dearest of friends. The happiest time of my life—I'm not embarrassed to say it."

I could imagine. All Ukashin's formidable personality and charm descending upon the poor undefended intellectual. It must have been overwhelming. It must have felt like love.

Finally he got the other ski off and handed it to me, but he slipped on the rocks coming down, scraping his cheek and tearing his pants. Down on the snowy river, I put his skis back on him, strapping him in. For a brief moment I imagined doing the same for my child, buckling his skis, tying his little skates. I would be a good mother. If I survived.

He picked up his ski poles and pushed off across the white expanse. "I introduced him to everyone he knows. They embraced him as one of their own. I opened every door for him. He never would have had access to those circles if wasn't for me."

It was with relief that I saw the red twigs of riverbank willows poking up through the snow. We were across. I could exhale.

Now it was as if he'd forgotten he was crossing a frozen river. He was back in that office in Petrograd, his own parallel stream. "My wife hated him, of course. She knew he was up to something. Well, I couldn't see it. I was mesmerized. He understands people, you see. He reads them like you read those tracks. He knows what you want. He makes you feel special, like you can do great things."

I knew the truth of that. It worked until he turned on you, as he had Andrei, and perhaps me as well.

"I don't know what people want. I don't understand people. I'll admit it. To have a friend in him...I felt like I'd been asleep my whole life, just imitating a human being, and now I was awake. I felt like anything was possible." *Understand why I trusted him,* he was saying. *Why I loved him.* And he still did. I eased my pace, and he stopped, inhaling a chugging breath, trying to calm himself. It wasn't exertion. But it was now only another half a mile to the house. I felt safer. I didn't think the wolf would follow us so far. So I let him talk. Why not?

Replacing the pistol in my pocket, I put on my mittens. "Tell me about the Laboratory."

He started moving again, climbing the little rise. They had discussed renting a dacha to conduct their research, in a resort town on the Gulf of Finland. Without the skeptical wife, no doubt. "Just a dream, I see that now. A toy. Before October, you couldn't find five people in Petrograd willing to give up their roles for such an experiment. But after, that was another thing. Taras came to my home. My boys were already asleep. He always came late—it drove my wife mad. 'He's a free man,' I told her. 'You don't know what to do with a free man.' 'I know what to do with him,' she said. 'Just give me half a chance.' Honestly, I wish I had."

But then they wouldn't have been here. The place would have been abandoned, in a shambles. I scanned the trees ahead through the falling snow, and I imagined I could smell dinner cooking. I had the rabbit and the hare in my bag; it was good enough.

Ukashin had been the one to find the dacha. "He told me he'd found the perfect place for our Laboratory. The Gromov dacha, you know where that is?"

A huge place with massive gardens on Aptekarsky Island.

"I thought it was far too large for our needs. There were only eight of us, after all. But he predicted there would be many more. Well, he was right about that. But I had pictured philosophers, scientists, authors. Cultured people. Not dancers and lunatics." Snow

gathered on his hat and shoulders, his brow and moustache. His glasses steamed over.

"And where was Mother in all this?"

"Vsevolod brought us to your old flat. She was down
to one room by then. It was a shame to see how low
she'd fallen. We took her to the dacha that very night.
Almost like old times." But by then, the Laboratory
was already out of control. "Shopgirls, spiritual thrill
seekers. Morphine addicts. His so-called *followers*. And
I was helpless to stop it."

"I'm sure you did what you could," I said, sounding
like Sofia Yakovlevna. We were almost within sight of
the house now. I took a couple of steps up the hill but
failed to entice him onward.

"I couldn't stem the tide," he said, growing more upset as he told the story, as if pleading his case before a
judge. "Who would follow Andrei Petrovin? By then it
was all Taras the Magus. He stole it from me! Imagine
how it feels to hold your dream in your hands only to
watch it fed to the dogs. Thrown into the fire, your
life's work!" A sob caught his voice.

Yes, I could imagine. I'd felt something similar when
I'd seen the lists of the executed in *Krasnaya Gazeta*.
Here's your revolution. See what we've done with it.

"We were supposed to be a circle of equals. All of
a sudden we had people who'd never heard of Steiner
or Blavatsky. They just wanted to open their mouths
like baby birds and have us feed them. They kissed the
hem of his coat. It was disgusting. By that point he was

styling himself as a holy man. He spent hours creating rituals for our little acolytes to enact. 'Go find five things the color green.' And they would do it! And the women—I shudder to tell you what went on there. 'How can you do this, Taras?' I asked. 'This isn't what we talked about at all.' He said, 'People are animals, my friend. They want to know where they stand. Are they up? Are they down? They don't come to us to have us ask them, 'Well, what do you think?' They're waiting to be told. Would you withhold that from them?"

He was weeping. I was afraid to get near him. I thought he might hit me.

"I know who I am. I don't need followers! I don't need to be called Master. That's his weakness. He needs them to love him, to fear him. He's Moloch. It's not about ideas. He needed my ideas to give him legitimacy. But once he had what he wanted, he didn't care about them at all."

A burst of wind blew snow in our faces. I could barely see the trees now. But soon we'd be safe. Or at least warm. So all the pretty girls, that was not a figment of my imagination. Yet I thought of that night in his *kabinyet*. He never touched me. "Why didn't you leave? Why did you come here, then?"

He hung his head. "Why indeed . . . fool that I am, I had nothing left. I'd destroyed everything that meant anything to me," he said bitterly.

"What about your wife? Couldn't you go back to her?"

He gazed behind him, toward the river, that blurry sleeve of white. I hoped he wasn't going to bolt. It had taken me forever to get him this far. "It turned out she was more attached to her roles than to me. She wanted to be the Publisher's Wife." He stabbed the snow as if lancing a bear. "She wanted me to renounce my research. Concentrate on publishing popular novels." He grimaced. "Romances. *Cookbooks.* Said if I moved to the dacha, I would never see my children again. She wanted me to choose between my work and my roles. What could I do? What would you have done?" His haunted, desperate face, begging me for an answer. Me, of all people. I was just nineteen.

I tugged the fox hat further down onto my head. "I don't know," I said. "I've never been in that position."

He leaned over the peeled birch ski poles and wept, great ragged sobs. It was terrible to hear. The months I'd watched him at dinner, accompanying us on the piano, shoveling snow, sitting like an Alsatian outside my mother's door. Why had we never talked before this? Perhaps, like me, he hadn't wanted to name his suffering, hadn't wanted to see it so clearly.

He bent back so his face was bared to the sky, snow falling like freed secrets. "What was I to do? I had to pursue my ideas. A man is not an animal, to wander the world without a question in his head, a moment of wonder. I had to see, to learn, to discover! She brought the children in that night. 'Kiss your father. He's going on a trip.' 'Oh, where, Papa? To Moscow? With

'Kashin'? A grown man, a father, I walked in with my eyes wide open." He struggled through the snow up to where I stood, slipped, fell against me, almost knocking me over. I pushed him back upright. "I'm such a fool," he said, weeping, clinging to me. "I didn't feel the noose around my neck until it was too late." He backed away from me, sidestepping. "Maybe I still hoped I had a place. That I could protect my ideas somehow." He took off his glasses. "I've been so blind!" And, disgusted, he pitched them out into snow.

That face, so full of pain. "Did I follow Ukashin, Marina? Have you noticed, only he gets a name? I have a name. Andrei Petrovin. Does that mean anything to you—Petrovin Press?"

He'd published poets I'd read. Ravich, Ivan Modal. And this is what had become of him.

"Andrei Petrovin!" He yelled into the falling snow, backing away from me. "Andrei Alexandrovich Petrovin!"

Without his glasses, he looked as unfocused and helpless as a worm writhing on a pavement.

I didn't know how to help him. I didn't want to embarrass him further, watching him sobbing so nakedly, so I moved in the direction he'd thrown his spectacles. I had little hope of finding them. Still, what else could I do? I couldn't bring back his children, his good name, his publishing house, his marriage, his dignity. *What would you have done?* I scanned the snow, and there! Two small circles in the fading light. A perfect imprint of the specs. Like a fox, I dug them out with both hands, flinging snow left and right, then held them aloft. "Andrei, I found them!"

I was turning when I heard the blast. My God.

He sagged halfway to his knees, then fell over sideways in the snow, his feet still tied to the skis. I raced back to him, my right snowshoe coming undone. I plunged in up to my thigh, struggling to get back to him with one foot on top of the drift, the other falling through. "Andrei! Andrei Petrovin!"

He was lying on his side, my gun in his mouth, his eyes shocked and staring out, and the back of his head was gone.

80 *Metel'*

DID I SCREAM? Did I weep? My words returned tenfold as I knelt beside him in the falling snow. *I've never been in that position.* He'd reached out to me, and this was my answer to his soul-deep despair? That was all I could say? I took off my scarf and laid it over his head. I knew I should do something—go to the house, get help—but I didn't want to leave him alone. It was not just the wolf. It was that he'd been alone so long already. I still had his glasses in my hand. *I found your glasses, Andrei Alexandrovich.* As if that was the important thing.

The crunch of snow. Pasha, flakes building up on his

hat and his black beard, had heard the blast. He took one look at Andrei, at me. "Stay there. I'll be right back." The snow fell, trying to cover the deed, the blood, a soft mercy. Too late, too late. *God forgive me, Andrei. I didn't know there wouldn't be another chance.*

Soon Pasha returned with Bogdan and Gleb and the sledge he used to carry his wood. They loaded Andrei's long, awkward body onto it. Bogdan didn't know what to do with the gun. He tried to hand it to me, that deadly piece of steel. I couldn't bear to look at it.

"I'll take it to the Master," he said, tucking it into his coat.

"No. Give it to me," I said. I put it back in my pocket. It was already cold, and it weighed more than it used to, heavy with death. Andrei had fallen against me on purpose. His desperate hand reaching into my pocket. How could I have saved him? Why hadn't I tried? Bogdan carried the skis while Pasha harnessed himself to the sled. Gleb held Andrei's limp legs so they didn't drag in the snow.

By the time we arrived at the house, the others had already gathered in the yard. They stared at the dead man, and at me, confused and wary. I had brought death to their camp.

Ukashin emerged from the house with his hairy dogs, buckling the belt of his greatcoat. The dogs ran to us, snuffled at the body. I kicked them away. This was a man, not a dead deer.

The Master approached. I didn't want to look at him.

Alive, so sturdy, so self-important. *Usurper.* He had stolen Andrei's ideas, made him a laughingstock, driven him to suicide. He lifted my scarf to gaze at the man who'd once been his friend. His face betrayed nothing. I had the gun in my pocket. I could have shot him right there and then.

He straightened, whispered something into Magda's ear, sending her into the house. Natalya hovered, scared, wanting to help, but her frightened eyes waited for Ukashin to signal his verdict. She would follow his lead. I glanced up to the second story, the windows overlooking the yard. *Are you up there, Mother? What do you think of your companion now?*

Magda returned with a sheet she laid out on the shoveled snow. The boys lifted the dead man onto it and wrapped him up. Natalya rested her arm around me. Ukashin avoided my gaze. My fellow sheep waited for their master to tell them what to think. He contemplated the broken figure of his compatriot. Did he realize that he'd taken it too far? Or was this what he wanted all along? For Andrei to eliminate himself, so he wouldn't have to do it. The Ionians shifted, brushing snow from their sad, innocent faces.

Then he turned to regard the group. "Our brother, Andrei Ionian, did a desperate thing," he said at last. He looked into the faces of his children, one by one, a hard extra moment for me. "Our life, what we're accomplishing here, it's a difficult path. He became trapped in his own darkness."

The acolytes nodded, like wooden heads on springs. The wrapped figure in the sheet on the hard-packed snow testified to the truth of that.

"We must not become lost," he said. "The path is twisting and hard to follow. It's easy to head in the wrong direction." His eyes met mine once again. "It's easy to fall."

Here came Avdokia, trotting across the snow. She pushed her way in at my elbow, crossing herself, murmuring a prayer for the dead.

"An idea without commitment to Practice is a dangerous thing," he said. "Farewell, brother Andrei." He nodded to the boys to lift him back onto the sledge.

"He had a name," I said, my voice too loud. It startled the others in the fading light. "It was Andrei Alexandrovich Petrovin, and Ionia was his life's work. It was all he had. And your Master took it from him. And now he's dead."

Avdokia held on to my arm. "Shh, shh," she whispered. "For the love of God."

I could hear the creak of the snow as the disciples shifted, backing away as if lightning bolts might come out of the Master's eyes and strike me dead, and they didn't want to be caught in the crossfire. But the face he showed me was one of mourning and concern. "Let us send a message of love to Marina Ionian, that she was the instrument of such a terrible loss. Her guilt and suffering are our own. But the universe supports all who need it."

He lifted his palms to me, and they all followed suit, their eyes closing, their heads tilting to the right, sending me their impersonal love on command. And I could feel his energy among them, a force like a flavor of spice in the midst of their pallid porridge. I could smell it, strong and musky. He had me. I was as trapped as Andrei Ionian.

"Take him to the icehouse," the Master told the boys. And they began to pull him back the way we'd come.

"*Vechnaya pamyat'*," said Avdokia. *Eternal memory.*

Murmurs echoing her sentiment moved through the group as they followed him down the path to cold storage.

I returned with Avdokia to her room, where I sat on her bed, still in my sheepskin. "Don't fight about this, Marinoushka, my angel," she said, kneeling, pulling off my boots, putting my slippers on, taking my hat. "It's not your business. This was between him and *that one*."

I told her what Andrei had said, that he had thrown his glasses. I showed them to her, warm from my pocket. An hour earlier they'd been on his face. "You saw how it was. Ukashin cut him down every day, so no one would ever listen to him. He killed him."

Her blue kerchief before me, she shook her head. "You have to think of yourself now. Your baby. This was not your quarrel."

"You want me just to forget? Like it never happened?" I could still see him, his face to the sky, praying for help, praying for release from his suffering. How he fell on me. The blood in the snow.

Avdokia sighed as she hauled herself to her feet. "You have such a tender heart, *milaya*. I pray for you." She sat on her bed next to me, her arm around my waist. I took a deep, shuddering breath. Her warm smell, so familiar. Oh couldn't we go back to the way it was? "Don't lose everything for that sad man. He's gone, poor thing. But you're still here. You have to live on. Ask yourself, who was he to you really?"

Who was he? Why would she ask such a question? In truth—an annoyance, a pedant. I knew nothing about him. But when a human being unburdens himself to you, you become part of his troubles. "Does it matter? He didn't deserve to be so reduced. You didn't hear him crying. Ukashin took everything from him."

"Listen to me." She pressed my face between the palms of her bent old hands, exactly as she used to do when I was a child and she needed to talk to me seriously. Her little eyes in their nest of wrinkles, her nose and her chin practically touching. "Things are going to happen to you in your life far worse than this, Marinoushka. It's a terrible thing to say to a young person, I know. You're still seeing him out there...God knows how he got your gun. But the thing is—where are you going to be when *that one* puts you out? What use will you be to anyone if you don't make it? Let Andrei go. He's in God's hands now." She crossed herself. "May God have mercy on the living and the dead."

But my old nanny hadn't been there. She hadn't heard him, hadn't seen his face when he talked about kissing his children goodbye. *What would you have done?*

I slept in her bed with his glasses curled in my hand.

I heard them through the door, making dinner. No one said a word. I didn't come out. I turned my face to the wall. Avdokia brought me soup with a good piece of meat in it. I ate it while she watched me, hoping I would talk to her, but I had nothing more to say. Not to her, not to anyone.

Later in the evening, Natalya's pretty face poked through the door, her water-brown hair, my swan. "Are you all right?"

"No," I said.

"Are you coming for Practice?"

"No."

"It's nobody's fault," she said. "He fell into doubt." As though he'd fallen from a tram. Belief was like that. When you fell, you cracked yourself open. And what would it take for this pretty butterfly to doubt her Master? Whose death would it take? Mine?

He sent for me, late. This time, Bogdan was the messenger. "He wants you." Avdokia was the one who made me get up, put my slippers on me. "You have to go. You can't hide in here forever." And so I went.

In the front parlor, I could feel the just-completed Practice, like a violin that was too high to hear, an invisible cloak of scented silk. I didn't want to feel its beauty, didn't want it to dissipate my disgust. Bogdan left me with a guilty shrug.

"Sit down," Ukashin said quietly. I was afraid of him. I tried to remember my courage, but where had it fled?

I sat on the carpet, and to my horror he came and sat right in front of me, our knees nearly touching. I was terrified to be so close to him. What was he going to do to me? He had already been threatening to put me out, and that was before my outburst.

"You've had a shock," he said. "To have him do this when he was with you. And with your own gun. I don't blame you for being upset. I'm upset, too."

I saw again the bright bloom of Andrei's blood, the way he'd crumpled to the ground, still strapped into his skis. A wave of comfort suffused me. I didn't want it. I knew it was a lie, that he was doing it to me, but I needed comfort, too. I was not as strong as I pretended to be.

"I know you're thinking you should have done something," he said, his voice low, confiding. "If you'd only said the right words. That you should have steadied him, brought him back to the light. Supported his path instead of fanning his doubt."

It was true. I didn't try to make him feel better. *I've never been in that position.*

"He trusted you," he went on in that kind voice. "He

liked you. That's why I sent him with you. To see if he would reach out. But you didn't help him. You failed him."

Oh God, that was true, too. But I had to remember, I wasn't the reason for his suffering. I was only a tool.

"I don't blame you," he said. "You didn't know what you were doing. I worried about this from the beginning. You act without thinking."

I gazed down at the carpet, the stylized pomegranates and deer. I didn't want him to confuse me. It was he who had betrayed his friend. Andrei had no one, and that was Ukashin's fault, not mine.

"Look at me, Marina Ionian." I lifted my eyes, so very weary. "Am I angry?" In his face, no anger, only tenderness, a little tiredness, that of a man with many responsibilities. For all of Ionia. How human he looked right now. It surprised me after my accusations. "Each of us is seeking something here, Marina. Some want a more radiant path. Others, fellowship. We all have our own reasons. Even you."

"I wasn't seeking anything." I wanted more than anything to push myself back from him, but then he would know how frightened I was.

"You wanted sanctuary," he said. "A home. A place in the world. And I gave it to you, didn't I?"

I had made this happen. Again, I had forced my way in. I was the one. He'd wanted to send me away that first day. Oh God, I wished he had.

"But you can't both tear down your home and have

it," he said. "And your child can't be born into a snow-drift. I want you to have it here."

In that exact moment, I felt a fluttering, like an eyelid's tic, in the depths of my body. The fetus had chosen this moment to awaken.

He was impossible to escape, those bull's eyes, sad, piercing, his drooping moustache, the big nose, the planes of his face, the mole on his forehead, the lines on the dome of his head. "The dead hold no grudges, Marina. They know everything, understand everything." Insistent, warm. "Andrei sought understanding," he continued. "It was his life's purpose. Now he's released from the blindness of this world into the Great Knowledge. A violent release, but he didn't know how else to accomplish it. He's where he always wanted to be. He has transcended to the upper dimensions."

How awful to say he was better off dead. But much of what this hard man was saying was true. The more he spoke, the less sure I was. I felt his words like a current, urging me onto the river of his story.

What would you have done?

He reached out and took my hand. His flesh like wood, denser than ordinary flesh. I felt a great rush of grief—for Andrei, and myself, and all the people caught in their traps, and those who don't know how to save them. What a world of suffering we live in. I felt unmoored, drifting and spinning in the tide.

*   *   *

Andrei's suicide lingered. It tapped the windows, clung to our faces and hands. The possibility of doom darkened the edges of the Ionian dream, and the weather did nothing to lessen it. *Metel'*, we say. Blizzard. The compressed savagery of the season came down as if trying to scrape us from the face of the earth. The nearness of death was a smell in my hair like gunpowder. How small and alone we were here, the country around us not Russia but Death.

The blizzard raged. Wind shrieked at the corners of the house; the trees streamed, tugging at their roots. Branches rattled against the walls. Bad luck had arrived. Ukashin's dogs mysteriously disappeared. Nightmares swept the dormitories. We no longer shared our dreams in public, teasing out their meaning. Ukashin met with each of us privately in his *kabinyet* to unburden us, to explain away the darkness.

I dreamed I was feasting with Taras Ukashin, gorging on dates and almonds, colored eggs and mulled wine. We made love on the sheepskins while Andrei Ionian stood outside in the cold, miserable, with only that sheet around him, his blue face pressed to the window.

The temperature continued to drop. Outside the kitchen, the glass tube with its mercury spine showed forty below. There's a hardness to the air when the thermometer falls this low. The cold is a knife gouging any bit of exposed skin. It slashes your cheeks. You have to close your eyes or your eyeballs freeze in your head.

The Master ordered everything to be brought into the house—meat from the smokehouse, chickens from the coop, everything edible carried down to the larder under the kitchen. I could not stop thinking about Andrei in the icehouse. I was not so sure that the dead forgive us everything.

Bad-tempered Lilya and I brought in the chickens from the henhouse, collecting them one by one and conveying them under our coats. She left the rooster to me. I tackled him, wrapped him in my sheepskin as he madly clawed me. I was afraid I'd break his neck or one of his feet. We stashed them under baskets weighted with wood in Avdokia's room and stood by the hot stove, waited for the shivering to die down before going out again. The boys brought firewood into the hall, and the girls melted snow in barrels in the kitchen. It was as if we were preparing for a siege.

No more could I escape to tramp the woods. I would experience Ionia undiluted, the full force of the communal mind.

We assembled in the Practice room. The Master had an announcement to make. "It is time to accelerate your advancement, the adept along with the novice. All together as one." He would introduce a new Practice— *vlivaniye. Inflowing.* It was a technique known only to a few dozen human beings on earth. The excitement in the faces of the acolytes was as if he'd announced to a bunch of children that the Sugar Plum Fairy was coming to visit. "A secret teaching," he said, "kept for thousands of years among the Brotherhood of the Sun." A sect of monks in the Tien Shan, the eastern Himalayas, where he had spent time learning their mysteries. They took in energy directly from the earth and sun right through their skins. Hale and hearty, they lived to a great age, and some had not eaten in fifty years.

"Imagine the freedom," he said. "To no longer have to feed on matter that feeds on other matter. To concentrate energy directly from the cosmos. If people knew, all wars would cease, all craving would vanish. People would know there was always enough to sustain them. That they were truly sons and daughters of the universe."

Vlivaniye became our lives. Sealed together by the storm, we were one body, one consciousness. And I went under like a diver, I plunged. In the end I could not bear the loneliness of being outside the circle. I had to trust that there was a boat rocking above me, my own rationality, and that when I returned to the surface it would still be there, and I would not be lost in a featureless sea.

Ukashin taught us that the material body wasn't solid but rather permeated with radiant matter capable of absorbing energy, as a sponge can be filled with water. We held on to his voice as if it were a rope across a vast chasm of space.

First we *inflowed* with the earth. I was surprised how much I enjoyed descending into the ground, passing the tunnels of moles and lairs of badgers, the nut-filled hideouts of squirrels and rabbits—how surprised they were to see me! I visited foxes with their tails around their noses, and sleeping bears, and proceeded down through the roots of trees, breathing through the earth, reaching the glowing gems and veins of metals. You were safe down there. Nothing could hurt you with the earth tucked in over you. Cross-legged on the carpet, we breathed in the planetary emanations, and they felt like kindness, forgiveness. All things began and ended in earth. Crops, trees, animals. How alive it was, how generous. At least I could say, *This was my home*. Safe from guilt, safe from the past, safe from Andrei, safe from the Master himself.

The sun's energy was brighter, clear and intelligent "Your light body is activated," he lectured. "Open your eyes, look around. You'll know this to be true." And when I looked, the Ionians had become floating bodies of light, suffused with bright handfuls of energy like glittering fistfuls of confetti.

I gazed at my own arms, astonished. I could have sworn I saw light like fine hairs rising from them. Movement in the hair and in the beards of my friends, light concentrating in their organs. Yet still I heard Andrei saying, *You don't care, as long as he keeps you fascinated*. Well, I was not Andrei, willing to sit in a corner while the others did their Practice, feeding on self-righteousness, alone, hungry, and miserable.

Those nights I lay on my pallet, trying to see if I

could still detect that glow, testing to see if it was only hypnosis. But it was becoming harder to tell what was suggestion and what was real. We were eating very little, and the near fasting exaggerated the effects. I turned over, trying to sleep, but the energy was far too high. I thought of Andrei in the icehouse, his blue face, his bloody head. *Don't listen to him,* he begged me. *Don't fall under his spell.*

But I couldn't be both here and there. *Andrei, you shot yourself with my gun, but I didn't shoot you. You made your choices long before. You should have left when people started kissing his hem, but you could not open your hand.*

I know I was a failure, he replied. *But don't succumb as I did.*

His feud was with Ukashin, but it wasn't my fight. The Earth Devi was supporting me now. It wasn't about the Master. The teaching wasn't the man. The former could be good while the other was corrupt, couldn't it? Andrei could not do the *inflowing,* dissolving himself, because he loved only ideas. And without a body, there was nowhere for the light to come in. It entered the skin, it filled you like a wineskin.

Though the days were dark and the wind shook the house, the sun grew inside us, rushing through the glowing sea anemones of our nerves, our blood vessels like rivers. Sometimes I jerked crazily. Ukashin said it was because I was leaping so far ahead of where I'd been in my Practice, bringing in far larger quantities of energy than my body was accustomed to. The energetic channels had to expand to accommodate the new current, and sometimes there were kinks. I sweated, I shook. Natalya created a dance—coiling in, then un-curling. When others joined her, it became a flower. But no more would Andrei accompany our dances on my mother's old piano.

We would not be ready for total *inflowing* for months, he said. But I could attest that the Practice was already making changes in us. For one thing, food seemed sick-ening now. We had to be urged to eat. When did that happen, in the Russia of 1919? Avdokia dropped the big pot onto the table with a clang, as if she wanted to startle us from our high vibrational hum. As we passed our bowls I could hear her grumble. "Living on light...we'll see how well that works."

Ukashin lowered his spoon. "The ignorant suffer most, because they brace for the worst. Fear closes you off. You have to be porous, like a sponge."

After she left, we could hear her clattering in the kitchen. I wanted to laugh, imagining her curses, her comments about sponges and the Master. She couldn't see what we saw—that we were feeding on radiance, living in radiance.

After the dishes were cleared, we brought out our projects, shoes and hats. Ukashin played his flute. The disciples sang. Though our voices were not as strong as before, they were purer. Small motions captured my eye. I was transfixed by the movement of the hanging spindle—long and slender, of carved wood like a top—that Anna used to spin flax. The spinning reminded me of the earth and the stars. Like a wedding ring hung over a pregnant belly—*will it be a boy or a girl?* I never did that. No wedding ring.

My head shimmered with strings of sound—the storm's vowels, *oooo ooo oooo.* The consonants: *Ts*, the sizzle of the peppering snow. *K*—Crack! Crash! The wind clawed the windows, battered the house as if shot from a fire hose. *Eeee.*

"Why shouldn't it storm?' said Ukashin, brandishing his flute like Aaron with his staff. "Why should nature cut itself down to fit our capacity for experience? Don't be afraid. Embrace it. Look at Marina. Tell us the storm, Marina Ionian. Be our bard." He leaned back in his chair.

I rose, the storm in my mouth. *I am the storm.* The size of it rose within me, the power. I felt its rage and envy, its hunger. I gloried in my own strength.

> *Far my reach my wreck my wrath . . .*
> *With my feet of iron and head of ice*
> *My name is Knife.*
> *My name is Rage*
> *Tear you apart like a loose-nailed roof.*
> > *Say you're not afraid?*
> > *You think this is a children's game?*

Their faces startled, mesmerized.

> *I kiss your lips—aniline blue*

Your hands freeze to the ax
I'm Winter's blade
A Tula sword,
I'll ride you down
With my twelve-legged horse.
Say you're not afraid?
Meet my children, wind and ice.
They set their shoulders to your door.
Dig you out of your hiding place.
Baba Yaga stores her mortar out of sight.
Stenka Razin flees with his brothers
Ilya Muromets cowers before my power.
The throne lies empty.
The house of ice awaits.

With Andrei, the house of death awaiting them all.

Say you're not afraid
When branches crack and fly?
When you're caught in Winter's grip?
I am the storm.
My name is Be Afraid.

The thrill and the heart of the chaos, its inhuman force and destructive joy surged within me. The throne, empty. Yes. He could not invite the devil in and stop it halfway. The storm served no one but itself.

Suddenly heads swiveled to the door.

My mother stood in the doorway, hovering, in an

aura of powder, like a moth. Her long white hair unbraided, her pale cloak awry. Ilya, at her side, her indecisive shadow, looked terrified. "Taras?" came the high, tremulous voice I knew so well.

Already Ukashin was moving toward her, taking her white hands.

It was as if some fantastic figure who lived across seas seven times seven had appeared in our humble izba, summoned by my words. "The wolf," she hissed. "Don't you hear it?" My mother's terror ratcheted up their anxiety, even higher than my poem had. "Scratching, scratching. Don't let it in!" She pointed toward the north, and the storm's volume rose at that moment, as if in reply. *Let me in.*

The Master held her thin hands between his own. "We won't let it, Mother. What shall we do? Tell us what you see."

"Rub the sills! Have them fetch fir and juniper. Lay them across the doorways. Don't let it in!"

Ukashin looked around. His eyes settled upon Pasha. "You. Cut some boughs, bring them in."

He was going to send Pasha out into that storm? Yes, he was the woodsman, but he was also guilty of a secret personal love, something that excluded the Master. This would be a two for one. It was not a joke to send someone out for the storm to eat. But Pasha rose without hesitation.

Katrina paled, her face a mask, but the woodcutter bowed to the will of his Master and the prophetess.

Mother's urgency breathed life into my metaphor, creating a shape—yes, a wolf, tearing at the windows, trying to get in. "I'll go, too," Bogdan volunteered. *"Davai,"* said Gleb, rising. Perhaps not wanting Pasha to get all the credit for bravery in Katrina's eyes. The three piled into the kitchen, grabbed their skis and snowshoes, coats and hats, and returned through the hall to the front door to prepare for the bitter cold, wrapping their scarves around their faces, leaving mere slits for their eyes.

I snatched at Bogdan's sleeve. "Please—don't risk your life for a handful of pine needles. If you die, he'll say it's because you didn't believe enough."

He stroked my face, gently. "It will be fine. You have to trust."

"Don't say *die*," Katrina snapped, trying to pull me back toward the workroom. "Can't you see you're just making it worse?" Her worried blue eyes followed Pasha out the door.

I yanked myself away from her grasp and stood in the cold vestibule after she returned to the others. They didn't know how quickly death could come. Just in a minute. Tree limbs flew faster than horses out there. Your skin froze in moments.

Avdokia appeared at my elbow. "You can't talk a fool out of a fire," she said and slipped something into my pocket—a packet wrapped in paper. Meat. She must have stolen it from the pot right under Katrina's nose. I choked it down, threw the paper into a corner so they wouldn't find it on me. "Can you smell me?" I held out my hands to her.

"Don't get too close," she said.

In the workroom, my lunatic mother now sat in Ukashin's chair, white as Snegurochka, the Snow Maiden, Winter's daughter. Maybe she really had seen a wolf, or a spirit, or a Dark Body from a far dimension only visible to her squid eyes, but you didn't send precious humans out when these creatures were stalking.

Katrina and I wiped off a window and peered out at the tiny flicker of lantern light swinging off in the lee of the house. Then it was swallowed by the storm. All because of a woman who hadn't been out of her room for months and talked to imaginary creatures in the dark. Ukashin sat by her side, knitting his brow like a priest at confession as she spoke into his ear. It was the first time I'd seen them together in the open, in the light. How reverently he was listening, his head bowed, nodding.

And then it struck me like a tree branch in the head. Taras Ukashin *believed in my mother*. This was no confidence game, not a clever use of her to appropriate her holdings or to lay further claim to the mystical Beyond. It was worse. He truly believed she was receiving insights from other worlds. I'd always assumed that he was controlling her—but what if it was the opposite? What if it was Vera Borisovna setting our course, not Taras Ukashin? *Bozhe moi.*

Mother continued speaking urgently to her—what?

Lover? Communicant? —while her devotees ranged around the table, nervously resuming their tasks. I noticed that Magda could not take her eyes off Ukashin, the way he practically knelt at Mother's feet, holding her hand. Jealousy burned in her like an empty pan on a hot stove. Ilya swallowed, his big Adam's apple rising and falling. I *saw* that he was ashamed to be inside and safe when the other boys risked their lives on this fool's errand.

Five minutes passed. Forty below, with a wind like frozen nails. My mother's glance slid briefly over the rest of us without interest, as if we were dolls in a shop window. Something struck the house, and we jumped. She jumped as well. Good, she was not so insensible as all that.

"There are no wolves, you know," I said. "It's too cold. They're asleep in their dens under the snow." The minnows of her attention hovered over my face, their tickling mouths in my eyes, in my ears.

"So much red," she pronounced. Evidently even *inflowing* had done nothing for my aura.

"Recent events have disturbed her energy, Mother," Ukashin defended me. "But she is one with us."

"She's one with no one," my mother said. "She'll never be one with anyone. It is her fate."

As if balling me into a lump like a greasy piece of paper and throwing me into a corner. So much for me. My lungs froze in my chest. I tried to think of people I *had* been one with—Genya, Kolya. The Poverty Artel. But a deeper truth uncoiled, like a fiddlehead fern. Around me, glances of pity. A ripple of unease traveled around the room—except for Magda. A pleased smile flickered around her lips.

"There's no such thing as Fate," I said. But what the high priestess said was oracle, and I had the horrible suspicion that she could be right. What if it was true? Damn her—why did she have to come downstairs when she'd been so happy in that creepy room with her weird icons and little polished stones?

Ukashin leaned toward her. "She's with us for now, Mother," he said. "In this time stream. And who can say more about anyone?"

I should have felt gratitude. Yet I still felt the teeth of the storm in my mouth, my horrible red aura, and wanted to hurt her for handing me such a fate like a slap. I wanted to wipe that otherworldly vagueness from her face. "Did your spirit guides tell you Andrei Petrovin shot himself?" I called down the table. "Your friend Andrei?" The attention swam back to me, regarding my outline as if it wavered in water. "That's right—Andrei Petrovin. Notice you haven't seen him around much? He's lying in the icehouse, rolled up like a carpet."

She turned away from me as she used to when I'd said something awkward to one of her guests, simply erased me from her attention. That was her answer. Her friend's death meant nothing. Ukashin had been more perturbed.

was going on inside our minds. Only in the window on the stairway landing could you see what was going on in the yard. Sometimes I stood there for hours, it seemed, in a trance, watching the trees lashing about like souls in some white hell.

Now that Mother had joined us, Ukashin more and more often turned his back on the others to focus entirely on his prophetess. He stopped leading the *inflowing* meditation, leaving it in the hands of Magda and Natalya. Instead he spent hours in communication with his priestess, meditating with her, or else painting or lying in his hammock, which he'd slung in the corner by the fire next to Mother's chair. Through the buildup of snow, the storm's roaring sounded more and more like the blood in my ears. The acolytes worked hard to regain their Master's favor, as if the blizzard were somehow their fault, as if they could make things better by being perfect little disciples. Mother sat communing with the paintings they'd fetched from her lair and rearranging her little stones with the clicking sounds like waves turning pebbles on a beach. Her spirit guides watched us night and day.

Pasha was the first to collapse. He crumpled during a meditation session. Katrina, surfacing from her trance, jumped to her feet. "Pasha?" she called out, leaning over him but afraid to touch him. "Master? Pasha's fainted!"

But the Master said nothing.

"He's all right," Magda said. "Let him be."

"What else didn't they tell you?" I shouted down the table. "Did you know I was pregnant? I'm going to have a child, Mama. This summer. Your grandchild."

The devotees shifted uncomfortably, embarrassed that their priestess was being dragged into a matter so unseemly and personal when they'd given up every family connection, even their names. I could see that Magda wanted to get her hands around my throat. Ukashin stared at me. I could almost hear him—*I can't save you forever.*

"Your grandchild, Mama. It's Kolya Shurov's."

Now her vision cleared, and she saw me. Oh, yes. She remembered me now. *Your daughter.* She regarded me with something resembling fear.

"Yes, Kolya. We've been lovers since I was sixteen. Did you see that in your multidimensional universe?"

But then her vision clouded over, and she was scanning me, as she had in the room upstairs, as if she were reading a wall poster, a playbill for a drama at the People's House. What was I, a little Ibsen? Or maybe Wilde?

"It won't live," she said.

The sound echoed like a gunshot in a long hall. When it faded, the only sound in the room was the roaring of the wind.

Doors slammed, and in a gust of frigid air, the trio of boys thundered into the hall. In walked Pasha, frosted white, hat, scarf, coat, boots, gloves, his arms piled high with fragrant fir, followed by Gleb and Bogdan equally laden. The relief was palpable. All uncertainty vanished, and the disciples beamed with the proof: their prophetess was wise, Ukashin was still in control, I was an alarmist and disrupter. *You see?* said the Master's sideways glance. *We know what we're doing here.* The others grabbed up the boughs and began rubbing the sills and doorways.

I lay on my pallet that night among the others, no longer marveling at our initiation into the mysteries of *inflowing*. Even hiding within the earth did me no good. I only heard my mother's voice. I thought of her face, her calm. I wanted to slap her even now. Was she punishing me for insisting that there was no wolf and that she was no seer, only a madwoman? Or was she so crazy that she didn't understand how terrible was her curse?

But what if it was true?

No. That I would not believe. I might never be one with anyone—fine—but I would not let her kill my baby. I rejected her spell, I spat on it, I walked on it, I pissed on it. I would not believe. To think of how I'd cared for her. She was the reason I'd broken with Genya, the reason I'd gone to Kamenny Island to sell that pin. She had not defended me against my father that October night. I turned over and over, settling the sheepskin back on top of the quilt. As long as I could have my baby, I would endure the rest.

I had not realized how passionately I wanted this child until my mother tried to take it away from me.

81 *The Hunter*

THE STORM DID NOT abate. If anything, it worsened. Ukashin moved us into the heart of the house, the back parlor, closing off all the other rooms to conserve heat and firewood. We squashed into the workroom like kittens in a sack. After what my mother had said to me, it was agony to have to see her every day. I thought I would go mad. Everyone breathing each other's breath and that sticky incense, the stove pushing smoke into the room as it would in a black izba. If it wasn't for *inflowing,* I would have had to stop breathing altogether. Only under the earth was it still possible to inhale. Meditation was the only escape from the oppressive togetherness. I supposed my mother's curse of eternal loneliness had not yet taken effect.

I sometimes ventured up the frost-coated stairs to the water closet just to be free of them all. The chamber pots we'd put there had frozen fast—we couldn't have them in the room with us. They didn't stink, though you had to wear your coat and hat and boots to visit the convenience. You might as well be outside. White rime built up on the bare risers of the stairs, showing our footprints. Outside, snow buried the first-floor windows, cutting us off from the world, mirroring what

It was frightening to see Pasha lying on the carpet. It reminded me of Andrei in the snow. Bogdan, our erstwhile doctor, knelt to tend to his fallen brother. Katrina hovered. She brought a cloth as white as her face and a jug of cold water. Wiping his face revived him, and he was terribly embarrassed. I myself was teetering on the tightrope between the need to *inflow* to keep hunger and terror at bay and my growing anger and anxiety about Ukashin's detachment from the world he'd built, the one he'd stolen from Andrei Ionian.

Inflowing went on. The meals lightened to suit our more rarefied systems—thin oatmeal, cabbage, kasha, soup with floating bits of meat. The more resentful I became about the figure in the hooded cloak, the less the meat sickened me and the hungrier I became.

It struck me one day—the *meat.*

Fresh meat.

Not salted. Not smoked. Where did it come from?

Surely those two rabbits I'd caught the night Andrei died hadn't lasted thirteen people this long, no matter how frugal we were. The *vlivaniye* was supposed to supply us with new ideas, but in fact I could see that the opposite was true. It kept us from thinking at all. As I fell out of step with the others and my dense body returned, I started to consider things more clearly. For one thing, I recalled the quiet departure of Bonya and Buyan. Ukashin never mentioned them, and no one asked, just as we'd never asked about Andrei's sorrows. Those dogs hadn't run off. We were consuming them, bit by bit.

There will always be enough if we believe. If we don't re-press the bounty with our doubts.

I wondered what else I'd missed amid so much *in-flowing*. Harmony was lovely but I was the hunter— the fox, not the lamb. And the fox in me wondered— what really lay in the larder beneath the kitchen floor? I thought of the profligacy of the Great Feast of the Golden Egg. That green-painted door beckoned. What secrets might be hidden in the cold room where we used to keep Annoushka's jams and the canned produce from our garden, barrels of apples and turnips in sand? That door made my palms itch. Nobody was allowed down there now but Katrina Ionian. Even en-tering the kitchen was a rationed act.

I woke in the night, squirmed into my coat, my hat, and quietly left the workroom. But instead of walk-ing upstairs to the icy water closet, I felt my way along the hall lined with Ukashin's spiritualist paint-ings toward the forbidden door. One painting, two, three. As children, we often played the game of Blind Man. You pretended to be blind and found your way about the house by touch alone. I found the kitchen door, and opened it. Inside, the oven was still warm from dinner, the air soup-perfumed. I felt along the soft wood of the chest, the table. I knew the door to the larder would be to the right. The iron knob was cool, and turned. Unlocked. Cold musty air rose from under the house as I slipped inside, closed the door behind me and inched down the steep stairs, holding the wooden railing.

Such a familiar smell enveloped me—mushrooms, cold dirt, apples, potatoes. I knew the shape of the room as I knew the shape of my lover's hand. Shelves along three sides for preserves, starting just underneath the low ceiling and stopping around hip height. Bags and barrels tucked underneath. Boxes of sand for the root vegetables. I began examining the shelves with my fingertips, moving from left to right, top to bottom. Empty. Empty. All empty. A crock. The faint tang of pickles. Two more cold crocks—maybe more of that green wine Bogdan had made. Something brushed my face and I jumped. Strings of dried mushrooms. The dry crunchy whisper of braided onions. More empty shelves. My felt boot found a sack. I dipped my hand. Grain, cool through my fingers. Another—grain, but only half full. String after string of wizened ears— dried apples. I tore off a few, ate them as I went. Pairs of dried fish hung together, and the urge to eat one was overwhelming, but I resisted. It would be stealing— they belonged to the group. *Hypocrite.* I let Avdokia steal for me almost every day. But I wouldn't do it my- self.

My worst fears had proved correct. The cellar held nothing but empty shelves, empty sacks. In the sand- boxes, a few cabbages lay buried like severed heads, along with some turnips, maybe, or beets. A barrel of apples. And that was all. Thirteen people could not live off this for the rest of the winter. Maybe there was more hidden away somewhere. Perhaps they'd only brought in what was needed to last through the storm.

But my Petrograd mind was already flying, calculating: half a pound of grain a day per person. How long could these sacks last? Two, maybe three weeks at most. Eight chickens at one chicken a day...fourteen fish, in soup...

We weren't going to make it.

No wonder he'd introduced *inflowing*. No wonder.

I was halfway up the stairs when I saw the flicker of a candle under the door. I flew back down and wedged myself behind the sandboxes and barrels, lay down on the cold earthen floor at full length, my head under the lowest stair. The smell of earth and apples. Childhood. The creak of the stairs under a soft-shod foot. "Marina, I know you're down there."

Magda Ionian. Did she know or was she just guessing? Had she seen me get up? Had she counted the sleeping bodies? I could hear her breathing. I *inflowed* through the earth, my breath just a wisp. She was examining the stores, rattling the crocks, counting the fish. I could hear their dried skins rasping together. I wasn't here, I told myself. I was within the earth, with just a siphon to the surface. I wasn't breathing; the earth was breathing me. She held the candle aloft, as if I might be clinging to the rafters. "If you're stealing, he'll put you out, Mother or no. She can only protect you for so long."

Then her shuffle on the earthen floor grew near. The candle threw its light over the sandboxes. *Theotokos, protect me.* Would she see where I'd left my handprints in the sand? She looked, but she didn't *see.* I could hear her sighs of frustration. *Yes, doubt, Magda. You're cross, you're tired, you're hearing things. It's so cold down here. Your pallet by the stove misses you.*

What was she waiting for? Did she think I would pop up like a rabbit in an amusement-park arcade?

She sneezed. Her candle's light was weak and unsteady, the dust and cobwebs thick under the stairs. At last the light moved off, and the old steps creaked. She closed the door behind her.

In the morning, she never took her eyes off me. I did nothing that would give myself away. I stretched, practiced *inflowing,* ate breakfast as innocently as a lamb. *I am the hunter.* She would not catch me asleep. "You've got cobwebs in your hair," she whispered, passing behind me.

"But not in my eyes," I said.

Avdokia caught our exchange. Her eyes shot a warning: *Don't bite the tiger's tail!* But my teeth craved it. My dense matter. My fury building as I watched Ukashin meditating with Mother, their backs to us. *It won't live,* she'd said. Not if I trusted that larder. We must have eaten half our stores the one night of the Great Feast of the Golden Egg. Without such an elaborate gesture, we might have made it. *What were you thinking, Taras*

Ukashin? No matter what his failings, I'd always considered him a practical man, but Andrei was right. The well-being of Ionia had never been foremost in his mind. It was fascination he sought, adulation, keeping us under his sway. I didn't know what he was planning or if indeed he had a plan at all. Maybe my mother told him the sky would open up and rain down *pirozhky* with meat or, better yet, roast beef. Maybe he really did believe in *inflowing*. Or had finally realized the enormity of what he'd done and was too guilty to face us. But I was past wanting his answers. Whatever he'd planned or hadn't planned, his future wouldn't include me or my child. Because this baby needed to live. It had to.

On each trip to the chamber pot now, I hid something on top of the wardrobe in the cold women's dormitory. All the things I'd brought with me—my Vikzhel papers, my clothes, my gun. The letter opener from Ukashin's campaign desk for good measure. I watched for the end of the storm. The wind still gusted, and snow flew, but I could feel the blizzard tiring, like a man continuing an argument long after his initial passion has faded. Now it was only habit. The gypsy caught me up there once. "What were you doing in here?"

I forced myself to peer through the windows and not look in the direction of the wardrobe. "Seeing if the storm's over yet. I'm sick of breathing everyone's farts. I need to get back to my traps. Soup's getting thin, don't you think?"

"The devis will provide," she told me.

"Believe what you want," I replied, pushing past her. "I prefer rabbit to dog meat."

"Doubt's a contagion," she called after me. "He should put you out now."

It was hard. I could no longer lose myself for hours *inflowing*. I felt every bit of my hunger, the need to leave while I could still walk. Now I saw them as they were. Natalya, becoming ghostly, paper thin. Ilya's hands shaking. They couldn't see they were fading away. *Inflowing* worked, but only because the trance lifted you out of your body. We were starving, though our spirits felt bright. It was a lie. They should kill off those chickens now and conserve the grain. But still the chickens clucked on in their overturned baskets. Pasha passed out again during dinner, Lilya during *inflowing*. Ukashin didn't even deign to turn around and see what had happened.

One morning I pleaded illness, refusing to get up off my pallet for the Practice. Natalya came to me, gazing down with great green eyes filled with anxiety. "You have to *inflow*, Marina. We're almost there." Her poor worried face, that I'd cut myself off from the invisible manna. Should the emperor wear a vest or a waistcoat?

"I will," I said. "I'm just going to sleep a little now."

She went back with the others. I could see their light,

their bliss. I wanted to shriek, "You're dying!" but not one of them would hear me. *Don't say "die."*

Avdokia, who'd seen Natalya come for me, padded over, asked, "Marinoushka, are you all right?"

I pulled her down to me. She lowered herself, stiff as a person born without joints, and stroked my hair, my cheeks, felt my temperature with the back of her soft hand. I winked. She stopped when she realized my illness was purely theatrical, then resumed her ministrations, glancing quickly around us. "How do you feel? You have a little fever," she said in a stage whisper.

"My snowshoes," I murmured in her ear. "Put them on top of the wardrobe in the dormitory." Magda watching my every twitch and cough. I didn't dare get anywhere near the kitchen. I could end up tied, wrist and ankle, in a cold room.

Avdokia nodded her old head. She was a master of conspiracy. "I'm going to get you some tea now," she announced. "Your lips are all dry. See if you can sleep a little."

After a while, she brought the tea back. I could feel the cold on her, the smell of unheated rooms. She propped me up, held the glass, just as she had when I was small. If only I could stay here forever, just like this, in her arms. But I had to get out. I had a baby to think about. She kissed me as I drank. "I made it *just the way you wanted*," she said.

My tears would betray me, so I closed my eyes, nestled at her breast. How could I leave her behind? How could I have this baby without her? "Come with me," I whispered between sips. "It's not that far. You could do it."

Her expression could have melted a heart of stone. "Forgive me," she whispered. "My strong, brave girl."

She would still sacrifice her life for my mother, her first love. I could take care of myself, yes, but who would take care of Avdokia? Maybe I should put this off another day or two. But no. I would never forget Arkady's lesson, taught to me with a shard of glass—I still bore the scar. *You waited. That was stupid. Only amateurs wait.*

My nanny snugged my scarf around my neck. "I only wish I could hold that baby," she said. "Yours and Kolya's—heaven help us." I rested against her, her arms around me as she tipped the last of the barley tea into my mouth.

"How can I leave you?" I said.

She smoothed my hair. "Go, while I can still stand it," she breathed in my ear.

My old love, my nanny, with her ancient gnarled hands. She helped me on with my sheepskin and felt boots for the trip to the icy loo. If I only could carry her—my Vasilisa doll—with me in my pocket, I would feed her crumbs, and she would teach me how to throw a comb that would become a forest, a towel that would become a river, and I would outwit all the sorcerers and stepmothers and Baba Yagas from here to Tikhvin. But I would have to do my best on my own.

From the windows in the dormitory, I could not see as far as the henhouse for the fog. The wild horse of the storm had finally run itself out, and the softness of the powdered air hid the damage. Below me, snowdrifts covered the roof of the kitchen porch. I opened the window and sat on the sill, strapped hard into my snowshoes, my game bag snug across my chest, my scarf wrapped around my face. In my pocket, I touched Andrei's glasses for memory, if not for luck. Without him, I might still be down there *inflowing* with the rest. I said a prayer and dropped into the unbroken white.

82 *Wonderworker*

I SMELLED THE village before I saw it. After the long fast, I was weak as any invalid. I struggled the last half mile, stopping every other minute to corral my last reserves of strength. The snow had hardened a bit with the wind, but was still incredibly deep, and often I'd had to strike out cross-country across fields where fallen trees barred the road. Finally I smelled chimney smoke—welcome as a brass band. People cooking, bread baking. Salvation. A dog barked. Peasants called to one another in the fog, exchanging thoughts about the storm as they dug out narrow walkways between snowbound izbas and the lane.

A sledge passed, loaded with hay. I trembled, leaning into a tree and fighting for consciousness, thinking of the girl I'd once been, waiting just here that evening after my long walk from Tikhvin. How strong I'd been then, how confident of my powers compared to this scarecrow, this ghost I'd become.

A burly man in a greasy coat and leather apron came out of the forge with another man. Together they stood smoking on the porch, shook hands and parted. Soon the clang of the blacksmith's hammer filled the morning. So much activity! In my half-starved, unreal state, this tiny village was dizzying as Petrograd.

Finally a brisk young woman appeared on the porch of a prosperous izba with four windows past the blacksmith's shop. She was eating an apple. I left the safety of the trees to approach her. It had been so long since I'd spoken to anyone not Ionian. She raised her head, squinting at me. I could only imagine what I looked like these days in my homemade fox hat and sheepskin and felt boots, my game bag, my patchwork *sarafan* with the trousers underneath, my face wrapped in a thick woolen scarf. I lowered the scarf.

I don't know what I expected. A smile, an embrace? At least the welcome I'd received the last time I was here. But it wasn't forthcoming. Her mouth gaped open in shock. Was I so changed? "What are you doing here? Are you crazy?" She lowered her head, her back half turned, checking up and down the lane. She tossed the apple, half-eaten, picked up a broom and swept the steps. "You've got to get out of here," she hissed. "Don't you know what's going on? I can't be seen with you. You've got to leave."

But I was too weak to leave. I needed to eat, to rest, to collect myself and make plans. "I can't go any farther. I'm pregnant. I need food. They're starving out there at Maryino."

"Well, what am I supposed to do about it?" She swept angrily. "They should have thought about that when they moved out there. We have our own problems now." A cluster of peasant women were watching us from the porch of another house. "Damn those busybodies," she said under her breath. "Now you've done it. Sveta!" she exclaimed, leaning her broom against the house. "Good to see you! Mama's going to be so happy!" She pulled me in for an embrace. In my ear, she whispered, "Go to Olya's. Two houses from the end. And don't come back. I can't do anything for you."

"Thanks." The smell of her apple followed me like a perfume as I headed down the lane. To think I'd taught Lyuda how to read. We'd swum in the river together, climbed trees, picked berries. But the revolution was still going on, and people had changed. I was the one who had to keep up. I walked down the lane, trying not to gape like a rube on Nevsky Prospect. But the colors were dazzling. I'd been locked away in another world. Here were children and horses and old people, but there were hidden worlds, too. I had to be the hunter, not blunder in, keep my wits about me. Lyuda's fear had been palpable. Why? Had there been an expropriation? Had the Cheka arrived? Something had changed since I'd been out at Maryino if she was afraid to even talk to me now.

So I was to be Sveta, some cousin or other, visiting Auntie Olya.

Avdokia's half sister's house was small, sad, with an old coating of blue paint worn mostly to the boards. The path had barely been cut—it looked stamped, not shoveled. Some neighbor had broken her out, but that was all. What had been a front porch was only a tunnel, the roof heavily laden. I took off my snowshoes and propped them by the door. It was private here at least, down the end of the lane, away from the village center. I was about to knock on Olya's door, then thought better of it. If I were truly some distant cousin, I wouldn't be standing on the front porch like a census taker.

It was warm inside and shockingly crowded. Little tables, pieces of lace, rugs, even an ugly chandelier with a milk-glass bowl crammed the small cabin to the rafters, all bits and pieces of our bourgeois life at Maryino. On the tables stood portraits of my family in silver frames. It was a museum of a former life, a former world. I could not even be angry at her. They were only things, and things had no feelings. What would I do with them, anyway—sell them? If anyone deserved the booty, it was Olya, who had washed and dusted and polished them all these years. And yet I couldn't deny a small sense of betrayal.

"Olya?"

The place was damp with steam, and a great pot boiled on the stove. "Olga Fomanovna?" I called from the doorway. I'd never used her patronymic. No one ever had, not in my hearing.

She looked up from a load of laundry she was ironing, a sheet on the board. She reminded me of a bigger, softer Avdokia, twenty years younger. Same father, different mother. Women wore out quickly in the villages. Her mouth made a perfect O.

"Sorry to barge in. Lyuda said you'd be here."

"Marina Dmitrievna! No, no, please, come in, come in!" She looked around the place, suddenly aware that I was seeing the extent of her plunder, and her hands flew to her mouth. The sheet started to burn. She put her iron upright just in time.

"It's been a while," I said.

"You've seen Lyuda, then?"

I nodded. "She didn't want to be seen with me, though. Class enemy and all." I took off my hat.

"Oh, don't mind her." Olya came away from the laundry, took my hat and bag, helped me off with my coat, hung it on the hook by the door. "Now that she's on the village committee she thinks she's Lenin's right arm." She nodded approvingly. "Married the blacksmith after all. That girl always had an eye to improving her lot. I told her the blacksmith would be good for her, didn't I? She runs him like a horse around a ring." The words poured out of her, probably in an attempt to distract me from the familial furniture and bric-a-brac. "Remember when she wanted to go to Petrograd and work in a factory? She certainly came to her senses. Sit down, sit down!" She pulled out a chair from the lace-covered table.

I recognized the chair, too. It was one that used to sit at the little desk in the front parlor where my mother opened the mail. Somehow the sight of that chair loosened the grief of having lost her. I settled down into it. Now I was glad to let Olya babble away.

"We don't get many visitors, as you can imagine. Can I make you some tea? Let me heat the samovar. Did she tell you she had a letter in the paper, my Lyuda? Imagine! Look, there on the table." She handed me a yellowed issue of *Bednota,* a badly printed newspaper intended for peasant consumption, folded back to a page of letters and reports from the villages. A complaint about a certain corrupt party official in Ryazan Oblast headed the page.

"Look—right there." Flushing with pride, she pointed to a report below the Ryazan one. From "Correspondent L. G. Fedeyeva." Lyuda, writing for *Bednota.* She described the cooperation of the Novinka Village Committee of Poor Peasants with a Red Army food detachment to expropriate the hoarded goods of the kulak Zuborin. How many poods of grain they had located under the floor of his barn and so on. It ended, *"The Speculators and Kulaks might think they've put One over on Soviet Power but they will not Succeed because we Know Them."*

Because we Know Them. I shuddered at the thought of the savagery behind that simple statement. One might think there would be safety in these tiny hamlets, but it was the opposite. "What did they do with him?"

"Zuborin?" Olya sighed, fishing coals from the stove to put in the samovar. "He really was a terrible man. Everyone was afraid of him. Up there safe and sound at Maryino, your people never knew what our lives were like here. We had to pay Zuborin to graze our animals. His grandfather bought up all the common land with Emancipation. Those bastards have lorded it over us ever since. Think they own the village. Only last year, he beat an old man to death, didn't he? An old man who owed him money."

The outrage on her face told me it was true. But then something crossed it, something not so pure, a slightly sly look. "And we owe so much more grain to the provisioning this year..." She began straightening the room, swatting her rag at the lamps and tabletops, squaring chairs, not looking at me. "The workers used to leave us grain and seed and take the rest. That was bad enough. But now it's different. The soldiers are hard, even the workers now, when they come through. They take their quota off the top, and if there's not enough left for planting, it's too bad for you. So what

are you supposed to plant in the spring? When Zuborin's got hundreds of poods hidden under his cow barn—everyone knew it. Why should we suffer for a man like that?" She shrugged. "The devil take him."

So now it was to be peasant against peasant, all the wounds of the village since Emancipation resurfacing. The villagers had offered up Zuborin. "Did they kill him?"

She went back to the stove to recover her iron, spat on it, began to iron the sheet again. "It's a hard world these days, Marina Dmitrievna, a hard life. At least they left the family. Except Motka. They took him for the army."

When she was done catching me up on village gossip, she put the iron up and went to fuss with the samovar, pouring tea. "How strong?"

"Medium," I said. I turned the fragile, soft pages of the newspaper back to the beginning. The issue was dated January 19. Epiphany. Two months ago. The broadsheet bawled about an English threat from the north. Blockade along the Baltic coast. Wrangel in the Caucasus—that was a new one. Joining forces with Denikin, threatening Moscow. Kolchak in the east. Soviet Russia, as far as I could tell, was surrounded, cut off not only from Europe but from the Ukraine, the Don, and Siberia. Only its red beating heart was left. Without Don coal, without Siberian grain, I couldn't imagine how Petrograd was suffering by now. Of course Kolya would be right in the middle of it. He

must have made a killing with our bags of grain. *And may he never have a day's peace with it.*

"And how is Avdokia? Still putting on airs?"

This was how her sister saw her—as the one who had escaped. My dear Avdokia, whom I'd left to Mother, to live or die. All depended upon what I could do with Olya right now.

I began to wonder, why hadn't anybody told the Red Army about us? The villagers owed us nothing. Why would Correspondent L. G. Fedeyeva, a rising revolutionary star, protect the Ionians in general and a former landowner in particular? No wonder she wanted to be rid of me. Maybe she was holding us in reserve, a card up her sleeve in case of emergency. More likely she was afraid of turning us in at this late date, afraid she would be accused of sheltering the aristocracy. A born politician, you had to give her that.

Olya finished the sheet she'd been ironing, folded it gently. No, not a sheet. It was a priestly gown. I couldn't help but smile. She was doing the priest's laundry. Didn't she see the contradiction—Lyuda on the committee, a party candidate, maybe even a member by now, with a mother who still did the priest's linens? Then I noted the icon in the red corner, the little flame. The family had one leg in the past, one in the future. Hedging their bets.

I sipped my tea—roasted barley—and she opened a tin with a flowered top. Oh that smell! Inside were the sweet fennel cookies she used to make at Maryino. I

took one, dipped it in my tea. The taste threw me into a parallel reality, one where I was a child of seven and bees hummed in the lilac bush out the kitchen window. Flowers on the cabinets, my doll Natasha having a tea party with me. "You still make these..." I could hardly speak or choke it down for the nostalgia of it.

"I don't have so many visitors anymore. Have another."

That licorice smell, the slight sweetness. How far I'd come to end up a half-starved pregnant woman of nineteen with my possessions in a stained game bag. It made me cry, my mouth full of longing. I wanted more. I wanted to eat the whole tin.

"So they're having a hard time out there, are they?" Olya asked, sitting down at the table, folding her strong, reddened hands before her.

I was relieved she'd brought it up herself. "How did you know?"

She raised her palm. *Isn't it obvious?* My gauntness was evidently clear, even in all these layers of clothes.

And here I'd been trying to think of a tactful way to work up to the desperate situation at Maryino. "They're not practical people, Olya."

She smoothed out the tablecloth. "I heard they have a wonderworker."

What on earth had Ukashin done when they came through in the spring? Thrown some energy into an old lady and convinced her to cast away her crutches? "I wouldn't exactly call him a wonderworker."

"Not him. *Her.*" She lowered her voice, as if the stove imp might hear us. "Vera Borisovna."

I almost dropped my tea glass.

"They say she has powers." There was awe in her voice, and her eyes were bright—so like her sister's, but with an innocence untainted by contact with the outside world. "The priest says she's a sorceress, that all them out there is devils."

My mother the wonderworker. Now, there was a pretty idea. The priest had a better sense of it. But what mattered was that Olya thought so. I pretended my heart wasn't pounding in my chest as I responded casually, "Well, she always did have the second sight. You remember when she wouldn't get in the trap with Slava? And the axle broke the same day?"

"We thought it was because she didn't like young Slava. He lost his leg. Kept him out of the army, though, so there's a blessing. But she knew it was going to happen."

"Last spring she saw of a tide of blood," I said, lowering my voice so she would come closer. "They moved out here a few weeks short of a cholera epidemic. Then Red Terror. They would have all been shot."

Olya's eyes were aglitter. "They say she makes cures."

She makes cures. The priest said she's a sorceress. Suddenly I *saw*, as if right through this opaque form seated before me, what the trouble was. Olya was ill, suffering from some hidden misery, and frightened. Her chances of obtaining medical help out here were just about nil—not in the best of times, and certainly not during a civil war. If there were any doctors, they would have been swept up when the army came through, leaving the old women to their diseases. Now Olya was holding out hope for a miracle worker.

I thought of those beautiful Ionians trying to live on promises and air. "I bet Avdokia could get you in to see her. You should go out there."

I knew what I was doing was wrong, duping the vulnerable, but if she went, she would bring offerings—a sack of grain, a *funt* of potatoes, maybe an old sheep—and with any luck the word would spread. The peasant women of Novinka and even the surrounding hamlets were capable of feeding the Ionians into spring. Avdokia would make sure the gifts kept coming, of that I had no doubt. And these women would raise no alarm. They knew better than anyone how to protect their old ways.

Grandfather Golovin glared out from his silver frame, beleaguered and outraged, bushy white eyebrows like snowy eaves over his beautiful old eyes. *Sorry, Dyedushka, but it's 1919, not 1875. You're going to be a great-grandfather. We've got to be practical, you and I.* At least he was here, in his village, where they knew him, with his family all around, if only in photographs. *All I pray is that I'm buried in Russia,* Avdokia liked to say. For myself, I had no idea how much longer I would sojourn, how many miles I would walk, how many years. To live was the thing.

I stayed at Olya's until she found a ride for me into Tikhvin, a neighbor with a load of wood to sell. I left Novinka on top of a sledge heading for town, pulled by a little swaybacked mare. For the food she fed me I paid cash but managed to cajole her into parting with one of my grandmother's silver salt cellars in exchange for the ride. "It's only pewter," I told her. Though I noticed she had no trouble convincing the old man it was sterling. How appropriate that my ride had been purchased with salt.

I sat atop the load and looked back—oh, yes I did—my hungry eyes drinking in every detail. The dogs sniffing the new drifts. A boy running out of a gate, red-cheeked, his young mother shouting, "Don't forget your brother!" Nostalgia gored me like a bull. The smaller child, so thickly clad he looked like a ball, arms sticking out on either side, toddled after him. When Seryozha was that age I had to take him with me everywhere. The load, redolent with the sticky smell of new-cut pine, shifted beneath me as the sledge slid and jolted in a lane freshly scored with runner marks.

Maryino—already lost. The house with its dark logs, the lilac bush, the painted cabinets, my mother wrapped in mists and visions. A fox running in the snow. Seryozha lying on his stomach in the front parlor, cutting figures from an old Paris fashion catalog.

A fallen tree over the river. Floating along in the lazy green—then crossing it again with Andrei Ionian. The larch proud in the yard, the larch cut down. Ionians spinning in perfect synchrony, an egg stained red with beet juice. I folded all these images in half, in quarters, over and over again, and pressed them, hard nuggets of memory, into the center of my forehead.

The horse labored hock deep through the new snow, its harness creaking. Olya's old neighbor lit his pipe. A woman came out onto her porch and threw a basin of water into the yard, and I saw Mother in white coming off the veranda at Maryino in a hat like a wheel. My governess in a straw boater, calling me as I drifted deeper into the trees. *Marina*... Volodya, standing on the back of a fat pony. And that young girl in green, walking barefoot along a rope tied between two trees.

Marina...

I would remember this: the brush of the runners over the new snow, the squeak of the sledge as the hamlet shrank into the past. First the pines disappeared, then the aspen-shingled church, the sooty barn of the blacksmith's shop, and Lyuda's pretty house. Now the dogs, the gates, the children. At last Novinka itself blurred and vanished into the fog, like a sketch in pencil rubbed out by a thumb.

End of Book I

Acknowledgments

The people to whom I owe gratitude in the writing of this book would populate a small but extremely beautiful city. First, I would like to offer thanks to the heroes of my writing life, my writers' group, David Francis, Rita Williams, and Julianne Ortale, whose unfailing support saw this book through its long gestation. Also to my daughter, Allison Strauss, whose sharp eye proved instrumental in shaping the version of the novel you hold in your hands today. To my tireless editor, Asya Muchnick, at Little, Brown, who took on Marina's epic journey without a backward look. Thanks to the rest of the team at Little, Brown, and especially Karen Landry, who moved mountains for this book. To my agent and champion, Warren Frazier at John Hawkins and Associates, ever in my corner as the book and I went eighty rounds, and to Bill Reiss, for changing my life. Thank you to Boris Dralyuk, gentle friend and sounding board, for your insights and for creating original translations for much of the Russian poetry that appears in this book. To the irreplaceable Dr. Judson Rosengrant, close reader and literary Virgil into the manners and mores of the Russian intelligentsia. And thank you to my earliest reader, Jane Chafin, for your curiosity and long friendship.

Depthless gratitude goes to the Likhachev Foundation of St. Petersburg, Russia, the research fellowship that opened Marina's world for me. Without you, I would still be pressing my nose to the windows of Revolutionary Petrograd. Instead, you swung wide the doors. Thank you with all my heart to Alexander Kobak, Elena Vitenberg, Inna Sviderskaya, Anna Shulgat, Sasha Vasiliev, Boris Poleschuk, and Ksenia Pikaliova (Kobak) for your generosity and care. Through my Likhachev fellowship, I was able to reach out to some of the most prestigious cultural institutions in St. Petersburg. At the Anna Akhmatova Museum, many thanks to director Nina Popova; Tatyana Poznyakova, head of the Education Department; and Masha Korosteleva, curator. At the Museum of Political History, my gratitude to curators Alexander Kalmyov and Alexey Kulegin. At the Museum of the City of St. Petersburg, I thank research secretary Irina Karpenko and deputy director Julia Demidenko. At the Dostoyevsky House Museum, thank you to deputy director Vera Biron for the tour of the Dostoyevsky district and having me speak about this project at the museum. And special thanks to translator Eireene Nealand for alerting me to the Likhachev Foundation, and for introducing me to contemporary St. Petersburg poets. And thanks to Tobin Auber, editor of the *St. Petersburg Times,* for your warm welcome and insider views. And abiding gratitude to Andrey Nesteruk and his parents for their memorable tour of hidden St. Petersburg.

Research was the oxygen in the water of this novel. I thank the eminent Russian historians Alexander Rabinowitch and Arch Getty, social historian Choi Chatterjee, and art historian John Bowlt for their precious help, as well as the H-Russia Listserv, and teacher and translator Natalya Pollack. I thank the USC libraries for the richness of their collection and my access to it, and Reed College, whose 2007 alumni trip under the guidance of Dr. Rosengrant informed so many aspects of this work.

Novelists not only require the world, they also require retreat from the world, and I have found many a kind harbor for myself and my crates of binders and books. Many thanks to those who offered me shelter and the gift of time—Eduardo Santiago and Mark Davis of Idyllwild, California; David Lewis and Liz Sandoval of Portland, Oregon; Brett Hall Jones, Louis Jones, and the Hall family of Squaw Valley, California; Andrew Tonkovich and Lisa Alvarez of Modjeska Canyon, California; Jan Rabson and Cindy Akers of Salt Spring Island, British Columbia; Wendy Goldstein and Sharon Smith of Manitou Springs, Colorado; Sally Wright of Idyllwild, California; and the Helen R. Whiteley Fellowship, University of Washington Friday Harbor Laboratories, San Juan Island, Washington.

Though they live only in my heart now, I would like to thank my father, Vernon Fitch, who long ago put

Dostoyevsky into my restless hands, leading me into a lifelong love of Russia, and my mother, Alma Fitch, who taught me that girls can do anything.

Most of all, I want to thank my most generous husband, Andrew John Nicholls, who stuck with me throughout this long labor, read so many drafts, calmed so many storms, cheered me when it looked bad, and encouraged me to celebrate prematurely whenever possible. "If you don't celebrate prematurely," he says, "you'll never taste champagne." I love you more than I can say.

For an overview of the books that shaped my understanding of the Revolution and Marina's world, please visit janetfitchwrites.com.

"What else didn't they tell you?" I shouted down the table. "Did you know I was pregnant? I'm going to have a child, Mama. This summer. Your grandchild."

The devotees shifted uncomfortably, embarrassed that their priestess was being dragged into a matter so unseemly and personal when they'd given up every family connection, even their names. I could see that Magda wanted to get her hands around my throat. Ukashin stared at me. I could almost hear him — *I can't save you forever.*

"Your grandchild, Mama. It's Kolya Shurov's."

Now her vision cleared, and she saw me. Oh, yes. She remembered me now. *Your daughter.* She regarded me with something resembling fear.

"Yes, Kolya. We've been lovers since I was sixteen. Did you see that in your multidimensional universe?"

But then her vision clouded over, and she was scanning me, as she had in the room upstairs, as if she were reading a wall poster, a playbill for a drama at the People's House. What was I, a little Ibsen? Or maybe Wilde?

"It won't live," she said.

The sound echoed like a gunshot in a long hall. When it faded, the only sound in the room was the roaring of the wind.

Doors slammed, and in a gust of frigid air, the trio of boys thundered into the hall. In walked Pasha, frosted white, hat, scarf, coat, boots, gloves, his arms piled high with fragrant fir, followed by Gleb and Bogdan equally laden. The relief was palpable. All uncertainty vanished, and the disciples beamed with the proof: their prophetess was wise, Ukashin was still in control, I was an alarmist and disrupter. *You see?* said the Master's sideways glance. *We know what we're doing here.* The others grabbed up the boughs and began rubbing the sills and doorways.

I lay on my pallet that night among the others, no longer marveling at our initiation into the mysteries of *inflowing*. Even hiding within the earth did me no good. I only heard my mother's voice. I thought of her face, her calm. I wanted to slap her even now. Was she punishing me for insisting that there was no wolf and that she was no seer, only a madwoman? Or was she so crazy that she didn't understand how terrible was her curse?

But what if it was true?

No. That I would not believe. I might never be one with anyone—fine—but I would not let her kill my baby. I rejected her spell, I spat on it, I walked on it, I pissed on it. I would not believe. To think of how I'd cared for her. She was the reason I'd broken with Genya, the reason I'd gone to Kamenny Island to sell that pin. She had not defended me against my father that October night. I turned over and over, settling the sheepskin back on top of the quilt. As long as I could have my baby, I would endure the rest.

I had not realized how passionately I wanted this child until my mother tried to take it away from me.

81 *The Hunter*

THE STORM DID NOT abate. If anything, it worsened. Ukashin moved us into the heart of the house, the back parlor, closing off all the other rooms to conserve heat and firewood. We squashed into the workroom like kittens in a sack. After what my mother had said to me, it was agony to have to see her every day. I thought I would go mad. Everyone breathing each other's breath and that sticky incense, the stove pushing smoke into the room as it would in a black izba. If it wasn't for *inflowing,* I would have had to stop breathing altogether. Only under the earth was it still possible to inhale. Meditation was the only escape from the oppressive togetherness. I supposed my mother's curse of eternal loneliness had not yet taken effect.

I sometimes ventured up the frost-coated stairs to the water closet just to be free of them all. The chamber pots we'd put there had frozen fast—we couldn't have them in the room with us. They didn't stink, though you had to wear your coat and hat and boots to visit the convenience. You might as well be outside. White rime built up on the bare risers of the stairs, showing our footprints. Outside, snow buried the first-floor windows, cutting us off from the world, mirroring what was going on inside our minds. Only in the window on the stairway landing could you see what was going on in the yard. Sometimes I stood there for hours, it seemed, in a trance, watching the trees lashing about like souls in some white hell.

Now that Mother had joined us, Ukashin more and more often turned his back on the others to focus entirely on his prophetess. He stopped leading the *inflowing* meditation, leaving it in the hands of Magda and Natalya. Instead he spent hours in communication with his priestess, meditating with her, or else painting or lying in his hammock, which he'd slung in the corner by the fire next to Mother's chair. Through the buildup of snow, the storm's roaring sounded more and more like the blood in my ears. The acolytes worked hard to regain their Master's favor, as if the blizzard were somehow their fault, as if they could make things better by being perfect little disciples. Mother sat communing with the paintings they'd fetched from her lair and rearranging her little stones with the clicking sounds like waves turning pebbles on a beach. Her spirit guides watched us night and day.

Pasha was the first to collapse. He crumpled during a meditation session. Katrina, surfacing from her trance, jumped to her feet. "Pasha?" she called out, leaning over him but afraid to touch him. "Master? Pasha's fainted!"

But the Master said nothing.

"He's all right," Magda said. "Let him be."

About the Author

Janet Fitch's first novel, *White Oleander*, a #1 bestseller and Oprah's Book Club selection, has been translated into twenty-eight languages and was made into a feature film. Her most recent novel, *Paint It Black*, hit bestseller lists across the country and has also been made into a film. She lives with her husband in Los Angeles. She is currently working on the second part of Marina's story.